Sōseki Natsume

I Am a Cat

translated by
Aiko Ito & Graeme Wilson

TUTTLE Publishing
Tokyo | Rutland, Vermont | Singapore

Published by Tuttle Publishing, an imprint of Periplus Editions (HK) Ltd. Originally published in three volumes by Tuttle Publishing in 1972 (Vol. I), 1979 (Vol. II), and 1986 (Vol. III). Volume I was originally published in Japan by the Asahi Shimbun Publishing Company in the Japan Quarterly, Vol. XVII, No. 4, and Vol. XVIII, Nos. 1 and 2. Chapter I of Volume II was originally published in Japan by the Asahi Shimbun Publishing Company in the Japan Quarterly, Vol. XII, No. 4.

www.tuttlepublishing.com

Library of Congress Catalog Card Number: 2002100535

ISBN 978-0-8048-3265-6
ISBN 978-4-8053-1097-7 (for sale in Japan only)

Distributed by:

North America, Latin American & Europe
Tuttle Publishing
364 Innovation Drive
North Clarendon, VT 05759-9436 U.S.A.
Tel: 1 (802) 773-8930
Fax: 1 (802) 773-6993
info@tuttlepublishing.com
www.tuttlepublishing.com

Japan
Tuttle Publishing
Yaekari Building, 3rd Floor
5-4-12 Osaki, Shinagawa-ku
Tokyo 141-0032
Tel: (81) 3 5437-0171
Fax: (81) 3 5437-0755
sales@tuttle.co.jp
www.tuttle.co.jp

Asia Pacific
Berkeley Books Pte. Ltd.
61 Tai Seng Avenue #02-12
#06-01/03 Olivine Building
Singapore 534167
Tel: (65) 6280-1330
Fax: (65) 6280-6290
inquiries@periplus.com.sg
www.periplus.com

16 15 14 13 12 11 10 20 19 18 17 16 15 14
Printed in the United States of America

contents

INTRODUCTION

SŌSEKI NATSUME is the pen name of Kin'nosuke Natsume (1867–1916), the eighth and youngest son of a family of minor town-gentry. The family's hereditary occupation as ward-chiefs in Tokyo under the Tokugawa shogunate disappeared with the Meiji Restoration of 1868, and thus they fell upon hard times, yet Sōseki received the compulsory modern education, both primary and at middle school level, which had been introduced in 1872.

In his mid-teens he switched to a private school for Chinese studies and, though upper-class tradition regarded literature as no more than a civilized diversion, he began to toy with the idea of adopting it as a working profession. However, extensively educated in both the Chinese and the Japanese literary traditions, Sōseki recognized early on the importance of English to any senior career under the westernizing influence of the restored regime and, specifically, to the entry requirements of Tokyo Imperial University—then the only university in the capital. Hoping to become an architect, he entered that university's Department of Engineering in 1881, but he soon transferred to the Department of Literature that same year. In September 1890, Sōseki joined the Department of English Literature as a loan-scholarship student of the Ministry of Education.

The English department, founded in 1888, had produced only one previous graduate, a student of the first year who became a customs inspector in Shanghai. Sōseki graduated in July 1893 and then briefly enrolled as a postgraduate student. He applied unsuccessfully for a post as a journalist with the English-language *Japan Mail* in Yokohama and taught for a time at Tokyo Normal College. In 1895 he suddenly left Tokyo to become a provincial teacher—first in Shikoku (where his university friend, the *haiku* poet Masaoka Shiki, resided) and later, in 1896, at Kumamoto in Kyushu. There, by formal arrangement, he married Nakane Kyōko, the eldest daughter of the chief secretary of the House of Peers.

In 1900 the Ministry of Education sent him on a miserable scholarship to London University. For two unhappy years in London, he seems to have done nothing but read an almost incredible number of books on every conceivable subject and, at the same time, make himself an authority on eighteenth-century literature. His only social contacts with the British appear to have been a weekly private English lesson with W. J. Craig—subsequently the editor of the *Arden Shakespeare*—and a single tea party given in Dulwich by the wife of a missionary whom he had met on the ship bringing him to England. It is, therefore, perhaps not surprising that Sōseki formed a poor opinion of English social life and that back in Japan he was widely rumored to have gone mad.

In 1903 he returned to Tokyo and, shortly thereafter, in fulfillment of the terms of his London scholarship, served four years as a lecturer in English literature at Tokyo Imperial University. During this period he began writing. He had formed various useful literary friendships while he was a student at the university, and, though his close friend Shiki had died in 1902, the editorial board of the influential literary magazine *Hototogisu* (*Cuckoo*), which Shiki had founded, still included many men who were Sōseki's personal friends.

Takahama Kyoshi—one of the editors of *Hototogisu*, but not a close friend of Sōseki—allegedly asked Sōseki to write something for the magazine. Accordingly, during 1904, Sōseki produced his first short story, which he called *I Am a Cat*. Takahama read it, told Sōseki that it was no good, and, when Sōseki asked for an explanation, provided comment in considerable detail. Today it seems ludicrous that one of the three or four best novelists ever to write in Japanese should have been glad to receive guidance from such a relatively insignificant figure as Takahama. However, we must remember that, at that time, Takahama was a well-known, well-established, and very influential editor (a man with the sensitivity to divine Sōseki's promise and the kindness to give him guidance), while Sōseki was a virtually unknown young man who had just produced his first, and really rather odd, short story. In any event, Sōseki appears to have accepted the advice (though he later stated that he could not remember what that advice had been) and rewrote the story. Takahama liked the second version and published it in the January 1905 issue of *Hototogisu*.

Sōseki had not intended to write more than that single short story, which is now the first chapter of a very long book, but Takahama was so pleased with its immediate success that he persuaded Sōseki to write further installments. The subsequent ten chapters that make up *I Am a*

Cat were thus successively published in *Hototogisu's* issues for February, April, June, July, and October 1905 and for January, March, April, and August 1906. The seventh and eighth chapters appeared together in the issue for January 1906. This somewhat curious account of the origin and development of Sōseki's famous novel rests primarily upon Takahama's testimony in his later book *Sōseki and I*, but there is no reason to doubt that it is substantially correct. The actual book of *I Am a Cat* was first published in three-volume form, the volumes appearing in October 1905, November 1906, and May 1907. The first single-volume edition was published in 1911.

Takahama's account of how this story came to be a novel explains the unevenness, even jerkiness, of the early parts of the book. Indeed, though the first chapter is adequately articulated into the total work, it is as clear from that chapter's ending as from Sōseki's own later remarks—"When the first chapter appeared in *Hototogisu*, it was my intention to stop there"—that he originally meant to write no more. There are, moreover, one or two minor points in that first chapter that an ungenerous critic might highlight as inconsistent with subsequent portions of the book. The second chapter, nearly the longest of them all, shows Sōseki still feeling his way towards the right chapter length. He did not really hit his stride until the third chapter, which finally established the tone, length, and character of the remaining eight.

The circumstances of the book's construction no doubt largely account for its rambling structure and discursive content; however, Sōseki must very quickly have realized that the technique used by Laurence Sterne for the construction of *The Life and Opinions of Tristram Shandy* would very neatly solve his own problems. Though Sōseki's total book is held together by the continuing theme of a nameless cat's observations on upper-middle-class Japanese society of the Meiji period, the essence of the book resides in the humor and the sardonic truth of those various observations, not in the development of the story. The cat's eventual drunken death in a water-butt comes without any particular reason or structural build-up, and one is forced to the conclusion that Sōseki simply drowned his hero because he had run out of sufficiently humorous observations to offer on Meiji society. Consequently, it is possible to take almost any single chapter of the book as an isolated short story.

It is also worth stressing the apparent oddity of choosing for the main character in one's first published writing a stray kitten, and a stray kitten world-weary from the moment of its birth. However, much of the charm of *I Am a Cat* resides in its diverting presentation of a cat's view of mankind. The satire is of man in general but the associated case for the superiority of cats, however entertainingly and persuasively put, is not inexhaustible; so that the unique cat-ness of the opening chapters simply could not be maintained in its original and beguiling purity throughout the further chapters demanded by a happily insulted public. Sōseki himself was clearly alive to these considerations, for as early as the opening paragraph of the third chapter the cat apologizes to readers for his growing resemblance to a human being and for his consequent new tendency to criticize humanity as though he, too, were human. Thus the satire beginning in Chapter 3 is less specifically feline. In yet later chapters the cat's viewpoint becomes almost totally human, while the object of satire narrows from mankind in general (albeit as exemplified in Meiji, middle-class society) to a concentrated satirization of the particularities of that particular society. By a combination of sheer literary skill and a seemingly endless inventiveness, Sōseki contrived to maintain the vitality of his book throughout eleven chapters and some quarter million words: but one understands why, eventually, he had no choice but to drown his hero. It would, however, be unreasonable to denigrate the first-rate satire of the later parts of *I Am a Cat* simply because they lack the full felinity, the quite exceptional beguilement, of the earlier parts of the book. Moreover, one has only to read Sōseki's other comic novel *Botchan* (*The Young Master*), of 1906, with its entirely human style of human satire, to realize that, however much humanity seeps in to soften the later portions of *I Am a Cat*, even their most uncat-like passages contain that glint, that claw-flash under velvet, which stamp them ultimately aluroid. In addition, choosing a kitten for the main character has a two-fold meaning as Sōseki was, in fact, himself a stray kitten. As soon as he was born, Sōseki's parents had put him out to nurse. In his first year he was adopted by the Shiobara family. He only rejoined his own family when the Shiobaras were divorced some eight years later. And even then he only learned that his parents were his parents from the whisperings of servants. Sōseki lived his life as do all those who feel themselves born middle-aged.

While at the university Sōseki wrote several other books, notably *Botchan* (a satire reflecting his teaching experience at Shikoku), but he disliked university life and, rightly, considered himself very poorly paid.

He accordingly resigned as soon as he could (1907) and became the literary editor of the *Asahi Shimbun*. He continued in that journal's employment, publishing several novels as serials in its pages, until his death in 1916 from complications arising from the stomach troubles that plagued the last ten years of his life.

* * *

Sōseki Natsume is generally recognized in Japan as the best writer of prose to have emerged during the century since contact was re-established with the outside world in 1868. Despite the lateness of his development as a novelist (he was only just short of forty when his first book was published), Sōseki rapidly achieved, and has since maintained, widespread recognition as the best of modern Japanese novelists. His literary reputation reflects not only the variety, quality, and modernity of his novels, but the high regard still paid to his works of scholarly criticism, to his enchanting essays, and, especially, to his poetry. His *haiku*, strongly influenced by his personal friend Masaoka Shiki, were once considered outstanding but, though they continue to be included in anthologies of modern *haiku*, their diminutive form was not the natural mode for the expression of his genius. His poems in English, poor imitations of the poorest style of Edwardian poetry, are appalling. But his many excellent poems in Chinese, some written even in the month before his death, are the last (or, rather, the most recent) flowering of a formidable tradition of such writing by Japanese poets which, unbroken, extends right back to the *Kaifūsō* of 751. Sōseki's deep scholarship, both in Chinese and in English literature, eminently qualified him for that marrying of Eastern and Western traditions, which was the declared objective of Meiji policy-makers. Unlike the majority of his contemporaries who had learned their English in mission schools, Sōseki approached Western literature with the wary sensitivity of a man deeply versed in the Chinese tradition.

Sōseki was, of course, also well-versed in Japanese literature. However, oddly enough for a man of gentle birth, the main Japanese influences upon his writing are found in the *rakugo*—comic recitations by professional storytellers—to which his childhood circle had been addicted. The *rakugo* techniques are especially noticeable in his masterly use of dialogue. It is also worth stressing that, though Sōseki's Chinese studies resulted in a style as concise as the language traditionally used in the composition of *tanka* and *haiku*, much of the vitality of his prose writing comes from his skilled exploitation of colloquial Japanese speech (*kōgotai*).

Sōseki's writing represents a continuation into modern times of the city-culture which first flowered in the late seventeenth century when the wealth of the towns prospering under the *Pax Tokugawa* provided the economic base for an urban and specifically non-aristocratic literature. Sōseki's writing contains an untraditional independence of thought and attitude—a rationalist and (in the best sense) liberal outlook—which is often contrasted with the very rigid *samurai* attitude that was also prevalent during Sōseki's time.

Sōseki's longer novels reflect his assiduous study of the construction and mechanisms of the English novel and, in particular, his liking for the works of Laurence Sterne, Jonathan Swift, and Jane Austen. He shared their sly, ironic turn of mind, and their influence on his work was more deep and lasting than that of George Meredith, as so frequently cited by contemporary critics.

There is an understandable tendency for critics of any literature to emphasize the dependence of a writer on his predecessors, but the "game of influences" is all too frequently played with an enthusiasm that leads to an unfair disregard of the writer's real originality. So far as Japan is concerned, there can be no doubt whatsoever that Sōseki's originality was a main factor in his popular success—but he also has genuine claims to originality in world literature. World literature has, of course, a long tradition of animal-fables, animal myths, and major groupings of stories around such figures as Renard the Fox and even Brer Rabbit. But Sōseki's device of dealing with a human world through animal eyes appears to be entirely original.

Sōseki's modernity is even more strikingly illustrated by the fact that sixty years ago the characters in *I Am a Cat* (notably "the aesthete") were all fully engaged in those comic ploys and counter-ploys of gamesmanship, lifemanship, and one upmanship that are now usually associated with the comparatively recent work of Stephen Potter. The passages in the first chapter of *I Am a Cat* about Gibbon's *History of the French Revolution* and Harrison's *Theophano* are both extremely fine examples of what Potter has called "rilking." Similarly, the description of the visit to a restaurant in the second chapter is a particularly well-developed example of Potter's comic techniques.

Perhaps the most significant aspect of Sōseki's work is that, while deeply conversant with Western literature and while sharply and persistently critical of Japanese society, he remained unswamped (even, perhaps, unimpressed) by Western enlightenment. Throughout his career he remained essentially and uncompromisingly Japanese; his deadly serious attitude is, typically, revealed in that comic, even coarse, account in *Koto no Sorane* (1905) of the protest by Japanese badgers against contemporary Japanese infatuation with routine badger-tricks (such as the "hypnotic method") whose sole novelty is that their names have been exported to Japan by "badgers in the West." Probably for this reason Sōseki's writings have retained their popularity and, perhaps, even extended their influence. In a public opinion survey conducted by the *Asahi Shimbun* among students and professors at four universities which still produce the social and intellectual elite of Japan, Sōseki's *Kokoro* (*The Heart of Things*) of 1914 was second only to Dostoievski's *Crime and Punishment* in the list of books which had most influenced the thinking of the interviewees. *Yukiguni* (*Snow Country*) by Nobel Prize winner Kawabata Yasunari was seventeenth.

* * *

Sōseki's brilliant and extremely concise use of the Japanese language makes all his writings difficult to translate. In the case of this particular book, difficulty arises with the very first word of its title, *Wagahai wa Neko de Aru*. There being no English equivalent for the Japanese word *Wagahai*, the main significance of that title, the comic incongruity of a mere cat, a mere stray mewling kitten, referring to itself in so lordly a manner, cannot be conveyed to the English reader. An additional difficulty that faces any translator of Sōseki's work is his individual literary style: its reflection of his deep scholarship in Chinese, Japanese, and English literature, its consequent exploitation of a singularly wide range of reference and its unique combination of classical and colloquial language. Such problems usually lead translators to beg the indulgence of their readers: but forgive them not, for they know what they do.

VOLUME I

I

I AM A CAT. As yet I have no name. I've no idea where I was born. All I remember is that I was miaowing in a dampish dark place when, for the first time, I saw a human being. This human being, I heard afterwards, was a member of the most ferocious human species; a *shosei*, one of those students who, in return for board and lodging, perform small chores about the house. I hear that, on occasion, this species catches, boils, and eats us. However as at that time I lacked all knowledge of such creatures, I did not feel particularly frightened. I simply felt myself floating in the air as I was lifted up lightly on his palm. When I accustomed myself to that position, I looked at his face. This must have been the very first time that ever I set eyes on a human being. The impression of oddity, which I then received, still remains today. First of all, the face that should be decorated with hair is as bald as a kettle. Since that day I have met many a cat but never have I come across such deformity. The center of the face protrudes excessively and sometimes, from the holes in that protuberance, smoke comes out in little puffs. I was originally somewhat troubled by such exhalations for they made me choke, but I learnt only recently that it was the smoke of burnt tobacco which humans like to breathe.

For a little while I sat comfortably in that creature's palm, but things soon developed at a tremendous speed. I could not tell whether the *shosei* was in movement or whether it was only I that moved; but anyway I began to grow quite giddy, to feel sick. And just as I was thinking that the giddiness would kill me, I heard a thud and saw a million stars. Thus far I can remember but, however hard I try, I cannot recollect anything thereafter.

When I came to myself, the creature had gone. I had at one time had a basketful of brothers, but now not one could be seen. Even my precious mother had disappeared. Moreover I now found myself in a painfully bright place most unlike that nook where once I'd sheltered. It was in fact so bright that I could hardly keep my eyes open. Sure that there was something wrong, I began to crawl about. Which proved painful. I had been snatched away from softest straw only to be pitched with violence into a prickly clump of bamboo grass.

After a struggle, I managed to scramble clear of the clump and emerged to find a wide pond stretching beyond it. I sat at the edge of the pond and wondered what to do. No helpful thought occurred. After a while it struck me that, if I cried, perhaps the *shosei* might come back to fetch me. I tried some feeble mewing, but no one came. Soon a light wind blew across the pond and it began to grow dark. I felt extremely hungry. I wanted to cry, but I was too weak to do so. There was nothing to be done. However, having decided that I simply must find food, I turned, very, very slowly, left around the pond. It was extremely painful going. Nevertheless, I persevered and crawled on somehow until at long last I reached a place where my nose picked up some trace of human presence. I slipped into a property through a gap in a broken bamboo fence, thinking that something might turn up once I got inside. It was sheer chance; if the bamboo fence had not been broken just at that point, I might have starved to death at the roadside. I realize now how true the adage is that what is to be will be. To this very day that gap has served as my shortcut to the neighbor's tortoiseshell.

Well, though I had managed to creep into the property, I had no idea what to do next. Soon it got really dark. I was hungry, it was cold and rain began to fall. I could not afford to lose any more time. I had no choice but to struggle toward a place which seemed, since brighter, warmer. I did not know it then, but I was in fact already inside the house where I now had a chance to observe further specimens of humankind. The first one that I met was O-san, the servant-woman, one of a species yet more savage than the *shosei*. No sooner had she seen me than she grabbed me by the scruff of the neck and flung me out of the house. Accepting that I had no hope, I lay stone-still, my eyes shut tight and trusting to Providence. But the hunger and the cold were more than I could bear. Seizing a moment when O-san had relaxed her watch, I crawled up once again to flop into the kitchen. I was soon flung out again. I crawled up yet again, only to be flung out yet again. I remember that the process was several times repeated. Ever since that time, I have been utterly disgusted with this O-san person. The other day I managed at long last to rid myself of my sense of grievance, for I squared accounts by stealing her dinner of mackerel-pike. As I was about to be flung out for the last time, the master of the house appeared, complaining of the noise and demanding an explanation. The servant lifted me up, turned my face to the master and said, "This little stray kitten is being a nuisance. I keep putting it out and it keeps crawling back into the kitchen." The master briefly studied my face, twisting the black hairs under his nostrils. Then, "In that case, let it stay," he said; and turned and went inside. The master seemed to be a person of few words. The servant resentfully threw me down in the kitchen. And it was thus that I came to make this house my dwelling.

My master seldom comes face-to-face with me. I hear he is a schoolteacher. As soon as he comes home from school, he shuts himself up in the study for the rest of the day; and he seldom emerges. The others in the house think that he is terribly hard-working. He himself pretends to be hard-working. But actually he works less hard than any of them think. Sometimes I tiptoe to his study for a peep and find him taking a snooze. Occasionally his mouth is drooling onto some book he has begun to read. He has a weak stomach and his skin is of a pale yellowish color, inelastic and lacking in vitality. Nevertheless he is an enormous gormandiser. After eating a great deal, he takes some taka-diastase for his stomach and, after that, he opens a book. When he has read a few pages, he becomes sleepy. He drools onto the book. This is the routine religiously observed each evening. There are times when even I, a mere cat, can put two thoughts together. "Teachers have it easy. If you are born a human, it's best to become a teacher. For if it's possible to sleep this much and still to be a teacher, why, even a cat could teach." However, according to the master, there's nothing harder than a teacher's life and every time his friends come round to see him, he grumbles on and on.

During my early days in the house, I was terribly unpopular with everyone except the master. Everywhere I was unwelcome, and no one would have anything to do with me. The fact that nobody, even to this day, has given me a name indicates quite clearly how very little they have thought about me. Resigned, I try to spend as much of my time as possible with the master, the man who had taken me in. In the morning, while he reads the newspaper, I jump to curl up on his knees. Throughout his afternoon siesta, I sit upon his back. This is not because I have any particular fondness for the master, but because I have no other choice; no one else to turn to. Additionally, and in the light of other experiments, I have decided to sleep on the boiled-rice container, which stays warm through the morning, on the quilted foot-warmer during the evening, and out on the veranda when it is fine. But what I find especially agreeable is to creep into the children's bed and snuggle down between them. There are two children, one of five and one of three: they sleep in their own room, sharing a bed. I can always find a space between their bodies, and I manage somehow to squeeze myself quietly in. But if, by great ill-luck, one of the children wakes, then I am in trouble. For the children have nasty natures, especially the younger one. They start to cry out noisily, regardless of the time, even in the middle of the night, shouting, "Here's the cat!" Then invariably the neurotic dyspeptic in the next room wakes and comes rushing in. Why, only the other day, my master beat my backside black and blue with a wooden ruler.

Living as I do with human beings, the more that I observe them, the more I am forced to conclude that they are selfish. Especially those children. I find my bedmates utterly unspeakable. When the fancy takes them, they hang me upside-down, they stuff my face into a paper-bag, they fling me about, they ram me into the kitchen range. Furthermore, if I do commit so much as the smallest mischief, the entire household unites to chase me around and persecute me. The other day when I happened to be sharpening my claws on some straw floor-matting, the mistress of the house became so unreasonably incensed that now it is only with the greatest reluctance that she'll even let me enter a matted room. Though I'm shivering on the wooden floor in the kitchen, heartlessly she remains indifferent. Miss Blanche, the white cat who lives opposite and whom I much admire, tells me whenever I see her that there is no living creature quite so heartless as a human. The other day, she gave birth to four beautiful kittens. But three days later, the *shosei* of her house removed all four and tossed them away into the backyard pond. Miss Blanche, having given through her tears a complete account of this event, assured me that, to maintain our own parental love and to enjoy our beautiful family life, we, the cat-race, must engage in total war upon all humans. We have no choice but to exterminate them. I think it is a very reasonable proposition. And the three-colored tomcat living next door is especially indignant that human beings do not understand the nature of proprietary rights. Among our kind it is taken for granted that he who first finds something, be it the head of a dried sardine or a gray mullet's navel, acquires thereby the right to eat it. And if this rule be flouted, one may well resort to violence. But human beings do not seem to understand the rights of property. Every time we come on something good to eat, invariably they descend and take it from us. Relying on their naked strength, they coolly rob us of things which are rightly ours to eat. Miss Blanche lives in the house of a military man, and the tomcat's master is a lawyer. But since I live in a teacher's house, I take matters of this sort rather more lightly than they. I feel that life is not unreasonable so long as one can scrape along from day to day. For surely even human beings will not flourish forever. I think it best to wait in patience for the Day of the Cats.

Talking of selfishness reminds me that my master once made a fool of himself by reason of this failing. I'll tell you all about it. First you must understand that this master of mine lacks the talent to be more than average at anything at all; but nonetheless he can't refrain from trying his hand at everything and anything. He's always writing *haiku* and submitting them to *Cuckoo*; he sends off new-style poetry to *Morning Star*; he has a shot at English prose peppered with gross mistakes; he develops a passion for archery; he takes lessons in chanting *No* play-texts; and sometimes he devotes himself to making hideous noises with a violin. But I am sorry to say that none of these activities has led to anything whatsoever. Yet, though he is dyspeptic, he gets terribly keen once he has embarked upon a project. He once got himself nicknamed "The Maestro of the Water-closet" through chanting in the lavatory, but he remains entirely unconcerned and can still be heard there chanting "I am Taira-no-Munemori." We all say, "There goes Munemori," and titter at his antics. I do not know why it happened, but one fine day (a payday roughly four weeks after I'd taken up residence) this master of mine came hurrying home with a large parcel under his arm. I wondered what he'd bought. It turned out that he'd purchased watercolor paints, brushes, and some special "Whatman" paper. It looked to me as if *haiku*-writing, and mediaeval chanting were going to be abandoned in favor of watercolor painting. Sure enough, from the next day on and every day for some long time, he did nothing but paint pictures in his study. He even went without his afternoon siestas. However, no one could tell what he had painted by looking at the result. Possibly he himself thought little of his work; for, one day when his friend who specializes in matters of aesthetics came to visit him, I heard the following conversation.

"Do you know it's quite difficult? When one sees someone else painting, it looks easy enough; but not till one takes a brush oneself, does one realize just how difficult it is." So said my noble master, and it was true enough.

His friend, looking at my master over his gold-rimmed spectacles, observed, "It's only natural that one cannot paint particularly well the moment one starts. Besides, one cannot paint a picture indoors by force of the imagination only. The Italian Master, Andrea del Sarto, remarked that if you want to paint a picture, always depict nature as she is. In the sky, there are stars. On earth, there are sparkling dews. Birds are flying. Animals are running. In a pond there are goldfish. On an old tree one sees winter crows. Nature herself is one vast living picture. D'you understand? If you want to paint a picturesque picture, why not try some preliminary sketching?"

"Oh, so Andrea del Sarto said that? I didn't know that at all. Come to think of it, it's quite true. Indeed, it's very true."The master was unduly impressed. I saw a mocking smile behind the gold-rimmed glasses.

The next day when, as always, I was having a pleasant nap on the veranda, the master emerged from his study (an act unusual in itself) and began behind my back to busy himself with something. At this point I happened to wake up and, wondering what he was up to, opened my eyes just one slit the tenth of an inch. And there he was, fairly killing himself at being Andrea del Sarto. I could not help but laugh. He's starting to sketch me just because he's had his leg pulled by a friend. I have already slept enough, and I'm itching to yawn. But seeing my master sketching away so earnestly, I hadn't the heart to move: so I bore it all with resignation. Having drawn my outline, he's started painting the face. I confess that, considering cats as works of art, I'm far from being a collector's piece. I certainly do not think that my figure, my fur, or my features are superior to those of other cats. But however ugly I may be, there's no conceivable resemblance between myself and that queer thing which my master is creating. First of all, the coloring is wrong. My fur, like that of a Persian, bears tortoiseshell markings on a ground of a yellowish pale grey. It is a fact beyond all argument. Yet the color which my master has employed is neither yellow nor black; neither grey nor brown; nor is it any mixture of those four distinctive colors. All one can say is that the color used is a sort of color. Furthermore, and very oddly, my face lacks eyes. The lack might be excused on the grounds that the sketch is a sketch of a sleeping cat; but, all the same, since one cannot find even a hint of an eye's location, it is not all clear whether the sketch is of a sleeping cat or of a blind cat. Secretly I thought to myself that this would never do, even for Andrea del Sarto. However, I could not help being struck with admiration for my master's grim determination. Had it been solely up to me, I would gladly have maintained my pose for him, but Nature has now been calling for some time. The muscles in my body are getting pins and needles. When the tingling reached a point where I couldn't stand it another minute, I was obliged to claim my liberty. I stretched my front paws far out in front of me, pushed my neck out low and yawned cavernously. Having done all that, there's no further point in trying to stay still. My master's sketch is spoilt anyway, so I might as well pad round to the backyard and do my business. Moved by these thoughts, I start to crawl sluggishly away. Immediately, "You fool" came shouted in my master's voice, a mixture of wrath and disappointment, out of the inner room. He has a fixed habit of saying, "You fool" whenever he curses anyone. He cannot help it since he knows no other swear words. But I thought it rather impertinent of him thus unjustifiably to call me "a fool." After all, I had been very patient up to this point. Of course, had it been his custom to show even the smallest pleasure whenever I jump on his back, I would have tamely endured his imprecations: but it is a bit thick to be called "a fool" by someone who has never once with good grace done me a kindness just because I get up to go and urinate. The prime fact is that all humans are puffed up by their extreme self-satisfaction with their own brute power. Unless some creatures more powerful than humans arrive on earth to bully them, there's just no knowing to what dire lengths their fool presumptuousness will eventually carry them.

One could put up with this degree of selfishness, but I once heard a report concerning the unworthiness of humans, which is several times more ugly and deplorable.

At the back of my house there is a small tea-plantation, perhaps some six yards square. Though certainly not large, it is a neat and pleasantly sunny spot. It is my custom to go there whenever my morale needs strengthening; when, for instance, the children are making so much noise that I cannot doze in peace, or when boredom has disrupted my digestion. One day, a day of Indian summer, at about two o'clock in the afternoon, I woke from a pleasant after-luncheon nap and strolled out to this tea-plantation by way of taking exercise. Sniffing, one after another, at the roots of the tea plants, I came to the cypress fence at the western end; and there I saw an enormous cat fast asleep on a bed of withered chrysanthemums, which his weight had flattened down. He did not seem to notice my approach. Perhaps he noticed but did not care. Anyway, there he was, stretched out at full length and snoring loudly. I was amazed at the daring courage that permitted him, a trespasser, to sleep so unconcernedly in someone else's garden. He was a pure black cat. The sun of earliest afternoon was pouring its most brilliant rays upon him, and it seemed as if invisible flames were blazing out from his glossy fur. He had a magnificent physique; the physique, one might say, of the Emperor of Catdom. He was easily twice my size. Filled with admiration and curiosity, I quite forgot myself. I stood stock-still, entranced, all eyes in front of him. The quiet zephyrs of that Indian summer set gently nodding a branch of Sultan's Parasol, which showed above the cypress fence, and a few leaves pattered down upon the couch of crushed chrysanthemums. The Emperor suddenly opened his huge round eyes. I remember that moment to this day. His eyes gleamed far more beautifully than that dull amber stuff which humans so inordinately value. He lay dead still. Focussing the piercing light that shone from his eyes' interior upon my dwarfish forehead, he remarked, "And who the hell are you?"

I thought his turn of phrase a shade inelegant for an Emperor, but because the voice was deep and filled with a power that could suppress a bulldog. I remained dumb-struck with pure awe. Reflecting, however, that I might get into trouble if I failed to exchange civilities, I answered frigidly, with a false *sang froid* as cold as I could make it, "I, sir, am a cat. I have as yet no name." My heart at that moment was beating a great deal faster than usual.

In a tone of enormous scorn, the Emperor observed, "You. . . a cat? Well, I'm damned. Anyway, where the devil do you hang out?" I thought this cat excessively blunt-spoken.

"I live here, in the teacher's house."

"Huh, I thought as much. 'Orrible scrawny aren't you." Like a true Emperor, he spoke with great vehemence.

Judged by his manner of speech, he could not be a cat of respectable background. On the other hand, he seemed well fed and positively prosperous, almost obese, in his oily glossiness. I had to ask him "And you, who on earth are you?"

"Me? I'm Rickshaw Blacky." He gave his answer with spirit and some pride: for Rickshaw Blacky is well-known in the neighborhood as a real rough customer. As one would expect of those brought up in a rickshaw-garage, he's tough but quite uneducated. Hence very few of us mix with him, and it is our common policy to "keep him at a respectful distance." Consequently when I heard his name, I felt a trifle jittery and uneasy but at the same time a little disdainful of him. Accordingly, and in order to establish just how illiterate he was, I pursued the conversation by enquiring, "Which do you think is superior, a rickshaw-owner or a teacher?"

"Why, a rickshaw-owner, of course. He's the stronger. Just look at your master, almost skin and bones."

"You, being the cat of a rickshaw-owner, naturally look very tough. I can see that one eats well at your establishment."

"Ah well, as far as I'm concerned, I never want for decent grub wherever I go. You too, instead of creeping around in a tea-plantation, why not follow along with me? Within a month, you'd get so fat nobody'd recognize you."

"In due course I might come and ask to join you. But it seems that the teacher's house is larger than your boss's."

"You dimwit! A house, however big it is, won't help fill an empty belly." He looked quite huffed. Savagely twitching his ears, ears as sharp as slant-sliced stems of the solid bamboo, he took off rowdily.

This was how I first made the acquaintance of Rickshaw Blacky, and since that day I've run across him many times. Whenever we meet he talks big, as might be expected from a rickshaw-owner's cat; but that deplorable incident which I mentioned earlier was a tale he told me.

One day Blacky and I were lying as usual, sunning ourselves in the tea-garden. We were chatting about this and that when, having made his usual boasts as if they were all brandnew, he asked me, "How many rats have you caught so far?"

While I flatter myself that my general knowledge is wider and deeper than Blacky's, I readily admit that my physical strength and courage are nothing compared with his. All the same, his point-blank question naturally left me feeling a bit confused. Nevertheless, a fact's a fact, and one should face the truth. So I answered "Actually, though I'm always thinking of catching one, I've never yet caught any."

Blacky laughed immoderately, quivering the long whiskers, which stuck out stiffly round his muzzle. Blacky, like all true braggarts, is somewhat weak in the head. As long as you purr and listen attentively, pretending to be impressed by his rhodomontade, he is a more or less manageable cat. Soon after getting to know him, I learnt this way to handle him. Consequently on this particular occasion I also thought it would be unwise to further weaken my position by trying to defend myself, and that it would be more prudent to dodge the issue by inducing him to brag about his own successes. So without making a fuss, I sought to lead him on by saying, "You, judging by your age, must have caught a notable number of rats?" Sure enough, he swallowed the bait with gusto.

"Well, not too many, but I must've caught thirty or forty," was his triumphant answer. "I can cope," he went on, "with a hundred or two hundred rats, any time and by myself. But a weasel, no. That I just can't take. Once I had a hellish time with a weasel."

"Did you really?" I innocently offered. Blacky blinked his saucer eyes but did not discontinue.

"It was last year, the day for the general housecleaning. As my master was crawling in under the floorboards with a bag of lime, suddenly a great, dirty weasel came whizzing out."

"Really?" I make myself look impressed.

"I say to myself, 'So what's a weasel? Only a wee bit bigger than a rat.' So I chase after it, feeling quite excited and finally I got it cornered in a ditch."

"That was well done," I applaud him.

"Not in the least. As a last resort it upped its tail and blew a filthy fart. Ugh! The smell of it! Since that time, whenever I see a weasel, I feel poorly." At this point, he raised a front paw and stroked his muzzle two or three times as if he were still suffering from last year's stench.

I felt rather sorry for him and, in an effort to cheer him up, said, "But when it comes to rats, I expect you just pin them down with one hypnotic glare. And I suppose that it's because you're such a marvelous ratter, a cat well nourished by plenty of rats, that you are so splendidly fat and have such a good complexion." Though this speech was meant to flatter Blacky, strangely enough it had precisely the opposite effect. He looked distinctly cast down and replied with a heavy sigh.

"It's depressing," he said, "when you come to think of it. However hard one slaves at catching rats. . . In the whole wide world there's no creature more brazen-faced than a human being. Every rat I catch they confiscate, and they tote them off to the nearest police-box. Since the copper can't tell who caught the rats, he just pays up a penny a tail to anyone that brings them in. My master, for instance, has already earned about half a crown purely through my efforts, but he's never yet stood me a decent meal. The plain fact is that humans, one and all, are merely thieves at heart."

Though Blacky's far from bright, one cannot fault him in this conclusion. He begins to look extremely angry and the fur on his back stands up in bristles. Somewhat disturbed by Blacky's story and reactions, I made some vague excuse and went off home. But ever since then I've been determined never to catch a rat. However, I did not take up Blacky's invitation to become his associate in prowling after dainties other than rodents. I prefer the cozy life, and it's certainly easier to sleep than to hunt for titbits. Living in a teacher's house, it seems that even a cat acquires the character of teachers. I'd best watch out lest, one of these days, I, too, become dyspeptic.

Talking of teachers reminds me that my master seems to have recently realized his total incapacity as a painter of watercolors; for under the date of December 1st his diary contains the following passage:

> At today's gathering I met for the first time a man who shall be nameless. He is said to have led a fast life. Indeed he looks very much a man of the world. Since women like this type of person, it might be more appropriate to say that he has been forced to lead, rather than that he has led, a fast life. I hear his wife was originally a geisha. He is to be envied. For the most part, those who carp at rakes are those incapable of debauchery. Further, many of those who fancy themselves as rakehells are equally incapable of debauchery. Such folk are under no obligation to live fast lives, but do so of their own volition. So I in the matter of watercolors. Neither of us will ever make the grade. And yet this type of debauchee is calmly certain that only he is truly a man of the world. If it is to be accepted that a man can become a man of the world by drinking *saké* in restaurants, or by frequenting houses of assignation, then it would seem to follow that I could acquire a name as a painter of watercolors. The notion that my watercolor pictures will be better if I don't actually paint them leads me to conclude that a boorish country-bumpkin is in fact far superior to such foolish men of the world.

His observations about men of the world strike me as somewhat unconvincing. In particular his confession of envy in respect of that wife who'd worked as a geisha is positively imbecile and unworthy of a teacher. Nevertheless his assessment of the value of his own watercolor painting is certainly just. Indeed my master is a very good judge of his own character but still manages to retain his vanity. Three days later, on December 4th, he wrote in his diary:

> Last night I dreamt that someone picked up one of my watercolor paintings which I, thinking it worthless, had tossed aside. This person in my dream put the painting in a splendid frame and hung it up on a transom. Staring at my work thus framed, I realized that I have suddenly become a true artist. I feel exceedingly pleased. I spend whole days just staring at my handiwork, happy in the conviction that the picture is a masterpiece. Dawn broke and I woke up, and in the morning sunlight it was obvious that the picture was still as pitiful an object as when I painted it.

The master, even in his dreams, seems burdened with regrets about his watercolors. And men who accept the burdens of regret, whether in respect of watercolors or of anything else, are not the stuff that men of the world are made of.

The day after my master dreamt about the picture, the aesthete in the gold-rimmed spectacles paid a call upon him. He had not visited for some long time. As soon as he was seated he inquired, "And how is the painting coming along?"

My master assumed a nonchalant air and answered, "Well, I took your advice and I am now busily engaged in sketching. And I must say that when one sketches one seems to apprehend those shapes of things, those delicate changes of color, which hitherto had gone unnoticed. I take it that sketching has developed in the West to its present remarkable condition solely as the result of the emphasis which, historically, has always there been placed upon the essentiality thereof. Precisely as Andrea del Sarto once observed." Without even so much as alluding to the passage in his diary, he speaks approvingly of Andrea del Sarto.

The aesthete scratched his head, and remarked with a laugh, "Well actually that bit about del Sarto was my own invention."

"What was?" My master still fails to grasp that he's been tricked into making a fool of himself.

"Why, all that stuff about Andrea del Sarto whom you so particularly admire, I made it all up. I never thought you'd take it seriously." He laughed and laughed, enraptured with the situation.

I overheard their conversation from my place on the veranda and I could not help wondering what sort of entry would appear in the diary for today. This aesthete is the sort of man whose sole pleasure lies in bamboozling people by conversation consisting entirely of humbug. He seems not to have thought of the effect his twaddle about Andrea del Sarto must have on my master's feelings, for he rattled on proudly, "Sometimes I cook up a little nonsense and people take it seriously, which generates an aesthetic sensation of extreme comicality which I find interesting. The other day, I told a certain undergraduate that Nicholas Nickleby had advised Gibbon to cease using French for the writing of his masterpiece, *The History of the French Revolution*, and had indeed persuaded Gibbon to publish it in English. Now this undergraduate was a man of almost eidetic memory, and it was especially amusing to hear him repeating what I told him, word for word and in all seriousness, to a debating session of the Japan Literary Society. And d'you know, there were nearly a hundred in his audience, and all of them sat listening to his drivel with the greatest enthusiasm! In fact, I've another, even better, story. The other day, when I was in the company of some men of letters, one of them happened to mention *Theofano*, Ainsworth's historical novel of the Crusades. I took the occasion to remark that it was a quite outstanding romantic monograph and added the comment that the account of the heroine's death was the epitome of the spectral. The man sitting opposite to me, one who has never uttered the three words 'I don't know,' promptly responded that those particular paragraphs were indeed especially fine writing. From which observation I became aware that he, no more than I, had ever read the book."

Wide-eyed, my poor dyspeptic master asked him, "Fair enough, but what would you do if the other party had in fact read the book?" It appears that my master is not worried about the dishonesty of the deception, merely about the possible embarrassment of being caught out in a lie. The question leaves the aesthete utterly unfazed.

"Well, if that should happen, I'd say I'd mistaken the title or something like that," and again, quite unconcerned, he gave himself to laughter.

Though nattily tricked out in gold-rimmed spectacles, his nature is uncommonly akin to that of Rickshaw Blacky. My master said nothing, but blew out smoke rings as if in confession of his own lack of such audacity. The aesthete (the glitter of whose eyes seemed to be answering, "and no wonder; you, being you, could not even cope with watercolors") went on aloud. "But, joking apart, painting a picture's a difficult thing. Leonardo da Vinci is supposed to have once told his pupils to make drawings of a stain on the Cathedral wall. The words of a great teacher. In a lavatory for instance, if absorbedly one studies the pattern of the rain leaks on the wall, a staggering design, a natural creation, invariably emerges. You should keep your eyes open and try drawing from nature. I'm sure you could make something interesting."

"Is this another of your tricks?"

"No; this one, I promise, is seriously meant. Indeed, I think that that image of the lavatory wall is really rather witty, don't you? Quite the sort of thing da Vinci would have said."

"Yes, it's certainly witty," my master somewhat reluctantly conceded. But I do not think he has so far made a drawing in a lavatory.

Rickshaw Blacky has recently gone lame. His glossy fur has thinned and gradually grown dull. His eyes, which I once praised as more beautiful than amber, are now bleared with mucus. What I notice most is his loss of all vitality and his sheer physical deterioration. When last I saw him in the tea garden and asked him how he was, the answer was depressingly precise: "I've had enough of being farted at by weasels and crippled with side-swipes from the fishmonger's pole."

The autumn leaves, arranged in two or three scarlet terraces among the pine trees, have fallen like ancient dreams. The red and white sasanquas near the garden's ornamental basin, dropping their petals, now a white and now a red one, are finally left bare. The wintry sun along the ten-foot length of the southwards-facing veranda goes down daily earlier than yesterday. Seldom a day goes by but a cold wind blows. So my snoozes have been painfully curtailed.

The master goes to school every day and, as soon as he returns, shuts himself up in the study. He tells all visitors that he's tired of being a teacher. He seldom paints. He's stopped taking his taka-diastase, saying it does no good. The children, dear little things, now trot off, day after day, to kindergarten: but on their return, they sing songs, bounce balls and sometimes hang me up by the tail.

Since I do not receive any particularly nourishing food, I have not grown particularly fat; but I struggle on from day to day keeping myself more or less fit and, so far, without getting crippled. I catch no rats. I still detest that O-san. No one has yet named me but, since it's no use crying for the moon, I have resolved to remain for the rest of my life a nameless cat in the house of this teacher.

II

SINCE New Year's Day I have acquired a certain modest celebrity: so that, though only a cat, I am feeling quietly proud of myself. Which is not unpleasing.

On the morning of New Year's Day, my master received a picture-postcard, a card of New Year greetings from a certain painter-friend of his. The upper part was painted red, the lower deep green; and right in the center was a crouching animal painted in pastel. The master, sitting in his study, looked at this picture first one way up and then the other. "What fine coloring!" he observed. Having thus expressed his admiration, I thought he had finished with the matter. But no, he continued studying it, first sideways and then longways. In order to examine the object he twists his body, then stretches out his arms like an ancient studying the *Book of Divinations* and then, turning to face the window, he brings it in to the tip of his nose. I wish he would soon terminate this curious performance, for the action sets his knees asway and I find it hard to keep my balance. When at long last the wobbling began to diminish, I heard him mutter in a tiny voice, "I wonder what it is." Though full of admiration for the colors on the picture-postcard, he couldn't identify the animal painted in its center. Which explained his extraordinary antics. Could it perhaps really be a picture more difficult to interpret than my own first glance had suggested? I half-opened my eyes and looked at the painting with an imperturbable calmness. There could be no shadow of a doubt: it was a portrait of myself. I do not suppose that the painter considered himself an Andrea del Sarto, as did my master; but, being a painter, what he had painted, both in respect of form and of color, was perfectly harmonious. Any fool could see it was a cat. And so skillfully painted that anyone with eyes in his head and the mangiest scrap of discernment would immediately recognize that it was a picture of no other cat but me. To think that anyone should need to go to such painful lengths over such a blatantly simple matter. . . I felt a little sorry for the human race. I would have liked to have let him know that the picture is of me. Even if it were too difficult for him to grasp that particularity, I would still have liked to help him see that the painting is of a cat. But since heaven has not seen fit to dower the human animal with an ability to understand cat language, I regret to say that I let the matter be.

Incidentally, I would like to take the occasion of this incident to advise my readers that the human habit of referring to me in a scornful tone of voice as some mere trifling "cat" is an extremely bad one. Humans appear to think that cows and horses are constructed from rejected human material, and that cats are constructed from cow pats and horse dung. Such thoughts, objectively regarded, are in very poor taste though they are no doubt not uncommon among teachers who, ignorant even of their ignorance, remain self-satisfied with their quaint puffed-up ideas of their own unreal importance. Even cats must not be treated roughly or taken for granted. To the casual observer it may appear that all cats are the same, facsimiles in form and substance, as indistinguishable as peas in a pod; and that no cat can lay claim to individuality. But once admitted to feline society, that casual observer would very quickly realize that things are not so simple, and that the human saying that "people are freaks" is equally true in the world of cats. Our eyes, noses, fur, paws—all of them differ. From the tilt of one's whiskers to the set of one's ears, down to the very hang of one's tail, we cats are sharply differentiated. In our good looks and our poor looks, in our likes and dislikes, in our refinement and our coarsenesses, one may fairly say that cats occur in infinite variety. Despite the fact of such obvious differentiation, humans, their eyes turned up to heaven by reason of the elevation of their minds or some such other rubbish, fail to notice even obvious differences in our external features, that our characters might be characteristic is beyond their comprehension. Which is to be pitied. I understand and endorse the thought behind such sayings as, the cobbler should stick to his last, that birds of a feather flock together, that rice-cakes are for rice-cake makers. For cats, indeed, are for cats. And should you wish to learn about cats, only a cat can tell you. Humans, however advanced, can tell you nothing on this subject. And inasmuch as humans are, in fact, far less advanced than they fancy themselves, they will find it difficult even to start learning about cats. And for an unsympathetic man like my master there's really no hope at all. He does not even understand that love can never grow unless there is at least a complete and mutual understanding. Like an ill-natured oyster, he secretes himself in his study and has never once opened his mouth to the outside world. And to see him there, looking as though he alone has truly attained enlightenment, is enough to make a cat laugh. The proof that he has not attained enlightenment is that, although he has my portrait under his nose, he shows no sign of comprehension but coolly offers such crazy comment as, "perhaps, this being the second year of the war against the Russians, it is a painting of a bear."

As, with my eyes closed, I sat thinking these thoughts on my master's knees, the servant-woman brought in a second picture-postcard. It is a printed picture of a line of four or five European cats all engaged in study, holding pens or reading books. One has broken away from the line to perform a simple Western dance at the corner of their common desk. Above this picture "I am a cat" is written thickly in Japanese black ink. And down the right-hand side there is even a *haiku* stating that "on spring days cats read books or dance." The card is from one of the master's old pupils and its meaning should be obvious to anyone. However my dim-witted master seems not to understand, for he looked puzzled and said to himself, "Can this be a Year of the Cat?" He just doesn't seem to have grasped that these postcards are manifestations of my growing fame.

At that moment the servant brought in yet a third postcard. This time the postcard has no picture, but alongside the characters wishing my master a happy New Year, the correspondent has added those for, "Please be so kind as to give my best regards to the cat." Bone-headed though he is, my master does appear to get the message when it's written out thus unequivocally: for he glanced down at my face and, as if he really had at last comprehended the situation, said, "hmm." And his glance, unlike his usual ones, did seem to contain a new modicum of respect. Which was quite right and proper considering the fact that it is entirely due to me that my master, hitherto a nobody, has suddenly begun to get a name and to attract attention.

Just then the gate-bell sounded: tinkle-tinkle, possibly even ting-ting. Probably a visitor. If so, the servant will answer. Since I never go out of my way to investigate callers, except the fishmonger's errand-boy, I remained quietly on my master's knees. The master, however, peered worriedly toward the entrance as if duns were at the door. I deduce that he just doesn't like receiving New Year's callers and sharing a convivial tot. What a marvellous way to be. How much further can pure bigotry go? If he doesn't like visitors, he should have gone out himself, but he lacks even that much enterprise. The inaudacity of his clam-like character grows daily more apparent. A few moments later the servant comes in to say that Mr. Coldmoon has called. I understand that this Coldmoon person was also once a pupil of my master's and that, after leaving school, he so rose in the world to be far better known than his teacher. I don't know why, but this fellow often comes round for a chat. On every such visit he babbles on, with a dreadful sort of coquettishness, about being in love or not in love with somebody or other; about how much he enjoys life or how desperately he is tired of it. And then he leaves. It is quaint enough that to discuss such matters he should seek the company of a withered old nut like my master, but it's quainter still to see my mollusk opening up to comment, now and again, on Coldmoon's mawkish maunderings.

"I'm afraid I haven't been round for quite some time. Actually, I've been as busy as, busy since the end of last year, and, though I've thought of going out often enough, somehow shanks' pony has just not headed here." Thus, twisting and untwisting the fastening-strings of his short surcoat, Coldmoon babbled on.

"Where then did shanks' pony go?" my master enquired with a serious look as he tugged at the cuffs of his worn, black, crested surcoat. It is a cotton garment unduly short in the sleeves, and some of its nondescript, thin, silk lining sticks out about a half an inch at the cuffs.

"As it were in various directions," Coldmoon answered, and then laughed. I notice that one of his front teeth is missing.

"What's happened to your teeth?" asks my master, changing the subject.

"Well, actually, at a certain place I ate mushrooms."

"What did you say you ate?"

"A bit of mushroom. As I tried to bite off a mushroom's umbrella with my front teeth, a tooth just broke off."

"Breaking teeth on a mushroom sounds somewhat senile. An image possibly appropriate to a *haiku* but scarcely appropriate to the pursuit of love," remarked my master as he tapped lightly on my head with the palm of his hand.

"Ah! Is that *the* cat? But he's quite plump! Sturdy as that, not even Rickshaw Blacky could beat him up. He certainly is a most splendid beast." Coldmoon offers me his homage.

"He's grown quite big lately," responds my master, and proudly smacks me twice upon the head. I am flattered by the compliment but my head feels slightly sore.

"The night before last, what's more, we had a little concert," said Coldmoon going back to his story.

"Where?"

"Surely you don't have to know where. But it was quite interesting, three violins to a piano accompaniment. However unskilled, when there are three of them, violins sound fairly good. Two of them were women and I managed to place myself between them. And I myself, I thought, played rather well."

"Ah, and who were the women?" enviously my master asks. At first glance my master usually looks cold and hard; but, to tell the truth, he is by no means indifferent to women. He once read in a Western novel of a man who invariably fell partially in love with practically every woman that he met. Another character in the book somewhat sarcastically observed that, as a rough calculation, that fellow fell in love with just under seven-tenths of the women he passed in the street. On reading this, my master was struck by its essential truth and remained deeply impressed. Why should a man so impressionable lead such an oysterish existence? A mere cat such as I cannot possibly understand it. Some say it is the result of a love affair that went wrong; some say it is due to his weak stomach; while others simply state that it's because he lacks both money and audacity. Whatever the truth, it doesn't much matter since he's a person of insufficient importance to affect the history of his period. What is certain is that he did enquire enviously about Coldmoon's female fiddlers. Coldmoon, looking amused, picked up a sliver of boiled fishpaste in his chopsticks and nipped at it with his remaining front teeth. I was worried lest another should fall out. But this time it was all right.

"Well, both of them are daughters of good families. You don't know them," Coldmoon coldly answered.

The master drawled "Is—th-a-t—," but omitted the final "so" which he'd intended.

Coldmoon probably considered it was about time to be off, for he said, "What marvellous weather. If you've nothing better to do, shall we go out for a walk? As a result of the fall of Port Arthur," he added encouragingly, "the town's unusually lively."

My master, looking as though he would sooner discuss the identity of the female fiddlers than the fall of Port Arthur, hesitated for a moment's thought. But he seemed finally to reach a decision, for he stood up resolutely and said, "All right, let's go out." He continues to wear his black cotton crested surcoat and, thereunder, a quilted kimono of hand-woven silk which, supposedly a keep-sake of his elder brother, he has worn continuously for twenty years. Even the most strongly woven silk, cannot survive such unremitting, such preternaturally, perennial wear. The material has been worn so thin that, held against the light, one can see the patches sewn on here and there from the inner side. My master wears the same clothes throughout December and January, not bothering to observe the traditional New Year change. He makes, indeed, no distinction between workaday and Sunday clothes. When he leaves the house he saunters out in whatever dress he happens to have on. I do not know whether this is because he has no other clothes to wear or whether, having such clothes, he finds it too much of a bore to change into them. Whatever the case, I can't conceive that these uncouth habits are in any way connected with disappointment in love.

After the two men left, I took the liberty of eating such of the boiled fishpaste as Coldmoon had not already devoured. I am, these days, no longer just a common, old cat. I consider myself at least as good as those celebrated in the tales of Momokawa Joen or as that cat of Thomas Gray's, which trawled for goldfish. Brawlers such as Rickshaw Blacky are now beneath my notice. I don't suppose anyone will make a fuss if I sneak a bit of fishpaste. Besides, this habit of taking secret snacks between meals is by no means a purely feline custom. O-san, for instance, is always pinching cakes and things, which she gobbles down whenever the mistress leaves the house. Nor is O-san the only offender: even the children, of whose refined upbringing the mistress is continually bragging, display the selfsame tendency. Only a few days ago that precious pair woke at some ungodly hour, and, though their parents were still sound asleep, took it upon themselves to sit down, face-to-face, at the dining-table. Now it is my master's habit every morning to consume most of a loaf of bread, and to give the children scraps thereof which they eat with a dusting of sugar. It so happened that on this day the sugar basin was already on the table, even a spoon stuck in it. Since there was no one there to dole them out their sugar, the elder child scooped up a spoonful and dumped it on her plate. The younger followed her elder's fine example and spooned an equal pile of sugar onto another plate. For a brief while these charming creatures just sat and glared at each other. Then the elder girl scooped a second spoonful onto her plate, and the younger one proceeded to equalize the position. The elder sister took a third spoonful and the younger, in a splendid spirit of rivalry, followed suit. And so it went on until both plates were piled high with sugar and not one single grain remained in the basin. My master thereupon emerged from his bedroom rubbing half-sleepy eyes and proceeded to return the sugar, so laboriously extracted by his daughters, back into the sugar-basin. This incident suggests that, though egotistical egalitarianism may be more highly developed among humans than among cats, cats are the wiser creatures. My advice to the children would have been to lick the sugar up quickly before it became massed into such senseless pyramids, but, because they cannot understand what I say, I merely watched them in silence from my warm, morning place on top of the container for boiled rice.

My master came home late last night from his expedition with Coldmoon. God knows where he went, but it was already past nine before he sat down at the breakfast table. From my same old place I watched his morose consumption of a typical New Year's breakfast of rice-cakes boiled with vegetables, all served up in soup. He takes endless helpings. Though the rice-cakes are admittedly small, he must have eaten some six or seven before leaving the last one floating in the bowl. "I'll stop now," he remarked and laid his chopsticks down. Should anyone else behave in such a spoilt manner, he could be relied upon to put his foot down: but, vain in the exercise of his petty authority as master of the house, he seems quite unconcerned by the sight of the corpse of a scorched rice-cake drowning in turbid soup. When his wife took taka-diastase from the back of a small cupboard and put it on the table, my master said, "I won't take it, it does me no good."

"But they say it's very good after eating starchy things. I think you should take some." His wife wants him to take it.

"Starchy or not, the stuff's no good." He remains stubborn.

"Really, you are a most capricious man," the mistress mutters as though to herself.

"I'm not capricious, the medicine doesn't work."

"But until the other day you used to say it worked very well and you used to take it every day, didn't you?"

"Yes, it did work until that other day, but it hasn't worked since then," an antithetical answer.

"If you continue in these inconsistencies, taking it one day and stopping it the next, however efficacious the medicine may be, it will never do you any good. Unless you try to be a little more patient, dyspepsia, unlike other illnesses, won't get cured, will it?" and she turns to O-san who was serving at the table.

"Quite so, madam. Unless one takes it regularly, one cannot find out whether a medicine is a good one or a bad one." O-san readily sides with the mistress.

"I don't care. I don't take it because I don't take it. How can a mere woman understand such things? Keep quiet."

"All right. I'm merely a woman," she says pushing the taka-diastase toward him, quite determined to make him see he is beaten. My master stands up without saying a word and goes off into his study. His wife and servant exchange looks and giggle. If on such occasions I follow him and jump up onto his knees, experience tells me that I shall pay dearly for my folly. Accordingly, I go quietly round through the garden and hop up onto the veranda outside his study. I peeped through the slit between the paper sliding doors and found my master examining a book by somebody called Epictetus. If he could actually understand what he's reading, then he would indeed be worthy of praise. But within five or six minutes he slams the book down on the table, which is just what I'd suspected. As I sat there watching him, he took out his diary and made the following entry.

> Took a stroll with Coldmoon round Nezu, Ueno, Ikenohata and Kanda. At Ikenohata, geishas in formal spring kimono were playing battledore and shuttlecock in front of a house of assignation. Their clothes beautiful, but their faces extremely plain. It occurs to me that they resemble the cat at home.

I don't see why he should single me out as an example of plain features. If I went to a barber and had my face shaved, I wouldn't look much different from a human. But, there you are, humans are conceited and that's the trouble with them.

> As we turned at Hotan's corner another geisha appeared. She was slim, well-shaped and her shoulders were most beautifully sloped. The way she wore her mauve kimono gave her a genuine elegance. "Sorry about last night, Gen-chan—I was so busy. . ." She laughed and one glimpsed white teeth. Her voice was so harsh, as harsh as that of

> a roving crow, that her otherwise fine appearance diminished in enchantment. So much so that I didn't even bother to turn around to see what sort of person this Gen-chan was, but sauntered on toward Onarimachi with my hands tucked inside the breast-fold of my kimono. Coldmoon, however, seemed to have become a trifle fidgety.

There is nothing more difficult than understanding human mentality. My master's present mental state is very far from clear; is he feeling angry or lighthearted, or simply seeking solace in the scribblings of some dead philosopher? One just can't tell whether he's mocking the world or yearning to be accepted into its frivolous company; whether he is getting furious over some piddling little matter or holding himself aloof from worldly things. Compared with such complexities, cats are truly simple. If we want to eat, we eat; if we want to sleep, we sleep; when we are angry, we are angry utterly; when we cry, we cry with all the desperation of extreme commitment to our grief. Thus we never keep things like diaries. For what would be the point? No doubt human beings like my two-faced master find it necessary to keep diaries in order to display in a darkened room that true character so assiduously hidden from the world. But among cats both our four main occupations (walking, standing, sitting, and lying down) and such incidental activities as excreting waste are pursued quite openly. We live our diaries, and consequently have no need to keep a daily record as a means of maintaining our real characters. Had I the time to keep a diary, I'd use that time to better effect; sleeping on the veranda.

> We dined somewhere in Kanda. Because I allowed myself one or two cups of *saké* (which I had not tasted for quite a time), my stomach this morning feels extremely well. I conclude that the best remedy for a stomach ailment is *saké* at suppertime. Taka-diastase just won't do. Whatever claims are made for it, it's just no good. That which lacks effect will continue to lack effect.

Thus with his brush he smears the good name of taka-diastase. It is as though he quarreled with himself, and in this entry one can see a last flash of this morning's ugly mood. Such entries are perhaps most characteristic of human mores.

The other day, Mr. X claimed that going without one's breakfast helped the stomach. So I took no breakfast for two or three days but the only effect was to make my stomach grumble. Mr. Y strongly advised me to refrain from eating pickles. According to him, all disorders of the stomach originate in pickles. His thesis was that abstinence from pickles so dessicates the sources of all stomach trouble, that a complete cure must follow. For at least a week no pickle crossed my lips, but, since that banishment produced no noticeable effect, I have resumed consuming them. According to Mr. Z, the one true remedy is ventral massage. But no ordinary massage of the stomach would suffice. It must be massage in accordance with the old-world methods of the Minagawa School. Massaged thus once, or at most twice, the stomach would be rid of every ill. The wisest scholars, such as Yasui Sokuken, and the most resourceful heroes, such as Sakamoto Ryoma, all relied upon this treatment. So off I went to Kaminegishi for an immediate massage. But the methods used were of inordinate cruelty. They told me, for instance, that no good could be hoped for unless one's bones were massaged; that it would be difficult properly to eradicate my troubles unless, at least once, my viscera were totally inverted. At all events, a single session reduced my body to the condition of cotton-wool and I felt as though I had become a lifelong sufferer from sleeping sickness. I never went there again. Once was more than enough. Then Mr. A assured me that one shouldn't eat solids. So I spent a whole day drinking nothing but milk. My bowels gave forth heavy plopping noises as though they had been swamped, and I could not sleep all night. Mr. B states that exercising one's intestines by diaphragmic breathing produces a naturally healthy stomach and he counsels me to follow his advice. And I did try. For a time. But it proved no good for it made my bowels queasy. Besides, though every now and again I strive with all my heart and soul to control my breathing with the diaphragm, in five or six minutes I forget to discipline my muscles. And if I concentrate on maintaining that discipline I get so midriff-minded that I can neither read nor write. Waverhouse, my aesthete friend, once found me thus breathing in pursuit of a naturally healthy stomach and, rather unkindly, urged me, as a man, to terminate my labor-pangs. So diaphragmic breathing is now also a thing of the past. Dr. C recommends a diet of buckwheat noodles. So buckwheat noodles it was, alternately in soup and served cold after boiling. It did nothing, except loosen my bowels. I have tried every possible means to cure my ancient ailment, but all of them are useless. But those three cups of *saké* which I drank last night with Coldmoon have certainly done some good. From now on, I will drink two or three cups each evening.

I doubt whether this *saké* treatment will be kept up very long. My master's mind exhibits the same incessant changeability as can be seen in the eyes of cats. He has no sense of perseverance. It is, moreover, idiotic that, while he fills his diary with lamentation over his stomach troubles, he does his best to present a brave face to the world; to grin and bear it. The other day his scholar friend, Professor Whatnot, paid a visit and advanced the theory that it was at least arguable that every illness is the direct result of both ancestral and personal malefaction. He seemed to have studied the matter pretty deeply for the sequence of his logic was clear, consistent, and orderly. Altogether it was a fine theory. I am sorry to say that my master has neither the brain nor the erudition to rebut such theories. However, perhaps because he himself was actually suffering from stomach trouble, he felt obliged to make all sorts of face-saving excuses. He irrelevantly retorted, "Your theory is interesting, but are you aware that Carlyle was dyspeptic?" as if claiming that because Carlyle was dyspeptic his own dyspepsia was an intellectual honor. His friend replied, "It does not follow that because Carlyle was a dyspeptic, all dyspeptics are Carlyles." My master, reprimanded, held his tongue, but the incident revealed his curious vanity. It's all the more amusing when one recalls that he would probably prefer not to be dyspeptic, for just this morning he recorded in his diary an intention to take treatment by *saké* as from tonight. Now that I've come to think of it, his inordinate consumption of rice-cakes this morning must have been the effect of last night's *saké* session with Coldmoon. I could have eaten those cakes myself.

Though I am a cat, I eat practically anything. Unlike Rickshaw Blacky, I lack the energy to go off raiding fishshops up distant alleys. Further, my social status is such that I cannot expect the luxury enjoyed by Tortoiseshell whose mistress teaches the idle rich to play on the two-stringed harp. Therefore I don't, as others can, indulge myself in likes and dislikes. I eat small bits of bread left over by the children, and I lick the jam from bean-jam cakes. Pickles taste awful, but to broaden my experience I once tried a couple of slices of pickled radish. It's a strange thing but once I've tried it, almost anything turns out edible. To say, "I don't like that" or "I don't like this" is mere extravagant willfulness, and a cat that lives in a teacher's house should eschew such foolish remarks. According to my master, there was once a novelist whose name was Balzac and he lived in France. He was an extremely extravagant man. I do not mean an extravagant eater but that, being a novelist, he was extravagant in his writing. One day he was trying to find a suitable name for a character in the novel he was writing, but, for whatever reason, could not think of a name that pleased him. Just then one of his friends called by, and Balzac suggested they should go out for a walk. This friend had, of course, no idea why, still less that Balzac was determined to find the name he needed. Out on the streets, Balzac did nothing but stare at shop signboards, but still he couldn't find a suitable name. He marched on endlessly, while his puzzled friend, still ignorant of the object of the expedition, tagged along behind him. Having fruitlessly explored Paris from morning till evening, they were on their way home when Balzac happened to notice a tailor's signboard bearing the name "Marcus." He clapped his hands. "This is it," he shouted. "It just has to be this. Marcus is a good name, but with a Z in front of Marcus it becomes a perfect name. It has to be a Z. Z. Marcus is remarkably good. Names that I invent are never good. They sound unnatural however cleverly constructed. But now, at long, long last, I've got the name I like." Balzac, extremely pleased with himself, was totally oblivious to the inconvenience he had caused his friend. It would seem unduly troublesome that one should have to spend a whole day trudging around Paris merely to find a name for a character in a novel. Extravagance of such enormity acquires a certain splendor, but folk like me, a cat kept by a clam-like introvert, cannot even envisage such inordinate behavior. That I should not much care what, so long as it's edible, I eat is probably an inevitable result of my circumstances. Thus it was in no way as an expression of extravagance that I expressed just now my feeling of wishing to eat a rice-cake. I simply thought that I'd better eat while the chance offered, and I then remembered that the piece of rice-cake which my master had left in his breakfast bowl was possibly still in the kitchen. So round to the kitchen I went.

The rice-cake was stuck, just as I saw it this morning, at the bottom of the bowl and its color was still as I remembered it. I must confess that I've never previously tasted rice-cake. Yet, though I felt a shade uncertain, it looks quite good to eat. With a tentative front paw I rake at the green vegetables adhering to the rice-cake. My claws, having touched the outer part of the rice-cake, become sticky. I sniff at them and recognize the smell that can be smelt when rice stuck at the bottom of a cooking-pot is transferred into the boiled-rice container. I look around, wondering, "Shall I eat it, shall I not?" Fortunately, or unfortunately, there's nobody about. O-san, with a face that shows no change between year end and the spring, is playing battledore and shuttlecock. The children in the inner room are singing something about a rabbit and a tortoise. If I am to eat this New Year speciality, now's the moment. If I miss this chance I shall have to spend a whole, long year not knowing how a rice-cake tastes. At this point, though a mere cat, I perceived a truth: that golden opportunity makes all animals venture to do even those things they do not want to do. To tell the truth, I do not particularly want to eat the rice-cake. In fact the more I examined the thing at the bottom of the bowl the more nervous I became and the more keenly disinclined to eat it. If only O-san would open the kitchen door, or if I could hear the children's footsteps coming toward me, I would unhesitatingly abandon the bowl; not only that, I would have put away all thought of rice-cakes for another year. But no one comes. I've hesitated long enough. Still no one comes. I feel as if someone were hotly urging me on, someone whispering, "Eat it, quickly!" I looked into the bowl and prayed that someone would appear. But no one did. I shall have to eat the rice-cake after all. In the end, lowering the entire weight of my body into the bottom of the bowl, I bit about an inch deep into a corner of the rice-cake.

Most things that I bite that hard come clean off in my mouth. But what a surprise! For I found when I tried to reopen my jaw that it would not budge. I try once again to bite my way free, but find I'm stuck. Too late I realize that the rice-cake is a fiend. When a man who has fallen into a marsh struggles to escape, the more he thrashes about trying to extract his legs, the deeper in he sinks. Just so, the harder I clamp my jaws, the more my mouth grows heavy and my teeth immobilized. I can feel the resistance to my teeth, but that's all. I cannot dispose of it. Waverhouse, the aesthete, once described my master as an aliquant man and I must say it's rather a good description. This rice-cake too, like my master, is aliquant. It looked to me that, however much I continued biting, nothing could ever result: the process could go on and on eternally like the division of ten by three. In the middle of this anguish I found my second truth: that all animals can tell by instinct what is or is not good for them. Although I have now discovered two great truths, I remain unhappy by reason of the adherent rice-cake. My teeth are being sucked into its body, and are becoming excruciatingly painful. Unless I can complete my bite and run away quickly, O-san will be on me. The children seem to have stopped singing, and I'm sure they'll soon come running into the kitchen. In an extremity of anguish, I lashed about with my tail, but to no effect. I made my ears stand up and then lie flat, but this didn't help either. Come to think of it, my ears and tail have nothing to do with the rice-cake. In short, I had indulged in a waste of wagging, a waste of ear-erection, and a waste of ear-flattening. So I stopped.

At long last it dawned on me that the best thing to do is to force the rice-cake down by using my two front paws. First I raised my right paw and stroked it around my mouth. Naturally, this mere stroking brought no relief whatsoever. Next, I stretched out my left paw and with it scraped quick circles around my mouth. These ineffectual passes failed to exorcize the fiend in the rice-cake. Realizing that it was essential to proceed with patience, I scraped alternatively with my right and left paws, but my teeth stayed stuck in the rice-cake. Growing impatient, I now used both front paws simultaneously. Then, only then, I found to my amazement that I could actually stand up on my hind legs. Somehow I feel un-catlike. But not caring whether I am a cat or not, I scratch away like mad at my whole face in frenzied determination to keep on scratching until the fiend in the rice-cake has been driven out. Since the movements of my front paws are so vigorous I am in danger of losing my balance and falling down. To keep my equilibrium I find myself marking time with my hind legs. I begin to tittup from one spot to another, and I finish up prancing madly all over the kitchen. It gives me great pride to realize that I can so dextrously maintain an upright position, and the revelation of a third great truth is thus vouchsafed me: that in conditions of exceptional danger one can surpass one's normal level of achievement. This is the real meaning of Special Providence.

Sustained by Special Providence, I am fighting for dear life against that demonic rice-cake when I hear footsteps. Someone seems to be approaching. Thinking it would be fatal to be caught in this predicament, I redouble my efforts and am positively running around the kitchen. The footsteps come closer and closer. Alas, that Special Providence seems not to last forever. In the end I am discovered by the children who loudly shout, "Why look! The cat's been eating rice-cakes and is dancing." The first to hear their announcement was that O-san person. Abandoning her shuttlecock and battledore, she flew in through the kitchen door crying, "Gracious me!" Then the mistress, sedate in her formal silk kimono, deigns to remark, "What a naughty cat." And my master, drawn from his study by the general hubbub, shouts, "You fool!" The children find me funniest, but by general agreement the whole household is having a good old laugh. It is annoying, it is painful, it is impossible to stop dancing. Hell and damnation! When at long last the laughter began to die down, the dear, little five-year-old piped up with an, "Oh what a comical cat," which had the effect of renewing the tide of their ebbing laughter. They fairly split their sides. I have already heard and seen quite a lot of heartless human behavior, but never before have I felt so bitterly critical of their conduct. Special Providence having vanished into thin air, I was back in my customary position on all fours, finally at my wit's end, and, by reason of giddiness, cutting a quite ridiculous figure. My master seems to have felt it would be perhaps a pity to let me die before his very eyes, for he said to O-san, "Help him get rid of that rice-cake." O-san looks at the mistress as if to say, "Why not make him go on dancing?" The mistress would gladly see my minuet continued, but, since she would not go so far as wanting me to dance myself to death, says nothing. My master turned somewhat sharply to the servant and ordered, "Hurry it up, if you don't help quickly the cat will be dead." O-san, with a vacant look on her face, as though she had been roughly wakened from some peculiarly delicious dream, took a firm grip on the rice-cake and yanked it out of my mouth. I am not quite as feeble-fanged as Coldmoon, but I really did think my entire front toothwork was about to break off. The pain was indescribable. The teeth embedded in the rice-cake are being pitilessly wrenched. You can't imagine what it was like. It was then that the fourth enlightenment burst upon me: that all comfort is achieved through hardship. When at last I came to myself and looked around at a world restored to normality, all the members of the household had disappeared into the inner room.

Having made such a fool of myself, I feel quite unable to face such hostile critics as O-san. It would, I think, unhinge my mind. To restore my mental tranquillity, I decided to visit Tortoiseshell, so I left the kitchen and set off through the backyard to the house of the two-stringed harp.

Tortoiseshell is a celebrated beauty in our district. Though I am undoubtedly a cat, I possess a wide general knowledge of the nature of compassion and am deeply sensitive to affection, kind-heartedness, tenderness, and love. Merely to observe the bitterness in my master's face, just to be snubbed by O-san, leaves me out of sorts. At such times I visit this fair, lady friend of mine and our conversation ranges over many things. Then, before I am aware of it, I find myself refreshed. I forget my worries, hardships, everything. I feel as if reborn. Female influence is indeed a most potent thing. Through a gap in the cedar-hedge, I peer to see if she is anywhere about. Tortoiseshell, wearing a smart new collar in celebration of the season, is sitting very neatly on her veranda. The rondure of her back is indescribably beautiful. It is the most beautiful of all curved lines. The way her tail curves, the way she folds her legs, the charmingly lazy shake of her ears—all these are quite beyond description. She looks so warm sitting there so gracefully in the very sunniest spot. Her body holds an attitude of utter stillness and correctness. And her fur, glossy as velvet that reflects the rays of spring, seems suddenly to quiver although the air is still. For a while I stood, completely enraptured, gazing at her. Then as I came to myself, I softly called, "Miss Tortoiseshell, Miss Tortoiseshell," and beckoned with my paw.

"Why, Professor," she greeted me as she stepped down from the veranda. A tiny bell attached to her scarlet collar made little tinkling sounds. I say to myself, "Ah, it's for the New Year that she's wearing a bell," and, while I am still admiring its lively tinkle, find she has arrived beside me. "A happy New Year, Professor," and she waves her tail to the left; for when cats exchange greetings one first holds one's tail upright like a pole, then twists it round to the left. In our neighborhood it is only Tortoiseshell who calls me Professor. Now, I have already mentioned that I have, as yet, no name; it is Tortoiseshell, and she alone, who pays me the respect due to one that lives in a teacher's house. Indeed, I am not altogether displeased to be addressed as a Professor, and respond willingly to her apostrophe.

"And a happy New Year to you," I say. "How beautifully you're done up!"

"Yes, the mistress bought it for me at the end of last year. Isn't it nice?" and she makes it tinkle for me.

"Yes indeed, it has a lovely sound. I've never seen such a wonderful thing in my life."

"No! Everyone's using them," and she tinkle-tinkles. "But isn't it a lovely sound? I'm so happy." She tinkle-tinkle-tinkles continuously.

"I can see your mistress loves you very dearly." Comparing my lot with hers, I hinted at my envy of a pampered life.

Tortoiseshell is a simple creature. "Yes," she says, "that's true; she treats me as if I were her own child." And she laughs innocently. It is not true that cats never laugh. Human beings are mistaken in their belief that only they are capable of laughter. When I laugh my nostrils grow triangular and my Adam's apple trembles. No wonder human beings fail to understand it.

"What is your master really like?"

"My master? That sounds strange. Mine is a mistress. A mistress of the two stringed harp."

"I know that. But what is her background? I imagine she's a person of high birth?"

"Ah, yes."

A small Princess-pine
While waiting for you. . .

Beyond the sliding paper-door the mistress begins to play on her two-stringed harp.

"Isn't that a splendid voice?" Tortoiseshell is proud of it.

"It seems extremely good, but I don't understand what she's singing. What's the name of the piece?"

"That? Oh, it's called something or other. The mistress is especially fond of it. D'you know, she's actually sixty-two? But in excellent condition, don't you think?"

I suppose one has to admit that she's in excellent condition if she's still alive at sixty-two. So I answered, "Yes." I thought to myself that I'd given a silly answer, but I could do no other since I couldn't think of anything brighter to say.

"You may not think so, but she used to be a person of high standing. She always tells me so."

"What was she originally?"

"I understand that she's the thirteenth Shogun's widowed wife's private-secretary's younger sister's husband's mother's nephew's daughter."

"What?"

"The thirteenth Shogun's widowed wife's private-secretary's younger sister's. . ."

"Ah! But, please, not quite so fast. The thirteenth Shogun's widowed wife's younger sister's private-secretary's . . ."

"No, no, no. The thirteenth Shogun's widowed wife's private-secretary's younger sister's. . ."

"The thirteenth Shogun's widowed wife's. . ."

"Right."

"Private-secretary's. Right?"

"Right."

"Husband's. . ."

"No, younger sister's husband's."

"Of course. How could I? Younger sister's husband's. . ."

"Mother's nephew's daughter. There you are."

"Mother's nephew's daughter?"

"Yes, you've got it."

"Not really. It's so terribly involved that I still can't get the hang of it. What exactly is her relation to the thirteenth Shogun's widowed wife?"

"Oh, but you are so stupid! I've just been telling you what she is. She's the thirteenth Shogun's widowed wife's private-secretary's younger sister's husband's mother's. . ."

"That much I've followed, but. . ."

"Then, you've got it, haven't you?"

"Yes." I had to give in. There are times for little white lies.

Beyond the sliding paper-door the sound of the two-stringed harp came to a sudden stop and the mistress' voice called, "Tortoiseshell, Tortoiseshell, your lunch is ready." Tortoiseshell looked happy and remarked, "There, she's calling, so I must go home. I hope you'll forgive me?" What would be the good of my saying that I mind? "Come and see me again," she said; and she ran off through the garden tinkling her bell. But suddenly she turned and came back to ask me anxiously, "You're looking far from well. Is anything wrong?" I couldn't very well tell her that I'd eaten a rice-cake and gone dancing; so, "No," I said, "nothing in particular. I did some weighty thinking, which brought on something of a headache. Indeed I called today because I fancied that just to talk with you would help me to feel better."

"Really? Well, take good care of yourself. Good-bye now." She seemed a tiny bit sorry to leave me, which has completely restored me to the liveliness I'd felt before the rice-cake bit me. I now felt wonderful and decided to go home through that tea-plantation where one could have the pleasure of treading down lumps of half-melted frost. I put my face through the broken bamboo hedge, and there was Rickshaw Blacky, back again on the dry chrysanthemums, yawning his spine into a high, black arch. Nowadays I'm no longer scared of Blacky, but, since any conversation with him involves the risk of trouble, I endeavor to pass, cutting him off. But it's not in Blacky's nature to contain his feelings if he believes himself looked down upon. "Hey you, Mr. No-name. You're very stuck-up these days, now aren't you? You may be living in a teacher's house, but don't go giving yourself such airs. And stop, I warn you, trying to make a fool of me." Blacky doesn't seem to know that I am now a celebrity. I wish I could explain the situation to him, but, since he's not the kind who can understand such things, I decide simply to offer him the briefest of greetings and then to take my leave as soon as I decently can.

"A happy New Year, Mr. Blacky. You do look well, as usual." And I lift up my tail and twist it to the left. Blacky, keeping his tail straight up, refused to return my salutation.

"What! Happy? If the New Year's happy, then you should be out of your tiny mind the whole year round. Now push off sharp, you back-end of a bellows."

That turn of phrase about the back-end of a bellows sounds distinctly derogatory, but its semantic content happened to escape me. "What," I enquired, "do you mean by the back-end of a bellows?"

"You're being sworn at and you stand there asking its meaning. I give up! I really do! You really are a New Year's nit."

A New Year's nit sounds somewhat poetic, but its meaning is even more obscure than that bit about the bellows. I would have liked to ask the meaning for my future reference, but, as it was obvious I'd get no clear answer, I just stood facing him without a word. I was actually feeling rather awkward, but just then the wife of Blacky's master suddenly screamed out, "Where in hell is that cut of salmon I left here on the shelf? My God, I do declare that hellcat's been here and snitched it once again! That's the nastiest cat I've ever seen. See what he'll get when he comes back!" Her raucous voice unceremoniously shakes the mild air of the season, vulgarizing its natural peacefulness. Blacky puts on an impudent look as if to say, "If you want to scream your head off, scream away," and he jerked his square chin forward at me as if to say, "Did you hear that hullaballoo?" Up to this point I've been too busy talking to Blacky to notice or think about anything else; but now, glancing down, I see between his legs a mud-covered bone from the cheapest cut of salmon.

"So you've been at it again!" Forgetting our recent exchanges, I offered Blacky my usual flattering exclamation. But it was not enough to restore him to good humor.

"Been at it! What the hell d'you mean, you saucy blockhead? And what do you mean by saying 'again' when this is nothing but a skinny slice of the cheapest fish? Don't you know who I am! I'm Rickshaw Blacky, damn you." And, having no shirtsleeves to roll up, he lifts an aggressive right front-paw as high as his shoulder.

"I've always known you were Mr. Rickshaw Blacky."

"If you knew, why the hell did you say I'd been at it again? Answer me!" And he blows out over me great gusts of oven breath. Were we humans, I would be shaken by the collar of my coat. I am somewhat taken aback and am indeed wondering how to get out of the situation, when that woman's fearful voice is heard again.

"Hey! Mr. Westbrook. You there, Westbrook, can you hear me? Listen, I got something to say. Bring me a pound of beef, and quick. O.K.? Understand? Beef that isn't tough. A pound of it. See?" Her beef-demanding tones shatter the peace of the whole neighborhood.

"It's only once a year she orders beef and that's why she shouts so loud. She wants the entire neighborhood to know about her marvellous pound of beef. What can one do with a woman like that!" asked Blacky jeeringly as he stretched all four of his legs. As I can find nothing to say in reply, I keep silent and watch.

"A miserable pound just simply will not do. But I reckon it can't be helped. Hang on to that beef. I'll have it later." Blacky communes with himself as though the beef had been ordered specially for him.

"This time you're in for a real treat. That's wonderful!" With these words I'd hoped to pack him off to his home.

But Blacky snarled, "That's nothing to do with you. Just shut your big mouth, you!" and using his strong hind-legs, he suddenly scrabbles up a torrent of fallen icicles which thuds down on my head. I was taken completely aback, and, while I was still busy shaking the muddy debris off my body, Blacky slid off through the hedge and disappeared. Presumably to possess himself of Westbrook's beef.

When I get home I find the place unusually springlike and even the master is laughing gaily. Wondering why, I hopped onto the veranda, and, as I padded to sit beside the master, noticed an unfamiliar guest. His hair is parted neatly and he wears a crested cotton surcoat and a duck-cloth *hakama*. He looks like a student and, at that, an extremely serious one. Lying on the corner of my master's small hand-warming brazier, right beside the lacquer cigarette-box, there's a visiting card on which is written, "To introduce Mr. Beauchamp Blowlamp: from Coldmoon." Which tells me both the name of this guest and the fact that he's a friend of Coldmoon. The conversation going on between host and guest sounds enigmatic because I missed the start of it. But I gather that it has something to do with Waverhouse, the aesthete whom I have had previous occasion to mention.

"And he urged me to come along with him because it would involve an ingenious idea, he said." The guest is talking calmly.

"Do you mean there was some ingenious idea involved in lunching at a Western style restaurant?" My master pours more tea for the guest and pushes the cup toward him.

"Well, at the time I did not understand what this ingenious idea could be, but, since it was *his* idea, I thought it bound to be something interesting and. . ."

"So you accompanied him. I see."

"Yes, but I got a surprise."

The master, looking as if to say, "I told you so," gives me a whack on the head. Which hurts a little. "I expect it proved somewhat farcical. He's rather that way inclined." Clearly, he has suddenly remembered that business with Andrea del Sarto.

"Ah yes? Well, as he suggested we would be eating something special. . ."

"What did you have?"

"First of all, while studying the menu, he gave me all sorts of information about food."

"Before ordering any?"

"Yes."

"And then?"

"And then, turning to a waiter, he said, 'There doesn't seem to be anything special on the card.' The waiter, not to be outdone, suggested roast duck or veal chops. Whereupon Waverhouse remarked quite sharply that we hadn't come a very considerable distance just for common or garden fare. The waiter, who didn't understand the significance of common or garden, looked puzzled and said nothing."

"So I would imagine."

"Then, turning to me, Waverhouse observed that in France or in

England one can obtain any amount of dishes cooked *à la Tenmei* or *à la Manyō* but that in Japan, wherever you go, the food is all so stereotyped that one doesn't even feel tempted to enter a restaurant of the so-called Western style. And so on and so on. He was in tremendous form. But has he ever been abroad?"

"Waverhouse abroad? Of course not. He's got the money and the time. If he wanted to, he could go off anytime. He probably just converted his future intention to travel into the past tense of widely traveled experience as a sort of joke." The master flatters himself that he has said something witty and laughs invitingly. His guest looks largely unimpressed.

"I see. I wondered when he'd been abroad. I took everything he said quite seriously. Besides, he described such things as snail soup and stewed frogs as though he'd really seen them with his own two eyes."

"He must have heard about them from someone. He's adept at such terminological inexactitudes."

"So it would seem," and Beauchamp stares down at the narcissus in a vase. He seems a little disappointed.

"So, that then was his ingenious idea, I take it?" asks the master still in quest of certainties.

"No, that was only the beginning. The main part's still to come."

"Ah!" The master utters an interjection mingled with curiosity.

"Having finished his dissertation on matters gastronomical and European, he proposed 'since it's quite impossible to obtain snails or frogs, however much we may desire them, let's at least have moat-bells. What do you say?' And without really giving the matter any thought at all, I answered, 'Yes, that would be fine.'"

"Moat-bells sound a little odd."

"Yes, very odd, but because Waverhouse was speaking so seriously, I didn't then notice the oddity." He seems to be apologizing to my master for his carelessness.

"What happened next?" asks my master quite indifferently and without any sign of sympathetic response to his guest's implied apology.

"Well, then he told the waiter to bring moat-bells for two. The waiter said, 'Do you mean meatballs, sir?' but Waverhouse, assuming an ever more serious expression, corrected him with gravity. 'No, not meatballs, moat-bells.'"

"Really? But is there any such dish as moat-bells?"

"Well I thought it sounded somewhat strange, but as Waverhouse was so calmly sure and is so great an authority on all things Occidental—remember it was then my firm belief that he was widely traveled—I too joined in and explained to the waiter, 'Moat-bells, my good man, moat-bells.'"

"What did the waiter do?"

"The waiter—it's really rather funny now one comes to think back on it—looked thoughtful for a while and then said, 'I'm terribly sorry sir, but today, unfortunately, we have no moat-bells. Though should you care for meatballs we could serve you, sir, immediately.' Waverhouse thereupon looked extremely put out and said, 'So we've come all this long way for nothing. Couldn't you really manage moat-bells? Please do see what can be done,' and he slipped a small tip to the waiter. The waiter said he would ask the cook again and went off into the kitchen."

"He must have had his mind dead set on eating moat-bells."

"After a brief interval the waiter returned to say that if moat-bells were ordered specially they could be provided, but that it would take a long time. Waverhouse was quite composed. He said, 'It's the New Year and we are in no kind of hurry. So let's wait for it?' He drew a cigar from the inside of his Western suit and lighted up in the most leisurely manner. I felt called upon to match his cool composure so, taking the *Japan News* from my kimono pocket, I started reading it. The waiter retired for further consultations."

"What a business!" My master leans forward, showing quite as much enthusiasm as he does when reading war news in the dailies.

"The waiter re-emerged with apologies and the confession that, of late, the ingredients of moat-bells were in such short supply that one could not get them at Kameya's nor even down at No. 15 in Yokohama. He expressed regret, but it seemed certain that the material for moat-bells would not be back in stock for some considerable time. Waverhouse then turned to me and repeated, over and over again, 'What a pity, and we came especially for that dish.' I felt that I had to say something, so I joined him in saying, 'Yes, it's a terrible shame! Really, a great, great pity!'"

"Quite so," agrees my master, though I myself don't follow his reasoning.

"These observations must have made the waiter feel quite sorry, for he said, 'When, one of these days, we do have the necessary ingredients, we'd be happy if you would come, sir, and sample our fare.' But when Waverhouse proceeded to ask him what ingredients the restaurant did use, the waiter just laughed and gave no answer. Waverhouse then pressingly enquired if the key-ingredient happened to be Tochian (who, as you know, is a *haiku* poet of the Nihon School); and d'you know, the waiter answered, 'Yes, it is, sir, and that is precisely why none is currently available even in Yokohama. I am indeed,' he added, 'most regretful, sir.'"

"Ha-ha-ha! So that's the point of the story? How very funny!" and the master, quite unlike his usual self, roars with laughter. His knees shake so much that I nearly tumble off. Paying no regard to my predicament, the master laughs and laughs. He seems suddenly deeply pleased to realize that he is not alone in being gulled by Andrea del Sarto.

"And then, as soon as we were out in the street, he said 'You see, we've done well. That ploy about the moat-bells was really rather good, wasn't it?' and he looked as pleased as punch. I let it be known that I was lost in admiration, and so we parted. However, since by then it was well past the lunch-hour, I was nearly starving."

"That must have been very trying for you." My master shows, for the first time, a sympathy to which I have no objection. For a while there was a pause in the conversation and my purring could be heard by host and guest.

Mr. Beauchamp drains his cup of tea, now quite cold, in one quick gulp and with some formality remarks, "As a matter-of-fact I've come today to ask a favor from you."

"Yes? And what can I do for you?" My master, too, assumes a formal face.

"As you know, I am a devotee of literature and art. . ."

"That's a good thing," replies my master quite encouragingly.

"Since a little while back, I and a few like-minded friends have got together and organized a reading group. The idea is to meet once a month for the purpose of continued studying in this field. In fact, we've already had the first meeting at the end of last year."

"May I ask you a question? When you say, like that, a reading group, it suggests that you engage in reading poetry and prose in a singsong tone. But in what sort of manner do you, in fact, proceed?"

"Well, we are beginning with ancient works but we intend to consider the works of our fellow members."

"When you speak of ancient works, do you mean something like Po Chu-i's *Lute Song*?"

"No."

"Perhaps things like Buson's mixture of *haiku* and Chinese verse?"

"No."

"What kinds of thing do you then do?"

"The other day, we did one of Chikamatsu's lovers' suicides."

"Chikamatsu? You mean the Chikamatsu who wrote *jōruri* plays?" There are not two Chikamatsus. When one says Chikamatsu, one does indeed mean Chikamatsu the playwright and could mean nobody else. I thought my master really stupid to ask so fool a question. However, oblivious to my natural reactions, he gently strokes my head. I calmly let him go on stroking me, justifying my compliance with the reflection that so small a weakness is permissible when there are those in the world who admit to thinking themselves under loving observation by persons who merely happen to be cross-eyed.

Beauchamp answers, "Yes," and tries to read the reaction on my master's face.

"Then is it one person who reads or do you allot parts among you?"

"We allot parts and each reads out the appropriate dialogue. The idea is to empathize with the characters in the play and, above all, to bring out their individual personalities. We do gestures as well. The main thing is to catch the essential character of the era of the play. Accordingly, the lines are read out as if spoken by each character, which may perhaps be a young lady or possibly an errand-boy."

"In that case it must be like a play."

"Yes, almost the only things missing are the costumes and the scenery."

"May I ask if your reading was a success?"

"For a first attempt, I think one might claim that it was, if anything, a success."

"And which lovers' suicide play did you perform on the last occasion?"

"We did a scene in which a boatman takes a fare to the red light quarter of Yoshiwara."

"You certainly picked on a most irregular incident, didn't you?" My master, being a teacher, tilts his head a little sideways as if regarding something slightly doubtful. The cigarette smoke drifting from his nose passes up by his ear and along the side of his head.

"No, it isn't that irregular. The characters are a passenger, a boatman, a high-class prostitute, a serving-girl, an ancient crone of a brothel-attendant, and, of course, a geisha-registrar. But that's all." Beauchamp seems utterly unperturbed. My master, on hearing the words "a high-class prostitute," winces slightly but probably only because he's not well up in the meanings of such technical terms as *nakai, yarite,* and *kemban*.

He seeks to clear the ground with a question. "Does not *nakai* signify something like a maid-servant in a brothel?"

"Though I have not yet given the matter my full attention, I believe that *nakai* signifies a serving-girl in a teahouse and that *yarite* is some sort of an assistant in the women's quarters." Although Beauchamp recently claimed that his group seeks to impersonate the actual voices of the characters in the plays, he does not seem to have fully grasped the real nature of *yarite* and *nakai*.

"I see, *nakai* belong to a teahouse while *yarite* live in a brothel. Next, are *kemban* human beings or is it the name of a place? If human, are they men or women?"

"*Kemban*, I rather think, is a male human being."

"What is his function?"

"I've not yet studied that far. But I'll make inquiries, one of these days."

Thinking, in the light of these revelations, that the play-readings must be affairs extraordinarily ill-conducted, I glance up at my master's face. Surprisingly, I find him looking serious. "Apart from yourself, who were the other readers taking part?"

"A wide variety of people. Mr. K, a Bachelor of Law, played the high-class prostitute, but his delivery of that woman's sugary dialogue through his very male mustache did, I confess, create a slightly queer impression. And then there was a scene in which this *oiran* was seized with spasms. . ."

"Do your readers extend their reading activities to the simulation of spasms?" asked my master anxiously.

"Yes indeed; for expression is, after all, important." Beauchamp clearly considers himself a literary artist *à l'outrance*.

"Did he manage to have his spasms nicely?" My master has made a witty remark.

"The spasms were perhaps the only thing beyond our capability at such a first endeavor." Beauchamp, too, is capable of wit.

"By the way," asks my master, "what part did you take?"

"I was the boatman."

"Really? You, the boatman!" My master's tone was such as to suggest that, if Beauchamp could be a boatman, he himself could be a geisha-registrar. Switching his tone to one of simple candor, he then asks: "Was the role of the boatman too much for you?"

Beauchamp does not seem particularly offended. Maintaining the same calm voice, he replies, "As a matter of fact, it was because of this boatman that our precious gathering, though it went up like a rocket, came down like a stick. It so happened that four or five girl students are living in the boarding house next door to our meeting hall. I don't know how, but they found out when our reading was to take place. Anyway, it appears that they came and listened to us under the window of the hall. I was doing the boatman's voice, and, just when I had warmed up nicely and was really getting into the swing of it—perhaps my gestures were a little over-exaggerated—the girl students, all of whom had managed to control their feelings up to that point, thereupon burst out into simultaneous cachinnations. I was of course surprised, and I was of course embarrassed: indeed, thus dampened, I could not find it in me to continue. So our meeting came to an end."

If this were considered a success, even for a first meeting, what would failure have been like? I could not help laughing. Involuntarily, my Adam's apple made a rumbling noise. My master, who likes what he takes to be purring, strokes my head ever more and more gently. I'm thankful to be loved just because I laugh at someone, but at the same time I feel a bit uneasy.

"What very bad luck!" My master offers condolences despite the fact that we are still in the congratulatory season of the New Year.

"As for our second meeting, we intend to make a great advance and manage things in the grand style. That, in fact, is the very reason for my call today: we'd like you to join our group and help us."

"I can't possibly have spasms." My negative-minded master is already poised to refuse.

"No, you don't have to have spasms or anything like that. Here's a list of the patron members." So saying, Beauchamp very carefully produced a small notebook from a purple-colour carrying-wrapper. He opened the notebook and placed it in front of my master's knees. "Will you please sign and make your seal-mark here?" I see that the book contains the names of distinguished Doctors of Literature and Bachelors of Arts of this present day, all neatly mustered in full force.

"Well, I wouldn't say I object to becoming a supporter, but what sort of obligations would I have to meet?" My oyster-like master displays his apprehensions. . .

"There's hardly any obligation. We ask nothing from you except a signature expressing your approval."

"Well, in that case, I'll join." As he realizes that there is no real obligation involved, he suddenly becomes lighthearted. His face assumes the expression of one who would sign even a secret commitment to engage in rebellion, provided it was clear that the signature carried no binding obligation. Besides, it is understandable that he should assent so eagerly: for to be included, even by name only, among so many names of celebrated scholars is a supreme honor for one who has never before had such an opportunity. "Excuse me," and my master goes off to the study to fetch his seal. I am tipped to fall unceremoniously onto the matting. Beauchamp helps himself to a slice of sponge cake from the cake-bowl and crams it into his mouth. For a while he seems to be in pain, mumbling. Just for a second I am reminded of my morning experience with the rice-cake. My master reappears with his seal just as the sponge cake settles down in Beauchamp's bowels. My master does not seem to notice that a piece of sponge cake is missing from the cake-bowl. If he does, I shall be the first to be suspected.

Mr. Beauchamp having taken his departure, my master reenters the study where he finds on his desk a letter from friend Waverhouse.

"I wish you a very happy New Year. . ."

My master considers the letter to have started with an unusual seriousness. Letters from Waverhouse are seldom serious. The other day, for instance, he wrote: "Of late, as I am not in love with any woman, I receive no love letters from anywhere. As I am more or less alive, please set your mind at ease." Compared with which, this New Year's letter is exceptionally matter-of-fact:

> I would like to come and see you, but I am so very extremely busy every day because, contrary to your negativism, I am planning to greet this New Year, a year unprecedented in all history, with as positive an attitude as is possible. Hoping you will understand. . .

My master quite understands, thinking that Waverhouse, being Waverhouse, must be busy having fun during the New Year season.

> Yesterday, finding a minute to spare, I sought to treat Mr. Beauchamp to a dish of moat-bells. Unfortunately, due to a shortage of their ingredients, I could not carry out my intention. It was most regrettable. . .

My master smiles, thinking that the letter is falling more into the usual pattern.

> Tomorrow there will be a card party at a certain Baron's house; the day after tomorrow a New Year's banquet at the Society of Aesthetes; and the day after that, a welcoming party for Professor Toribe; and on the day thereafter. . .

My master, finding it rather a bore, skips a few lines.

> So you see, because of these incessant parties—*nō*-song parties, *haiku* parties, *tanka* parties, even parties for New Style Poetry, and so on and so on, I am perpetually occupied for quite some time. And that is why I am obliged to send you this New Year's letter instead of calling on you in person. I pray you will forgive me. . .

"Of course you do not have to call on me." My master voices his answer to the letter.

> Next time that you are kind enough to visit me, I would like you to stay and dine. Though there is no special delicacy in my poor larder, at least I hope to be able to offer you some moat-bells, and I am indeed looking forward to that pleasure. . .

"He's still brandishing his moat-bells," muttered my master, who, thinking the invitation an insult, begins to feel indignant.

> However, because the ingredients necessary for the preparation of moat-bells are currently in rather short supply, it may not be possible to arrange it. In which case, I will offer you some peacocks' tongues. . .

"Aha! So he's got two strings to his bow," thinks my master and cannot resist reading the rest of the letter.

> As you know, the tongue meat per peacock amounts to less than half the bulk of the small finger. Therefore, in order to satisfy your gluttonous stomach. . .

"What a pack of lies," remarks my master in a tone of resignation.

I think one needs to catch at least twenty or thirty peacocks. However, though one sees an occasional peacock, maybe two, at the zoo or at the Asakusa Amusement Center, there are none to be found at my poulterer's, which is occasioning me pain, great pain. . .

"You're having that pain of your own free will." My master shows no evidence of gratitude.

The dish of peacocks' tongues was once extremely fashionable in Rome when the Roman Empire was in the full pride of its prosperity. How I have always secretly coveted after peacocks' tongues, that acme of gastronomical luxury and elegance, you may well imagine. . .

"I may well imagine, may I? How ridiculous." My master is extremely cold.

From that time forward until about the sixteenth century, peacock was an indispensable delicacy at all banquets. If my memory serves me, when the Earl of Leicester invited Queen Elizabeth to Kenilworth, peacocks' tongues were on the menu. And in one of Rembrandt's banquet scenes, a peacock is clearly to be seen, lying in its pride upon the table. . .

My master grumbles that if Waverhouse can find time to compose a history of the eating of peacocks, he cannot really be so busy.

Anyway, if I go on eating good food as I have been doing recently, I will doubtless end up one of these days with a stomach weak as yours. . .

"'Like yours' is quite unnecessary. He has no need to establish me as the prototypical dyspeptic," grumbles my master.

According to historians, the Romans held two or three banquets every day. But the consumption of so much good food, while sitting at a large table two or three times a day, must produce in any man, however sturdy his stomach, disorders in the digestive functions. Thus nature has, like you. . .

"'Like you,' again, what impudence!"

But they, who studied long and hard simultaneously to enjoy both luxury and exuberant health, considered it vital not only to devour disproportionately large quantities of delicacies, but also to maintain the bowels in full working order. They accordingly devised a secret formula. . .

"Really?" My master suddenly becomes enthusiastic.

They invariably took a post-prandial bath. After the bath, utilizing methods whose secret has long been lost, they proceeded to vomit up everything they had swallowed before the bath. Thus were the insides of their stomachs kept scrupulously clean. Having so cleansed their stomachs, they would sit down again at the table and there savor to the uttermost the delicacies of their choice. Then they took a bath again and vomited once more. In this way, though they gorged on their favorite dishes to their hearts' content, none of their internal organs suffered the least damage. In my humble opinion, this was indeed a case of having one's cake and eating it.

"They certainly seem to have killed two or more birds with one stone." My master's expression is one of envy.

Today, this twentieth century, quite apart from the heavy traffic and the increased number of banquets, when our nation is in the second year of a war against Russia, is indeed eventful. I, consequently, firmly believe that the time has come for us, the people of this victorious country, to bend our minds to study of the truly Roman art of bathing and vomiting. Otherwise, I am afraid that even the precious people of this mighty nation will, in the very near future, become, like you, dyspeptic. . .

"What, again like me? An annoying fellow," thinks my master.

Now suppose that we, who are familiar with all things Occidental, by study of ancient history and legend contrive to discover the secret formula that has long been lost; then to make use of it now in our Meiji Era would be an act of virtue. It would nip potential misfortune in the bud, and, moreover, it would justify my own everyday life which has been one of constant indulgence in pleasure.

My master thinks all this a trifle odd.

Accordingly, I have now, for some time, been digging into the relevant works of Gibbon, Mommsen, and Goldwin Smith, but I am extremely sorry to report that, so far, I have gained not even the slightest clue to the secret. However, as you know, I am a man who, once set upon a course, will not abandon it until my object is achieved. Therefore my belief is that a rediscovery of the vomiting method is not far off. I will let you know when it happens. Incidentally, I would prefer postponing that feast of moat-bells and peacocks' tongues, which I've mentioned above, until the discovery has actually been made. Which would not only be convenient to me, but also to you who suffer from a weak stomach.

"So, he's been pulling my leg all along. The style of writing was so sober that I have read it all, and took the whole thing seriously. Waverhouse must indeed be a man of leisure to play such a practical joke on me," said my master through his laughter.

Several days then passed without any particular event. Thinking it too boring to spend one's time just watching the narcissus in a white vase gradually wither, and the slow blossoming of a branch of the blue-stemmed plum in another vase, I have gone around twice to look for Tortoiseshell, but both times unsuccessfully. On the first occasion I thought she was just out, but on my second visit I learnt that she was ill. Hiding myself behind the aspidistra beside a wash-basin, I heard the following conversation which took place between the mistress and her maid on the other side of the sliding paper-door.

"Is Tortoiseshell taking her meal?"

"No, madam, she's eaten nothing this morning. I've let her sleep on the quilt of the foot-warmer, well wrapped up." It does not sound as if they spoke about a cat. Tortoiseshell is being treated as if she were a human.

As I compare this situation with my own lot, I feel a little envious but at the same time I am not displeased that my beloved cat should be treated with such kindness.

"That's bad. If she doesn't eat she will only get weaker."

"Yes indeed, madam. Even me, if I don't eat for a whole day, I couldn't work at all the next day."

The maid answers as though she recognized the cat as an animal superior to herself. Indeed, in this particular household the cat may well be more important than the maid.

"Have you taken her to see a doctor?"

"Yes, and the doctor was really strange. When I went into his consulting room carrying Tortoiseshell in my arms, he asked me if I'd caught a cold and tried to take my pulse. I said 'No, Doctor, it is not I who am the patient, this is the patient,' and I placed Tortoiseshell on my knees. The doctor grinned and said he had no knowledge of the sicknesses of cats, and that if I just left it, perhaps *it* would get better. Isn't he too terrible? I was so angry that I told him, 'Then, please don't bother to examine her, *she* happens to be our precious cat.' And I snuggled Tortoiseshell back into the breast of my kimono and came straight home."

"Truly so."

"Truly so" is one of those elegant expressions that one would never hear in my house. One has to be the thirteenth Shogun's widowed wife's somebody's something to be able to use such a phrase. I was much impressed by its refinement.

"She seems to be sniffling. . ."

"Yes, I'm sure she's got a cold and a sore throat; whenever one has a cold, one suffers from an honorable cough."

As might be expected from the maid of the thirteenth Shogun's somebody's something, she's quick with honorifics.

"Besides, recently, there's a thing they call consumption. . ."

"Indeed these days one cannot be too careful. What with the increase in all these new diseases like tuberculosis and the black plague."

"Things that did not exist in the days of the Shogunate are all no good to anyone. So you be careful too!"

"Is that so, madam?"

The maid is much moved.

"I don't see how she could have caught a cold, she hardly ever went out. . ."

"No, but you see she's recently acquired a bad friend."

The maid is as highly elated as if she were telling a State secret.

"A bad friend?"

"Yes, that tatty-looking tom at the teacher's house in the main street."

"D'you mean that teacher who makes rude noises every morning?"

"Yes, the one who makes the sounds like a goose being strangled every time he washes his face."

The sound of a goose being strangled is a clever description. Every morning when my master gargles in the bathroom he has an odd habit of making a strange, unceremonious noise by tapping his throat with his toothbrush. When he is in a bad temper he croaks with a vengeance; when he is in a good temper, he gets so pepped up that he croaks even more vigorously. In short, whether he is in a good or a bad temper, he croaks continually and vigorously. According to his wife, until they moved to this house he never had the habit; but he's done it every day since the day he first happened to do it. It is rather a trying habit. We cats cannot even imagine why he should persist in such behavior. Well, let that pass. But what a scathing remark that was about "a tatty-looking tom." I continue to eavesdrop.

"What good can he do making that noise! Under the Shogunate even a lackey or a sandal-carrier knew how to behave; and in a residential quarter there was no one who washed his face in such a manner."

"I'm sure there wasn't, madam."

That maid is all too easily influenced, and she uses "madam" far too often.

"With a master like that what's to be expected from his cat? It can only be a stray. If he comes round here again, beat him."

"Most certainly I'll beat him. It must be all his fault that Tortoiseshell's so poorly. I'll take it out on him, that I will."

How false these accusations laid against me! But judging it rash to approach too closely, I came home without seeing Tortoiseshell.

When I return, my master is in the study meditating in the middle of writing something. If I told him what they say about him in the house of the two-stringed harp, he would be very angry; but, as the saying goes, igno-rance is bliss. There he sits, posing like a sacred poet, groaning.

Just then, Waverhouse, who has expressly stated in his New Year letter that he would be too busy to call for some long time, dropped in. "Are you composing a new-style poem or something? Show it to me if it's interesting."

"I considered it rather impressive prose, so I thought I'd translate it," answers my master somewhat reluctantly.

"Prose? Whose prose?"

"Don't know whose."

"I see, an anonymous author. Among anonymous works, there are indeed some extremely good ones. They are not to be slighted. Where did you find it?"

"The *Second Reader,*" answers my master with imperturbable calmness.

"The *Second Reader*? What's this got to do with the *Second Reader*?"

"The connection is that the beautifully written article which I'm now translating appears in the *Second Reader*."

"Stop talking rubbish. I suppose this is your idea of a last minute squaring of accounts for the peacocks' tongues?"

"I'm not a braggart like you," says my master and twists his mustache. He is perfectly composed.

"Once when someone asked Sanyo whether he'd lately seen any fine pieces of prose, that celebrated scholar of the Chinese classics produced a dunning letter from a packhorse man and said, 'This is easily the finest piece of prose that has recently come to my attention.' Which implies that your eye for the beautiful might, contrary to one's expectations, actually be accurate. Read your piece aloud. I'll review it for you," says Waverhouse as if he were the originator of all aesthetic theories and practice. My master starts to read in the voice of a Zen priest, reading that injunction left by the Most Reverend Priest Daitō. "'Giant Gravitation,'" he intoned.

"What on earth is giant gravitation?"

"'Giant Gravitation' is the title."

"An odd title. I don't quite understand."

"The idea is that there's a giant whose name is Gravitation."

"A somewhat unreasonable idea but, since it's a title, I'll let that pass. All right, carry on with the text. You have a good voice. Which makes it rather interesting."

"Right, but no more interruptions." My master, having laid down his prior conditions, begins to read again.

> Kate looks out of the window. Children are playing ball. They throw the ball high up in the sky. The ball rises up and up. After a while the ball comes down. They throw it high again: twice, three times. Every

time they throw it up, the ball comes down. Kate asks why it comes down instead of rising up and up. "It is because a giant lives in the earth," replies her mother. "He is the Giant Gravitation. He is strong. He pulls everything toward him. He pulls the houses to the earth. If he didn't they would fly away. Children, too, would fly away. You've seen the leaves fall, haven't you? That's because the Giant called them. Sometimes you drop a book. It's because the Giant Gravitation asks for it. A ball goes up in the sky. The giant calls for it. Down it falls.

"Is that all?"

"Yes, isn't it good?"

"All right, you win. I wasn't expecting such a present in return for the moat-bells."

"It wasn't meant as a return present, or anything like that. I translated it because I thought it was good. Don't you think it's good?" My master stares deep into the gold-rimmed spectacles.

"What a surprise! To think that you of all people had this talent. . . Well, well! I've certainly been taken in right and proper this time. I take my hat off to you." He is alone in his understanding. He's talking to himself. The situation is quite beyond my master's grasp.

"I've no intention of making you doff your cap. I translated this text simply because I thought it was an interesting piece of writing."

"Indeed, yes! Most interesting! Quite as it should be! Smashing! I feel small."

"You don't have to feel small. Since I recently gave up painting in watercolors, I've been thinking of trying my hand at writing."

"And compared with your watercolors, which showed no sense of perspective, no appreciation of differences in tone, your writings are superb. I am lost in admiration."

"Such encouraging words from you are making me positively enthusiastic about it," says my master, speaking from under his continuing misapprehension.

Just then Mr. Coldmoon enters with the usual greeting.

"Why, hello," responds Waverhouse, "I've just been listening to a terrifically fine article and the curtain has been rung down upon my moat-bells." He speaks obliquely about something incomprehensible.

"Have you really?" The reply is equally incomprehensible. It is only my master who seems not to be in any particularly light humor.

"The other day," he remarked, "a man called Beauchamp Blowlamp came to see me with an introduction from you."

"Ah, did he? Beauchamp's an uncommonly honest person, but, as he is also somewhat odd, I was afraid that he might make himself a nuisance to you. However, since he had pressed me so hard to be introduced to you. . ."

"Not especially a nuisance. . ."

"Didn't he, during his visit, go on at length about his name?"

"No, I don't recall him doing so."

"No? He's got a habit at first meeting of expatiating upon the singularity of his name."

"What is the nature of that singularity?" butts in Waverhouse, who has been waiting for something to happen.

"He gets terribly upset if someone pronounces Beauchamp as Beecham."

"Odd!" said Waverhouse, taking a pinch of tobacco from his gold-painted, leather tobacco pouch.

"Invariably he makes the immediate point that his name is not Beecham Blowlamp but Bo-champ Blowlamp."

"That's strange," and Waverhouse inhales pricey tobacco-smoke deep into his stomach.

"It comes entirely from his craze for literature. He likes the effect and is inexplicably proud of the fact that his personal name and his family name can be made to rhyme with each other. That's why when one pronounces Beauchamp incorrectly, he grumbles that one does not appreciate what he is trying to get across."

"He certainly is extraordinary." Getting more and more interested, Waverhouse hauls back the pipe smoke from the bottom of his stomach to let it loose at his nostrils. The smoke gets lost en route and seems to be snagged in his gullet. Transferring the pipe to his hand, he coughs chokingly.

"When he was here the other day, he said he'd taken the part of a boatman at a meeting of his Reading Society, and that he'd gotten himself laughed at by a gaggle of schoolgirls," says my master with a laugh.

"Ah, that's it, I remember." Waverhouse taps his pipe upon his knees. This strikes me as likely to prove dangerous, so I move a little way farther off. "That Reading Society, now. The other day when I treated him to moat-bells, he mentioned it. He said they were going to make their second meeting a grand affair by inviting well-known literary men, and he cordially invited me to attend. When I asked him if they would again try another of Chikamatsu's dramas of popular life, he said no and that they'd decided on a fairly modern play, *The Golden Demon*. I asked him what role he would take and he said, 'I'm going to play O-miya.' Beauchamp as O-miya would certainly be worth seeing. I'm determined to attend the meeting in his support."

"It's going to be interesting, I think," says Coldmoon and he laughs in an odd way.

"But he is so thoroughly sincere, which is good, and has no hint of frivolousness about him. Quite different from Waverhouse, for instance." My master is revenged for Andrea del Sarto, for peacocks' tongues, and for moat-bells all in one go. Waverhouse appears to take no notice of the remark.

"Ah well, when all's said and done, I'm nothing but a chopping board at Gyōtoku."

"Yes, that's about it," observes my master, although in fact he does not understand Waverhouse's involved method of describing himself as a highly sophisticated simpleton. But not for nothing has he been so many years a schoolteacher. He is skilled in prevarication, and his long experience in the classrooms can be usefully applied at such awkward moments in his social life.

"What is a chopping board at Gyōtoku?" asks the guileless Coldmoon. My master looks toward the alcove and pulverizes that chopping board at Gyōtoku by saying, "Those narcissi are lasting well. I bought them on my way home from the public baths toward the end of last year."

"Which reminds me," says Waverhouse, twirling his pipe, "that at the end of last year I had a really most extraordinary experience."

"Tell us about it." My master, confident that the chopping board is now safely back in Gyōtoku, heaves a sigh of relief. The extraordinary experience of Mr. Waverhouse fell thus upon our ears:

"If I remember correctly, it was on the twenty-seventh of December. Beauchamp had said he would like to come and hear me talk upon matters literary, and had asked me to be sure to be in. Accordingly, I waited for him all the morning but he failed to turn up. I had lunch and was seated in front of the stove reading one of Pain's humorous books, when a letter arrived from my mother in Shizuoka. She, like all old women, still thinks of me as a child. She gives me all sorts of advice; that I mustn't go out at night when the weather's cold; that unless the room is first well-heated by a stove, I'll catch my death of cold every time I take a bath. We owe much to our parents. Who but a parent would think of me with such solicitude? Though normally I take things lightly and as they come, I confess that at that juncture the letter affected me deeply. For it struck me that to idle my life away, as indeed I do, was rather a waste. I felt that I must win honor for my family by producing a masterwork of literature or something like that. I felt I would like the name of Doctor Waverhouse to become renowned, that I should be acclaimed as a leading figure in Meiji literary circles, while my mother is still alive. Continuing my perusal of the letter, I read, 'You are indeed lucky. While our young people are suffering great hardships for the country in the war against Russia, you are living in happy-go-lucky idleness as if life were one long New Year's party organized for your particular benefit!' Actually, I'm not as idle as my mother thinks. But she then proceeded to list the names of my classmates at elementary school who had either died or had been wounded in the present war. As, one after another, I read those names, the world grew hollow, all human life quite futile. And she ended her letter by saying, 'since I am getting old, perhaps this New Year's rice-cakes will be my last. . .' You will understand that, as she wrote so very dishearteningly, I grew more and more depressed. I began to yearn for Beauchamp to come soon, but somehow he didn't. And at last it was time for supper. I thought of writing in reply to my mother, and I actually wrote about a dozen lines. My mother's letter was more than six feet long, but, unable myself to match such a prodigious performance, I usually excuse myself after writing some ten lines. As I had been sitting down for the whole of the day, my stomach felt strange and heavy. Thinking that if Beauchamp did turn up he could jolly well wait, I went out for a walk to post my letter. Instead of going toward Fujimicho, which is my usual course, I went, without my knowing it, out toward the third embankment. It was a little cloudy that evening and a dry wind was blowing across from the other side of the moat. It was terribly cold. A train coming from the direction of Kagurazaka passed with a whistle along the lower part of the bank. I felt very lonely. The end of the year, those deaths on the battlefield, senility, life's insecurity, that time and tide wait for no man, and other thoughts of a similar nature ran around in my head. One often talks about hanging oneself. But I was beginning to think that one could be tempted to commit suicide just at such a time as this. It so happened that at that moment I raised my head slightly, and, as I looked up to the top of the bank, I found myself standing right below that very pine tree."

"That very pine tree? What's that?" cuts in my master.

"The pine for hanging heads," says Waverhouse ducking his noddle.

"Isn't the pine for hanging heads that one at Kōnodai?" Coldmoon amplifies the ripple.

"The pine at Kōnodai is the pine for hanging temple bells. The pine at Dotesambanchō is the one for hanging heads. The reason why it has acquired this name is that an old legend says that anyone who finds himself under this pine tree is stricken with a desire to hang himself. Though there are several dozen pine trees on the bank, every time someone hangs himself, it is invariably on this particular tree that the body is found dangling. I can assure you there are at least two or three such danglings every year. It would be unthinkable to go and dangle on any other pine. As I stared at the tree I noted that a branch stuck out conveniently toward the pavement. Ah! What an exquisitely fashioned branch. It would be a real pity to leave it as it is. I wish so much that I could arrange for some human body to be suspended there. I look around to see if anyone is coming. Unfortunately, no one comes. It can't be helped. Shall I hang myself? No, no, if I hang myself, I'll lose my life. I won't because it's dangerous. But I've heard a story that an ancient Greek used to entertain banquet parties by giving demonstrations of how to hang oneself. A man would stand on a stool and the very second that he put his head through a noose, a second man would kick the stool from under him. The trick was that the first man would loosen the knot in the rope just as his stool was kicked away, and so drop down unharmed. If this story is really true, I've no need to be frightened. So thinking I might try the trick myself, I place my hand on the branch and find it bends in a manner precisely appropriate. Indeed the way it bends is positively aesthetic. I feel extraordinarily happy as I try to picture myself floating on this branch. I felt I simply must try it, but then I began to think that it would be inconsiderate if Beauchamp were waiting for me. Right, I would first see Beauchamp and have the chat I'd promised; thereafter I could come out again. So thinking, I went home."

"And is that the happy ending to your story?" asks my master.

"Very interesting," says Coldmoon with a broad grin.

"When I got home, Beauchamp had not arrived. Instead, I found a postcard from him saying that he was sorry he could not keep our appointment because of some pressing but unexpected happening, and that he was looking forward to having a long interview with me in the near future. I was relieved, and I felt happy, for now I could hang myself with an easy mind. Accordingly, I hurry back to the same spot, and then. . ." Waverhouse, assuming a nonchalant air, gazes at Coldmoon and my master.

"And then, what happened?" My master is becoming a little impatient.

"We've now come to the climax," says Coldmoon as he twists the strings of his surcoat.

"And then, somebody had beaten me to it and had already hanged himself. I'm afraid I missed the chance just by a second. I see now that I had been in the grip of the God of Death. William James, that eminent philosopher, would no doubt explain that the region of the dead in the world of one's subliminal consciousness and the real world in which I actually exist, must have interacted in mutual response in accordance with some kind of law of cause and effect. But it really was extraordinary, wasn't it?" Waverhouse looks quite demure.

My master, thinking that he has again been taken in, says nothing but crams his mouth with bean-jam cake and mumbles incoherently.

Coldmoon carefully rakes smooth the ashes in the brazier and casts down his eyes, grinning; eventually he opens his mouth. He speaks in an extremely quiet tone.

"It is indeed so strange that it does not seem a thing likely to happen. On the other hand, because I myself have recently had a similar kind of experience, I can readily believe it."

"What! Did you too want to stretch your neck?"

"No, mine wasn't a hanging matter. It seems all the more strange in that it also happened at the end of last year, at about the same time and on the same day as the extraordinary experience of Mr. Waverhouse."

"That's interesting," says Waverhouse. And he, too, stuffs his mouth with bean-jam cake.

"On that day, there was a year-end party combined with a concert given at the house of a friend of mine at Mukōjima. I went there taking my violin with me. It was a grand affair with fifteen or sixteen young or married ladies. Everything was so perfectly arranged that one felt it was the most brilliant event of recent times. When the dinner and the concert were over, we sat and talked late, and as I was about to take my leave, the wife of a certain doctor came up to me and asked in whisper if I knew that Miss O was unwell. A few days earlier, when last I saw Miss O, she had been looking well and normal. So I was surprised to hear this news, and my immediate questions elicited the information that she had become feverish on the very evening of the day when I'd last seen her, and that she was saying all sorts of curious things in her delirium. What was worse, every now and again in that delirium, she was calling my name."

Not only my master but even Waverhouse refrain from making any such hackneyed remark as "you lucky fellow." They just listen in silence.

"They fetched a doctor who examined her. According to the doctor's diagnosis, though the name of the disease was unknown, the high fever affecting the brain made her condition dangerous unless the administration of soporifics worked as effectively as was to be hoped for. As soon as I heard this news, a feeling of something awful grew within me. It was a heavy feeling, as though one were having a nightmare, and all the surrounding air seemed suddenly to be solidifying like a clamp upon my body. On my way home, moreover, I found I could think of nothing else, and it hurt. That beautiful, that gay, that so healthy Miss O. . ."

"Just a minute, please. You've mentioned Miss O about two times. If you've no objection, we'd like to know her name wouldn't we?" asks Waverhouse turning to look at my master. The latter evades the question and says, "Hmm."

"No, I won't tell you her name since it might compromise the person in question."

"Do you then propose to recount your entire story in such vague, ambiguous, equivocal, and noncommittal terms?"

"You mustn't sneer. This is a serious story. Anyway, the thought of that young lady suffering from so odd an ailment filled my heart with mournful emotion, and my mind with sad reflections on the ephemerality of life. I felt suddenly depressed beyond all saying, as if every last ounce of my vitality had, just like that, evaporated from my body. I staggered on, tottering and wobbling, until I came to the Azuma Bridge. As I looked down, leaning on the parapet, the black waters—at neap or ebb, I don't know which—seemed to be coagulating, only just barely moving. A rickshaw coming from the direction of Hanakawado ran over the bridge. I watched its lamp grow smaller and smaller until it disappeared at the Sapporo Beer factory. Again, I looked down at the water. And at that moment I heard a voice from upstream calling my name. It is most improbable that anyone should be calling after me at this unlikely time of night, and, wondering whom it could possibly be, I peered down to the surface of the water, but I could see nothing in the darkness. Thinking it must have been my imagination, I had decided to go home, when I again heard the voice calling my name. I stood dead-still and listened. When I heard it calling me for the third time, though I was gripping the parapet firmly, my knees began to tremble uncontrollably. The voice seemed to be coming either from far away or from the bottom of the river, but it was unmistakably the voice of Miss O. In spite of myself I answered, 'Yes.' My answer was so loud that it echoed back from the still water, and, surprised by my own voice, I looked around me in a startled manner. There was no one to be seen. No dog. No moon. Nothing. At this very second I experienced a sudden urge to immerse myself in that total darkness from which the voice had summoned me. And, once again, the voice of Miss O pierced my ears painfully, appealingly, as if begging for help. This time I cried, 'I'm coming now,' and, leaning well out over the parapet, I looked down into the somber depths. For, it seemed to me that the summoning voice was surging powerfully up from beneath the waves. Thinking that the source of the pleading must lie in the water directly below me, I at last managed to clamber onto the parapet. I was determined that, next time the voice called out to me, I would dive straight in; and, as I stood watching the stream, once again the thin thread of that pitiful voice came floating up to me. This, I thought, is it; jumping high with all my strength, I came dropping down without regret like a pebble, or something."

"So, you actually did dive in?" asks my master, blinking his eyes.

"I never thought you'd go as far as that," says Waverhouse pinching the tip of his nose.

"After my dive I became unconscious, and for a while I seemed to be living in a dream. But eventually I woke up, and, though I felt cold, I was not at all wet and did not feel as if I had swallowed any water. Yet I was sure that I had dived. How very strange! Realizing that something peculiar must have taken place, I looked around me and received a real shock. I'd meant to dive into the water but apparently I'd accidentally landed in the middle of the bridge itself. I felt abysmally regretful. Having, by sheer mistake, jumped backwards instead of forwards, I'd lost my chance to answer the summons of the voice." Coldmoon smirks and fiddles with the strings of his surcoat as if they were in some way irksome.

"Ha-ha-ha, how very comical. It's odd that your experience so much resembles mine. It, too, could be adduced in support of the theories of Professor James. If you were to write it up in an article entitled 'The Human Response,' it would astound the whole literary world. But what," persisted Waverhouse, "became of the ailing Miss O?"

"When I called at her house a few days ago, I saw her just inside the gate playing battledore and shuttlecock with her maid. So I expect she has completely recovered from her illness."

My master, who for some time has been deep in thought, finally opens his mouth, and, in a spirit of unnecessary rivalry, remarks, "I too have a strange experience to relate."

"You've got what?" In Waverhouse's view, my master counts for so little that he is scarcely entitled to have experiences.

"Mine also occurred at the end of last year."

"It's queer," observed Coldmoon, "that all last year," and he sniggers. A piece of bean-jam cake adheres to the corner of his chipped front tooth.

"And it took place, doubtless," added Waverhouse, "at the very same time on the very same day."

"No, I think the date is different: it was about the 20th. My wife had earlier asked me, as a year's-end present to herself, to take her to hear Settsu Daijō. I'd replied that I wouldn't say no, and asked her the nature of the program for that day. She consulted the newspapers and answered that it was one of Chikamatsu's suicide dramas, *Unagidani*. 'Let's not go today, I don't like *Unagidani*,' said I. So we did not go that day. The next day my wife, bringing out the newspaper again, said, 'Today he's doing the *Monkey Man at Horikawa*, so, let's go.' I said let's not, because *Horikawa* was so frivolous, just *samisen*-playing with no meat in it. My wife went away looking discontented. The following day, she stated almost as a demand, 'Today's program is *The Temple With Thirty-Three Pillars*. You may dislike the *Temple* quite as strongly as you disliked all the others, but since the treat is intended to be for me, surely you won't object to taking me there.' I responded, 'If you've set your heart on it so firmly, then we'll go, but since the performance has been announced as Settsu's farewell appearance on the stage, the house is bound to be packed full, and since we haven't booked in advance, it will obviously be impossible to get in. To start with, in order to attend such performances there's an established procedure to be observed. You have to go to the theatre-teahouse and there negotiate for seat reservations. It would be hopeless to try going about it in the wrong way. You just can't dodge this proper procedure. So, sorry though I am, we simply cannot go today.' My wife's eyes glittered fiercely. 'Since I am a mere woman, I do not understand your complicated procedures, but both Ōhare's mother and Kimiyo of the Suzuki family managed to get in without observance of any such formalities, and they heard everything very well. I realize that you are a teacher, but surely you don't have to go through all that troublesome rigmarole just to visit a theatre? It's too bad. . . you are so. . .' and her voice became tearful. I gave in. 'All right. We'll go to the theatre even if we can't get into it. After an early supper we'll take the tram.' She suddenly became quite lively. 'If we're going, we must be there by four o'clock, so we mustn't dilly-dally.' When I asked her why one had to be there by four o'clock, she explained that Kimiyo had told her that, if one arrived any later, all the seats would be taken. I asked her again, to make quite sure, if it would be fruitless to turn up later than four o'clock; and she answered briskly, 'Of course it would be no good.' Then, d'you know, at that very moment the shivering set in."

"Do you mean your wife?" asks Coldmoon.

"Oh, no, my wife was as fit as a fiddle. It was me. I had a sudden feeling that I was shriveling like a pricked balloon. Then I grew giddy and unable even to move."

"You were taken ill with a most remarkable suddenness," commented Waverhouse.

"This is terrible. What shall I do? I'd like so much to grant my wife her wish, her one and only request in the whole long year. All I ever do is scold her fiercely, or not speak to her, or nag her about household expenses, or insist that she cares more carefully for the children; yet I have never rewarded her for all her efforts in the domestic field. Today, luckily, I have the time and the money available. I could easily take her on some little outing. And she very much wants to go. Just as I very much want to take her. But much indeed as I want to take her, this icy shivering and frightful giddiness make it impossible for me even to step down from the entrance of my own house, let alone to climb up into a tram. The more I think how deeply I grieve for her, the poor thing, the worse my shivering grows and the more giddy I become. I thought if I consulted a doctor and took some medicine, I might get well before four o'clock. I discussed the matter with my wife and sent for Mr. Amaki, Bachelor of Medicine. Unfortunately, he had been on night duty at the university hospital and hadn't yet come home. However, we received every assurance that he was expected home by about two o'clock and that he would hurry round to see me the minute he returned. What a nuisance. If only I could get some sedative, I know I could be cured before four. But when luck is running against one, nothing goes well. Here I am, just this once in a long, long time, looking forward to seeing my wife's happy smile, and to be sharing in that happiness. My expectations seem sadly unlikely to be fulfilled. My wife, with a most reproachful look, enquires whether it really is impossible for me to go out. 'I'll go; certainly I'll go. Don't worry. I'm sure I'll be all right by four. Wash your face, get ready to go out and wait for me.' Though I uttered all these reassurance, my mind was shaken with profound emotions. The shivering strengthens and accelerates, and my giddiness grows worse and worse. Unless I do get well by four o'clock and implement my promise, one can never tell what such a pusillanimous woman might do. What a wretched business. What should I do? As I thought it possible that the very worst could happen, I began to consider whether perhaps it might be my duty as a husband to explain to my wife, now while I was still in possession of my faculties, the dread truths concerning mortality and the vicissitudes of life. For if the worst should happen, she would then at least be prepared and less liable to be overcome by the paroxysms of her grief. I accordingly summoned my wife to come immediately to my study. But when I began by saying, 'Though but a woman you must be aware of that Western proverb which states that there is many a slip "twixt the cup and the lip,"' she flew into a fury. 'How should I know anything at all about such sideways-written words? You're deliberately making a fool of me by choosing to speak English when you know perfectly well that I don't understand a word of it. All right. So I can't understand English. But if you're so besotted about English, why didn't you marry one of those girls from the mission schools? I've never come across anyone quite so cruel as you.' In the face of this tirade, my kindly feelings, my husbandly anxiety to prepare her for extremities, were naturally damped down. I'd like you two to understand that it was not out of malice that I spoke in English. The words sprang solely from a sincere sentiment of love for my wife. Consequently, my wife's malign interpretation of my motives left me feeling helpless. Besides, my brain was somewhat disturbed by reason of the cold shivering and the giddiness; on top of all that, I was understandably distraught by the effort of trying quickly to explain to her the truths of mortality and the nature of the vicissitudes of life. That was why, quite unconsciously and forgetting that my wife could not understand the tongue, I spoke in English. I immediately realized I was in the wrong. It was all entirely my fault. But as a result of my blunder, the cold shivering intensified its violence and my giddiness grew ever more viciously vertiginous. My wife, in accordance with my instructions, proceeds to the bathroom and, stripping herself to the waist, completes her make-up. Then, taking a kimono from a drawer, she puts it on. Her attitudes make it quite clear that she is now ready to go out any time, and is simply waiting for me. I begin to get nervous. Wishing that Mr. Amaki would arrive quickly, I look at my watch. It's already three o'clock. Only one hour to go. My wife slides open the study door and putting her head in, asks, 'Shall we go now?' It may sound silly to praise one's own wife, but I had never thought her quite so beautiful as she was at that moment. Her skin, thoroughly polished with soap, gleams deliciously and makes a marvelous contrast with the blackness of her silken surcoat. Her face has a kind of radiance both externally and shining from within; partly because of the soap and partly because of her intense longing to listen to Settsu Daijō. I feel I must, come what may, take her out to satisfy that yearning. All right, perhaps I will make the awful effort to go out. I was smoking and thinking along these lines when at long last Mr. Amaki arrived. Excellent. Things are turning out as one would wish. However, when I told him about my condition, Amaki examined my tongue, took my pulse, tapped my chest, stroked my back, turned my eyelids inside out, patted my skull, and thereafter sank into deep thought for quite some time. I said to him, 'It is my impression that there may be some danger. . .' but he replied, 'No, I don't think there's anything seriously wrong.' 'I imagine it would be perfectly all right for him to go out for a little while?' asked my wife. 'Let me think.' Amaki sank back into the profundities of thought, reemerging to remark, 'Well, so long as he doesn't feel unwell. . .' 'Oh, but I do feel unwell,' I said. In that case I'll give you a mild sedative and some liquid medicine. . .' 'Yes please. This is going to be something serious, isn't it?' 'Oh no, there's nothing to worry about. You mustn't get nervous,' said Amaki, and thereupon departed. It is now half past three. The maid was sent to fetch the medicine. In accordance with my wife's imperative instructions, the wretched girl not only ran the whole way there, but also the whole way back. It is now a quarter to four. Fifteen minutes still to go. Then, quite suddenly, just about that time, I began to feel sick. It came on with a quite extraordinary suddenness. All totally unexpected. My wife had poured the medicine into a teacup and placed it in front of me, but as soon as I tried to lift the teacup, some keck-keck thing stormed up from within the stomach. I am compelled to put the teacup down. 'Drink it up quickly' urges my wife. Yes, indeed, I must drink it quickly and go out quickly. Mustering all my courage to imbibe the potion I bring the teacup to my lips, when again that insuppressible keck-keck thing prevents my drinking it. While this process of raising the cup and putting it down is being several times repeated, the minutes crept on until the wall clock in the living room struck four o'clock. Ting-ting-ting-ting. Four o'clock it is. I can no longer dilly-dally and I raise the teacup once again. D'you know, it really was most strange. I'd say that it was certainly the uncanniest thing I've ever experienced. At the fourth stroke my sickliness just vanished, and I was able to take the medicine without any trouble at all. And, by about ten past four—here I must add that I now realized for the first time how truly skilled a physician we have in Dr. Amaki—the shivering of my back and the giddiness in my head both disappeared like a dream. Up to that point I had expected that I was bound to be laid up for days, but to my great pleasure the illness proved to have been completely cured."

"And did you two then go out to the theatre?" asks Waverhouse with the puzzled expression of one who cannot see the point of a story.

"We certainly both wanted to go, but since it had been my wife's reiterated view that there was no hope of getting in after four o'clock, what could we do? We didn't go. If only Amaki had arrived fifteen minutes earlier, I could have kept my promise and my wife would have been satisfied. Just that fifteen minute difference. I was indeed distressed. Even now, when I think how narrow the margin was, I am again distressed."

My master, having told his shabby tale, contrives to look like a person who has done his duty. I imagine he feels he's gotten even with the other two.

"How very vexing," says Coldmoon. His laugh, as usual, displays his broken tooth.

Waverhouse, with a false naivety, remarks as if to himself. "Your wife, with a husband so thoughtful and kind-hearted, is indeed a lucky woman." Behind the sliding paper-door, we heard the master's wife make an harumphing noise as though clearing her throat.

I had been quietly listening to the successive stories of these three precious humans, but I was neither amused nor saddened by what I'd heard. I merely concluded that human beings were good for nothing, except for the strenuous employment of their mouths for the purpose of whiling away their time in laughter at things which are not funny, and in the enjoyment of amusements which are not amusing. I have long known of my master's selfishness and narrowmindedness, but, because he usually has little to say, there was always something about him which I could not understand. I'd felt a certain caution, a certain fear, even a certain respect toward him on account of that aspect of his nature that I did not understand. But having heard his story, my uncertainties suddenly coalesced into a mere contempt for him. Why can't he listen to the stories of the other two in silence? What good purpose can he serve by talking such utter rubbish just because his competitive spirit has been roused? I wonder if, in his portentous writings, Epictetus advocated any such course of action. In short, my master, Waverhouse, and Coldmoon are all like hermits in a peaceful reign. Though they adopt a nonchalant attitude, keeping themselves aloof from the crowd, segegrated like so many snake-gourds swayed lightly by the wind, in reality they, too, are shaken by just the same greed and worldly ambition as their fellow men. The urge to compete and their anxiety to win are revealed flickeringly in their everyday conversation, and only a hair's breadth separates them from the Philistines whom they spend their idle days denouncing. They are all animals from the same den. Which fact, from a feline viewpoint, is infinitely regrettable. Their only moderately redeeming feature is that their speech and conduct are less tediously uninventive than those of less subtle creatures.

As I thus summed up the nature of the human race, I suddenly felt the conversation of these specimens to be intolerably boring, so I went around to the garden of the mistress of the two-stringed harp to see how Tortoiseshell was getting on. Already the pine tree decorations for the New Year and that season's sacred festoons have been taken down. It is the 10th of January. From a deep sky containing not even a single streak of cloud the glorious springtime sun shines down upon the lands and seas of the whole wide world, so that even her tiny garden seems yet more brilliantly lively than when it saw the dawn of New Year's Day. There is a cushion on the veranda, the sliding paper-door is closed, and there's nobody about. Which probably means that the mistress has gone off to the public baths. I'm not at all concerned if the mistress should be out, but I do very much worry about whether Tortoiseshell is any better. Since everything's so quiet and not a sign of a soul, I hop up onto the veranda with my muddy paws and curl up right in the middle of the cushion, which I find comfortable. A drowsiness came over me, and, forgetting all about Tortoiseshell, I was about to drop off into a doze when suddenly I heard voices beyond the paper-door.

"Ah, thanks. Was it ready?" The mistress has not gone out after all.

"Yes, madam. I'm sorry to have taken such a long time. When I got there, the man who makes Buddhist altar furniture told me he'd only just finished it."

"Well, let me see it. Ah, but it's beautifully done. With this, Tortoiseshell can surely rest in peace. Are you sure the gold won't peel away?"

"Yes, I've made sure of it. They said that as they had used the very best quality, it would last longer than most human memorial tablets. They also said that the character for 'honor' in Tortoiseshell's posthumous name would look better if written in the cursive style, so they had added the appropriate strokes."

"Is that so? Well, let's put Myōyoshinnyo's tablet in the family shrine and offer incense sticks."

Has anything happened to Tortoiseshell? Thinking something must be wrong, I stand up on the cushion. Ting! "Amen! Myōyoshinnyo. Save us, merciful Buddha! May she rest in peace." It is the voice of the mistress.

"You, too, say prayers for her."

Ting! "Amen! Myōyoshinnyo. Save us, merciful Buddha! May she rest in peace." Suddenly my heart throbs violently. I stand dead-still upon the cushion, like a wooden cat; not even my eyes are moving.

"It really was a pity. It was only a cold at first."

"Perhaps if Dr. Amaki had given her some medicine, it might have helped."

"It was indeed Amaki's fault. He paid too little regard to Tortoiseshell."

"You must not speak ill of other persons. After all, everyone dies when their allotted span is over."

It seems that Tortoiseshell was also attended by that skilled physician, Dr. Amaki.

"When all's said and done, I believe the root cause was that the stray cat at the teacher's in the main street took her out too often."

"Yes, that brute."

I would like to exculpate myself, but realizing that at this juncture it behoves me to be patient, I swallow hard and continue listening. There is a pause in the conversation.

"Life does not always turn out as one wishes. A beauty like Tortoiseshell dies young. That ugly stray remains healthy and flourishes in devilment. . ."

"It is indeed so, Madam. Even if one searched high and low for a cat as charming as Tortoiseshell, one would never find another person like her."

She didn't say 'another cat,' she said 'another person.' The maid seems to think that cats and human beings are of one race. Which reminds me that the face of this particular maid is strangely like a cat's.

"If only instead of our dear Tortoiseshell. . ."

". . . that wretched stray at the teacher's had been taken. Then, Madam, how perfectly everything would have gone. . ."

If everything had gone that perfectly, I would have been in deep trouble. Since I have not yet had the experience of being dead, I cannot say whether or not I would like it. But the other day, it happening to be unpleasantly chilly, I crept into the tub for conserving half-used charcoal and settled down upon its still-warm contents. The maid, not realizing I was in there, popped on the lid. I shudder even now at the mere thought of the agony I then suffered. According to Miss Blanche, the cat across the road, one dies if that agony continues for even a very short stretch. I wouldn't complain if I were asked to substitute for Tortoiseshell; but if one cannot die without going through that kind of agony, I frankly would not care to die on anyone's behalf.

"Though a cat, she had her funeral service conducted by a priest and now she's been given a posthumous Buddhist name. I don't think she would expect us to do more."

"Of course not, madam. She is indeed thrice blessed. The only comment that one might make is that the funeral service read by the priest was, perhaps, a little wanting in gravity."

"Yes, and I thought it rather too brief. But when I remarked to the priest from the Gekkei Temple 'you've finished very quickly, haven't you?' he answered 'I've done sufficient of the effective parts, quite enough to get a kitty into Paradise.'"

"Dear me! But if the cat in question were that unpleasant stray. . ."

I have pointed out often enough that I have no name, but this maid keeps calling me "that stray." She is a vulgar creature.

"So very sinful a creature. Madam, would never be able to rest in peace, however many edifying texts were read for its salvation."

I do not know how many hundreds of times I was thereafter stigmatized as a stray. I stopped listening to their endless babble while it was still only half-run, and, slipping down from the cushion, I jumped off the veranda. Then,simultaneously erecting every single one of my eighty-eight thousand, eight hundred, eighty hairs, I shook my whole body. Since that day I have not ventured near the mistress of the two-stringed harp. No doubt by now she herself is having texts of inadequate gravity read on her behalf by the priest from the Gekkei Temple.

Nowadays I haven't even energy to go out. Somehow life seems weary. I have become as indolent a cat as my master is an indolent human. I have come to understand that it is only natural that people should so often explain my master's self-immurement in his study as the result of a love affair gone wrong.

As I have never caught a rat, that O-san person once proposed that I should be expelled; but my master knows that I'm no ordinary common or garden cat, and that is why I continue to lead an idle existence in this house. For that understanding I am deeply grateful to my master. What's more, I take every opportunity to show the respect due to his perspicacity. I do not get particularly angry with O-san's ill-treatment of me, for she does not understand why I am as I now am. But when, one of these days, some master sculptor, some regular Hidari Jingorō, comes and carves my image on a temple gate; when some Japanese equivalent of the French master portraitist, Steinlein, immortalizes my features on a canvas, then at last will the silly purblind beings in shame regret their lack of insight.

III

TORTOISESHELL is dead, one cannot consort with Rickshaw Blacky, and I feel a little lonely. Luckily I have made acquaintances among humankind so I do not suffer from any real sense of boredom. Someone wrote recently asking my master to have my photograph taken and the picture sent to him. And then the other day somebody else presented some millet dumplings, that speciality of Okayama, specifically addressed to me. The more that humans show me sympathy, the more I am inclined to forget that I am a cat. Feeling that I am now closer to humans than to cats, the idea of rallying my own race in an effort to wrest supremacy from the bipeds no longer has the least appeal. Moreover, I have developed, indeed evolved, to such an extent that there are now times when I think of myself as just another human in the human world; which I find very encouraging. It is not that I look down on my own race, but it is no more than natural to feel most at ease among those whose attitudes are similar to one's own. I would consequently feel somewhat piqued if my growing penchant for mankind were stigmatized as fickleness or flippancy or treachery. It is precisely those who sling such words about in slanderous attacks on others who are usually both drearily straight-laced and born unlucky. Having thus graduated from felinity to humanity, I find myself no longer able to confine my interests to the world of Tortoiseshell and Blacky. With a haughtiness not less prideful than that of human beings, I, too, now like to judge and criticize their thoughts and words and deeds. This, surely, is equally natural. Yet, though I have become thus proudly conscious of my own dignity, my master still regards me as a cat only slightly superior to any other common or garden moggy. For, as if they were his own and without so much as a by-your-leave to me, he has eaten all the millet dumplings; which is, I find, regrettable. Nor does he seem yet to have dispatched my photograph. I suppose I would be justified if I made this fact a cause for grumbling, but after all, if our opinions—my master's and mine—are naturally at difference, the consequences of that difference cannot be helped. Since I am seeking to behave with total humanity, I'm finding it increasingly difficult to write about the activities of cats with whom I no longer associate. I must accordingly seek the indulgence of my readers if I now confine my writing to reports about such respected figures as Waverhouse and Coldmoon.

Today is a Sunday and the weather fine. The master has therefore crept out of his study, and, placing a brush, an ink stone, and a writing pad in a row before him, he now lies flat on his belly beside me, and is groaning hard. I watch him, thinking that he is perhaps making this peculiar noise in the birth pangs of some literary effort. After a while, and in thick black strokes, he wrote, "Burn incense." Is it going to be a poem or a *haiku*? Just when I was thinking that the phrase was rather too witty for my master, he abandons it, and, his brush running quickly over the paper, writes an entirely new line: "Now for some little time I have been thinking of writing an article about Mr. the-late-and-sainted Natural Man." At this point the brush stops dead. My master, brush in hand, racks his brains, but no bright notions seem to emerge for he now starts licking the head of his brush. I watched his lips acquire a curious inkiness. Then, underneath what he had just written, he drew a circle, put in two dots as eyes, added a nostrilled nose in the center, and finally drew a single sideways line for a mouth. One could not call such creations either *haiku* or prose. Even my master must have been disgusted with himself, for he quickly smeared away the face. He then starts a new line. He seems to have some vague notion that, provided he himself produces a new line, maybe some kind of a Chinese poem will evolve itself. After further moonings, he suddenly started writing briskly in the colloquial style. "Mr. the-late-and-sainted Natural Man is one who studies Infinity, reads the *Analects* of Confucius, eats baked yams, and has a runny nose." A somewhat muddled phrase. He thereupon read the phrase aloud in a declamatory manner and, quite unlike his usual self, laughed. "Ha-ha-ha. Interesting! But that 'runny nose' is a shade cruel, so I'll cross it out," and he proceeds to draw lines across that phrase. "Though a single line would clearly have sufficed, he draws two lines and then three lines. He goes on drawing more and more lines regardless of their crowding into the neighboring line of writing. When he has drawn eight such obliterations, he seems unable to think of anything to add to his opening outburst. So he takes to twirling his mustache, determined to wring some telling sentence from his whiskers. He is still twisting them up and twirling them down when his wife appears from the living room, and sitting herself down immediately before my master's nose, remarks, "My dear."

"What is it?" My master's voice sounds dully like a gong struck under water. His wife seems not to like the answer, for she starts all over again. "My dear!" she says.

"Well, what is it?"

This time, cramming a thumb and index finger into a nostril, he yanks out nostril hairs.

"We are a bit short this month. . ."

"Couldn't possibly be short. We've settled the doctor's fee and we paid off the bookshop's bill last month. So this month, there ought in fact to be something left over." He coolly examines his uprooted nostril hairs as though they were some wonder of the world.

"But because you, instead of eating rice, have taken to bread and jam. . ."

"Well, how many tins of jam have I gone through?"

"This month, eight tins were emptied."

"Eight? I certainly haven't eaten that much."

"It wasn't only you. The children also lick it."

"However much one licks, one couldn't lick more than two or three shillings worth." My master calmly plants his nostril hairs, one by one, on the writing pad. The sticky-rooted bristles stand upright on the paper like a little copse of needles. My master seems impressed by this unexpected discovery and he blows upon them. Being so sticky, they do not fly away.

"Aren't they obstinate?" he says and blows upon them frantically.

"It is not only the jam. There's other things we have to buy." The lady of the house expresses her extreme dissatisfaction by pouting sulkily.

"Maybe." Again inserting his thumb and finger, he extracts some hairs with a jerk. Among these hairs of various hue, red ones and black ones, there is a single pure white bristle. My master who, with a look of great surprise, has been staring at this object, proceeds to show it to his wife, holding it up between his fingers right in front of her face.

"No, don't." She pushes his hand away with a grimace of distaste.

"Look at it! A white hair from the nostrils." My master seems to be immensely impressed. His wife, resigned, went back into the living room with a laugh. She seems to have given up hope of getting any answer to her problems of domestic economy. My master resumes his consideration of the problems of Natural Man.

Having succeeded in driving off his wife with his scourge of nostril hair, he appears to feel relieved, and, while continuing that depilation, struggles to get on with his article. But his brush remains unmoving. "That 'eats baked yams' is also superfluous. Out with it." He deletes the phrase. "And 'incense burns' is somewhat over-abrupt, so let's cross that out too." His exuberant self-criticism leaves nothing on the paper but the single sentence "Mr. the-late-and-sainted Natural Man is one who studies Infinity and reads the *Analects* of Confucius." My master thinks this statement a trifle over-simplified. "Ah well, let's not be bothered: let's abandon prose and just make it an inscription." Brandishing the brush crosswise, he paints vigorously on the writing pad in that watercolor style so common among literary men and produces a very poor study of an orchid. Thus all his precious efforts to write an article have come down to this mere nothing. Turning the sheet, he writes something that makes no sense. "Born in Infinity, studied Infinity, and died into Infinity. Mr. the-late-and-sainted Natural Man. Infinity." At this moment Waverhouse drifts into the room in his usual casual fashion. He appears to make no distinction between his own and other people's houses; unannounced and unceremoniously, he enters any house and, what's more, will sometimes float in unexpectedly through a kitchen door. He is one of those who, from the moment of their birth, discaul themselves of all such tiresome things as worry, reserve, scruple, and concern.

"'Giant Gravitation again?'" asks Waverhouse still standing.

"How could I be always writing only about 'Giant Gravitation?' I'm trying to compose an epitaph for the tombstone of Mr. the-late-and-sainted Natural Man," replied my master with considerable exaggeration.

"Is that some sort of posthumous Buddhist name like Accidental Child?" inquires Waverhouse in his usual irrelevant style.

"Is there then someone called Accidental Child?"

"No, of course there isn't, but I take it that you're working on something like that."

"I don't think Accidental Child is anyone I know. But Mr. the-late-and-sainted Natural Man is a person of your own acquaintance."

"Who on earth could get a name like that?"

"It's Sorosaki. After he graduated from the University, he took a postgraduate course involving study of the 'theory of infinity.' But he overworked, got peritonitis, and died of it. Sorosaki happened to be a very close friend of mine."

"All right, so he was your very close friend. I'm far from criticizing that fact. But who was responsible for converting Sorosaki into Mr. the-late-and-sainted Natural Man?"

"Me. I created that name. For there is really nothing more philistine than the posthumous names conferred by Buddhist priests." My master boasts as if his nomination of Natural Man were a feat of artistry.

"Anyway, let's see the epitaph," says Waverhouse laughingly. He picks up my master's manuscript and reads it out aloud. "Eh . . . 'Born into infinity, studied infinity, and died into infinity. Mr. the-late-and-sainted Natural Man. Infinity.' I see. This is fine. Quite appropriate for poor old Sorosaki."

"Good, isn't it?" says my master obviously very pleased.

"You should have this epitaph engraved on a weight-stone for pickles and then leave it at the back of the main hall of some temple for the practice-benefit of passing weight lifters. It's good. It's most artistic. Mr. the-late-and-sainted may now well rest in peace."

"Actually, I'm thinking of doing just that," answers my master quite seriously. "But you'll have to excuse me," he went on, "I won't be long. Just play with the cat. Don't go away." And my master departed like the wind without even waiting for Waverhouse to answer.

Being thus unexpectedly required to entertain the culture-vulture Waverhouse, I cannot very well maintain my sour attitude. Accordingly, I mew at him encouragingly and sidle up on to his knees. "Hello," says Waverhouse, "you've grown distinctly chubby. Let's take a look at you." Grabbing me impolitely by the scruff of my neck he hangs me up in midair. "Cats like you that let their hind legs dangle are cats that catch no mice. . . Tell me," he said, turning to my master's wife in the next room, "has he ever caught anything?"

"Far from catching so much as a single mouse, he eats rice-cakes and then dances." The lady of the house unexpectedly probes my old wound, which embarrassed me. Especially when Waverhouse still held me in midair like a circus-performer.

"Indeed, with such a face, it's not surprising that he dances. Do you know, this cat possesses a truly insidious physionomy. He looks like one of those goblin-cats illustrated in the old storybooks." Waverhouse, babbling whatever comes into his head, tries to make conversation with the mistress. She reluctantly interrupts her sewing and comes into the room.

"I do apologize. You must be bored. He won't be long now." And she poured fresh tea for him.

"I wonder where he's gone."

"Heaven only knows. He never explains where he's going. Probably to see his doctor."

"You mean Dr. Amaki? What a misfortune for Amaki to be involved with such a patient."

Perhaps finding this comment difficult to answer, she answers briefly: "Well, yes."

Waverhouse takes not the slightest notice, but goes on to ask, "How is he lately? Is his weak stomach any better?"

"It's impossible to say whether it's better or worse. However carefully Dr. Amaki may look after him, I don't see how his health can ever improve if he continues to consume such vast quantities of jam." She thus works off on Waverhouse her earlier grumblings to my master.

"Does he eat all that much jam? It sounds like a child."

"And not just jam. He's recently taken to guzzling grated radish on the grounds that it's a sovereign cure for dyspepsia."

"You surprise me," marvels Waverhouse.

"It all began when he read in some rag that grated radish contains diastase."

"I see. I suppose he reckons that grated radish will repair the ravages of jam. It's certainly an ingenious equation." Waverhouse seems vastly diverted by her recital of complaint.

"Then only the other day he forced some on the baby."

"He made the baby eat jam?"

"No, grated radish! Would you believe it? He said, 'Come here, my little babykin, father'll give you something good. . .' Whenever, once in a rare while, he shows affection for the children, he always does remarkably silly things. A few days ago he put our second daughter on top of a chest of drawers."

"What ingenious scheme was that?" Waverhouse looks to discover ingenuities in everything.

"There was no question of any ingenious scheme. He just wanted the child to make the jump when it's quite obvious that a little girl of three or four is incapable of such tomboy feats."

"I see. Yes, that proposal does indeed seem somewhat lacking in ingenuity. Still, he's a good man without an ill wish in his heart."

"Do you think that I could bear it if, on top of everything else, he were ill-natured?" She seems in uncommonly high spirits.

"Surely you don't have cause for such vehement complaint? To be as comfortably off as you are is, after all, the best way to be. Your husband neither leads the fast life nor squanders money on dandified clothing. He's a born family man of quiet taste." Waverhouse fairly lets himself go in unaccustomed laud of an unknown way of life.

"On the contrary, he's not at all like that. . ."

"Indeed? So he has secret vices? Well, one cannot be too careful in this world." Waverhouse offers a nonchalantly fluffy comment.

"He has no secret vices, but he is totally abandoned in the way he buys book after book, never to read a single one. I wouldn't mind if he used his head and bought in moderation, but no. Whenever the mood takes him, he ambles off to the biggest bookshop in the city and brings back home as many books as chance to catch his fancy. Then, at the end of the month, he adopts an attitude of complete detachment. At the end of last year, for instance, I had a terrible time coping with the bill that had been accumulating month after month."

"It doesn't matter that he should bring home however many books he may like. If, when the bill collector comes, you just say that you'll pay some other time, he'll go away."

"But one cannot put things off indefinitely." She looks cast down.

"Then you should explain the matter to your husband and ask him to cut down expenditure on books."

"And do you really believe he would listen to me? Why, only the other day, he said, 'You are so unlike a scholar's wife: you lack the least understanding of the value of books. Listen carefully to this story from ancient Rome. It will give you beneficial guidance for your future conduct.'"

"That sounds interesting. What sort of story was it?" Waverhouse becomes enthusiastic, though he appears less sympathetic to her predicament than prompted by sheer curiosity.

"It seems there was in ancient Rome a king named Tarukin."

"Tarukin? That sounds odd in Japanese."

"I can never remember the names of foreigners. It's all too difficult. Maybe he was a barrel of gold. He was, at any rate, the seventh king of Rome."

"Really? The seventh barrel of gold certainly sounds queer. But, tell me, what then happened to this seventh Tarukin."

"You mustn't tease me like that. You quite embarrass me. If you know this king's true name, you should teach me it. Your attitude," she snaps at him, "is really most unkind."

"I tease you? I wouldn't dream of doing such an unkind thing. It was simply that the seventh barrel of gold sounded so wonderful. Let's see. . . a Roman, the seventh king. . . I can't be absolutely certain but I rather think it must have been Tarquinius Superbus, Tarquin the Proud. Well, it doesn't really matter who it was. What did this monarch do?"

"I understand that some woman, Sibyl by name, went to this king with nine books and invited him to buy them."

"I see."

"When the king asked her how much she wanted, she stated a very high price, so high that the king asked for a modest reduction. Whereupon the woman threw three of the nine books into the fire where they were quickly burnt to ashes."

"What a pity!"

"The books were said to contain prophecies, predictions, things like that of which there was no other record anywhere."

"Really?"

"The king, believing that six books were bound to be cheaper than nine, asked the price of the remaining volumes. The price proved to be exactly the same; not one penny less. When the king complained of this outrageous development, the women threw another three books into the fire. The king apparently still hankered for the books and he accordingly asked the price of the last three left. The woman again demanded the same price as she had asked for the original nine. Nine books had shrunk to six, and then to three, but the price remained unaltered even by a farthing. Suspecting that any attempt to bargain would merely lead the woman to pitch the last three volumes into the flames, the king bought them at the original staggering price. My husband appeared confident that, having heard this story, I would begin to appreciate the value of books, but I don't at all see what it is that I'm supposed to have learnt to appreciate."

Having thus stated her own position, she as good as challenges Waverhouse to contravert her. Even the resourceful Waverhouse seems to be at a loss. He draws a handkerchief from the sleeve of his kimono and tempts me to play with it. Then, in a loud voice as if an idea had suddenly struck him, he remarked, "But you know, Mrs. Sneaze, it is precisely because your husband buys so many books and fills his head with wild notions that he is occasionally mentioned as a scholar, or something of that sort. Only the other day a comment on your husband appeared in a literary magazine."

"Really?" She turns around. After all, it's only natural that his wife should feel anxiety about comments on my master.

"What did it say?"

"Oh, only a few lines. It said that Mr. Sneaze's prose was like a cloud that passes in the sky, like water flowing in a stream."

"Is that," she asks smiling, "all that it said?"

"Well, it also said 'it vanishes as soon as it appears and, when it vanishes, it is forever forgetful to return.'"

The lady of the house looks puzzled and asks anxiously "Was that praise?"

"Well, yes, praise of a sort," says Waverhouse coolly as he jiggles his handkerchief in front of me.

"Since books are essential to his work, I suppose one shouldn't complain, but his eccentricity is so pronounced that. . ."

Waverhouse assumes that she's adopting a new line of attack. "True," he interrupts, "he is a little eccentric, but any man who pursues learning tends to get like that." His answer, excellently noncommittal, contrives to combine ingratiation and special pleading.

"The other day, when he had to go somewhere soon after he got home from school, he found it too troublesome to change his clothes. So do you know, he sat down on his low desk without even taking off his overcoat and ate his dinner just as he was. He had his tray put on the footwarmer while I sat on the floor holding the rice container. It was really very funny. . ."

"It sounds like the old-time custom when generals sat down to identify the severed heads of enemies killed in battle. But that would be quite typical of Mr. Sneaze. At any rate he's never boringly conventional." Waverhouse offers a somewhat strained compliment.

"A woman cannot say what's conventional or unconventional, but I do think his conduct is often unduly odd."

"Still, that's better than being conventional." As Waverhouse moves firmly to the support of my master, her dissatisfaction deepens.

"People are always saying this or that is conventional, but would you please tell what makes a thing conventional?" Adopting a defiant attitude, she demands a definition of conventionality.

"Conventional? When one says something is conventional. . . It's a bit difficult to explain. . ."

"If it's so vague a thing, surely there's nothing wrong with being conventional." She begins to corner Waverhouse with typically feminine logic.

"No, it isn't vague, it's perfectly clear-cut. But it's hard to explain."

"I expect you call everything you don't like conventional." Though totally uncalculated, her words land smack on target. Waverhouse is now indeed cornered and can no longer dodge defining the conventional.

"I'll give you an example. A conventional man is one who would yearn after a girl of sixteen or eighteen but, sunk in silence, never do anything about it; a man who, whenever the weather's fine, would do no more than stroll along the banks of the Sumida taking, of course, a flask of *saké* with him."

"Are there really such people?" Since she cannot make heads or tails of the twaddle vouchsafed by Waverhouse, she begins to abandon her position, which she finally surrenders by saying, "It's all so complicated that it's really quite beyond me."

"You think that complicated? Imagine fitting the head of Major Pendennis onto Bakin's torso, wrapping it up and leaving it all for one or two years exposed to European air."

"Would that produce a conventional man?" Waverhouse offers no reply but merely laughs.

"In fact it could be produced without going to quite so much trouble. If you added a shop assistant from a leading store to any middle school student and divided that sum by two, then indeed you'd have a fine example of a conventional man."

"Do you really think so?" She looks puzzled but certainly unconvinced.

"Are you still here?" My master sits himself down on the floor beside Waverhouse. We had not noticed his return.

" 'Still here' is a bit hard. You said you wouldn't be long and you yourself invited me to wait for you."

"You see, he's always like that," remarks the lady of the house leaning toward Waverhouse.

"While you were away I heard all sorts of tales about you."

"The trouble with women is that they talk too much. It would be good if human beings would keep as silent as this cat." And the master strokes my head.

"I hear you've been cramming grated radish into the baby."

"Hum," says my master and laughs. He then added "Talking of the baby, modern babies are quite intelligent. Since that time when I gave our baby grated radish, if you ask him 'where is the hot place?' he invariably sticks out his tongue. Isn't it strange?"

"You sound as if you were teaching tricks to a dog. It's positively cruel. By the way, Coldmoon ought to have arrived by now."

"Is Coldmoon coming?" asks my master in a puzzled voice.

"Yes. I sent him a postcard telling him to be here not later than one o'clock."

"How very like you! Without even asking us if it happened to be convenient. What's the idea of asking Coldmoon here?"

"It's not really my idea, but Coldmoon's own request. It seems he is going to give a lecture to the Society of Physical Science. He said he needed to rehearse his speech and asked me to listen to it. Well, I thought it would be obliging to let you hear it, too. Accordingly, I suggested he should come to your house. Which should be quite convenient since you are a man of leisure. I know you never have any engagements. You'd do well to listen." Waverhouse thinks he knows how to handle the situation.

"I wouldn't understand a lecture on physical science," says my master in a voice betraying his vexation at his friend's high-handed action.

"On the contrary, his subject is no such dry-as-dust matter as, for example, the magnetized nozzle. The transcendentally extraordinary subject of his discourse is 'The Mechanics of Hanging.' Which should be worth listening to."

"Inasmuch as you once only just failed to hang yourself, I can understand your interest in the subject, but I'm. . ."

". . .The man who got cold shivers over going to the theatre, so you cannot expect not to listen to it." Waverhouse interjects one of his usual flippant remarks and Mrs. Sneaze laughs. Glancing back at her husband, she goes off into the next room. My master, keeping silent, strokes my head. This time, for once, he stroked me with delicious gentleness.

Some seven minutes later in comes the anticipated Coldmoon. Since he's due to give his lecture this same evening, he is not wearing his usual get-up. In a fine frock-coat and with a high and exceedingly white clean collar, he looks twenty per cent more handsome than himself. "Sorry to be late." He greets his two seated friends with perfect composure.

"It's ages that we've now been waiting for you. So we'd like you to start right away. Wouldn't we?" says Waverhouse, turning to look at my master. The latter, thus forced to respond, somewhat reluctantly says, "Hmm." But Coldmoon's in no hurry. He remarks, "I think I'll have a glass of water, please."

"I see you are going to do it in real style. You'll be calling next for a round of applause." Waverhouse, but he alone, seems to be enjoying himself.

Coldmoon produced his text from an inside pocket and observed, "Since it is the established practice, may I say I would welcome criticism." That invitation made, he at last begins to deliver his lecture.

"Hanging as a death penalty appears to have originated among the Anglo-Saxons. Previously, in ancient times, hanging was mainly a method of committing suicide. I understand that among the Hebrews it was customary to execute criminals by stoning them to death. Study of the *Old Testament* reveals that the word 'hanging' is there used to mean 'suspending a criminal's body after death for wild beasts and birds of prey to devour it.' According to Herodotus, it would seem that the Jews, even before they departed from Egypt, abominated the mere thought that their dead bodies might be left exposed at night. The Egyptians used to behead a criminal, nail the torso to a cross and leave it exposed during the night. The Persians. . ."

"Steady on, Coldmoon," Waverhouse interrupts. "You seem to be drifting farther and farther away from the subject of hanging. Do you think that wise?"

"Please be patient. I am just coming to the main subject. Now, with respect to the Persians. They, too, seemed to have used crucifixion as a method of criminal execution. However, whether the nailing took place while the criminal was alive or simply after his death is not incontrovertibly established."

"Who cares? Such details are really of little importance," yawned my master as from boredom.

"There are still many matters of which I'd like to inform you but, as it will perhaps prove tedious for you . . ."

" 'As it might prove' would sound better than 'as it will perhaps prove.' What d'you think, Sneaze?" Waverhouse starts carping again but my master answers coldly, "What difference could it make?"

"I have now come to the main subject, and will accordingly recite my piece."

"A storyteller 'recites a piece.' An orator should use more elegant diction." Waverhouse again interrupts.

"If to 'recite my piece' sounds vulgar, what words should I use?" asks Coldmoon in a voice that showed he was somewhat nettled.

"It is never clear, when one is dealing with Waverhouse, whether he's listening or interrupting. Pay no attention to his heckling, Coldmoon, just keep going." My master seeks to find a way through the difficulty as quickly as possible.

"So, having made your indignant recitation, now I suppose you've found the willow tree?" With a pun on a little known *haiku,* Waverhouse, as usual, comes up with something odd. Coldmoon, in spite of himself, broke into laughter.

"My researches reveal that the first account of the employment of hanging as a deliberate means of execution occurs in the *Odyssey*, volume twenty-two. The relevant passage records how Telemachus arranged the execution by hanging of Penelope's twelve ladies-in-waiting. I could read the passage aloud in its original Greek, but, since such an act might be regarded as an affectation, I will refrain from doing so. You will, however, find the passage between lines 465 and 473."

"You'd better cut out all that Hellenic stuff. It sounds as if you are just showing off your knowledge of Greek. What do you think, Sneaze?"

"On that point, I agree with you. It would be more modest, altogether an improvement, to avoid such ostentation." Quite unusually my master immediately sides with Waverhouse. The reason is, of course, that neither can read a word of Greek.

"Very well, I will this evening omit those references. And now I will recite. . . that is to say, I will now continue. Let us consider, then, how a hanging is actually carried out. One can envisage two methods. The first method is that adopted by Telemachus who, with the help of Eumaeus and Philoetios, tied one end of a rope to the top of a pillar: next, having made several loose loops in the rope, he forced a woman's head through each such loop, and finally hauled up hard on the other end of the rope."

"In short, he had the women dangling in a row like shirts hung out at a laundry. Right?"

"Exactly. Now the second method is, as in the first case, to tie one end of a rope to the top of a pillar and similarly to secure the other end of the rope somewhere high up on the ceiling. Thereafter, several other short ropes are attached to the main rope, and in each of these subsidiary ropes a slip-knot is then tied. The women's heads are then inserted in the slipknots. The idea is that at the crucial moment you remove the stools on which the women have been stood."

"They would then look something like those ball-shaped paper-lanterns one sometimes sees suspended from the end-tips of rope curtains, wouldn't they?" hazarded Waverhouse.

"That I cannot say," answered Coldmoon cautiously. "I have never seen any such ball as a paper-lantern-ball, but if such balls exist, the resemblance may be just. Now, the first method as described in the *Odyssey* is, in fact, mechanically impossible; and I shall proceed, for your benefit, to substantiate that statement."

"How interesting," says Waverhouse.

"Indeed, most interesting," adds my master.

"Let us suppose that the women are to be hanged at intervals of an equal distance, and that the rope between the two women nearest the ground stretches out horizontally, right? Now $\alpha 1$, $\alpha 2$ up to $\alpha 6$ become the angles between the rope and the horizon. T_1, T_2, and so on up to T_6 represent the force exerted on each section of the rope, so that $T_7 = X$ is the force exerted on the lowest part of the rope. W is, of course, the weight of the women. So far so good. Are you with me?"

My master and Waverhouse exchange glances and say, "Yes, more or less." I need hardly point out that the value of this "more or less" is singular to Waverhouse and my master. It could possibly have a different value for other people.

"Well, in accordance with the theory of averages as applied to the polygon, a theory with which you must of course be well acquainted, the following twelve equations can, in this particular case, be established:

$T_1 \cos \alpha l = T_2 \cos \alpha 2$......(1)

$T_2 \cos \alpha 2 = T_3 \cos \alpha 3$......(2)"

"I think that's enough of the equations," my master irresponsibly remarks.

"But these equations are the very essence of my lecture." Coldmoon really seems reluctant to be parted from them.

"In that case, let's hear those particular parts of its very essence at some other time." Waverhouse, too, seems out of his depth.

"But if I omit the full detail of the equations, it becomes impossible to substantiate the mechanical studies to which I have devoted so much effort. . ."

"Oh, never mind that. Cut them all out," came the cold-blooded comment of my master.

"That's most unreasonable. However, since you insist, I will omit them."

"That's good," says Waverhouse, unexpectedly clapping his hands.

"Now we come to England where, in *Beowulf*, we find the word 'gallows': that is to say 'galga.' It follows that hanging as a penalty must have been in use as early as the period with which the book is concerned. According to Blackstone, a convicted person who is not killed at his first hanging by reason of some fault in the rope should simply be hanged again. But, oddly enough, one finds it stated in *The Vision of Piers Plowman* that even a murderer should not be strung up twice. I do not know which statement is correct, but there are many melancholy instances of victims failing to be killed outright. In 1786 the authorities attempted to hang a notorious villain named Fitzgerald, but when the stool was removed, by some strange chance the rope broke. At the next attempt the rope proved so long that his legs touched ground and he again survived. In the end, at the third attempt, he was enabled to die with the help of the spectators."

"Well, well," says Waverhouse becoming, as was only to be expected, re-enlivened.

"A true thanatophile." Even my master shows signs of jollity.

"There is one other interesting fact. A hanged person grows taller by about an inch. This is perfectly true. Doctors have measured it."

"That's a novel notion. How about it, Sneaze?" says Waverhouse turning to my master. "Try getting hanged. If you were an inch taller, you might acquire the appearance of an ordinary human being." The reply, however, was delivered with an unexpected gravity.

"Tell me, Coldmoon, is there any chance of surviving that process of extension by one inch?"

"Absolutely none. The point is that it is the spinal cord which gets stretched in hanging. It's more a matter of breaking than of growing taller."

"In that case, I won't try." My master abandons hope.

There was still a good deal of the lecture left to deliver and Coldmoon had clearly been anxious to deal with the question of the physiological function of hanging. But Waverhouse made so many and such capriciously-phrased interjections and my master yawned so rudely and so frequently that Coldmoon finally broke off his rehearsal in mid-flow and took his leave. I cannot tell you what oratorical triumphs he achieved, still less what gestures he employed that evening, because the lecture took place miles away from me.

A few days passed uneventfully by. Then, one day about two in the afternoon, Waverhouse dropped in with his usual casual manners and looking as totally uninhibited as his own concept of the "Accidental Child." The minute he sat down he asked abruptly, "Have you heard about Beauchamp Blowlamp and the Takanawa Incident?" He spoke excitedly, in a tone of voice appropriate to an announcement of the fall of Port Arthur.

"No, I haven't seen him lately." My master is his usual cheerless self.

"I've come today, although I'm busy, especially to inform you of the frightful blunder which Beauchamp has committed."

"You're exaggerating again. Indeed you're quite impossible."

"Impossible, never: improbable, perhaps. I must ask you to make a distinction on this point, for it affects my honor."

"It's the same thing," replied my master assuming an air of provoking indifference. He is the very image of a Mr. the-late-and-sainted Natural Man.

"Last Sunday, Beauchamp went to the Sengaku Temple at Takanawa, which was silly in this cold weather, especially when to make such a visit nowadays stamps one as a country bumpkin out to see the sights."

"But Beauchamp's his own master. You've no right to stop him going."

"True, I haven't got the right, so let's not bother about that. The point is that the temple yard contains a showroom displaying relics of the forty-seven ronin. Do you know it?"

"N-no."

"You don't? But surely you've been to the Temple?"

"No."

"Well, I am surprised. No wonder you so ardently defended Beauchamp. But it's positively shameful that a citizen of Tokyo should never have visited the Sengaku Temple."

"One can contrive to teach without trailing out to the ends of the city." My master grows more and more like his blessed Natural Man.

"All right. Anyway, Beauchamp was examining the relics when a married couple, Germans as it happened, entered the showroom. They began by asking him questions in Japanese, but, as you know, Beauchamp is always aching to practice his German so he naturally responded by rattling off a few words in that language. Apparently he did it rather well.

Indeed, when one thinks back over the whole deplorable incident, his very fluency was the root cause of the trouble."

"Well, what happened?" My master finally succumbs.

"The Germans pointed out a gold-lacquered pill-box which had belonged to Ōtaka Gengo and, saying they wished to buy it, asked Beauchamp if the object were for sale. Beauchamp's reply was not uninteresting. He said such a purchase would be quite impossible because all Japanese people were true gentlemen of the sternest integrity. Up to that point he was doing fine. However, the Germans, thinking that they'd found a useful interpreter, thereupon deluged him with questions."

"About what?"

"That's just it. If he had understood their questions, there would have been no trouble. But you see he was subjected to floods of such questions, all delivered in rapid German, and he simply couldn't make head or tail of what was being asked. When at last he chanced to understand part of their outpourings, it was something about a fireman's axe or a mallet—some word he couldn't translate—so again, naturally, he was completely at a loss how to reply."

"That I can well imagine," sympathizes my master, thinking of his own difficulties as a teacher.

"Idle onlookers soon began to gather around and eventually Beauchamp and the Germans were totally surrounded by staring eyes. In his confusion Beauchamp fell to blushing. In contrast to his earlier self-confidence he was now at his wit's end."

"How did it all turn out?"

"In the end Beauchamp could stand it no longer, shouted *sainara* in Japanese and came rushing home. I pointed out to him that *sainara* was an odd phrase to use and inquired whether, in his home-district, people used *sainara* rather than *sayonara*. He replied they would say *sayonara* but, since he was talking to Europeans, he had used *sainara* in order to maintain harmony. I must say I was much impressed to find him a man mindful of harmony even when in difficulties."

"So that's the bit about *sainara*. What did the Europeans do?"

"I hear that the Europeans looked utterly flabbergasted." And Waverhouse gave vent to laughter. "Interesting, eh?"

"Frankly, no. I really can't find anything particularly interesting in your story. But that you should have come here specially to tell me the tale, that I do find much more interesting." My master taps his cigarette's ash into the brazier. Just at that moment the bell on the lattice door at the entrance rang with an alarming loudness, and a piercing woman's voice declared, "Excuse me." Waverhouse and my master look at each other in silence.

Even while I am thinking that it is unusual for my master's house to have a female visitor, the owner of that piercing voice enters the room. She is wearing two layers of silk crepe kimono, and looks to be a little over forty. Her forelock towers up above the bald expanse of her brow like the wall of a dyke and sticks out toward heaven for easily one half the length of her face. Her eyes, set at an angle like a road cut through a mountain, slant up symmetrically in straight lines. I speak, of course, metaphorically. Her eyes, in fact, are even narrower than those of a whale. But her nose is exceedingly large. It gives the impression that it has been stolen from someone else and thereafter fastened in the center of her face. It is as if a large, stone lantern from some major shrine had been moved to a tiny ten-square-meter garden.

It certainly asserts its own importance, but yet looks out of place. It could almost be termed hooked: it begins by jutting sharply out, but then, halfway along its length, it suddenly turns shy so that its tip, bereft of the original vigour, hangs limply down to peer into the mouth below. Her nose is such that, when she speaks, it is the nose rather than the mouth which seems to be in action. Indeed, in homage to the enormity of that organ, I shall refer hence forward to its owner as Madam Conk. When the ceremonials of her self-introduction had been completed, she glared around the room and remarked, "What a nice house."

"What a liar," says my master to himself, and concentrates upon his smoking. Waverhouse studies the ceiling. "Tell me," he says, "is that odd pattern the result of a rain leak or is it inherent in the grain of the wood?"

"Rain leak, naturally" replies my master. To which Waverhouse coolly answers, "Wonderful."

Madam Conk clearly regards them as unsociable persons and boils quietly with suppressed annoyance. For a time the three of them just sit there in a triangle without saying a word.

"I've come to ask you about a certain matter." Madam Conk starts up again.

"Ah." My master's response lacks warmth.

Madam Conk, dissatisfied with this development, bestirs herself again. "I live nearby. In fact, at the residence on the corner of the block across the road."

"That large house in the European style, the one with a godown? Ah, yes. Of course. Have I not seen 'Goldfield' on the nameplate of that dwelling?" My master, at last, seems ready to take cognizance of Goldfield's European house and his incorporated godown, but his attitude toward Madam Conk displays no deepening of respect.

"Of course my husband should call upon you and seek your valued advice, but he is always so busy with his company affairs." She puts on a "that ought to shift them" face, but my master remains entirely unimpressed. He is, in fact, displeased by her manner of speaking, finding it too direct in a woman met for the first time. "And not of just one company either. He is connected with two or three of them and is a director of them all, as I expect you already know." She looks as if saying to herself, "Now surely he should feel small." In point of fact, the master of this house behaves most humbly toward anyone who happens to be a doctor or a professor, but, oddly enough, he offers scant respect toward businessmen. He considers a middle school teacher to be a more elevated person than any businessman. Even if he doesn't really believe this, he is quite resigned, being of an unadaptable nature, to the fact that he can never hope to be smiled upon by businessmen or millionaires. For he feels nothing but indifference toward any person, no matter how rich or influential, from whom he has ceased to hope for benefits. He consequently pays not the faintest attention to anything extraneous to the society of scholars, and is almost actively disinterested in the goings-on of the business world. Had he even the vaguest knowledge of the activities of businessmen, he still could never muster the slightest feeling of awe or respect for such abysmal persons. While, for her part, Madam Conk could never stretch her imagination to the point of considering that any being so eccentric as my master could actually exist, that any corner of the world might harbor such an oddity. Her experience has included meetings with many people and invariably, as soon as she declares that she is wife to Goldfield, their attitude towards her never fails immediately to alter. At any party whatsoever and no matter how lofty the social standing of any man before whom she happens to find herself, she has always found that Mrs. Goldfield is eminently acceptable. How then could she fail to impress such an obscure old teacher? She had expected that the mere mention of the fact that her house was the corner residence of the opposite block would startle my master even before she added information about Mr. Goldfield's notable activities in the world of business.

"Do you know anyone called Goldfield?" my master inquires of Waverhouse with the utmost nonchalance.

"Of course I know him. He's a friend of my uncle. Only the other day he was present at our garden party." Waverhouse answers in a serious manner.

"Really?" said my master. "And who, may I ask, is your uncle?"

"Baron Makiyama," replied Waverhouse in even graver tones. My master is obviously about to say something, but before he can bring himself to words, Madam Conk turns abruptly toward Waverhouse and subjects him to a piercing stare. Waverhouse, secure in a kimono of the finest silk, remains entirely unperturbed.

"Oh, you are Baron Makiyama's. . . That I didn't know. I hope you'll excuse me. . . I've heard so much about Baron Makiyama from my husband. He tells me that the Baron has always been so helpful. . ." Madam Conk's manner of speech has suddenly become polite. She even bows.

"Ah yes," observes Waverhouse who is inwardly laughing. My master, quite astonished, watches the two in silence.

"I understand he has even troubled the Baron about our daughter's marriage. . ."

"Has he indeed?" exclaims Waverhouse as if surprised. Even Waverhouse seems somewhat taken aback by this unexpected development.

"We are, in fact, receiving proposal after proposal in respect of marriage to our daughter. They flood in from all over the place. You will appreciate that, having to think seriously of our social position, we cannot rashly marry off our daughter to just anyone. . ."

"Quite so." Waverhouse feels relieved.

"I have, in point of fact, made this visit precisely to raise with you a question about this marriage matter." Madam Conk turns back to my master and reverts to her earlier vulgar style of speech. "I hear that a certain Avalon Coldmoon pays you frequent visits. What sort of a man is he?"

"Why do you want to know about Coldmoon?" replies my master in a manner revealing his displeasure.

"Perhaps it is in connection with your daughter's marriage that you wish to know something about the character of Coldmoon," puts in Waverhouse tactfully.

"If you could tell me about his character, it would indeed be helpful."

"Then is it that you want to give your daughter in marriage to Coldmoon?"

"It's not a question of my wanting to give her." Madam Conk immediately squashes my master. "Since there will be innumerable proposals, we couldn't care less if he doesn't marry her."

"In that case, you don't need any information about Coldmoon," my master replies with matching heat.

"But you've no reason to withhold information." Madam Conk adopts an almost defiant attitude.

Waverhouse, sitting between the two and holding his silver pipe as if it were an umpire's instrument of office, is secretly beside himself with glee. His gloating heart urges them on to yet more extravagant exchanges.

"Tell me, did Coldmoon actually say he wanted to marry her?" My master fires a broadside pointblank.

"He didn't actually say he wanted to, but. . ."

"You just think it likely that he might want to?" My master seems to have realized that broadsides are best in dealing with this woman.

"The matter is not yet so far advanced, but. . . well, I don't think Mr. Coldmoon is wholly averse to the idea." Madam Conk rallies well in her extremity.

"Is there any concrete evidence whatsoever that Coldmoon is enamored of this daughter of yours?" My master, as if to say, "now answer me if you can," sticks out his chest belligerently.

"Well, more or less, yes." This time my master's militance has failed in its effect. Waverhouse has hitherto been so delighted with his self-appointed role of umpire that he has simply sat and watched the scrap, but now his curiosity seems suddenly to have been aroused. He puts down the pipe and leans forward. "Has Coldmoon sent your daughter a love letter? What fun! One more new event since the New Year and, at that, a splendid subject for debate." Waverhouse alone is pleased.

"Not a love letter. Something much more ardent than that. Are you two really so much in the dark?" Madam Conk adopts a disbelieving attitude.

"Are you aware of anything?" My master, looking nonplussed, addresses himself to Waverhouse.

Waverhouse takes refuge in banter. "I know nothing. If anyone should know, it would be you." His reaction is disappointingly modest.

"But the two of you know all about it," Madam Conk triumphs over both of them.

"Oh!"The sound expressed their simultaneous astonishment.

"In case you've forgotten, let me remind you of what happened. At the end of last year Mr. Coldmoon went to a concert at the Abe residence in Mukōjima, right? That evening, on his way home, something happened at Azuma Bridge. You remember? l won't repeat the details since that might compromise the person in question, but what I've said is surely proof enough. What do you think?" She sits bolt-upright with her diamond-ringed fingers in her lap. Her magnificent nose looks more resplendent than ever, so much so that Waverhouse and my master seem practically obliterated.

My master, naturally, but Waverhouse also, appear dumbfounded by this surprise attack. For a while they just sit there in bewilderment, like patients whose fits of ague have suddenly ceased. But as the first shock of their astonishment subsides and they come slowly back to normality, their sense of humor irrepressibly asserts itself and they burst into gales of laughter. Madam Conk, baulked in her expectations and, ill-prepared for this reaction of rude laughing, glares at both of them.

"Was that your daughter? Isn't it wonderful! You're quite right. Indeed Coldmoon must be mad about her. I say, Sneaze, there's no point now in trying to keep it secret. Let's make a clean breast of everything." My master just says "Hum."

"There's certainly no point in your trying to keep it secret. The cat's already out of the bag." Madam Conk is once more cock-a-hoop.

"Yes, indeed, we're cornered. We'll have to make a true statement on everything concerning Coldmoon for this lady's information. Sneaze! you're the host here. Pull yourself together, man. Stop grinning like that or we'll never get this business sorted out. It's extraordinary. Secretiveness is a most mysterious matter. However well one guards a secret, sooner or later it's bound to come out. Indeed, when you come to think of it, it really is most extraordinary. Tell us, Mrs. Goldfield, how did you ever discover this secret? I am truly amazed." Waverhouse rattles on.

"I've a nose for these things." Madam Conk declares with some self-satisfaction.

"You must indeed be very well informed. Who on earth has told you about this matter?"

"The wife of the rickshawman who lives just there at the back."

"Do you mean that man who owns that vile black cat?" My master is wide-eyed.

"Yes, your Mr. Coldmoon has cost me a pretty penny. Every time he comes here I want to know what he talks about, so I've arranged for the wife of the rickshawman to learn what happens and to report it all to me."

"But that's terrible!" My master raises his voice.

"Don't worry, I don't give a damn what you do or say. I'm not in the least concerned with you, only with Mr. Coldmoon."

"Whether with Coldmoon or with anyone else. . . Really, that rickshaw woman is a quite disgusting creature." My master begins to get angry.

"But surely she is free to stand outside your hedge. If you don't want your conversations overheard, you should either talk less loudly or live in a larger house." Madam Conk is clearly not the least ashamed of herself. "And that's not my only source. I've also heard a deal of stuff from the Mistress of the two-stringed harp."

"You mean about Coldmoon?"

"Not solely about Coldmoon." This sounds menacing but, far from retreating in embarrassment, my master retorts. "That woman gives herself such airs. Acting as though she and she alone were the only person of any standing in this neighborhood. A vain, an idiotic fellow. . ."

"Pardon me! It's a woman you're describing. A fellow, did you say? Believe me, you're talking out of the back of your neck." Her language more and more betrays her vulgar origin. Indeed, it now appears as if she has only come in order to pick a quarrel. But Waverhouse, typically, just sits listening to the quarrel as if it were being conducted for his amusement. Indeed, he looks like a Chinese sage at a cockfight: cool and above it all.

My master at last realizes that he can never match Madam Conk in the exchange of scurrilities, and he lapses into a forced silence. But eventually a bright idea occurs to him.

"You've been speaking as though it were Coldmoon who was besotted with your daughter, but from what I've heard, the situation is quite different. Isn't that so, Waverhouse?"

"Certainly. As we heard it, your daughter fell ill and then, we understand, began babbling in delirium."

"No. You've got it all wrong." Madam Conk gives the lie direct.

"But Coldmoon undoubtedly said that that was what he had been told by Dr. O's wife."

"That was our trap. We'd asked the Doctor's wife to play that trick on Coldmoon precisely in order to see how he'd react."

"Did the doctor's wife agree to this deception in full knowledge that it was a trick?"

"Yes. Of course we couldn't expect her to help us purely for affection's sake. As I've said, we've had to lay out a very pretty penny on one thing and another."

"You are quite determined to impose yourself upon us and quiz us in detail about Coldmoon, eh?" Even Waverhouse seems to be getting annoyed for he uses some sharpish turns of phrase quite unlike his usual manner.

"Ah well, Sneaze," he continues, "what do we lose if we talk? Let's tell her everything. Now, Mrs. Goldfield, both Sneaze and I will tell you anything within reason about Coldmoon. But it would be more convenient for us if you'd present your questions one at a time."

Madam Conk was thus at last brought to see reason. And when she began to pose her questions, her style of speech, only recently so coarsely violent, acquired a certain civil polish, at least when she spoke to Waverhouse. "I understand," she opens, "that Mr. Coldmoon is a bachelor of science. Now please tell me in what sort of subject has he specialized?"

"In his post-graduate course, he's studying terrestrial magnetism," answers my master seriously.

Unfortunately, Madam Conk does not understand this answer. Therefore, though she says, "Ah," she looks dubious and asks: "If one studies that, could one obtain a doctor's degree?"

"Are you seriously suggesting that you wouldn't allow your daughter to marry him unless he held a doctorate?" The tone of my master's inquiry discloses his deep displeasure.

"That's right. After all, if it's just a bachelor's degree, there are so many of them!" Madam Conk replies with complete unconcern.

My master's glance at Waverhouse reveals a deepening disgust.

"Since we cannot be sure whether or not he'll gain a doctorate, you'll have to ask us something else." Waverhouse seems equally displeased.

"Is he still just studying that terrestrial something?"

"A few days ago," my master quite innocently offers, "he made a speech on the results of his investigation of the mechanics of hanging."

"Hanging? How dreadful! He must be peculiar. I don't suppose he could ever become a doctor by devoting himself to hanging."

"It would of course be difficult for him to gain a doctorate if he actually hanged himself, but it is not impossible to become a doctor through study of the mechanics of hanging."

"Is that so?" she answers, trying to read my master's expression. It's a sad, sad thing but, since she does not know what mechanics are, she cannot help feeling uneasy. She probably thinks that to ask the meaning of such a trifling matter might involve her in loss of face. Like a fortuneteller, she tries to guess the truth from facial expressions. My master's face is glum. "Is he studying anything else, something more easy to understand?"

"He once wrote a treatise entitled 'A Discussion of the Stability of Acorns in Relation to the Movements of Heavenly Bodies.'"

"Does one really study such things as acorns at a university?"

"Not being a member of any university, I cannot answer your question with complete certainty, but since Coldmoon is engaged in such studies, the subject must undoubtedly be worth studying." With a deadpan face, Waverhouse makes fun of her.

Madam Conk seems to have realized that her questions about matters of scholarship have carried her out of her depth, for she changes the subject. "By the way," she says, "I hear that he broke two of his front teeth when eating mushrooms during the New Year season."

"True, and a rice-cake became fixed on the broken part." Waverhouse, feeling that this question is indeed up his street, suddenly becomes light-hearted.

"How unromantic! I wonder why he doesn't use a toothpick!"

"Next time I see him, I'll pass on your sage advice," says my master with a chuckle.

"If his teeth can be snapped on mushrooms, they must be in very poor condition. What do you think?"

"One could hardly say such teeth were good. Could one, Waverhouse?"

"Of course they can't be good, but they do provide a certain humor. It's odd that he hasn't had them filled. It really is an extraordinary sight when a man just leaves his teeth to become mere hooks for snagging rice-cakes."

"Is it because he lacks the money to get them filled or because he's just so odd that he leaves them unattended to?"

"Ah, you needn't worry. I don't suppose he will continue as Mr. Broken Front Tooth for any long time." Waverhouse is evidently regaining his usual bouyancy.

Madam Conk again changes the subject. "If you should have some letter or anything which he's written, I'd like to see it."

"I have masses of postcards from him. Please have a look at them," and my master produces some thirty or forty postcards from his study.

"Oh, I don't have to look at so many of them. . . perhaps two or three would do. . ."

"Let me choose some for you," offers Waverhouse, adding as he selects a picture postcard, "Here's an interesting one."

"Gracious! So he paints pictures as well? Rather clever that," she exclaims. But after examining the picture she remarks "How very silly! It's a badger! Why on earth does he have to paint a badger of all things! Strange. But it does indeed look like a badger." She is, albeit reluctantly, mildly impressed.

"Read what he's written beside it," suggests my master with a laugh. Madam Conk begins to read aloud like a servant-girl deciphering a newspaper.

"On New Year's Eve, as calculated under the ancient calendar, the mountain badgers hold a garden party at which they dance excessively. Their song says, 'This evening, being New Year's Eve, no mountain hikers will come this way.' And bom-bom-bom they thump upon their bellies. What is he writing about? Is he not being a trifle frivolous?" Madam Conk seems seriously dissatisfied.

"Doesn't this heavenly maiden please you?" Waverhouse picks out another card on which a kind of angel in celestial raiment is depicted as playing upon a lute.

"The nose of this heavenly maiden seems rather too small."

"Oh no, that's about the average size for an angel. But forget the nose for the moment and read what it says," urges Waverhouse.

"It says 'Once upon a time there was an astronomer. One night he went as was his wont high up into his observatory, and, as he was intently watching the stars, a beautiful heavenly maiden appeared in the sky and began to play some music; music too delicate ever to be heard on earth. The astronomer was so entranced by the music that he quite forgot the dark night's bitter cold. Next morning the dead body of the astronomer was found covered with pure white frost. An old man, a liar, told me that this story was all true.' What the hell is this? It makes no sense, no nothing. Can Coldmoon really be a bachelor of science? Perhaps he should read a few literary magazines." Thus mercilessly does Madam Conk lambaste the defenseless Coldmoon.

Waverhouse for fun selects a third postcard and says, "Well then, what about this one?" The card has a sailing boat printed on it and, as usual, there is something scribbled underneath the picture.

Last night a tiny whore of sixteen summers
Declared she had no parents.
Like a plover on a reefy coast,
She wept on waking in the early morning.
Her parents, sailors both, lie at the bottom of the sea.

"Oh, that's good. How very clever! He's got real feeling," erupted Madam Conk.

"Feeling?" says Waverhouse.

"Oh yes," says Madam Conk. "That would go well on a *samisen*.

"If it could be played on the *samisen*, then it's the real McCoy. Well, how about these?" asks Waverhouse picking out postcard after postcard.

"Thank you, but I've seen enough. For now, at least I know that Coldmoon's not a straight-laced prude." She thinks she has achieved some real understanding and appears to have no more queries about Coldmoon, for she remarks, "I'm sorry to have troubled you. Please do not report my visit to Mr. Coldmoon." Her request reflects her selfish nature in that she seems to feel entitled to make a thorough investigation of Coldmoon whilst expecting that none of her activities should be revealed to him. Both Waverhouse and my master concede a half-hearted "Y-es," but as Madam Conk gets up to leave, she consolidates their assent by saying, "I shall, of course, at some later date repay you for your services."

The two men showed her out and, as they resumed their seats, Waverhouse exclaimed, "What on earth is that?" At the very same moment my master also ejaculated, "Whatever's that?" I suppose my master's wife could not restrain her laughter any longer, for we heard her gurgling in the inner-room.

Waverhouse thereupon addressed her in a loud voice through the sliding door. "That, Mrs. Sneaze, was a remarkable specimen of all that is conventional, of all that is 'common or garden.' But when such characteristics become developed to that incredible degree the result is positively staggering. Such quintessence of the common approximates to the unique. Don't seek to restrain yourself. Laugh to your heart's content."

With evident disgust my master speaks in tones of the deepest revulsion. "To begin with," he says, "her face is unattractive."

Waverhouse immediately takes the cue. "And that nose, squatting, as it were, in the middle of that phiz, seems affectedly unreal."

"Not only that, it's crooked."

"Hunchbacked, one might say. A hunchbacked nose! Quite extraordinary." And Waverhouse laughs in genuine delight.

"It is the face of a woman who keeps her husband under her bottom." My master still looks resentful.

"It is a sort of physiognomy that, left unsold in the nineteenth century, becomes in the twentieth shop-soiled." Waverhouse produces another of his invariably bizarre remarks. At which juncture my master's wife emerges from the inner-room and, being a woman and thus aware of the ways of women, quietly warns them, "If you talk such scandal, the rickshaw-owner's wife will snitch on you again."

"But, Mrs. Sneaze, to hear such tattle will do that Goldfield woman no end of good."

"But it's self-demeaning to calumniate a person's face. No one sports that sort of nose as a matter of choice. Besides, she is a woman. You're going a little too far." Her defense of the nose of Madam Conk is simultaneously an indirect defense of her own indifferent looks.

"We're not unkind at all. That creature isn't a woman. She's just an oaf. Waverhouse, am I not right?"

"Maybe an oaf, but a formidable character nonetheless. She gave you quite a tousling, didn't she just?"

"What does she take a teacher for, anyway?"

"She ranks a teacher on roughly the same level as a rickshaw-owner. To earn the respect of such viragoes one needs to have at least a doctor's degree. You were ill-advised not to have taken your doctorate. Don't you agree, Mrs. Sneaze?" Waverhouse looks at her with a smile.

"A doctorate? Quite impossible." Even his wife despairs of my master.

"You never know. I might become one, one of these days. You mustn't always doubt my worth. You may well be ignorant of the fact, but in ancient times a certain Greek, lsocrates, produced major literary works at the age of ninety-four. Similarly, Sophocles was almost a centenarian when he shook the world with his masterpiece. Simonides was writing wonderful poetry in his eighties. I, too. . ."

"Don't be silly. How can you possibly expect, you with your stomach troubles, to live that long." Mrs. Sneaze has already determined my master's span of life.

"How dare you! Just go and talk to Dr. Amaki. Anyway, it's all your fault. It's because you make me wear this crumpled black cotton surcoat and this patched-up kimono that I am despised by women like Mrs. Goldfield. Very well then. From tomorrow I shall rig myself out in such fineries as Waverhouse is wearing. So get them ready."

"You may well say 'get them ready,' but we don't possess any such elegant clothes. Anyway, Mrs. Goldfield only grew civil to Waverhouse after he'd mentioned his uncle's name. Her attitude was in no way conditioned by the ill-condition of your kimono." Mrs. Sneaze has neatly dodged the charge against her.

The mention of that uncle appears to trigger my master's memory, for he turns to Waverhouse and says, "That was the first I ever heard of your uncle. You never spoke of him before. Does he, in fact, exist?"

Waverhouse has obviously been expecting this question, and he jumps to answer it. "Yes, that uncle of mine, a remarkably stubborn man. He, too, is a survival from the nineteenth century." He looks at husband and wife.

"You do say the quaintest things. Where does this uncle live?" asks Mr. Sneaze with a titter.

"In Shizuoka. But he doesn't just live. He lives with a top-knot still on his head. Can you beat it? When we suggest he should wear a hat, he proudly answers that he has never found the weather cold enough to don such gear. And when we hint that he might be wise to stay abed when the weather's freezing, he replies that four hour's sleep is sufficient for any man. He is convinced that to sleep more than four hours is sheer extravagance, so he gets up while it's still pitch-dark. It is his boast that it took many long years of training so to minimize his sleeping hours. 'When I was young,' he says, 'it was indeed hard because I felt sleepy, but recently I have at last achieved that wonderful condition where I can sleep or wake, anywhere, anytime, just as I happen to wish.' It is of course natural that a man of sixty-seven should need less sleep. It has nothing to do with early training, but my uncle is happy in the belief that he has succeeded in attaining his present condition entirely as a result of rigorous self-discipline. And when he goes out, he always carries an iron fan."

"Whatever for?" asks my master.

"I haven't the faintest idea. He just carries it. Perhaps he prefers a fan to a walking stick. As a matter of fact an odd thing happened only the other day." Waverhouse speaks to Mrs. Sneaze.

"Ah yes?" she noncommittally responds.

"In the spring this year he wrote to me out of the blue with a request that I should send him a bowler hat and a frock-coat. I was somewhat surprised and wrote back asking for further clarification. I received an answer stating that the old man himself intended to wear both items on the occasion of the Shizuoka celebration of the war victory, and that I should therefore send them quickly. It was an order. But the quaintness of his letter was that it enjoined me 'to choose a hat of suitable size and, as for the suit, to go and order one from Daimaru of whatever size you think appropriate.'"

"Can one get suits made at Daimaru?"

"No. I think he'd got confused and meant to say at Shirokiya's."

"Isn't it a little unhelpful to say 'of whatever size you think appropriate'?"

"That's just my uncle all over."

"What did you do?"

"What could I do? I ordered a suit which I thought appropriate and sent it to him."

"How very irresponsible! And did it fit?"

"More or less, I think. For I later noticed in my home-town newspaper that the venerable Mr. Makiyama had created something of a sensation by appearing at the said celebration in a frock coat carrying, as usual, his famous iron fan."

"It seems difficult to part him from that object."

"When he's buried, I shall ensure that the fan is placed within the coffin."

"Still it was fortunate that the coat and bowler fitted him."

"But they didn't. Just when I was congratulating myself that everything had gone off smoothly, a parcel came from Shizuoka. I opened it expecting some token of his gratitude, but it proved only to contain the bowler. An accompanying letter stated, 'Though you have taken the trouble of making this purchase for me, I find the hat too large. Please be so kind as to take it back to the hatter's and have it shrunk. I will of course defray your consequent expenses by postal order.'"

"Peculiar, one must admit." My master seems greatly pleased to discover that there is someone even more peculiar than himself. "So what did you do?" he asks.

"What did I do? I could do nothing. I'm wearing the hat myself."

"And is that the very hat?" says my master with a smirk.

"And he's a Baron?" asks my master's wife from her mystification.

"Is who?"

"Your uncle with the iron fan."

"Oh, no. He's a scholar of the Chinese classics. When he was young he studied at that shrine dedicated to Confucius in Yushima and became so absorbed in the teachings of Chu-Tzu that, most reverentially, he continues to wear a top-knot in these days of the electric light. There's nothing one can do about it." Waverhouse rubs his chin.

"But I have the impression that in speaking just now to that awful woman you mentioned a Baron Makiyama."

"Indeed you did. I heard you quite distinctly, even in the other room." Mrs. Sneaze for once supports her husband.

"Oh, did I?" Waverhouse permits himself a snigger. "Fancy that. Well, it wasn't true. Had I a Baron for an uncle I would by now be a senior civil servant." Waverhouse is not in the least embarrassed.

"I thought it was somehow queer," says my master with an expression half-pleased, half-worried.

"It's astonishing how calmly you can lie. I must say you're a past master at the game." Mrs. Sneaze is deeply impressed.

"You flatter me. That woman quite outclasses me."

"I don't think she could match you."

"But, Mrs. Sneaze, my lies are merely tarrydiddles. That woman's lies, every one of them, have hooks inside them. They're tricky lies. Lies loaded with malice aforethought. They are the spawn of craftiness. Please never confuse such calculated monkey-minded wickedness with my heaven-sent taste for the comicality of things. Should such confusion prevail, the God of Comedy would have no choice but to weep for mankind's lack of perspicacity."

"I wonder," says my master, lowering his eyes, while Mrs. Sneaze, still laughing, remarks that it all comes down to the same thing in the end.

Up until now I have never so much as crossed the road to investigate the block opposite. I have never clapped eyes on the Goldfield's corner residence so I naturally have no idea what it looks like. Indeed today is the first time that I've even heard of its existence. No one in this house has ever previously talked about a businessman and consequently I, who am my master's cat, have shared his total disinterest in the world of business and his equally total indifference to businessmen. However, having just been present during the colloquy with Madam Conk, having overheard her talk, having imagined her daughter's beauty and charm, and also having given some thought to that family's wealth and power, I have come to realize that, though no more than a cat, I should not idle all my days away lying on the veranda. Nor only that, I cannot help but feel deep sympathy with Coldmoon. His opponent has already bribed a doctor's wife, bribed the wife of the rickshaw-owner, bribed even that highfalutin mistress of the two-stringed harp. She has so spied upon poor Coldmoon that even his broken teeth have been disclosed, while he has done no more than fiddle with the fastenings of his surcoat and, on occasion, grin. He is guileless even for a bachelor of science just out of the university. And it's not just anyone who can cope with a woman equipped with such a jut of nose. My master not only lacks the heart for dealing with matters of this sort, but he lacks the money, too. Waverhouse has sufficient money, but is such an inconsequential being that he'd never go out of his way merely to help Coldmoon. How isolated, then, is that unfortunate person who lectures on the mechanics of hanging. It would be less than fair if I failed at least to try and insinuate myself into the enemy fortress and, for Coldmoon's sake, pick up news of their activities. Though but a cat, I am not quite as other cats. I differ from the general run of idiot cats and stupid cats. I am a cat that lodges in the house of a scholar who, having read it, can bang down any book by Epictetus on his desk. Concentrated in the tip of my tail there is sufficient of the spirit of chivalry for me to take it upon myself to venture upon knight-errantry. It is not that I am in any way beholden to poor Coldmoon, nor am I engaging in foolhardy action for the sake of any single individual. If I may be allowed to blow my own trumpet, I am proposing to take magnificent unself-interested action simply in order to realize the will of Heaven that smiles upon impartiality and blesses the happy medium. Since Madam Conk makes impermissible use of such things as the happenings at Azuma Bridge; since she hires underlings to spy and eavesdrop on us; since she triumphantly retails to all and sundry the products of her espionage; since by the employment of rickshaw-folk, mere grooms, plain rogues, student riff-raff, crone daily-help, midwives, witches, masseurs, and other trouble-makers she seeks to trouble a man of talent; for all these reasons even a cat must do what can be done to prevent her getting away with it.

The weather, fortunately, is fine. The thaw is something of nuisance, but one must be prepared to sacrifice one's life in the cause of justice. If my feet get muddy and stamp plum blossom patterns on the veranda, O-San may be narked but that won't worry me. For I have come to the superlatively courageous, firm decision that I will not put off until tomorrow what needs to be done today. Accordingly, I whisk off around to the kitchen, but, having arrived there, pause for further thought. "Softly, softly," I say to myself. It's not simply that I've attained the highest degree of evolution that can occur in cats, but I make bold to believe my brain is as well-developed as that of any boy in his third year at a middle school. Nevertheless, alas, the construction of my throat is still only that of a cat, and I cannot therefore speak the babbles of mankind. Thus, even if I succeed in sneaking into the Goldfield's citadel and there discovering matters of moment, I shall remain unable to communicate my discoveries to that Coldmoon who so needs them. Neither shall I be able to communicate my gleanings to my master or to Waverhouse. Such incommunicable knowledge would, like a buried diamond, be denied its brilliance and my hard-won wisdom would all be won for nothing. Which would be stupid. Perhaps I should scrap my plan. So thinking, I hesitated on the very doorstep.

But to abandon a project halfway through breeds a kind of regret, that sense of unfulfillment which one feels when the slower one had so confidently expected drifts away under inky clouds into some other part of the countryside. Of course, to persist when one is in the wrong is an altogether different matter, but to press on for the sake of so-called justice and humanity, even at the risk of death uncrowned by success, that, for a man who knows his duty, can be a source of the deepest satisfaction. Accordingly, to engage in fruitless effort and to muddy one's paws on a fool's errand would seem about right for a cat. Since it is my misfortune to have been born a cat, I cannot by turns of the tip of my tail convey, as I can to cats, my thinking to such scholars as Coldmoon,

Sneaze, and Waverhouse. However, by virtue of felinity, I can, better than all such bookmen, make myself invisible. To do what no one else can do is, of itself, delightful. That I alone should know the inner workings of the Goldfield household is better than if nobody should know. Though I cannot pass my knowledge on, it is still cause for delight that I may make the Goldfields conscious that someone knows their secrets. In the light of this succession of delights, I boldly make to believe my brain is as delightful as well. All right then. I will go.

Coming to the side street in the opposite block, there, sure enough, I find a Western-style house dominating the crossroads as if it owned the whole area. Thinking that the master of such a house must be no less stuck up than his building, I slide past the gate and examine the edifice. Its construction has no merit. Its two stories rear up into the air for no purpose whatever but to impress, even to coerce, the passersby. This, I suppose, is what Waverhouse means when he calls things common or garden. I slink through some bushes, take note of the main entrance to my right, and so find my way round to the kitchen. As might be expected, the kitchen is large—at least ten times as large as that in my master's dwelling. Everything is in such apple pie order, all so clean and shining, that it cannot be less splendid than that fabulous kitchen of Count Ōkuma so fulsomely described in a recent product of the national press. I tell myself, as I slip inside on silent muddy paws, that this must be "a model kitchen." On the plastered part of its floor the wife of the rickshaw-owner is standing in earnest discussion with a kitchen-maid and a rickshaw-runner. Realizing the dangers of this situation, I hide behind a water-tub.

"That teacher, doesn't he really even know our master's name?" the kitchen-maid demands.

"Of course he knows it. Anyone in this district who doesn't know the Goldfield residence must be a deaf cripple without eyes," snaps the man who pulls the Goldfield's private rickshaw.

"Well, you never know. That teacher's one of those cranks who know nothing at all except what it says in books. If he knew even the least little thing about Mr. Goldfield he might be scared out of his wits. But he hasn't the wits to be scared out of. Why," snorts Blacky's bloody-minded mistress, "he doesn't even know the ages of his own mis-managed children."

"So he's not afraid of our Mr. Goldfield! What a cussed clot he is! There's no call to show him the least consideration. Let's go around and give him something to be scared about."

"Good idea! He says such dreadful things. He was telling his crackpot cronies that, since Madam's nose is far too big for her face, he finds her unattractive. No doubt he thinks himself a proper picture, but his mug's the spitting image of a terra-cotta badger. What can be done, I ask you, with such an animal?"

"And it isn't only his face. The way he saunters down to the public bathhouse carrying a hand towel is far too high and mighty. He thinks he's the cat's whiskers." My master Sneaze seems notably unpopular, even with this kitchen-maid.

"Let's all go and call him names as loud as we can from just outside his hedge."

"That'll bring him down a peg."

"But we mustn't let ourselves be seen. We must spoil his studying just with shouting, getting him riled as much as we can. Those are Madam's latest orders."

"I know all that," says the rickshaw wife in a voice that makes it clear that she's only too ready to undertake one-third of their scurrilous assignment. Thinking to myself, "So that's the gang who're going to ridicule my master," I drift quietly past the noisesome trio and penetrate yet further into the enemy fortress.

Cat's paws are as if they do not exist. Wheresoever they may go, they never make clumsy noises. Cats walk as if on air, as if they trod the clouds, as quietly as a stone going light-tapped under water, as an ancient Chinese harp touched in a sunken cave. The walking of a cat is the instinctive realization of all that is most delicate. For such as I am concerned, this vulgar Western house simply is not there. Nor do I take cognizance of the rickshaw-woman, manservant, kitchen-maids, the daughter of the house, Madam Conk, her parlor-maids or even her ghastly husband. For me they do not exist. I go where I like and I listen to whatever talk it interests me to hear. Thereafter, sticking out my tongue and frisking my tail, I walk home self-composedly with my whiskers proudly stiff. In this particular field of endeavor there's not a cat in all Japan so gifted as am I. Indeed, I sometimes think I really must be blood-kin to that monster cat one sees in ancient picture books. They say that every toad carries in its fore-head a gem that in the darkness utters light, but packed within my tail I carry not only the power of God, Buddha, Confucius, Love, and even Death, but also an infallible panacea for all ills that could bewitch the entire human race. I can as easily move unnoticed through the corridors of Goldfield's awful mansion as a giant god of stone could squash a milk-blancmange.

At this point, I become so impressed by my own powers and so conscious of the reverence I consequently owe to my own most precious tail that I feel unable to withhold immediate recognition of its divinity. I desire to pray for success in war by worshiping my honored Great Tail Gracious Deity, so I lower my head a little, only to find I am not facing in the right direction. When I make the three appropriate obeisances I should, of course, as far as it is possible, be facing toward my tail. But as I turn my body to fulfill that requirement, my tail moves away from me. In an effort to catch up with myself, I twist my neck. But still my tail eludes me. Being a thing so sacred, containing as it does the entire universe in its three-inch length, my tail is inevitably beyond my power to control. I spun round in pursuit of it seven and a half times but, feeling quite exhausted, I finally gave up. I feel a trifle giddy. For a moment I lose all sense of where I am and, deciding that my whereabouts are totally unimportant, I start to walk about at random. Then I hear the voice of Madam Conk. It comes from the far side of a paper-window. My ears prick up in sharp diagonals and, once more fully alert, I hold my breath. This is the place which I set out to find.

"He's far too cocky for a penny-pinching usher," she's screaming in that parrot's voice.

"Sure, he's a cocky fellow. I'll have a bit of the bounce taken out of him, just to teach him a lesson. There are one or two fellows I know, fellows from my own province, teaching at his school."

"What fellows are those?"

"Well, there's Tsuki Pinsuke and Fukuchi Kishago for a start. I'll arrange with them for him to be ragged in class."

I don't know from what province old man Goldfield comes, but I'm rather surprised to find it stiff with such outlandish names.

"Is he a teacher of English?" her husband asks.

"Yes. According to the wife of the rickshaw-owner, his teaching specializes in an English Reader or something like that."

"In any case, he's gotta be a rotten teacher."

I'm also struck by the vulgarity of that "gotta be" phraseology.

"When I saw Pinsuke the other day he mentioned that there was some crackpot at his school. When asked the English word for *bancha*, this fathead answered that the English called it, not 'coarse tea' as they actually do, but 'savage tea.' He's now the laughing stock of all his teaching colleagues. Pinsuke added that all the other teachers suffer for this one's follies. Very likely it's the self-same loon."

"It's bound to be. He's got the face you'd expect on a fool who thinks that tea can be savage. And to think he has the nerve to sport such a dashing mustache!"

"Saucy bastard."

If whiskers establish sauciness, every cat is impudent.

"As for that man Waverhouse—Staggering Drunk I'd call him—he's an obstreperous freak if ever I saw one. Baron Makiyama, his uncle indeed! I was sure that no one with a face like his could have a baron for an uncle."

"You, too, are at fault for believing anything which a man of such dubious origins might say."

"Maybe I was at fault. But really there's a limit and he's gone much too far." Madam Conk sounds singularly vexed. The odd thing is that neither mentions Coldmoon. I wonder if they concluded their discussion about him before I sneaked up on them or whether perhaps they had earlier decided to block his marriage suit and had therefore already forgotten all about him. I remain disturbed about this question, but there's nothing I can do about it. For a little while I lay crouched down in silence but then I heard a bell ring at the far end of the corridor. What's up down there? Determined this time not to be late on the scene, I set out smartly in the direction of the sound.

I arrived to find some female yattering away by herself in a loud unpleasant voice. Since her tones resemble those of Madam Conk, I deduce that this must be that darling daughter, that delicious charmer for whose sake Coldmoon has already risked death by drowning. Unfortunately, the paper-windows between us make it impossible for me to observe her beauty and I cannot therefore be sure whether she, too, has a massive nose plonked down in the center of her face. But I infer from her mannerisms, such as the way she sounds to be turning up her nose when she talks, that that organ is unlikely to be an inconspicuous pug-nose. Though she talks continuously, nobody seems to be answering, and I deduce that she must be using one of those modern telephones.

"Is that the Yamato? I want to reserve, for tomorrow, the third box in the lower gallery. All right? Got it? What's that? You can't? But you must. Why should I be joking? Don't be such a fool. Who the devil are you? Chōkichi? Well, Chōkichi, you're not doing very well. Ask the proprietress to come to the phone. What's that? Did you say you were able to cope with any possible inquiries? How dare you speak to me like that? D'you know who I am? This is Miss Goldfield speaking. Oh, you're well aware of that, are you? You really are a fathead. Don't you understand, this is *the* Goldfield. Again? You thank us for being regular patrons? I don't want your stupid thanks. I want the third box in the lower gallery. Don't laugh, you idiot. You must be terribly stupid. You are, you say? If you don't stop being insolent, I shall just ring off. You understand? I can promise you you'll be sorry. Hello. Are you still there? Hello, hello. Speak up. Answer me. Hello, hello, hello." Chōkichi seems to have hung up, for no answer is forthcoming. The girl is now in something of a tizzy and she grinds away at the telephone handle as though she's gone off her head. A lapdog somewhere around her feet suddenly starts to yap, and, realizing I'd better keep my wits about me, I quickly hop off the veranda and creep in under the house.

Just then I hear approaching footsteps and the sound of a paper-door being slid aside. I tilt my head to listen.

"Your father and mother are asking for you, Miss." It sounds like a parlor-maid.

"So who cares?" was the vulgar answer.

"They sent me to fetch you because they've something they want to tell you."

"You're being a nuisance. I said I just don't care." She snubs the maid once more.

"They said it's something to do with Mr. Coldmoon." The maid tries tactfully to put this young vixen into a better humor.

"I couldn't care less if they want to talk about Coldmoon or Piddlemoon. I abominate that man with his daft face looking like a bewildered gourd." Her third sour outburst is directed at the absent Coldmoon. "Hello," she suddenly goes on, "when did you start dressing your hair in the Western style?"

The parlor-maid gulps and then replies as briefly as she can "Today."

"What sauce. A mere parlor-maid, what's more." Her fourth attack comes in from a different direction. "And isn't that a brand new collar you've got on?"

"Yes, it's the one you gave me recently. I've been keeping it in my box because it seemed too good for the likes of me, but my other collar became so grubby I thought I'd make the change."

"When did I give it you?"

"It was January you bought it. At Shirokiya's. It's got the ranks of sumō wrestlers set out as decoration on the greeny-brown material. You said it was too somber for your style. So you gave it me."

"Did I? Well, it certainly looks nice on you. How very provoking!"

"I'm much obliged!"

"I didn't intend a compliment. I'm very much put out."

"Yes, Miss."

"Why did you accept something which so very much becomes you without letting me know that it would?"

"But Miss. . ."

"Since it looks that nice on you, it couldn't fail, could it, to look more nice on me?"

"I'm sure it would have looked delightful on you."

"Then why didn't you say so? Instead of that, you just stand there wearing it when you know I'd like it back. You little beast." Her vituperations seem to have no end. I was wondering what would happen when, from the room at the other end of the house, old man Goldfield himself suddenly roared out for his daughter. "Opula," he bellowed. "Opula, come here." She had no choice but to obey and mooched sulkily out of the room containing the telephone. Her lapdog, slightly bigger than myself with its eyes and mouth all bunched together in the middle of its revolting mug, slopped along behind her.

Thereupon, with my usual stealthy steps, I tiptoed back to the kitchen and, through the kitchen-door, found my way to the street, and so back home. My expedition has been notably successful.

Coming thus suddenly from a beautiful mansion to our dirty little dwelling, I felt as though I had descended from a sunlit mountaintop to some dark dismal grot. Whilst on my spying mission. I'd been far too busy to take any notice of the ornaments in the rooms, of the decoration of the sliding-doors and paper-windows or of any similar features, but as soon as I returned and became conscious of the shabbiness of home, I found myself yearning for what Waverhouse claims to despise. I am inclined to think that, after all, there's a good deal more to a businessman than there is to a teacher. Uncertain of the soundness of this thinking, I consult my infallible tail. The oracle confirms that my thinking is correct.

I am surprised to find Waverhouse still sitting in my master's room.

His cigarette stubs, stuffed into the brazier, make it look like a beehive. Comfortably cross-legged on the floor, he is, as usual, talking. It appears, moreover, that during my absence Coldmoon has dropped in. My master, his head pillowed on his arms, lies flat on his back rapt in contemplation of the pattern of the rainmarks on the ceiling. It is another of those meetings of hermits in a peaceful reign.

"Coldmoon, my dear fellow, I seem to remember that you insisted upon maintaining as the darkest of dark secrets the name of that young lady who called your name from the depths of her delirium. But surely the time has now come when you could reveal her identity?" Waverhouse begins to niggle Coldmoon.

"Were it just solely my concern, I wouldn't mind telling you, but since any such disclosure might compromise the other party. . ."

"So you still won't tell?"

"Besides, I promised the Doctor's wife. . ."

"Promised never to tell anyone?"

"Yes," says Coldmoon back at his usual fiddling with the strings of his surcoat. The strings are a bright purple, objects of a color one could never nowadays find in any shop.

"The color of those strings is early nineteenth century" remarks my supine master. He is genuinely quite indifferent to anything that concerns the Goldfields.

"Quite. It couldn't possibly belong to these times of the Russo-Japanese War. That kind of string would be appropriate only to the garments worn by the rank and file of soldiers under the Shogunate. It is said that on the occasion of his marriage, nearly four hundred years ago, Oda Nobunaga dressed his hair back in the fashion of a tea whisk, and I have no doubt his projecting top-knot was bound with precisely such a string." Waverhouse goes, as usual, all around the houses to make his little point.

"As a matter of fact, my grandfather wore these strings at the time, not forty years back, when the Tokugawa were putting down the last rebellion before the restoration of the Emperor." Coldmoon takes it all dead seriously.

"Isn't it then about time you presented those strings to a museum? For that well-known lecturer on the mechanics of hanging, that leading bachelor of science, Mr. Avalon Coldmoon to go around looking like a relic of mediaevalism would scarcely help his reputation."

"I myself would be only too ready to follow your advice. However, there's a certain person who says that these strings do specially become me. . ."

"Who on earth could have made such an imperceptive comment?" asks my master in a loud voice as he rolls over onto his side.

"A person not of your acquaintance."

"Never mind that. Who was it?"

"A certain lady."

"Gracious me, what delicacy! Shall I guess who it is? I think it's the lady who whimpered for you from the bottom of the Sumida River. Why don't you tie up your surcoat with those nice purple strings and go on out and get drowned again?" Waverhouse offers a helpful suggestion.

Coldmoon laughs at the sally. "As a matter of fact she no longer calls me from the riverbed. She is now, as it were, in the Pure Land, a little northwest from here. . ."

"Don't hope for too much purity. That ghastly nose looks singularly unwholesome."

"Eh?" says Coldmoon, looking puzzled.

"The Archnose from over the way has just been round to see us. Yes, right here. I can tell you we had quite a surprise. Hadn't we, Sneaze?"

"We had," replies my master still lying on his side but now sipping tea.

"Whom do you mean by the Archnose?"

"We mean the honorable mother of your ever-darling lady."

"Oh!"

"A woman calling herself Mrs. Goldfield came round here asking all sorts of questions about you." My master, clarifying the situation, speaks quite seriously.

I watch poor Coldmoon, wondering if he will be surprised or pleased or embarrassed, but in fact he looks exactly as he always does. And in his accustomed quiet tones he comments "I suppose she's asking if I'll marry the daughter? Was that it?" and he goes on twisting and untwisting his purple strings.

"Far from it! That mother happens to own the most enormous nose. . ." But before Waverhouse could finish his sentence my master interrupted him with a sudden irrelevance.

"Listen," he chirps, "I've been trying to compose a new-style *haiku* on that snout of hers." Mrs. Sneaze begins to giggle in the next room.

"You're taking it all extremely lightly! And have you composed your poem?"

"I've made a start. The first line goes 'A Conker Festival takes place in this face.'"

"And then?"

"'At which one offers sacred wine.'"

"And the concluding line?"

"I've not yet got to that."

"Interesting," says Coldmoon with a grin.

"How about this for the missing line?" improvises Waverhouse. "'Two orifices dim.'"

Whereupon Coldmoon offers, "'So deep no hairs appear.'"

They were thus thoroughly enjoying themselves by proposing wilder and wilder lines when from the street beyond the hedge came the voices of several people shouting "Where's that terra-cotta badger? Come on out, you terra-cotta badger. Terra-cotta badger! Yah!"

Both my master and Waverhouse look somewhat startled and they peer out through the hedge. Loud hoots of derisive laughter are followed by the sound of footsteps running away.

"Whatever can they mean by a terra-cotta badger?" Waverhouse asks in puzzled tones.

"I've no idea," replies my master.

"An unusual occurrence," says Coldmoon.

Waverhouse suddenly gets to his feet as if he had remembered something. "For some several lustra," he declaims in parody of the style of public lecturers, "I have devoted myself to the study of aesthetic nasofrontology and I would accordingly now like to trespass on your time and patience in order to present certain interim conclusions at which I have arrived." His initiative has been so suddenly taken that my master just stares up at him in silent blank amazement.

Coldmoon's tiniest voice observes, "I'd love to hear your interim conclusions."

"Though I have made a thorough study of this matter, the origin of the nose remains, alas, still deeply obfuscated. The first question that arises reflects the assumption that the nose is intended for use. The functional approach. If that premise is valid, would not two mere vent-holes meet the case? There is no obvious need either for such arrogant profusion or for the nasal arrogation of a median position in the human physiognomy. Why then should the nasal organ thus," and he paused to pinch his own, "thrust itself forward?"

"Yours doesn't stick out much," cuts in my master rather rudely.

"At any rate it has no indentations, no incurvations; still less could it be described as countersunk or infundibular. I draw your attention to these facts because if you fail to make the necessary distinction between having two holes in the medio-frontal area of the face and having two such holes in some form of protuberance, you will inevitably be unable to follow the quintessential drift of my dissertation. Now, it is at least my own, albeit humble, opinion that it is by an accumulation of human actions trifling in themselves, for who could attach major importance to the blowing of one's nose, that the organ in question has developed into its present phenomenal form."

"How very humbly you do hold your humble views," interjects my master.

"As you will know, the act of blowing the nose involves the coarctation of that organ. Such stenosis of the nose, such astrictive and, one might even venture to say, pleonastic stimulation of so localized an area results, by response to that stimulus and in accordance with the well-established principles of Lamarckian evolutionary theory, in the development of that specific area to a degree disproportionate to the development of other areas. The epidermis of the affected area inevitably indurates and the subcutaneous material so coagulates as eventually to ossify."

"That's a bit extreme. Surely you can't turn flesh to bone just by blowing your nose." Coldmoon, as behoves a bachelor of science, lodges a protest. Waverhouse continues to deliver his speech with the utmost nonchalance.

"I can well appreciate your natural dubieties, but the proof of the pudding is the eating. For, behold, there is bone there, and that bone has demonstrably been molded. Nevertheless, and despite that bone, one snivels. If one snivels one has to blow the nose, and in the course of that action both sides of the bone get worn away until the nose itself acquires the shape of a high and narrow bulge. It is indeed a terrifying process. But just as little taps of dropping water will eventually bore through granite, so has the high, straight ridge of the nasal organ been smithied by incessant nose-blows. Thus painfully was fangled the hard straight line on one's face."

"But yours is flabby."

"I deliberately refrain from any discussion of this particular feature as it may be observed in the physiognomy of the lecturer himself; for such a purely personal approach involves the dangers of self-exculpation, the temptation to gloss over, even to defend, one's individual defects or deficiencies. But the nose of the honorable Mrs. Goldfield is such that I would wish to bring it to your attention as the most highly developed of its kind, the most egregiously rare object, in the world."

Coldmoon cries out in spontaneous admiration. "Hear, hear."

"But anything whatever that develops to an extreme degree becomes thereby intimidating. Even terrifying. Spectacular it may be, but simultaneously awesome, unapproachable. Thus the bridge of that lady's nose, though certainly magnificent, appears to me unduly rigid, unacceptably steep. If one pauses to consider the nature of the noses of the ancients, it seems probable that those of Socrates, Oliver Goldsmith, and William Thackeray were strikingly imperfect from the structural point of view, but those very imperfections had their own peculiar charms. This is, no doubt, the intellection behind the saying that a nose, like a mountain, is not significant because it is high but because it is odd. Similarly, the popular catch-phrase that 'dumplings are better than nosegays' is no doubt a corruption of some yet more ancient adage to the effect that dumplings are better than noses. From which it follows that, viewed aesthetically, the nose of Citizen Waverhouse is just about right."

Coldmoon and my master greet this fantastication with peals of appreciative laughter, and even Waverhouse joins in.

"Now, the piece I have just been reciting. . ."

"Distinguished speaker, I must object to your use of the phrase 'reciting a piece': a somewhat vulgar word one would only expect from a storyteller." Coldmoon, catching Waverhouse in the use of language which only recently Waverhouse had criticized, feels himself revenged.

"In which case, sir, and having with your gracious permission purged myself of error, I would now like to touch upon the matter of the proper proportion between the nose and its associated face. If I were simply to discuss noses in disregard of their relation to other entities, then I would declare without fear of contradiction that the nose of Mrs. Goldfield is superb, superlative, and, though possibly supervacaneous, one well-placed to win first prize at any exhibition of nasal development which might be organized by the long-nosed goblins on Mount Kurama.

But alas! And even alack! That nose appears to have been formed, fashioned, dare I say fabricated, without any regard for the configuration of such other major items as the eyes and mouth. Julius Caesar was undoubtedly dowered with a very fine nose. But what do you think would be the result if one scissored off that Julian beak and fixed it on the face of this cat here? Cats' foreheads are proverbially diminutive. To raise the tower of Caesar's boned proboscis on such a tiny site would be like plonking down on a chessboard the giant image of Buddha now to be seen at Nara. The juxtaposing of disproportionate elements destroys aesthetic value. Mrs. Goldfield's nose, like that of Caesar's, is, as a thing in itself, a most dignified and majestic protuberance. But how does it appear in relation to its surroundings? Of course those circumjacent areas are not quite so barren of aesthetic merit as the face of this cat. Nevertheless, it is a bloated face, the face of an epileptic skivvy whose eyebrows meet in a sharp-pitched gable above thin tilted eyes. Gentlemen, I ask you, what sort of nose could ever survive so lamentable a face?"

As Waverhouse paused, a voice could be heard from the back of the house. "He's still going on about noses. What a spiteful bore he is."

"That's the wife of the rickshaw-owner," my master explains to Waverhouse.

Waverhouse resumes. "It is a great, if unexpected, honor for this present lecturer to discover at, as it were, the back of the hall an interested listener of the gentle sex. I am especially gratified that a gleam of charm should be added to my arid lecture by the bell-sweet voice of this new participant. It is, indeed, a happiness unlooked for, a serendipity. To be worthy of our beautiful lady's patronage I would gladly alter the academic style of this discourse into a more popular mode, but, as I am just about to discuss a problem in mechanics, the unavoidably technical terminology may prove a trifle difficult for the ladies to comprehend. I must therefore beg them to be patient."

Coldmoon responds to the mention of mechanics with his usual grin.

"The point I wish to establish is that such a nose and such a face will never harmonize. In brief, they cannot conform to Zeising's rule of the Golden Section, a fact which I propose to prove by use of a mechanical formula. We should first designate H as the height of the nose, and α as the angle between the nose and the level surface of the face. Please note that W is, of course, the weight of the nose. Are you with me thus far?"

"Hardly," breathes my master.

"Coldmoon, what about you?"

"I, too, am slightly at a loss."

"You distress me, Coldmoon. Sneaze doesn't matter, but I'm shocked that you, a bachelor of science, should fail to understand. This formula is a key part of my lecture. To abandon this portion of my argument must render the whole endeavor pointless. However, such things can't be helped. I'll omit the formula and merely deliver the peroration."

"Is there a peroration?" asks my master in genuine curiosity.

"Why, naturally! A lecture without a peroration is like a Western dinner shorn of the dessert. Now, listen, both of you, carefully. I am launching on my peroration. Gentlemen, if one reflects upon the theory which I have advanced on this occasion and gives due weight to the related theories of Virchow and of Wisemen, one is bound also to take appropriate account of the problem of the heredity of congenital form. Furthermore, though there is a substantial body of evidence to support the contention that acquired characteristics are not hereditarily transmissible, one cannot lightly dismiss the view that the mental conditions associated with hereditarily transmissible forms are themselves also transmissible. It is consequently reasonable to assume that a child born to the possessor of a nose of such enormity will have an abnormal nose. Because Coldmoon is still young, he has not noticed any particular abnormality in the structure of Miss Goldfield's nasal organ. But the genes lurk. The products of heredity take long to incubate. One never knows. Perhaps it would need no more than a sharp change of climate for the daughter's snout suddenly to germinate and, in a mere instant, to tumesce into a replica of that of her most honorable mother. In sum, I believe that in the light of my theoretical demonstration, it would seem prudent to forswear any idea of this marriage. Now, while it is still possible to do so. I would go so far as to claim that, quite apart from the master of this house, even his monstrous cat asleep among us, would not dissent my conclusions."

My master sits up at last. "Of course," he says "no one in his senses would ever marry a daughter of that creature! Really, my dear Coldmoon," he insists in real earnest, "you simply must not marry her."

I seek in my own humble way to second all these sentiments by mewing twice. Coldmoon, however, does not seem to be particularly alarmed. "If you two sages share that opinion, I would be prepared to give her up, but it would be cruel if the consequent distress brought the person in question into poor health."

"That," burbled Waverhouse happily, "might even be regarded as a sort of sex crime."

Only my master continues to take the matter seriously. "Don't joke about such things. That girl wouldn't wither away, not if she's the daughter of that forward and presumptuous creature who strove to humiliate me from the moment she set an uninvited foot in my house." My master again works himself up into a great huff.

At which point there is a further outbreak of laughter from, by the sound of it, three or four people on the far side of the hedge. A voice says, "You're a stuck-up blockhead." Another jeers, "I bet you'd like to live in a bigger house." A third loud voice announces, "Ain't it a pity! You swagger around but you're only a silly old windbag."

My master goes out on to the veranda and shouts with matching violence, "Hold your tongues. What do you think you're doing making this sort of disturbance so close to my property?"

The laughter gets even louder. "Hark at him. It's silly old Savage Tea. Savage Tea. Savage Tea." They set up an abusive chant.

My master, looking furious, turns abruptly, snatches up his stick and rushes out into the street.

Waverhouse claps his hands in pure delight. "Up guards and at 'em" he shouts, urging my master on.

Coldmoon sits and grins, twisting his purple fastening-strings.

I follow my master and, as I crawl out through a gap in the hedge, find him standing in the middle of the street with his stick held awkwardly in his hand. Apart from him, the street is empty. I cannot help but feel that he's been made to make a ninny of himself.

VOLUME II

I

IT HAS become my usual practice to I sneak into the Goldfields' mansion. I won't expand upon the meaning of my use of "usual," which is merely a word expressing the square of "often." What one does once, one wants to do again, and things tried twice invite a third experience. This sense of enquiry is not confined to humanity, and I must ask you to accept that every cat born into this world is endowed with this psychological peculiarity. Just as in the human case, so with cats: once we've done a thing more than three times over, the act becomes a habit and its performance a necessity of our daily life. If you should happen to wonder why I so often visit the Goldfield place, let me first address a modest enquiry to mankind. Why do human beings breathe smoke in through the mouth and then expel it through the nose? Since such shameless inhalation and exhalation can do little to ease the belly's hunger and less to cure giddiness, I do not see why a race of habitual smokers should dare to offer criticism of my calls on the Goldfields. That house is my tobacco.

To say that I "sneak in" gives a misleading impression: it sounds vaguely reprehensible, a term to be used for the self-insinuations of thieves and clandestine lovers. Though it is true that I am not an invited guest, I do not go to the Goldfields' in order to snitch a slice of bonito or for a cozy chat with that disgusting lapdog whose eyes and nose are convulsively agglomerated in the center of its face. Hardly! Or are you suggesting that I visit there for the sheer love of snooping? Me, a detective? You must be out of your mind! Among the several most degrading occupations in this world, there are, in my opinion, none more grubby than those of the detective and the money-lender. It is true that once, for Coldmoon's sake, I displayed a chivalrous spirit unbecoming in a cat and kept an indirectly watchful eye on the Goldfields' goings on. It was but once that I acted with such ill-placed kind-heartedness, and since that isolated occasion I have done nothing whatsoever that could bring a twinge to the conscience of the most pernickety cat. In which case, you may ask, why did I describe my own actions with such an unpleasantly suggestive phrase as "to sneak in?" I have my own good reasons, but their explanation involves analysis in depth.

In the first place it is my opinion that the sky was made to shelter all creation, and that the earth was made so that all things created that were able to stand might have something to stand on. Even those human beings who love argument for the arguing's sake could surely not deny this fact. Next we may ask to what extent did human effort contribute to the creation of heaven and earth, and the answer is that it contributed nothing. What right, then, do human beings hold to decide that things not of their own creation nevertheless belong to them? Of course the absence of right need not prevent such creatures from making that decision, but surely there can be no possible justification for them prohibiting others from innocent passage in and out of so-called human property. If it be accepted that Mr. So-and-so may set up stakes, fence off sections of this boundless earth, and register that area as his own, what is to prevent such persons from roping off blue sky, from staking claims on heaven, an enclosure of the air? If natural law permitted proprietorial parceling-out of the land and its sale and purchase at so much the square foot, then it would also permit partition of the air we breathe at so much the cubic unit and its three-dimensional sale. If, however, it is not proper to trade in sky, if enclosure of the empyrean is not regarded as just in natural law, then surely it must follow that all land-ownership is unnatural and irrational. That, in fact, is my conviction, therefore I enter wherever I like. Naturally, I do not go anywhere where I do not want to go: but, provided they are in the direction I fancy, all places are alike to me. I slope along as it suits me, and feel no inhibition about entering the properties of people like the Goldfields if I happen to want to. However, the sad fact is that, being no more than a cat, I cannot match mankind in the crude matter of simple physical strength. In this real world the saying that "might is right" has very real force; so much so that no matter how sound my arguments may be, the logic of cats will not command respect. Were I to press the argument too far, I should be answered, like Rickshaw Blacky, with a swipe from a fishmonger's pole. In situations where reason and brute force are opposed and one may choose either to submit by a perversion of reason or to achieve one's reasonable ends by outwitting the opposition, I would, of course, adopt the latter course. If one is not to be maimed with bamboo poles, one must put up with things: one must press on. Thus, since the concept of trespass is irrational, and since "sneaking in" is only a form of "pressing on," I am prepared to describe my visits as sneaking in.

Though I have no wish whatsoever to spy upon the Goldfields, inevitably, as the number of my visits mount, I get to know things about that family which I'd rather not have known and I see happenings which, willy-nilly, I cannot purge from my memory. I am, for instance, regretfully aware that when Madam Conk dabs water on her face she wipes her nose with inordinate care; that Miss Opula persistently gluts herself on rice-cakes dusted with bean-flour; and that old man Goldfield, in striking contrast with his wife, has a nose as flat as a pancake. Indeed, not just his nose, but his whole face is flat. It is a face so leveled one suspects that when he was a lad he must have got into a fight with the strong boy of some children's gang who, grabbing him by the scruff of the neck, rammed his face so hard against a plaster wall that even now, forty years on, his squashed and crumpled features are a living memento of that unlucky day. Though it is certainly an extremely peaceful, even a harmless, face, it is somewhat lacking in variety. However much that face becomes infuriated, still it stays flat. I came to learn, moreover, that old man Goldfield likes tuna fish, sliced and raw, and that whenever he eats that delicacy, he pats himself on his own bald pate with a plashy, pattering sound. Further, because his body is as squat as his face is flat, he affects tall hats and high-stepped wooden clogs; facts which his personal rickshawman finds so vastly entertaining that he's always yattering on about them to the houseboy who, for his part, finds such sharp accuracy of observation impressively remarkable. I could go on forever with such details of the Goldfields' goings-on.

It has become my practice to enter the garden by the back-gate and to survey the lie of the land from the cover of a small artificial mound helpfully constructed there for decorative purposes. Having made sure that everything is quiet and that all the paper-windows are slid shut, I gingerly creep forward and hop up onto the veranda. But if I hear lively voices or consider there's a risk that I might be seen from within, I mosey off eastward around the pond, nip past the lavatory and finish up, safe and unobserved, under the veranda. My conscience is in no way troubled, I've nothing to hide and no reason to be scared of anything whatsoever, but I've learnt what to expect if one should have the vile ill-luck to run up against one of those lawless and disorderly bipeds. Were the human world cram-jammed with robber-toughs as violent as that long-departed villain, Kumasaka Chōhan, then even the most illustrious and virtuous of men would act as cautiously as I do. Inasmuch, as old man Goldfield is a dignified sort of businessman, I wouldn't expect him to come after me with any such dirty great sword, five feet, three inches of it they tell me, as Kumasaka was wont to brandish. However, from what I've seen and heard, Goldfield has his own unpleasant quirks and is certainly not disposed to accept that a man's a man for a' that. If Goldfield is overbearing with his fellowmen, how would he treat a cat? A cat, as I keep on saying, is also a cat for a' that, but given Goldfield's nature, even a feline of the most upright virtues would be wise to adopt a low posture and a very cautious attitude once inside the Goldfield premises. This very need to be constantly on the *qui vive* is, I find, delightful, and my taste for danger explains why I make these frequent risky visits. I will give further and careful thought to this fascinating point and, when I have completed my analysis of cat-mentality, I will publish the results.

What's up today, I wonder, as I settle my chin against the grass on top of the garden-hillock and survey the prospect spread below me. The doors of their ample drawing room are open wide to the full spring day and I can see, inside, the Goldfields busily engaged in conversation with a guest. I am somewhat daunted by the fact that Madam Conk's proboscis is pointed directly in my direction: it glares across the pond straight at my unprotected forehead. This is my first experience of being glared at by a nose. Facing his guest, old man Goldfield presents himself to my gaze in full profile. My eyes are spared one half of his flattened features but, for the same profilic reason, the location of his nose is indeterminable, and it is only because one can see where his grayish-white moustache sprouts raggedly from the flesh that one can deduce that the vent-holes of his nostrils must be gaping closely thereabove. I amuse myself with the reflection that the light spring breeze might well blow on forever if it encountered no more formidable obstruction than that jutless physiognomy. Of the three, the Goldfields' guest has the most normal features but, precisely because of their regularity, there's no facial peculiarity I see reason to point out. For anything to be regular suggests that the thing's all right, but regularity can be so utterly regular as to become, by its very ulteriority, mediocre and of no account, which is extremely pitiable.

I wonder who he is, this unfortunate fellow fated to be born in this glorious reign behind so meaningless a phiz. My curiosity can't be satisfied unless I crawl more close and, in my accustomed manner, establish myself underneath the veranda and listen to what is said. So under it I go.

". . .and my wife actually took the trouble to call on the man to ask for information." As usual, old man Goldfield speaks in an arrogant manner. The manner is certainly prideful, but his voice contains no hint of sharpness. It gives, like his face, an impression of massive flatness.

"I see. So he's the fellow who used to teach your Mr. Avalon Coldmoon. I see, I see. Yes, yours is a good idea. . . Indeed, I see." This guest is positively overflowing with "I see's."

"But somehow my wife's approaches all proved pretty pointless."

"No wonder. Sneaze is not strong on point. Even in the days when he and I shared digs and looked after ourselves, his lack of point, his lack of resolution, were painfully extreme. You must," he said, turning to Madam Conk, "have had a difficult time."

"Difficult! That's hardly the word. Never in my life have I made a visit and been so badly treated." As is her ugly custom, Madam Conk snorts storm-winds down her snout.

"Did he say anything rude to you? He's always been obstinate, a real old stick-in-the-mud. He's been teaching that English Reader for years without a break, so you can imagine. . ." With what charm and tact this guest is making himself agreeable.

"He is beyond help. I understand that every time my wife asked a question, she received a blunt rebuff."

"What impudence! As I see it, persons of some small education tend to grow conceited and, if they happen also to be poor, their characters become as bitter as sour grapes. Indeed, some people in that condition turn truly quite absurd. For no reason at all, they flare up at persons of wealth as if unconscious of their own total ineffectiveness. It's quite astonishing how they behave; as if the rich had robbed them personally of things they never owned." The guest's laughter rang out affectedly, but he certainly seems delighted with himself.

"Scandalous behavior! It's because they know nothing of the world that they carry on so outrageously. So I thought I'd have him taken down a peg or two. It's time he learned how many beans make six."

"I see. Splendid. That should have shaken him up a bit. Done him no end of good." Goldfield is smothered in his guest's congratulations, even though that sycophant still lacks the least idea of the kind of rod which Goldfield's put in pickle for poor Sneeze.

"But really, Mr. Suzuki, Sneaze is impossible. D'you know," said Madam Conk, "down at his school he won't exchange two words with our friend, Mr. Fukuchi? Nor, come to think of it, with Mr. Tsuki either. We'd thought he'd learnt his lesson and was keeping quiet because he knew he's been sat on, but, would you believe it, only the other day we heard he'd been chasing after our harmless houseboy with a walking stick! Just imagine that. He's a man of thirty. No sane grown-up could act in such a way. Perhaps," she ended hopefully, "despair has driven him dotty."

"But what can have driven him to such an act of violence?" Their guest seems mystified that Sneaze could act so firmly.

"Nothing much really. It seems that our houseboy happened to be passing Sneaze's place, made some innocent remark, and, before you could say Jack Robinson, Sneaze came rushing out in his bare feet and began lashing around with his stick. Whatever the houseboy may have said, he is, after all, no more than a boy. But Sneaze is a bearded man and, what's more, supposed to be a teacher."

"Some teacher," says the guest.

"Some teacher," echoed Goldfield.

It would seem that this precious trio has reached complete agreement that, if one happens to be a teacher, one should, like some wooden statue, grin and bear whatever insults anyone cares to offer.

"And then," said Madam Conk, "there's that fibbing crank called Waverhouse. I've never heard a man tell such a stream of whoppers. All quite pointless, but all flat lies. Really, I've never clapped eyes on such a loony in my life."

"Waverhouse? Yes, he seems to be bragging on as usual. Was he also there when you called on Sneaze? He, too, can be a tricky customer. He was another of our group in digs. I remember I was always having rows with him on account of his incessant, ill-judged mockery and his warped sense of humor."

"A man like that would rile a saint. We all, of course, tell lies, sometimes out of loyalty, sometimes by demand of the occasion, and in such circumstances anyone may fairly bend the truth. But that man Waverhouse tells his lies for no good reason at all. What can one do with a man like that? I just can't see how he brings himself to rattle off such reams of barefaced balderdash. What does he expect to gain by it?"

"You've hit the nail on the head. There's nothing one can do when a man tells lies for a hobby."

"I made a special visit to that miserable house to ask no more than the normal questions about Avalon that any mother would, but all my efforts came to nothing; they vexed me and they put me down. But all the same, I felt obliged to do the decent thing, so afterward I sent our rickshawman around with a dozen bottles of beer. Can you imagine what happened? That saucy usher Sneaze had the cheek to order our man to take the bottles away because, so he said, he saw no reason why he should accept them. Our fellow pressed him to take the bottles as a token of our appreciation. So then Sneaze said that he liked jam but reckoned beer too bitter. Then he just shut the door and went off back to his room. Now can you beat that? How damned rude can one get?"

"That's terrible." The guest seems, this time genuinely, to think it's really terrible.

After a brief pause I hear the voice of old man Goldfield. "And that's, in fact, precisely why we've asked you here today. It's something, of course, to make fun of that fool Sneaze behind his back, but that sort of thing doesn't entirely suit our present purpose. . ." Splash, spatter; spatter, spatter, splash. He's patting his pate as though he's just been eating sliced, raw tuna fish. Of course, being tucked away underneath the veranda, I cannot actually see him beating that wet tattoo on the skin of his hairless head, but I've seen so much of him lately that, just as a priestess in a temple gets to recognize the sound of each particular wooden gong, so I can tell, from the quality of the sound, even though I'm under the floor, when old man Goldfield takes to drumming on his skull.

"And it occurred to me to ask for your assistance in this matter. . ."

"If I can be of any service, please don't hesitate to ask me. After all, it's entirely due to your kind influence that I have had the great good fortune to be transferred to the Tokyo office." Their guest is so obviously anxious to oblige that he must be another of those many persons under obligation to return some form of help to Goldfield. Well, well, so the plot thickens. I wandered out today simply because the weather was so wonderful, and I certainly had not expected to stumble upon such exciting news of planned skulduggery. It is as though one had gone to the family temple dutifully intending to feed the Hungry Dead, only to find oneself invited to a right old lash-up of rice-cake dumplings and bean-paste jam in the private room of a priest. Wondering what kind of assistance will be sought from this client-guest, I prick my ears to listen.

"Don't ask me to explain it, but that nitwitted teacher keeps planting crazy notions in the head of young Coldmoon: like, for instance, hinting that he shouldn't marry any daughter of mine." He turned to his wife. "That's what he hinted, didn't he?"

"Hinting's not the word. He said flat out 'No one in his senses would ever marry a daughter of that creature. Coldmoon,' he said, 'you simply mustn't marry her.'"

"Well, blow me down. Did he really have, the brazen cheek to speak of me as a creature? Did he really pitch it as strong as that?"

"Not half he didn't. The wife of the rickshaw-man came around double-quick just to be sure I knew."

"Well, there you are, Suzuki. That man Sneaze is getting to be a nuisance, wouldn't you agree?"

"How extremely irritating. Marriage negotiations are not matters in which to meddle lightly. Surely even a dunderhead like Sneaze ought to have the common sense to know that. Really, the whole thing's beyond my comprehension."

"In your undergraduate days you lived in the same boarding-house as Sneaze, and, though things may have changed by now, I understand that you two then used to be pretty pally. Now, what I want you to do is to go and see Sneaze and try to talk some reason into him. He may be feeling offended, but if he is, it's really all his own fool fault. If he plays ball, I'd be willing to give him generous help with his personal affairs, and we would, of course, lay off annoying him. But if he keeps on gumming things up the way he's so far done, it will only be natural if I find ways of my own to settle his meddlesome hash. In short, it just won't pay him to go on acting obstinate."

"How very right you are. Continued resistance on his part would be idiotic. It could bring him no possible profit and could well cause him loss. I'll do my best to make him understand."

"One more thing. Since there are many other suitors for our daughter, I can't make any firm promise of giving her to Coldmoon, but you could usefully go so far as to hint that, if he studies hard and gets his degree in the near future, he stands a chance of winning her."

"That should encourage him to buckle down to study. All right, I'll do as you wish."

"One last thing. It may sound odd, but what especially sticks in my gullet is the way that Coldmoon, who's supposed to be so smart, laps up everything that Sneaze lets drop, and even goes around addressing that crack-brained ninny as though he were some kind of sage professor. Of course, since Coldmoon's not the only man we are considering for Opula, such unbecoming conduct is not of vast importance. Nevertheless. . ."

"You see," squawked Madam Conk, butting in on her husband's careful sentence, "it's just that we're sorry for Coldmoon."

"I've never had the pleasure of meeting the gentleman, but, since to marry into your distinguished family would be to ensure a lifetime's happiness, I'm quite convinced that he himself could not possibly wish other than the marriage."

"You're absolutely right," said Madam Conk. "Coldmoon's keen to marry her. It's only that numbskull Sneaze and his crackpot crony Waverhouse who keep throwing spanners in the works."

"Most reprehensible. Not the style of behavior one expects from any reasonable, well-educated person. I'll go and talk with Sneaze."

"Please do, we'd be most grateful. Remember, too, that Sneaze knows better than anyone else what Coldmoon's really like. As you know, during her recent call my wife failed to dig out anything much worth knowing. If in addition to ascertaining details of his scholastic talent and all that stuff, you could also find out more about Coldmoon's character and conduct, I'd be particularly obliged."

"Certainly. Since it's Saturday today, Sneaze must be home by now. Where does he live, I wonder," says Suzuki.

"You turn right from our place, then turn left at the end of the road. About one block along, you'll see a house with a tumbled down black fence. That," said Madam Conk, "is it."

"So it's right here in this neighborhood! Then it should be easy. I'll go and see him on my way home. It will be simple to identify the house by the name plate."

"You may, or you may not, find his name plate on display. I understand he uses one or two grains of cooked rice to stick his visiting card on his wooden gate. When it rains, of course, the cardboard comes unstuck. Then on some convenient sunny day he'll paste another card in place. So you can't be sure that his name plate will be up. It's hard to see why he keeps to such a trouble some routine when the obvious thing to do is to hang up a wooden name board. But that," sighed Madam Conk, "is just another example of his general cussedness."

"Astonishing," remarked Suzuki, "but I'll find the place in any case by asking for the house with the black fence in a state of disrepair."

"Oh yes, you'll find it easily enough. There's not another house in the whole neighborhood quite so filthy-looking. Wait a minute! I've just remembered something else. Look for a house with weeds growing out of the roof. It's impossible to miss."

"In fact, a quite distinguished residence," said Suzuki and, laughing, took his leave.

It would not suit my book to have Suzuki beat me home. I've already overheard as much as I need to know; so, still concealed beneath the veranda, I retrace my steps to the lavatory where, turning west, I briefly break cover to get back behind the hillock and, under its concealment, regain the safety of the street. A brisk cat-trot soon brings me to the house with the weed-grown roof where, with the utmost nonchalance, I hopped up onto our own veranda.

My master had spread a white woolen blanket on the wooden boards and was lying there, face down, with the sunshine of this warm spring day soaking into his back. Sunshine, unlike other things, is distributed fairly. It falls impartially upon the rich and the poor. It makes a squalid hut, whose only distinctions are the tufts of shepherd's purse sprouting from its roof, no less gaily warm than, for all its solid comfort, the Goldfields' mansion. I am, however, obliged to confess that that blanket jars with the day's spring feeling. No doubt its manufacturer meant that it should be white. No doubt, too, it was sold as white by some haberdasher specializing in goods imported from abroad. No less certainly, my master must have asked for a white blanket at the time he bought it. But all that happened twelve or thirteen years ago, and since that far-off Age of White, the blanket has declined into a Dark Age where its present color is a somber gray. No doubt the passage of time will eventually turn it black, but I'd be surprised if the thing survived that long. It is already so badly worn that one can easily count the individual threads of its warp and woof. Its wooliness is gone and it would be an exaggeration, even a presumption, to describe this scrawny half-eroded object as a blanket. A "blan," possibly; even a "ket," but a full-blown "blanket," no. However, my master holds, or at least appears to hold, that anything which one has kept for a year, two years, five years, and eventually for a decade, must then be kept for the rest of one's natural life. One would think he were a gypsy. Anyway, what's he doing, sprawled belly-down on that remnant of the past? He lies with his chin stuck out, its jut supported on a crotch of hands, with a lighted cigarette projecting from his right-hand fingers. And that is all he's doing. Of course inside his skull, deep below the dandruff, universal truths may be spinning around in a shower of fiery sparks like so many Catherine Wheels. It's possible but, judging from his external appearance, not likely even in one's wildest imaginings.

The cigarette's lit tip is steadily burning down and an inch of ash, like some gray caddis-case, plopped down onto the blanket. My master, ignoring that declension, stares intently at the rising smoke. Stirred by the light spring breeze, the smoke floats up in loops and vortices, finally to gather in a kind of clinging haze around the ends of his wife's just-washed black hair. Gentle reader, please accept my apologies. I had completely forgotten to mention that lady's presence.

Mrs. Sneaze is sitting so that her bottom presents itself before her husband's face. You think that impolite? Speaking for myself I would not call it so. Both courtesy and discourtesy depend on one's point of view. My master is lying perfectly at ease with his cupped face in close proximity to his wife's bottom: he is neither disturbed by its proximity nor concerned at his own conduct. His wife is equally composed to position her majestic bum bang in her husband's face. There is neither the slightest hint nor intention of discourtesy. They are simply a much-married couple who, in less than a year of wedlock, sensibly disengaged themselves from the cramps of etiquette. Mrs. Sneaze seems to have taken advantage of the exceptionally fine weather to give her pitch-black hair a really thorough wash with a concoction made from raw eggs and some special kind of seaweed. Somewhat ostentatiously, she has let her long straight hair hang loose around her shoulders and all the way down her back, and sits, busy and silent, sewing a child's sleeveless jacket. In point of fact, I believe it is purely because she wants to dry her hair that she's brought both her sewing-box and a flattish cushion made from some all-woolen muslin out here. It is similarly to present her hair at the best angle to the sun that, deferentially, she presents her bottom to her spouse. That's my belief, but it may, of course, be that my master moved to intrude his face where her bum already was.

Now, to return to that business of the cigarette smoke, my master lay watching with fascinated absorption the way in which the smoke, floating upward through his wife's abundant and now loosened hair, was itself combed into an appearance of filaments of blue-gray air. However, it is in the nature of smoke to go on rising, so that my master's fascination with this singular spectacle of hair-entangled smoke compels him, lest he miss any phase of its development, steadily to lift his gaze. His eyes, first leveled on her hips, move up her back, over her shoulders, and along her neck. And it was after his concentrated stare had completed the ascent of her neck and was focused on the very crown of her head that he suddenly let out an involuntary gasp of surprise.

For there, on the very summit of the lady whom he had promised to love and cherish till death did them part, was a large round patch of baldness. That unexpected nakedness, catching the clear spring sunshine, threw back the light and shone with an almost braggart self-confidence. My master's eyes remain fixed open in surprise at this dazzling discovery and, disregarding the danger of such brightness to his own uncovered retinal tissue, he continues to goggle at her skin's bright mirror. The image that then immediately shot into my master's mind was of that dish on which stood the taper set before the altar in the household shrine handed down in his family for untold generations. My master's family belongs to the Shin sect of Buddhism, a sect in which it is the established custom to lay out substantial sums, more indeed than most of its adherents can afford, on household shrines. My master suddenly remembers how, when he was a very small boy, he first saw the shrine in the family safe-room. It was a miniature shrine, somber though thickly gilded, in which a brass taper-dish was hanging. From the burning taper a faint light shone, even in the day time, on the rounded dish. Bright against the shrine's general darkness, that image of the shining dish, seen in his childhood time and time again, leapt back into his mind as he gaped at his wife's bald patch. But that first remembrance quickly vanished, to be replaced by memories of the pigeons at the Kannon Temple in Asakusa. There seems no obvious connection between temple doves and Mrs. Sneaze's gleaming scalp, but in my master's mind the association of images is clear and very close. It, again, is an association deriving from his early childhood. Whenever then he was taken to that temple, he would buy peas for the pigeons. The peas cost less than a farthing a saucer. The saucers, made of an unglazed reddish clay, were remarkably similar, both in size and color, to his wife's bare patch.

"Astonishingly similar." The words escape from his lips in tones of an awed wonder.

"What is?" says his wife without even turning toward him.

"What is? There's a big bald patch on the crown of your head. Did you know?"

"Yes," she answers, still not interrupting her sewing. She seems not the least embarrassed by his discovery. A model wife, at least in point of imperturbability.

"Was it there before we married or did it crop up later?" Though my master does not come out with an open accusation, he clearly sounds as if he would regard himself as having been tricked into marriage if the bald patch was, in fact, present in her maidenhood.

"I don't remember when I got it. Not that it matters. Whatever difference could a bald patch make?" Quite the philosopher, isn't she just.

"Not that it matters! But it's your own hair that we're talking about." My master speaks with a certain sharpness.

"It's just because it is my own hair that it doesn't matter." An effective answer, but she may have been feeling slightly self-conscious for she lifted her right hand gently to stroke the spot. "Oh dear," she said, "it's got much bigger. I hadn't realized that." Her tone conceded that the patch was larger than would be normal at her age and, now driven onto the defensive, she added, "Once one starts doing one's hair in the married style, the strands at the crown come under a very real strain. All married women lose hair from the top of the head."

"If all married women lost hair at your rate, by the time they were forty they'd be bald as kettles. You must have caught some kind of disease. Maybe it's contagious. You'd better go round and have it looked at by Dr. Amaki before things go too far," says my master, carefully stroking his own head.

"That's all very well, but what about you? White hairs in your nostrils! If baldness is contagious, white hairs will be catching." Mrs. Sneaze begins to go over to the attack.

"A single, white hair in the nostrils is obviously harmless, and it doesn't even show. But fox-mange on the crown of the head cannot be ignored. It is, especially in the case of a young woman, positively unsightly. It's a deformity."

"If you think I'm deformed, why did you marry me? It was you who wanted the marriage, yet now you call me deformed. . ."

"For the simple reason that I didn't know. Indeed, I was unaware of your condition until this very day. If you want to make an issue of it, why didn't you reveal your naked scalp to me before we got married?"

"What a silly thing to say! Where in the world would you find a place where girls had to have their scalps examined before they could get married?"

"Well, the baldness might be tolerable but you're also uncommonly dumpy, and that is certainly unsightly."

"There's never been anything hidden about my height. You knew perfectly well when you married me that I'm slightly on the short side."

"Of course I knew, but I'd thought you might extend a bit, and that's why I married you."

"How could anyone grow taller after the age of twenty? Are you trying to make a fool of me? Eh?" She drops the sleeveless jacket and, twisting around to face her husband, gives him a threatening look as if to say, "Now watch your step, you go too far, and you'll be sorry."

"There is surely no law forbidding people from growing taller after the age of twenty. I cherished a faint hope that, if I fed you up on decent food, you might prolong yourself." With every appearance of meaning what he said, my master was about to develop his curious reasoning, when he was cut off by a sharp ringing of the doorbell followed by a loud shout of "Hello." Snuffling after the scent of that shepherd's purse on the roof, the dogged Suzuki seems at last to have tracked down Sneaze's den.

My master's wife, temporarily postponing their domestic row, snatches up the jacket and her sewing-box and vanishes into an inner room. My master scrabbles his gray blanket up into a ball and slings it into the study. The maid brings in the visitor's card and gives it to my master, who, having read it, looks a little surprised. Then, having told the maid to show the visitor in, he goes off into the lavatory with the card still clasped in his hand. If it is beyond one's comprehension that he should thus suddenly take to the loo, it is even more difficult to explain why he should have taken with him the visiting-card of Suzuki Tōjūrō. It is, in any case, very hard luck on the soul of that visiting-card that it should have to accompany him to that noisome place.

The maid deposits a printed, cotton cushion on the floor in front of the alcove-recess, invites the guest to be seated in that place of honor, and then removes herself. Suzuki first inspects the room. He begins by examining the scroll displayed in the alcove: its Chinese characters, allegedly written by Mokuan, that master calligrapher of the Zen sect, are, of course, faked, but they state that flowers are in bloom and that spring is come to all the world. He next tarns his attention to some early-flowering cherry-blossoms arranged in one of those celadon vases which they turn out cheap in Kyoto. Then, when his roving glance chances to fall upon the cushion provided for his particular convenience, what should he find but, planted serenely smack in its center, a squatting cat. I need hardly add that the cat in question is my lordly self.

It was at this point that the first quick tremor of tension, a ripple so small it did not show on his face, quaked in Suzuki's mind. That cushion had undoubtedly been provided for himself but before he could sit down on it, some strange animal, without so much as a by-your-leave, had dispossessed him of the seat of honor and now lay crouched upon it with an air of firm self-confidence. This was the first consideration to disturb the composure of his mind. In point of fact, had the cushion remained unoccupied, Suzuki would probably have sought to demonstrate his modesty by resting his rump on the hard matfloor until such time as my master himself invited its transfer to the comfort of the cushion. So who the hell is this that has so blithely appropriated the cushion which was destined, sooner or later, to have eased Suzuki buttocks? Had the interloper been a human being, he might well have given way. But to be preempted by a mere cat, that is intolerable. It is also a little unpleasant. This minor animality of his dis-sedation was the second consideration to disturb the composure of Suzuki's mind. There was, moreover, something singularly irritating about the very attitude of the cat. Without the least small twitch-sign of apology, the cat sits arrogantly on the cushion it has filched and, with a cold glitter in its unamiable eyes, stares up into Suzuki's face as if to say, "And who the hell are you?" This is the third consideration to ruffle Suzuki's composure. Of course if he's really irked, he ought to jerk me off the cushion by the scruff of my neck. But he doesn't. He just watches me in silence. It is inconceivable that any creature as massive and muscular as man could be so afraid of a cat as not to dare to bring crude force to bear in any clash of wills. So why doesn't Suzuki express his dislike by turfing me off the cushion with summary dispatch? The reason is, I think, that Suzuki is inhibited by his own conception of the conduct proper to a man. When it comes to the use of force any child three feet tall can, and will, fling me about quite easily. But a full-grown man, even Suzuki Tōjūrō, Goldfield's right-hand man, cannot bring himself to raise a finger against this Supreme Cat Deity ensconced upon the holy ground of a cotton cushion two feet square. Even though there were no witnesses, a man would regard it as beneath his dignity to scuffle with a cat for possession of a cushion. One would make oneself ridiculous, even a figure of farce, if one degraded oneself to the level of arguing with a cat. For Suzuki, the price of this human estimate of human dignity is to endure a certain amount of discomfort in the nates, but precisely because he feels he must endure it, his hatred of the cat is proportionately increased. When, every now and again he looks at me, his face exudes distaste. Since I find it amusing to see such wry distortion of his features, I do my best myself to maintain an air of innocence and resist the temptation to laugh.

While this pantomime was still going on, my master left the lavatory and, having tidied himself up, came in and sat down. "Hello," he said. Since the visiting card is no longer in his hand, the name of Suzuki Tōjūrō must have been condemned to penal servitude for life in that evil-smelling place. Almost before I could feel sorry for the visiting card's ill-luck, my master, saying, "Oh, you!" grabs me by the scruff of my neck and hurls me out to land with a bang on the veranda.

"Do take this cushion. You're quite a stranger. When did you come up to Tokyo?" My master offers the cushion to his old friend, and Suzuki, having turned it catside-down, dumps himself upon it.

"As I've been so busy I haven't let you know, but I was recently transferred back to our main office in Tokyo."

"That's splendid. We haven't seen each other for quite a long while. This must be the first time since you went off to the provinces?"

"Yes, nearly ten years ago. Actually, I did sometimes come up to Tokyo, but as I was always flooded with business commitments, I simply couldn't manage to get round to see you. I do hope you won't think too badly of me. But, unlike your own profession, a business firm is honestly very busy."

"Ten years make big changes," observes my master, looking Suzuki up and down. His hair is neatly parted. He wears an English-made tweed suit enlivened by a gaudy tie. A bright gold watch chain glitters from his waistcoat. All these sartorial touches make it hard to credit that this can really be one of Sneaze's friends.

"Well, one gets on. Indeed, I'm now virtually obliged to sport such things as this. . ." Suzuki seems a little self-conscious about the vulgarly fashionable display of his watch chain.

"Is that thing real?" My master poses his question with the minimum of tact.

"Solid gold. Eighteen carat," Suzuki answers, smilingly smug. "You, too," he continued, "seem to have aged. Am I right in thinking you've children now? One? Am I right?"

"No."

"Two?"

"No."

"What, more? Three, then, is it?"

"Yes, I have three children now, and I don't know how many more to come in the future."

"Still as whimsical as ever. How old is your eldest? Quite big, I suppose."

"Yes, I'm not quite sure how old, but probably six or seven."

Suzuki laughed. "It must be pleasant to be a teacher, everything so free and easy. I wish I too had taken up teaching."

"Just you try. You'd be sorry in three days."

"I don't know. It seems a good kind of life: refined and not too stressful, plenty of spare time, and the opportunity to really study one's own special interest. Being a businessman is not bad, either, though at my present level things aren't particularly satisfactory. If one becomes a businessman, one has to get to the top. Anywhere lower on the ladder, you have to go around spouting idiotic flatteries and drinking *saké* with the boss when there's nothing you want less. Altogether, it's a stupid way of life."

"Ever since my school days I've always taken a scunner to businessmen. They'll do anything for money. They are, after all, what they used to be called in the good old days: the very dregs of society." My master, with a businessman right there in front of him, indulges in tactlessness.

"Oh, have a heart. They aren't always like that. Admittedly, there's a certain coarseness about them; for there's no point in even trying to be a businessman unless your love for money is so absolute that you're ready to accompany it on the walk to a double suicide. For money, believe you me, is a hard mistress and none of her lovers are let off lightly. As a matter of fact, I've just been visiting a businessman and, according to him, the only way to succeed is to practice the 'triangled technique': try to escape your obligations, annihilate your kindly feelings, and geld yourself of the sense of shame. Try-an-geld. You get it? Jolly clever, don't you think?"

"What awful fathead told you that?"

"He's no fathead. Smart as a whip, in fact. And increasingly respected in business circles. I rather fancy you know him. He lives up a side street just around the corner."

"You mean that frightful Goldfield?"

"Goodness me, but you're really getting worked up. He only meant it, you know, as a kind of joke. It's simply a way of summarizing the fact that to make money one must go through hell. So please don't take a joke too seriously."

"His 'triangled technique' may, I grant, be a joke: let's say it's screamingly funny. But what about his wife and her nauseating nose? If you've been to their house you could hardly have avoided colliding with that beak."

"Ah, Mrs. Goldfield. She seems a sensible woman of broad understanding."

"Damn her understanding. I'm talking about her nose. Her nose, Suzuki, it's a positive monstrosity. Only the other day I composed a *haitai* poem about it."

"What the dickens is a *haitai* poem?"

"Do you mean to say you've never heard of the current experiments in the composition of extended *haiku*? You do seem cut off from what's going on in the world."

"True. When one is as busy as I am, it's absolutely impossible to keep up with things like literature. Anyway, even when a lad, I never liked it much."

"Are you aware of the shape of Charlemagne's nose?"

"You are indeed in a whimsical mood." Suzuki laughed quite naturally. "Of course I haven't the faintest idea of the shape of Charlemagne's nose."

"Well, what about Wellington then? His troops used to call him Nosey. Did you know that?"

"Why on earth are you so batty about noses? Surely it doesn't matter if a nose happens to be round or pointed."

"On the contrary, it matters very much. D'you know about Pascal?"

"Questions, questions! Am I supposed to be taking an exam or something? No, I don't know about Pascal. What did he do?"

"He had this to say."

"What to say?"

"'Had Cleopatra's nose been a little bit shorter, the history of the world would have been changed.'"

"Did he now!"

"Perhaps now you see why one can't afford to underestimate the importance of noses."

"All right, I'll be more careful in future. By the way, I dropped in today because there's something I'd like to ask you. It's about a chap you used to teach. Avalon something or other. I can't remember his other name, but I understand that you and he see a lot of each other."

"You mean Coldmoon?"

"That's it, Coldmoon. Well, I've really come to make enquiries about him."

"About a matrimonial matter?"

"One might say that. You see, I called in earlier on the Goldfields. . ."

"The Nose herself came sniffing round here only the other day."

"Did she? Well, as a matter of fact she mentioned that she'd called. She said she'd paid a visit in order to present her respects to Mr. Sneaze and to entreat his assistance in a matter of information, but that Waverhouse was present and made so many and such frivolous interruptions that she just got muddled."

"It was all her own fault. Coming round here with a nose like that."

"She spoke of you with the deepest respect. She's just regretful that the performance put on by Waverhouse made it impossible to ask you certain personal questions about Coldmoon, and she has therefore asked me to speak on her behalf. For what it's worth, I've never before played the part of an honest broker in matters of this sort, but if the two parties most directly concerned are not against the idea, it's not a bad thing to serve as a go-between and so bring about a marriage. Indeed, that's the reason for my present visit."

"How kind of you to call," commented my master somewhat acidly. But, though he could not explain his feeling, he was inwardly a little moved by that phrase about "the two parties most directly concerned." Its slightly sentimental appeal made him feel as though a wraith of cool air had drifted through his sleeves on a hot and humid summer's night. It is true that my master's character is based on so firm an inborn bedrock of cold reserve and obstinacy that he is, by nature, one of this world's wet blankets. Nevertheless, his nature is of a completely different type from that of the vicious, heartless products of modern civilization. The antique mold of his nature is clearly evidenced in the way in which he flares up at the slightest provocation. The sole reason for his barney with Madam Conk was that he could not stand her modern-day approach. But his flat dislike of the mother was no fault of her daughter. Similarly, because he abominates all businessmen, he finds Goldfield acutely distasteful: yet here again, no blame can be laid on the daughter. Sneaze bears no real ill-will toward her, and Coldmoon is his favorite pupil and he loves that lad more deeply than he would a brother. If Suzuki is correct in his statement that the two parties most directly concerned do, in fact, love each other, then it would be an act unworthy of a gentleman even indirectly to hinder true love's course. Sneaze is quite convinced that he himself is a gentleman, so his only remaining question is whether Coldmoon and Miss Goldfield are in love. He must, if he is to amend his attitude, first be sure of the facts.

"Tell me, does that girl really want to marry Coldmoon? I don't care what Goldfield or the Nose feel about the matter, but what are the girl's own feelings?"

"Well, you see. . . that is, I understand. . . well, yes, I suppose she does." Suzuki's answer is not exactly clear-cut. Thinking that all he had to do was to find out more about Coldmoon, he came unbriefed on Opula's view of the match; so even this slippery lad now finds himself in a bit of a jam.

"The word 'suppose' implies some measure of uncertainty." My master, tactless as ever and not a man to be put off, goes in again like a bull at a gate.

"True enough. Perhaps I should have expressed myself more clearly. Now, the daughter certainly has a certain inclination. Indeed, that's true. What? Oh yes, Mrs. Goldfield told me so herself, though I gather she sometimes says some awful things about Coldmoon."

"Who does? D'you mean the daughter?"

"Yes."

"What impudence! That snip of a girl disparaging Coldmoon! Well, it can hardly mean that she cares for him."

"But that's just it. Odd you may think it, but sometimes people do run down precisely those they love."

"I can't conceive that anyone could be so deranged as to behave like that." Such intricate convolutions of human nature are quite beyond my master's blunt and simple mind.

"In fact the world is full of such people. Certainly that's how Mrs. Goldfield interprets her daughter's comments. She said to me 'My daughter must be quite taken with that young Coldmoon, for I've even heard her say he looks like a bewildered gourd.'"

These revelations of the strangeness of the human heart leave my master dumbstruck. Wide-eyed and wordless, he stares in astonishment at Suzuki as though he were some soothsayer wandered in from the street. Suzuki seems to have the mind to sense the danger implicit in my master's unbelief and, fearful lest further discussion should wreck his whole approach, quickly changes the subject to aspects of the matter which even my master cannot fail to understand.

"Consider these facts," he said. "With her good looks and money that girl can marry almost where she chooses. Now Coldmoon may be a splendid fellow, but comparing their relative social positions. . . No, such comparisons are always odious and could be taken as offensive. So let me put it this way: that, in terms of personal means, the couple are obviously ill-matched. Surely then, you can see that if the Goldfields are so worried that they ask me to come round here and talk to you, that very fact indicates the strength and nature of their daughter's yearnings?" One can't deny Suzuki's clever. He is relieved to notice that my master seems impressed by his latest line of argument, but realizing that the question of the degree of bleeding in Miss Goldfield's heart is likely to be re-opened if he allows the conversation to loiter on her feelings about Coldmoon, he concludes that the best way to complete his mission is to drive the discussion forward as quickly as possible.

"So, you see, as I've just explained, the Goldfields aren't expecting money or property; what they'd like instead is that Coldmoon should have some status of his own, and by status they mean the public recognition of qualification that is symbolized in a senior degree. It's not that they're so stuck-up as to say that they'll only consider giving him their daughter if he holds a doctorate. You mustn't misunderstand them. Things got jumbled up the other day when Mrs. Goldfield called on you purely because Waverhouse chose to amuse himself with his usual display of verbal fireworks and distorting mirrors. No, no, please don't protest. I know it was none of your fault. Mrs. Goldfield spoke in admiration of you as a frank and honest man. I'm certain that the blame and any awkwardness that may have arisen must be laid at Waverhouse's door. Anyway, you see, the nub of the matter is this: if Coldmoon can get a doctorate, he would have independent status. People would naturally look up to Dr. Coldmoon, and the Goldfields would be proud of such a son-in-law. So what are the chances of Coldmoon's making an early submission of his thesis and receiving his doctorate? You see, so far as the Goldfields themselves are concerned, they'd be the last to demand a doctor's degree, they wouldn't even ask for a bachelor's. But they have to consider what the world and his wife will say, and when dealing with the world one simply cannot be too careful."

So presented, the Goldfields' request for a doctorate seems not altogether unreasonable, and anything he deems not altogether unreasonable qualifies for my master's support. He feels inclined to act as Suzuki suggests. Suzuki, it is clear, can twiddle my master around his artful little finger. I recognize my master as indeed a simple, honest man.

"Well, in that case, next time Coldmoon drops around, I'll urge him to get on with his thesis. However, I feel that I must first question him closely to ascertain whether or not he really wants to marry that Goldfield girl."

"Question him closely! If you act with such meticulous formality, the business will never get settled. The quickest way to a happy ending is to sound his mind, casually, in the course of an ordinary conversation."

"To sound his mind?"

"Yes, but perhaps the word 'sound' is not quite right since it can be thought to smack of indirection. Of course I'm not suggesting deception of any kind. What I mean is that you would understand the drift of his mind in this matter from simply talking with him about generalities."

"You might understand, but I wouldn't unless I ask him point-blank."

"Ah well, I suppose that's up to you. But I don't think it would be reasonable to ruin a romance by slinging cold water on it, quite unnecessarily and even for fun, like Waverhouse. Perhaps one doesn't need actually to jostle them into marriage, but surely in matters of this sort, the two parties most directly concerned should be left undistracted by irrelevant outside influences to settle their future for themselves. So next time Coldmoon calls, try, please, not to interfere. Of course I don't mean you yourself. I'm referring to Waverhouse; nobody emerges scatheless whom Waverhouse discusses." Since Suzuki could not very well speak ill of my master, he spoke thus bitterly against Waverhouse, when, talk of the devil, who should come floating unexpectedly in on a spring breeze through the kitchen but Waverhouse himself.

"Hello," he said, throwing the accent onto the second syllable, "a visitor from the past! I haven't seen you in years. You know," he rattled on,

"Sneaze treats intimate friends like me with scant ceremony. Shocking behavior! One ought to visit him roughly once a decade. Those sweets, for instance, you wouldn't get those if you called here often." Scanting all ceremony, Waverhouse reaches over and crams his mouth with a large piece of red-bean sugar-paste confection from the well-known Fujimura shop. Suzuki fidgets. My master grins. Waverhouse munches. As from the veranda I watched this interlude, I realized that good theater need not depend upon speech, that high dramatic effect can be achieved with mime. The Zen sect practices instantaneous mental communication of truth from mind to mind in dialogues of silence. The dumb show going on within the room is, no doubt, a version of that practice; and the dialogue, though brief is pretty sharply worded. It was, of course, Waverhouse who broke the silence.

"I'd thought, Suzuki, that you'd become a bird of permanent passage, always coming or going somewhere, but I see you've landed back. The longer one lives, the greater the chance that something odd will turn up." Waverhouse babbles away to Suzuki with that same complete absence of reserve which characterizes his conversations with my master. Though they lodged together in their student days, still it would be normal for a man to address someone whom he hasn't seen for at least ten years with a little more formality. Except when that man is Waverhouse. That he pays not the least regard to the requirements of convention marks him out as either a superior soul or a rightdown jobbernowl. But which one cannot say.

"That's a little hard. Aren't you being a trifle pessimistic," commented Suzuki noncommittally, but his way of fingering his watch-chain betrayed a continuing unease.

"Tell me, have you ever ridden on a tram?" My master shot this sudden and peculiar enquiry at Suzuki.

"It seems that I've come here today simply to provide you two city-wits with a laughingstock on which to hone your singular sense of humor. Though it's true that I'm very much up from the provinces, I actually happen to own some sixty shares in the Tram Company of your precious city."

"Well, that's not to be sneezed at! I myself once used to own eight hundred and eighty-eight and a half of them. But I'm sorry to say that the vast majority have now been eaten by insects, so that I've nothing but one single half-share left. If you'd come up to Tokyo a little bit earlier, I would gladly have given you some ten shares that, until very recently, the moths had not yet got at. What a sad misfortune."

"I see you haven't changed your personal style of ridicule. But joking apart, you're bound to do well if you just hang on to stocks of that quality. They cannot fail, year after year, to climb in value."

"Quite right. Even half a share, provided one holds it for roughly a thousand years, will end up making you so rich you'll need three strongrooms. You and I, razor-minded fellows with our senses keyed to the economic inwardness of these stirring times, are, of course, keenly conscious of the significance of stocks. But what about poor Sneaze? Just look at him. To him," said Waverhouse, conferring on my master a look of withering pity, "stocks are no more than some vague kind of gillyflower." He helped himself to another piece of confectionery. His appetite is contagious, for my master, too, stretches out his arm toward the sweet dish. It is in the immutable nature of the human world that positivity should triumph, that initiative be aped.

"I do not care two hoots about stocks or shares, but I do wish poor old Sorosaki had lived to ride, if only once, on a tram." With morose concentration my master studies the pattern cut by his teeth in his half-eaten sweet.

"Had Sorosaki ever got into a tram, sure as egg is egg, he'd have finished up at the end of the line in Shinagawa. He was an absent-minded man. He's better off where he is now, engraved upon a weight-stone as Mr. the-late-and-sainted Natural Man. At least he knows where he is."

"I'd heard that Sorosaki had died. I'm sorry. He was a brainy chap," says Suzuki.

"Brainy, all right," Waverhouse chipped in, "but when it came to cooking rice he was a positive imbecile. Every time it came round to Sorosaki's turn to do the cooking, I contrived to keep body and soul together by eating out on noodles."

"True, Sorosaki's rice had the peculiar characteristics of smelling burnt yet being undercooked. I, too, used to suffer. What's more, he had an odd way with the accompanying bean-curds. Uncooked and so cold that one could not eat them." Suzuki dredges up a grievance ten years old.

"Even in those days Sneaze was Sorosaki's closest friend. They used to trot off together every evening to gulp down rice-cakes swamped in red-bean soup, and, as a proper and inevitable result, Sneaze is now a martyr to dyspepsia. As a matter of fact, since it was Sneaze who always guzzled most, he should by rights have predeceased his crony."

"What extraordinary chains of logic do run around in your contraption of a mind. Anyway," remarked my master, "there was nothing particularly reprehensible about my going out for sweet-bean soup. As I remember it, your own evening expeditions took the form of haunting a graveyard in order to beat up tombstones with a bamboo stick. You called it physical exercise, but that didn't save you from a right old rap on the knuckles when the priest came out and caught you." In this exchange of student reminiscence I thought my master's counter-swipe with the tombstones far more telling than that dribble of soup from Waverhouse. Indeed, by his laughter, Waverhouse himself acknowledged the defeat.

"Indeed," he said, "I well remember that priest. He told me I was thumping on the noddles of the dear departed, which would disturb their sleep. So, would I please desist. All I did was to make some practice passes with a bamboo wand, but General Suzuki here, training his body with wrestlers' drills, engaged those stones in violent personal combat. I recall that on one occasion he wrestled loose and overthrew three monuments of assorted sizes."

"That did annoy the priest. He got quite fierce about it, insisting I restore my victims to their original positions. I asked him to hold his horses for a moment while I went and hired some navvies for the job, but he wouldn't hear of it. 'Navvies,' he said, 'won't do. Only your own hands can purge the evil they have done. The dead will accept no penitence but yours.'"

"And what a sight you were! Moaning and groaning through those muddy puddles in a calico shirt and a loincloth tied with string. . ."

"And I remember you, with a coldly serious face you stood and sketched me as I struggled with those goddam stones. Such utter heartlessness. I'm very slow to anger, but at that time, from the bottom of my heart, I ached to kill you for your insultingly dispassionate detachment. I can still remember what you said that day. Can you, I wonder?"

"How could anyone remember what was said ten years ago. I do, however, recall the words engraved on one of the stones: Returning Fountain Hall, Lord Yellow Crane the Great Deceased, January 1776. The stone, moreover, was antique and elegant. I was tempted to make off with it. Its general style was Gothic and chimed entrancingly with those aesthetic principles I cherish." Waverhouse is off again, flaunting his gimcrack knowledge of aesthetics. Whoever heard of Japanese Gothic from 1776. . .

"That's as may be, but listen to what you said. These are your very words. 'Since I propose to devote my days to the study of aesthetics, I must, for future reference, grasp each and every opportunity to set down upon paper any event of interest in this universe which comes before my eyes.' What's more, you were kind enough to dispassionately add 'A man such as I, one totally and exclusively committed to the pursuit of learning, cannot permit himself the luxury of such personal feelings as those of pity or compassion.' I could have done you in for such nonchalance. But all I did, in fact, was to grab your sketchbook with my muddied hands and rip the thing to ribbons."

"And it was from precisely that moment that my talent as a creative artist, up until then widely accepted as remarkably promising, was nipped in the bud, never to bloom again. I have my own whole skeleton of bones still to pick with you."

"Don't be so daft. If anyone's entitled to a grudge, it's me."

"Waverhouse, from as far back as my mind can reach, has always been a windbag." My master, having munched his sweet to extinction, rejoins the conversation. "He never means what he says and has never been known to keep a promise. Pressed hard for an explanation, he never apologizes but trots out endless pretexts and prevarications. Once when the myrtles were in bloom in the temple yard, he told me that he would complete a treatise he was writing, on those same old cherished principles of aesthetics, before the flowers fell. 'Impossible,' I said. Can you guess his answer? He claimed, despite appearances, to be of iron will. 'If you doubt my word,' he said, 'just name your bet.' I took him up on it and we agreed that the loser should stand a dinner at a Western restaurant over in Kanda. I took the bet because I was certain that he'd never get his writing done in time, but I confess that, not in fact having the cash to pay for the dinner if I lost, I remained a little nervous that he still might work a miracle. Anyway, he showed no signs of getting down to work. A week went by, three weeks went by, and still he hadn't written a single page. At last the flowers of the myrtle fell, and, though the tree stood empty, Waverhouse stood calm. Looking forward to my Western meal, I pressed our friend to meet his obligation. Not to put too fine a point upon his answer, he told me to get lost."

"No doubt," chimed in Suzuki, "he offered this, that and the other reason?"

"Indeed he did, the barefaced rogue. You can't imagine how obstinate he was. 'Say what you will,' he said, 'about my other flaws and faults. I admit them all, and readily. But the fact remains that in strength of will I'm stronger than the pack of you.'"

"Do you mean," asked Waverhouse himself, "that, having written nothing, I still claimed not to have lost the bet?"

"Of course you did. You said the bet was not about finishing the treatise but about your iron will. And in respect of that iron quality, so you most willfully informed me, you would yield to none. You conceded that your memory might be poor; so poor indeed that you had next day forgotten that you intended to write a paper on the principles of aesthetics; but you maintained that your will to write it remained ferric to the core. The fault lay in your memory, not in your will. So, though the myrtle flowers were fallen and the treatise still unwritten, you made it painfully clear that you saw no reason why you should come across with my dinner."

"Now that's very interesting. And so very typical of Waverhouse." I can't see what in that rather tedious story should so particularly interest Suzuki, but the tone of his comments is markedly different from that which he used before Waverhouse came in. Perhaps such variousness is a sign of a clever man.

"Not in the least interesting." My master interjects a sharpish contradiction.

"It distresses me that you should still be feeling so put out about it, but is it not for that very reason that I've had men out with lanterns searching high and low for those peacocks' tongues I promised you? Don't be so huffy, Sneaze. Just wait a while and all shall be made up. Incidentally, this talk about writing a treatise reminds me that I've called today with some especially odd news."

"Since you bring round odd news every time you visit, I'll take that statement with a pinch of salt."

"But today's odd news truly is sensational. Cross my heart and hope to die, it's stunning. Coldmoon's started writing his thesis. What about that? Since in his own quaint way Coldmoon has a fairly elevated opinion of himself, I wouldn't have expected him to engage in such a mundane, tasteless chore as getting a thesis actually written, but it appears that he, too, is tainted with wordly ambition. Now don't you think that odd? You'd better let that Goldfield woman know that she may now start dreaming of decking her family tree with a full-blown doctor of acorns."

At the first mention of Coldmoon's name, Suzuki begins jerking his chin and twitching his eyes at my master in silent pleas that nothing should be said of their recent conversation. My master fails to notice these entreating galvanisms. A short while back, under the suasion of Suzuki's moral lecture, he had felt sufficiently sorry for the love-lorn daughter not to indulge his unabated antipathy toward her mother. But as soon as Waverhouse referred to Madam Conk, his recollection of his recent row with that virago came flooding back in full spate. That the row had had its comic aspects did not make it any the less provoking. But the news that Coldmoon had started to write his thesis, that was really marvelous. He was grateful to Waverhouse, who had more than fulfilled his boast of having something startling to say, for bringing such a welcome present. It was, indeed, a stunning piece of news; stunning but singularly pleasant. It doesn't greatly matter, one way or the other, whether Coldmoon marries the girl, but it is certainly an excellent thing for the lad to get his doctorate. In surprising ways my master knows himself, and would with absolute humility accept that not a tear need fall if a botched wooden statue is left undecorated to rot away in some dark back-corner of a sculptor's shop. But when a statue is superbly carved, when its basic quality is noble, then no effort should be spared and no time wasted in ensuring that it be given gilding of appropriate splendor.

"Are you really telling me that Coldmoon's started writing?" my master enquires eagerly and paying no attention at all to the jittering Suzuki.

"What a suspicious mind you've got! Don't you ever believe what I tell you? Yes, he's started, but I regret I cannot tell you whether his thesis will be concerned with the stability of acorns or with the mechanics of hanging. Whatever the subject, a Coldmoon thesis must be a glorious snub for the Nose."

Suzuki has been getting more and more restive as Waverhouse repeats and develops his discourteous references to Madam Conk; Waverhouse, not noticing, sails unconcernedly on.

"I have," he said, "carried out some further research into noses and am happy to advise you of an interesting treatment of the subject in the *Life and Opinions of Tristram Shandy, Gentleman*. Had Sterne but known of that mountain of relevant material, how greatly it would have helped him. The sadness of chronology! To think that that staggering organ, eminently qualified as it is to gain immortal nose-fame, should be born, like many another nosegay, to blush unseen! One's heart is filled with an immense compassion. When next it thrusts itself upon us, I shall sketch that vast promontory of flesh for my future reference in the study of aesthetics." There's no restraining Waverhouse.

"But I hear that the Goldfield girl is yearning to be Coldmoon's bride." My master makes a fair summary of Suzuki's representations, while the latter, annoyance twitching from every feature on his face and electric messages flashing from his eyes, signals desperately for disengagement. My master, like some nonconducting substance, remains immune to these distraught discharges.

"How bizarre. It strains the mind to think that the daughter of such a man might fall in love. . . Not, I would imagine, that it could be love of any quality, just rubbing noses."

"Whatever its nature," my master commented, "let's hope that Coldmoon marries her."

"What's that?" said Waverhouse. "Who's now hoping Coldmoon marries her? Only the other day you were dead against such a disastrous match. Have you gone soft or something?"

"It's not a matter of going soft. I never go soft, but. . ."

"But something's happened? That's it, isn't it? Now look here, Suzuki, since you're some kind of lower life-form in the business jungle, let me give a piece of advice to guide your future slitherings. It's with reference to that grunting Goldfield and his piglet daughter. The idea that reasonable persons might be called upon to treat that creature with the respect due to the wife of Mr. Avalon Coldmoon, that talented national figure, why, man, the thing's impossible. They'd no more balance each other than would a paper-lantern and a big bronze bell. No one who calls himself a friend to Coldmoon could stand by and not speak against the folly of such a misalliance. Surely, Suzuki, even you, looking at it as a businessman, can see the sense in what I'm saying."

"What a kerfuffle you do still manage to kick up! Always something stirring, eh? You haven't changed one little bit in all of these ten years. Really, it's remarkable." Suzuki tries to slither round the question.

"Since you compliment me as being remarkable, let me display some more remarkable dollops of learning appropriate to this case. The ancient Greeks set very high store by physical prowess and encouraged its pursuit by awarding valuable prizes to the winners of all sorts of athletic contests. But, strangely enough, there is no record that they ever offered prizes for intellectual prowess. Until recently this curious circumstance incessantly puzzled me."

"I see," says Suzuki still trying to make himself agreeable. "That does seem odd."

"However, just the other day, I chanced, in the course of my researches into aesthetics, to light upon the explanation. Years of accumulated worrying fell instantly away from me and, in that blessed trice, as though disburdened of all errors and earthly delusions, I found myself transported to that pure realm of infinite enlightenment where my soul rejoiced in its transcendence of the world and its attainment of pansophic self-awareness." Waverhouse departs on such a flight of gongoristic drivel that even the toadying Suzuki allows his face to slip into the lineaments of having had enough. "He's at it again" may be read in my master's resigned expression as, with eyes cast down, he sits there tapping, kan-kan-kan, on the rim of the cake-dish with his ivory chopsticks. Nowise disconcerted, Waverhouse blathers on.

"And to whom do you think we are indebted for that brilliant logical analysis, which, by its simple explanation of this seeming anomaly, has rescued us forever from the dark abyss of doubt? It was that famous Greek philosopher, the greatest of all scholars since scholarship began, the renowned founder of the Peripatetic School, Aristotle himself. His explanation—I say, Sneaze, please stop flogging that cake-dish and pay a little more attention—may be summarized thus. The prizes awarded at Greek contests were worth more than the performances that earned them, for the prizes were intended not only to stimulate effort but to reward achievement. Consequently, if one were to give a prize for intellectual prowess, for knowledge itself, one would have to find something to award which was more valuable than knowledge. But knowledge already is the rarest gem in the world. The Greeks, unwilling to debase the value of knowledge, piled up chests all crammed with gold to the height of Mount Olympus. They gathered in the wealth of Croesus, and wealth beyond that wealth, but in the end they recognized that the value of knowledge cannot be matched, let alone exceeded. So, masters of reason that they were, they decided that the prize should be nothing at all. From this, Suzuki, I trust you will have learnt that, whatever the color of your money, it is worthless stuff compared with learning. Let us accordingly apply this revealed truth, this fundamental principle, to the particular problem that has arisen today. Surely you're bound to see that Goldfield's merely a paper man, a bill of exchange with eyes and a nose scrawled onto it. If I may put it epigrammatically, the man's no more than an animated banknote. And if he's money in motion, currency one might say, his daughter's nothing but a circulating promissory note. In contrast, now, let us consider Coldmoon. With consummate ease he graduated with the best degree of his year from the highest seat of learning in our land. On leaving the Imperial University, he showed no sign of slackening of effort. On the contrary, fiddling with the antique fastening-strings of his short surcoat, he devotes himself both day and night to intensive study of the thorny problem of the stability of acorns. And in addition to all that, this indefatigable servant of learning is just about to publish a thesis which, unquestionably, will embody intellectual concepts beside whose depth, originality, and scope those adumbrated by the great Lord Kelvin must pale into insignificance. It is true he was concerned in an abortive attempt at suicide, but that was no more than a passing fancy of a kind common among lads of spirit. Certainly the incident can cast no serious doubt upon his reputation as a vast repository of learning and intelligence. If I may adapt to Coldmoon's case one of my own earlier turns of phrase, I should describe him as a circulating library. He is a high-explosive shell, perhaps only a twenty-eight centimeter, but compactly charged with knowledge. And when at the properly chosen time this projectile makes its impact upon the world of learning, then, if it detonates, detonate it will."

Waverhouse, unbelievably, seems to have run out of steam. Confused by his own jumble of metaphors, he almost flinches, and his flow of language peters pointlessly out. As the saying goes, the dragon's head of his opening remarks has dwindled down to a snake's tail of an ending. However, though Waverhouse may falter, he's unlikely to shut up. In a matter of seconds he's off again.

"In that inevitable explosion things like promissory notes, though there be thousands of them, will all be blasted into dust. It follows that, for Coldmoon, such a female simply will not do. I cannot consent to so ill-suited an alliance. It would be as though an elephant, that wisest and most noble of all animals, were to marry the greediest piglet of a greedy farrow." With a final burst of speed Waverhouse breasts the tape. "That's so, isn't it, Sneaze?" My master, silent, resumed his melancholy tapping on the cake-dish.

Looking a bit depressed and obviously at his wit's end for a suitable answer, Suzuki mumbles something about not being able to entirely agree. His position is, indeed, delicate. His hands, as it were, are still wet with blood from his verbal assassination, barely a half-hour back, of Waverhouse's character, and a man as outrageously tactless as my master might, at any moment, come straight out with anything. Suzuki's soundest tactic is to receive, and if possible smother, the Waverhouse attack, and then, in the general confusion, to wriggle away to safety as quickly as he can. Suzuki's clever. Very much a man cast in the modern mold, he seeks to avoid head-on collisions and considers it positively medieval to enter into arguments that, of their nature, can have no practical result. In his opinion the purpose of life is not to talk, but to act. If events develop as one wishes, then life, its purpose thus fulfilled, is good. But if events not only develop as one wishes but do so without difficulties, fret, or altercation, then life, its purpose slitheringly fulfilled, is paradisal. Suzuki's unwavering devotion to this Elysian principle of slithering had brought him great success in the business world he'd entered after graduating from the university. It had brought him a watch of eighteen-carat gold. It had brought him a request from the Goldfields that he should do them a small favor.

It had even enabled him to maneuver Sneaze nine-tenths of the way toward doing what the Goldfields wished. Then Waverhouse descends upon the scene. Out of the ordinary, careless of all conventions, totally eccentric, he manifests himself as an incarnation of capriciousness operating in accordance with a psychological pattern never previously observed in the human creature. No wonder that Suzuki feels a bit bewildered. Though Suzuki's principle was invented by a variety of clever gentlemen seeking success in Meiji circumstances, its prime practitioner is Suzuki Tōjūrō himself, and it is consequently he who is most signally stumped when the principle proves inapplicable.

"It's only because you're out of your depth," Waverhouse pressed on, "that you sit there looking supercilious and offer no more useful contribution than the cool comment that you can't entirely agree. But if you'd been here the other day when that Nose came throwing her weight around, even you, businessman to the backbone though you are, even you would have felt like throwing up. It's true, Sneaze, isn't it? Go on, tell him. I thought you handled the situation magnificently."

"But I'm told," my master almost smirked, "that my conduct on that occasion created a more favorable impression than did yours."

The answering laugh was a mixture of pity and scorn. "What incredible self-confidence! I begin to understand how you manage to sail along at school unperturbed by the mockery of your colleagues and your pupils' shouts of Savage Tea. In matters of willpower I'm a match for anyone, but when it comes to sheer nerve, I'm just not even in your class. I humble myself in the presence of such staggering self-confidence."

"Why on earth should I be moved by such puerile carryings-on? Their grumbles don't scare me. Though Sainte-Beuve was perhaps the greatest of all critics, his lectures at the Sorbonne proved so unpopular that, whenever he walked in the streets, he was obliged to carry a dagger up his sleeve to defend himself against attacks from students. Similarly, when Brunetière's lectures attacked the novels of Zola. . ."

"Come off it, Sneaze. You're not a professor or a university lecturer. For a mere teacher of the English Reader to start comparing himself with world-famous professors is like a minnow demanding to be treated as a whale. If you keep on saying things like that, you're bound to be laughed at."

"That's just your opinion. As I see it, Sainte-Beuve and I, considered as scholars, are of roughly the same standard."

"What fantastic self-esteem! But if I were you, I'd give up any idea of going around with a dagger. You might cut yourself. Of course, if university professors do go armed with dirks, it might be reasonable for a teacher of the English Reader to carry a folding penknife. But even so, any edged tool is dangerous. What you ought to do is to toddle along to the Nakamise arcade down in Asakusa and get yourself a toy pop-gun. You could carry it slung from your shoulder. You'd make a charming picture. What d'you think, Suzuki?"

Suzuki's feeling better. Relieved that the conversation has at long last veered away from the subject of the Goldfields, he feels it safe to venture a few, and preferably flattering, sentences.

"As it always was, it's been great fun to take part again in such a lively but good-natured discussion. Not having seen you two for a full ten years, I feel as though I had just walked back into a spacious sunny landscape out of some dark and narrow alley. As you'll understand, conversations among business associates tend to be pretty tricky. One has to watch one's step, constantly minding one's p's and q's, and ever alert for a stab in the back. The never-ending worry and strain is genuinely painful. But I myself enjoy frank and open conversation, and it's marvelous to be talking again with one's student-chums in the same old style of uninhibited honesty. I'm delighted that my visit brought me the added and unexpected pleasure of running into Waverhouse. Well," he concluded, "I must leave you now. I've got a man to meet."

Having delivered himself of these slithery sentences, Suzuki was beginning to lever himself loose from my cushion, when Waverhouse remarked, "I'll come along, too. They're waiting for me at the Entertainment Temperance Union over in Nihombashi. Let's run along together."

"Fine," said Suzuki. "Part of the way we'll be going in the same direction." So, arm in arm, they left.

II

TO WRITE down every event that takes place during a period of twenty-four hours, and then to read that record would, I think, occupy at least another twenty-four hours. Though I am all in favor of realistically descriptive literature, I must confess that to make a literal record of all that happened in a day and a night would be a *tour de force* quite beyond the capacities of a cat. Therefore, however much my master's paradoxical words and eccentric acts may merit being sketched from life at length and in exhaustive detail, I regret that I have neither the talent nor the energy to set them all down for my readers. Regrettable as it is, it simply can't be helped. Even a cat needs rest.

After Suzuki and Waverhouse had taken their departure, it became as quiet as a night when winter's icy wind suddenly drops and the snow falls soundlessly. My master, as usual, shuts himself up in his study. In their six-mat sleeping-room, side-by-side in a bumpy row, the children lie asleep. Mrs. Sneaze in the adjoining room, a room that faces south, lies in bed giving suck to Menko, her one-year-old baby daughter. It has been a hazy day of the type we often get in springtime, and dusk has fallen early. The sound of wooden clogs passing in front of the house can be heard quite distinctly in the living room and the sound of a Chinese flute, played in random snatches by someone in the boarding-house on the next street, falls lullingly in broken drifts upon my sleepy ears. Outside it must still be hazy. Having filled my stomach with that dinner of rice with fish gravy which O-san had provided in my abalone-shell, I feel that a little shut-eye is precisely what I need.

It has come to my ears that *haiku* poets have taken to using the phrase "cat's love" as a means of indicating that a poem is concerned with the season of spring. Indeed, I have myself observed that there are nights in early spring when my fellow cats in this neighborhood set up such a caterwauling that sleep is well-nigh impossible. As it happens, I personally have not yet experienced such a derangement of my senses. Nevertheless, love is a universal stimulant. It is the way of all things, from Olympian Zeus right down to the very humblest of the earthworms and mole-crickets that chirrup on this earth, to wear themselves out in this exhausting field of endeavor. It is, therefore, only natural that cats, too, dreamily joyful, should indulge themselves in the risk-fraught search for love. Indeed, on looking back, I remember that I myself once pined away for love of Tortoiseshell. I hear that even Opula, that gormandizer of rice-cakes dusted with bean-flour, that daughterly extension of the very baseline of the triangled technique, old man Goldfield, I hear that even she is smitten with love for the unlikely person of Coldmoon. I, consequently, would not dream of sneering at those tomcats and their lady consorts who, throughout the whole wide world, are so inspired by the ineffable magic of these evenings of the spring that they run amuck under the excruciations of their lusts and loneliness. However, and to my infinite regret, even when invited to participate, I just don't have the urge. In my present condition all that I need is rest. I am so utterly sleepy that I simply couldn't perform. Accordingly, I sidle sluggishly around the children's bedding, set paw on that forbidden territory at the end where their own feet lie and, finding a suitable space, curl up comfortably and drop off into slumber.

I happen to open my eyes and, looking round, find that my master is lying asleep inside the bedding spread beside his wife's. When he goes to bed, it is his invariable habit to bring along some small Western book from his collection, but I've never seen him actually read so much as two consecutive pages. Sometimes he just brings the book, places it beside his pillow, and makes no faintest attempt to read it. Though it seems peculiarly unnecessary to bring a book of which not one line will be read, such actions are quite typical of my master. However much his wife laughs at him, however suasively she begs him to give up this stupid habit, still he persists. Every evening he makes a point of going to bed with a book which he does not read. Sometimes he makes a positive beast of himself and shuffles in with three or four books tucked under his arms. For several days until a little while ago, it was his nightly practice to tote in *Webster's* whacking great dictionary. I suppose this behavior reflects some kind of psychological ailment. Just as some men of peculiarly extravagant taste can only get to sleep to the gentle simmering singing of one of Ryūbundō's special iron kettles, so too, perhaps, my master cannot sleep without a book beside his pillow. It would seem that for my master a book is not a thing to be read, but a device to bring on slumber: a typographical sleeping-pill, a paginated security-blanket.

I take a peep to see what he's brought tonight and find that he's fallen asleep with a slim, red volume lying half-open on his chin, with its top edge almost brushing his moustache. Judging by the fact that his left-hand thumb is sandwiched between the pages, he must tonight have made a praiseworthy improvement on his usual performance to the extent of reading at least a line or two. Beside the bed, in its accustomed place, its cold, gray surface a dull reflection of this warm spring night, his nickel watch lies gleaming.

My master's wife, the nursling baby tumbled about a foot away from her, lies open-mouthed and snoring. Her head has slipped down from the pillow. In my opinion, there is nothing more unbecoming in the human type than its indecent habit of sleeping with the mouth left open. Never in a lifetime would a cat be caught in such degenerate conduct. The mouth and the nose have their separate functions: the former is provided for the making of sounds and the latter for respiratory purposes. However, in northern lands the human creature has grown slothful and opens its mouth as seldom and as little as possible. One obvious result of this muscular parsimony is that northern style of tight-lipped speech in which the words would seem to be enunciated through the nostrils. That is bad, but it's even worse when the nose is kept closed and the mouth assumes the respiratory function. The result is not only unsightly, but could indeed, when rat shit drops from the rafters, involve real risk to health.

As for the children, they too, small-scale reproductions of the indignities of their parents, lie sprawled about on their bedding. Tonko, the elder daughter, as if to demonstrate the monstrous regiment of elder sisters, lies with her right arm stretched out full so that her fist is firmly planted against her sister's ear. In a kind of sleeping counterattack, Sunko lies flat on her back with one leg flung across her elder's stomach. Both have managed to revolve through ninety degrees since, properly positioned, they drifted off to sleep. But, perfectly at ease in their unnatural dispositions, they slumber deeply on.

There is something peculiarly moving about the faint illumination of a night-lamp in the dark hours of the spring. Over the unpretentious, but sadly inelegant interior-scene of our dwelling, it casts a flickering radiance so sweet and gentle that it seems to be inviting our gladdest marvelment at the beauty of this night. Wondering what the time is, I look around the room. Dead silence reigns, broken only by the ticking of the wall clock, the snores of Mrs. Sneaze, and, despite the distance, the relentless grinding of the servant's teeth. Whenever they tell that O-san woman of her grinding ways, she swears it isn't true. Obstinately, flatly, she takes her oath that, never from the day since she was born, not that many babies turn up tusked, has she ever ground a tooth. She neither apologizes nor attempts to break the habit, just stubbornly insists that she doesn't remember ever having done such a thing. Since she does it in her sleep, it's probably true that she doesn't remember doing it. But facts, remembered or not, are all, alas, still facts. There are persons in this world who, having perpetrated villainies, remain assured of their own absolute saintliness. They really do convince themselves that they're pure of any guilt. Such utter self-deception is, I dare say, a form of simple-mindedness, but however genuine the self-deception, if the actuality is objectionable to other people it should be put down. As I lay there thinking that there's no real difference between our grinding skivvy and those evil-doing gentlefolk who think themselves so righteous, the night wore peacefully on.

Suddenly I hear a light double-tapping on the wooden shutters of the kitchen entrance. Odd. People would hardly come visiting at this time of the night. It must be one of those damnable rats. So let it bump. As I mentioned earlier, I long ago decided never to catch rats. Then, once again, I heard a double-tapping. Somehow it doesn't sound like a rat. If it is a rat, it must be an extremely cautious one. For the rats in my master's house, like the students at his school, devote their entire energies, both day and night, to the practice of riotous behavior and seem to believe that they were only brought into this world to disrupt as violently as possible the dopey dreamings of that pitiable man. No rat of ours would make such modest noises. No, it is not a rat. Far too timid. The other night we had a rat come boldly into my master's bedroom, nip off a snippet from the tip of his already stunted nose and then depart in squeaking triumph. It just can't be a rat. As if to confirm my suspicions, the next sound that I hear is the scraping creak of the wooden shutter being lifted from its groove, and then I hear the sliding screen being eased sideways as quietly as possible. Beyond all doubt, it's not a rat. It can then but be human. Even Waverhouse or Suzuki would hesitate at this late hour to lift the latch and walk in unannounced, and neither, I think would go so far as to dismantle a wooden shutter. Could it, I wonder, be one of those gentleman-burglars of whom I've heard so much? If it really is a burglar, I'd like to see what he looks like.

As far as I can judge, two steps with muddy feet have so far been taken across the kitchen floor. The third step must have been planted on one of the removable floorboards for there was a sharp thwacking sound loud enough to echo through the silence of the night. I feel as if the fur on my back were being rubbed in the wrong direction with a boot brush. For a while there was no further sound, not even the stealthiest footstep. Mrs. Sneaze snores gently on, sucking in and blowing out through her gaping gob the beneficent air of this peaceful era. My master is probably dreaming some dream in which his thumb is trapped in a scarlet book. After a while, there comes the sound of a match being struck in the kitchen. Even a gentleman-thief cannot, as I can, see in the dark. It must be very inconvenient for him.

At this point I crouched well down and tried to work out what moves the intruder would next make. Will he proceed hither from the kitchen by way of the living room, or will he, turning left through the hall, make his way to the study? I hear the sound of a sliding door, and then footsteps on the veranda. He's gone to the study. Dead silence followed.

It then occurred to me that it would be kind, while there was still time, to wake my master and his wife. But how? A few impractical notions spin around inside my skull like water-wheels, but I am not visited with any sensible ideas. It struck me that I might possibly rouse them by tugging at the bedcovers. Two or three times I tried, worrying away at the lower end of the material, but my efforts had no effect. I then thought I might do better if I rubbed my wet cold nose against my master's cheek. I accordingly put my muzzle to his face, but all I got for my trouble was a sharp smack in the snoot. He didn't even wake but, lifting his arm in his sleep, rapped me hard on the nose. The nose, even in cats, is a vulnerable area and I suffered agonies. Nevertheless, I persisted. Since I could think of nothing else, I tried miaowing at them. Indeed I tried. At least twice, but somehow my throat just failed to function and no sound emerged. When at long last, and by enormous self-discipline I did manage to emit a single feeble mew, I was quickly shocked back into silence. For, though my master continued just to lie there like a log, suddenly I heard the interloper once more on the move. I hear the little creakings of his inexorable approach along the veranda. This, I think, is it. There's nothing more I can do. So, slipping in between the sliding door and a wickerwork trunk, I get myself into a position suitable at least for this stage of the proceedings: a hidey-hole from which, in the safety of concealment, I can spy upon a criminal at work.

The footsteps advance along the veranda until they are immediately outside the paper-door of my master's bedroom. There they stop dead. I dare not even breathe. My every nerve is at full stretch as I hunch down waiting for the thief's next move. I realized later that my feelings at that time were precisely those which I could expect to feel if I ever hunted rats. It was as though my very soul were about to pounce from my eyes. I am indebted to this thief that, though long ago I resolved never to turn ratter, nevertheless I have been enlightened, this once in my lifetime, as to the nature of the hunting thrill.

The next moment a tiny area in the very middle of the third frame of the paper-door began to change color, to darken as though it had been struck by a raindrop. As I stare at that dampened spot, I can see behind its darkening an object of pale scarlet. Suddenly the paper gives and through it pokes the bare length of a wet red tongue. The tongue seems just to pulse there for a second, and then it vanishes into the darkness. In its place a shining thing, something menacingly glittery, appears in the tongue-licked hole. The eye of a thief. Strangely enough, that gleaming eye seems to disregard all other objects in the room and to be concentrating its gaze directly upon the place where I lurk behind the wickerwork trunk. Though that terrifying inspection cannot have lasted for even so much as a minute, I have never endured a stare so baleful or intense. So to be stared at burns away whole stretches of one's life-expectancy. The scorching of that eye became intolerable, and I had just made up my mind to jump out from behind the trunk when the paper-door slid gently sideways and the thief was at last disclosed to my fascinated sight.

Though at this point it would be normal, in accordance with the established customs of the storyteller's art, to offer a description of this rare and unexpected visitor, I must beg the reader's indulgence for a small digression of which the point and pertinence will, in due course, become clear. My digression takes the form of a statement of my humble views upon the nature of omnipotence and omniscience, both human and divine; views upon which I would invite the discerning comment of all my honored readers.

From time immemorial God has been worshiped as omniscient and omnipotent. In particular, the Christian God, at least up until the twentieth century, was honored for his alleged possession of those qualities.

However, that alleged omniscience and omnipotence could well be regarded by the ordinary man in the street as, in fact, their precise opposites: nescience and impotence. I believe that, not since the world was first created, has anyone preceded me in identifying this extraordinary paradox. It is consequently unavoidable that I should feel a certain pride of self-discovery, pride in this revelation that I am indeed no ordinary cat. It is accordingly to drive home to numbskull human beings the unwisdom of sneering at cats that I offer the following analysis of the paradox which, if I had a name, would be named after its inimitable discoverer. I am informed that God created all things in this universe, from which it must follow that God created men. In fact, I am advised that this proposition is specifically stated as a fundamental truth in some fat book which human beings call the *Bible*. Now, mankind has been engaged for several thousands of years in the accumulation of human observations about the facts of humanity. From which mass of data one particular fact has emerged which not only causes human beings to wonder at and admire themselves, but also inclines them to acquire ever-deepening credence in the omniscience and omnipotence of God. The particular fact in question is the fact that, although mankind now teems upon this earth, no two human creatures have identical faces. The constituents of the human face are, of course, fixed: two eyes, two ears, a nose and a mouth. Further, the general dimensions of those constituent items are, more or less, the same. Nevertheless, though the myriads of human faces are thus all constructed from the same basic materials, all the final products differ from each other. The human reaction to this state of affairs is not only to rejoice in how bloody marvelous it is that each and every one of them commands an individuality of appearance, but also to admire the miraculous skill of the Creator who, using such simple and uniform materials, has yet produced such an infinite variety of result. For surely only a power of infinite originality of imagination could have created such almost incredible diversity. Even the greatest of painters cannot produce, however strenuously he exerts himself in pursuit of variety, more than twelve or thirteen individual masterpieces. So it is natural that mankind should marvel at God's astonishing and singlehanded achievement in the production of people. Since such a protean creativity cannot be matched by men as themselves creators, inevitably they regard the process as a manifestation of divinity and, in particular, of divine omnipotence. For which reasons human beings stand in endless awe of God, and, of course, considered from the human viewpoint, it is entirely understandable that they should.

However, considered from the feline viewpoint, the same facts lead to the opposite conclusion: that God, if not entirely impotent, is at least of limited ability, even incompetent. Certainly of no greater creative capability than muddle-headed man. God is supposed to have created, of intent, as many faces as there are people. But surely one cannot just dismiss the possibility that, in fact, he lacked sureness of touch; that, though he originally intended to create every man-jack of mankind with the same face, he found the task impossible, and that he consequently produced so long a string of botched appearances as to end up with the present disorderly state of the human physiognomy. Thus the variformity of the human face can equally well be regarded either as a demonstration of God's success or as evidence of his failure. Lacking knowledge of his original creative intent, one can only say that the evidence of the human face argues no more strongly for God's omnipotence than it does for his incompetence.

Consider human eyes. They are embedded in pairs within a flat surface and their owners, therefore, cannot simultaneously see to both their left and right. It is regrettable, but only one side of any object can, at any one time, enter their field of vision. Being thus incapable of seeing in the round, even the daily happenings of life in his own society, it is perhaps not surprising that man should get so excited about certain one-sided aspects of his limited view of reality, and, in particular, should allow himself to fall into awe of God. Any creature capable of seeing things whole must recognize that, if it is difficult to create infinite variation, it is equally difficult to create absolute similitude. Had Raphael ever been asked to paint two absolutely identical portraits of the Madonna, he would have found it no less irksome than to be pressed for two pictures of that subject in which every single detail was totally different. Indeed, it is probable that the painting of identical portraits would prove the harder task. Kōbō Daishi was not only the Great Teacher but also a master calligrapher. But had he been asked one morning to inscribe the two characters of his own name in exactly the same style as he had done the day before, he would have found it more difficult than to write them differently. Consider, too, the nature of language-learning. Human beings learn their various tongues purely by imitation. They reproduce, without any display of initiative or inventiveness, the noises made by the daily mouthings of their mothers, nurses, and whomsoever else they may happen to hear. To the best of their ability, they imitate. Nevertheless, in the course of one or two decades, the languages thus produced by imitation show distinct changes in pronunciation. Which amply demonstrates the human inability to make perfect imitations. Exact imitation is extremely difficult to achieve. Now if God had shown himself able to create human beings indistinguishable from each other, that would have been impressive. If every single one of them appeared with the self-same features, like so many mold-cast masks of a fat-faced woman, then indeed would God's omnipotence have been tellingly demonstrated. But the actual state of affairs, a situation in which God has let loose under the sun all manner of different faces, could well be taken to prove the limited competence of his creative power.

I must confess that I have now forgotten why I embarked upon this digression. However, since similar forgetfulness is common among mankind, I trust such a lapse will be found pardonable in a cat. The fact is that the foregoing thoughts leapt naturally to my mind the moment that the paper-door slid open and I at last clapped eyes upon the thief. Why so? you may ask. Why should the sudden appearance of a thief upon the threshold prompt this closely reasoned, this irrefutable critique of divine omnipotence? As I said, I have forgotten why. But if I may have a moment to recollect my train of thought, I'm sure I can find the reason. Ah yes, I have it.

When I looked at the thief's calm face, I was so struck by one peculiarity that my long-held theories about God's incompetence as a face-creator seemed in that instant to he crumbling down to nothing. For the peculiarity was that the thief's face was the spitting image of the handsome face of our much-loved Avalon Coldmoon. Naturally, I lack acquaintances among the burglaring fraternity, but, basing my judgment on their outrageous behaviors, I had formed my own private picture of a burglar's face. But the face of this particular burglar did not match my image. I had always assumed that a burglar's nostrils would be widely splayed to left and right, that his eyes would be as big and round as copper coins, and that his hair would be close-cropped. But there's a vast difference between the fancied and the fact, so vast one should always be wary of giving free rein to one's imagination. This thief is tall and slimly built, with a charmingly darkish complexion and straight, level eyebrows: altogether a very modish sort of burglar. He seems, again like Coldmoon, to be about twenty-six or twenty-seven. Indeed a God so deft as to be able to produce this startling likeness cannot possibly be regarded as incompetent. To tell the truth, the resemblance is so close that my immediate and astonished reaction was to wonder whether, bursting in like this in the middle of the night, Coldmoon had gone mad. It was only when I noticed the absence of any sign of a budding moustache that I realized that the intruder could not possibly be Coldmoon.

Coldmoon is both masculine and handsome. He has been manufactured by God with such especial care that it is proper he should so easily besot that walking credit card, Miss Opula Goldfield. Yet, to judge from his appearance, this thief's power to attract women can be no less strong than Coldmoon's. If that Goldfield girl is besotted by Coldmoon's eyes and mouth, it would be no more than a matter of courtesy that she should go into similarly ardent raptures over those of this burglar. Quite apart from the question of courtesy, it would be contrary to logic if she failed to love him. Being so naturally quick-minded and intelligent, she would, of course, immediately grasp the point, and it would follow that, if she were offered the burglar as a substitute for Coldmoon, she would, body and soul, adore him and live with him in conjugal felicity till death did them part. Even if Coldmoon so succumbs to the wiles of Waverhouse that this very rare and excellent match is broken off, still, so long as the burglar remains alive and well, there is no real cause for concern. Having thus projected the possible train of future events, I felt, purely for Miss Goldfield's sake, relieved and reassured. That this noble burglar exists as a husband-in-reserve is, I think, likely to be important to her happiness in life.

The thief is carrying something under his arm. Peering, I discover that it's that decrepit blanket which, a little earlier on, my master had pitched away into his study. The thief is dressed in a short coat of cotton drawn tight below his bottom with a sash of blue-gray silk. His pallid legs are bare from the knees down. Gently he extends one foot from the veranda and sets it softly on the bedroom matting. At which moment my dozing master, no doubt still dreaming that his finger is being savaged by a scarlet book, turns over in his sleep and, as he slumps with a heavy thud into a new position, suddenly shouts, "It's Coldmoon!" The burglar drops the blanket and whips back as though he'd trodden on a scorpion. Through the flimsy paper of the sliding door, I see the silhouette of two long legs a-tremble. My master grunts in his sleep, mumbles something meaningless and knocks his red book sideways. He then begins a noisy scratching of his dark-skinned arm as though he'd caught the scurvy. He suddenly goes quiet, and lies there fast asleep with his head off the pillow. His shout of Coldmoon-recognition relates, not to reality, but to some incident of dream. Nevertheless, for quite a little while the burglar stood silent on the veranda watching the room for any further liveliness. Satisfied at last that my master and his wife are safely deep in sleep, he reintrudes one cautious foot. There is, this time, no commentary on Coldmoon. Almost at once the second foot appears.

The glow of the night lamp, which hitherto had bathed the whole of this six-mat bedroom, is now sharply segmented by the shadow of the thief. An utter darkness has fallen upon the wickerwork trunk and reaches halfway up the wall behind it. I turn my head and see the shadow of the intruder's skull drifting about the wall some two-thirds of the way up to the ceiling. Though the man is certainly handsome, the misshapen shadow of his head, like some deformed potato, is positively ludicrous. For a while he stood there staring down at Mrs. Sneaze's face and then, suddenly and for goodness knows what reason, broke into a grin. I was surprised to find that even in such aimless grinning he was a twin to Coldmoon. Lying close to Mrs. Sneaze's pillow there is an oblong box, perhaps fifteen inches long and some four inches broad. The lid is nailed down fast and the box itself so placed as to suggest that its contents must be precious. It is in fact that box of yams which, just the other day, Mr. Tatara Sampei presented to the Sneazes on his return from holiday at his family's country place in Karatsu. It is, one must admit, rather unusual to go to sleep with yams to decorate one's bedside, but Mrs. Sneaze is a lady little troubled by notions of propriety of placement. She keeps high-quality cooking sugar in her chest of drawers, so the presence in her bedroom of pickles, let alone of yams, would hardly even ruffle her placid unconcern. But the burglar, a non-participant in the alleged omniscience of God, could hardly be expected to have such knowledge of her nature and it is consequently understandable that he should jump to the conclusion that a box so carefully kept within hand's reach of a sleeping woman is certain to be worth removing. He lifts and hefts the box. Finding its weight matches his expectations, he nods in satisfaction. It suddenly struck me as extremely funny that this gentleman-thief this very prepossessing burglar, was about to waste his expert skills in vegetable furacity. However, since it could be dangerous to make my presence heard, I hold back the laughter bursting to escape.

The burglar wraps the yam box carefully in the blanket and looks round the room for something with which to tie the bundle. His eye lights upon the sash that my master threw down on the floor when he was undressing for bed. The burglar ties and knots the sash around the yam box and hoists it smoothly onto his back. I doubt if women would be attracted to the figure he now presents. He proceeds to stuff two of the children's sleeveless jackets into my master's knitted underpants. Each of the leg parts looks like a snake that has swallowed a frog. Perhaps their swollen ugliness could be better compared to the shape of some pregnant serpent. At all events the shape produced was odd and rather ugly. If you don't believe me, try it for yourself. The thief then tied the pant legs round his neck, leaving his hands free for further rummage. Wondering what he'll nobble next, I watch him closely. He spreads out my master's silk kimono on the floor and neatly, quickly, piles upon it Mrs. Sneaze's *obi*, my master's *haori,* and his remaining underwear together with various bits and bobs which he finds about the room. I am deeply impressed by the sheer professionalism of his larceny, the technical polish of his packaging and parcel work. First he fashions a long silk cord by knotting Mrs. Sneaze's *obi*-string to her waistband-fastener. With this cord he ties his loot into a tidy package, and lifts the lot with one hand. Taking a last look round, he spots a packet of cheap gaspers lying beside my master's head. He shoves the packet into his sleeve but, on second thought, takes it out again and, carefully selecting a cigarette, bends to light it at the flame of the night lamp. He inhales deeply, like a man content with a job well done. Before the exhaled smoke had thinned to nothingness around the milky glass of the night lamp's chimney, the sound of the burglar's footfalls had faded away into silent distance. Husband and wife remain deep-sunk in slumber. Contrary even to their own idea of themselves, human beings are a careless and unwary lot. I myself feel quite worn out by the night's excitements and, if I now continue this account of them, I shall have some kind of break-down. . .

I slept both deep and late, so that, when I finally awoke, the sun was already bright in the blue spring sky. My master and his wife were talking to a policeman at the kitchen entrance.

"I see. You reckon he entered here and then worked round toward the bedroom? And you two were asleep and noticed nothing at all?"

"That's right." My master seems a bit embarrassed.

"And about what time did this burglary take place?" The policeman asks the usual silly question. If one could he in a position to state the hour of such an offense, the chances are that no offense would have occurred.

My master and his wife seem not to realize this point and take the question in real earnest.

"I wonder whenabouts it was."

"Well now, let me think," says Mrs. Sneaze. She seems to imagine that by taking thought one can fix the time of events that took place when one was unconscious. "What was the time," she asks her husband, "when you went to bed?"

"It was after you that I went to bed."

"Yes," she agrees, "I went to bed before you did."

"I wonder what time I woke up."

"I think it was at half past seven."

"So what time would that make it when the thief broke in?"

"It must, I suppose, have been sometime in the dead of night."

"Of course it was sometime in the dead of night. But what I'm asking you about is the particular time."

"Well, that I can't just say for certain. Not until I've had a good think." She's still committed to her thinking ways.

The policeman had only asked his potty question as a matter of form, and he is in fact totally indifferent as to the precise time at which the burglar broke in. All he wants is that my master and his wife should give some kind of an answer: any answer, never mind whether true or not, would do. But the victims engage in such pointless and protracted dialogue that the policeman shows signs of irritation. Eventually he snaps at them. "Right then. So the time of the burglary is not known. Is that correct?"

"I suppose it does come down to that," my master answers in his usual drily pedagogic manner.

The policeman was not amused. He plodded stolidly on in accordance with his own routine of police procedure.

"In that case you should send in a written statement of complaint to the effect that on such and such a date in this the thirty-eighth year of the Meiji Era, you, having fastened the entrances to your dwelling, retired to bed, and that subsequently a burglar, having removed such and such a sliding wooden shutter, sneaked into such and such a room or rooms and there stole such and such items of property. Remember, this paper is not just a statement of lost goods but constitutes a formal complaint which may later be used as an accusation. You'd be advised not to address it to anyone in particular."

"Do we have to identify every single item that's been stolen?"

"Yes. Set it all out in a detailed list. Coats, for instance, set down how many have gone, and the value of each one taken. No," he went on in answer to my master's next suggestion, "I don't think it would help much if I stepped inside. The burglary has already taken place." With which unhelpful comment he took himself off.

My master, having planted himself with his writing brush and inkstone in the very center of the room, calls his wife to come and sit beside him. Then, almost in belligerence, he announces, "I shall now compose a written statement of complaint. Tell me what's been stolen. Item by item. Sharp, if you please."

"What cheek! Who d'you think you are to tell me to look sharp? If you talk to me in that dictatorial manner, I shall tell you nothing." Her toilet incomplete, she plonks herself down sulkily beside him.

"Just look at yourself! You might be some cheap tart at a post-town inn. Why aren't you wearing an *obi*?"

"If you don't like how I look, buy me decent clothes. A post-town tart, indeed! How can I dress correctly when half my stuff's been stolen?"

"He took your *obi?* What a despicable thing to do! All right then, we'll start with that. What kind of *obi* was it?"

"What d'you mean? What kind? How many *obi* do you think I've got? It was my black satin with the crêpe lining."

"One *obi* of black satin lined with crêpe. . . And what would you say it cost?"

"About six yen, I think."

"Six yen! That's far too expensive. You know we can't afford to fling our money about on fripperies. Don't spend more than one yen fifty sen on the replacement."

"And where do you think you'd find a decent *obi* at that price? As I always say, you're totally heartless. You couldn't care less how wretchedly your wife may be dressed, so long as you yourself look reasonably turned out."

"All right. We'll drop the matter. Now, what's next?"

"A surcoat woven with thrown silk. It was given to me as a keepsake of Aunt Kōno. You won't find surcoats these days of that quality."

"I didn't ask for a lecture on the decline of textiles. What would it cost?"

"Not less than fifteen yen."

"You mean you've been going around in a surcoat worth not less than fifteen yen? That's real extravagance. A standard of living miles beyond our means."

"Oh, what does it matter? You didn't even buy it."

"What's the next item?"

"One pair of black foot-gloves."

"Yours?"

"Don't be silly. Whoever heard of a woman wearing black ones? They're yours, of course. And the price, twenty-seven sen."

"Next?"

"One box of yams."

"Did he even filch the yams? I wonder how he'll eat them. Stewed, d'you think? Or in some kind of soup?"

"How the devil should I know? You'd better run along and ask him."

"What were they worth?"

"I wouldn't know the price of yams."

"In that case, let's say twelve yen fifty sen."

"That's ridiculous. How could a box of yams, even ones grown down in Kyushu and then transported here, cost as much as that?"

"You said you didn't know what they would cost."

"I did, and I don't. But twelve yen fifty sen would be plain absurd. Far, far too much."

"How can you say in one and the same breath that you don't know their price but that twelve yen fifty sen is absurd? It makes no sense at all. Except to prove that you're an Otanchin Palaeologus."

"That I'm a what?"

"That you're an Otanchin Palaeologus."

"What's that?"

One can hardly blame the lady. Though long experience has given me a certain facility in decoding my master's thoughts as expressed in vile puns and twisted references to Japanese provincial slang and the mustier tracts of Western scholarship, this particular demonstration of his skills is both sillier and more obscure than usual. I'm still not sure that I understand his full intention, but I suspect he meant no more than that he thought his wife a blockhead. Why then didn't he just leave it at "Otanchin?" Because, despite his temerarious attack on her balding pate, he lacks the guts to risk a head-on clash, and he's not entirely certain that she's never heard that slang-term for a fool. So what does he do? He sees a similarity of sound between "Otanchin" and "Konstantin," the name of the last Palaeologue Emperor of Byzantium. Not that the sounds are sufficiently similar to justify a pun. Not that Constantine the Eleventh has any remote connection with the price of yams. Not that such truths would sway my master. He simply wants to call his wife a blockhead without having to cope with the consequences of doing so. No wonder Mrs. Sneaze is foxed and no wonder she presses for an explanation.

"Never mind about that. What's next on the list? You haven't yet mentioned my own kimono."

"Never mind about what's next. Just tell me what 'Otanchin Palaeologus' means."

"It hasn't got any meaning."

"You're so excessively clever that I'm sure you could explain what it means if you wanted to. What kind of a fool do you take me for? I bet you've just been calling me names by taking advantage of the fact that I can't speak English."

"Stop talking nonsense and get on with the rest of the list. If we aren't quick in lodging this complaint, we'll never get our property returned."

"It's already too late to make an effective complaint. I'd rather you told me something more about Otanchin Palaeologus."

"You really are making a nuisance of yourself. As I said before, it has no meaning whatsoever. There's nothing more to be said."

"Well, if that's how you feel, I've nothing more to say about the list."

"What pigheadedness! Have it your own way. I won't then write out this complaint for you."

"Suit yourself. But don't come bothering me for details of what's missing. It's you, not me, who's lodging the complaint. I just don't care two hoots whether you write it or you don't."

"Then let's forget it," snaps my master. In his usual abrupt manner he gets up and stalks off into his study. Mrs. Sneaze retires to the living room and dumps herself down in front of her sewing-box. For some ten minutes, this precious pair sit glaring in silence at the paper-door between them.

That was the situation when Mr. Tatara Sampei, donor of yams, came bustling gaily in through the front door. This Tatara was once the Sneazes' houseboy, but nowadays, having received his degree in law, he works in the mining department of some big company or other. Like, but junior to, the slippery Suzuki, he's another budding businessman. Nevertheless, because of his former connection with the family, he still occasionally visits the humble dwelling of his erstwhile benefactor. Indeed, having once been almost one of that family, he sometimes spends whole Sundays in the house.

"What wonderful weather, Mrs. Sneaze." He sits on the floor in front of her, with his trousered knees drawn up, and speaks as ever in his own Karatsu dialect.

"Why, hello, Mr. Tatara."

"Is the master out?"

"No, he's in the study."

"It's bad for the health to study as hard as he does. Today's a Sunday, and Sundays don't come every day of the week. Now do they?"

"There's no point in telling me. Go and say it to my husband."

"Yes, but. . ." He looks around the room and then half-asks his hostess, "The girls, now, they're not in?" But the words are hardly out of his mouth when Tonko and Sunko both run in from the next room.

"Mr. Tatara, have you brought the goodies?" Tonko, the elder daughter, wastes no time in reminding him of a recent promise.

Tatara scratches his head. "What a memory you've got! I'm sorry I forgot them, but really, next time, I promise to remember."

"What a shame," says Tonko, and her younger sister immediately echoes "What a shame." Mrs. Sneaze, in a modest revival of her natural good humor, smiles slightly.

"I confess I forgot the raw fish goodies, but I did bring around some yams. Have you two girls yet tried them?"

"What's a yam?" asks Tonko, and little Miss Echo pipes up with, "What's a yam?"

"Ah, so you've not yet eaten them. Ask your mother to cook you some at once. Karatsu yams are especially delicious, quite different from those you get in Tokyo." As Tatara tootles away on his provincial trumpet, Mrs. Sneaze remembers to thank him again for his kindness.

"It really was kind of you, Mr. Tatara, to bring us yams the other day. And so many of them. Such a generous thought."

"Well, have you eaten them? I had the box I made specially so that they wouldn't get broken. I hope you found them undamaged and in their full length."

"I'm sure we would have. But I'm sorry to say that, only last night, the whole lot were stolen by a burglar."

"You've been burgled for yams? What a peculiar criminal. I'd never have dreamt that the passion for yams, even Karatsu yams, could be carried so far." Tatara is enormously impressed.

"Mother," says Tonko, "Was there a burglar here last night?"

"Yes," Mrs. Sneaze answers lightly.

"A burglar? Here? A real, real burglar?" Sunko voices wonderment, but immediately goes on to ask, "What sort of face did he have?"

Mrs. Sneaze, stumped by this curious question, finds something suitable to say, "He had," she says, looking over at Tatara for sympathetic understanding, "a most fear-some face."

"Do you mean," asks the tactless Tonko, "that he looked like Mr. Tatara?"

"Really, Tonko, that's very rude of you."

"Dear, oh dear," laughs the visitor, "is my face as fearsome as all that?" He once more scratches his head. There's a bald patch, about an inch across, on the back of his head. It began to appear not much more than a month ago and, though he's taken it round to the quack, it shows no sign of improvement. It is, of course, Tonko who draws attention to the patch.

"Why look," she says, "Mr. Tatara's head is shiny just like mother's."

"Tonko, behave yourself. I told you to be quiet."

"Was the thief's head shiny, too?" Sunko innocently asks. In spite of themselves, the adults burst out laughing. Still, the children's chatter so interrupts all conversation that Mrs. Sneaze decides to pack them off. "Run along now and play in the garden. Be good girls and later on I'll find you both some sweeties."

After the girls had gone, Mrs. Sneaze turned to Tatara and with all the gravity of a fellow-sufferer enquired, "Mr. Tatara, what has happened to your head?"

"Some kind of skin-infection. Not exactly moth, but a bug of some sort which takes ages to clear up. Are you having the same trouble?"

"Ugh! don't talk about bugs. In my case the trouble's the usual female problem of the hair thinning because it's drawn so tight in the married woman's hairstyle."

"All baldness is caused by bacteria."

"Well, mine's not."

"Come, come, Mrs. Sneaze, you're being obstinate. One cannot fly in the face of the Scientific facts."

"Say what you like, it's not bacteria. But tell me, what's the English word for baldness?"

Tatara said he wasn't sure, but he answered her correctly.

"No, no," she said, "Not that, it's a very much longer word."

"Why not ask your husband? He could tell you straight off."

"I'm asking you precisely because he refuses to help."

"Well, all I know is 'baldness.' You say the word you want's much longer. Can you give me an idea of its sound?"

"'Otanchin Palaeologus.' I have an idea that 'Otanchin' means bald and 'Palaeologus' head."

"Possibly. I'll pop into the master's study a little later and look it up for you in *Webster's Dictionary*. By the way, the master is eccentric, isn't he? Fancy staying indoors and doing nothing on such a lovely day! No wonder his stomach-troubles never get better. Why don't you persuade him to go and view the flowers at Ueno?"

"Please, you ask him. He never listens to what a woman says."

"Is he still licking jam?"

"Yes, as always."

"The other day he was complaining that you're always telling him he overdoes it. 'But she's wrong,' he said, 'I really don't eat all that much.' So I told him the obvious answer was that you and the girls are also fond of jam. . ."

"Mr. Tatara, how could you say such a thing!"

"But, Mrs. Sneaze, you've got a jam-licker's face."

"How can you tell a thing like that by looking at someone's face?"

"I can't, of course. But, honestly, Mrs. Sneaze, don't you ever take any?"

"Well, naturally I sometimes take a little. And why shouldn't I? After all, it's ours."

Tatara laughed right out. "I thought that was the answer. But seriously," he said, adopting a more sober tone, "that really was bad luck about the burglar. Was it only yams that he filched?"

"If it were only yams, we wouldn't be so upset. But he's taken all of our everyday clothing."

"Then you really are in trouble. Will you have to borrow money again? If only this thing here were a dog, not just an idle cat. . . What a difference that might have made. Honestly, you ought to keep a dog, a big sturdy dog. Cats are practically useless. All they do is eat. This cat, for instance, has it ever even caught a rat?"

"Not a single one. It's a very lazy and impudent cat."

"Ah! that's terrible. You must get rid of it at once. Shall I take it along with me? Boiled, you know, they're really quite good eating."

"Don't tell me you eat cats!"

"Yes, indeed, every now and again. They taste delicious,"

"You must have a remarkably strong stomach."

I have heard that among these degraded houseboys there are some so close to outright barbarism that they do, in fact, eat cats: but not until now had I ever dreamt that our Tatara, a person with whom I'd long been on terms of quite some coziness, could be so base a creature. Of course he's not our houseboy any longer. Far from it. Though barely out of university, he is now not only a distinguished Bachelor of Law but also a rising executive in that well-known limited company, Mutsui Products. I was, therefore, more than surprised. The proverb says, "When you see a man, take him for a felon;" the truth of that adage has been well-demonstrated by the thieving conduct of last night's pseudo-Coldmoon. Thanks now to Tatara, I have just invented another proverb: "When you see a man, take him for a felophage." The longer one lives in this wicked world, the more one learns. It is always good to learn, but as one accumulates knowledge of the world's wickedness, one grows ever the more cautious, ever the more prepared for the worst. Artfulness, uncharitableness, self-defensive wariness: these are the fruits of worldly learning. The penalty of age is this rather ugly knowingness. Which would seem to explain why one never finds among the old a single decent person. They know too much to see things straight, to feel things cleanly, to act without compromise.

Thinking that there might then be some merit in departing this world while still in my prime, I was making myself small in a corner lest such a departure should be forced upon me in the company of onions stewing in Tatara's pot, when my master, drawn from his study by the sound of Tatara's voice, slouched back into the living room.

"I hear, sir, you've been burgled. What a stupid thing to have happen." Tatara opens the conversation somewhat bluntly.

"That yam-purloiner was certainly stupid." My master has no doubt whatsoever of his own profound intelligence.

"Indeed, the thief was stupid, but his victim wasn't exactly clever."

"Perhaps those with nothing worth stealing, people like Mr. Tatara, are the cleverest of all." Rather surprisingly Mrs. Sneaze comes out on her husband's side.

"Anyway, one thing's clear. That this cat's totally useless. Really, one can't imagine what it thinks it's for. It catches no rats. It sits calmly by while a burglar breaks in. It serves no purpose whatsoever. How about letting me take it?"

"Well," says My master, "maybe I will. What would you do with it?"

"Cook it and eat it."

On hearing that ferocious proposition, my master gave vent to a minister wail of dyspeptic laughter, but he answered neither yes nor no. This, to my mingled surprise and glad relief, seemed to satisfy Tatara for he pressed no further with his disgusting proposal. After a brief pause, my master, changing the subject, remarks, "The cat doesn't matter, but I do object most strongly to anyone stealing my clothes. I feel so cold." He looks indeed dispirited, and no wonder he feels cold. Until yesterday he was wearing two quilted kimonos: but today, wearing only a single lined-kimono and a short-sleeved shirt, he's been sitting about since morning and has taken no exercise. What little blood he has is totally engaged in keeping his miserable stomach going, so naturally it doesn't get round to his arms and legs.

"It's hopeless being a teacher. Your world gets turned upside-down by a mere burglar. It's still not too late to make a change. Why not come into the business world?"

"Since my scholarly spouse just doesn't care for businessmen, it's a waste of time even to suggest the idea." Mrs. Sneaze, of course, would be delighted to see him go into business.

"How many years is it," Tatara asks, "since you took your degree?"

"Eight years, I think," answers Mrs. Sneaze looking toward her husband. My master neither confirms nor denies the period.

"Eight years and your pay's the same as on the day you started. However hard you study, no one appreciates your merits. 'All by himself the master is, and lonely.'" For Mrs. Sneaze's benefit Tatara quotes a scrap of Chinese poetry remembered from his days in middle school. Since she fails to understand him she makes no answer.

"Of course I don't like teaching, but I dislike commerce even more." My master seems to be a bit uncertain in his own mind what it is he does like.

"He dislikes everything," says Mrs. Sneaze.

"Well, anyway I'm sure he doesn't dislike his wife." Tatara makes an unexpected sally.

"I dislike her most of all." My master's comment is extremely terse.

Mrs. Sneaze turns slightly away and her face stiffens, but she then looks back at her husband and says, as if she thought she were getting a good dig in at him, "I suppose you'll be saying next that you dislike living."

"True," came his off-hand answer, taking the wind clean out of her sails, "I don't like living much." He's way past praying for.

"You should go for a brisk walk every now and again. Staying indoors all day must be ruining your health. And what's more, you really should become a businessman. Making money is simple as pie."

"Look who's talking. You yourself aren't exactly rolling in it."

"Ah, well. But I only joined the company last year. Even so, I've more saved up than you have."

"How much have you saved?" Inevitably, Mrs. Sneaze rises to such bait, and puts her question with real earnestness.

"Fifty yen, already."

"And how much is your salary?" Again it's Mrs. Sneaze who asks the question.

"Thirty yen a month. The company retains five yen and saves it up for me. In an emergency, I can draw on the accumulated capital. Really, why don't you buy some tramway shares with your pin-money? Their value will double within three or four months. Indeed anyone with a bit of capital could double, even triple, his money in next to no time."

"If I had any pin-money," Mrs. Sneaze somewhat sourly observes, "I wouldn't now be up a gum tree all on account of some petty theft."

"That's why I keep saying your husband should go into business. For instance, if he'd studied law and then joined a company or a bank, he would by now be earning three or four hundred yen a month. It seems a shame he didn't. By the way, sir, do you happen to know a man called Suzuki Tōjūrō who got his degree in engineering?"

"Yes, he called here only yesterday."

"So you've seen him then. I ran into him a few days back at a party and your name cropped up. I said I'd once been a member of your household, and he replied that he and you had once shared lodgings at some temple in Koishikawa. 'Next time you see him,' he said, 'please give him my kindest regards and say I'll be looking him up one of these days.'"

"I gather he's recently been transferred back to Tokyo."

"That's right. Until the other day he was pining away somewhere down in Kyushu, but he's just been moved up to the head office here in Tokyo. He's a smooth lad, that one.

Smooth as a keg of lacquer. He even takes the trouble to speak engagingly to me. . . Have you any idea how much he earns?"

"Not the foggiest."

"Well, on top of his basic monthly pay of 250 yen, he'll be getting bonuses twice a year, in July and December, so that his overall income can't be less than four or five hundred yen each month. To think that a man like that can be coining the stuff while you, a teacher of the English Reader, can scarcely make ends meet. It's a lunatic state of affairs."

"Lunatic's the word." Even a man as snooty and superior as my master is no different from the herd of his fellow men when it comes to matters of money. Indeed, the very fact that he's skint the whole year long makes him rather more keen than most to get his claws on a copper. However, having spoken at such length on the marvels of making money, Tatara has now exhausted his stock of slogans about the beatitudes of the business life: so he turns to Mrs. Sneaze on a totally different tack.

"Does a man called Coldmoon come visiting your husband?"

"Yes, often."

"What sort of fellow is he?"

"I'm told he's a brilliant scholar."

"Handsome, would you say?"

Mrs. Sneaze permits herself an unbecoming titter. "I'd say that in looks he's just about as good looking as you,"

"Is that so? About as good-looking as me. . . "

"How do you come to be interested in Coldmoon?" enquires my master.

"The other day someone asked me to ask around about him. Is he a man worth making enquiries about?" Even before he gets an answer, Tatara shows by his condescending tone that he doesn't think much of Coldmoon.

"As a man," says my master, "he's a great deal more impressive than you."

"Is he, now? More impressive than me?" Characteristically, Tatara neither smiles nor seems offended. A sensitive man of the utmost self-control? A dense unfeeling dullard? Need one ask? He eats cats, doesn't he? "But tell me, will this Coldmoon fellow be getting a doctorate one of these days?"

"I'm told he's writing a thesis now."

"So he's a fool after all. . . Writing a thesis for a doctorate indeed! I'd expected him to be brighter than that."

"You don't half fancy yourself," says Mrs. Sneaze with a laugh. "You always did reckon yourself the bee's knees and the cat's whiskers. But what's so foolish about being well educated?"

"Someone told me that once this Coldmoon gets his doctorate, then he'll be given someone's daughter. Something like that. So of course I said, 'A man's a fool who works for a doctorate just to marry a girl. Someone should not marry someone's daughter to anyone so foolish. Better for,' I said, 'someone's daughter to marry me.'"

My master wobbled his head. "To whom did you say all that?"

"To the Man who asked me to ask around about Coldmoon."

"Suzuki?"

"Golly, no. I wouldn't be bandying words with a big shot like that on such a delicate matter. At least, not yet I wouldn't."

"A lion at home, a wood louse in the open!" says Mrs. Sneaze. "You talk big, Mr. Tatara, when you're here with us, but I bet you curl up small and quiet when you talk to Mr. Suzuki."

"Of course I do. It would be foolhardy to do anything else. One wrong word and I could be out on my ear."

"Tatara," my master suddenly breaks in, "let's go out for a walk." Sitting there in the scanty remnants of his wardrobe he's grown to feel downright frozen, and the thought has just filtered through that the exercise of walking might warm him up a bit. There can be no other explanation for such an unprecedented suggestion.

Tatara, that unpetrine person, that seaweed in the tide-flows of the world, that reed which bends to its lightest wind, doesn't even hesitate. "Yes, indeed, let's go. How about Ueno? Let's go try some of Imozaka's famous dumplings. Have you ever tried those dumplings? You, too, Mrs. Sneaze, sometime you really ought, if only just once, to try them. They're beautifully soft and even more beautifully cheap. They serve *saké* as well." Tatara was still babbling away about dumplings when my master, his hat on his head, was ready on the doorstone waiting to leave. . .

Myself, I need rest. There's no conceivable reason why I should keep watch upon, still less record, how my master and Tatara behaved at Ueno Park, how many plates of dumplings they consumed, and what other pointless happenings transpired. In any case, I lack the energy to trail along after them. I shall therefore skip all mention of their afternoon doings and, instead, relax. All created things are entitled to demand of their Creator some rest for recreation. We are born with an obligation to keep going while we can, and if, like maggots wriggling in the fabric of this world, we are to keep on thrashing about down here, we do need rest to do it. If the Creator should take the line that I am born to work and not to sleep, I would agree that I am indeed born to work but I would also make the unanswerable point that I cannot work unless I also rest. Even my master, that timid but complaining crank in the grinding mechanism of our national education, sometimes though it costs him money, takes a weekday off. I am no human cog. I am a cat, a being sensitive to the most subtle shades of thought and feeling. Naturally, I tire more quickly than my master. Naturally, I need more sleep. But I confess I'm a little worried by Tatara's recent travesty of my case, his wicked misrepresentation of my natural need for sleep as evidence of my practical uselessness. Philistines such as he, creatures responsive only to the crudest material phenomena, cannot appreciate anything deeper than the surface appearances recorded by their five coarse senses. Unless one is rigged out in a navvy's clobber and the sweat can be seen and smelt as it pours from one's brow and armpits, such persons can't conceive that one is working. I have heard there was a Zen priest called, I fancy, Bodhidharma, who remained so long immobilized in spiritual meditation that his legs just rotted away. That he made no move, even when ivies crept through the wall and their spreading suckers sealed his eyes and mouth, did not mean that the priest was sleeping or dead. On the contrary, his mind was very much alive. Legless in the bonds of dusty vegetation, Bodhidharma came to grasp such brilliantly stylish truths as the notion that, since Zen is of itself so vast and so illumining, there can be no appreciable distinction between saints and mediocrities. What's more, I understand that the followers of Confucius also practice forms of meditation though not perhaps to the extent of self-immurement and of training their flesh to crippledom by idleness.

All such meditants have powers burning in the brain that are a lot more fierce than anything non-meditants could possibly conceive. But because the outward appearance of these spiritual giants is so solemn, calm, unutterably serene, the fathead nincompoops who come and stare at them can see nothing more than ordinary persons in states of coma, catatonia, or even simple syncope. Such mediocrities slander their betters as drones and layabouts. But the fault lies in the very ordinariness of the eyes of ordinary people, for, in truth, their eyesight is defective in that their glances merely slither over external appearances, never pierce through to spiritual inwardness. Now it is understandable that a man like Tatara Sampei, that personification of all things superficial, would only see shit on a shovel if, undergoing the Zen test of a man's ability to find purity among impurities, he were so shown a shitten shovel. But it grieves me to the core to find that my master who, after all, has read fairly widely and ought to be able to see some little way beyond the mere surface of things, should nevertheless so readily concur in the flippertigibbet fancies of his shallow houseboy; at least to the extent of failing to raise objections to his casserole of cat.

However, when I think things over and see them in perspective, I can understand that it's not altogether unreasonable that my master and his houseboy should thus look down on me. Two relevant sayings by ancient Chinese sages occur to my mind. "Elevated and noble music cannot penetrate the ears of the worldly wise" and "Everyone sings street-songs but very few can join in singing such learned airs as 'Shining Spring' and 'White Snow.'" It's a waste of effort to try and force those incapable of seeing more than outer forms to understand the inner brilliance of their own souls. It is like pressing a shaven priest to do his hair in a bun, like asking a tunny-fish to deliver a lecture, like urging a tram to abandon its rails, like advising my master to change his job, like telling Tatara to think no more about money. In short, it is exorbitant to expect men to be other than they are. Now the cat is a social animal and, as such, however highly he may rate his own true worth, he must contrive to remain, at least to some extent, in harmony with society as a whole. It is indeed a matter for regret that my master and his wife, even such creatures as O-san and Tatara, do not treat me with that degree of respect which I properly deserve, but nothing can be done about it. That's the way things are, and it would be very much worse, indeed fatal, if in their ignorance they went so far as to kill me, flay me, serve up my butchered flesh at Tatara's dinner table, and sell my emptied skin to a maker of cat-banjos. Since I am a truly unusual cat, one born into this world with a mission demanding purely mental activity, I am responsible for safeguarding the inestimable worth of my own rarity. As the proverb says, "The rich man's son is never seated at the edge of the raised hall." I, too, am far too precious to be exposed to the danger of a tumble into calamity. If sheer vainglory led me to run such risks, I would not only be inviting personal disaster but flouting the evident will of Heaven. However, even the fiercest tiger, once installed in a zoo, settles down resignedly next to some filthy pig. Even the largest of wild geese, once in the poulterer's hands, must finish up on the selfsame chopping board as the scrawniest chickling. Consequently, for as long as I consort with ordinary men, I must conduct myself as if I were an ordinary cat. Ordinary cats catch rats. This long but faultless chain of logic leads to but one conclusion. I have finally decided to catch a rat.

I understand that, now for some time, Japan has been at war with Russia. Being a Japanese cat, I naturally side with Japan. I have even been cherishing a vague ambition to organize some kind of Cats Brigade which, if only a scratch formation, could still inflict claw-damage on the Russian horde. Being thus magnificently militant, why should I dither over a miserable rat or two? So long as the will to catch them burns within me, why, I could rake them in with my eyes shut. Long ago, when someone asked a well-known Zen priest of that ancient time how to attain enlightenment, the priest replied "You should proceed like a cat stalking a rat." Indeed, such utter concentration on one's objective is always certain to bring success. There is, of course, that other proverb which warns against over-cleverness. The over-clever woman may well have failed to sell her cow, but I've never heard it suggested that an over-clever cat might fail to catch a rat. Thus a cat of my outstanding qualities should have no trouble in catching any rat around. Indeed, I cannot see how I could fail to catch one. The fact that up until now I've not caught any, reflects no more than my erstwhile disinclination to do so. Nothing more than that.

Just as yesterday, the spring sun sets and flurries of falling cherry-blossoms, whirled on occasional gusts of the evening wind, burst in through the broken kitchen door. Floating on the water in a kitchen pail, they glimmer whitely in the dim light of a kitchen lamp. Now that I have decided to surprise the entire household with the feat of arms which I purpose to achieve during the coming night, I realize that some preliminary reconnaissance of the battlefield is needed to ensure my proper grasp of the topography of the ground. The field of maneuver is not particularly large, covering perhaps an area of four mats. Of that area a full eighth is occupied by the sink, while another eighth consists of that unfloored space where roundsmen from the wine shop and the greengrocer's stand to wait for the day's order. The stove is unexpectedly grand for a poor man's kitchen and it even boasts a brilliantly shiny copper kettle. Behind the stove, on a strip of wooden boarding about two feet wide, stands the abalone-shell in which I am served my meals. Close to the living room there is a cupboard for plates and bowls, which, being six feet long, severely reduces the already limited space. Beside the cupboard and reaching roughly up to the level of its top, shelves extend along the wall, and on one of two lower shelves there is an earthenware mortar with a small pail placed inside it upside-down. A wooden pestle and a radish-grater hang side-by-side from hooks, and ranged beside them there's a dreary-looking pot for extinguishing live charcoal. From the point where the blackened rafters cross, a pot-hook is suspended, and on that hook a large flat basket floats in midair. Every now and again, under the pressure of the kitchen's drafts, the basket moves with a certain magnanimity. When I was a newcomer to this house, I simply could not understand why this basket hung where it did, but, learning later that it was so placed specifically to prevent cats getting at the food which it contained, I realized once again how thoroughly mean, how preternaturally bloody-minded, are the hearts and heads of humankind. The reconnaissance completed, one must plan a campaign appropriate to the site. But a battle with rats can only take place where rats are available to be fought. However brilliantly one may position one's forces, they can achieve nothing if they are alone upon the field. It was thus obviously vital to determine the rats were most likely to appear. Standing in the middle of the kitchen, I look around and wonder from what direction they would probably emerge. I feel as Admiral Tōgō must have done as he pondered the likeliest course of the Russian fleet.

That awful O-san went off to a bathhouse a little while ago and she hasn't yet come back. Long ago the children went to sleep. My master ate dumplings at Imozaka, came home and has now vanished into his study. His wife, I don't know what she's doing but I would guess she's dozing somewhere deep in yammy dreams. An occasional rickshaw can be heard passing along the street in front of the house: each subsequent silence makes the night more deep, its desolation lonelier. My decision to take action, my sense of resolute high spirit, the waiting kitchen-battlefield, the all-pervading feeling of loneliness: it is the perfect setting and atmosphere for deeds of high renown. There's no doubt about it. I am the Admiral Tōgō of the cats. Anyone so placed must feel, however terrifying the situation, a certain wild exhilaration, but I confess that, underneath that pleasurable excitement, I was persistently nagged by one disquieting consideration. I have decided to do battle with rats, so I care nothing for the mere number of the rats to be fought, but I do find it worryingly inconvenient not to know from which direction or directions the rats will make their appearance. I have collated and analyzed the results of my recent reconnaissance, and have concluded that there are three lines of advance by which these robber riffraff might debouch upon the field. If they are gutter rats, they'll come sneaking up the drainpipe to the sink and thence nip round behind the stove. In which case, my correct tactic is to be in hiding behind the charcoal extinguisher and thence interdict their line of retreat. Alternatively, such villains might slide in through the hole cut at the base of the washroom's plaster-wall for the escape of dirty water into the outside drain: if they adopt that point of entry, they could then sneak across the washroom and so pop out into the kitchen. In which case, my best tactic is to station myself on the lid of the rice-cooker from which position, as the filthy brutes glide past below me, I could drop upon them from the sky. Finally, my visual check of the terrain has revealed, at the bottom right-hand corner of the cupboard, a gnawed halfmoon of a hole which looks suspiciously convenient for raiding rats. Putting my nose to the place, I sniff the ground. It smells a little ratty. If a rat comes dashing out to battle from that curved sally-port, my best tactic is to lurk behind the pillar and pounce upon him from the side as he scuttles by.

A further thought then struck me. Suppose the rats should find some line of advance along unexpectedly higher ground. I look up and the soot-black ceiling gleams evilly in the glow of the lamp. It looks like hell hung upside-down. It is plain that with my limited strength and skills I could neither climb up there, still less climb down. Either because if I can't, rats can't, or because if I can't, rats wouldn't, I decide that there's no likelihood that they will descend from those infernal altitudes, and I accordingly abandon any attempt to make plans to cope with that threat. Even so, there's danger of being simultaneously attacked from three directions. If they come from only a single direction, with one eye shut I could wipe the whole lot out. If from two directions, still I'd be able to cope. But if they come from three directions, however confident I may be of my instinctive aptitude for catching rats, the situation would be distinctly dicey. It would be an affront to my own dignity to go beg help from such as Rickshaw Blacky. What on earth shall I do? When, having wondered what on earth to do, one still can't think of anything, it is, I've found, the shortest way to peace of mind to decide that what one fears won't happen. In point of fact, everyone chooses to assume that the insupportable will never occur. Look around at the world. Today's delighted bride holds no guarantee against death tomorrow, but the bridegroom, happily chanting auspicious texts, displays no sign of worry. The fact that he doesn't worry is not because there's nothing to be worried about. The reason is that, however much he worries, it will not make the slightest difference. So, too, in my case. I've no reason whatsoever to assert that simultaneous triple-pronged attacks will certainly never be launched, but to decide that they won't sorts best with my self-assurance. All things need assurance. Not least myself. I have, consequently, reached the firm conclusion that attacks from three directions will not happen.

Even so I still feel tweaks of doubt. I pondered the cause of this continuing uneasiness and worried away at the problem until at last I understood the source of my disquiet. It is the agony of not being able to find a single clear-cut answer to a problem: in my case, to the problem of deciding which of three strategies will prove most profitable. If rats emerge from the cupboard, I have a plan to deal with the situation. If they appear from the bathroom, I have another scheme to cope with that. And if they come sneaking up through the sink, I have yet another wheeze worked out to settle their slithery hash. But to choose one of these three courses of action and then stick firmly to my choice, that I find excruciatingly difficult. I hear that Admiral Tōgō was similarly excruciated as he pondered whether the Russian Baltic Fleet would pass through the Straits of Tsushima, or would steer a more easterly course for the Straits of Tsugaru, or would take the longest way around by heading out into the Pacific and then swinging back through the Straits of La Pérouse between Hokkaido and Sakhalin. My own predicament enabled me fully to appreciate just how worried the noble Admiral must have been. Not only am I placed in a similar situation, but I share his agony of choice.

While I was thus absorbed in contriving a solution to my problem of major strategy, the damaged paper-door was suddenly slid open, and the ugly face of O-san loomed into view. I do not intend that turn of phrase to imply that that creature lacks arms and legs; simply that the remainder of her carcass was so indistinguishable from the background darkness that only her face, hectically bright and savagely colored, struck upon my eyes. She has just returned from the public bathhouse, and her normally red cheeks look positively scarlet. Even though it is still quite early, she proceeds, probably in belated wisdom learnt from last night's happenings, carefully to fasten up the kitchen door. From the study comes my master's voice enjoining her to place his walking stick at hand's reach by his bedside. Really, I fail to see why such a man should want to decorate his bedside with a walking stick. Can it be that he's started to fancy himself in the role of that heroic assassin who, so the classics tell us, attacked the first of the Chinese Emperors? Can it be that he sees his walking stick as that tomb-treasure sword which, at a robber's touch, roared like a tiger, growled like a dragon, and then flew upward into the sky? Surely not even my perplexed master could harbor such daft delusions. But yesterday it was the yams. Now it's a walking stick. What will it be tomorrow?

The night is still young. The rats are not likely to appear for some time yet. I need repose before the coming battle.

There are no windows in my master's kitchen. Instead, just below the level of the ceiling there's a sort of transom about one foot wide, which, left open all the year round, serves as a skylight. I was brought suddenly out of my sleep by a flurry of blossoms from the early-flowering cherries blown through that opening on a gust of wind. A hazy moonlight slants into the kitchen and casts a shadow of the stove sidelong across the wooden floor. Wondering if I have overslept, I shake my ears two or three times and then look carefully around to see if anything's developed. Dead silence reigns, through which, as was the case last night, the clock ticks steadily on. It's high time that the rats came out. I wonder where they will appear. It's not long before gentle noises start-up inside the cupboard. It sounds as though rats are trying to get at something on a plate and are scrabbling at the plate's edge with their horny claws. In the expectation that these cupboard rats will eventually emerge from the gnawed half-moon at the bottom of its door, I hunker down to wait beside that opening. The rats seem in no hurry to come out. Eventually the plate noise stopped, but was soon succeeded by sounds of rat feet on some sort of bowl or basin. Every now and again there were heavy humpings on the other side of the cupboard door, only a bare three inches distant from the tip of my waiting nose. Sometimes the sounds come even closer to the hole, but then they scamper away again and not one single rat so much as shows its face. Just beyond that door the foe is rampaging through the cupboard, but all I can do is lurk here quietly at the half-moon exit. Which calls for patience; very great patience. The rats, like the Russians in the basin of Port Arthur, seem to be having a rare old shindig in their bowl. I wish that that fool O-san had the mind to leave the cupboard door at least sufficiently ajar to allow me to slip through, but what can one expect from so thick-skulled a country bumpkin.

From behind the stove my abalone-shell emits a sound of gentle rocking. Aha! The enemy is also coming from that direction. Very well, then. I creep forward on the stealthiest of paws but catch only a glimpse of a tail among the buckets before it whisks away below the sink. A short while later I hear the clink of my master's gargling glass against the metal of the wash-basin. So! Now they are behind me. As I turn to face this new danger, a whopping great rat, at least six inches long, adroitly tips a small bag of tooth-powder off the shelf above the basin, and then itself goes skittering away to safety under the floorboards. Determined not to let him escape, I spring down after him, but even before I'd landed, the filthy beast had vanished. Catching rats, I find, is trickier than I'd thought. Perhaps I am congenitally inculpable of catching them.

When I advance upon the bathroom, rats pop out of the cupboard. When I take post by the cupboard, rats erupt from the sink. And when I plant myself firmly in the center of the kitchen, rats shoot racketing up on all three fronts together. Never have I seen such impudent bravado combined with such poltroonery! Their skittering evasion of fair fight brands them unworthy adversaries for a gentleman. Fifteen, maybe sixteen times I darted hither and thither until, all to no purpose, I had exhausted myself both physically and mentally. I am ashamed to confess my failure, but against such mean-souled adversaries even the resourceful Admiral Tōgō would have found himself stumped. I had launched upon this venture with high courage, a determination to subdue the foe, and even a certain elevated sense of the spiritual beauty of my undertaking, but now, tired out and downright sleepy, I find it merely fatuous and irksome. I cease to rush around and squat down right in the center of the kitchen. But, though utterly motionless, if I maintain a sharp lookout all around me, the enemy, being such miserable dastards, will never dare to try on anything serious. When, unexpectedly, one's enemy turns out to be so pettily paltry, the sense of war as an honorable activity cannot be sustained and one is left with nothing but a feeling of naked hatred. When that acrid animosity dulls, one becomes downhearted and even absent-minded. And after that general dimness fades away, one just feels sleepy. So deep is the lethargy of complete disdain that one feels prepared to let one's foes do anything they like. For what of any possible significance, so one asks oneself, are beings so debased capable of doing? Having myself gone through all those stages, I, too, eventually grew sleepy, and dozed off. All that lives must rest, even in the midst of enemies.

I woke to find a violent wind blowing around me. Again, a gust was pitching handfuls of petals through the open transom running along below the eaves. At the very moment of my waking, something, shooting out from the cupboard like a bullet from a gun, sliced across the blowing wind and, quick as a flash, fastened its snapping teeth into my left ear. I'd barely time to realize what was happening before another black shadow flickered around behind me and closed its jaws upon my tail. This all took place within the batting of an eye. Taking no thought whatsoever, by simple reflex action I spring to my feet. Converting all my strength into a shuddering paroxysm of my skin, I try to shake these monsters off. The demon anchored to my ear, yanked off his feet as I sprang to mine, dangles down beside my face. The end of his tail, spongily soft like a rubber tube, falls unexpectedly into my mouth. I take a firm grip on the beastly object and, teeth clamped fast upon it, I waggle my head from side-to-side as hard as I can go. The tail came off in my jaws, while the jactitated body, slung first against the wall plastered with old newspapers, bounced off onto the floor-boards. While the rat still struggles to regain his balance, quick to seize my chance I pounce upon him, but, like some rebounding ball, he whizzes up past my descending muzzle and lands surprisingly high on one of the upper shelves. Tucking in his legs, he stares down at me over the edge of his shelf. I stare up at him from the wooden floor. The distance between us is about five feet. Clean across that distance, the moonlight slants from the transom like a woman's broad white sash stretched out along the air.

Concentrating all my strength in my legs, I leapt up at the shelf. My front paws grasp its edge but, weighted down by the rat still riveted to my tail, my hindlegs are left scrabbling in midair. I am in danger. I try to clamber upward by judicious adjustment of the positions of my paws, but each such effort, by reason of the rat weight on my tail, merely results in a weakening of my pawhold. If my paws slip just one further quarter of an inch I shall be lost. I am really in great danger. My claws scrape noisily along the wooden ledge. In a last effort, I try to advance my left paw, but its claws fail to gain purchase in the smooth wood surface and I finish up hanging by a single claw of my right paw. My body, dragged fully out under its own and the rear rat's weight, begins both to swing and to rotate. The monster on the shelf, which has hitherto been content to sit motionless and glare at me, now hops down onto my forehead. My last claw loses hold.

Melded into one black lump, the three bodies plummet downward through the slanted moonlight. Objects on the shelf below, the earthenware mortar, the small pail standing inside it, and an empty tin, swell the falling lump which, further swollen by the dislodgement of a charcoal extinguisher, finally splits in two. Half the ugly mass falls straight into a water jar, while the rest disintegrates into bodies wildly rolling across the kitchen floor. In the dead quiet of night the noise was truly appalling. Even my own already frantic soul was further shaken by the din.

"Burglars!" Hoarsely bellowing, my master comes rushing out from the bedroom. He carries a lamp in one hand and a walking stick in the other. From his sleepy eyes there flashes as much of the light of battle as such a man could be expected ever to muster. I crouch down silently beside my abalone-shell. The two rat-monsters vanish into the cupboard. "What's going on here? Who made all that hideous noise?" My master, looking vaguely sheepish, shouts in his angriest voice questions that no one's there to answer.

The westering moon sank steadily lower and lower, and its broad white sash of light across the kitchen narrowed and narrowed as it sank.

III

THIS HEAT is quite unbearable, especially for a cat. An English clergyman, a certain Sydney Smith, once remarked that the weather was so intolerably hot that there was nothing left for it but to take off his skin and sit about in his bones. Though to be reduced to a skeleton might be going too far, I would at least be glad to slip out of my fur of spotted, palish gray and send it to be washed or even popped temporarily into pawn. To human eyes, the feline way of life may seem both extremely simple and extremely inexpensive, for a cat's face looks the same all the year round and we wear the same old only suit through each of the four seasons. But cats, I can assure you, just like anyone else, feel the heat and feel the cold. There are times when I consider that I really wouldn't mind, just that once, soaking myself in a bath, but if I got hot water all over my fur, it would take ages to get dry again and that is why I grin and bear the stink of my own sweat and have never in all my life yet passed through the entrance of a public bathhouse. Every now and again I think about using a fan but, since I cannot hold one in my paws, the thought's not worth pursuing.

Compared with our simplistic style, human manners are indeed extravagant. Some things should be eaten either raw or as they are, but humans go quite unnecessarily out of their way to waste both time and energy on boiling them, grilling them, pickling them in vinegar, and smarming them over with bean-paste. The horrible results of all these processes appear to tickle them to death. In matters of dress they are similarly absurd. Inasmuch as they are born imperfect, it might be asking too much if one expected them to wear, as is the custom of cats, the same clothes all year long but, surely to goodness, they cannot need to swaddle their skins in such a heterogeneity of sheer clobber. Since it seems not to shame them to be indebted to sheep, to be dependent on silkworms, and even to accept the charity of cotton shrubs, one could almost assert that their extravagance is an admission of incompetence.

Even if one overlooks their oddity and allows them their perversities in matters of food and clothing, I completely fail to see why they have to exhibit this same crass idiosyncrasy in matters that have no bearing whatsoever on their continuing existence. Take, for instance, their hair. Since, willy-nilly, it grows, I would have thought it simplest and best for any creature just to leave it alone. But no. Not for humans. Totally unnecessarily, they trick themselves out in every conceivable sort and kind of hair-do. And even take pride in their idiot variations. Those who call themselves priests keep their heads clean-shaven blue: blue in summer, winter blue. Yet when it's hot they put on sunhats, and when it's cold they hood themselves in bits of blanket. Given all this hatting and hooding, why do they shave their heads? It's absolutely senseless. Again, there are some who, using a sawlike instrument called a comb, part their hair down the middle and look as pleased as punch with the result. Others rake out an artificial separation of the hair three-sevenths of the way across their cranial bones, and some of these extend that scraped division right over the top of their skulls so that the hair flops out at the back like false banana-leaves. Some have the hair on their crowns shorn flat but cut the hair at the sides, both left and right, to hang down straight. This creation of a square frame for a round head makes them look, if they can be said to look like anything, as though they were staring out on the world through a cedar hedge just trimmed by a maniac gardener. In addition to these styles there are those based on cutting every hair to a standard length: the five-inch cut, the three-inch cut, and even the one-inch cut. Who knows, if such close cropping is continued, they'll finish up with a cut inside their skulls. Maybe the minus-one-inch cut, even a minus-three-inch cut will be the ultimate fashion. In any event, I cannot understand why mankind becomes enslaved to such fool fads.

Why, for instance, do they use two legs when they all have four available? Such waste of natural resources! If they used four legs to get about, they'd all be a great deal nippier; nevertheless, they persist in the folly of using only two and leave the other pair just hanging from their shoulders like a couple of dried codfish that someone brought around as a present. One can only deduce that human beings, having so very much more spare time than do cats, lighten their natural boredom by putting their minds to thinking up such nonsenses. The odd thing is not simply that these creatures of endless leisure assure each other, whenever two of them get together, of just how busy they are, but that their faces do in fact look busy. Indeed they look so fussed that one wonders just how many men get eaten by their business. I sometimes hear them say, when they have the good fortune to make my acquaintance, how nice and easy life could be if one lived it like a cat. If they really want their lives to be nice and easy, it's already in their own good power to make them so. Nothing stands in the way. Nobody insists that they should fuss about as they do. It is entirely of their own free will that they make more engagements than they can possibly keep and then complain about being so horribly busy. Men who build themselves red-hot fires shouldn't complain of the heat. Even we cats, if we had to think up twenty different ways of scissoring our fur, would not for long remain as carefree as we are. Anyone who wants to be carefree must train himself to be, like me, able to wear a fur coat in the summer. Still. . . I must admit it is a little hot. Really, it is too hot, a fur coat in the summer.

In this appalling heat I can't even get that afternoon nap which is my sole and special pleasure. How then shall I while the time away? Since I have long neglected my study of human society, I thought I might usefully devote a few hours to watching them toiling and moiling away in their usual freakish fashions. Unfortunately, my master's character, at least in the matter of napping, is more than a little aluroid. He takes his afternoon siestas no less seriously than I do and, since the summer holidays began, he has not done a stroke of what humans would call work. Thus, however closely I may observe him, I should learn nothing new about the human condition. If only someone like Waverhouse would drop in, then there'd be some chance of a twitch in my master's depressingly dyspeptic skin, some hope of him stirring from his catlike languor. Just is I was thinking it is indeed about time that Waverhouse dropped by, I hear the sound of somebody splashing water in the bathroom. And it's not just splashing water that I hear, for the splasher punctuates his aquatics with loud expressions of his appreciation. "Perfect. How wonderfully refreshing. One more bucketful, if you please!" The voice rings brashly through the house. There's only one man in the world who would speak so loudly and who would make himself, unbidden, so very much at home in my master's dwelling. It must, thank God, be Waverhouse.

I was just thinking, "Well, at least today I shall be eased of half the long day's tedium," when the man himself walks straight into the living room. His shoulders re-covered beneath kimono sleeves, he's wiping sweat from his face as, without any ceremony at all, he pitches his hat down on the matting and calls out, "Hello there. Tell me, Mrs. Sneaze, how's your husband bearing up today?" Mrs. Sneaze had been comfortably asleep in the next room. Hunkered down on her knees with her gormless face bent over onto her sewing-box, she was shocked awake as Waverhouse's yelpings pierced deep into her ears. When, trying to lever her sleepy eyes wide open, she came into the room, Waverhouse, already seated in his fine linen kimono, was happily fanning himself.

"Good afternoon," she says and, still looking somewhat confused, almost shyly adds, "I'd no idea you were here." As she bowed in greeting a bead of sweat glissades to gather at the tip of her nose.

"I've only this minute arrived. With your servant's kind assistance I've just been having a most splendid shower in the bathroom. As a result I now feel greatly refreshed. Hot, though, isn't it?"

"Very hot. These last few days one's been perspiring even when sitting still. . . But you look as well as ever." Mrs. Sneaze has not yet wiped the sweat-drop from her nose.

"Thank you, yes I am. Our usual spells of heat hardly affect me at all, but this recent weather has been something special. One can't help feeling sluggish."

"How very true. I've never before felt need of a nap but in this weather, being so very hot. . ."

"You had a nap? That's good. If one could only sleep during the daytime and then still sleep at night. . . why, nothing could be more wonderful." As always, he rattles along as the mood of the moment takes him. He seems, however, this time faintly dissatisfied with what's popped out of his mouth, for he hurries to add, "Take me, for example. By nature I need no sleep. Consequently, when I see a man like Sneaze who is invariably sleeping whenever I call, I feet distinctly envious. Well, I expect such heat is pretty rough on a dyspeptic. On days like this even a healthy person feels too tired to balance his head on his shoulders. However, since one's head is fixed tight, one can't just wrench it off." Rather unusually, Waverhouse seems uncertain what to do with his head. "Now you, Mrs. Sneaze, with all that hair on your head, don't you find it hard even to sit up? The weight of your chignon alone must leave you aching to lie down."

Mrs. Sneaze, thinking that Waverhouse is referring again to her nap by drawing attention to her disordered hair, giggles with embarrassment. Touching her hand to her hair, she mumbles "How unkind you are!"

Waverhouse, totally unconscious of her reaction, goes off at a tangent. "D'you know," he says, "yesterday I tried to fry an egg on the roof."

"How's that?"

"The roof tiles were so marvelously baking-hot that I thought it a pity not to make practical use of them. So I buttered a tile and broke an egg onto it."

"Gracious me!"

"But the sun, you know, let me down. Even though I waited for ages, the egg was barely half-done. So I went downstairs to read the newspapers. Then a friend dropped in, and somehow I forgot about the egg. It was only this morning that I suddenly remembered and, thinking it must be done by now, went up to took at it."

"How was it?"

"Far from being ready to eat, it had gone completely runny. In fact, it had run away, all down the side of the house."

"Oh dear." Mrs. Sneaze frowned to show she was impressed.

"But isn't it strange that all through the hot season the weather was so cool and then it should turn so hot now."

"Yes, indeed. Right up until recently we've been shivering in our summer clothes and then, quite suddenly, the day before yesterday, this awful heat began."

"Crabs walk sideways but this year's weather walks backward. Maybe it's trying to teach us the truth of that Chinese saying that sometimes it is reasonable to act contrary to reason."

"Come again," says Mrs. Sneaze who's not much up on Chinese proverbs.

"It was nothing. The fact is that the way this weather is retrogressing is really just like Hercules' bull." Carried away on the tide of his crankiness, Waverhouse starts making ever more odd remarks. Inevitably, my master's wife, marooned in ignorance, is left behind as Waverhouse drifts off beyond the horizons of her comprehension. However, having so recently burnt her fingers over that bit of unreasonable Chinese reason, she was not out looking for a further scorching. So, "Oh," she says, and sits silent. Which doesn't, of course, suit Waverhouse. He hasn't gone to the trouble of dragging in Hercules' bull not to be asked about it.

"Mrs. Sneaze," he says, driven to the direct question, "do you know about 'Hercules' bull'?"

"No," she says, "I don't."

"Ah, well if you don't, shall I tell you about it?"

Since she can hardly ask him to shut up, "Please do," she answers.

"One day in ancient times Hercules was leading a bull along."

"This Hercules, was he some sort of cowherd?"

"Oh no, not a cowherd. Indeed he was neither a cowherd nor yet the owner of a chain of butcher-shops. In those far days there were, in fact, no butcher-shops in Greece."

"Ah! So it's a Greek story? You should've told me so at the start. . . " At least Mrs. Sneaze has shown that she knows that Greece is the name of a country.

"But I mentioned Hercules, didn't I?"

"Is Hercules another name for Greece?"

"Well, Hercules was a Greek hero."

"No wonder I didn't know his name! Well, what did he do?"

"Like you, dear lady, he felt sleepy. And in fact he fell asleep. . . "

"Really! Mr. Waverhouse!"

"And while he slept, along came Vulcan's son."

"Now who's this Vulcan fellow?"

"Vulcan was a blacksmith, and his son stole Hercules' bull, but in a rather special way. Can you guess what he did? He dragged the bull off by its tail. Well, when Hercules woke up he began searching for his bull and bellowing, 'Bull, where are you?' But he couldn't find it and he couldn't track it down because, you see, the beast had been hauled off backward so there weren't any hoofmarks pointing to where it had gone. Pretty smart, don't you agree? For a blacksmith's son?" Dragged off track by his own tale, Waverhouse has already forgotten that he had been discussing the unseasonable heat.

"By the way," he rattled on, "what's your husband doing? Taking his usual nap? When such noddings-off are mentioned in Chinese poetry they sound refined, even romantic, but when, as in your husband's case, they happen day in, day out, the whole concept becomes vulgarized. He has reduced an eternal elegance of life to a daily form of fragmentary death. Forgive my asking you," he brings his speech to a sudden conclusion, "but please do go and wake him up."

Mrs. Sneaze seems to agree with the Waverhouse view of naps as a form of piecemeal perishing for, as she gets to her feet, she says, "Indeed he's pretty far gone. Of course it's bad for his health. Especially right on top of his lunch."

"Talking of lunch, the fact is I've not had mine yet." Waverhouse drops broad hints composedly, magnanimously, as though they were pearls of wisdom.

"Oh, I am sorry. I never thought of it. It's lunchtime, of course. . . Well, would you perhaps like some rice, pickles, seaweed, things like that, and a little hot tea?"

"No thanks. I can manage without them."

"Well, as we hadn't realized you would be honoring us today, we've nothing special we can offer you." Not unnaturally, Mrs. Sneaze responds with an edge of sarcasm, which is all quite wasted on Waverhouse.

"No and indeed no," he imperturbably replies, "neither with hot tea nor with heated water. On my way here, I ordered a lunch to be sent to your house and that's what I'm going to eat." In his most matter-of-fact manner Waverhouse states his quite outrageous actions.

Mrs. Sneaze said, "Oh!" But in that one gasped sound three separate "oh's" were mingled: her "oh" of blank surprise, her "oh" of piqued annoyance, and her "oh" of gratified relief. At which moment my master comes tottering in from the study. He had just begun to doze off into sleep when it became so unusually noisy that he was hauled back into consciousness, like something being scraped against its natural grain. "You're a rowdy fellow," he grumbles sourly through his yawns. "Always the same. Just when I was getting off to sleep, feeling so pleasant and relaxed. . ."

"Aha! So you're awake! I'm extremely sorry to have disturbed your heavenly repose, but missing it just once in a while may even do you good. Please come and be seated." Waverhouse makes himself an agreeable host to my master in my master's house. My master sits down without a word, and, taking a cigarette from a box of wooden crazy-work, begins to puff at it. Then, happening to notice the hat which Waverhouse had tossed away into a corner, he observes, "I see you've bought a hat."

"What d'you think of it?" Waverhouse fetches it and holds it proudly out for the Sneazes to inspect.

"Oh, how pretty. It's very closely woven. And so soft." Mrs. Sneaze strokes it almost greedily.

"This hat, dear lady, is a handy hat. And as obedient as a man could wish. Look." He clenched his hand into a knobbly fist and drove it sharply into the side of his precious panama. A fist-shaped dent remained, but before Mrs. Sneaze could finish her gasp of surprise, Waverhouse whipped his hand inside the hat, gave it a sharpish shove, and the hat popped back into shape. He then grasped the hat by opposite sides of its brim and squashed it flat as dough beneath a rolling pin. Next he rolled it up, as one might roll a light straw mat. Finally, saying, "Didn't I say it was handy," be tucked it away into the breast-fold of his kimono.

"How extraordinary!" Mrs. Sneaze marvels as if she were watching that master magician Kitensai Shoichi performing one of his most dazzling sleights of hand. Waverhouse himself appears to be bitten by the spirit of his own act for, producing from his left-hand sleeve the tube of hat he'd thrust into the breast of his kimono, he announces, "Not a scratch upon it." He then bats the hat back into its original shape and, sticking his forefinger into its crown, spins it around like a conjuror's plate. I thought the act was over, but Waverhouse proceeded neatly to flip his whirling headgear over his head and onto the floor behind him, where, as the climax of his performance, he sat down squarely on it with a heavy solid whump.

"You're sure it's all right?" Even my master looks somewhat concerned. Mrs. Sneaze, genuinely anxious, squeaks, "Please, you'd better stop. It would be terrible to spoil so fine a hat."

Only its owner wants to keep going. "But it can't be spoiled. That's the wonder of it." He heaves the crumpled object out from under his bottom and jams it on his head. It sprang back into shape.

"Indeed it's a very strong hat. Isn't it extraordinary? Quite amazing." Mrs. Sneaze is more and more impressed.

"Oh, there's nothing extraordinary about it. It's just that kind of hat," says Waverhouse smirking out from under its brim.

A moment later Mrs. Sneaze turns to her husband. "I think you, too, had better buy a hat like that."

"But he's already got a splendid boater."

"Just the other day the children trampled on it and it's all squashed out of shape." Mrs. Sneaze persists.

"Oh dear. That was a pity."

"That's why I think he should buy a hat like yours, strong and splendiferous." She has no idea what panama hats can cost, so nothing moderates the urgency of her proddings. "Really, my dear, you must get one, just like this. . . "

At this point Waverhouse produces from his right sleeve a pair of scissors in a scarlet sheath. "Mrs. Sneaze," he says, "forget the hat for a moment and take a look at these scissors. They, too, are fantastically handy. You can use them in fourteen different ways." If it hadn't been for those scissors my master would have succumbed to wifely pressure in the matter of the hat. He was extremely lucky that the inborn female sense of curiosity diverted his wife's attention. It crossed my mind that Waverhouse had acted of intent, helpfully and tactfully, but after careful consideration I've concluded that it was pure good luck that saved my master from painful outlay on a panama hat.

No sooner has Mrs. Sneaze responded with a, "What are the fourteen ways?" than Waverhouse is off again in triumphantly full flow. "I shall explain each of them, so listen carefully. All right? You see here a crescent-shaped opening? One sticks one's cigar in here to nip its lip-end before smoking. This gadget down here by the handle can cut through wire as though it were mere noodle. Now if you put the scissors flat down upon paper, there's a ruler for you. Here, on the back-edge of this blade, there's a scale engraved so the scissors can be used as a measure. Over here there's a file for one's fingernails. Right? Now then, if you push this blade-tip out, you can twist it around and around to drive screws. Thus, it serves as a hammer. And you can use this blade-tip to lever open with the greatest of case even the most carefully nailed lid. Furthermore, the end of this other blade, being ground to so fine a point, makes an excellent gimlet. With this thing you can scrape out any mistakes in your writing. And finally, if you take the whole thing to pieces, you get a perfectly good knife. Now, Mrs. Sneaze, there's actually one more especially interesting feature. Here in the handle there's a tiny ball about the size of a fly. You see it? Well, take a peep right into it."

"No. I'd rather not. I'm sure you're going to make fun of me again."

"I'm grieved that you should have so little confidence in me. But, just this once, take me at my word and have a little look. No? Oh, please, just one quick squint." He handed her the scissors.

Mrs. Sneaze takes them very gingerly and, setting her eyeball close to the magic spot, does her best to see into it.

"Well?"

"Nothing. It's all black."

"All black? That won't do. Turn a little toward the paper-window and look against the light. Don't tilt the scissors like that. Right, that's it. Now you can see, can't you?"

"Oh, my! It's a photograph, isn't it? How can a tiny photograph be fixed in here?"

"That's what's so remarkable." Mrs. Sneaze and Waverhouse are now absorbed in their conversation. My master, silent now for some time but intrigued by the idea of the photograph, seems suddenly possessed by an urge to see it. He asks his wife to let him but she, her eye still glued to the scissors, just babbles on. "How very lovely. What a beautiful study of the nude." She won't be parted from the scissors.

"Come on, let me see it."

"You wait. What lovely tresses, all the way down to her hips. How movingly her face is lifted. Rather a tall girl, I'd say, but indeed a beauty!"

"Damn it, let me see." My master, now distinctly marked, flares up at his wife.

"There you are then. Gawp away to your heart's content." As she was handing the scissors over, the servant trundles in from the kitchen with an announcement that Waverhouse's meal has been delivered. Indeed she carries with her two lidded bamboo plates loaded with cold buckwheat noodles.

"Aha," says Waverhouse, "so here, Mrs. Sneaze, is the lunch I bought myself. With your permission, I propose to eat it now." He bows respectfully. As he seems to have spoken half in earnest and half in jest, Mrs. Sneaze is at a loss how best to answer, so she just says lightly, "Please do," and settles back to watch.

At long last my master drags his eyes away from the photograph and remarks, "In weather as hot as this, noodles are bad for one's health."

"No danger. What one likes seldom upsets one. In fact I've heard," says Waverhouse, lifting one of the lids, "that a little of what you fancy does you good." He appears satisfied by what he's seen on the plate for he goes straight on to observe, "In my opinion noodles that have been left to stand are, like heavily bearded men, never to be relied upon." He adds green horseradish to his dish of soy sauce and stirs away like mad.

"Steady on," says my master in genuinely anxious tones, "if you put in that much spice it'll be too hot to eat."

"Noodles must be eaten with soy sauce and green horse-radish. I bet you don't even like noodles."

"I do indeed. The normal kind."

"That's the stuff for pack-horse drivers. A man insensitive to cold buckwheat noodles spiced like this is a man to be devoutly pitied." So saying, Waverhouse digs his cedar-wood chopsticks deep into the mass of noodles, scoops up a hefty helping and lifts it some two inches. "Did you know, Mrs. Sneaze, that there are several styles for eating noodles?

Raw beginners always use too much sauce and then they munch this delicacy like so many cattle chewing the cud. That way, the exquisite savor of the noodles is inevitably lost. The correct procedure is to scoop them up like this. . . " Waverhouse raises his chopsticks above the bamboo plate until a foot-long curtain of noodles dangles in the air. He looks down at the plate to check that he's lifted his lading clear of the plate but finds a dozen or so of the tail-ends still lying coiled within it.

"What very long noodles! Look, Mrs. Sneaze, aren't they the longest that you ever saw?" Waverhouse demands that his audience should participate, if only by interjections.

"Indeed, they are lengthy!" she answers, as if impressed by his dissertation.

"Now, you dip just one-third of these long strands in the sauce, then swallow them in a single gulp. You mustn't chew them. Mastication destroys their unique flavor. The whole point of noodles is in the way they slither down one's throat." He thereupon raises his chopsticks to a dramatic height and the ends of the longest strands at last swing clear of the plate. Then, as he starts to lower his arm again, the tail-ends of the noodles slowly start submerging into the sauce dish held in his left hand. Which, in accordance with Archimedes' Law, causes the sauce slowly to rise in the dish as its volume is displaced by noodles. However, since the dish was originally eight-tenths full of sauce, the level of the liquid reached its brim before Waverhouse could get even one-quarter, let alone the connoisseur's one-third, of the length of his wriggling noodles into the sauce. The chopsticks appear paralyzed about five inches above the dish and so remain for an awkward pause while Waverhouse considers his dilemma. If he lowers the noodles one more fraction of an inch, the sauce must overflow, but if he does not lower them, he must fail to conform with the standards he has established for the proper style of stuffing oneself with noodles. No wonder he looks moithered and half-hesitates. Then, suddenly, jerking his head and neck forward and downward like a striking snake, he jabbed his mouth at the chopsticks, There was a slushy slurping sound, his throttle surged and receded once or twice and the noodles were all gone. A few tears oozed from the corners of his eyes. To this day I am not sure whether those tear drops were a tribute to the strength of the green horseradish or evidence of the painful effort such gurgitation must involve.

"What an extraordinary performance! How on earth," enquires my flabbergasted master, "do you contrive to gulp down such a mass of vermicelli in one consuming go?"

"Amazing, isn't he!" Mrs. Sneaze is equally lost in admiration.

Waverhouse says nothing, puts down the chopsticks, and pats his chest an easing couple of times. "Well, Mrs. Sneaze," he eventually answers, "a plate of noodles should be consumed in three and a half, at most in four, mouthfuls. If you drag out the process longer than that, the noodles will not taste their best." He wipes his face with a handkerchief and sits back to take a well-earned breather.

At this point who should walk in but Coldmoon. His feet are soiled with summer dust but, for no reason I can offer, despite the broiling heat he's wearing a winter hat.

"Hello! Here comes our handsome hero! However, since I'm still in the middle of eating, you must excuse me." Waverhouse, totally unabashed, settles down to finishing off the noodles. This time, rather sensibly, he makes no effort to give a repeat performance as a vermicelli virtuoso, and is consequently spared the indignities of needing support from handkerchiefs and breathers between mouthfuls. Eating normally he empties both the bamboo plates in a matter of minutes.

"Coldmoon," says my master, "how's your thesis coming along?" And Waverhouse adds, "Since the delectable Miss Goldfield is yearning to be yours, you should in common kindness submit the finished text as fast as possible."

Coldmoon breaks as usual into his disconcertingly idiot grin. "Inasmuch as waiting is a cruelty to her, I'd like indeed to finish it quickly," he replies, "but the nature of its subject is such that a great deal of drudging research is unavoidable." He spoke with measured seriousness of things he couldn't possibly himself be taking seriously.

"Quite so," says Waverhouse adopting Coldmoon's style with contrapuntal skill. "The subject being what it is, naturally it cannot be handled just as Coldmoon wishes. Nevertheless, that nasality her mother being the snorter that she is, naturally it would be prudent to trim one's sails to the way she blows."

The only relatively sensible comment comes from my master. "What did you say was the subject of your thesis?"

"It is entitled 'The Effects of Ultraviolet Rays upon Galvanic Action in the Eyeball of the Frog.'"

"Remarkable. Just what one might expect from Coldmoon. I like both the rhythm and the substantial originality of that last bit, the electrifying shock in that 'eyeball of the frog.' How about it, Sneaze? Ought we not to inform the Goldfields of at least the title before our scholar finishes his paper?"

My master, disregarding these waggeries from Waverhouse, asks Coldmoon, "Can such a subject really involve much drudgery of research?"

"Oh yes, it's a complicated question. For one thing, the structure of the lens in the eyeball of the frog is by no means simple. Hundreds, even thousands, of experiments will have to be carried out. For a start I'm planning to construct a round glass ball."

"A glass ball? Surely, you could find one quite easily in a glass shop?"

"Oh, no, far from it," says Coldmoon, throwing out his chest a little. "To begin with, things like circles and straight lines are pure geometrical concepts, and neither actual circles nor actual straight lines can, in this imperfect world, ever realize such idealities."

"If they can never exist, hadn't you better abandon the attempt to create them?" butts in Waverhouse.

"Well, I thought I'd begin by making a ball suitable for my experiments and, in fact, I started on it the other day."

"And have you finished it?" asks my master as if the task were an easy matter.

"How could I?" says Coldmoon, but then, realizing perhaps that he's getting close to self-contradiction, hurries on to explain. "It's really frightfully difficult. After I've filed it for some time, I notice that the radius on one side is too long, so I grind it fractionally shorter, but this leads on to trouble, because now I find the radius on the other side excessive. When, with great effort I grind that excess off, the entire ball becomes misshapen. After I've at last corrected that distortion, I discover that the diametrical dimensions have, somehow or other, once more gone agley. The glass ball, originally the size of an apple, soon becomes a strawberry and, as I patiently struggle for perfection, it rapidly shrinks to no more than a bean. Even then, it's not a perfect sphere. Believe me, I have striven. . . I have dedicated my whole life to the grinding of glass balls. Since New Year's Day no less than six of them, admittedly of differing sizes, have melted away to nothing in these hands. . ." He speaks with such rare passion that no one could say whether or not he's telling the truth.

"Where do you do this grinding?"

"In the university laboratory of course. I start grinding in the morning. I take a short rest for lunch, and then continue grinding until the light fails. It's not an easy job."

"D'you mean to say that you go down to the university day after day, including Sundays, simply to grind glass balls? Is that what keeps you, as you're always telling us, so inexorably busy?"

"That's correct. At this stage in my studies I have no choice but to grind glass balls morning, noon, and night."

"I seem to recall," says Waverhouse, now very much in his element, "a Kabuki play in which one character gains his ends by disguising himself as a gardener." He strikes an attitude and quotes, "'As I was luckily brought up among civilian non-officials, no one knows my face: so I enter as a cultivator of chrysanthemums.' You, Coldmoon, seem bent on gaining your ends disguised as a cultivator of crystals. For I'm sure that when the mother of all noses learns of your ardor, your single-minded dedication to your work, your selfless devotion to the grinding of glass balls, she cannot fail to warm toward you. Incidentally, the other day I had some work to do in the university library and, as I was leaving, I chanced to bump into an old colleague, Knarle-Damson, at the door. Thinking it peculiar that, years after his graduation, he should still be using the library, I said to him, 'Knarle-Damson,' I said, 'I'm most impressed, Knarle-Damson, to find you still imbibing at the fount of learning.' He gave me a very odd look and explained that, far from wanting to consult a book, he'd been caught short as he passed the university and had just popped in for a pee. A curious use for a seat of learning. However, it's just occurred to me that you and Knarle-Damson both exemplify, though in contrasting styles, how to misuse a university. You will, of course, have read that Chinese classic which is constructed from pairs of parallel anecdotes, one ancient and one modern, about famous men. I am proposing to bring out a new selection along similar lines and, with your permission, will include therein a short section on glass balls and urinals."

My master, however, took a more serious view of the matter. "It's all very well," he said, "to pass your days frotting away at glass but when do you expect to finish your thesis and get your doctorate?"

"At my present rate of progress, maybe in ten years." Coldmoon seems far less concerned than my master about the doctorate.

"Ten years, eh? I think you'd better bring your grinding to a halt rather sooner than that."

"Ten years is an optimistic estimate. It could well take me twenty."

"That's terrible. You can't, then, hope for a doctorate for a long time."

"No. Of course I'd be only too happy to get it quickly, and so set the young lady's mind at rest, but until I've got the glass ball properly ground, I can't even launch out on my first experiment." Coldmoon's voice trailed off into silence as though his mind were staring into the lens of a frog's eyeball but, after a brief pause, he continued. "There's no need, you know, to get so worried about it. The Goldfields are fully aware that I do nothing but grind away at these glass balls. As a matter of fact, I gave them a fairly detailed explanation when I saw them just a few days back." He smiled in quiet complacence.

Mrs. Sneaze who, though hardly understanding a word of it, has been listening to the three men's conversation, interjects in a puzzled voice, "But the whole Goldfield family has been away at the seaside, out at Oiso, since last month."

This flummoxes even Coldmoon, but he maintains a pretense of innocence. "How very odd," he says, "I can't understand it."

There are occasions when Waverhouse fulfills a useful social function. When a conversation flags, when one is embarrassed, when one becomes sleepy, when one is troubled, then, as on all other occasions, Waverhouse can be relied upon to have something immediate and diverting to say. "To have met someone a few days back in Tokyo who had gone to Oiso last month is engagingly mysterious. It is an example, is it not, of the exchange of souls. Such a phenomenon is likely to occur when the sentiment of requited love is particularly poignant. When one hears of such a happening, it sounds like a dream, but, even if it is a dream, it is a dream more actual than reality. For someone like you, Mrs. Sneaze, who were married to Sneaze not because you loved him or because he loved you, life has never given an opportunity for you to understand the extraordinary nature of love: so it is only natural that you should find odd the disparities you mentioned. . ."

"I don't know why you should say such nasty things. Why are you always getting at me like this?" Mrs. Sneaze rounds snappishly on Waverhouse.

"What's more, you yourself don't look like a man who has any experience of the pangs of love." My master brings up reinforcements in surprising support of the frontline position manned by his wife.

"Well, since all my love affairs were over long before the nine days back that might have made them wonders, you doubtless don't remember them. But it remains a fact that it was a disappointment in love that has made me, to this day, a lonely bachelor." Waverhouse leveled a steady look upon each of his listeners, one after the other.

It was Mrs. Sneaze who laughed, though she added, "But how interesting."

My master said, "Bosh," and turned to stare off into the garden.

Coldmoon, though he grinned, said politely, "I would like, for my own future benefit, to hear the story of your ancient love."

"My story, too, contains elements of the mysterious. So much so that, if he were not lamentably dead, it must have moved the interest of the late Lafcadio Hearn. I am, I must confess, a little reluctant to tell this painful tale but, since you insist, I'll confide in you all on the sole condition that you listen carefully to the very end." They promised, and he starts.

"As well as I can recollect. . . it was. . . hum. . . how many years ago was it, I wonder. . . Never mind, let's say it was maybe fifteen or sixteen years ago."

"Incorrigible," snorts my master.

"You do have a very poor memory, don't you, Mr. Waverhouse?" Mrs. Sneaze puts in a jabbing oar.

Coldmoon is the only person who, keeping the promise, says nothing but wears the expression of a man eagerly waiting for the remainder of a story.

"Anyway, it was in the winter, some years back. Having passed through the Valley of the Bamboo Shoots at Kambara in Echigo, I was climbing up through the Pass of the Octopus Trap on my way to the Aizu territory."

"What odd-named places!" My master interrupts again.

"Oh, do keep quiet and listen. This is getting interesting." Mrs. Sneaze reins back her husband.

"Unfortunately, it was getting dark. I lost my way. I was hungry. So, in the end, I was obliged to knock at the door of a hut way up in the middle of the Pass. Explaining my predicament, I begged for a night's lodging. And do you know, the minute that I saw the face of the girl who, thrusting a lit candle out toward me, answered, 'Of course, please enter,' my whole body began to tremble. Since that moment I've been very acutely conscious of the supernatural power of that blind force we call love."

"Fancy that," says Mrs. Sneaze. "Are there really, I wonder, many beautiful girls living up there in those godforsaken mountains?"

"It hardly matters that I found her in the mountains. It might just as well have been beside the seaside. But, oh Mrs. Sneaze, would that you could have seen her, if only for a glance. . . She wore her hair in the high-dressed fashion of a marriageable girl. . ."

Mrs. Sneaze, rendered speechless by the wonder of it all, gives vent to a long-drawn sigh.

"On entering the hut, I found a big fireplace sunk in the center of an eight-mat room, and soon the four of us—the girl, her grandfather, her grandmother, and myself—were sitting comfortably around it. They said I must be very hungry. And I was. Very. So I asked for some food, anything, no matter what, so long as I might have it quickly. The old man said, 'It's seldom we have visitors, so let's prepare snake-rice in honor of our guest.' Now then, this is where I come to the story of my disappointment in love, so listen carefully."

"Of course we'll listen carefully," says Coldmoon, "but I find it hard to believe that even out in the wilds of Echigo there are snakes around in the winter."

"Well, that's a fair observation. But in a romantic story such as this, one shouldn't be too scrupulous over the logic of its details. Why, in one of Kyoka's novels, you'll find a crab crawling out of the snow."

"I see," said Coldmoon who thereupon resumed his serious attitude of listening.

"In those days I was outstandingly capable, really in the champion class, of eating ugly foods, but, being more or less wearied of locusts, slugs, red frogs, and such like, I thought snake-rice sounded like a welcome change. So I told the old man I'd be delighted. He then set a pot on the fire and put some rice inside it. Slowly it began to cook. The only oddity was that there were about ten holes of various sizes in the lid of the pot. Through these holes, the steam came fuffing up. I was really fascinated by the effect and I remember thinking how ingenious these country people were. Just then, the old man suddenly stood up and went out of the hut. A while later, he came back with a large basket under his arm and, when he put it casually down beside the hearth, I took a look inside. Well, there they were. Snakes, and all of them long ones, coiled up tight, as Coldmoon will appreciate, in their winter torpor."

"Please stop talking about such nasty things. It's quite revolting," says Mrs. Sneaze with a girlish shudder.

"Oh I can't possibly stop, for all these matters lie at the bottom of my broken-heartedness. Well, by and by, the old man lifted the pot's lid with his left hand while with his other he nimbly grabbed up a wad of snakes from the basket. He threw them into the pot and popped the lid back on. And I must admit that, though I'm neither squeamish nor particularly scared of snakes, the old man's nonchalant action did, at that moment, leave me gasping."

"Oh, please do stop. I can't stand gruesome stories." Mrs. Sneaze is actually quite frightened.

"Very soon now I'll be coming to the broken-hearted bit, so please just do be patient. Well, barely a minute had passed when, to my great surprise, a snake's head popped out of a hole in the lid. I'd barely realized what it was before another one popped its face out from a neighboring hole, and I'd barely registered that second head before another and another and another erupted into view until the whole lid was studded with snakes' faces."

"Why did they stick their heads out?" asks my master.

"Because, in agony, they were trying to crawl away from the heat building up inside the pot. After a while the old man said, speaking, naturally, in his local dialect, something like, 'Right then, give 'em the old heave-ho.' His wife said, 'Aye' and the girl said, 'Yes' and each of them, grasping a snake's head firmly, gave it a savage yank. While the flesh remained in the pot, the head and a length of bones came waggling free in their hands."

"What you might call boned snake?" asks Coldmoon with a laugh.

"Yes, indeed. Boned, or even spineless. But wasn't it all exceedingly clever? They lifted the lid, took a ladle, stirred the rice and the snake-flesh into one great wonderful mishmash and then invited me to tuck in."

"Did you actually eat it?" asks my master in a slightly edgy sort of voice.

His wife makes a sour face and grumblingly complains. "I do so wish you'd all stop talking about it. I'm feeling sick right down to my stomach, and I shan't dare eat for days."

"You only say that, Mrs. Sneaze, because you've never had the luck to taste snake-rice. If you but tried it once, you'd never forget its exquisite flavor."

"Never. Nothing on earth could induce me to touch the nasty stuff."

"Anyway, I dined well. I forgot the bitter cold. I studied the girl's face to my heart's content and, though I could happily have stared at her forever, when they suggested I should go to sleep, I remembered that I was in fact dog tired from my traveling. So I took their advice and laid down, and before long everything blurred and I was fast asleep."

"And what happened then?" This time it's Mrs. Sneaze who urges him to continue.

"When I woke up next morning, heart-ache had set in."

"Did anything happen to you?" asks Mrs. Sneaze.

"No, nothing special happened to me. I just woke up and, while I was smoking a cigarette, I chanced to look out through the back window, and there I saw, washing its face in the water flowing from a bamboo-pipe, someone as bald as a kettle."

"The old man," asks my master, "or the old woman?"

"At first I couldn't tell. I sat there watching it in vague distaste for quite some time and, when at last the kettle turned towards me, I got the shock of my life. For it was the girl to whom I had already lost my heart."

"But you said earlier that she wore her hair in the style of a marriageable girl," my master promptly objects.

"The night before, unmitigated beauty: in the morning, unmitigated kettle."

"Really! What balderdash will you trot out next." As is usual when he feels put out, my master stares at the ceiling.

"Naturally, I was most deeply shocked, even a little frightened, but, making myself inconspicuous, I continued to watch. At long last the kettle finished washing its face, featly donned the wig waiting on a nearby stone and then came tripping primly back to the hut. I understood everything. But though I understood, I have from that moment been a man incurably wretched, a man with a broken heart."

"The silliest broken heart that ever was. Observe, my dear Coldmoon, how gay and lively he contrives to be despite his broken heart." Turning toward Coldmoon, my master registers his low opinion of his friend's disastrous love affair.

"But," says Coldmoon, "if the girl had not been bald, and if Waverhouse had brought her back with him to Tokyo, he might now be livelier than he is. The fact remains that it is infinitely pitiable that the young lady happened to be bald. But tell me, Waverhouse, how did it come about that a girl so young should have lost her hair?"

"Well, naturally I've thought about that too, and I'm certain now that the depilation must be due entirely to over-indulgence in snake-rice. It goes to the head, you know. It drives the blood upward, damaging the capillaries in the follicles of the scalp."

"I'm so glad nothing so terrible happened to you," says Mrs. Sneaze with an undertone of sarcasm.

"It is true that I was spared the affliction of going bald, but instead, as you can see, I have become a presbyope." Taking off his goldrimmed spectacles, he polishes them carefully with his pocket handkerchief.

There was a short silence. To be a presbyope sounded so awful that none dared ask for an explanation. But my master, possibly being made of sterner stuff, possibly because he knows that nearsightedness is more often caused by the passing of the years than by one night's meal of snake-rice, was not yet done.

"I seem to remember," he eventually said, "that you mentioned some mystery that would have moved the interest of Lafcadio Hearn. What mystery?"

"Did she buy the wig or simply pick it up, and, if she picked it up, where? That," said Waverhouse, replacing his spectacles on his nose, "is the mystery. To this day I cannot work it out."

"It's just like listening to a comic storyteller," says Mrs. Sneaze.

As Waverhouse's improbable tale had come to its conclusion, I thought he might shut-up. But no. He appears by nature incapable of keeping quiet unless actually gagged. For he's at it again already.

"My disappointment in love was, of course, a bitter experience: but had I married that heavenly girl in ignorance of kettledom, the matter would have remained a lifelong cause of friction. One has to be careful. In matters like marriage, one tends only to discover at the very last moment hidden defects in unexpected places. I therefore advise you, Coldmoon, not to waste your youth in futile yearnings or in pointless despair but to keep on grinding away at your balls of glass with an easy mind and heart."

"I'd be happy," answers Coldmoon, "to do nothing more. However, the Goldfield ladies, to my considerable botheration, do keep on at me." He grimaces in exaggerated annoyance.

"True. You are, in your case, somewhat put upon. But there are many comic cases of people thrusting themselves forward to invite disquiet. Take, for example, the case of Knarle-Damson, that well-known piddler upon seats of learning. His was extremely odd."

"What did he do?" asks my master, entering into the swing of the conversation.

"Well, it was like this. Once upon a long, long time ago, he stayed at the East-West Inn in Shizuoka. Just for one night, mind you, but that same evening he offered marriage to one of the servants working there. I myself am pretty easy-going, but I would not find it easy to go as far as that. The fact was, that in those days one of the maids at that Inn, they called her Summer, was a raving beauty, and it just so happened that she looked after Knarle-Damson's room, so he could not help but meet her."

"The meeting was no doubt fated, just like yours in that something-or-other pass," observes my master.

"Yes, there is some resemblance between the cases. Indeed, there are obvious similarities between Knarle-Damson and myself. Anyway, he proposed to this Summer girl but, before she gave her answer, he felt a need for watermelon."

"Huh?" My master looks puzzled. And not only he, for both his wife and Coldmoon cock their heads sideways as they try to see the connection. Waverhouse disregards them all and proceeds blithely with his story.

"He summoned the girl and asked her if one could get a watermelon in Shizuoka. She replied that, though the town was not as up-to-date as Tokyo, even in Shizuoka watermelons could be had, and almost immediately she brought him a tray heaped high with slices of the fruit. So, while waiting for her answer, Knarle-Damson scoffed the lot. But before she gave her answer, Knarle-Damson got the gripes. He groaned away like mad but, since that didn't help, he summoned the girl again and this time asked if there was a doctor available. The girl replied that, though the town was not as up-to-date as Tokyo, still, even in Shizuoka, doctors were available, and in a matter of minutes she ushered one in to his room. The doctor, incidentally, had a very odd name, something like Heaven-and-Earth, anyway something obviously cribbed, for effect, from the Chinese classics. Well, next morning when Knarle-Damson woke up, he was to find his gut-ache gone, and, some fifteen minutes before he was due to leave, he again summoned the Summer girl and asked for her answer to his proposal of marriage. The girl replied with laughter. She then said that down in Shizuoka it is possible to find doctors and watermelons at very short notice but that, even in Shizuoka, few find brides in a single night. She turned, went out of the room and that was the last he saw of her. And ever since that day, Knarle-Damson has remained, like me, a man scarred by a disappointment in love.

Almost a recluse, he'll only go to a library when pressed there by his bladder. Which all goes to show the wickedness and cruelty of women."

My master, most unusually, comes out this time in strong support of Waverhouse's theme. "How right you are," he says, "how very right. Just the other day I was reading one of de Musset's plays in which some character quoted Ovid to the effect that, lighter than a feather is dust; than dust, wind; than wind, woman; but than woman, nothing. A very penetrating observation, isn't it? Women are indeed the dreaded end." My master adopts an exceedingly cavalier attitude, but his wife, of course, is not going to let these flourishes pass unchallenged.

"You complain about women being light, but I can't see any particular merit in the fact that men are heavy."

"What do you mean by heavy?"

"Heavy is just heavy. Like you."

"Why d'you say I'm heavy?"

"Because you are heavy. Very heavy."

They're off on one of their crazy arguments again. For a time Waverhouse just sits there, listening with amusement to their increasingly bitter bickering, but eventually he opens his mouth.

"The way you two go on at each other, hammering away until you're red in the face, is perhaps the clearest possible demonstration that you truly are husband and wife. I'm inclined to think that marriage in the old days was a less meaningful thing than it is today." None of his listeners could tell whether he was teasing or complimenting his host and hostess but, since their bickering was halted, he could with profit have just stopped there. But that's not the way of a Waverhouse, who always has more to say.

"I hear that in the old days no woman would have dreamt of answering back to her husband. From the man's point of view it must have been like marriage to a deaf-mute. I wouldn't have liked that. Not one little bit. I certainly prefer women who, like you, Mrs. Sneaze, have the spirit to retort, 'Because you are heavy,' or something else in the same vein. If one is to be married, it would be insupportably boring never to have the liveliness of an occasional spat. My mother, for instance, spent her whole life saying, 'Yes' and 'You're right' to my frequently foolish father. She lived with him for twenty or so assenting years, and in all that stretch she never set foot outside the house except to go to a temple. Really, it's too pitiful. There were, of course, advantages. Thus my mother has the enormous satisfaction of knowing that she knows by heart the full posthumous names of all my family's ancestors. This hideous sort of relationship did not exist simply between man and wife but extended to cover the whole range of relations between the sexes. When I was a lad it was quite out of the question for a young man and a young woman even to play music together. There was no such thing as a lovers' meeting. They couldn't even meet in the world of the spirit, like Coldmoon here, by a long range swap of souls."

"It must have been awful," says Coldmoon with a sort of shrinking bow.

"Indeed it was. One weeps for one's ancestors. Still, women in those days were not necessarily any better behaved than the women of today. You know, Mrs. Sneaze, people talk down their noses about the depraved conduct of modern, girl students, but the truth is that things were very much worse in those so-called good old days."

"Really?" Mrs. Sneaze is serious.

"Of course. I'm not just making it up. I can prove what I say. You, Sneaze, will probably remember that when we were maybe five or six there were men going about in the streets with two panniers hanging down from each end of their shoulder-poles, and in the panniers, like so many pumpkins, they had little girls for sale. You remember?"

"I don't remember anything of the sort."

"I don't know how things were in your part of the country, but that's most certainly the way it was in Shizuoka."

"Surely not," murmurs Mrs. Sneaze.

"Do you mean that for a fact?" asks Coldmoon in a tone of voice that shows he can't quite credit it.

"For an absolute, rock hard fact. I can even remember how once my father haggled over the price of one. I must then have been about six. As my father and I were coming out of a side street into the main thoroughfare, we saw a man approaching us who was bawling out, 'Girls for sale! Girls for sale! Anyone want a baby girl?' When we reached the corner of the second block in the street, we came face-to-face with this hawker, just in front of the draper's. Isegen's it was. Isegen is quite the biggest draper in Shizuoka with a sixty-foot frontage and five warehouses. Have a look at it the next time you're down there. It's just the same today as it was then. Quite unaltered. A fine building. The chief clerk's name is Jimbei, and he sits at his counter with the invariable expression of a man who's lost his mother only three days back. Sitting right beside Jimbei you'll find a young man of twenty-four, maybe twenty-five, whose name is Hatsu. Hatsu's very pale. He looks like one of those novices who, in demonstration of their devotion to the thirty-third priest-prince of the Shingon Sect, take nothing but buckwheat-water for twenty-one days at a stretch. And next to Hatsu there's Chodon. Chodon's the one who's hunched dejectedly above his abacus as though but yesterday he lost his home in a fire. And next to Chodon. . ."

"Come off it, Waverhouse," snaps my master. "Is this a chanting of the genealogy of your draper or is it a tale about the maiden-mongers of Shizuoka?"

"Ah yes. I was telling you the story of the maiden-mongers. As a matter of fact, there's an extremely strange story I was going to tell you about that draper's, but I'll cut it out and concentrate on the sellers of little girls."

"Why not cut that too?" suggests my master.

"Oh no! I wouldn't feel right if I abandoned that story. For it provides exceedingly valuable data by which to compare the characters of modern women with those of their predecessors in the early Meiji Era. Now, as I was saying, when my father and I arrived in front of Isegen, the maiden-monger addressed my father in these terms: ''ow about one of these 'ere little leftovers? Take a toddler, sir, and I'll make 'er special cheap.' He's put his shoulder-pole down on the ground and is wiping sweat from his brow. In each of the two dumped panniers there's a little girl about two-years-old. My father says, 'If they're really cheap, I might, but is this all you've got?' The man replies respectfully, 'Yes, sir, I'm afraid so. Today I've sold I 'em all, 'cept for these two little 'uns. Take your choice.' He holds the little girls up in his hands like, as I told you, pumpkins, and he pushes them under my father's nose. My father taps on their heads as one might rap a melon and says, 'Yes, they sound quite good.' The negotiations then begin in earnest and, after a great deal of chaffering, my father finally says, 'That's all very well, but can you guarantee their quality?' 'Yes,' says the man. 'That 'un in the leading basket, I can take me oath is sound, 'cos I've 'ad 'er all day long right in front of me own two peepers, but t'other in the back-side basket could be a wee mite cracked. I've not got eyes in the back of me 'ead, so I won't go making no promises. Tell you what, just for you, I'll knock a bit more off for that 'un.' To this day I can clearly remember every word of their dickering and, though only a nipper myself, I did then learn how insidiously cracked a little girl can be. However, in this thirty-eighth year of the Emperor's reign there's none so foolish now as to go trotting through the streets with little girls for sale. So one no longer hears people saying how those at the back, those that one can't keep one's own sharp watchful eye on, are liable to be damaged. It is consequently my opinion that, thanks to the beneficent influx of Western civilization, the conduct of women has in fact improved. What do you think, Coldmoon?"

Coldmoon hesitated, cleared his throat and then gave his opinion in a low and measured tone. "Women today, on their way to and from schools, at concerts, at charity parties and at garden parties, are, in effect, already selling themselves. Their light behavior is tantamount to such statements as, 'Hey, how about buying me?' or 'Oh, so you're not much interested!' There is accordingly no contemporary need for hawkers or other middlemen selling on commission, and the street cries of our modern cities are of course the poorer by the disappearance of maiden-mongers shouting their wares. Such changes are bound to follow from the introduction and dissemination of modern ideas of the individual's independence. The older generation get unnecessarily worked up and moan and groan as though the world were coming to its end, but that's the trend of modern civilization and I, for one, welcome and encourage these changes. For instance, there's no need nowadays for anyone to go tapping poor tots on the skull to see if they're good enough to buy. In any case, no one ever gets anywhere in this hard world by being unduly choosey. That way, one can easily end up husbandless and, even after fifty or sixty years of assiduous search, still not be a bride."

Coldmoon, very much a bright young man of this twentieth century, spoke for his generation and, having so spoken, blew cigarette smoke into Waverhouse's face. But Waverhouse is not a man to flinch from a mere residue of burnt tobacco. "As you say," he responded, "among schoolgirls and young ladies, nowadays their very flesh and bones are permeated with, if not actually manufactured out of, self-esteem and self-confidence, and it is indeed admirable that they should prove themselves a match for men in every possible field. Take, for instance, the girls at the high school near my house. They're terrific. Togged out in trousers, they hang themselves upside-down from iron wall-bars. Truly, it's wonderful. Every time that I look down from my upstairs window and see them catapulting about at their gymnastics, I am reminded of ancient Grecian ladies pursuing strength and beauty through the patterns of calisthenics."

"Oh, no. Not the Greeks again," says my master with something like a sneer.

"It's unavoidable. It just so happens that almost everything aesthetically beautiful seems to have originated in Greece. Aesthetics and the Greeks: you speak of one and you are speaking of the other. When I see those dark-skinned girls putting their whole hearts into their gymnastics, into my mind, invariably, leaps the story of Agnodice." He's wearing his font-of-all-wisdom face as he babbles on and on.

"So you've managed to find another of those awkward names," says Coldmoon with his usual, witless grin.

"Agnodice was a wonderful woman. When I look back at her across the gulf of centuries, still I am impressed. In those far days the Laws of Athens forbade women to be midwives. It was most inconvenient. One can easily see why Agnodice thought it unreasonable."

"What's that? What's that word?"

"Agnodice. A woman. It's a woman's name. Now this woman said to herself, 'It's really lamentable that women cannot be midwives, inconvenient, too. I wish to God I could become a midwife. Isn't there any way I can?' So she thought and thought, doing nothing else for three straight days and nights, and just at dawn on the third day, as she heard the yowling of a babe newborn next door, the solution flashed upon her. She immediately cut off her long hair, dressed herself as a man, and took to attending the lectures on childbirth then being given by the eminent Hierophilus. She learnt all that he could teach and, feeling her time had come, set up as a midwife. D'you know, Mrs. Sneaze, she was a great success. Here, there, and everywhere yowling babies put in their appearance, and, since they were all assisted by Agnodice, she made a fortune. However, the ways of Heaven are proverbially inscrutable. For seven ups there are eight downs. And it never rains but it pours. Her secret was discovered. She was hauled before the courts. And she stood in danger of the direst punishment for breaking the laws of Athens."

"You sound just like a professional storyteller," says Mrs. Sneaze.

"Aren't I good? Well then, at that point all the women of Athens got together and signed such an enormous round robin in support of Agnodice that the magistrates felt unable to ignore it. In the end she was let off, and the laws were changed to allow women to become midwives, and they all lived happily ever after."

"You do know about so many things. It's wonderful," sighs Mrs. Sneaze.

"True. I know almost everything about almost everything. Perhaps the only thing I don't know all about is the real extent of my own foolishness. But even on that, I can make a pretty good guess."

"You do say such funny things. . ." Mrs. Sneaze was still chortling away when the front doorbell, its tone unchanged since the day it was first installed, began to tinkle.

"What! another visitor!" squeaked Mrs. Sneaze and scuttled off into the living room.

And who should it be but our old friend Beauchamp Blowlamp. With his arrival the entire cast of the eccentrics who haunt my master's house was gathered upon stage. Lest that should sound ungracious, perhaps I could better emphasize that sufficient eccentrics are gathered to keep a cat amused, and it would indeed be ungracious if I were not satisfied with that. Had I had the misfortune to dwell in some other household, I might have lived nine lives and never known that such remarkable scholars, that even one such remarkable scholar, could be found among mankind. I count myself fortunate to be sitting here, his adopted cat-child, beside my noble master. It is, moreover, a rare privilege to be numbered among the disciples of Professor Sneaze: for only thus am I enabled, comfortably lying down, to observe the manners and actions not only of my master but of such heroic figures, such matchless warriors, as Waverhouse, Coldmoon, and the bold Sir Beauchamp. Even in this vast city, such personages are rare, and I take it as the highest accolade that I am accepted by them as one of their company. It is only the consciousness of that honor that enables me to forget the hardship of being condemned to endure this heat in a fur bag. And I am especially grateful thus to be kept amused for a whole half-day. Whenever the four of them get together like this, something entertaining is bound to transpire, so I watch them respectfully from that draft-cooled place by the door to which I have retired.

"I'm afraid I haven't been around to see you for quite some time," says Beauchamp with a modest bow. His head, I notice, shines as brightly as it did the other day. Judged by his head alone, he might be taken for a second-rate actor, but the ceremonious manner in which he wears his very stiff white cotton *hakama* makes him look like nothing so much as a student-swordsman from the fencing-school of Sakakibara Kenkichi. Indeed, the only part of Beauchamp's body which looks in the least bit normal is the section between his hips and his shoulders.

"Well, how nice of you to call. In this hot weather, too. Come right in." Waverhouse, as usual, plays the host in someone else's home.

"I haven't seen you for a long time, sir," Beauchamp says to him.

"Quite so. Not, I believe, since that Reading Party last spring. Are you still active in that line? Have you again performed the part of a high-class prostitute? You did it very well. I applauded you like mad. Did you notice?"

"Yes, I was much encouraged. Your kind appreciation gave me the strength to carry on until the end."

"When are you having your next meeting?" interjects my master.

"We rest during July and August but we hope to be livening up again in September. Can you suggest anything interesting we might tackle?"

"Well," my master answers half-heartedly.

"Look here, Beauchamp," says Coldmoon suddenly, "Why don't you try my piece?"

"If it's yours, it must be interesting, but what's this piece you've written?"

"A drama," says Coldmoon with all the brass-faced equanimity he could muster. His three companions are dumbfounded, and stare upon him with looks of unanimous wonder.

"A drama! Good for you! A comedy or tragedy?" Beauchamp was the first to recover and find his tongue. With the utmost composure. Coldmoon gives his reply.

"It's neither a comedy nor a tragedy. Since people these days are always fussing about whether a play should be old-style drama or new-style drama, I decided to invent a totally new type and have accordingly written what I call a *haiku*-play."

"What on earth's a *haiku*-play?"

"A play imbued with the spirit of *haiku*." My master and Waverhouse, apparently dazed by the concept of an essentially tiny poem blown out to the length of a play, say nothing, but Beauchamp presses on.

"How do you implement that interesting idea?"

"Well, since the work is of the *haiku* mode, I decided it should not be too lengthy or too viciously clear-cut. It is accordingly a one act play, in fact a single scene."

"I understand."

"Let me first describe the setting. It must, of course, be very simple. I envisage one big willow in the center of the stage. From its trunk a single branch extends stage-right. And on that branch there's a crow."

"Won't the crow fly off?" says my master worriedly, as if talking to himself.

"That's no problem. One just ties the crow's leg to the branch with a stoutish bit of string. Now, underneath the branch there's a wooden bathtub. And in the bathtub, sitting sideways, there's a beautiful woman washing herself with a cotton towel."

"That's a bit decadent. Besides, who could you get to play the woman?" asks Waverhouse.

"Again, no problem. Just hire a model from an art school."

"The Metropolitan Police Bureau will undoubtedly prove sticky." My master's worriment is not allayed.

"But it ought to be all right so long as one doesn't present this work of art as some form of show. If this were the sort of thing that the police get sticky about, it would be impossible ever to draw from the nude."

"But nude models are provided for students to study, not just to stare at."

"If you scholars, the intellectual cream of Japan, remain so straight-laced in your ancient bigotry, there's no real hope for the future of Japan. What's the distinction between painting and drama? Are they not both arts?" Coldmoon, very evidently enjoying himself, lashes out at the prudery of his listeners.

"Well, let's leave all that for the moment," says Beauchamp, "but tell us how your play proceeds." He may not intend to use the play, but he clearly wants to know how that promising opening scene will be developed.

"Enter the *haiku*-poet Takahama Kyoshi. He advances along the ramp leading to the stage carrying a walking stick and wearing a white pith-helmet. Under his silk-gauze surcoat, his white kimono, patterned with colored splashes, is tucked up at the back, and he wears shoes in the Western style. He is thus costumed to look like a contractor of Army supplies but, being a *haiku*-poet, he must walk in a leisurely manner looking as though deeply absorbed in the composition of a poem. When he reaches the main stage, he notices first the willow tree and then the light-skinned lady in her bath. Startled, he looks up and sees the crow peering down at her from its long branch. At this point the poet strikes a pose, which should be held for at least fifty seconds, to indicate how deeply he is moved by the refined *haiku*-like effect of the scene before him. Then in a deep resonant voice he declaims:

"A crow
Is in love
With a woman in a bath"

As soon as the last word has been spoken, the clappers are cracked and the curtain falls. Well now, what do you think of it? Don't you like it? I need hardly say that any sensible man would rather play the part of a *haiku*-poet than that of a high-class tart."

Beauchamp, however, looks undecided and comments with a serious face, "It seems too short. I think it needs a little more action, something that will add real human interest."

Waverhouse, who has so far been keeping comparatively quiet, can hardly be expected indefinitely to pass up such a splendid opportunity for the display of his peculiar talents. "So that wee bit of a thing is what you call a *haiku*-play? Quite awful! Ueda Bin is constantly pointing out in his essays and articles that the spirit of *haiku*, as also indeed the comic spirit, lacks constructive positivism. He argues that they undermine the morals and hence the morale of the Japanese nation. And, as one would expect, whatever Bin points out is very much to the point. He'd have you laughed out of town if you dared risk staging such an artsy-craftsy bit of rubbish. In any case, it's all so uncleancut that no one could tell whether it's meant to be straight theater or burlesque. A thing so indeterminate could, in fact, be anything. Forgive me that I take the liberty of saying so, my dear Coldmoon, but I really do think you'd do better to stay in your laboratory and limit your creativity to the grinding of glass balls. You could, I'm sure, write hundreds of such plays but, since they could achieve nothing but the ruin of our nation, what would be the point?"

Coldmoon looks slightly huffed. "Do you think its effect is as demoralizing as all that? Myself, I think it's constructive, positivist, definitely yea-saying." He is seeking to vindicate something too unimportant to merit vindication. "The point is that Kyoshi actually makes the crow fall in love with the woman. His lines having that effect are, I consider, an affirmation of life, and that, I think, is very positivist."

"Now that," says Waverhouse, "is a totally new approach. A novel concept casting fresh light upon dramatic theory. We must listen with the deepest attention."

"As a bachelor of science, such an idea as that of a crow falling in love with a woman strikes me as illogical."

"Quite so."

"But this illogicality is expressed with such consummate artistry that it does not seem in the least illogical to the audience. The effect of great dramatic artistry is, in fact, to impose upon the listener a willing suspension of disbelief."

"I doubt it," says my master in tones of the deepest dubiety, but Coldmoon pays him no heed.

"You ask why the unreasonable should not sound unreasonable? Well, when I have given the psychological explanation, you will understand why. Of course, the emotion of being in love, or of not being in love can only be experienced by the poet. It has nothing whatsoever to do with the crow. Similarly, the concept of a crow in love is not a concept likely to cross the mind of a crow. In short, it is the poet himself who is in love with the woman. The moment Kyoshi clapped eyes on her he must have fallen head over heels in love. He then sees the crow sitting immobile on the branch and staring down at her. Being himself smitten with love for the lady, he assumes that the crow is similarly moved. He is, of course, mistaken, but nevertheless, indeed for that very reason, the basic idea of the play is not simply literary, but positivist as well. I would in particular suggest that the manner in which the poet, while still contriving himself to appear objective and heart-free, transposes his own sentiments to become crow-sentiments is indisputably yea-saying and positivist. I ask you, gentlemen, am I not right?"

"It's a well-turned argument," says Waverhouse, "but I bet it would leave Kyoshi, if he ever heard it, distinctly taken aback. I accept that your exposition of the play is positivist but, if the play were to be staged, the audience reaction would undoubtedly be negative. Don't you agree, Beauchamp?"

"Yes, I confess I think it's a little too negative." Beauchamp confesses with due critical gravity.

My master seems to think things have gone far enough and, to ease the pressure upon his favorite disciple, he seeks to lead the conversation away from Coldmoon's ill-received venture into the literary field. "But tell me, Beauchamp," he says, "have you perhaps written any new masterpieces recently?"

"Nothing really worth showing you, but I am, in fact, thinking of publishing a collection of them. Luckily, I chance to have the manuscript with me, and I'd welcome your opinion of these trifles I've composed." He thereupon produced from his breast a package wrapped in a cloth of purple crepe. Loosening the material, he carefully extracted a notebook some fifty or sixty pages thick which he proceeded to deposit, reverently, before my master. My master assumes his most magisterial mien and then, with a grave "Allow me," opens the book. There, on the first page, stands an inscription:

Dedicated
To the frail Opula

My master stared at the page, wordless and with an enigmatic expression on his face, for such a long time that Waverhouse peered across from beside him.

"What have we here? New-style poetry? Aha! Already dedicated! How splendid of you, Beauchamp," he says with all the enthusiasm of a hound on the scent, "to come out bang with so bold a dedication. To, if my eyes do not deceive me, a certain Opula?"

My master, now looking more puzzled than enigmatic, turns to the poet. "My dear Beauchamp," he says, "this Opula, is she a real person?"

"Oh yes indeed. She's one of the young ladies whom I invited to our last Reading Party, the one where Waverhouse so generously applauded me. She lives, in fact, in this neighborhood. Actually, I called at her home on my way here but learnt, to my sorrow, that she's been away since last month. I gather that the whole family is spending the summer at Oiso." Beauchamp looks peculiarly solemn as, with corroborative detail, he affirms the reality of his dedication.

"Come now, Sneaze, don't go pulling a long face like that. This is the twentieth century and you'd best get used to it. Let's get down to considering the masterpiece. First of all, Beauchamp, this dedication seems a bit of a bosh shot. What do you mean by 'frail'?"

"Well, I meant 'frail' in the romantic sense, to convey the idea of a person infinitely delicate, infinitely refined and ethereal."

"Did you now. Well, the word can, of course, be so used but it does have other, coarser connotations. Especially if it were read as an adjectival noun, you could be thought to be calling her some sort of franion. So if I were you, I'd rephrase it."

"Could you suggest how? I'd like it to be unmisinterpretably poetic."

"Well, I think I'd say something like 'Dedicated to all that's frail beneath the nares of Opula.' It wouldn't involve much change in wording, but yet it makes an enormous difference in the feeling."

"I see," says Beauchamp. While it is quite clear that he doesn't understand the balderdash proposed by Waverhouse, he is trying hard to look as though he had grasped, considered, and accepted it.

My master, who has been sitting silently, turns the first page and begins to read aloud from the opening section.

> "In the fragrance of that incense which I burn.
> When I am weary, seemingly
> Your soul trails in the smoky twist and turn
> Of love requited. Woe, ah woe is me,
> Who in a world as bitter as is this
> Must in a mist of useless yearning yearn
> For the sweet fire of your impassioned kiss.

"This, I'm afraid," he says with a sigh, "is a bit beyond me," and he passes the notebook along to Waverhouse.

"The effect is strained, the imagery too heightened," says Waverhouse passing it on to Coldmoon.

"I . . . s . . . e . . . e," says Coldmoon, and returns it to the author.

"It's only natural that you should fail to understand it." Beauchamp leaps to his own defense. "In the last ten years the world of poetry has advanced and altered out of all recognition. Modern poetry is not easy. You can't understand it if you do no more than glance through it in bed or while you're waiting at a railway station. More often than not, modern poets are unable to answer even the simplest questions about their own work. Such poets write by direct inspiration, and are not to be held responsible for more than the writing. Annotation, critical commentary, and exegesis, all these may be left to the scholars. We poets are not to be bothered with such trivia. Only the other day some fellow with a name like Sōseki published a short story entitled 'A Single Night.' But it's so vague that no one could make head or tail of it. I eventually got hold of the man and questioned him very seriously about the real meaning of his story. He not only refused to give any explanation, but even implied that, if the story happened in fact to have any meaning at all, he couldn't care less. His attitude was, I think, typical of a modern poet."

"He may be a poet, but he sounds, doesn't he, downright odd," observes my master.

"He's a fool." Waverhouse demolishes this Sōseki in one curt breath.

Beauchamp, however, has by no means finished defending the merits of his own daft poem. "Nobody in our poetry group is in any way associated with this Sōseki fellow, and it would be unreasonable if you gentlemen were to condemn my poems by reason of some such imagined association. I took great pains with the construction of this work, and I would like in particular to draw your attention to my telling contrast of this bitter world with the sweetness of a kiss."

"The pains you must have taken," says my master somewhat ambiguously, "have not gone unremarked."

"Indeed," says Waverhouse, "the skill with which you have made 'bitter' and 'sweet' reflect each other is as interesting as if you had spiced each syllable of a *haiku* with seventeen different peppery tastes. The saying speaks of only seven such peppery tangs but, so tasteful, Beauchamp, is the concoction you've cooked up, that no saying is sufficient to say how inimitable it is, and how totally lost I am in admiration of your art." Rather unkindly, Waverhouse diverts himself at the expense of an honest man. Possibly for that reason, my master suddenly got to his feet and went off into his study. Possibly not, for he quickly re-emerged with a piece of paper in his hand.

"Now that we've considered Coldmoon's play and Beauchamp's poem, perhaps you will grant me the boon of your expert comments on this little thing here that I've written." My master looks as if he means what he says to be taken seriously. If so, he is to be immediately disappointed.

"If it's that epitaph thing for Mr. the-late and-sainted Natural Man, I've heard it twice already. If not thrice," says Waverhouse dismissingly.

"For heaven's sake, Waverhouse, why don't you just pipe down. Now, Beauchamp, I'd like you to understand that this is not an example of my best and serious work. I wrote it just for fun, so I'm not especially proud of it. But let's just see if you like it."

"I'd be delighted to hear it."

"You too, Coldmoon. Since you're here, you might as well listen."

"Of course, but it's not long, is it?"

"Very short. I doubt," says my master quite untruthfully, "whether it contains as many as three score words and ten," whereupon, giving no opportunity for further interruptions, he launches out upon a recital of his homespun master-work.

"'The Spirit of Japan,' cries Japanese man;
'Long may it live,' cries he
But his cry breaks off in that kind of cough
Which comes from the soul's T.B."

"What a magnificient opening," burbles Coldmoon with real enthusiasm. "The theme rises before one, immediate, undodgeable, and imposing, like a mountain!"

"'The Spirit of Japan,' scream the papers,
Pickpockets scream it too:
In one great jump the Japanese Spirit
Crosses the ocean blue
And is lectured upon in England,
While a play on this staggering theme
Is a huge success on the German stage.
A huge success? A scream!"

"Splendid," says Waverhouse, letting his head fall backwards in token of his approbation. "It's even better than that epiphanic epitaph."

"Admiral Tōgō has the Japanese Spirit,
So has the man in the street:
Fish shop managers, swindlers, murderers,
None would be complete,
None would be the men they are,
None would be a man
If he wasn't wrapped up like a tuppenny cup
In the Spirit of Japan"

"Please," breathes Coldmoon, "please do mention that Coldmoon has it too."

"But if you ask what this Spirit is
They give that cough and say
'The Spirit of Japan is the Japanese Spirit,'
Then they walk away
And when they've walked ten yards or so
They clear their throats of phlegm,

And that clearing sound is the Japanese Spirit
Manifest in them."

"Oh I like that," says Waverhouse, "that's a very well-turned phrase. Sneaze, you've got talent, real literary talent. And the next stanza?"

"Is the Spirit of Japan triangular?
Is it, do you think, a square?
Why no indeed! As the words themselves
Explicitly declare,
It's an airy, fairy, spiritual thing
And things that close to God
Can't be defined in a formula
Or measured with a measuring-rod."

"It's certainly an interesting composition and most unusual in that, defying tradition, it has a strong didactic element. But don't you think it contains too many Spirits of Japan. One can have," says Beauchamp mildly, "too much of the best of things."

"A good point. I agree." Waverhouse chips in yet again with two-pennyworth of tar.

"There's not one man in the whole of Japan
Who has not used the phrase,
But I have not met one user yet
Who knows what it conveys.
The Spirit of Japan, the Japanese Spirit,
Could it conceivably be
Nothing but another of those long-nosed goblins
Only the mad can see?"

My master comes to the end of his poem and, believing it pregnant with eminently debatable material, sits back in expectation of an avalanche of comment. However, though the piece is undoubtedly that masterpiece for which the anthologists have been waiting, its endless Western form and its lack of clear meaning have resulted in the present audience not realizing that the recitation is over. They, accordingly, just sit there. For a long time. Eventually, no more verses being vouchsafed them, Coldmoon ventures "Is that all?"

My master answers with a noncommittal, I thought falsely carefree, kind of throaty grunt.

Very much contrary to my own expectations, Waverhouse failed to rise to the occasion with one of his usual flights of fantastication.

Instead, after a brief interval, he turned to my master and said, "How about collecting some of your shorter pieces into a book? Then you, too, could dedicate it to someone."

"How about to you?" my master flippantly suggests.

"Not on your life," says Waverhouse very firmly. He takes out the scissors which he had earlier analyzed for the benefit of Mrs. Sneaze and begins clipping away at his fingernails.

Coldmoon turns to Beauchamp and, somewhat cautiously, enquires, "Are you closely acquainted with Miss Opula Goldfield?"

"After I invited her to our Reading Party last spring, we became friends and we now see quite a lot of each other. Whenever I'm with her I feel, as it were, inspired, and even after we've parted, I still feel, at least for quite a time, such a flame alight within me that poems, both in the traditional forms and in the modern style, come singing up like steam from a kettle. I believe that this little collection contains so high a proportion of love poems precisely because I am so deeply stirred by women and, in particular, by her. The only way I know by which to express my sincere gratitude is by dedicating this book to the source of its inspiration. I stand at the end of a long tradition inasmuch as, since time immemorial, no poet wrote fine poetry save under the inspiration of some deeply cherished woman."

"Is that indeed so?" says Coldmoon as though he had just learnt a fact of imponderable gravity. But deep behind the sober skin of his face I could see him laughing at the folly of his friend.

Even this gathering of gasbags cannot wheeze on forever, and the pressure of their conversation is now fast whimpering down toward exhaustion. Being under no obligation to listen all day long to their endless blather, their carping and flapdoodle, I excused myself and went out into the garden in search of a praying mantis.

The sun is going down. Its reddened light, filtered through the green foliage of a sultan's parasol, flecks the ground in patches. High up on the trunk of the tree, cicadas are singing their hearts out. Tonight, perhaps, a little rain may fall.

IV

I HAVE, of late, taken to taking exercise. To those who may sneer at me saying, "What sauce, a mere cat taking exercise indeed!" I would like to address you with the few following words. It was not until recently that human beings, previously content to regard eating and sleeping as their only purposes in life, began to grasp the point of taking exercise. Let all mankind remember in what self-complacent idleness they used to pass their days; how passionately they once believed that impassivity of mind and body were the signs of a noble soul, and that the honor of a nobleman resided in his ability to do nothing more strenuous than to plant his bum on a cushion that there it might, in comfort, rot away. It is only recently that, like some infectious disease brought from the West to this pure land of the gods, a stream of silly injunctions has been sprayed upon us to take exercise, to gulp milk, to shower ourselves with freezing water, to plonk ourselves in the sea, and, in the summertime, to sequester ourselves in the mountains on a diet, allegedly healthy, of nothing more solid than mist. Such importations seem to me about as salubrious as the black plague, tuberculosis, and that very Western malady, neurasthenia. However, since I am only one year old, born as I was last year, I cannot personally testify as to the state of affairs when human beings here first began to suffer from these sicknesses. It happened at a time before I came to float along in this vale of tears. Nevertheless, one may fairly equate a cat's one year, with ten for human beings: and though our span of life is two or three times shorter than theirs, a cat may still therein achieve full feline self-development. It follows that any evaluation of a cat's life and a man's life by reference to a common time-scale must result in grievous error.

That point is surely proven by the fact that I, who am but a year and a few months old, possess the discernment to make such an analysis. In contrast, the third daughter of my master, whom I understand to be already in her third year, is lamentably backward, a laggard in all learning, a slow-coach in development. Her accomplishments are limited. She yowls, she mucks her bed and she sucks milk from her mother. Compared with someone like myself who am distressed by the state of the world and deplore the degeneracy of the age, that girl is truly infantile. It is consequently not in the least surprising that I should have stored away, deep within my mind, the entire history of taking exercise, of sea-bathing, and of going away for a change of air. If there should be anyone surprised at a thing so trifling as this vast extent of my knowledge, it could only be another of those handicapped humans, those stumbling creatures whom heaven has retarded with the gift of no more than a measly couple of legs. From time immemorial man has been a slow-coach, so it is only very recently that such inveterate sluggards have begun to recommend the virtues of exercise, and, as if the notion were their own incredible discovery, to babble endlessly of the benefits of bobbing about in the sea. *Per contra*, I was aware of such things in my prenatal condition, and to fully realize the benisons of brine one needs but walk on a beach.

Precisely how many fish are frolicking about in so vast a volume of water, I would not care to guess; however it is certain that not a single specimen has ever fallen so sick as to need the attentions of a doctor. There they all are, swimming about in the best of health. When a fish does catch some illness, its body first becomes helpless. But let it be remembered that the death of a fish is described in Japanese as an ascension. Birds, we say, drop dead, become mere fallen things. Men are simply said to have kicked the bucket. But fish, I stress, ascend. Now, just ask anyone who's journeyed overseas, anyone who's crossed the Indian Ocean, whether they've seen a dying fish. Of course they haven't. And no wonder. However often you might plow back and forth across that endless waste of water, never would you see afloat upon its waves one single fish that had just given up its last breath. Given up, I should perhaps fish-pertinently say, its last seawater gulp. Had you assiduously searched since time began, were you now to go on steaming day and night up and down that wide and boundless expanse of water, not one solitary fish would ever be seen to ascend. Since fish do not ascend, their undying strength, their hardihood, indeed their deathlessness, is easily deduced.

How comes it, then, that fish should be so death defyingly hardy? Here once again, mankind can give no answer. But the answer, as I shortly shall disclose, is simplicity itself. The answer is that fish are hardy because they incessantly bathe in the sea, because they swill saltwater. It's as simple as that. Now, since the benefits of sea bathing are so evidenced by fish, surely it must follow that the practice would be beneficial to mankind. Lo and behold, in 1750 a certain Dr. Richard Russell came out with the humanly exaggerated pronouncement that anyone who jumped into the sea at Brighton would find that all his various diseases would be cured on the spot. Is it not laughable that it took mankind so long to arrive at so simple a conclusion? Even we cats, when the time is ripe, intend to go down to the seaside, to some place like Kaniakura. But *now* is not the time. There is always a right time for everything. Just as the Japanese people before the Restoration of the Emperor, both lived and died without benefit of sea bathing, so cats today have not yet reached the appropriate stage for leaping naked into the briny deep. Timing is all important, and a hurried job is a job half-botched. Consequently, since no cat taken today to be drowned in some shrine's canal will ever come home safely, it would be most imprudent indeed for me to go plunging in. Until by the laws of evolution we cats have developed the characteristics needed to resist the rage of overwhelming waves; until, in fact, a dead cat can be said not to have died but, like fish, to have ascended, until that happy day, I won't go near the water.

Postponing my sea bathing to some later date, I have anyway decided to make a start on some sort of exercise. In this enlightened twentieth century, any failure to take exercise is likely to be interpreted as a sign of pauperdom. Which would be bad for one's reputation. If you don't take exercise, you will be judged incapable of taking it by reason of an inability to afford either the time or the expense, or both. It is thus no longer a simple question of not taking exercise. In olden times those who did take physical exercise, persons such as the riffraff of male servants in an upper-class household, were regarded with a proper scorn. But nowadays it is precisely those who do not take some form of physical exercise at whom the world turns up its nose. The world's evaluations of an individual's social worth, like the slits in my eyeballs, change with time and circumstance. In point of fact my pupil-slits vary but modestly between broad and narrow, but mankind's value judgements turn somersaults and cartwheels for no conceivable reason. Still, now that I come to think of it, there may perhaps be sense in such peculiar topsy-turvydom. For just as there are two ends to every string, there are two sides to every question. Perhaps in its extreme adaptability mankind has found a way to make apparent opposites come out with identical meanings. Thus, if one takes the symbols meaning "idea" and turns them upside-down, one finds oneself with the symbols meaning "plan." Charming, isn't it? A similar conception can be seen at work in the Japanese practice of viewing the so-called Bridge of Heaven by bending down and peering backward between one's parted legs. Seen thus, the sea and its reflection of the pine-trees on the sandbar appear like true pines reared into the sky, whereas the true pines and the sky appear as trees reflected upon the water. It is indeed a remarkable effect. Even the works of Shakespeare might be more thoroughly appreciated if they were re-examined from unorthodox positions. Someone, once in a while, should take a good long look at Hamlet through his legs. Presented upside-down, that tragedy might earn the bald remark "Ye Gods, this play is bad." How else, except by standing on their heads, can the critics in our literary world make any progress?

Considered against that background, it is hardly surprising that those who once spoke ill of physical exercise should suddenly go crazy about sports, that even women should walk about on the streets with tennis rackets clutched in their hands. So far as I'm concerned, I have no criticisms to offer on any of these matters provided no misguided human being has the effrontery to criticize a cat for the sauciness of its interest in taking physical exercise. That said, perhaps I ought to satisfy your probable curiosity, to offer some explanation of the exercise I take.

As you are aware, it is my misfortune that my paws cannot grasp any kind of implement. I am consequently unable to pick up balls or to grip such things as bats and bloody rackets. Moreover, even could I handle them, I cannot buy them for I don't have any money. For these two reasons, I have chosen such kinds of exercise as cost nothing and need no special equipment. I suppose you might consequently assume that my idea of exercise must be limited to merely walking about, or to running away like Rickshaw Blacky with a slice of stolen tuna fish jammed in my jaws. But to swagger about on the ground by the mere mechanical movement of four legs and in strict obedience to the laws of gravity, that is all too simple; simple and therefore totally uninteresting. There is indeed one kind of exercise called "movements" in which my master occasionally indulges. But it is, in fact, no more than its name suggests, a matter of mere mechanical movements. Which, to my mind, is a desecration of the sanctity of exercise. Of course, if some true incentive is involved, I do not always scorn the simplicities of mere movement. For example, I get real pleasure from racing for dried bonito and from going on salmon hunts. But those activities are related to specific objectives. If the incentives are removed, the activities become mere waste of spirit, ashes in the mouth.

When there is no prize to provide the needed stimulus, then my preference is for exercises that demand some kind of genuine skill. I have devised a variety of exercises satisfying that requirement. One is jumping from the kitchen-eaves up and onto the main roof of the house. Another is standing with all four legs together on the plum-blossom shape of the narrow tile at the very top of the roof. An especially difficult feat is walking along the laundry pole, which usually proves a failure because my claws can't penetrate the hard and slippery surface of bamboo. Perhaps my most interesting exercise is jumping suddenly from behind onto the children's backs. However, unless I am extremely careful about the method and timing of such exploits, the penalties involved can be uncommonly painful. Indeed, I derive so very little pleasure from having my head stuffed deep in a paperbag that I only risk this splendid exercise three times, at most, in a month. One must also recognize the disadvantage that any success in this form of exercise depends entirely, and unsatisfactorily, upon the availability of some human partner. Yet another form of exercise is clawing the covers of books. In this case two kinds of snags arise. First, there is the invariable drubbing administered by my master whenever he catches me at it. Secondly, though the exercise undoubtedly develops a certain dexterity of finger, it does nothing at all for the remaining muscles of my body.

I have so far only described those comparatively crude activities which I would choose to call old-fashioned exercises. However, my newfangled sports include a few of the most exquisite refinement. First among such sports comes hunting the praying mantis, which is only less noble than hunting rats by the lesser degree of its dangers. The open season, with the quarry in superb condition, runs from high mid-summer until early in the autumn. The hunting rules are as follows. First one goes to the garden to flush one's quarry out. Given the proper weather, one may expect to find at least a brace of them browsing in the open. Next, having chosen one particular mantis, a sudden dash, a regular windslicer, is made towards the quarry. The mantis, thus alerted to its danger, rears its head and readies for the fray. For all its puniness, the mantis, at least until it realizes the hopelessness of any further resistance, is a plucky little beast, and its fatuous readiness to make a fight of it adds zest to the fun. I, accordingly, open by patting him lightly on the head with the flat of my right, front paw. The head is soft and is generally cocked to one side. At this point, the expression on the quarry's face adds singular edge to my pleasure. The beast is clearly puzzled. I immediately spring around behind him and, from that new position, lightly claw at his wings. These wings are normally folded carefully close but, if clawed with exactly the right degree of scratchiness, they can be harrowed loose, and from beneath the beast a disheveled flurry of underwear, a yellowish tatter of stuff like thin transparent paper, droops flimsy into view. Oh, what an elegant fellow! Tricked out in double lined clothing even at the height of summer! And may it bring him luck!

Invariably, at this moment the mantis twists his long, green neck around to face me. Then, turning his whole body in the same direction, sometimes he defiantly advances and sometimes simply stands there like some dwarf-annoyed giraffe. If he remains transfixed in that latter attitude I shall be cheated of my exercise. Accordingly, having given him every chance to take the initiative, I then give him a stimulating smack. If the mantis happens to have the least intelligence, he will now attempt escape, but some, ill-schooled and of a barbarous ferocity, will persevere in derring-do, even to the point of launching an attack. When dealing with such savages, I carefully calculate the precisely proper moment to strike back and then, suddenly, deliver a really heavy blow as he advances at me. I would say that on such occasions the beast is usually batted sideways for a distance of between two and three feet. However, if my quarry displays a civilized recognition of its plight and drags away in pitiful retreat, then I am moved to pity. Off I go, racing along like a flying bird, two or three times around a convenient tree in the garden. Yet, when I return I rarely find that the mantis has managed to crawl away more than five or six inches. Now conscious of my power, he has no stomach for continued battle. He staggers away, tottering first left and then right in dazed attempts to escape me. Matching his movements, this way and that, I harry him back and forth. Sometimes in his ultimate despair, he makes the ultimate effort of fluttering his wings. It is the nature of the wings, as of the neck, of a praying mantis to be exceedingly long and exceedingly slender. Indeed, I understand that these wings are entirely ornamental and are of no more practical use to a praying mantis than are, to a human being, the English, French, and

German languages. It follows that, however ultimate his effort, however grand his pitiful remonstrance, no fluttering of those ineffectual wings can have on me the very least effect. One speaks of his effort but, in reality, there's nothing so purposeful about it. One should not use a word so energetic to describe the shambling totter, torn wings a-drag along the ground, of this pathetic creature. For I confess that I really do feel a wee mite sorry for my miserable antagonist. However, my need for physical exercise outweighs all other considerations, and into every life, even that of a mantis, a little rain must fall. My conscience salved, I dart beyond him from behind, twist, and so confront him. In his condition, having committed himself to forward movement, he has no choice but to keep coming. Equally and naturally, faced with such aggression, I have no choice but to give him a whack on the nose. My foe collapses, falls down flat with his wings spread out on either side. Extending a front paw, I hold him down in that squashed-face position whilst I take a little breather. Myself at ease again, I let the wretched perisher get up and struggle on. Then, again, I catch him. My strategy is based, of course, on the classic Chinese methods of Kung Ming, that military marvel of the Shu Kingdom in the third century, who, seven times in succession, first caught, then freed, his enemy. For maybe thirty minutes I pursue that classic alternation. Eventually, the mantis abandons hope and, even when free to drag himself away, lies there motionless. I lift him lightly in my mouth and spit him out again. Since, even then, he just lies loafing on the ground, I prod him with my paw. Under that stimulus the mantis hauls himself erect and makes a kind of clumsy leap for freedom. So once again, down comes my quick immobilizing paw. In the end, bored by the repetitions, I conclude my exercise by eating him. Incidentally, for the benefit of those who've never munched mantis, I would report that the taste is rather unpleasant and I have been led to understand that the nutrimental value is negligible.

Next to mantis hunting, my favorite sport is cricketing. In exactly the same way as, among the varieties of man, one can find oily creatures, cheeky chaps, and chatterboxes, so among the species of cicada there are oily cicadas, pert cicadas, and chatterboxes, too. The oily ones are not much fun, being in fact too greasily importunate. The cheeky chaps annoy one, being a sight too uppity. And I am consequently most interested in silencing the chatterboxes. They do not appear until the end of summer. There comes a day when, unexpectedly, the first cool wind of autumn blows through the gaps torn in the sleeves of one's kimono, making one feel a sniffling cold is surely on its way. Just about then the chatterboxes, tails cocked up behind them, start their singing din. And a deal of din they make. So much noise, in fact, one could almost believe they have no purposes in life except to chatter at the top of their rowdy voices and to be caught by cats. It is in early autumn that I catch them, and cricketing is what I call this form of taking exercise. I must first emphasize that in hunting for live chatterboxes there's no point in questing on the ground. Any that are on the ground will invariably be found half-buried under ants. Those which I stalk are not the perished relics at the mercy of the pismires, but those alive and chattering away in the branches of tall trees. Whilst I am on this general subject, it occurs to me to query whether these noisy creatures are shouting o-shi-i-tsuku-tsuku or tsuku-tsuku-o-shi-i. I suspect there could be real significance in the difference, a difference no doubt capable of casting much-needed light on the whole field of cicada studies. It is a topic that cries out for the exercise of the particular gifts of humankind. Indeed, man's natural proclivity for this kind of investigation is the sole characteristic by which he is superior to a cat. Which is, of course, precisely the reason that human beings, proud of their singularity, attach so much importance to such pettifogging points. Consequently, if men can't offer an immediate answer, I suggest that for all our sakes they think the matter over very carefully. Of course, so far as my cricketing is concerned, the outcome of their ponderings, whatever that may be, could hardly matter less.

Now, with respect to the practice of cricketing, all I have to do is to climb toward the source of noise and catch the so-called singer while he is totally absorbed in his so-called act of singing. Superficially the simplest of all exercises, it is in fact quite difficult. Since I have four legs, I do not regard myself as inferior to any other animal in the matter of moving about on the surface of this planet. Indeed, by mathematical deduction of comparative mobility by reference to the number of legs involved, the average cat would seem to be at least twice as nimble as the average man. But when it comes to climbing trees, there are many animals more dexterous than the cat. Apart from monkeys, those absolute professionals, one is bound to concede that men, descended as they are from tree-conditioned apes, sometimes display a truly formidable skill at climbing trees. I hasten to add that, since climbing trees is unnatural, being a direct defiance of the laws of gravity, I cannot consider a failure to shine in such unreasonable activity as in any way shameful. But it is a disadvantage to a cricketer. Luckily, I happen to possess this useful set of claws which makes it possible for me, however clumsily, to get up trees, but it's not as easy as you might think. What's more, a chatterbox, unlike the pitiable mantis, really can fly. And once it takes to the wing, all my painful climbing profits me nothing. Indeed a dismal outcome. It has, moreover, the dangerous and ugly habit of pissing in one's eye. One can't complain of its taking flight, but such filthy micturition is hardly playing the game. What psychological pressure induces this incontinence at the moment immediately prior to an act of aviation? Is it, perhaps, that the thought of flying is too unbearable to bear? Or is it simply that a pissed-on prowler is so shockedly surprised that his intended prey gains ample time to escape? If that latter hypothesis is correct, this urinating insect falls into a common category with the ink-ejecting squid, with the tattoo-flashing brawler in the alleyways of Tokyo, and with my poor old idiot master spouting clouds of protective Latin. Again, I would stress that this question of urination at take-off is no mere piddling matter, but an issue of possibly fundamental relevance to the study of cicadas. The problem certainly merits the detailed study of a doctoral dissertation. But I digress too far. Let us return to the practicalities of cricketing.

The spot where the cicadas most thickly concentrate (if you object to my use in this context of the word "concentrate," then I was originally prepared to substitute the word "assemble," but I find that latter word so banal that I have decided to stick to "concentrate") is the green paulownia, the so-called Sultan's Parasol which, I am reliably informed, is known to the Chinese as the Chinese Parasol. Now, the green paulownia is densely foliaged and each of its leaves is as big as a big, round fan. It is consequently hard to see the branches where my quarry lurks; a fact which constitutes another hazard for the keen cricketer. I sometimes think that it was with my predicament in mind that the author of that popular song wrote those words of yearning for "one, though heard, invisible." In any event, the best I can do is to work my way toward that place from which the song appears to emanate.

About six feet up from the ground, the trunks of all green paulownias fork conveniently into two. Within that crotch I rest from the exertion of my initial climb and, peering upward between the backs of the leaves, try to see where the chatterboxes are. Sometimes, however, before I even get to the crotch, one or two of my potential victims grow alarmed and, with a curious rustling sound, impatiently take flight. Then I've really had it. For, judging them by their readiness to be led, and their mindless passion for conformity of conduct, these chatterboxes are no less imbecile than men. As soon as the first one flies away, all the others follow. There are occasions, therefore, when by the time I've reached the fork, the whole tree stands deserted in a dead dispiriting silence. On one such day I'd climbed up to the fork only to find, however hard I peered and however much I pricked my ears, no faintest sign or sound of a chatterbox. Deciding it would be too much of a bore to start all over again in some other tree, I concluded that the sensible thing would be to stay where I was, enjoy the relaxation and wait for a second chance when the refugees returned. Before long I grew sleepy, and soon was happily far away in the pleasant land of Nod. My awakening was unpleasant, for I'd fallen thuddingly down onto a flagstone in the garden.

Nevertheless, I usually manage to catch one chatterbox for every tree I climb. It is, alas, an unavoidable characteristic of this sport, one which sadly reduces my interest in it, that, so long as I'm up in the tree, I have to hold my captive in my mouth; for, by the time I've descended and can spit him out on the ground, he is usually dead. However hard I may thereafter play with him and scratch him, he offers no response. The most exquisite moment in cricketing occurs when, after sneaking quietly upon a chatterbox whose whole vibrating being is concentrated upon song, upon the soul-absorbing business of scraping his tail parts in and out of the main shell of his body, suddenly I pounce and my paws clamp down upon him. How piercingly he shrieks, with what a threshing ecstasy of terror he shakes his thin transparent wings in efforts to escape. The sheer speed and intensity of these happenings creates an aesthetic experience impossible to describe. One can only say that the magnificence of its death-throes is the supreme achievement of a cicada's life. Every time I catch a chatterbox I ask, in suitably pressing terms, for a demonstration of his thrilling artistry. When tired of his performance, I beg his pardon for the interruption and pop him into my mouth. Occasional virtuosi have been known to continue with their act even after my mouth has closed behind them.

After cricketing, my next most favored form of physical exercise is pine sliding. A detailed explanation would be too much, so I'll offer only the minimum of comment needed for an understanding of this sport. Its name suggests that it is sliding down pine trees, but, in fact, it doesn't. It is, indeed, another form of climbing trees. But whereas when cricketing I climb to catch a chatterbox, when pine sliding I climb purely for the climbing. Ever since Genzaemon warmed the room for laypriest Saimyoji, that one-time Regent at Kamakura, by burning those trees to which Genzaemon in his own happier days had been particularly attached, the pine tree has been not only, as the song about that incident assures us, naturally an evergreen, but also most unnaturally rough-barked to one's touch. Whatever the explanation, there is certainly no tree less slippery than the pine, and no trunk in the world affords a better climbing surface either for hands or for feet. Clearly, when it comes to claws, nothing is more clawable and I can consequently run up a pine trunk in one breath.

Having run up, I run down. Now there are two styles of downward running. One way is to descend, effectively upside-down, with one's head facing the ground; the other is to descend tail-first in the normal attitude for an ascending climb. And which, I would ask you know-it-all human beings, would you suppose is the more difficult style of the two? Being but shallow brained, you probably think that one would find it easier to position one's head so as to lead in the direction of desired movement; you'd be wrong. When you heard me speak of running downward, no doubt you thought immediately of Yoshitsune's headlong horse charge down the cliff at Hiyodori-goe. And I can imagine you thinking to yourself that anything good enough for a human hero like Yoshitsune must be more than sufficient for some unnamed, unknown cat. But such disdain would be entirely misplaced. Just to begin with, do you know how cats' claws grow, their directional positioning in accordance with their function? They are, in fact, retrorsely curved so that, like firemen's hooks, they are peculiarly suited to catching hold of things and drawing them chestward. They are virtually useless for pushing things away. Now, since I am a terrestrial creature, it would be a breach of natural law if, having dashed up a pine tree trunk, I were to remain indefinitely and unsupported at the swaying top of the tree. I would certainly fall down. And, if that fall were nowise checked, the rate of my descent could well prove lethal. Thus, when I take measures to mitigate the potentially disastrous effects of the laws of gravity and nature, I call the consequent process of descent "descending." Though there may seem to be a substantial difference between descending and free falling, it isn't as great as one might fondly imagine; indeed, no more than a single letter's worth. Since I do not care to free all out of a pine tree top, I must find some means to check the natural acceleration of my body. And that's where my claws come in; or rather, out. Being retrorsely curved, all my twenty claws, appropriately extended from my heaven-facing body, provide a gripping power and frictional resistance sufficient to transform the hazards of free fall into the relative safety of descent. Simple, isn't it? But you just try to come down from a pine tree like a wolf on the fold in the headlong Yoshitsune style, and that's not simple at all. Claws are useless. Nothing retards the slithering acceleration of your body's weight, and those who'd hoped thus safely to descend, finish up by plummeting earthward like boulders dropped by rocs. You will, accordingly, appreciate that the headlong descent of Hiyodori-goe was an exceptionally difficult feat, one which only a veritable hero could successfully accomplish. Among cats, probably only I, the Yoshitsune of my kind, can pull it off. I accordingly feel I have earned my right to give a name to this particular sport, and I have chosen "pine sliding."

I cannot conclude these few words on the subject of sport without at least some mention of "going around the fence." My master's garden, rectangular in shape, is on all sides separated from neighboring properties by a bamboo fence about three feet high. The section running parallel to the veranda is some fifty feet long, and the two side-sections are each about half that length. The object of the aforementioned sport is to walk right around the whole property without falling off the thin top edge of the fence. There are times, I confess, when I do topple off, but, when successful, I find such tours of the horizon eminently gratifying. Really, great fun. The fence is supported here and there, and particularly at the corners, by sturdy cedar stakes, fire hardened at each end, on the tops of which I can conveniently take breathers in the course of my circumambulation. I found myself today in really rather good form. Before lunch I managed three successful tours, and on each occasion my performance improved. Naturally, every improvement adds to the fun. I was just about halfway home on my fourth time around when three crows, gliding down from the next-door roof, settled on the fence-top, side-by- side, some six short feet ahead of me. Cheeky bastards! Quite apart from the fact that they're interrupting my exercise, such low-born, ill-bred, rain-guttersnipes have no right whatsoever to come trespassing, indeed seemingly to start squatting, on my fence-property. So I told them, in terms of hissing clarity, to get lost. The nearest crow, turning its head toward me, appears to be grinning like a half-wit. The next one unconcernedly studies my master's garden. And the third continues wiping his filthy beak on a projecting splinter of the fence bamboo. He had all too evidently just finished eating something rather nasty. I stood there balanced on the fence, giving them a civilized three minutes grace to shove off. I've heard that these birds are commonly called Crowmagnons, and they certainly look as daft and primitively barbarous as their uncouth nickname would suggest. Despite my courteous waiting, they neither greeted me nor flew away. Becoming at last inpatient, I began slowly to advance; whereupon the nearest Crowmagnon tentatively stirred his wings. I thought he was at last backing off in face of my power, but all he did was to shift his posture so as to present his arse, rather than his head, toward me. Outright insolence! Conduct unbecoming even a Crow-magnon. Were we on the ground, I would call him to immediate account, but, alas, being as I am engaged upon a passage both strenuous and perilous, I really can't be bothered to be diverted from my purpose by such aboriginal naiseries. On the other hand, I do not greatly care for the idea of being stuck here while a trey of brainless birds waits for whatever impulse will lift them into the air. For one thing, there's my poor tired feet. Those feathered lightweights are used to standing around in such precarious places so that, if my fence-top happens to please them, they might perch here forever. I, on the other hand, am already exhausted. This is my fourth time around today, and this particular exercise is anyway no less tricky than tightrope-walking. At the best of times, each teetering step I take could throw me clean off-balance, which makes it all the more unpardonable that these three blackamoors should loaf here blocking the way. If it comes to the worst, I shall just have to abandon today's exercises and hop down from the fence. It's a bore, of course, but perhaps I might as well hop down now. After all, I am heavily outnumbered by the enemy. Besides, the poor simple things do seem to be strangers in these parts. Their beaks, I notice, are almost affectedly pointed, the sort of savage, stabbing snout that, found amongst his sons, would make its foul possessor the most sharply favored member of a long-nosed goblin's brood. The signs are unmistakable that these Crow-magnon louts will be equally ill-natured. If I start a fight and then, by sheer mischance, happen to lose my footing, the loss of face will be much greater than if I just chose to disengage. Consequently, thinking that it might be prudent to avoid a showdown, I had just decided to hop down when the arse-presenting savage offered me a rudery. “Arseholes,” he observed. His immediate neighbor repeated this coarse remark, while the last one of the trio took the trouble to say it twice. I simply could not overlook behavior so offensive. First and foremost, to allow myself to be grossly insulted in my own garden by these mere crows would reflect adversely upon my good name. Should you object that I do not have a name to be reflected upon, I will amend that sentence to refer to reflections upon my honor. When my honor is involved, cost what it may, I cannot retreat. At this point it occurred to me that a disorderly rabble is often described as a “flock of crows;” so it is just possible that, though they outnumber me three to one, when it comes to the crunch they’ll prove more weak than they look. Thus comforted, thus grimly resolute, I began slowly to advance. The crows, oblivious to my action, seem to be talking among themselves. They *are* exasperating! If only the fence were wider by five or six inches, I’d really give them hell. But as things are, however vehemently vexed I may feel, I can only tiptoe slowly forward to avenge my injured honor. Eventually, I reached a point a bare half-foot away from the nearest bird and was urging myself onward to one last final effort when, all together and as though by prearrangement, the three brutes suddenly flapped their wings and lumbered up to hang a couple of feet above me in the air. The down-draught gusted into my face. Unsportingly surprised, I lost my balance and fell off sideways into the garden.

Kicking myself for permitting such a shameful mishap to occur, I looked up from the ground to find all three marauders safely landed back again where they had perched before. Their three sharp beaks in parallel alignment, they peer down superciliously into my angry eyes. The bloody nerve of them! I responded with a glowering scowl. Which left them quite unmoved. So next I snarled and arched my back. Equally ineffective. Just as the subtlety of symbolic poetry is lost on a materialist, so were the symbols of my anger quite meaningless to the crows. Which, now that I reflect upon the matter, is perfectly understandable. Hitherto, and wrongly, I have been seeking to cope with crows as if they had been cats. Had that been the case, they would by now, most certainly, have reacted. But crows are crows, and what but crow behavior can anyone expect of them? My efforts have, in fact, all been as pointless as the increasingly short-tempered arguments of a businessman trying to budge my master; as pointless as Yoritomo’s gift of a solid silver cat to the unworldly Saigyo; as pointless as the bird shit that these fools and their fool cousins fly over to Ueno to deposit on the statue of poor Sai-o Takamori. Once I have conceived a thought, I waste no time before I act upon it. It were better to give up than to persist in a dialogue with dunces, so I abandoned my endeavors and withdrew to the veranda.

It was time for dinner anyway.

Exercise has merits, but one mustn't overdo it. My whole body felt limp and almost slovenly. What's more I feel horribly hot. We are now at the beginning of autumn, and during my exercise my fur seems to have become saturated with afternoon sunshine. The sweat which oozes from the pores in my skin refuses to drop away, but clings in greasy clots around the roots of every separate hair. My back itches. One can clearly distinguish between itches caused by perspiration and itches caused by creeping fleas. If the site of the itch lies within reach of my mouth, I can bite the cause, and if within reach of my feet, I know precisely how to scratch it. But if the irritation is at the midpoint of my spine, I simply can't get at it. In such a case, one must either frot oneself on the first available human being or scrape one's back against a pine tree's bark. Since men are both vain and stupid, I approach them in a suitably ingratiating manner using, as they would say, "tones that would wheedle a cat." Such are the tones men sometimes use to me, but, seen from my position, the phrase should be "tones by which a cat may be wheedled." Not that it matters. Anyway, human beings being the nitwits that they are, a purring approach to any of them, either male or female, is usually interpreted as proof that I love them, and they consequently let me do as I like, and on occasions, poor dumb creatures, they even stroke my head. Of late, however, just because some kind of parasitic insect, fleas, in fact, have taken to breeding in my fur, even my most tentative approaches to a human being evoke a gross response. I am grabbed by the scruff of the neck and pitched clean out of the room. It seems that this sudden aversion stems from human disgust with those barely visible and totally insignificant insects which I harbor. A heartless and most callous attitude! How can such inconsiderate behavior possibly be justified by the presence in my coat of one or two thousand footling fleas? The answer is, of course, that Article One of those Laws of Love (by which all human creatures regulate their lives) specifically enjoins that "ye shall love one another for so long as it serves thine individual interest."

Now that the human attitude towards me has so completely changed, I cannot exploit manpower to ease my itching, however virulent it may become. I therefore have no choice but to resort to the alternative method of finding relief in scraping myself on pine bark. To that end I was just going down the veranda steps when I realized that even this alternative solution was a silly idea and would not work. The point is that pines secrete an extremely sticky resin which, once it has gummed the ends of my fur together, cannot be loosened even if struck by lightning, or fired upon by the whole Russian Baltic Fleet. What's more, as soon as five hairs stick together, then ten, then thirty hairs get inextricably stuck. I am a dainty cat of candid temperament, and any creature as clinging, poisonous, and vindictive as this tenacious resin is an anathema to me. I cannot stand persons of that kind, and even if one such particular person were the most beautiful cat in the world, let alone a creature loathsome as resin, still I'd be revolted. It is outrageous that my charmingly pale gray coat can be ruined by a substance whose social and evolutionary status is no higher than that of the gummy muck which streams in the cold north wind from the corners of Rickshaw Blacky's eyes. Resin ought to realize the impropriety of its nature, but will, of course, do no such thing. Indeed, the very moment my back makes contact with a pine tree, great clots of resin gather on my fur. To have anything to do with so insensitive, so inconsiderate a creature would not only be beneath my personal dignity, but would be a defilement to anyone in my coat and lineage. I conclude that, however fleasome I may feel, I have no choice but to grin and bear it. Nonetheless, it is extremely disheartening to find that the two standard means of alleviating my discomfort are both unavailable. Unless I can quickly find some other solution, the irritation in my skin, and the thought of gumminess in my mind, will bring me to a nervous breakdown.

Sinking down upon my hind-legs into a thinking posture, I had scarcely begun my search for bright ideas when an illuminating memory flashed upon me. Every so often my scruffy master saunters off out of the house with a cake of soap and a hand towel. When he returns some thirty or forty minutes later, his normally dull complexion, while not exactly glowing, has nevertheless acquired a certain modest liveliness. If such expeditions can confer a sheen of vitality upon that shabby sloven, what wonders they might work upon myself. It is, of course, true that I am already so extremely handsome that improvements, if possible, are hardly necessary, but if by some misfortune I were to fall sick and perish at this very tender age of one year and a few odd months,

I could never forgive myself for allowing so irremediable a loss to be inflicted upon the populace of the world. I believe that the object of my master's sorties is one of those devices invented by mankind as a means of easing the tedium of its existence. Inasmuch as the public bath is an invention of mankind, it can hardly be much use to anyone but, clutching as I am at straws, I might as well investigate the matter. If it's as pointless as I anticipate, nothing would be simpler than to drop my enquiries; but I remain unsure whether human beings are sufficiently broadminded to give a cat, a member of another species, even a chance to investigate the efficacy of an institution devised for human purposes. I cannot imagine that I could be refused entry when nobody dreams of questioning the casual comings and goings of my master, but it would be socially most embarrassing to find myself turned from the door. Prudence suggests the wisdom of reconnaissance and, if I like the look of the place, then I can hop in with a hand towel in my mouth. My plan of action formed, I set off for the public bath at a properly leisurely pace.

As one turns left around the corner from our side street, one may observe a little further up the road an object like an upended bamboo waterpipe puffing thin smoke-fumes straight up into the sky. That fuming finger marks the site of the public bathhouse. I stole in through its back entrance. That style of entry is usually looked down upon as mean-spirited or cowardly, but such criticisms are merely the tedious grumbles spiced with jealousy which one must expect from persons only capable of gaining access by front doors. It is abundantly clear from the records of history that persons of high intelligence invariably launch attacks both suddenly and from the rear. Furthermore, I note from my study of *The Making of a Gentleman* (volume two, chapter one, pages five and six) that a backdoor, like a gentleman's last will and testament, provides the means whereby an individual establishes his true moral excellence. Being a truly twentieth-century cat, I have had included in my education, more than sufficient of such weighty learning, to make it inappropriate for anyone to sneer at my selected mode of entry. Anyway, once I was inside, I found on my immediate left a positive mountain of pine logs cut into eight-inch lengths and, next to it, a heaped-up hill of coal. Some of my readers may wonder what the subtle significance of my careful distinction between a mountain of logs and a mere hill of coal is. There is, in fact, no subtle significance whatsoever. I simply used the two words, "hill" and "mountain," as they should correctly be used. Far from having time to think about literary niceties, I am overwhelmed with pity for the human race which, having regularly dieted on such revolting objects as rice, birds, fish, and even animals, is now apparently reduced to munching lumps of coal. Right in front of me I see an open entrance about six feet wide. I peep through and find everything dead quiet but, from somewhere beyond, there comes a lively buzz of human voices and I deduce that the bath must be where the sound originates. I move forward between the woodpile and the coal heap, turn left and find a glazed window to my right. On the ledge below, a considerable number of small round tubs is piled up into a pyramid. My heart goes out to them, for it must be painfully contrary to a round thing's concept of reality to be constricted within a triangular world. To the south of these piles the sill juts out for a few feet with, as if to welcome me, wooden boarding on it. Since the board is roughly three feet up from the ground, it is, from my point of view, at an ideal hopping height. "All right," I said to myself, and, as I flew up nimbly to the board, the public bath, like something dangled, suddenly appeared beneath my very nose.

There is nothing in the world more pleasant than to eat something one has never yet eaten, or to see something one has never seen before. If my readers, like my master, spend thirty or forty minutes on three days of every passing week in the world of the public bath, then of course that world can offer them few surprises: but if, like me, they have never seen that spectacle, they should make immediate arrangements to do so. Don't worry about the deathbed of your parents, but at all costs do not miss the grand show of the public bath. The world is wide, but in my opinion it has no sight more startlingly remarkable to offer.

Wherein, you ask, resides its crass spectacularity? Well, it is so variously spectacular that I hesitate to particularize. First of all, the human beings vociferously swarming about beyond the window-glass are all stark naked. As totally unclothed as Formosan aborigines. Primeval Adams still prancing about in this twentieth century. I am moved by so much nudity to preface my comments with a history of clothing, but it would take so long that I will spare my readers any rehash of the learned observations of Herr Doktor Diogenes Teufelsdrockh in his monumental study on this subject (*Die Kleider, Werden und Wizken*) and simply refer them to a slightly less learned commentary on that work, Mr. Thomas Carlyle's *Sartor Resartus*. The essential fact remains that the clothes are the man, that the ungarbed man is nothing. Skipping centuries of sartorial civilization, indeed a tautological phrase, I would remind my readers that Beau Nash, in the heyday of his social regulation of eighteenth-century Bath, a royally patronized hotsprings spa in the west of England, established the inflexible rule that men and women submerging themselves in those salutary waters should, nevertheless, be clothed from their shoulders down to their feet. A further relevant incident occurred, again in a certain English city, just after the mid-point of the nineteenth century. It so happened that this city then founded a School of Art and, quite naturally, the school's function involved the presence and display of various studies, drawings, paintings, models, and statues of the naked human figure. But the inauguration of this school placed both its own staff and the city fathers in a deeply embarrassing situation. There could be no question but that the leading ladies of the city must be invited to the opening ceremony. Unfortunately, all civilized females of that era were unshakably sure that human beings are clothes-animals having no relationship whatsoever, let alone blood-kinship, with the skin-clad apes. A man without his clothes, they knew it for a fact, was like an elephant shorn of its trunk, a school without its students, soldiers devoid of courage. Anyone without the other of these pairs would be so totally decharacterized as to become, if not a complete nonentity, at least an entity of a basely tran-substantiated nature, and a man so transubstantiated would be, at best, a beast. The ladies, as the saying is, laid it on the line. "For us to consort with such beast-humans, even though those bestialities were only present in the form of drawings and statues, would compromise our honor. If they are to be present at the ceremony, we will not attend." The school authorities thought the ladies were all being a little silly but, in the West as in the East, women, however physically unfit for the hard slog of pounding rice or of slashing about on the battlefield, are indispensably ornamental features of any opening ceremony. What, then, could be done? The school authorities took themselves off to a draper's shop, bought thirty-five and seven-eighths rolls of suitable black material and clothed their beastly prints, their less-than-human statues, in a hundred yards of humanizing huckaback. Lest any lady's modesty might be outraged accidentally, they even masked the faces of their statues in swathes of sable stuffs. European marble and Hellenic plaster thus yashmaked out of the animal kingdom, I am happy to record that the ceremony went off to the complete satisfaction of all concerned.

From those remarkable accounts the importance of clothes to

mankind may be deduced. But, very recently, there has been a swing in the opposite direction and people may now be found who go about incessantly advocating nudity, praising nude pictures and generally making a naked menace of themselves. I think they are in error. Indeed, since I have remained decently clothed from the moment of my birth, how could I think otherwise? The craze for the nude began when, at the Renaissance, the traditional customs of the ancient Greeks and Romans were repopularized, for their own lewd ends, by the Italianate promoters of that cultural rebirth. The ancient Greeks and Romans were culturally accustomed to nudity, and it is highly unlikely that they recognized any connection between nakedness and public morality. But in northern Europe the prevailing climate is cold. Even in Japan there is a saying that "one cannot travel naked," so that, by natural law, in Germany or England, a naked man is very soon a dead one. Since dying is daft, northerners wear clothes. And when everyone wears clothes, human beings become clothes-animals. And having once become clothes-animals, they are unable to conceive that any naked animal whom they may happen to run across could possibly also be human. Its absence of clobber immediately identifies its brutish nature. Consequently, it is understandable that Europeans, especially northern Europeans, might regard nude pictures and nude statues as essentially bestial. In other words, Europeans and Japanese have the good sense to recognize nudes and representations of nudity as life-forms inferior to cats. But nudes are beautiful, you say? What of it? Beasts, though beautiful, are beasts. Some of my more knowledgeable readers, seeking to catch me in an inconsistency, may possibly ask whether I've ever seen a European lady in evening dress? Inevitably, being only a cat, I've never had that honor. But I am reliably advised that Western ladies in formal evening wear do in fact expose their shoulders, arms, and even breasts, which is, of course, disgusting. Before Renaissance times, women's dress styles did not sink to such scandalous levels, to such ridiculous decolletages. Instead, at all times women wore the clothes one would normally expect on any human being. Why, then, have they transformed themselves to look like vulgar acrobats? It would be far too wearisome to set down all the dreary history of that decadence. Let it suffice that those who know the reasons, know them, and that those who don't, don't need to. In any event, whatever the historical background, the fact remains that modern women, each and every night, trick themselves out in virtual undress and evince the deepest self-satisfaction with their bizarre appearances. However, it would seem that somewhere under that beastly brazenness, they retain some spark of human feeling, because, as soon as the sun comes up, they cover their shoulders, sleeve their arms, and tuck away their breasts. It is all the more odd in that, not only do they sheathe themselves by day to the point of near invisibility, but they carry their lunacy to the extreme of considering it extremely disgraceful to expose so much as a single day-lit toenail to the public view. Such inane contrariety surely proves that women's evening dresses are the brainchild of some gibbering conference of brain-damaged freaks. If women resent that logic, why don't they try walking about in the daytime with bared shoulders, arms, and breasts? The same type of enquiry should also be addressed to nudists. If they are so besotted with the nude, why don't they strip their daughters? And why, while they're about it, don't they and their families stroll around Ueno Park in no more than that nakedness they so affect to love? It can't be done, they say? But of course it can. The only reason why they hesitate is not, I bet, because it can't be done, but simply because Europeans don't do it. The proof of my point is in their dusk behavior. There they are, swaggering down to the Imperial Hotel, all dolled-up in those crazy evening dresses. What origin and history do such cockeyed costumes have? Nothing indigenous. Our bird-brained ladies flaunt themselves in goose-skinned flesh and feathers solely because that is the mode in Europe. Europeans are powerful, so it matters not how ridiculous or daft their goings on, everyone must imitate even their daftest designs. Yield to the long, and be trimmed down; yield to the powerful, and be humbled; yield to the weighty, and be squashed. Prudence demands a due degree of yielding, but surely only dullards yield all along the line, surely only chimpanzees ape everything they see. If my readers answer that they can't help being dullards, can't help being born without ability to discriminate in imitation, then of course I pardon them. But in that case, they must abandon all pretense that the Japanese are a great nation. I might add that all my foregoing comments apply with equal force in the field of academic studies, but, since I am here only concerned with questions of clothing, I will not now press the scholastic parallels.

I think I have established the importance of their clothes to human beings. Indeed, their clothing is so demonstrably all-important to them that one may reasonably wonder whether human beings are clothes, or clothes are the current acme of the evolutionary process. I am tempted to suggest that human history is not the history of flesh and bone and blood, but a mere chronicle of costumes. Things have indeed come to a pretty pass when a naked man is seen, not as a man, but as a monster. If by mutual agreement all men were to become monsters, obviously none would see anything monstrous in the others. Which would be a happy situation, were it not that men would be unhappy with it. When mankind first appeared upon the earth, a benign nature manufactured them to standard specifications, and all, equally naked, were pitched forth into the world. Had mankind been created with an inborn readiness to be content with equality, I cannot see why, born naked, they should have been discontent to live and die unclothed. However, one of these primeval nudists seems to have communed with himself along the following lines. "Since I and all my fellowman are indistinguishably alike, what is the point of effort? However hard I strive, I cannot of myself climb beyond the common rut. So, since I yearn to be conspicuous, I think I'll drape myself in something that will draw the eyes and blow the minds of all these clones around me." I would guess that he thought and thought for at least ten years before he came up with a stupendous idea, that glory of man's inventiveness, pants. He put them on at once and, puffed up with pride and all primordial pompousness, paraded about among his startled fellows. From him descend today's quaintclouted rickshawmen. It seems a little strange to have taken ten long years to think up something as simple, and as brief, as shorts, but the strangeness is only a kind of optical illusion created by time's immensely long perspective. In the days of man's remote antiquity, no such breathtaking invention as pants had ever been achieved. I've heard that it took Descartes, no intellectual slouch, a full ten years to arrive at his famous conclusion, obvious surely to any three-year-old, that I think and therefore I am. Since original thought is thus demonstrably difficult, perhaps one should concede that it was an intellectual feat, even if it took ten years, for the wits of proto-rickshawman to formulate the notion of knickers. In any event, ennobled by their knickers, the breed of rickshawmen became lords of creation and stalked the highways of the world with such overweening pride that some of the more spirited among the cloutless monsters were provoked into competition. Judging by its uselessness, I would guess that they spent a mere six years in planning their particular invention, the good-for-nothing surcoat. The knickers' glory faded and the golden age of surcoats shone upon the world, and from those innovators are descended all the green-grocers, chemists, drapers, and haberdashers of today. When twilight fell, first upon knickers and then upon surcoats, there came the dawn of Japanese skirted-trousers. These were designed by monsters peeved by the surcoat boom, and the descendants of their inventors include both the warriors of medieval times and all contemporary government officials. The plain, if regrettable, fact is that all the originally naked monsters strove vaingloriously to outdo each other in the novelty and weirdness of their gear. The ultimate grotesquerie has only recently appeared in swallow-tailed jackets. Yet if one ponders the history of these quaint manifestations, one recognizes that there is nothing random in their occurrence. The development was neither haphazard nor aimless. On the contrary, it is man's deathless eagerness to compete, the driving stretch of his intrepid spirit, his resolute determination to outdo all other members of his species, which has guided the production of successive styles of clothing. A member of this species does not go around shouting aloud that he or she differs in himself (or herself) from others of the species: instead each one goes about wearing different clothes. From this observed behavior a major psychological truth about this race of forked destroyers may be deduced: that, just as nature abhors a vacuum, "mankind abhors equality." Being thus psychologically determined, they now have no choice whatsoever but to continue enveloping themselves in clothes and would regard a deprivation thereof with as much alarm as they would face a cutting off of flesh or the removal of a bone. To them it would be absolute madness to cast their various clouts, a ripping away of their essential human substance, and as unthinkable to attempt a return to their original condition of equality. Even if they could bear the shame of being accounted lunatics, it would not be feasible to return to a state of nature in which, by all civilized standards, they would automatically become not merely lunatics but monsters. Even if all the billions of human inhabitants of this globe could be rehabilitated as monsters, even if they were purged of their shame by total reassurance that, since all were monsters, none were monsters, believe you me, it still would do no good. The very next day after the reign of equality among monsters had been re-established, the monsters would be at it once again. If they can't compete with their clothes on, then they will compete as monsters. With every man-jack stark-staring naked, they would begin to differentiate between degrees of staring starkness. For which reason alone, it would, I think, be best if clothes were not abandoned.

It is consequently incredible that the assorted human creatures now displayed before my very eyes should have taken off their clothes. Surcoats, skirted trousers, even their smallest smalls, things from which their owners would as soon be parted as from their guts and bladders, are all stacked up on shelves while the recreated monsters are, with complete composure, even chatting, scandalously exposing their archetypal nudity to the public view. Are you surprised then, gentle readers, that some time back I described this scene as genuinely spectacular? Shocked as I was, and am, it will be my honor to record for the benefit of all truly civilized gentlemen as much as I can of this extraordinary sight.

I must start by confessing that, faced by such mind-boggling chaos, I don't know how to start describing it. The monsters show no method in their madness, and it consequently is difficult to systematize analysis thereof. Of course, I can't be sure that it actually is a bath, but I make the wild surmise that it can't be anything else. It is about three feet wide and nine feet long, and is divided by an upright board into two sections.

One section contains white-colored bathwater. I understand that this is what they call a medicated bath: it has a turbid look, as though lime had been dissolved in it. Actually, it looks not only turbid with lime, but also heavily charged and scummed with grease. It's hardly a wonder that it looks so whitely stale, for I'm told that the water is changed but once a week. The other section comprises the ordinary bath, but, here again, by no stretch of the imagination could its water be described as crystal clear or pellucid. It has the peculiarly repulsive color of stirred rainwater which, against the danger of fire, has stood for months in a rain tank on a public street. Next, though the effort kills me, I will describe the monsters themselves. I see two youngsters standing beside that tank of dirty water. They stand facing each other and are pouring pail after pail of hot water over each other's bellies. Which certainly seems a worthwhile occupation. The two men are faultlessly developed, so far as the sun-burnt blackness of their skin is concerned. As I watch them, thinking that these monsters have remarkably sturdy figures, one of them, pawing at his chest with a hand towel, suddenly speaks to the other. "Kin, old man, I've got a pain right here. I wonder what it is."

"That's your stomach. Stomach pains can kill you. You'd better watch it carefully," is Kin's most earnest advice.

"But it's here, on my left," says the first one, pointing at his left lung.

"Sure, that there's your stomach. On the left, the stomach, and on the right, the lung."

"Really? I thought the stomach was about here," and this time he taps himself lightly on the hip.

"Don't be silly, that's the lumbago," Kin mockingly replies.

At this point, a man of about twenty-five or twenty-six and sporting a thin moustache jumped into the bath with a plop. Next minute, the soap and loosened dirt upon his body rose to the surface, and the water glinted richly as if it might be mined for mineral wealth. Right beside him a bald-headed old man is talking to some close-cropped crony. Only their heads are visible above the water.

"Nothing's much fun anymore when you get to be old like me. Once one gets decrepit, one can't keep up with the youngsters. But when it comes to a hot bath, even though they say that only lads can take real heat, that, for me, must still be really hot. Otherwise," the old man boastfully observed, "I don't feel right."

"But you, sir, are in spanking health. Not bad at all to be as energetic as you are."

"I'm not all that energetic, you know. I only manage to keep free from illness. A man, they say, should live to be a hundred and twenty provided he does nothing bad."

"What! Does one live as long as that?"

"Of course. I guarantee it up to a hundred and twenty. In the days before the Restoration there was a family called Magaribuchi-they were personal retainers of the Shogun—they used to live up here in Tokyo at Ushigome—and one of their male servants lived to a hundred and thirty."

"That's a remarkable age."

"Yes, indeed. He was in fact so old that he'd clean forgotten his age. He told me he could remember it until he turned a hundred, but then he just lost count. Anyway, when I knew him he was a hundred and thirty and still going strong. I don't know what's become of him. For all I know, he may be out there still, still alive and kicking." So saying, he emerged from the bath. His whiskered friend remained in the water, grinning to himself and scattering all around him suds that glittered like small flecks of mica. The man who thereupon got into the bath was certainly no ordinary monster; for all across his back was spread a vast tattoo. It seemed to represent that legendary hero, lwami Jutarō, about to decapitate a python with a huge high-brandished sword. For some sad reason, the tattoo has not yet been completed and the python must be guessed at. The great Jutarō looks a mite discomfited. As this illustrated man jumped into the water, "Much too tepid," he remarked. The man entering immediately behind him seems disposed to agree. "Oh dear," he says, "they ought to heat it up a bit." Just the same his features crack into a strained grimace, as though the water were in fact too hot for him. Finding himself right next to the tattooed monster, "Hello, chief," he greets him.

The tattooed monster nodded and, after a while, enquired "And how is Mr. Tami?"

"Couldn't say. He's gone so potty about gambling. . . "

"Not just gambling. . . "

"So? There's something wrong with that one. He's always bloody-minded. I don't know, but no one really likes him. Can't quite put a finger on it. Somehow one can't quite trust him. A man with a trade just shouldn't be like that."

"Exactly. Mr. Tami is rather too pleased with himself. Too damn stuck up, I'd say. That's why folk don't trust him. Wouldn't you say?"

"You're right. He thinks he's in a class by himself. Which never pays."

"All the old craftsmen around here are dying off. The only ones left are you, Mr. Moto the cooper, the master brickmaker, and that's about it. Of course, as you know, I too was born in these parts. But just take Mr. Tami. Nobody knows where he sprang from."

"True. It's a wonder that he's come as far as he has."

"Indeed it is. Somehow nobody likes him. Nobody even wants to pass the time of day with such an awkward bastard." Poor old Mr. Tami is getting it in the neck from all and sundry.

Shifting my gaze away from the section filled with filthy rainwater, I now concentrate upon the section filled with limey goo. It proves to be packed with people. Indeed, it would be more exact to describe it as containing hot water between men rather than as containing men in its hot water. All the creatures here are, moreover, quite remarkably lethargic. For quite some time now, men have been climbing in but none has yet climbed out. One cannot wonder that the water gets fouled when so many people use it and a whole week trundles by before the water's changed. Duly impressed by the turmoil in that tub, I peered more deeply among its tight-squeezed monsters and there I found my wretched master cowering in the left-hand corner, squashed and parboiled poppy-red. Poor old thing! Someone ought to make a gap and let him scramble out. But no one seems willing to budge an inch, and indeed my master himself appears perfectly happy to stay where he is. He simply stands there motionless as his skin climbs through the graduations of red to a vile vermilion. What a ghastly ordeal! I guess his readiness to suffer such dire reddening reflects a determination to extract his full two farthings worth in return for the bathhouse fee. But, devoted as I am to that dim monster of mine, I cannot sit here comfy on my ledge without worrying lest, dizzied by steam and medicating chemicals, he drown if he dallies longer. As these thoughts drifted through my mind, the fellow floating next to my master frowns and then remarks, "All the same, this is a bit too strong. It's boiling up, really scorching, from somewhere here behind me." I deduce that, reluctant to come out with a flat complaint which might impugn his manliness, he is trying indirectly to rouse the sympathy of his boiling fellow-monsters.

"Oh no, this is just about right. Any cooler, and a medicinal bath has no effect at all. Back where I come from we take them twice as hot as this." Some braggart speaks from the depths of swirling steam.

"Anyway, what the hell kind of good can these baths do?" enquires another monster who has covered his knobbly head with a neatly folded hand towel.

"It's good for all sorts of things. They say it's good for everything. In fact, it's terrific," replies a man with a face one could mistake, as much by reason of its color as of its shape, for a haggard cucumber. I thought to myself that if these limey waves are truly so effective, he ought to at least look a little more plump, a little more firm on the vine.

"I always say that the first day, when they put the medicine in, is not the best for results. One needs to wait until the third day, even the fourth. Today, for instance, everything's just about right." This knowing comment, accompanied by an equally knowing look, came from a fattish man. Perhaps his chubbiness is really no more than layers of dirt deposited by the water.

"Would it, d'you think, be good to drink?" asks a high-pitched querulous voice which quavers up from somewhere unidentifiable.

"If you feel a cold coming on, down a mugful just before going to bed. If you do that, you won't need to wake up in the night to go for a pee. It's quite extraordinary. You ought to try it." Again, I cannot tell from which of the steam-wreathed faces this wisdom bubbled out.

Turning my gaze from the baths, I stare down at the duckboards on the bathhouse floor where rows of naked men are sitting and sprawling in ugly disarray. Each adopts the posture that best suits him for scrubbing away at whichsoever portion of his body occupies his attention. Among these seriously contorted nudists, two attract my most astonished stare. One, flat on his back gawping up at the skylight; the other, flat on his stomach, is peering down the drainhole in the floor. Their utter self-abandonment, the totality of their idleness, is somehow deeply impressive. In another part of the forest, as Shakespeare pleasantly put it, a man with a shaven head squats down with his face to the stone of the wall while a younger, smaller man, also shaven-pated, stands behind him pounding away at his shoulders. They seem to have some kind of master-pupil relationship, and the pupil-type is busy playing the part of an unpaid bath attendant. There is, of course, a genuine bath attendant also somewhere on the scene. He is, in fact, not giving anyone a massage but merely tilting heated water out of an oblong pail over the shoulders of a seated patron. He looks as though he must have caught a cold because, despite the fearful hotness of the place, he's wearing a sort of padded sleeveless vest. I notice that, by a crooking of his right big toe, his foot is gripped on a camlet rag.

My glance drifts away to light upon a selfish monster hoarding no less than three wash pails for himself. Oddly enough, he keeps pressing his neighbor to make use of his soap; perhaps in order to inflict upon that defenseless creature a long and slightly loony flow of talk. I strain my ears to catch the conversation, which is, in truth, a monologue. "A gun is an imported thing. Something foreign, not something Japanese. In the good old days it was all a matter of sword against sword. But foreigners are cowards, so they dreamt up something dastardly like guns. They don't come from China, though. Long-range fighting with guns is what you'd expect from one of those Western countries. There weren't any guns in the days of Coxinga who, for all his Chinese name, was descended from the Emperor Seiwa through the Minamoto line. Yoshitsune, the best of the Minamotos, was not killed when they say he was. No, indeed. Instead he fled from Hokkaido to Manchuria, taking with him a Hokkaido man especially good at giving advice. Then Yoshitsune's son, calling himself a Manchurian, attacked the Emperor of China and the Great Ming was flat flummoxed. So what did he do? He sent a messenger to the third Tokugawa Shogun begging for the loan of three thousand soldiers. But the Shogun kept the messenger waiting in Japan for two whole years. I can't remember the messenger's name, but he had some name or other. In the end the Shogun sent him down to Nagasaki where he got mixed up with a prostitute. She then had a son. And that son was Coxinga. Of course, when the messenger at last got home to China, he found that the Emperor of the Ming had been destroyed by traitors. . ." I can't make heads or tails of this amazing rigmarole. It sounds so totally barmy, so crazed a mixture of garbled legends and historical untruths, that my attention again drifts away to focus on a gloomy looking fellow, maybe twenty-five or twenty-six years old, who appears to be steaming his crotch in the medicated water. He wears a vacant expression and seems to be suffering from a swelling or something. The very young man of seventeen or eighteen who sits beside him, talking in an affected manner, is presumably some houseboy from the neighborhood. Next to this mincing youth I see an odd looking back. Each joint in its spine sticks jaggedly out as though a knotted, bamboo rod had been rammed up under the skin from somewhere down between the buttocks. On either side of the spine, perfectly aligned, are four black marks like peg holes on a piquet board. All eight places are inflamed, some of them oozing pus.

Though I've tried to describe each thing as it appeared before my eyes, I now realize that there's still so much to write about that, with my limited skill, I can never set down more than a fraction of the totality. I was quietly flinching from the consequences of my own rash undertaking to describe in every detail the more spectacular features of a bathhouse when a bald-skulled oldster, maybe seventy years old and dressed in a light-blue, cotton kimono, suddenly appeared at the entrance. This hairless apparition bowed reverentially to his drove of naked monsters and then addressed them with the greatest fluency. "Good sirs," he says, "I thank you for your regular and daily visits to my humble establishment. Today it is, beyond these friendly walls, more than a little chilly; so please, I beg of you, take your time, both within and without my spotless baths, to warm yourselves at comfortable leisure. Hey, you there you in charge of the baths, make quite sure that the water is kept at precisely the proper temperature."

To which the bath attendant briefly answers, "Right."

"Now there's an amiable fellow," says the cracked historian of the doings of Coxinga, speaking admiringly of the aged proprietor. "To run this kind of business, you have to have his knack for it."

I was so struck by the sudden appearance of this strange old man that I decided to discontinue my overall surveillance of the bathhouse scene while I concentrated upon a more particularized scanning of so rum an individual. As I watched him, the old man, catching sight of a child some four years old who has just finished bathing, extends a mottled hand and, in that wheedling voice with which the old present their false advances to the young, calls out, "Come over here, my master." The child, frightened by that trampled pudding of a face which the gaffer bent upon him, promptly began to scream. The old man looked surprised. "Why! you're crying! What's the matter? Frightened of the old man? Well, I never!" His voice showed that he was genuinely astonished but, soon giving up this coaxing as a bad job, he quickly switched his attentions to the child's father. "Hello, Gen-san! How are you? A bit cold today, eh? And what about that burglar who broke into the big shop round the corner? Must have been a fathead. He cut a square hole in the wooden side-gate but then, can you believe it, took off without nicking a thing. Must have seen a copper or a watchman, I suppose. But what a waste of effort, eh!" Still grinning at the idea of the burglar's rash stupidity, he turns to someone else. "Isn't it cold, though! Perhaps, being young, you don't yet feel how it bites." It seems to me that, unique in his antiquity, he's the only person in the building who feels the cold at all.

Having been thus absorbed for several minutes in studying the old man's antics, I had virtually forgotten about all the other monsters, including my own master who was presumably still wedged in his boiling corner. I was jerked from my absorption by a sudden loud shouting in the middle of the room. And who should be the source of it but Mr. Sneaze himself. That my master's voice should be overloud and disagreeably indistinct is nothing new, but I was a little surprised to hear it raised in this particular place. I guessed in a flash that his raucous yawping had been caused by a rush of blood to his noddle in consequence of his unwisely protracted immersion in water heated up to cure all ills. Naturally, no one would object to such a hullaballoo, however raspingly unpleasant, if it were brought on by physical distress: but, as grew obvious soon enough, my beloved master, far from being geyser-dizzied out of his normal senses, was in fact being very much his own true self when he started bawling in that thickly violent voice. For the cause of the nasty uproar was a childishly idiotic squabble which he had started with some conceited pup, some totally insignificant houseboy.

"Get away from here! Go on, further off! You're splashing water into my pail." His shouting scraped one's eardrums. One's attitude to such outbursts depends, of course, upon one's point of view. One could, for instance, as I had done, conclude he had just gone potty with the heat. Another, perhaps one generous-minded person in ten thousand, might see a parallel with that courageous tongue lashing which Takayama Hikokuro dared to inflict upon a bandit. For all I know, that may have been precisely how my master saw himself. But since the houseboy clearly does not see himself in the bandit's role, we are unlikely to witness a successful repetition of that historic encounter.

"I was sitting here long before you came and plumped yourself down." The boy's reply, calmly delivered over his shoulder, was not unreasonable. But, since that answer made it clear that the lad was not prepared to budge, it did not please my master. My master, even though his blood was up, must have realized that neither the words nor the style of their delivery could really be picked upon as those of a bandit, but his howling outburst was not in fact occasioned by the boy's propinquity or any splashing of water. The truth was that, for some considerable time, the boy and his equally young companion had been swapping remarks in a pertly unpleasing manner utterly inappropriate to their age. My master had endured their prattle for as long as he could but, more and more exasperated, had finally blown up. Consequently, even though he had been perfectly civilly answered, the real cause of his fury remained unsoothed and he could not bring himself to leave the place without a last explosion of his heart. "Hobbledehoys," he shouted. "Damned young idiots. Splashing your dirty water in other people's pails."

In my own heart of hearts I felt considerable sympathy for my master, because I, too, had found the boys' behavior actively distasteful. Nevertheless, I was bound to regard my master's behavior during the incident as conduct unbecoming in a teacher. The trouble is that he is, by nature, something of a dry, old stick. Far too strict and far too rigid. Not only is he as rough and dessicated as a lump of coke, but he's also cinder-hard. I'm told that years ago when Hannibal was crossing the Alps, the advance of his army was impeded by a gigantic rock inconveniently blocking the mountain path. Hannibal is said to have soused the stone with vinegar and then to have lit a bonfire underneath it. The rock thus softened, he sawed it into segments, like someone slicing fish-paste, and so passed all his army safely on its way. A man like my master, on whom no effect whatsoever is produced by hours of steady boiling in a medicated bath, ought perhaps to be soused with vinegar and then grilled on an open fire. Failing some such treatment, his granitic obstinacy will not be softened though hordes of houseboys niggle away at the igneous rock of his nature for a hundred thousand years.

The objects floating in the bath and lazing about on the bathroom's floor are all monsters, teratoids dehumanized by the husking of their clothes; as such, they cannot be judged by normal civilized standards. In their teratical world anyone can do what he likes, anything can happen. A stomach can resite itself in a pulmonary location; Coxinga can be blood-kin to the Seiwa Minamotos; and that Mr. Tami, much maligned, may well be unreliable. But as soon as those naked objects emerge from their bathhouse into the normal world, they garb themselves in obedience to the requirements of civilization and, once robed, they resume the nature and behavior patterns of human beings. My master stands on the threshold between two worlds. Standing as he does between the bathroom and the changing room, he is poised at the verge of his return to worldliness, to the sad mundanities of man, to the suavities of compromise, the specious words, and the accommodating practices of his species in society. If, on the verge of returning to that world, he yet maintains so brute an obstinacy, surely his mokelike stubbornness must be a deep-rooted disease; a disease, indeed, so very firmly rooted as to be virtually ineradicable.

In my humble opinion, there is only one cure for his condition, and that would be to get the principal of his school to give him the sack. My master, being unable to adapt himself to any change of circumstances, would, if sacked, undoubtedly end up on the streets, and, if thus turned adrift, would equally certainly die in the gutter. In short, to sack him would be to kill him. My master loves being ill, but he would very much hate to die. He welters in hypochondriacal orgies of self-pity, but lacks the strength of soul to seriously look on death. Consequently, if anyone scares him with the news that some continued illness must lead to his demise, my craven master will immediately be both terrified out of his wits and, as I see it, terrified also into the best of health. Only the terror of death by dismissal can shrivel the roots of his almost ineradicable stubbornness. And if dismissal doesn't do the trick, well then, that, I'm afraid, is that, and the poor old perisher will perish. Still, in all, that foolish, fond old man, sick or well, remains my master. It was he who in my kittenhood took me in and fed me. I recall the tale of the Chinese poet who, given a meal when starving, later repaid that debt by saving his benefactor's life, and I consider it should not be impossible for a cat at least to be moved by his master's fate.

My soul brims full with pity and I become so preoccupied with the internal spectacle of the generous workings of my own deep-feeling heart that, once again, my attention wandered from the scene sprawled out below me. I was sharply brought back to reality by a hubbub of abuse coming from the medicinal bath. Thinking that maybe another squabble has broken out, I shift my gaze to find the throng of monsters all shoving and shouting as they struggle to get out of the narrow cleft of the adit to the bath. Horribly hairy legs and horrible hairless things are juxtaposed and tangled in a horrible squirm to escape. It is the early evening of an autumn day, and a red-gold flattish light burns here and there upon the boiling steam which rises up to the ceiling. Through the hot, foggy veils whose swirlings fill the room I catch appalling glimpses of wild stampeding monsters. Their shrieks and bellows pierce my ears, and from all sides their agonized shouting that the bloody water's boiling, mix in my skull as one loud howl of anguish. The shouts were multicolored: some yellow with sheer fear, some a despairing blue, some furiously scarlet, some a revengeful black. They spilt across each other, filling the bathroom with crashing columns of indescribable noise, the din of pandemonium, such sounds as have no context but Hell and the public bathhouse. Fascinated by this truly awful sight, I just stood there as though riveted to my ledge. The hideous roar climbed to a sort of blubbering climax where the pressure of mindless sound seemed just about to burst the walls apart when, from the swaying mass of turnbling naked bodies, a veritable giant lifted into view. He stands a good three inches taller than the tallest of his fellows. Not only that, but his radish-colored face is thickly bearded. The effect is so remarkable that one daren't affirm that the beard is actually growing on that face. It might be that the face has somehow got entangled in that beard. This apparition emits a booming sound like a large, cracked temple bell struck in the heat of noon. "Pour in cold water. Quick," he thundered. "This bath is on the boil." Both voice and face towered above the squawking rabble around him, and for a moment a sort of silence reigned. The giant had become the only person in the room. A superman; a living embodiment of Nietzsche's vision of Uebermensch; the Demon King among his swarm of devils; the master-monster; Tyrannosaurus Rex. As I stood goggling at him, someone beyond the bath answered through the sudden calm with a grunting cry of, "Yah." Assent? Derision? I shall never know. All I can say is that when I peered through the dark haze to identify the source of that ambiguous response, I could just make out the figure of the bathhouse attendant, padded still in his sleeveless vest, using all his strength to heave a whacking great lump of coal into the opened lid of the furnace. The coal made cracking sounds, and the attendant's profile came radiantly alight. Behind his body the brick wall gleamed with fire and the reflected glare burned at me through the darkness.

Thoroughly alarmed, I reared back from the window and, with one turning spring, hopped down and ran off home. But as I ran I pondered what I'd seen and the conclusions were clear. Although the human creatures in that bathhouse had been seeking a monstrous equality by stripping off their clothes, even from that leveling stark-nakedness a hero had emerged to tower above his fellows. I did not know what had happened to that hero, but I was certainly sure that equality is unachievable, however stark things may become.

On reaching home, I find that all is peaceful. My master, his face still glowing from the bath, is quietly eating supper: but, catching sight of me as I jump up onto the veranda, he breaks his silence to remark, "What a happy-go-lucky cat! I wonder what he's been up to, coming home as late as this."

My master has little money, but I note that on the table tonight there are laden dishes for a three-course meal. Grilled fish will be one of them. I don't know what the fish is called, but I guess it was probably caught in the sea off Shinagawa sometime yesterday. I have already expatiated at length upon the natural healthiness of fish as fostered by their salt environment; however, once a fish has been caught and boiled or, like this one, grilled, questions of environmental advantage are just no longer relevant. This fish would have done much better to stay alive in the sea, even if, in the course of time, it had eventually to suffer such ills as all fish-flesh is heir to. So thinking, I sat myself down beside the table. I pretended not to look while looking; looking, in particular, for a chance to snatch a piece of anything edible. Those who do not know how to look while not looking must give up any hope of ever eating good fish. My master pecked in silence at the fish, but soon put down his chopsticks as if to say that he didn't much like the taste. His wife, seated directly opposite him in matching silence, is anxiously watching how his chopsticks move up and down and whether my master's jaws are opening and closing.

"I say," he suddenly asked her, "give that cat a whack on the head."

"What happens if I whack it?"

"Never you mind what happens: just whack it."

"Like this?" asks his wife, tapping my head with the palm of her hand. It didn't hurt at all.

"Well, look at that! It didn't give the least miaow."

"No," she says, "it didn't."

"Then whack it again."

"It'll be just the same, however often I try." She gave me another tap on the head.

Since I still felt nothing, I naturally kept quiet. But what could be the point of these peculiar orders? As a prudent and intelligent cat, I find my master's behavior utterly incomprehensible. Any person who could understand what he's driving at, would then know how to react, but it's not that easy. His wife is simply told to "whack it," but she, the whacker, is self-statedly at a loss to know why she should whack; I, the unfortunate whackee, am no less lost to understand what it's all about. My master is becoming a little edgily impatient, for twice already his instructions have failed to produce the result which he only knows that he desires. It is therefore almost sharply that he says, "Whack it so that it miaows."

His wife assumed a resigned sort of expression and wearily asking, "Why on earth should you want to make the wretched thing miaow?" gave me another, slightly harder, slap. Now that I know what he wants, it's all absurdly easy. I can satisfy my master with a mere miaow, but it's really rather depressing, not just to witness but actually to participate in, yet another demonstration of his addlepated conduct. If he wanted me to miaow, he should have said so. His wife would have been spared two or three totally unnecessary efforts, and I would not have needed to endure more than a single whack. An order to whack should only be given when only a whack is wanted, but in this case what was wanted was simply a miaow. Now whacking may indeed fall within his sphere of responsibility, but miaowing lies in mine. It's a damned impertinence that he should dare to assume that an instruction to whack includes, or implies, an instruction to miaow, which is a matter totally within my discretion. If he is taking my miaows for granted, indeed he presumes too far. Such failure to respect another person's personality, a deadly insult to any cat, is the sort of crude insensitivity which one must expect from creatures like my master's own particular pet aversion, the nauseous Mr. Goldfield. But the same behavior on the part of my master, a man so confident of his open-heartedness that he struts about stark-naked, can only be seen as an act of unwonted weakness. Yet, as I know, my master is not mean. From which it follows that his venture into whacking was not motivated by any deviousness or malice. In my opinion, his orders were hatched in a brain as guileless and dim as that of a mosquito larva. If one gobbles rice, one's stomach becomes full. If one is cut, one bleeds. If one is killed, one dies. Therefore, such reasoning runs, if one is whacked, one must perforce miaow. Though I have done my best to justify my master's ways toward me, I regret to be bound to point out the clottish absurdity of such a style of logic. For if one were to concur in that logic, it would follow that if one falls in a river, one is required to drown; that if one eats fried fish, one must then get the squatters; that if one gets a salary, one must turn up for work; and that if one studies books, one cannot fail to make oneself a great name in the world. If that were the way things worked, there'd be some a bit embarrassed. I, for instance, would find it annoying to be obliged to miaow when whacked. What, I ask, would be the point of being born a cat if, like the bell-clock at Mejiro, one is expected to give off sounds every time one's struck? Having thus mentally reprimanded my presumptuous master, then and then only I obliged him with a mew.

As soon as I miaowed, my master turned to his wife. "Hear that?" he said. "Now tell me, is a miaow an interjection or an adverb?"

The question was so abrupt that Mrs. Sneaze said nothing. To tell the truth, my own immediate reaction was to think that, after all, he really had been driven out of his mind by his experiences in the bathhouse. He is, of course, well-known in the neighborhood for his eccentricities. I've even heard him called a clear case of neurosis. However, my master's self-conceit is so unshakable that he insists that, far from being a neurotic himself, it is his detractors in whom neurotic tendencies are clear. When his neighbors call him a dog, he calls them, in mere fairness, so he puts it, filthy pigs. He seems, indeed, besotted with maintaining his ideas of fairness: to the point of being a positive public nuisance. He really sees nothing odd in asking questions as ludicrous as that last enquiry to his wife about the proper parsing of a cat's miaow, but to the general run of his listeners his questions do suggest a certain mental instability. In any event, his wife, understandably mystified, makes no attempt to answer him. For obvious reasons, I too can offer nothing in reply.

My master waited for a moment and then, in a loud voice, suddenly shouted out, "Hey!"

His wife looked up in surprise and answered, "Yes?"

"Is that 'yes' an interjection or an adverb? Tell me now, which is it?"

"Whichever it is, it surely doesn't matter. What a silly thing to ask!"

"On the contrary, it matters a very great deal. That grammatical problem is an issue currently preoccupying the best brains among leading authorities on linguistics in Japan."

"Gracious me! You mean that our leading authorities are bending their brains to a cat's miaow? What a dreadful state of affairs. Anyway, cats don't speak in Japanese. Surely, a miaow is a word from the language of cats."

"That's precisely the point. The problem is a hard one in the very difficult field of comparative linguistics."

"Is that indeed so?" It is clear that she is sufficiently intelligent to be disinterested in such silly matters. "And have these leading authorities yet discovered what part of speech compares with a cat's miaow?"

"It's so serious a problem that it can't immediately be resolved." He munches away at that fish, and then proceeds to tuck into the next course of stewed pork and potatoes.

"This will be pork, won't it?"

"Yes, it's pork."

"Huh," he grunted in tones of deep disdain. "Huh," and then guzzled it down. Thereafter, holding out a *saké* cup, "I'll have another cup."

"You're drinking rather a lot today. Already you look quite red."

"Certainly I'm drinking," he began, but broke off to veer away on a new mad tack. "Do you know," he demanded, "the longest word in the world?"

"I think I've heard it somewhere. Let me think now. Yes. Isn't it 'Hoshoji-no-Nyudo-Saki-no-Kampaku-dajodaijin?'"

"No, I don't mean a title like that 'Former Chief Adviser to the Emperor and Prime Minister.' I mean a true, long word."

"Do you mean one of those crab-written sideways words from the

West?"

"Yes."

"Well then, no. That I wouldn't know. But I do know that you've had quite enough *saké*. You'll have some rice now, won't you? Right?"

"Wrong. First I'll drink some more. Would you like to know that longest word?"

"All right. But after, you'll have some rice?"

"The word is 'Archaiomelesidonophrunicherata.'"

"You made it up."

"Of course I didn't. It's Greek."

"What does it mean in Japanese?"

"I don't know what it means. I only know its spelling. Even if written sparingly it will cover about six and a quarter inches."

It is my master's singularity that he makes this sort of statement, which most men would vouchsafe in their cups, in dead cold sobriety. All the same, it's certainly true that he's drinking far too much tonight. He normally limits himself to no more than a couple of cups of *saké*, and he's already tossed back four. His normal dosage turns his face quite red, so the double dosage has inevitably flushed his features to the color of red-hot tongs. He looks to be in some distress, but he keeps on knocking them back. He extends the cup again. "One more," he says.

His wife, finding this really too much, makes a wry face. "Don't you think you've had enough? You'll only get a pain."

"Never mind the pain. From now on, I'm going to train myself into a steady drinker. Oinachi Keigetsu has recommended that I devote myself to drink."

"And who may this Keigetsu be?" Great and famous though he is, in the eyes of Mrs. Sneaze he isn't worth a ha'penny.

"Keigetsu is a literary colleague, a first-rate critic of these present times. He has advised me to spend less time at home communing with a cat, to get out and about, and to drink on all occasions. Since he's almost a doctor, albeit one of literature, it would seem all right to drink on doctor's orders."

"Don't be so ridiculous! I don't care what he's called or who he is. It's none of his business to urge other people to drink; especially people who happen to have weak stomachs."

"He didn't just recommend drinking. He also said I ought to be more sociable and take a fling at the fast life: wine, women, song, even travel."

"Are you actually trying to tell me that a so-called first-class critic has been making such outrageous suggestions? What kind of a man can he be? Truly, I'm shocked to learn that presumably responsible literary figures would recommend that a married man should go out on the loose."

"There's nothing wrong with living it up. If I had the money, I wouldn't need Keigetsu's encouragement before giving it a try."

"Well then, I'm very glad that you don't have the money. It would be quite awful if a man your age started gallivanting about with wanton girls and drunken half-wit critics."

"Since the idea seems to shock you, I'll scrap my plans for kicking over the traces. However, in consideration of that connubial self-sacrifice, you'll have to take better care of your husband and, in particular, serve him better dinners."

"I'm already doing the best I can on what you give me."

"Really? Well in that case, I'll postpone my investigation of the fast life until I can afford it, and, for tonight, I won't take any more *saké*." With what might just pass for a smile, he held out his rice bowl for his wife to fill from the container. As I remember it, he thereupon got through three great bowlfuls of mixed rice and tea.

My meal that night consisted of three slices of pork and the grilled head of that nameless fish.

VOLUME III

I

WHEN I WAS describing my fence trotting exercises, I must have mentioned that bamboo fence which encloses my master's garden. Beyond that fence to the south of us there is another dwelling, but it would be an error to assume that our neighbors are just anybody. Admittedly, it is a low-rent area, but Mr. Sneaze is a person of some standing, and certainly not the sort of man to establish chatty relationships across a backyard fence with any old Tom, Dick, or Harry. On the other side of our particular fence there is an open space about thirty feet deep at the far end, in which stands a dark green row of five or six heavily foliaged cypresses. If one looks at this scene from our veranda, the impression it creates is of a deep and thickly wooded forest, and one feels that here is a lonely house in a glade where some learned sage, indifferent to fame, and wealth, leads out his solitary life with only a nameless cat for his companion. However, the cypresses do not, in fact, grow quite as thickly as I'd like to make out, for through their greenery one can, with hurtful clarity, descry the undistinguished roof of a cheap boarding house of which the only redeeming feature is its soul-astounding name: Crane Flock Manor. You will appreciate that it consequently takes a real effort of the imagination to fit my master as I've hitherto described him into such a high-falutin' background. Yet, if that crumby boarding house can bear so grand a name, then surely my master's home deserves at least to be known as the Cave of the Sleeping Dragon. Since there's no tax on house names, one might as well select a name which sounds impressive. Anyway, this open space to the south of us, of a north-south depth of some thirty feet, extends on an east-west axis for about sixty feet along our bamboo fence, and then turns at a right angle northward to run along the eastern side of the Cave of the Sleeping Dragon. Now it is in this northern area that trouble has arisen.

One might dare boast that this open space, stretching as it does around two whole sides of our dwelling, is big enough to please anyone, but in point of fact not only the master of the house but even I, the dragon's resident sacred cat, are often at our wits' end to know what to do with so much emptiness. Just as the cypress trees lord it to the south, so to the north the scene is dominated by some seven or eight paulownias standing in a row. Since those trees have each now grown to be a good twelve inches around, one could make a pretty packet by selling their highly fancied wood to the first clog-maker whom one pared to call in. Unfortunately, even if my unworldly dragon could rise to such an idea, being no more than a tenant of his cavern, he couldn't put it into practice. My heart bleeds for my half-wit master. Especially so when I recall that only the other day some lowly drudge of a porter at his school came around and calmly cut a large branch from one tree. On his next visit he was sporting an exceedingly fancy pair of paulownia-wood clogs and was boasting to everyone within earshot that his clogs were made from the branch he'd stolen. Such cunning villains flourish; but for me and for the rest of my master's household, though those valuable paulownias are within our daily grasp, they profit us nothing. There's an old adage that to hold a gem invites misfortune, which is generally interpreted to mean that it is opportunity which creates a thief. But in our sad case the plain fact is that growing paulownias earn no money. There they are, as pointlessly valuable as gold left in the ground, but the numbskull in this matter is neither myself nor my master. It's the landlord, Dembei, a man so dense, so deaf that even when his trees are positively shouting for a clog-maker, begging aloud to be cut, he takes not the slightest notice, but just comes and collects his rent. However, since I bear no grudge against our landlord, I'll say no more about his crazy conduct and revert to my main theme, that is to say, to the odd series of events whereby that open space came to be the cause of so much strife and tribulation. But if I tell you the inwardness of it all, you mustn't, ever, let on to my master. These words of mine, remember, are between you and me and the gatepost.

The immediately obvious snag about that open space is that it is indeed entirely open: unenclosed, no kind of fence around it. It is a breezy, easy, go-as-you-pleasy sort of right-of-way: it is, in short, a good, honest open space. I must, however, confess that my use of the present tense is misleading, for, more precisely, I should have said that it *was* a good honest open space. As always, one cannot understand the present situation without tracing its development back to causes rooted in the ancient past. Since even doctors cannot prescribe cures unless they first have diagnosed the causes of disorder, I will take my time and, beginning my story from its true beginning, go back to those days when my master first moved into his present home.

It's always pleasant in the humid days of summer to have plenty of airy space around one's house. Of course such open sites offer to burglars the advantage of easy access, but there's little risk of burglary where there's nothing worth the thieving. Hence my master's house has never stood in need of any kind of outer wall, thorn-hedge, stockade, or even the flimsiest fence. However, it seems to me that the need for such defensive structures is really determined by the nature of whatever creatures, human or animal, which happen to live on the other side of any such open space. From which it follows that I must clarify the nature of the gentlemen dwelling to the north of us. It may seem rather rash to call them gentlemen before I have clearly established whether those beings are human or animal, but it's usually safer to start by assuming that everyone's a gentleman. After all, we have the authority of the Chinese classics for calling a sneak-thief hiding in the rafters a "gentleman on the beam." However, the gentlemen in our particular case are not, at least individually, criminal characters such as trouble the police. Instead, the criminality of these neighbors seems to be a function of their enormous number. For there are swarms of them. Swarms and swarms of pupils at a private middle school which, rejoicing in the name of the Hall of the Descending Cloud, collects two yen a month from each of eight hundred young gentlemen in return for training them to become even yet more gentlemanly. But you'd be making a serious mistake if you deduced from the elegant name of their school that all its students were gentlemen of elegance and taste. Just as no crane ever flocks to the seedy roosts in Crane Flock Manor, just as the Cave of the Sleeping Dragon in fact contains a cat, so the tasteful name of our neighboring school is an unreliable indicator of the true degree of its occupants' refinement. Since you have already learnt that a madman like my master can be held to be included within the ranks of university men, even of lecturers, you should have no difficulty in grasping what louts may well be numbered among the inferentially polished gentlemen in the Hall of the Descending Cloud. If my point is still not clear, a three-day visit to my master's house will certainly drive it home.

As I've already mentioned, when my master first moved into his house there was no fence around the empty space; consequently, the gentlemen of the Hall, just like Rickshaw Blacky, used to saunter about among the paulownias, chatting, eating from their lunchboxes, lying down on the clumps of bamboo-grass, doing, in fact, whatever they fancied. After a while they began using the paulownia grove for dumping their discardable rubbish—first the corpses of their lunch-boxes (that is to say, the bamboo wrapping-sheaths and odd sheets of old newspaper)—but soon they took to dumping worn-out sandals, broken clogs, anything in fact that needed pitching out. My master, typically indifferent, showed no concern about these developments and did not even bother to lodge a protest. I don't know whether he failed to notice what was going on or whether, noticing, he decided not to make a fuss. In any event, those gentlemen from the Hall seem to have grown ever more like gentlemen as they advanced in their education, for they gradually extended their disgusting activities on the northern side of the open space to encroach upon its southern area. If you object that a word like "encroach" should be used in reference to gentlemen, I am willing to abandon it; however, there is in truth no other word to describe the process whereby these gentlemen, like so many desert nomads, emerged from their paulownia wastes to advance upon the cypresses. Inasmuch as the cypress trees stand right in front of our living room, it was at first only the most daring of these elegant young men who dared to venture so far, but, within a matter of days, such daring had grown general, and the more sturdy of the venturers had moved on to greater things. There is nothing quite so terrifying as the results of education.

Having thus successfully advanced to the actual side of the house, these educated youths then launched upon us an assault of song. I have forgotten the name of their song, but it was certainly not a classical composition, being distinctly lively in the catchy style of certain popular ditties. My master was not the only person who was surprised, for I, too, was so much impressed by the range of talents displayed by these young gentlemen that I found myself listening to their singing in spite of myself. However, as my readers may already know, it is perfectly possible to be both impressed and seriously disturbed by the same occurrences. Indeed, upon reflection, it strikes me as regrettable that, as in the present case, the two reactions should so often be simultaneously evoked; I have no doubt that my master shared my sense of regret. Nevertheless, he had no real choice but, on two or three occasions, to come rushing out of his study and drive them off his property with such stern rebukes as, "This is not the place for you" and "I'd be obliged if you'd go."

Of course, since the offenders are educated gentlemen, they show no disposition to meekly obey my master's exhortations; no sooner have they been turned out but back they come again. And once they're back they start again on their less than seemly singing interspersed with loud-voiced chat and banter. What's more, and of course because they're gentlemen, their language differs from that in common use. They use such words as "youse" and "dunno." Such words, I understand, were, until the Restoration, part of the professional vocabulary of footmen, palanquin-carriers, and bathhouse attendants; however, in the present century, they have become the only style of language deserving study by an educated gentleman. I've heard it said that a similar social climb can be observed in the matter of taking physical exercise, for physical jerks, once generally scorned as an activity proper only to the lower classes, are now most warmly smiled upon at the highest levels of society. However, on the occasion when one of my master's frantic sallies from his study actually resulted in the capture of a student skilled in this new language of the gentry, the prisoner, no doubt frightened into forgetting the subtleties of modern educated speech, offered an explanation for his intrusion in such extremely vulgar terms as, "Please accept my most sincere apologies, but I had, Sir, the mistaken impression that this area was the school's botanical garden."

Having subjected his victim to a cautionary lecture, my master turned him loose. Which is a silly sounding form of words, more suited to the liberation of newly hatched baby turtles, but nevertheless appropriate in that my master kept a firm grip on his prisoner's sleeve throughout the process of his reprehension. Naturally enough, my master confidently expected that the force of his winged words would be sufficient to halt the nomadic inroads, but, as has been well known since the earliest days of recorded Chinese history, there is a vast difference between expectation and reality. In any event, my master's expectations were quickly proved misplaced. The young gentlemen now began to enter the open space from their northern side, walk boldly straight across it, then across our garden, and complete their short cut into the road beyond by use of our front gate. The sound of its opening naturally led us to expect the pleasure of visitors, so it was all the more infuriating to, in fact, receive nothing more than the noise of vulgar laughter from the direction of the paulownias. Things were clearly going from bad to worse. The effects of education grew daily more apparent until, recognizing that the situation had gone beyond his own powers of control, my master shut himself up in his study and there composed a politely worded letter to the headmaster of the Hall asking that a little closer control be exercised over the high spirits of his students. The headmaster, in similarly courteous terms, replied with an expression of regret for past intrusions and a plea for a little more patience pending the construction, for which he had already arranged, of a fence between the two properties. Shortly thereafter, a few workmen turned up and, in a scant half day, set up along the borderline a so-called four-eye fence of open-work bamboo approximately three feet high. My master, poor old duffer, was delighted. Daft as ever, he glowed in the false conviction that the nomadic raids had now been walled away, but what man in his right mind could possibly believe that a real change in the behavior of gentlemen can be wrought by the flimsy magic of a dwarfish bamboo fence?

One must, of course, recognize that there is a vast fund of pleasure to be drawn from the provocation of human beings. Even a cat like myself sometimes derives amusement from teasing my master's otherwise uninteresting daughters. So it is entirely understandable that the bright young gentlemen at the Hall should have found it rewarding to tease such a dimwit as my master. The only person who objects to teasing is, of course, the person teased. Analysis of the psychology of teasing reveals two major aspects of its successful pursuit. First, the person or persons teased must never be allowed to remain calm. Secondly, the person or persons teasing must be stronger than the teasee(s) both in sheer power and in mere number. Only the other day my master, who had gone off to gawp in some zoo, came home to recount an incident there which had particularly impressed him. He had, apparently, taken time to watch some idiotic rumpus between a small dog and a camel. The small dog, barking like mad, had scampered like a whirlwind around and around the camel, while the camel, paying no whit of attention, had simply stood there, stolidly patient under the burden of its hump. Unable to provoke the slightest stir of interest from the camel, the little dog had eventually barked itself into a disgusted silence. My master, too dull to see the relevance of that experience to his own circumstances, had seen the camel's dull insensitivity as nothing more than comic; and he laughed a lot as he told his tale. However, that incident does clearly illustrate one major facet of the business of teasing. No matter how skilled the teaser, his efforts will be wasted if the teasee happens to be as dull (or as intelligent) as a camel. Of course, should the victim happen to be as inordinately strong as a lion or a tiger, the teaser will quickly find himself involved in the yet more total disappointment of being ripped to shreds. But when the teaser has accurately determined that his victim, however deeply angered, still can do nothing in effective retaliation, then indeed the joys of provocation can be drawn from a bottomless well.

Why, one may ask, does teasing offer such endless pleasure? There are several reasons. First and foremost, it is the most marvelous way for killing time, better for the bored than counting one's whiskers. Of all the tribulations in this world, boredom is the one most hard to bear. I've even heard that, long ago, there was a prisoner so crazed by solitary confinement that he passed his days in drawing triangles, one upon another, all over the walls of his cell. For unless one does something, indeed anything, to incite a sense of purpose in one's life, one cannot go on living. Thus, the amusement in teasing derives in no small part from the stir, the stimulus, which it gives to the teaser. But it is, of course, obvious that it's worthless as a stimulant unless it successfully provokes in others a sufficient degree of that irritation, anger, even distress, which makes the teaser's life worth living.

Study of the annals of history discloses that there are two main types of people disposed to indulge in teasing: those of an utterly bored or witless mind and those who need to prove to themselves their superiority to others. The first group includes such creatures as those bored feudal lords who neither understood nor cared about the fellings of other people, a group which is nowadays best represented by boys so infantile, so mentally stunted, that, while having no time to think of anything but their own fool pleasures, they have insufficient intelligence to see how, even in that sub-puerile pursuit, best to employ their vitality. The second main group of teasers realizes that one can demonstrate superiority by killing, hurting, or imprisoning other people, but that such a proof only occurs as a sort of by-product from situations where the real objective is to hurt, kill, or jail. Consequently, should one wish to demonstrate superiority without going to the lengths (or running the risks) of inflicting major damage; the ideal method is by teasing. In practice it is impossible to prove one's superiority without inflicting some degree of injury, and the proof has to be practical because no one derives adequate or pleasurable confidence in his prowess from mere conviction thereof within the privacy of his own mind. It is of course true that the human creature characteristically prides itself on its self-reliance. However, it would be more exact to say that the creature, knowing it can't rely upon itself, would very much like to believe that it could and is consequently never at ease with itself until it can give a practical demonstration to some other such creature of how much it can rely upon itself. What's more, those endowed with the least intelligence and those least sure of themselves are precisely those who seize upon the slightest opportunity to demonstrate their entitlement to some sort of certificate of prowess. One can observe the same phenomenon in the world of judo, whose devotees, every so often, feel the need to heave someone or other over their buttocks and smack them down on the ground. The least proficient of these dedicated cross-buttockers wander about their neighborhoods looking for someone, even for someone not of their quaint fraternity, upon whose weaker person they can demonstrate their superiority in using their bottoms to sling the upright flat on their backs.

There are many other considerations which make teasing a popular and admirable activity, but, since it would take a long time to set them all down here, I will say no more upon the topic. However, anyone interested in deepening his understanding of this fascinating subject is always welcome to call upon me, bearing a proper fee in dried bonito, for further instruction.

Perhaps I might usefully offer the following succinct conclusion based upon my foregoing remarks, namely, that in my opinion the ideal subjects for teasing are zoo monkeys and school teachers. It would be disrespectful to compare a school teacher with a monkey in the Asakusa Zoo, disrespectful, that is, not to monkeys but to teachers. But truths will always come out, and no one can deny how close the resemblance is. As you know, the Asakusa monkeys are restricted by link-chain leashes so that, though they may snarl and screech to their hearts' content, they cannot scratch a soul. Now, though teachers are not actually kept on chains, they are very effectively shackled by their salaries. They can be teased in perfect safety. They won't resign or use their teeth on their pupils. Had they sufficient spunk to resign, they would not originally have allowed themselves to sink into the slavery of teaching. My master is a teacher. Though he does not teach at the Hall, still he is a teacher and just the man for the job: inoffensive, salary-shackled, a man designed by nature for schoolboys to torment in total safety. The pupils at the Hall are gentlemanly youths who not only consider it proper to practice teasing as a part of their rite of passage into the superiority of manhood, but who also believe that they are by right entitled to be tormentors as a due fruit by their education. Moreover, a sizable proportion of these lively lads would not know how to occupy their limbs and brains through the long ten minutes of the morning break if a kindly nature failed to provide them with a target for persecution. In such circumstances it is as inevitable that my wretched master should be teased as it is that the yobbos from the Hall should do the teasing. Given that inevitability, it seems to me quite ludicrous, a new high point in his long ascent to the thin-aired peaks of pure fatuity, that my master should have allowed himself to be provoked into so much pointless anger. Nonetheless, I shall now recount in detail how those pupils teased him and with what boorish folly he responded.

I assume my readers need no description of a four-eye fence. I, for instance, can move back and forth through its lattices with such complete freedom that it might as well not be there. However, the headmaster of the Hall did not have cats in mind when he arranged for the fence to be erected. His only concern was to provide a fence through which the young gentlemen of his school could not pass; I must confess that, freely as the winds may move between its bamboo laths, I see no way in which a man or boy could do the same. Even for such an accomplished contortionist as Chang Shih-tsun, that Chinese magician who flourished in the days of the Ch'ing, it would be hard to weasel a way through a wall of apertures each no more than a tight four inches square. Being thus impenetrable by human beings, it is understandable that the fence when first erected left my master happy with the thought that he was safe at last. However, there's a hole in the logic of my master's thinking, a hole far bigger than the squares in the four-eye fence. Indeed, the hole's so vast that it could easily let through even that monster fish which, in Chinese legend, once swallowed a whole ship. The point is this. My master assumes that a fence is something not to be crossed, from which follows his second assumption that no schoolboy worthy of that name would force his way past any fence which, however humble, can be recognized as indeed a fence and, as such, a clear identifier of a boundary-line. Even if my master were able to temporarily set aside those two assumptions, he would nevertheless still calculate that the smallness of the open-work squares provided genuine protection even against any such improbable youth as might dare to contemplate forcing his way through them. He all too hastily concluded he was safe simply because it was obvious that not even the smallest and most determined boy, unless he happened to be a cat, could possibly squeeze through the fence. But the massive flaw in his analysis lay in the fact that nothing is more easy than to climb or jump a fence but three feet high. Which, quite apart from the fun of it, also offers excellent physical exercise.

From the day following the erection of the fence, the young gentlemen from the Hall began jumping into the northern portion of the open space with the same regularity as they had previously just walked across. But they no longer advance to their earlier forward positions right in front of our living room because, if they are now chased, it will take them a little longer to reach the safety of school land by reason of the new need to get back over the four-eye fence. So they loaf about in the middle distance where they run no risk whatever of being caught. From his detached room on the east side of our house my master cannot see what the boys are doing. For that purpose one must either go out to the garden gate and there look at a right angle into the open space or else one must go to the inside lavatory and peer out through its little window. From that latter position my master can very clearly see what is going on, but, however many the intruders upon his property, nothing can be done to catch them. All he can do is to shout unheeded scoldings through the window grille. If he tries a sally through the garden gate into enemy-occupied territory, the sound of his approaching footsteps gives them ample time to scoot away, nimbly clear the fence, and continue their hooting from the safety of school land. My master's tactics of creep-and-rush are much like those adopted by sea-poachers trying to surprise seals as they bask in the sun. Naturally, my master cannot spend his whole life either peering from the loo or dashing out through the garden gate in response to every stimulus of sound from the open space. He would have to give up teaching and concentrate on full-time self-employment as a yobbo-hunter. The weakness of his position is that from his study he can hear, but not see his enemies, while from the lavatory he has them in plain view but can do nothing more effective than yell his silly head off. His enemies, full aware of his dilemma, have shaped their strategy to exploit his difficulties.

When the young gentlemen are sure that my master is in his study, they set up a racket of talk so deliberately loud that my master cannot avoid hearing the cracks they make about him. To salt his mortification, they vary the volume of their comments so that he can never be certain whether their babble originates from his or their side of the four-eye fence. When my master makes one of his forays, they either scuttle off or, if they happen already to be in their own territory, they stare at him with insolent indifference. When my master is lurking in his lavatory—I regret, indeed I would normally disparage, this constant use of that somewhat indelicate word, but in battle reports one is duty-bound to be topographically accurate—his tormentors loaf about under the paulownias and take pains to draw his attention to their unwelcome presence. Then, as soon as he starts raving at them through the window-grille, they, cool as little cucumbers, let the roar of his abuse flow over their heads to disturb the whole neighborhood with its ugly echos while, utterly unconcerned, they drift away into the home ground of their Hall. These tactics are reducing my master to a gibbering idiot. Sometimes, sure that the little louts are on his property, he dashes out with his walking stick at the ready, only to find the open space deserted. At other times, confident of their absence, he nevertheless takes a quick peep from his lavatory window, and there they are, a loathly gaggle of them, loitering on his land. So he nips around to his garden gate and he squinnies from the john. He squinnies from the john and he nips around to his garden gate. Over and over and over again. If you find my account repetitive, the simple reason is that I am committed to recounting endless repetitions of the same inane and equally pointless alternative behaviors. My master, worn to a frazzle, is clearly approaching the point of nervous breakdown. He has become so frenziedly obsessed with his problem that one hardly knows whether he is still a professional teacher or now regards this crazy oscillation between peep and sally as his sole true calling. And then, as the tides of his frenzy rose ever closer to the neap of madness, the following incident occurred.

Some kind of incident almost always does occur when frenzy, brainstorm, wrong-way-upness, a rush of blood to the head—call the condition what you will—impairs the human power to reason clearly. All the authorities, Galen, Paracelsus, even such ancient Chinese quacks as Pien Ch'üeh, are at one in this prognosis. There does, of course, remain some scope for debate as to where the "inverse up-rush" actually starts and as to what it is that rushes. The long outmoded lore of European medicine men held that there are four different liquids, or humors, washing around in the human body. The first such liquid was that of choler which, when it rose inversely, produced fury. The second liquid, that of dullness, if inversely risen, brought on lethargy. The third, the fluid of melancholy, produced, as one might have expected, melancholia. While the fourth, blood, was responsible for the activity of arms and legs. The progress of civilization appears, for no discernible reason, to have drained away the fluids of choler, dullness, and melancholia, so that, as I understand it, nothing now remains to circulate in our bodies but residual blood. Consequently, if any inverse rising does indeed take place, it must be a wrong-way-up-ness of the blood. There is, of course, a limit to the amount of blood containable in the human body and the precise volume varies slightly as between individual specimens, but, on average, every human being contains some 9.9 liters of the stuff. Now when that literage rises inversely, the head, beyond which it cannot rise, becomes heated and inordinately active, whilst the rest of the body, drained of blood, numbs with cold. One may reasonably compare this process to the happenings in September 1905 when the populace of Tokyo, dissatisfied with the terms of the Treaty of Portsmouth, took to burning police boxes. On that occasion all the police conglomerated at headquarters, leaving no single officer out on the streets or even to defend their various police boxes. That rush to headquarters could well, medically, be diagnosed as a rush of blood to the head. And in both cases the proper cure is to re-establish the normal balanced distribution of blood (or of bloody cops) throughout the body (or body politic). To achieve that balance the blood, inversely risen, must be drawn back down from the head, and there are various treatments available.

For instance, I understand that my master's deceased father was in the habit of wrapping a cold, wet towel around his head and then toasting his feet on a charcoal foot-warmer; practices whose efficacy would seem to be well warranted by those passages in that Chinese medical classic, *Some Thoughts on Typhoid Fever*, which states that keeping the head cold and the feet warm ensures good health and guarantees longevity. A towel a day keeps the doctor away. Another much-favored method of treatment is that in common use among the priesthood. Indeed, it appears that, when on pilgrimage, wandering Zen priests would invariably pick out a place to rest or sleep where there was "a tree above and a stone beneath." That slogan refers neither to any aesthetic ideal nor to the self-mortifications of penitents but to a particular technique for reversing rushes of blood to the head, which was first worked out, no doubt in his early days as a rice-pounding, kitchen scullion, by the Sixth Patriarch of the Zen sect, His Ineffable Holiness Hui Neng. Test the method for yourself. Sit on a stone and, in the nature of things, your bottom will grow cold. As the buttocks chill, any heady sensations associated with risen blood will sink away to nothing. That too, beyond all shadow of doubt, is also in the nature of things. One marvels, does one not, at the percipience of the Sixth Patriarch.

Thus, while a number of methods have been devised for cooling down rushes of blood to the head, I regret to report that, as of the present time, no satisfactory way to incite them has yet been invented. It is, perhaps, natural that people should generally assume that there's nothing to be gained from rushes of blood to the head, but there's at least one context where any such sweeping judgement is likely to prove unduly hasty. Indeed, many of those engaged in the activity I have in mind would swear blind that without such rushes they could not even begin to pursue their profession. I am speaking of poets. Just as coal is indispensable to a steamship, so to poets are rushes of blood to the head. Bereft of that energy source for so little as one day, poets would debate into mediocrities capable of nothing but eating and drinking in a lifelong haze of idleness. In sober truth, a rush of blood to the head is simply an attack of lunacy, but since no professional would care to admit that he cannot pursue his profession except when in a state of mental derangement, poets, even amongst themselves, do not call their madness madness. By an arrangement privately arrived at, a sort of literary conspiracy, they all seek to dazzle the foolish public by describing their derangement as inspiration. The fact remains that we are speaking of madness. Nevertheless, poets do have Plato on their side, for he called their ailment a sacred madness, a divine afflatus. Even so, and no matter what degree of divinity may really be involved, people would refuse to regard poetry with any measure of respect if it were openly identified with lunacy, and I therefore conclude that poets are wise to cling to their inspiration because, though "inspiration" sounds to me like the name of some newly invented patent medicine, it remains an all impressive word, one behind which the pottiness of poets can most splendidly be sheltered. When exotic-sounding delicacies in fact consist of nothing more unusual than yams, when images of the Goddess of Mercy consist of nothing more than two brief inches of rotten wood, when game soup specialities are cooked from common crow, when the best stewed beef in boarding houses is horse flesh in hot water, why should one question the reality of inspiration? If its reality is, as it must be, madness, at least it quickly spends itself—lunacy by fits (especially fits) and starts. Indeed it is only because their manic possession is so signally short lived that poets are not all shut away in the loony bin at Colney Hatch.

I think it fair to add that these short-term maniacs, these inspired idiots, appear to be extraordinarily difficult to produce. It is painfully easy to manufacture lifelong loonies, but even the most artful God seems to have trouble fashioning beings whose manic spells are limited to those periods during which the lunatic is holding a means to write and is confronted with blank paper. In any event, God seldom creates such specimens. Consequently, they have to be manufactured without divine assistance, and all down the ages, scholars have been obliged to devote as much time and effort to finding the best way to generate the flow of inspiration as they have to the problems of preventing rushes of blood to the head. One seeker after inspiration, convinced that the secret of its attainment lay in constipation, assiduously strove for that prior condition by eating a dozen unripe persimmons every day for fruitless years on end. Another aspirant to inspiration believed he could achieve his objective by literal hotheadedness and accordingly spent his days in an iron bathtub, heated from below, consuming enormous quantities of hot *saké*. Failing to achieve immediate success, he concluded that the flaw in his scheme must lie with the bath water, but unfortunately, he died before he could gather sufficient money to afford the expense of bathing in boiling port. Yet another would-be poet placed his hopes for an inspiring rush of blood to the head in the long-received concept of acquisition through imitation. It is an ancient idea that imitation of the conduct of some acknowledged master will produce in the ape the same mental state as graced the model. According, to this theory a man who behaves like a drunkard will eventually feel what a drunkard feels, while a man who squats sufficiently long in the attitudes of a Zen master, enduring the agony while a joss stick burns itself to nothing, will, somehow or other, experience the master's experience of enlightenment. The adoption of that theory of imitation to the search for inspiration led to the conclusion that, if one imitated the conduct of some literary giant, one would experience the same rushes of blood to the head as had inspired his literary achievements. I am reliably advised that Victor Hugo used to think up his finest prose effects while lying on his back in a sailing boat, from which it would follow that if one can board a yacht, lie on one's back and stare at the blue of sky, one may confidently expect an upflow of stupendous prose. Since Robert Louis Stevenson is said to have written his novels while lying flat on his belly, it should be possible by worming around on the floor to have one's brush construct whole archipelagoes of treasured islands.

You can deduce, even from the modest number of examples which I've cited, that many persons have devised methods for generating inspiration, but none has so far proved successful, and current opinion holds that its artificial generation is impossible. Which is, of course, sad, but nothing can be done about it. However, I am quite certain that, sooner or later, someone will find a way to produce the divine afflatus on demand and, for the sake of dull humanity, I sincerely hope that that desirable discovery is not too long delayed.

I feel that I have spoken at more than sufficient length about rushes of blood to the head, and I will therefore now revert to my account of the crisis mounting within my master. I must, however, first observe that any major event is invariably preceded by a series of minor happenings, tremors and smoke puffs clearly indicative of the coming explosion, and that throughout the ages, the admirable efforts of a long succession of historians have all been flawed by their concentration upon major events to the near total disregard of the minor forewarnings in any developing situation. Thus, in my master's case, the vehemence of the rush of blood to his head increased with every minor brush with his tormentors, and that steady rise in pressure made the eventual eruption entirely predictable. If I am to properly convey the real extent of my wretched master's sufferings, if I am to avoid the possibility that my readers should look down upon his rushes of blood to the head as trifling bubbles popping in his veins, if the world at large is not to sneer at his conduct as an exaggerated reaction to petty pin-pricks, surely I must not scamp the ordered details of the development of his frenzy. Indeed, when one considers what agony is involved in the generation of the most modest inspiration, it would be a discouragement to many a budding talent if any manifestation of wrong-way-upness should be disparaged. However, I must confess that the chain of incidents, minor and major, which I am about to relate reflects no honor upon Mr. Sneaze. Nonetheless, though the incidents themselves are, by and large, disgraceful, I must make it clear that the frenzy is no whit less genuine, less pure, than the flow of inspiration in the very greatest of the madmen of the arts. Since my own old master has nothing else remarkable about him, were I not to laud his frenzy, I, his life's recorder, would have nothing much to record.

Our enemies who swarm all over the Hall of the Descending Cloud have recently invented a new sort of dumdum bullet which they mercilessly fire into the northern part of the open space not only during their ten-minute breaks between classes, but also after their school hours end. This new dumdum is apparently called a ball and it is discharged at the foe by being struck with an object resembling a bloated pestle or rolling pin. However, powerful as that weapon may be, the range from its point of discharge in the Hall's playground to the study where my master is normally entrenched is too far for him to be in any personal danger. Our enemies are, of course, fully aware of the range problem and have accordingly developed a tactic which exploits the limitations of their weapon. I understand that the Japanese triumph at the battle of Port Arthur was due in no small part to the indirect gunfire of our Navy. Correspondingly, even a dumdum struck no further than into the open space must surely contribute something to the discomforture of my master; especially when, presumably as an expression of the solidarity of the swarm, every missile is accompanied by a loud and menacing cry of "Wow" uttered in unison from every hostile throat. You can imagine with what terror my master is overwhelmed, how pitifully contracted are the blood conduits to his arms and legs, and how inevitably, under the pressures of agony, all the blood at large within him begins to flow in the wrong direction upwards to his head. One must concede the artful ingenuity of those young schemers in the Hall.

Long ago in Greece there lived a writer named Aeschylus whose head was of the kind common to all scholars and writers—that is to say, it was bald. If you should wonder why such persons should all lack head hair, the reason is that scholars and writers are usually poor (and therefore ill nourished) and that their work is all in the head (so that what little nourishment reaches their heads is all so rapidly there consumed that only a very small proportion of it survives to nourish the hair roots in their scalps). Writers and scholars are all characteristically both undernourished and bald. It follows that Aeschylus, being a writer, had no hair on his head. Indeed, he was renowned for his magnificently smooth pate, hairless as a kumquat. One day, with his usual head (I do not mean to imply that one can change heads as one changes hats, wearing at will a party head or an everyday head or a Sunday-go-to-meeting head, but simply that on this occasion the head of Aeschylus was as bald as ever), this famous writer went out walking in the streets, where he allowed the brilliant Grecian sunshine to be reflected from his scalp. Which was a very bad mistake. Bright light reflected from a smooth bald head can be seen from an enormous distance. It is the top of the tallest tree which takes the wind's worst force, so the top of earth's most shining man may well expect attentions no less fierce. In any event, it then so happened that an eagle with a captured tortoise clutched in its talons came cruising through the skies directly above the scintillating Aeschylus. Tortoises and turtles make delicious eating, but even in the days of the early Greeks they had already so far evolved as to be very hard-shelled creatures; shells so hard, however delicious the meat within, make it equally hard for meals to be made of tortoises or turtles. It is perfectly true that lobsters grilled in the shell are a popular dish today, but no one's ever heard of tortoise stewed in the carapace, and I doubt if they ever will. Certainly no such item appeared on the menus of ancient Greece, and that cruising eagle was beginning, somewhat embarrassedly, to wonder what on earth he should do with his pendant tortoise when his eye was caught by a brilliant glittering from the distant earth below him. "I've got it," thought the eagle. "If I drop this tortoise on that shiny thing, its shell must surely break, and, once the shell is broken, I can plummet down and gorge to my heart's content on the so-unshielded meat. Nothing more simple. Here we go!" And, aiming skillfully for the effulgent center of the Aeschylean skull, he straightway dropped the tortoise. Unfortunately, both for Aeschylus and for the disappointed eagle, the skulls of writers are softer than the carapace of a tortoise; so it was that, with his bright head smashed in smithereens, that luminary of literature came to his pitiful death.

My readers may be wondering how this long digression into death from the sky relates to my master's troubles, but I have reasonable hope that all in good time the connections will declare themselves. First, however, I feel bound to comment that I find it hard to determine the true intent of that eagle. Did he drop the tortoise in full awareness that the shiny object was the head of a writer, or did he genuinely believe his target was bare rock? Depending on the way in which one interprets the bird's intention, one either can or cannot draw a useful parallel between the eagle and those boy-faced harpies from the Hall. Moreover, any attempt fully to understand the problem must take due account of a variety of conflicting factors. For instance, it is a matter of fact that my master is not bald, and consequently, his head, unlike those of Aeschylus and other distinguished writers and scholars, emits no brilliant light. However, he does possess (though it is a pitiably small example) that *sine qua non* of any writer or scholar, a study. In addition, though he is normally to be found asleep in front of it, he does actually spend much of his time with some difficult book propped up before his nose. One must accordingly regard him as a person of at least the scholarly type. The fact that his head is not of a scholarly baldness does not necessarily mean that he is unqualified for such nudity: it could simply be that he is not yet fully unfledged. However, at his present rate of losing his wig, he can confidently expect to soon be as bald as any coot of a professor. If his depilation is the battle objective of those hooligans at the Hall, one must acknowledge that they would be acting shrewdly if they concentrated their dumdum fire on my master's head. Two weeks of such bombardment would so terrify the man that his contracted veins would cease to nourish him properly and his head would quickly come to resemble a kumquat or a kettle or a bright, round, copper pot. Two further weeks of bombardment and the kumquat would be squashed, the kettle spring a leak, and the copper pot crack open. Faced with such a battle plan, the only person who could fail to predict its inevitable success, the only fathead who would soldier on regardless, would be, of course, my madman of a master.

There came an afternoon when, taking my usual snooze on the veranda, I dreamt I was a tiger. "Bring me," I growl at my master, "buckets brimming with chicken meat," which he, crawling toward me in a pleasing tremble of terror, immediately supplied. Waverhouse then appeared and I promptly snarl, "Get yourself down to the Wild Goose Restaurant, for I want, and you shall fetch, goose flesh of the best."

"Pickled turnip and rice-crackers," comes the expectable blather of Waverhouse response, "have a savor strikingly similar to that of the wild goose."

Not deigning even to comment on his presumptuous prevarication, I simply open wide my cavern of a mouth and shake him silly with a single shattering roar.

Waverhouse turns pale and placatingly continues, "The Wild Goose Restaurant on Yamashita Street has, I much regret to report, just gone out of business. What other fare, most honored sir, would you allow me to procure for you?"

"Shut, is it? Well, in that case I'll let you off with beef. Don't just stand there. Be off to Westbrooks and hurry back here with a pound of the finest roasting beef. Hurry," I said, "or I'll gulp you where you stand." Waverhouse shoots out of the house at the double, the back of his gown tucked up into his girdle to free his legs for a truly astonishing turn of speed. My enormous body sprawled at ease along the veranda, I am lying there waiting for the return of Waverhouse when, all of a sudden, a hideous shouting fills the house, and, without so much as a nibble of beef, I was jerked awake from my flesh-delicious dream. For my master, who only a moment back had been prostrating himself before me in a cringe of juddering terror, came rocketing out of the lavatory, kicked me aside with a savage toe in the ribs and, before I even recovered from that shock, had slipped on his outdoor clogs, whizzed out through the garden gate and was off at his ungainliest gallop toward the Hall of the Descending Cloud. It is distinctly disconcerting to find oneself so quickly shrunken from a tiger to a cat, but I confess I was also somewhat tickled by this latest weird development. Indeed, the combination of the sight of my master's ferocious countenance with the pain of his vicious kick soon wiped from my mind all memory of tiger-time. My lightheartedness derives from the likelihood that, if my master is, at last, really going into action, there'll be some fun when the sparks start flying. So disregarding my aching ribs, I limp along in his wake and, as I come to the backyard gate, I hear him barking, "Thief!"

Up ahead, just scrambling over the four-eye fence with his Hall school cap still stuck on his head, there's a sturdy lad aged about eighteen or nineteen. As the intruder drops into safety and scampers off to his base camp in the playground, I sigh that he's got away, but my master, encouraged by the success of his shout of "Thief," shouts it once again and thunders on in hot pursuit. Which brings him to the fence. If he keeps on going, he too will trespass into thievery and, in his present transport of frenzy, it looks as though the passion of the chase and his own Dutch courage may actually carry him up and over the barricades. Certainly he shows no sign of wavering as his spindly legs bring him to the point where the bamboo stakes stand planted on the border. One more climbing step and my normally craven master will have graduated into villainy. At that moment one of the enemy generals, some scurvy usher with a droopy thin moustache, moved up to the frontier, where he and my master, each on his own side of the fence, engaged in the following utterly fatuous parlay.

"Yes, he is a student of the Hall."

"Then, like all good students, he should conduct himself correctly. How does he come to be trespassing on someone else's premises?"

"He was collecting a ball that had rolled onto your land."

"Why, then, did he not simply come and ask my permission to retrieve it?"

"I will ensure that the boy is reproved."

"Well, in that case, all right."

The negotiations which I had happily anticipated developing into outright battle thus quickly petered out in a dull exchange of the prosiest kind of chicken chat. My master's fire-breathing threats are mere bravado. When it comes to action, nothing ever happens. It's not unlike my own reversion from a dream tiger to an actual cat. In any event, the foregoing happenings constitute that "minor incident" of which I wished to tell you, and I will now proceed to the tale of the major incident which followed.

My master is lying flat on his belly in the living room with the sliding door left open. He is deep in thought, probably devising ways to defend himself against those hooligans at the Hall where, it would seem, classes must be in progress because no noise whatsoever is coming from the playground. Instead, through the unwonted quiet comes a voice, which by its resonance I immediately recognize as the voice of the enemy general at yesterday's conference, delivering a clear and closely reasoned lecture upon ethics.

"Thus, public morality is so important that you will find it practiced everywhere: in Europe, in France, in Germany, in England, everywhere. Furthermore, everyone in Europe, even the most humble persons, pays deep respect to this public morality. It is all the more regrettable that we, in Japan, are still unable to match the civilizations of foreign countries in this matter. Some of you may perhaps think that public morality is an unimportant concept newly imported from abroad, but if you do so think, you are mistaken. Our own forebears were proud to be guided by the teachings of Confucius, which in every context emphasize the importance not only of faithfulness, but of true understanding of the needs of other beings; it is upon precisely such an understanding that public morality is founded. Since I am human, there are times when I feel like singing in a loud voice. But if I were studying, and someone in the next room started singing loudly, I'd find it impossible to concentrate on my reading. Therefore, even though I would like to refresh my mind by quoting aloud from some anthology of classical Chinese poetry, I restrain myself from doing so because I know how infuriating I would find such a disturbance of my own studies. In brief, your own national tradition of public morality must always be observed and you should never do things which might be a nuisance to others. . ."

At that point my master, who had been listening carefully to the lecture, broke into so broad a grin that I feel I must explain the inwardness of his reaction. A cynical reader might well suspect some element of sarcasm in my master's grinning, but the reality is that his nature is too simple, even too sweet, to accommodate the sour subtleties of doubt. He simply does not have the brainpower to be bad. He grinned for no more complicated reason than that he was pleased by what he'd heard, and, in his pitiful simplicity, he genuinely believed that since the ethics teacher had given such a poignant exhortation to the students, the hail of dum-dums would now cease and he could snooze along forever in the recovered safety of his study. He need not yet, he reasoned, lose his hair. His frenzies may not instantly be cured, but, with the passing of the days, their violence will abate. He can dispense with wet towels around his brows and a charcoal-burner for his feet. And he need not sleep with a tree for his only shelter and a stone beneath his bum. Cozy in such delusions, of course the fathead grinned. It is in the not unworthy nature of the man that my master should have taken that lecture seriously. Indeed, though he lives in the twentieth century, he still quite honestly believes even that debts should be repaid.

In due time the school's class hours must have ended, for the lecture on ethics came to a sudden stop. I assume all the other classes finished at the same time, for quite suddenly, with hideous whoops and shouts, some eight hundred young gentlemen came tumbling out of the building. Buzzing and whirring like a swarm of bees whose hive has been knocked over, they poured from the windows, doorways, and indeed from every least gap in the fabric of the school. And it was with that eruption that the major incident began.

Let me begin with an account of the battle formation of these human bees; should you think it overblown to use specialized military terms to describe such a piffling business as my master's scufflings with mere schoolboys, well, you'd be quite wrong. When ordinary people think of warfare, their idea of battle is of such bitter encounters as those which took place during our recent war with Russia at Shaka, Mukden and Port Arthur. Less ordinary persons, notably those barbarians who have some feel for poetry, associate warfare with particular colorful incidents or feats of derring-do: with Achilles in his chariot dragging the corpse of Hector around the walls of Troy, or with Chang Fei of Yen standing alone with his four-yard, snake-shaped halberd on the Ch'ang-pan Bridge and glaring down the milling hordes of Ts'ao Ts'ao's army. However, though every man is perfectly entitled to fashion his individual notion of the nature of warfare, it would be outrageous to lay down that the only real wars are those of the kinds to which I've just referred. One would like to think that totally foolish wars only took place in antiquity and that today, in the capital city of Imperial Japan and during a period of peace, such barbaric behavior were inconceivable. Even though riots do occasionally occur, there's no real danger of the disorder going beyond the burning of a few police boxes. Against that background there can be no doubt that the battle between Mr. Sneaze, Captain General of the Cave of the Sleeping Dragon, and the eight hundred stalwart youths from the Hall of the Descending Cloud must be recognized as one of the most important conflicts fought out in Tokyo since the foundation of that city.

Tso Shih's account of the battle of Yen Ling opens with a description of the enemy's forces and their disposition; since all subsequent historians of any repute have followed his example, I see no reason not to begin with a description of the battle formation of the Bees. In the van, disposed in line close against their own side of the four-eye fence, there is an advance guard of students whose probable function is to lure my master forward into artillery range. "D'you think the old nut knows when he's beaten?" "Too much of a fool." "Hasn't the guts to come against us." "Where's he skulking now?" "You'd think he had enough of his stinking loo." "Not him." "Maybe he's stuck there." "Silly old twerp." "Let's try barking." "Bow-wow-wow." "Yap-yap-yap." "Bow-wow-wow." These educated observations culminated in a long yowling war cry of derision from the whole detachment. Stationed slightly apart to the right and rear of the advance unit in the general direction of the playground, a battery of artillery has taken up a commanding position on a bump of higher ground. The chief gunner, armed with an enormous rolling pin, stands facing toward the Dragon's den; a second officer, with his back to the den, faces his colleague at a distance at some forty feet; and directly behind the bludgeon-bearer, similarly facing toward both the den and the second officer, a third artillery man crouches like a frog. I have been told that persons so aligned are not necessarily preparing for battle and are probably practicing a game newly imported from America which is called baseball. Being myself an ignorant creature, I know nothing whatsoever about that game, but it is said to have become the most popular of all sporting activities in the middle schools, high schools and universities of modern Japan. America has a peculiar bent for the invention of fantastic things and I suppose it was only in kindness of heart that she taught Japan a game which can so easily be mistaken for gunnery and which causes so much annoyance in an otherwise peaceful neighborhood. I imagine the Americans honestly think their game is no more than that; however, even the most gamesome game, if it is able to disrupt an entire neighborhood, can hardly avoid being regarded as bombardment. In my view the lads at the Hall schemed for the results of bombardment under the guise of good clean fun. The truth is that by the infinite flexibility of interpretation one can get away with anything. Some people perpetrate fraud in the name of charity, others justify their obvious lunacy by calling it inspiration. Could it not be that others practice warfare in the guise of baseball? Baseball as I've hitherto described it is the normal form of the game, but the variety which I'll now describe is nothing less than the gunnery aspects of siege warfare. I shall commence with an account of the gunnery drill for firing dumdums. The second officer in the three-man crew that I've already described takes a dumdum in his right hand and slings it straight at the bludgeoneer. None but the initiated know the precise contents of the dumdum, so, as a non-professional, I can only say that the missile is round and hard like a stony dumpling and that its contents are extremely carefully sewn tight within a leather casing. As I was saying, this dumdum comes whistling through the wind toward the bludgeoneer who, brandishing his rolling pin, slams the missile back. Every so often there is a misfire when bludgeon and dumdum fail to connect and the frog-like figure is then supposed to stop the ball and toss it back for the first officer again to start the firing procedure. However, in most cases the connection is achieved, and, with a savage cracking sound, the dumdum is discharged. The force thus generated is truly enormous and the kinetic energy stored in the missile could easily smash the thin skull of a neurotic dyspetic like my master. The main three-man gun crew is all that is fundamentally necessary for the weapon to go into action, but the master gunners are supported by droves of reinforcements who stand around the gunsite and, whenever the crack of pestle on sturdy dumpling reports a successful firing, burst into a chorus of raucous shouts and a rapid fire of hand claps.

"Strike," they bellow.

"A real home-slam."

"Had enough yet?"

"We've got you licked."

"Go, go, go!"

"Get on back, you fool!"

Such a tempest of insults to my master would be bad enough, but injury is added to that offensiveness by the fact that, out of every three struck dumdums, at least one rolls onto the dragon's land. And that penetration is not accidental. On the contrary, it is the entire reason for the use of the baseball weapon. The weapon's bullets are nowadays manufactured all over the world, but they still remain extremely expensive, so that even in times of war, their supply is limited. Normally each artillery unit is provisioned with no more than one or two dumdums, and they cannot afford to lose their precious missile every time it's fired. These units consequently always include a platoon of ball pickers, whose sole duty is to retrieve fallen balls. That duty is relatively easy when the dumdums happen to fall in plain view on accessible ground, but when they land in long grass or on hostile territory, the platoon has an unenviable task demanding speed, ingenuity, and often a willingness to face real danger. It is thus the gunners' normal tactic to aim the weapon in such a way that its projectile can be readily recovered, but, in the present context, their usual practice is deliberately reversed. They are no longer playing a game: they are engaged in warfare. They aim to fire their dumdum into my master's property so as to provide an excuse, the need to retrieve it, for crossing the four-eye fence. The constant irritation of dumdums landing in his property, immediately to be followed by hordes of howling schoolboys, leaves my master with a hideous choice between unventable anger and that resignation to fate which is surrender. Under such strain his baldness, surely, can only be a matter of time.

Then it was that a particularly well-struck dumdum came whistling over the four-eye fence, slashed off a few leaves from the lower branches of a paulownia, and, with tremendous noise, landed full-toss against our inner castle wall; that is to say, against that bamboo fence around our garden which I use for my exercises. We know from Newton's First Law of Motion that a body remains in its state of rest or of uniform motion unless acted upon by some external force. If the movement of matter were governed only by that law, my master's skull would at this very moment be sharing the fate of Aeschylus, so he was fortunate that Newton was kind enough to save him from such a shattering experience by the establishment of a Second Law to the effect that change in motion is proportional to, and in the same direction as, the applied force. This, I'm afraid, is all a bit too difficult to follow, but the fact that the dumdum failed to pierce our garden fence, failed to rip on through our paper-window, and failed to smash my master's skull must, with our deepest gratitude, be attributed to Newton. In next to no time, as was only to be expected, the intrepid ball pickers were in action on our property. One could hear them thrashing about with sticks in the clumps of bamboo grass to the accompaniment of such screeched comment as, "it landed about here" and "rather more to the left." All enemy penetrations of the frontier in hot pursuit of their dumdums are conducted with maximum noise, since to sneak in for a secret retrieval would be to fail in their real mission. It is, of course, important to recover a costly missile, but it is even more important to tease my master into frenzy. Thus, on this particular occasion the ball pickers knew perfectly well where to look for their ball. They'd seen its original line of flight, they'd heard it smack against our garden fence, and, therefore knowing the point of impact, they also knew precisely where it must have dropped to the ground; so it need have been no trouble at all to pick it up quietly and to depart in peace. We are indebted to Leibuiz for the observation that any form of coexistence depends upon the maintenance of formal order. Thus, the letters of the alphabet, like the symbols of a syllabary, must always, in accordance with his Law of Systematic Order, occur in the same sequential relationship. Similarly, the relationships established by convention, proverb and received wisdom should not be disturbed: good luck demands that under a willow tree there should always be a loach, while a bat and the evening moon are necessarily linked. There is no such obvious connection between a ball and a fence, but persons who have accustomed themselves by daily baseball practice to regular inroads into our property do acquire a sense of order in such a relationship, from which it follows that they always know exactly where to spot their fallen dumdums. It further follows that, since Leibuiz has told them where to look, their unwillingness to do so clearly shows that the fuss they make is directed not toward finding their ball but to provoking my master into warfare.

Things have now gone so far that even a man as mild and as naturally sluggish as my master cannot fail to respond to the challenge. Can it only have been yesterday that this suddenly berserk man of action was grinning so amiably to himself as he eavesdropped upon ethics? Swept to his feet by pure rage, he ran out roaring from the house, and so savagely sudden was his counter-attack that he actually took a prisoner. One cannot deny the brilliance, for my master, of this feat, but a beardless little lad of fourteen, maybe fifteen, summers makes a captive unbecoming to a fully whiskered man. Unbecoming or not, it was good enough for my master as, despite its pitiful pleas for mercy and forgiveness, he dragged the wretched child into his very den and onto the veranda.

At this point I should perhaps offer some further clarification of the enemy's tactics. They had in fact deduced from my master's ferocious behavior on the previous day that he was now close to the breaking point and that it was a near certainty that today he could easily be needled into another lunatic charge. If such a sally led to the capture of some laggard senior boy, there would obviously be trouble. But they calculated that the risk of trouble would be minimized to virtually nothing if they used as ball pickers only the smallest of their first- and second-year juniors. If my master succeeded in catching such a minnow and then kicked up a whale of a fuss, he would merely succeed in disgracing himself for childish behavior, and no reflection whatsoever would be cast upon the honor of the Hall. Such were the calculations of the enemy and such would be the calculations of any normal person; however their planning failed to take account of the fact that they were not dealing with an ordinary human being, and they should have realized from his extraordinary performance yesterday that my master lacks the common sense to see anything ludicrous in a full grown man pitting himself against some squitty little schoolboy. A rush of blood to the head will lift a normal person into flights of abnormality and transmute level headed creatures into raving loonies; so long as a victim of frenzy remains capable of distinguishing between women, children, packhorse drivers and rickshawmen, his frenzy remains a paltry possession. True frenzy, the divine afflatus, demands that its possessed possessor should, like my frenzied master, be capable of capturing alive some snotty, little schoolchild and of keeping him close as a prisoner of real war. The capture has been made. The trembling captive had been ordered forth to pick up balls like a common soldier ordered into battle by his senior officers, only to be cornered by the inspired battlecraft of a mad opposing general. Cut off from escape home across the frontier, he is caught and held in durance vile on the garden veranda of his captor. In such circumstances, my master's enemies cannot just sit back and watch their friend's disgrace. One after another, they come storming back over the four-eye fence and through the garden gate until some dozen doughties are lined up in front of my master. Most of them are wearing neither jacket nor vest. One, standing with his white shirt-sleeves rolled up above his elbows, folds defiant arms. Another carries a worn-out cotton-flannel shirt slung across one shoulder. In striking contrast, yet another, a right young dandy, wears a spotless shirt of whitest linen hem-piped in black with its owner's initials in tasteful matching black embroidered as large capital letters above his heaving chest. Every member of the detachment holds himself like a soldier, and, from the tanned darkness of their sturdy bulge of muscle, one might guess them to have arrived no later than last night from the rough, warrior-breeding uplands of the Sasayama mountains. It seems a shame to waste such splendid material on a middle school education. What an asset to the nation they could be as fishermen or boatmen. They were all barefooted with their trouser ends tucked high, as though interrupted on their way to fight some fire in the neighborhood. Lined up in front of my master, they glared at him in silence, and he, equally silent, glared belligerently back. Through what seemed hours of steadily increasing tension their eyes remained locked and the atmosphere built up toward a pressure only to be relieved by the letting of blood.

"Are you," suddenly snarled my master with truly draconian violence, "also thieves?" His fury, like a blast of flame, vented itself from nostrils flared back from the sear of passion. The nose of the lion mask used in lion dances must have been modeled from an angered human face, for I can think of nowhere else where one could find so vicious an image of the mindless savagery of anger.

"No, we are not thieves. We are students of the Hall of the Descending Cloud."

"Not just thieves but liars too! How could students of that school you mention break into someone else's garden without permission?"

"But you can see the school badge on the caps we're wearing."

"Those could be stolen, too. If you are what you claim to be, explain how pupils at such a respectable school could be such thieves, such liars, such disgusting trespassers?"

"We only came to get our ball."

"Why did you allow the ball to come upon my property?"

"It just did."

"What a disgraceful lot you are."

"We shall be more careful in future. Please forgive us this time."

"Why on earth should I forgive a gang of young hooligans, all complete strangers, who come rampaging over fences to muck about on my property?"

"But we really are students of the Hall."

"If you are indeed students, in what grade are you?"

"The third year."

"Are you certain of that?"

"Yes."

My master turned his head toward the house and shouted for the maid, and almost immediately, with a questioning, "Yes?" that idiot O-san stuck her head out of the door.

"Go over to the Hall of the Descending Cloud and fetch someone."

"Whom shall I fetch?"

"Anyone, but get him here."

Though O-san acknowledged these instructions, the scene in the garden was so odd, the meaning of my master's orders so insufficiently clear, and the general conduct of the matter so inherently silly that, instead of setting off for the school, she simply stood there with a half-baked grin on her face.

We must remember, however, that my master thinks he is directing a major war operation in which his inspired genius is in fullest flower. He naturally expects that his own staff should be flat out in his support and is far from pleased when some menial orderly not only seems blissfully unaware of the seriousness of warfare but, infinitely worse, reacts to action orders with a vacuous grin. Inevitably his frenzy mounts.

"I'm telling you to fetch someone from the Hall, anyone, no matter who. Can't you understand? One of the teachers, the school secretary, the headmaster, anybody."

"You mean the schoolmaster?" In respect of school matters that oaf O-san knows nothing of hierarchy and no school title save schoolmaster.

"Yes, any of the schoolmasters, or the secretary, or the head. Can't you hear what I'm saying?"

"If none of those are there, how about the porter?"

"Don't be such a fool. How could a porter cope with serious matters?"

At this point, O-san, probably thinking there was nothing more she could usefully do on the veranda, just said, "Right," and withdrew. Quite plainly she hadn't the foggiest idea of the purpose of her mission, and, while I was pondering the likelihood of her returning with the porter, I was surprised to see the lecturer on ethics come marching in by the front-gate. As soon as the new arrival had composedly seated himself, my master launched out upon his pettifogging impeachment.

"The clepsydera has barely dripped two shining drops since these brute fellows here broke in upon my land. . ." My master opened his indictment in such archaic phraseology as one hears at kabuki plays about the forty-seven masterless *samurai* who attracted so much attention by their carryings-on in the early days of the eighteenth century, and wound his wailings up with a modest touch of sarcasm: ". . .as if indeed such persons could possibly be students of your school."

The ethics instructor evinced no obvious signs of surprise. He glanced over his shoulder at the bravos in the garden and then, returning his eyes to focus on my master, indifferently answered, "Yes, they are all students from the Hall. We have repeatedly instructed them not to behave in the manner of which you complain. I deeply regret this occurrence. . . Now, boys, for what conceivable reason do you even want to go beyond the school fence?"

Well, students are students, everywhere the same. Confronted with their lecturer on ethics, they seem to have nothing to say. Silent and huddled together in a corner of the garden, they stand as though frozen, like flock of sheep trapped by snowfall.

Self-defeatingly, my master proved unable to hold his tongue. "Since this house stands next to the school, I realize it's inevitable that balls from the playground will sometimes roll in here. But, the boys are really too rowdy. If they must come over the fence, if they only collected their balls in decent silence and left without disturbing us, then I might be content not to pursue the matter, but. . ."

"Quite so. I will most certainly caution them yet again. But you'll appreciate there are so many of them sculling about all over the place that it's difficult for us teachers to. . . Listen, you lot: you must take far more care to behave properly. If a ball flies into this property, you must go right around to the front door and seek the master's permission to retrieve it. Understand?" He turned again to my master. "It is, good sir, a big school and our numbers give us endless, endless trouble. Since physical exercise is now an integral part of the educational system, we can hardly forbid them playing baseball even though we realize that the particular game can so easily prove a nuisance to your good self. We can thus only entreat you to overlook their intrusions in a benign awareness that high spirits do sometimes overflow into misconduct. For our part, we will ensure that they always present themselves at your front entrance and request your generous permission to enter upon your land and retrieve their balls."

"That will be perfectly satisfactory. They may throw in as many balls as they wish. If in future the boys will present themselves properly at the front door and properly ask permission, everything will be fine. Perhaps I may now hand these particular miscreants back into your charge for supervised conduct back to school. I am only sorry that it has proved necessary to put you personally to the inconvenience of coming over here to cope with this business." As always, my master, though he went up with the dash and sizzle of a rocket, came down like a dull old stick. The teacher of ethics led off his mountain troopers through the front gate, and so this major incident drooped to its tame conclusion.

If you laugh at me for calling it a major event, well, you are free to laugh. Should it, for you, seem trivial, then so indeed it is, but I have been describing what seemed to my master, not perhaps to anyone else, events of enormous magnitude. Anyone who sneers at him as, at best, an arrow shot from a possibly once strong bow but now so far gone as to be spent and feeble, should be reminded that such spent-arrowness is the essence of the man, and, moreover, that his peculiar character has made him the star figure in a popular comic novel. Those who call him a fool for wasting his days in crazy quarrels with the younger kinds of teenage schoolboys command my immediate assent, for he is undoubtedly a fool. Which, of course, is why certain critics have said that my master has not yet grown out of his babyhood.

Having now described the minor and major events in my master's war with the Hall, I shall close that history with an account of their aftermath. Some of my readers may choose to believe that I'm having them on with a history of pure balderdash but, I do assure you, no cat, and least of all myself, would be so irresponsible. Every single letter, every single word that I set down implies and reflects a cosmic philosophy and, as these letters and words cohere into sentences and paragraphs, they become a coordinated whole, clear and consistent, with beginnings and ends skillfully designed to correspond and, by that correspondence, to provide an overall world view of the condition of all creation. Thus, these close written pages, which the more superficial minds amongst you have seen as nothing better than a tiresome spate of trivial chit-chat, shall suddenly reveal themselves as containing weighty wisdom, edifying homilies, guidance for you all. I would therefore be obliged if you would have the courtesy to sit up straight, stop lolling about like so many sloppy sacks, and, instead of skimming through my text, study it with close attention. May I remind you that Liu Tsung-yüan thought it proper to actually lave his hands with rose-water before touching the paper lucky enough to carry the prose of his fellow poet and fellow scholar, Han T'ni-chih. The prose which I have written deserves a treatment no less punctiliously respectful. You should not disgrace yourselves by reading it in some old dog-eared copy of a magazine filched or borrowed from a friend. Have at least the grace to buy a copy of the magazine with your own money. As I indicated at the beginning of this well-constructed paragraph, I am about to describe an aftermath. If you think an aftermath could not possibly be interesting and consequently propose to skip reading it, you will most bitterly regret your decision. You simply must read on to the end.

On the day following the major showdown I took myself off for a walk. I had barely set out when, on the corner across from my master's house where a side street joins the road, whom should I see but Goldfield and his toady Suzuki engaged in earnest conversation. Lickspittle Suzuki had in fact just left the Goldfield mansion after some obsequious visit there, when its 'flat-faced' owner, homebound in his rickshaw, stopped to speak with him. Though I have lately come to find old Goldfield's household something of a bore and have therefore discontinued calling there, the sight of the old rogue himself stirred in my heart an odd warmth toward him. I even feel sufficient interest in Suzuki, whom I haven't seen for several weeks, to sidle across for a closer look; it was thus natural that, as I drifted toward them, their conversation should fall upon my ears. It's not my fault, but theirs, if in a public place I happen to hear their talk. Goldfield, a man whose broad concept of decency permits him to hire marks to spy upon my master, would, I feel quite sure, extend his sympathetic understanding to any chance coincidence of presence which narrower minds might consider common eaves-dropping. I'd be disappointed if he displayed such lack of balance as to cut up rough. In any event, I heard their conversation—not, I repeat, of my own will or by my own scheming, simply because their talking was rammed into my ears.

"I've just been to your house. How fortunate to have met you here." Suzuki performs his usual series of overhumble bows.

"Fortunate indeed. As a matter of fact, I've been wanting to see you."

"Have you, Sir? How lucky then. Is there anything I can do for you?"

"Well, nothing serious. Quite unimportant really. But it's something only you could do."

"You may be assured that anything I can do, most happily I will. What have you in mind?"

"Well now. . ." grunted Goldfield as he searched for the right words.

"If you prefer, I could come back any time which happens to suit you. Would you care to suggest a time?"

"No, no, it's not all that important. Indeed, I might as well tell you now."

"Please don't hesitate."

"That crazy fellow, that friend of yours. . . what's his name now. . . Sneaze I think it was. . ."

"Oh, him. What's Sneaze been up to now?"

"Nothing really, but I've not entirely gotten over that last annoying business. It's left a nasty taste in my mouth."

"I quite understand. Vainglory such as his is positively sickening. He should see himself and his social status realistically; but no, stupid and stuck-up, he carries on like the lord of all creation."

"That's just it. His insolent disparagement of the business community gets my goat. All that rant about never bowing to the might of money. So I thought I'd let him see what a businessman can do. For quite some time now I've been putting spokes in his wagon, modest irritations involving no more than modest expenditure, but the man's incredibly stubborn and I find myself stumped by his sheer block-headedness. He can't, apparently, grasp that he's being got at."

"The trouble is that he has no real understanding of profit and loss. He is incapable of appreciating, let alone weighing, the balance of his own advantage and disadvantage. So he goes his own mad road, feeble but persistent in resisting redirection, totally oblivious to his own best interest. He's always been like that. A hopeless case."

Goldfield burst into genuine laughter at the portrait drawn by Suzuki of a character so ludicrous to them both that cachinnation was their only possible reaction. "You've hit the nail on the head. I've tried all sorts of tricks to shake him up. Knowing the level of his intelligence, I've even hired schoolkids to play him up with pranks."

"That was a bright idea! Did it work?"

"I think it's working. Certainly it's put him under strain, and I fancy it's now only a matter of time before he cracks under the pressure."

"Under sheer weight of numbers! How clever you are."

"Yes, I think that he's beginning to feel the effects of his singularity. Anyway, he's pretty weakened and I want you to go along and see how he is."

"Gladly. I'll call on him right away and let you have a report on my way back. This should be interesting. It must be quite a sight to see that bull-headed fellow down in the dumps."

"Very well, then. See you later. I'll be expecting you."

"All right, Sir."

Well, well! So here we are again with another pretty plot. The power of a businessman is indeed formidable. By its frightening force my clinker of a master has been set afire with frenzy; his thatch of hair is well on its agonized way to becoming a skating rink for flies, and his skull can soon expect an Aeschylean bashing. Considering how much has been achieved by the power of a single businessman, I am obliged to conclude that, though I'll never know why the earth spins around on its axis, it's certainly cash that motivates this world. None know better than businessmen what power money buys. It is by their nod that the sun comes up in the east and, by their decision, goes down in the west. I have been very slow to learn the divine right of businessmen, and I attribute my backwardness to the atmosphere, the cultural effluvia from a poor pig-headed schoolie, in which I have been reared. The time has clearly come when my dimwitted bigot of a master simply must wake up to the realities of this world. To persevere in his present attitudes could well prove dangerous; dangerous, even, to that dreary, dull, dyspeptic life which he so desperately treasures. How, I wonder, will my master cope with the coming visitation of Suzuki? Believing that the style in which that visitor is received will be an accurate indicator of the degree to which my master has learnt to recognize and accept the power of businessmen, I know I must not loiter. Though merely a cat, I accept the imperatives of loyalty and am worried for my master's safety. I slink around the nauseating Suzuki and, at a scamper, got back home before him.

Suzuki proves as smooth and slippery as ever. No mention of the Goldfields soils his subtle lips, but he chats away, amused and even amusing, on matters of no importance.

"You don't look too well. Is anything wrong?"

"No, I'm quite well."

"But you're pale. Must take care of yourself. The weather's not been good. Are you sleeping all right?"

"Yes."

"Perhaps you have some worry. If there's anything I can do, just tell me."

"Worry? What worry?"

"Oh, if you're so lucky as to be quite worry-free, that's fine. I only spoke of worry in the hope that I might help. Worry, you know, is the worst of poisons. It's much more profitable to live one's life with gaiety and laughter. You seem to me a bit depressed, gloomy even."

"Laughter's no joke, sometimes positively harmful. Men have died from too much laughter."

"Nonsense. Remember the saying that luck arrives through a merry gate."

"It sounds to me as though you've never heard of Chrysippus. Have you? An ancient Greek philosopher?"

"Never heard of him. What did he do?"

"He died of laughter."

"Really? How extraordinary! But that was long ago."

"What difference does that make? Chrysippus saw a donkey eating figs from a silver bowl and thought the sight so funny he laughed and laughed and couldn't stop laughing. Eventually he laughed himself to death."

"Well, that's certainly a very funny story, but I'm not suggesting you should laugh your life away. But laugh a little, moderately, a little more than you do, and you'll find you feel wonderful."

Suzuki was watching my master through intently narrowed eyes, but his concentration was broken by the noise of the front gate opening. I thought, with pleased relief that one of my master's friends had chosen this happy moment to drop in. But I was wrong.

"Our ball's come in. May I go and get it?"

O-san answered from the kitchen, "Yes, you may," and the schoolboy pads around to the back garden.

Suzuki distinctly puzzled, asks, "What was all that about?"

"The boys from the school next door have batted one of their balls into my garden."

"Schoolboys next door? Do you have schoolboys for neighbors?"

"There's a school out back, the Hall of the Descending Cloud."

"Oh, I see. A school. It must be very noisy."

"You've no idea how noisy it is. I can't even study. If I were the Minister of Education, I'd order it closed forthwith."

Suzuki permitted himself a burst of laughter sufficiently long to increase my master's irritation. "My goodness," he observed when his cackling ceased, "you really are worked up. Do the schoolboys bother you all that much?"

"Bother me! They certainly do! They bother me from morning until night."

"If you find it all so irritating, why don't you move away?"

"You dare suggest that I should move away! What impertinence!"

"Steady on, now. There's no point in getting angry with me. Anyway, they're only little boys. If I were you, I'd simply disregard them."

"Yes, I expect you would; but I wouldn't. Only yesterday I summoned one of the teachers here and lodged a formal complaint."

"What a lark! He must have been ashamed."

"He was."

Just then, we heard again a voice and the sound of the front door opening. "Our ball's rolled in. May I please go and fetch it."

"Golly," said Suzuki, "not another with another lost ball."

"Yes, I've agreed that they should come by the front gate."

"I see, I see. They do keep coming, don't they? One after the other! I've got it. Yes, I see."

"What is it that you see?"

"Oh, I meant I see the reason for this stream of schoolboys coming to collect lost balls,"

"That's the sixteenth time today."

"Don't you find it a nuisance? Why don't you keep them out?"

"Keep them out? How can I keep them out when their ball keeps flying in? They'd come in anyway."

"Well, if you say you can't help it, I suppose you can't. But why get so tense and stiff-necked about it? A man with jagged edges is permanently handicapped: he can never roll smoothly along in this rough world. Anything rounded and easy going can easily go anywhere, but angular things not only find it hard to roll but, when they do roll, get their corners snagged and chipped and blunted, which hurts. You see, old chap, the world's not made simply and solely for you. You can't always have things your way. In a nutshell, it doesn't pay to defy the wealthy. All you'll achieve are strained nerves, damaged health, and an ill name from everyone. Whatever you do and however much you suffer, those with money won't care a damn. All they have to do is to sit back and hire others to work for them, including whatever dirty work they happen to want done. It's obvious that you can't stand up to people like that. Dogged adherence to high moral principle is all very well in its way, but it seems to me that the price you might have to pay, indeed the price you are apparently paying, is a total disruption of both your private studies and your daily employment. You'll finish up completely worn out for no gain whatsoever."

"Excuse me, but another ball's come in. May I go around to the back and get it?"

"Look," said Suzuki with a knowing laugh, "here they are again."

"The impudent brats," my master shouted from a face stung red with rage.

The purpose of his mission now achieved, Suzuki made polite excuses and, as he left the house, invited my master to call upon him sometime.

No sooner had Suzuki gone but we had another visitor, the family physician, Dr. Amaki. The record of history since the most ancient times shows very few persons describing themselves as frenzied, and it's obvious that when they can recognize themselves as a bit odd, they've passed the peak of their derangement. My master reached and passed that peak during yesterday's major incident, and, though he started off all flame and fury only to settle down in dust and ashes, the fact remains that he did achieve a settlement. Yesterday evening, as he ruminated over the business of that busy day, he recognized there had been something odd about it. Whether the oddness lay with himself or with the inmates of the Hall—that, naturally, remained in doubt. But there was no doubt at all that something very odd was going on. In the course of his ruminations, he even realized that, despite the constant provocation that having a middle school for a neighbor must inevitably generate, it was nevertheless a bit peculiar to have lost his temper, to have been dispossessed of his self-possession, day in day out, for weeks on end. If the oddity lay in himself something must be done about it. But what, he wondered, what? In the end he concluded he had no choice but to seek some drug or medicine which would suppress or tranquilize his irritation at its internal source. Having reasoned thus far, my master decided that he'd call in Dr. Amaki and ask for a physical checkup. We need not concern ourselves with the wisdom or folly of that decision, but my master's determination to cope with his frenzy once he'd noticed it commands, unquestionably, respect and praise.

Dr. Amaki is his usual smiling self as he serenely asks, "And how are we today ?" Most physicians ask that curious question in the plural, and I wouldn't trust a doctor who didn't.

"Doctor, I'm sure my end is near."

"What? Nonsense. That's impossible."

"Tell me frankly, do doctors' medicines ever do one good?"

Dr. Amaki was naturally taken aback by the form of that question but, being a man of courteous disposition, he answered gently without showing any annoyance: "Medicines usually do some good."

"Take my stomach trouble for instance. No amount of medicine produces the least improvement."

"That's not quite true."

"No? Do you think my medicine is making me feel better?" He's off again about his blessed stomach, inviting external opinions on an internal condition about which his nervous system sends him regular on-site reports.

"Well," says the doctor, "no cure comes in the twinkling of an eye. These things take time. But you're already better now than you used to be."

"Really? Do you think so?"

"Are you still easily irritated?"

"Of course I am. I fly off the handle even in my dreams."

"Perhaps you'd better take more exercise."

"If I do that, I'll lose my temper yet more quickly."

Dr. Amaki must have felt exasperated, for he said, "Let's take a look at you," and began examining my master. As soon as the examination was over, my master suddenly asked in a very loud voice, "Doctor, the other day I was reading a book about hypnotism which claimed that all sorts of ailments, including kleptomania and other strange disorders, respond well to hypnotic treatment. Do yon think it's true?"

"Yes, that treatment has been known to effect cures."

"Is it still practiced today?"

"Yes."

"Is it difficult to hypnotize a person?"

"No, quite easy. I often do it."

"What? You do it?"

"Yes, shall I try it on you? Anyone can be hypnotized, at least in theory. Would you like me to try?"

"Very interesting! Yes, please do try. I've always wanted to be hypnotized, but I wouldn't care to remain in a permanent trance, never to wake up."

"You needn't worry about that. Right then, shall we start?"

Knowing my master, I was surprised at the speed with which he had agreed to this somewhat unusual form of treatment. I've never seen a hypnotist in action, so, thrilled by this exciting chance to witness a wonder for myself, I settled to watch from a corner of the room. Dr. Amaki began by stroking my master's upper eyelids in a downward direction. Though my master kept his eyes shut tight, the doctor continued his downward stroking as though endeavoring to close the lids. After a while, the doctor asks, "As I stroke your eyelids down, like this, you feel the eyes are getting heavy, don't you?"

"True, they are becoming heavy," answers my master.

The doctor continues stroking and stroking, and eventually says, "Heavier and heavier, your eyes feel heavier and heavier, you feel that heaviness, don't you?"

My master, no doubt feeling just as the doctor suggests, is silent. The stroking continues for a further three or four minutes, and then the doctor murmurs, "Now you can't open your eyes."

My wretched master! Blinded by his own physician!

"You mean my eyes won't open."

"That's right. You can't open them."

My master, his eyes closed, makes no reply. And I watch this fearful scene in the compassionate conviction that he has now become blind. After a while the doctor says, "Just try to open them—I bet you can't."

"No," replies my master. No sooner had he spoken than both his eyes pop open, and, with a happy smirk, he comments, "You didn't do me, did you?"

"No," says Dr. Amaki, laughing in reply, "it seems I couldn't." So the experiment with hypnotic healing proved a flop, and Dr. Amaki left on some other mission of medical mercy.

Soon another visitor arrived. Since my master has very few friends, it's almost unbelievable that so many of those he has should choose to call today: indeed, I've never known such numbers visit in the space of a single day. Still, there it is. The visitors did come, and this particular visitor was a very rare specimen. I hasten to clarify that I shall be writing about him at some length not because of his rarity but because he has a significant part to play in that promised aftermath which I am still in process of describing. I do not know the man's name, but he looks about forty and sports a smart goatee on his long face. Just as I think of Waverhouse as an aesthete, I see this new arrival as a philosopher. It's not that he's laid any kind of claim to philosophic status or blown his own trumpet in the Waverhouse style, but simply that, as he talks to my master, he looks to me as a philosopher should look. I deduce that he must be another of my master's school mates, for they speak to each other in the familiar manner of very close old friends.

"You mentioned Waverhouse. Now there's an extraordinary man, as light and flossy as goldfish food floating around on a pond. Don't you agree? Someone was telling me that only the other day he went out walking with a friend and, as they passed the gates of some peer or other, no one of course whom Waverhouse had ever met, he dragged his companion right into the house on the grounds that it would be pleasant to call on the owner and take a dish of tea. He really is the giddy limit!"

"And what happened?"

"I didn't bother to find out. Something eccentric, I've no doubt. The man was born that way, not a thought in his head; unadulterated goldfish food. And Suzuki? You see him here? Well, well. That one's clever all right, but not a man of the mind, not the kind I'd have thought you'd care to have around. He's the type to whom money and a gold watch seem to gravitate. Worldly wise but ultimately worthless. A shallow man, and restless. He's always talking about the importance of smoothness, of doing things smoothly, smoothing one's way through life. But he understands nothing. Nothing at all. Not even the meaning of smoothness. If Waverhouse is goldfish food, Suzuki's common jelly paste: a thing unpleasantly smooth which shakes and trembles, a thing fit only to be strung on straw, available for sale to any passerby."

My master seems to be much impressed by this flow of denigrating simile for, which he rarely does, he broke into hearty laughter and enquires, "That's Waverhouse and Suzuki. Now what about you?"

"Me? Well, maybe I'm a yam—long in shape and buried in mud."

"At least you seem carefree, always so self-controlled and self-composed. How I envy you."

"But I'm much the same as anyone else. There's nothing about me particularly to be envied. Still, I have the luck not to envy anyone. Which is just about the only good thing about me."

"Financially, are you now well off?"

"No, the same as ever. Little enough, but just sufficient to eat, so there's nothing to worry about."

"Myself, I feel so deeply discontented that I'm always losing my temper. I grouse and grumble and hardly anything else."

"There's nothing wrong with grumbling. When you feel like grumbling, grumble away. At least it brings one interim relief. You see, everyone is different. You can't refashion others to be like you. Consider chopsticks and bread: you've got to hold chopsticks as everyone does or you'll find it hard to eat rice; however, bread can be cut, and is best cut, in accordance with your own particular liking. A suit made by a good tailor fits like a glove from the moment you put it on, but something run up by a shoddy craftsman takes years of tiresome wearing before it adjusts itself to your own particular bone structure. If competent parents produced children all neatly shaped to fit the ways of our present world, all would be happily well. But if you have the misfortune to be born bungled, your only choice is either to suffer as a misfit or to hang on grimly until the world so changes its shape as to suit yours."

"I see no prospect that I shall ever fit in. It's a depressing prospect."

"If one forces one's way into a suit too small for one's body, of course one tears the stitchings, by which I mean that persons violently ill suited to the world they seek to inhabit are those who pick quarrels, commit suicide, even incite real riots. But you, to be frank, are merely discontented. You're not going to do yourself in and you're not a natural brawler. You could be a lot worse off than you are."

"On the contrary, I find I'm picking quarrels morning, noon, and night. When I lack a subject on whom to vent my spleen, I live in a constant fume of anger. Even such undirected ire amounts to brawling, doesn't it?"

"I see, you brawl with yourself. Interesting. But what's wrong with that? Brawl away to your heart's content."

"But I've grown bored with brawling."

"Then just stop it."

"I understand what you're driving at, but whatever you may say, one cannot do what one likes with one's own mind."

"My point is that one can. But leaving that aside, what do you think is the root cause of your self-wounding discontent?"

In response to that sympathetic invitation, my master poured out before his friend the long sad catalogue of his woes and grievances. Beginning with an account of his war with the schoolboys, he proceeded to list, in manic detail and a neatly ordered, reverse chronology, every single fretfulness, right back to the days of the terracotta badger, Savage Tea, and his petty provocations by conniving colleagues on the staff of his own school.

The visiting philosopher listened in complete silence, but, allowing a long pause after Mr. Sneaze had finished his jeremiad to add its weight to his response, offered the following sagacities. "You should pay no regard whatsoever to the things said by your staff colleagues, which were anyway all complete rubbish. The schoolkids from the Hall are not to be taken seriously, grubby little vermin, existences not worthy even to be noticed by a man at your level of intellectual attainment. What? You insist that they disturb you? Tell me then, have your demeaning counter-activities, even your formal complaint, even that so-called settlement of the matter led to any lessening of disturbance? In all such matters I believe that the ways of our ancestors are wiser and much more effective than the ways of Europe, that so-called positivism which has lately attracted so much faddish attention. The main snag with positivism is that it acknowledges no limits. However long you may persist in positive action, the craving for ultimate satisfaction remains unsatisfied, the quest for the ideal eternally unrealized. You see those cypresses over there? Let us suppose you decide that they obstruct your view and you clear them away. Then you'll find the boarding house behind them has become a new interruption of your view. When you've eliminated the boarding house, the next building beyond begins to niggle you. There's no end to your search for a perfect view, and your ultimate dissatisfaction is the fate implicit in the European hankering for incessant progress toward an imagined ideal. Nobody at all, not even Alexander the Great or Napoleon, has ever felt satisfied with his conquests. Take a more homespun case. You meet a man, you take a scunner to him, you get into a quarrel, you fail to squash him, you take him to court, you win your case: but if you imagine that that's an end to the matter, you're most lamentably mistaken. For the real issue, the problem in your mind, remains unsettled, however hard you wrestle it around, until your dying day. The same truth applies in every context you may care to posit. You happen, perhaps, to live under an oligarchic government which you dislike so much that you replace it with a parliamentary democracy, but, finding you've only hopped out of a frying pan into a fire, you run the risks of civil commotion merely to find another, no less searing, form of government. Or you find a river troublesome, so you bridge it; you are blocked by a mountain, so you tunnel through; it's a bore to walk or ride, so you build a railway. On and on it goes, with no solution solving the real problem of a positivist's dissatisfaction. Surely it's obvious that no human individual can ever have the whole of his heart's desire. The progressive positivism of Western civilization has certainly produced some notable results, but, in the end, it is no more than a civilization of the inherently dissatisfied, a culture for unhappy peoples. The traditional civilization of Japan does not look for satisfaction by some change in the condition of others but in that of the self. The main difference between the West and Japan is that the latter civilization has developed on the basic assumption that one's external environment cannot be significantly changed. If father and son cannot get along together, Westerners seek to establish domestic peace and quiet by changing the parent-child relationship, whereas we in Japan accept that relationship as immutable and strive, within that fixed relationship, to find a workable pattern for the restoration of domestic harmony. We take the same attitude toward any difficulties that may arise in such other fixed relationships as those between husband and wife, between master and servant, between the merchant and the warrior classes. We hold our attitude to be consonant with, indeed a reflection of, nature itself. If some mountain range blocks our free passage to a neighboring country, we do not seek to flatten the mountain, to restructure the natural order. Instead we work out some arrangement under which the need to visit that neighboring country no longer arises.

"This method of fostering happiness, whereunder a man becomes perfectly content not to cross mountains, is perhaps best understood by Confucianists and Buddhists of the Zen sects. Nobody, however mighty, can do as he likes with the world. None can stop the sun from setting, none reverse the flow of rivers. But any man is able to do as he likes with his own mind. Thus, if you are prepared to undergo the disciplines that lead to control of the mind, indeed to its ultimate liberation, you would never even hear the racket kicked up by those graceless imps at the Hall; you would care no whit to be called a terracotta badger; and, knowing your fellow teachers for mere fools, you would smile your disconcern upon their pitiful pavinities. As an example of the efficacy of the course of conduct I suggest, may I remind you of the story of the Zen priest Sogan who, in the turbulent times of thirteenth-century China, was threatened with decapitation by some berserk Mongol swordsman. Sitting unmoved in the posture of meditation, Sogan spoke, extempore, this verse which, in my opinion, can never be too often quoted.

> Though, like a lightning flash, some sword
> May lop my head, it were as though
> Spring winds were slashed. One is not awed
> By threats of such a blowless blow.

"As you will recall, the Mongol swordsman was so discountenanced by that calm asservation of the power of Mind, of the life no killing sword can kill, that he simply ran away. Perhaps, after years of the hardest training of the mind, we, too, might reach that ultimate passivity where, with the same empowered disconcern so spiritedly shown by Sogan, we too might understand how, like a flash of lightning, the sword cuts through the breeze of spring. I do not pretend yet to understand anything so difficult, but of this I'm certain: that it is dangerously mistaken to place your entire trust in Western positivism. Your own case proves my point. However positively you struggle, you can't stop the schoolboys teasing you. Of course, if you had the power to close the school or could prove such serious wrong doing as would merit police attention, things might be different. But things are not that different and, as things actually are, you have no chance, however positivist your actions, of coming out on top. Any positivist approach to your problem involves the question, and the power, of money; it also involves the fact that you are in a minority of one against heavy odds. In brief, if you continue to behave as a Westerner would, you'll be forced to knuckle under to the rich man and, by sheer weight of their numbers, to be humiliated by the little boys. The basic reason for your baleful discontent lies in the fact that you are a man of no wealth seeking, all on your own, to pursue a quarrel on positivist lines. There," he concluded his lengthy dissertation, "you have it in a nutshell. Do you understand what I've been saying?"

My master, who had listened in attentive silence, said neither that he understood nor that he didn't. But after this extraordinary visitor had taken his leave, my master retired to sit in his study where, without even opening a book, he seemed to be lost in thought. Suzuki had preached that the wise man goes with the tide and always truckles to the wealthy. Dr. Amaki had given his professional opinion that jangled nerves may be steadied by hypnotism. And our last visitor had made it very clear that in his remarkable view that a man can only attain to peace of mind by training himself to be passive. It remains for my master to decide which course of action or inaction he wishes to follow. But one thing's certain: he cannot go on as he is, and something must be done.

II

MY MASTER is pockmarked. Though I hear that pockmarked faces were well regarded in the days before the restoration of the Emperor, in these enlightened times of the Anglo-Japanese Alliance, such cratered features look distinctly out of date. The decline of the pockmark began precisely when the birthrate started to climb, so one may confidently expect that it will soon become extinct. This conclusion is an inescapable deduction from medical statistics; these, being thus scientifically established, even a cat, a creature as penetrating critical as myself, would not dare cast doubt upon it. I cannot, offhand, quote statistics of the current incidence of pockmarks among the population of the world, but in my own district and among my many associates, no single cat and only one human being is so grievously afflicted. That human oddity is, I am deeply sorry to say, my poor, old, pitted master.

Every time I catch sight of it, I am moved by that pot-holed visage to reflect upon the dire ill luck which brought my master to live and breathe the air of this twentieth century through a face so anachronistic. Once upon a long time back, he might have made a brave showing of his disastrous dimples. But in these present times when, by virtue of the vaccination laws of 1870, all pockmarks have been ordered into reservations on the upper arms, the determined squatting of such sunkennesses on the wan wastes of his cheeks and on the very tip of his nose, while perhaps admirable for their resistance to the drifts of change, is in fact a slur upon the honor of all pockmarks. I think it would be best if my master just got rid of them as quickly as he can. It seems to me that those pockmarks must feel lonely. Or could it be that they crowd together in a clutter on his face as for some final gathering of doomed clans still driven by a mad ambition to restore their fallen fortunes to a former state of glory? If that should be the case, one should not slight these pockmarks. There they are, a rallying of eternal dents, last-ditch indentations entrenched to block the march of time and rapid change. Such deep redoubts deserve our deep respect. The only snag is that they are also so deeply dirty.

Now, there flourished in the days of my master's childhood a certain noted physician of Chinese medicine, Asada Sōhaku, who lived in Ushigome. When that old man went out upon his rounds, he invariably traveled, very, very slowly, in a palanquin. As soon as he was dead, and his adopted son had taken over the practice, the palanquin was put away in favor of a rickshaw. No doubt in time's due course the adopted son's adopted son will put away the invariable herb tea of his predecessors and start prescribing aspirin; however, even in the first Sōhaku's heyday, it was regarded as shabbily old-fashioned to be troudled through the streets of Tokyo in a palanquin. Only long established ghosts, dead pigs on their way to freight yards, and, of course, Sōhaku's doddering self saw nothing unpresentable about it. I tell you this because my master's pockmarks are as datedly unseemly as Sōhaku's palanquin. Persons who clap eyes upon my blighted patron naturally feel a little sorry for him. But every day my master, no less obstinate and insensitive than that trundled quack of an herbalist, serenely saunters off to school, his lone and helpless pockmarks bared to a dumb struck world, there to instruct his dullard students in the mysteries of the English Reader. And precisely because he is their teacher, the lessons to be learnt from a now departed era, deeply graven on his hapless face, are, in addition to his intended instruction, usefully imparted to his pupils. Again and again, reading from his treasured texts, his mouth transmits the precious truth that "monkeys have hands," but all the time his silent skin gives out its clear and frightening answer to unasked questions about the effect of smallpox on the face. Were men as warningly disfigured as my master to abandon the teaching profession, students concerned with the smallpox problem would be obliged to hie themselves off to libraries and museums, there to expend as much mental energy on visualizing pockmarks as we are forced to expend in our attempts to visualize the men of ancient Egypt by staring at their mummies. Considered from this angle, my master's blemishes, albeit unintentionally, are virtuous in performance.

However, it was not as an act of virtuous performance that my master plowed his face and scattered thereupon the tiny seeds of smallpox. It's barely credible, but the fact is that my master was actually once vaccinated. Unfortunately, the vaccine planted in his arm contrived, I know not how, to evade the intended localization and, instead, burst forth in ugly flower all over his face. Since this apparently happened when, being a child, he had neither the least romantic inclination nor any consciousness of our present high evaluation of a clear complexion, he consequently scratched away at his face wherever it felt itchy. Like volcanoes his many boils erupted and, as their yellow lava trickled down all over his face, the original appearance given him by his parents was irremediably wrecked. Every now and again my master still assures his wife that, before that business of the smallpox, he was a striking boy. At times he even boasts that he was indeed so remarkably beautiful that Europeans were wont to turn around in the street simply to take a second look at him. It is, of course, quite possible. But, sad to say, there's no one who can vouch for it.

Nevertheless, no matter how virtuous or how pregnant with admonitory truths a thing may be, if it is a dirty thing it still remains disgusting. Consequently, from as far back as his memory can reach, my master has been niggled by his pockmarks and has examined every conceivable method by which his tangerine appearance might be chamfered down to a texture less offensive. However, his pockmarks cannot just be garaged out of sight like Sōhaku's palanquin. They manifest themselves, and their blatant self-exposure so weighs upon his mind that, every time he walks along a street, he carefully counts the number of pockmarked persons he may be so lucky as to see. His diary logs the details. How many pockmarked persons, male or female, met that day, the place of the encounter, perhaps the general store at Ogawamachi, perhaps in Ueno Park. Sometimes he cheats with a specific count of pockmarks, but usually contents himself with a slight exaggeration of the general intensity of the pocking. Where pockmarks are concerned, he reckons himself an authority second to none. The subject so obsesses him that the other day, when one of his friends, just back from foreign travels, called around to see him, he opened their conversation with the question, "Are there pockmarks to be seen in Europe?"

His friend first answered, "Well," and then, tilting his head, gave himself up to long consideration before replying, "They are very seldom seen."

"Very seldom," repeated my master in despondent tones, "but," and a note of hope strengthened his voicing of the question, "there are, aren't there, just a few?"

"If there are, their owners will be either beggars or tramps. I doubt whether any pockmarks can be found on members of the educated classes," came the indifferent reply.

"Really?" said my master. "Then it must be very different from how things are in Japan."

Accepting the philosopher's advice, my master has given up quarreling with those little louts from Cloud Descending Hall and, since that act of abrogation, has secluded himself in his study to brood about something else. He may indeed be following the philosopher's recommendation that he should sit in silence and by negative activity advance the mental training of his soul; whatever he's up to, I'm sure no good can come of encouraging a cabbage, that creature born to craven passiveness, to indulge himself in loafing gloomy idleness. I have come to the conclusion that he'd be far better off if he pawned his English books and took up with some geisha who might at least teach him how far it is to Tipperary. But bigots such as he would never listen to a cat's advice; so I decided to let him stew in his own dull juice and have accordingly not been near the man for the last six days.

Today's the seventh day since I left him stewing. Since Zen practice includes the discipline of sitting in cross-legged meditation for a week long stretch, a discipline designed to bring divine enlightenment by sheer determination, I thought it possible that, by now, my master, dead or alive, might have meditated to some real effect. Accordingly, I slouched my way from the veranda and, peering in through the entrance to his study, looked for any sign of movement in the room. The study, a modest area of some hundred square feet, faces south with a big desk planted in its sunniest spot. "Big" is an understatement, for the desk is truly vast. Six feet long and nearly four feet wide, it stands proportionately high. Naturally, this mammoth object was not ready made but, the bespoke handiwork of a neighboring cabinet maker, it was most curiously required to serve both as a desk and as a bed. Never having discussed the matter with my master, I cannot possibly tell you how he came to order such an acreage of wood or why he ever contemplated sleeping on it. It may have been some passing whim which led to this enormity, the product of that process whereby certain types of lunatic associate two unassociable ideas. Certainly the association of the concept of a desk with the concept of a bed is genuinely remarkable. The trouble is that, for all its striking remarkability, the thing is virtually useless. Some time ago I happened to be watching while my master lay at snooze upon this ludicrous contraption. As I watched, he turned in his sleep, tumbled off and rolled out onto the veranda. Since that day he seems only to have used it as a desk.

In front of the desk lies a skimpy cushion whose cover of pure wool muslin is decorated with three or four small holes, all in one area, burnt there by his cigarettes. The cotton stuffing leaking through these holes looks distinctly grimed. The man so ceremoniously sitting on this cushion, with his back and foot soles turned toward us, is, of course, my master. His sash is knotted just above his bottom, and the two sash ends of some grubby gray material dangle down limply against his staring soles. Only the other day he gave me a savage smack just because I tried to play with those dangling ends. Those ends are ends strictly not to be touched.

He seemed still to be lost in meditation, and, as I moved to look beyond his shoulder, I recalled the saying that pointless pondering is a waste of time. I was accordingly surprised to see something gleaming strangely on his desk. In spite of myself I blinked and blinked again. Very strange it was, indeed a thing to blink at. Withstanding the glare as best I could, I studied this glittering object and suddenly realized that I was being dazzled by his manipulation of a mirror on his desk. What on earth, I naturally wondered, is my master doing with a mirror in the study? Mirrors belong in the bathroom. Indeed, it was only this morning that, visiting the bathroom, I saw this mirror there. My powers of recognition are, of course, remarkable; I hardly needed to exercise them, for the bathroom mirror is the only one in the house. My master uses it every morning when, having washed his face, he proceeds to comb a parting into his hair. My readers may well wonder that a man of my master's character should bother to part his hair but, though he is indeed bone-idle about all other aspects of personal grooming, he really does take trouble with his hair. Never since I joined this household, not even in the broiling beat of summer, have I seen my master's hair cropped close against his skull. Invariably, his hair is long, three inches long, carefully parted on the left with an inappropriately cocky quiff turned up in a ducktail on the right side of his scalp. This hairstyle may, of course, be nothing more than another symptom of mental disease. However, though this flash coiffure hardly accords with the antique dignity of his desk, it harms nobody and no one ever carps about it. Leaving aside all further discussion of the weird modernity of his parting, one may more usefully turn to consider the reason for his bizarre behavior. The fact is that his pockmarks do not merely pit his open face but, ever since early childhood, have extended their erosions right up over his scalp. Consequently, if he cut his hair like a normal man to a mere half inch or less, dozens and dozens of pockmarks would then be visible among the roots of his crop. No matter how hard he brushed or smoothed a close-cut head of hair, the spotty dots of his pockmarks would still shine whitely through. The effect could well be quite poetic, like a swarm of glow worms in a stubble field, but certainly his wife would not appreciate the spectacle. With his hair long, his scalp could be inalveolate. Why then should he go out of his way to expose his pitiable deformity? Indeed, he would, if he could, grow whiskers all over his face. Would it not then be crazy to spend good money on haircuts that can only expose his pitted pate to general derision, when hair that grows cost-free will hide what best were hid? That, then, is the reason why my master keeps his hair long. Because it's long, he must part it. Because he parts it, he must peer in a mirror and keep that mirror in the bathroom. Hence also why the bathroom mirror is the only pier glass in the house. How then comes that sole existing mirror, that characteristically bathroom feature, to be glinting about in the study? Unless the glass has sickened into somnabulism, my master must have brought it there. And if so, why? Could it be that he needs a mirror as an adjunct to his spiritual training in negative activity? I am led to recall the ancient story of the scholar who visited a Buddhist priest, far famed for his great virtue and enlightenment, only to find him sweating away at polishing a tile. "What are you doing?" asked the scholar. "I'm doing my best to make a mirror." In some surprise the scholar pointed out that, though the priest was a man of marvelous parts, no man in the world could ever polish a tile to be a mirror. "In that case," said the priest, "I'll stop the polishing. But," and he burst out laughing, "the parallel would seem to be that no man learns enlightenment by scholarly perusal of whole libraries of books." It may be that my master has heard some version of this tale about the uselessness of scholarship and, armed with the bathroom mirror, now seeks triumphantly to demonstrate that nothingness is all. I watch him cautiously, suddenly conscious that his mental instability may well be taking a dangerous turn.

My master, oblivious of my presence and my thinking, continues to stare, transfixedly and with an air of wild enthusiasm, into our one and only mirror. Actually, a mirror is a sinister thing. I'm told it takes real courage, alone at night, in a large room lit by a single candle, to stare into a mirror. Indeed the first time that my master's eldest daughter shoved a mirror in front of my face, I was so simultaneously startled and alarmed that I ran around the house three times without stopping. Even in broad daylight, anyone who stares into a mirror with the fixed absorption now being displayed by my master will end up terrified of his own reflected face; I am bound to observe that my master's face, even at first glance, is not exactly lacking in immediate sinisterity. I sat and watched. After a while my master began talking to himself. "Yes," he said, "I can see that it's a dirty face." I must say his acknowledgement of his own repulsiveness merits praise. Judging by appearances, his behavior is that of a madman, but what he says rings true. It struck me that if he goes one step further down this thorny path, he will be horrified by his own ugliness. Unless in his heart of hearts a man knows himself for a blackguard, he will never be wise in the ways of this world; a man who lacks that wisdom will never sufficiently rid himself of passion as to attain enlightenment. My master, having come thus far toward recognizing his intrinsic blackguardism, should now be shuddering back from the mirror with some cry from the heart such as, "Ah, how terrifying." He has, as you know, said nothing of the sort. Instead, having gotten so far as to admit out loud the nastiness of his face, he does no more than to start puffing out his cheeks. I cannot tell why he so ballooned himself. Next, with the palms of both hands, two or three times, he slapped his bloated chops. Perhaps, I thought, some ritual act of sorcery. And at the moment of so thinking I had the feeling that, somewhere I had seen that pursy face before. From my ransacked memory the sudden truth emerged. His is the face of O-san.

It would, I think, be proper if I here devoted a few lines to describing the face of my master's female servant. It is a tumid face, a face like that bulbous lantern made from a dried and gutted blowfish which someone bought while visiting a fox god's shrine, and then, when visiting this house, unloaded on my master. Her face is so malignly puffy that both her eyes are sunken out of sight. Of course the puffiness of a blowfish is evenly distributed all over its globular body; in the case of O-san's mug, the underlying bone-structure is angularly fashioned so that its overlying puffiness creates the effect of an hexagonal clock far gone in some dread dropsy. If O-san were to hear these comments, she'd be so actively angered that I deem it prudent to resume my interrupted account of my seemingly sorcerous master.

As I have already mentioned, first he blew his cheeks out, then he started slapping them. That done, he began once more to babble to himself. "When the skin is stretched," he said, "one hardly sees the pockmarks." Next, turning sideways to present his profile to the light, he pored upon his image in the glass. "This way, very bad. The side light shows them up. It seems that, after all, they look least there when the light's from dead in front. But even then," and he spoke as if quite genuinely impressed, "they're still extremely nasty." He then stretched out his right hand holding the mirror as far as it would go. He scrutinized the glass. "At a distance, not so bad. As I thought, it's the close-up view that's awful. Still, that's true of most things. Not," his mumblings came out clearly as though he'd lighted upon some marvelous, long hid truth, "just of pockmarked faces." Next, he suddenly laid the mirror, glass upward, flat on the desk and began contracting his facial muscles so that his brows, his eyebrows, even his very eyes, all seemed drawn in one wild whorl of wrinkles around the crease where his nose springs out from his skull. How hideous, I thought. My master, too, seemed shaken by the sight, for he muttered, "That won't do," and ceased his vile contractions. "I wonder," he went on, lifting the mirror up to a point but three short inches from his pot-holed skin, "why my face is so extraordinarily repulsive." He sounded as though honestly perplexed. With his right index finger he begins to stroke the wings of his nose. Breaking off, he presses his fingertip hard down on his blotting pad. The grease appeared as a round blob on the blotter. He has indeed some charming little ways. Next he raises his nose-greased fingertip and hauls down on his right lower eyelid daringly to produce a red-fleshed goblin look, an ugly trick which, very understandably, is commonly described as making a hare's face. It is not entirely clear whether he is studying his pockmarks or merely trying to stare his mirror down.

Let us, however, be generous. He is a quirky man, but at least it seems that in his case such staring at a bathroom mirror does induce original ideas, even original actions. Nor is that all. Such quaint behavior could be seen, by well-disposed and drolly natured persons, as the means by which my master moves, madly gesticulating and with a mirror for companion, toward a revelation of his inmost nature—toward, in Zen terms, his Original Face. All studies undertaken by human beings are always studies of themselves. The proper study of mankind is self. The heavens, earth, the mountains and the rivers, sun and moon and stars—they are all no more than other names for the self. There is nothing a man can study which is not, in the end, the study of the self. If a man could jump out of his self that self would disappear at the moment of his jumping. Nor is that all. Only oneself can study one's self It is totally impossible for anyone else to do it. Totally impossible, no matter how earnestly one may wish either to study another or to be studied by another. Which explains why all great men invariably achieve greatness solely by their own efforts. If it were true that you could learn to understand yourself by virtue of someone else's helping effort, then you could, for instance, declare whether some hunk of meat were tough or tender by getting someone else to eat it for you. But hearing truths preached in the morning, listening all evening to learned expositions of the Way, reading scholarly tomes the night long in your study—all these worthy activities are nothing but disciplines designed to facilitate your perception of your own true self. Yet that true self of yours cannot conceivably exist in the truth preached at you by some other person, or in the Way some other man expounds, or in ancient books however heaped upon you. If your own self exists, it is your personal phantom, a kind of doppelganger. Indeed, it's often the case that a phantom has more substance than a soulless person. For if you dog a shadow, one fine day you may well find its substance. Indeed, as a general rule, shadows adhere to their substances. If it is as a reflection of such concepts that my master's toying with the bathroom mirror should be seen, then he may be someone to be reckoned with. For surely those who seek the truth in themselves are wiser, better men than such fool scholars whose only claim to wisdom is that they have gulped down all that Epictetus scribbled on that subject.

A mirror is a vat for brewing self-conceit, yet, at the same time, a means to neutralize all vanity. Nothing shows up the absurd pretensions of a show-off more incitingly than a mirror. Since time began, the pretentious and the vainglorious have gone about the world inflicting damage both upon themselves and upon others, and the first cause of at least two-thirds of that injury undoubtedly lay in mirrors. Like that wretched Dr. Guillotin, who unintentionally caused himself, quite apart from many others, so much painful inconvenience during the French Revolution by inventing an improved method of decapitation, the man who invented the mirror must almost certainly have lived to regret it. On the other hand, for persons beginning to sicken into self-disgust and for persons already feeling spiritually shriveled, there's nothing quite so tonic as a good long look in a mirror. For any such observer cannot fail to realize as a staggering fact the effrontery of his having dared to go about for years with such an appalling face. The moment of that realization is the most precious moment in any man's life, and none looks more exaltedly transfigured than a fool grown self-enlightened to his own intrinsic folly. Before this self-enlightened fool all the world's vainglorious ninnies should, in the deepest awe, abase themselves. Such ninnies may indeed sneer in contempt at the enlightened one, but in reality their triumphing contempt is an expression, however unwitting, of an awed submission. I doubt whether my master has the depth to realize his foolishness by staring into a mirror, but he is at least capable of acknowledging the ugly truth pox-graven on his phiz. Recognition of the loathliness of one's face often proves a first step forward toward realizing the depravity of one's soul. My master shows promise. But this glint of wisdom may, of course, be nothing more than a fleeting consequence of his having been put down in his recent encounter with that Zen-bent chum of his.

Musing idly along these lines, I went on watching my master. Unaware of my surveillance, he continued happily tugging at his eyelids to produce a series of increasingly horrible caricatures of his naturally nasty features. "They seem," he suddenly said, "distinctly bloodshot. Chronic conjunctivitis." He closed his eyes and thereupon began to frot their reddened lids with the flank of his index finger. I imagine they must be itching, but eyes already so irksomely inflamed are hardly likely to be soothed by such vigorous abrasion. If he keeps it up, it won't be long before his eyes just decompose like those of a salted bream. After a bit he reopened his lids and peered back into the mirror. Just as I'd feared, his eyes have all the glassy leadenness of the winter sky of some northern country. As a matter of fact, whatever the season, his eyes are never exactly bright or even clear. They are, to coin a term, nubeculoid: so muzzily inchoate that nothing differentiates their pupils and their whites. Just as his mind is dim and vaporous, so too his eyes, cloudily unfocused, drift pointlessly around. Some say this eye defect was caused by infection contracted when still in the womb, others that it is an after effect of his childhood smallpox. In any event, he was thoroughly dosed as a tot with decoctions of red frogs and of those insects found on willow trees. Perhaps because such cures are properly intended to eradicate peevishness in children, the doubtless loving care of his doubtless loving mother seems to have been wasted upon him, for, to this day, his eyes have remained as swimmingly vacuous as on the day he was born. My personal conviction is that neither antenatal poisoning nor infantile smallpox are in any way responsible for his inner blear of eye. That lamentable condition, the persistent drifting of his gaze, the dark turbidity of his eyeballs, are all no more than external signs of the darkly turbid content of his mind. Indeed, since he is responsible for the long, gray drizzle of his own dismal thoughts, he should be chided for their outward manifestations which occasioned so much needless worry to his innocent mother. Where there's a drift of smoke, there you will find a fire. Where there are drifting eyes, there you will find a half-wit. Since his eyes reflect his mind, which is about as much use as a hole in the head, I can understand why his goggle eyes, the shape and size of those old-time coins with holes right through them, are as totally vacuous as they are unsuited to these times.

My master next began to twirl his moustache. It is, by nature, an unruly growth, each individual hair sticking out in whatever direction happens to take its surly fancy. Though individualism is currently very much the fashion, if every moustache hair behaved thus egotistically, gentlemen so adorned would be sadly inconvenienced. Having given the matter considerable thought, my master has recently begun trying to train his various tufts into some sort of general order and, to be fair, he's had a modest measure of success, for his whiskers have of late shown signs of acquiring a certain sense of cooperative discipline. Originally, the growth was a mere haphazard extension of hair through the skin of his upper lip, but now it is possible for him to claim with pride that he keeps a moustache. All determination is strengthened by success. And my master, conscious that his moustache has a promising future, gives it every encouragement, not just in the mornings and at bedtime, but on every possible occasion. His dearest ambition is to sport twin upturned spikes like those on Kaiser Bill, so, disregarding the random inclinations of his pores, some pointed sideways, some straight down, he hauls his tuft growths hideously heavenward. Which must be very painful for those wretched hairs. Indeed, it's clear that even my master sometimes finds it painful. But that, of course, is the essence of training. Willing or not, in pain or not, the tufts are being disciplined to stick straight up. To any objective observer this drill must seem a silly sort of occupation, but to my master it makes good sense; one can hardly reproach him when the whole educational system of this country is similarly designed so that teachers may go about bragging that they can twist their student's real characters into upward aspirations as daft as a waxed moustache.

My master was thus brutally drilling his whiskers when the hexagonal O-san advanced from the kitchen and, sticking a raw red hand into the study with her customary lack of ceremony, abruptly stated, "The mail, master." My master, still holding his moustache uptwisted in his right hand and the mirror in his left, turned round toward the entrance. As soon as O-san, who knows that growth for the ragged flop it is, clapped eyes upon what looked like two fish snuggled under my master's nose with their tails frisked up on either side of it, she threw down some letters and scuttled off back to the kitchen where, her whole fat body bent across the lid of the rice-cooker, she lay convulsed with laughter. My master, nowise perturbed by her performance, put down the mirror with the utmost composure and gathered up the scattered post.

The first letter is a printed communication imposingly heavy with formal Chinese characters. It reads as follows:

Dear Sir,

May we offer you the compliments of the season. Please permit us to congratulate you upon your present prosperity, and long may it continue. As we are all aware, the Russo-Japanese War has ended in our complete and total victory, and peace has been restored. Most of our officers and men, loyal, brave, and gallant, are singing victory-songs amidst that incessant cheering which signifies the heart-felt joy of all our people. At the call to arms, these officers and men, selflessly sacrificing themselves for the public good, went forth to endure the broiling heat and the piercing cold in foreign parts thousands of miles from home. There, unstintingly, they risked their lives, fighting on our behalf. Such faithful devotion to duty must never be forgotten. We should carry a living consciousness thereof always, close to our hearts.

By the end of this month the last of our triumphant troops will have returned. Accordingly, our association, which represents this district, proposes to hold, on the 25th instant, a major victory celebration honoring the thousand or so officers, noncommissioned officers, petty officers, and private soldiers who hail from our district. We would also wish to welcome to this occasion all those bereaved families whose dear ones fell on the field of battle. We desire thus

> to express with human warmth our sympathy with them in their loss and our sincere gratitude to them for their menfolk's sacrifice and valor.
>
> It would give our association the greatest pleasure, indeed it would do us credit, if we could carry out the proposed ceremony in the knowledge of your approval. We therefore sincerely hope you will signify your approval of our proposal by a generous subscription to this worthy cause.

The letter is signed by a peer. My master, having read it through in silence, replaces it in the envelope. He looks quite unconcerned and shows no sign whatsoever of any readiness to cough up cash. The other day he did actually contribute a few pence for the relief of those whom the poor crops in the northeast had exposed to famine. But ever since he made that gift he has bombarded everyone he meets with complaints that the subscription was a robbery. If he voluntarily subscribed, he can't possibly call it robbery. It is, indeed, most improper to use a word with such criminal implications. However, my master really does seem to think he really was robbed. I consequently think it most unlikely that he will part with his precious money in response to a mere printed letter, certainly not to a letter so civilly written and unperemptory, even though the cause is as noble as a victory celebration, and its canvasser as noble as a nobleman can be. As my master sees it, before honoring the army, he'd like to be honored himself. After he has been sufficiently honored, he well might honor almost anything; so long as he continues having to scrape along in penny-pinched obscurity, he seems content to leave the honoring of armies to peers who can afford it.

"Oh dear," he said as he picked up the second envelope, "another printed letter." He then began, with steadily growing interest, to read what it said.

> We offer our congratulations that you and your family should be enjoying good prosperity at this season of chilly autumn.
>
> As you are aware, over the past three years the operation of our school has been greatly hindered by a few overacquisitive men. Indeed at one stage, things looked very serious. However, having realized that all those difficulties originated in certain of my own failings, I, your humble servant Shinsaku, communed and expostulated

most deeply with myself in respect of those regrettable deficiencies and, having endured unspeakable self-criticism, hardships, and privations, I have at long last found a way unaided to obtain sufficient funds to construct the new school building in a style compatible with my own ideals. The fact is that I am about to publish a book entitled *The Essentials of the Secret Art of Sewing: A Separate Volume*. This book, which I, your humble servant Shinsaku, have composed at immense trouble, is written in strict accordance with that theory and those principles of industrial art which, for many years, I have so painfully been studying. I hope that every household will buy a copy of this book, the price of which is no more than the actual cost of producing it with little or nothing added as profit. For I am convinced that this book will serve to advance the art of sewing. At the same time, the modest profits I anticipate from its sale should be sufficient to finance the needed extensions to the school buildings.

Therefore, I should be most grateful and honored if you would, by way of making a donation toward the construction expenses of the school house, be so kind as to purchase a copy of the aforementioned *Essentials of the Secret Art of Sewing*, a book which you could, for instance, advantageously put in the hands of your maidservant. I do most humbly and sincerely hope you will grant me your support in this matter.

With the utmost respect and good will, and with nine respectful bows,

Nuida Shinsaku
Principal
Great Japan Women's High Graduate School of Sewing

My master indifferently crumpled this courteous letter into a ball and pitched it lightly into the waste-paper basket. I am sorry to say that Mr. Shinsaku's nine respectful bows and his many unspeakable hardships all came to nothing.

My master then took up his third letter. This one gleams with quite extraordinary luster. Its envelope is brightly colored with red and white stripes and looks as gay as a signboard advertising boiled sweets. Right in the center of these dazzling slats there is written in a thickly, flowery calligraphic style, "O Rare Dr. Sneaze! With Deep Respect." Whatever this envelope may contain, its externalities are extremely grand.

Sir,

If I am to dominate the universe, then I would, in one swift go, swallow up the whole world. But if the universe is to rule over me, then I would become no more than a mote of dust. Tell me, I entreat you, what is the correct relation between myself and the universe.

The person who first ate sea slugs deserves respect for his daring. The man who first ate blowfish should be honored for his bravery. He who added sea slugs to our diet performed a service for the nation comparable to Shinran's founding of the Pure Land sect, and the contributor of blowfish may be fairly compared with such a courageous religious innovator as the great Priest Nichiren. But you, dear Dr. Sneaze, your gastronomic genius stretches no further than to dried gourd shavings dressed with vinegared bean-paste. I have yet to meet a man of parts whose prowess was advanced by eating dried gourd shavings dressed with vinegared bean-paste.

Your closest friend might betray you. Your very parents might turn cold toward you. Even your own true love might cast you off. No man, naturally, can put his trust in wealth or worldly honors. Lands and peerages can vanish in the twinkling of an eye. Even a lifetime's scholarship treasured in one's head goes moldy in the end. On what, then, Dr. Sneaze, do you intend to rely? What is there in the whole, wide universe on which you dare depend? God? God is a mere clay figure fabricated in the depths of their despair by dreggy persons, by beings themselves so terrified as to be nothing more than stinking lumps of shit. Could it be that you claim nevertheless to find some ease of mind by putting your trust in objects that you know to be untrustworthy? Ah, what a depth of folly! A staggering drunkard, babbling senseless words, totters, however weavingly, straight toward his grave. The oil is all used up. As the wick gutters into darkness, so even one's passions die down and are gone. When your destined course is run, what flicker of your self will remain or be remembered? Respected sir, had you not better take a sip of tea?

If you disdain others, you have nothing to fear. Why is it, then, that you, who do disdain all others, are nonetheless enraged at the world which disdains you? High-ranking and distinguished persons seem to be puffed up by their disdain for people. However, as soon as they feel themselves disdained, they flare up in real anger. Let them flare up. They are all idiots!

When due regard is given to other people but those other people do not reciprocate, then, instead of just complaining, the discontented are liable, every now and again, to seek redress of their grievance by some positive action. Such spasmodic action is called revolution. Revolutions are not the work of mere grumblers, but are the happy handiwork of high-ranking and distinguished persons who enjoy promoting them.

Honored sir, there is a great deal of ginseng in Korea. Why, dear Dr. Sneaze, don't you give it a try?

Written from Colney Hatch
and dispatched with two respectful bows
by Providence Fair

The needle-plying Shinsaku had offered nine such bows, but Providence Fair produces only a measly brace, and, since his letter does not ask for money, he must, to the extent of seven respectful bobbings, be that much the more arrogant. Still, even though the letter does not scrounge for cash, its vile construction and indigestible contents make it equally painful to receive. Were it submitted to a magazine, even the scurviest, it would undoubtedly be rejected, and I felt consequently sure that my master, who never likes to put the least strain on his gray matter, would just tear it up. To my immense surprise he reads it over and over again. Perhaps he cannot credit that a posted letter might actually have no meaning and is determined to discover what this one seeks to convey. The world is crammed with conundrums, but none of them are totally meaningless. No matter how incomprehensible a phrase may be, a willing listener can always wring some kind of message out of it. You can say mankind is stupid or that mankind is astute: either way, the statement makes some sense. Indeed, one can go much further. It is not incomprehensible if one says that human beings are dogs or pigs. Nor would it occasion any surprise if one stated that a mountain was low; or that the universe is small. One could well get away with claiming that crows are white, that living dolls are dead ugly, even that my master is a man of worth. It follows that even a letter as weird as Mr. Fair's could, if one really bent one's mind to the effort, be twisted to make sense. And a man like my master, who has spent his whole life explaining the meanings of English words which he does not understand, naturally has small difficulty in wrenching meaning out of mumbo-jumbo totally uninterpretable by anyone else. He is, after all, the very fellow who, when one of his pupils asked why people still say "Good morning" when the weather happens to be bad, pondered that knotty problem for seven days at a stretch. I remember, too, that he once devoted three whole days and three long nights to an attempt at establishing the correct way for a Japanese to pronounce the name of Columbus. Such a man finds no trouble at all in making free interpretations of anything he comes across: he could, for instance, interpret a habit of eating dried gourd shavings dressed with vinegared bean-paste as a sure indicator of inherent ability to achieve world fame, and with similar ease he could identify ginseng-eaters as the instigators of revolutions. In any event, it soon became clear that my master, demonstrating yet again that perspicacity and depth of mind which he once bought to bear on the knotty matter of saying "Good morning" at times of nasty weather, has penetrated to the inner meanings of the crazy letter sent him with two respectful bows. "This letter," he breathed in tones of the deepest admiration, "is fraught with profound significance. Whoever wrote these words is an adept of philosophies. The sweep, the range, the grasp of the mind behind this letter are truly stupendous." Which only goes to show how daft my master is. But, on second thought, perhaps he isn't quite so stupid at all. Habitually he values whatever he does not understand, but he is by no means alone in that behavior. Something unignorable lurks in whatever passes our understanding, and there is something inherently noble in that which we cannot measure. For which reason laymen are loud in their praises of matters they do not understand and scholars lecture unintelligibly on points as clear as day. This lesson is daily demonstrated in our universities, where incomprehensible lectures are both deeply respected and popular, while those whose words are easily understood are shunned as shallow thinkers. My master admired his third letter, not because its meaning was clear, but precisely because large tracts of it were utterly incomprehensible. He was touched, I would say, by the total lack of reason for the letter's sudden irrelevant sallies into such matters as the first consumption of sea slugs and its description of theists as terror-frantic shit. Thus, as Taoists are most deeply ravished by the most gnomic sayings of Lao-tzu, as followers of Confucius laud the *Book of Changes,* and as Zen priests dote on the *Collected Thoughts* of Lin Chi, so my master admires that letter because he hasn't the faintest idea what it means. Of course, it wouldn't do not to understand it at all; so, reading its nonsense in accordance with his gift for free interpretation, he manages to convince himself that he's grasped its real intent. Well, it's always pleasant to admire something incomprehensible when you think you understand it. So it was with understandable reverence that my master refolded the florid calligraphy of that precious letter and placed it gently down upon the desk before him. He sits there, lost in meditation, head bowed and his hands sunk deep within his clothing.

Suddenly, there came a loud voice from the entrance. "Hello there! Can I come in?" It sounds like that of Waverhouse, but most uncharacteristically, it keeps on asking for admission. My master obviously hears the constant calling, but, keeping his hands buried in his clothes, makes no move whatsoever. Perhaps he holds it as a principle that the master of a house should not answer a caller, for in my experience he has never, at least not from his study, ever cried, "Come in." The maidservant has just gone out to buy some soap and Mrs. Sneaze is busy in the lavatory, so that leaves only me to answer the door. But, frankly, I do not care to. The matter was, however, settled when the visitor, grown impatient, stepped up onto the veranda by the door, walked in uninvited and left the door wide open. In the matter of civilities, my master and his visitor seem a perfect match. The visitor first went into the living room but, having fruitlessly opened and shut various of its sliding doors, then marched into the study.

"Well, really! What on earth are you doing? Don't you know you've got a visitor?"

"Ah, so it's you."

"Is that all you have to say? You should've answered if you were in. The house seemed positively deserted."

"Well, as it happens, I've got something on my mind."

"Even so, you could at least have said, 'Come in.'"

"I could have."

"The same old iron nerves."

"The fact is that lately I've been concentrating on training my mind."

"Fantastic! And what will become of your visitors if your trained mind makes you incapable of answering the door? I wish you wouldn't sit there looking so smugly cool. The point is that I'm not alone today.

I've brought along someone very unusual. Won't you come out and meet him?"

"Whom have you brought?"

"Never mind that. Just come out and meet him. He's most anxious to meet you."

"Who is it?"

"Never mind who. Just get up. . . There's a good fellow."

My master stood up without removing his hands from his clothing. "I'll bet you're pulling my leg again," he grumbled as, passing along the veranda, he walked into the drawing room with the clear expectation of finding it empty. But there, politely facing the alcove in the wall, sat an old man whose stiffly upright posture expressed both a natural courtesy and a certain solemnity of mind. Involuntarily, my master first brought his hands into view and then immediately sat down with his bottom pushed hard up against the sliding-door. By this precipitate action my master finished up facing in the same westerly direction as the old man, so that it was now impossible for them to bow to each other in formal greeting. And the older generation remains extremely rigid in matters of etiquette.

"Please be seated there," said the old man urging my master to take his proper place with his back to the alcove.

Up until a few years ago, my master assumed that it did not matter where one sat in a room; but since the day when someone told him that an alcove is a modified form of that upper room where envoys of the Shogun were accustomed to seat themselves, he avoids that place like the plague. Consequently, and especially now that an unfamiliar elderly person is present, nothing will induce him to sit down in the place of honor. Indeed, he cannot even manage a proper greeting. He just bowed once and then exactly repeated the words used by his visitor. "Please be seated there."

"I beg of you. I am at a loss to greet you properly unless you sit over there."

"Oh no, I beg of you. Please, you sit over there." My master seems unable to do anything but parrot his guest.

"Sir, your modesty overwhelms me. I am unworthy. Please don't stand on ceremony. And please do sit there."

"Sir, your modesty. . . overwhelms you. . . please," came the jumbled answer from my scarlet faced master. His mental training does not seem to have had much useful effect. Waverhouse, who has been delightedly watching this ridiculous performance from a position just outside the door, evidently thought it had gone on long enough.

"Move over. If you plant yourself so close to the door, I shan't be able to find a place to sit down. Get along with you, don't be shy." He prodded my master with his foot and then, bending down, unceremoniously shoved at my master's bottom from behind until he was able to force himself between the two seated figures facing the alcove. My master reluctantly slid forward.

"Sneaze, this is my uncle from Shizuoka of whom you've often heard me speak. Uncle, this is Mr. Sneaze."

"How do you do? Waverhouse tells me that you have been very kind and that you let him come on frequent visits. I've been meaning myself to call on you for a long time and today, as I happened to be in the neighborhood, I decided to come and thank you. I beg to be favored with your acquaintance." The old man delivers his old-fashioned speech of greeting with great fluency.

Not only is my master taciturn by nature and possessed of few acquaintances, but he has rarely, if ever, met anyone of this antiquated type. He was thus ill at ease from the start, and became increasingly scared as the old man's flood of language washed about his ears. All thoughts of Korean ginseng, of the shining stripes of that red and white envelope, or of other aids to mental discipline have slipped from his mind, and his incoherent stutter of response betrays his desperation. "I, too. . . yes, I also. . . just meant to call on you. . . pleased. . . yes, indeed. . . most glad to make your acquaintance." This babble was delivered with his head bowed down to the floor. When he fell silent, he half-lifted his nut only to find the old man still bent politely flat. Jittering with embarrassment, he promptly lowered his head back onto the floor.

The old man, timing it beautifully, lifts his head. "In the old days," he remarked, "I, too, had a place up here in Tokyo and for many years used to live close to the Shogun's residence. However, when the shogunate collapsed, I left for the country and have, since then, only seldom visited the capital. Indeed, I find that things have changed so much that now I cannot even find my way around. If Waverhouse is not there to help, I'm as good as lost. Great, great changes." He shook his head and sighed. "The shogunate, you know, had been established in the castle here for over three hundred years. . ."

Waverhouse seems to feel that the old man's observations are taking a tiresome turn, so he quickly interupts. "Uncle, though the shogunate was no doubt a very excellent institution, the present government is also to be praised. In the old days, for instance, there was no such thing as the Red Cross, was there?"

"No, there wasn't. Such things as the Red Cross didn't exist at all. There are other welcome innovations. Only in this present time has it become possible actually to lay one's eyes on members of the imperial family. I'm lucky to have lived so long and I'm especially fortunate to have attended today's general meeting of the Red Cross where, with my own two ears, I heard the voice of the Crown Prince. If I die tonight, I shall die a happy man."

"It's good that, once again, you can see the sights of Tokyo. D'you know, Sneaze, my uncle came up from Shizuoka specially for today's general meeting of the Red Cross in Ueno, from which we are in fact now on the way home. It's because of the meeting that he's wearing that splendid frock coat that I recently ordered for him at Shirokiya's."

He is wearing a frock coat all right. Not that it fits him anywhere. The sleeves are too long, the lapels are strained back too far, there's a dent in the back as big as a pond, and the armpits are too tight. If one tried for a year to make an ill-cut coat, one could not match the mis-shapen marvel on Waverhouse's uncle. I should add that the old man's white wing-collar has come adrift from the front stud in his spotless shirt so that, whenever he lifts his head, his Adam's apple bobbles out between the shirt top and the levitating collar. At first I couldn't be sure whether his black bow tie was fastened around his collar or his flesh. Moreover, even if one somehow could contrive to overlook the enormities of his coat, his topknot of white hair remains a spectacle of staggering singularity. I notice, too, that his famous iron fan, more precisely his famous iron-ribbed fan, is lying close beside him.

My master has now, at last, managed to pull himself together, and I observed that, as he applied the results of his recent mental training to his study of the old man's garb, he looked distinctly shaken. He had naturally taken Waverhouse's stories with several pinches of salt but now, with the old man dumped down before his very eyes, he recognizes that the truth of the man is stronger than any of Waverhouse's fictions. I could see my master's thoughts moving behind his cloudy eyes. If my wretched pockmarks, he was thinking, constitute valuable material for historical research, then this old man's get-up, his topknot and his iron fan, must be of yet more striking value. My master was obviously yearning to pose a thousand questions about the history of the iron fan, but equally obviously believed it would be rude to make a blunt enquiry. He also thought it would be impolite to say nothing, so he asked a question of the uttermost banality. "There must," he said, "have been a lot of people there?"

"Oh, an awful lot of people, and all of them just staring at me. It seems that men have grown too greatly and far too blantantly inquisitive. In the old days of the shogunate, things were very different."

"Quite so. In the old days things were not like that at all," says my master as if he, too, were venerable with years. To be fair, however, I must assert that, in speaking as he did, my master was not trying to show off. It's just that the words came out like that, random fume drifts from the dingy cloud-wastes of his brain.

"What's more, you know, all those people kept gawping at this helmet cracker."

"Your iron fan? It must be very heavy," says my master.

"Sneaze, you try it. It is indeed quite heavy. Uncle, do let him hold it."

Slowly the old man lifts it up and, with a courteous "Please," hands it to my master. He, like some worshiper at the Kurodani Temple who has been allowed briefly to hold the long sword treasured there, holds the iron fan for several minutes and finally says, "Indeed." Then, reverently, he passed the ancient weapon back to its ancient owner.

"People call it an iron fan but actually it's a helmet cracker. A thing quite different from an iron fan."

"Ah yes? And what was it used for?"

"For cracking helmets. And while your enemy is still dazed, you just finish him off. I believe this particular fan was in use as long ago as the early fourteenth century, possibly even by the great General Masashige himself."

"Really, Uncle? Masashige's helmet cracker?"

"It is not known for certain to whom this beauty belonged. But it's certainly an old one. Probably fangled in 1335."

"It may be quite as ancient as you say, but it surely had that bright young Coldmoon worried. You know, Sneaze, since we happened today to be passing through the university grounds on our way back from Ueno, I thought it would be pleasant and convenient to drop in at the Science Department. We asked to be shown around the physics laboratory and, because this helmet cracker happens to be made of iron, every magnetic device in the place went completely crazy. We caused a most almighty stir."

"It couldn't have been the fan. It's pure iron of the Kemmu period. Iron of superior quality. Absolutely safe."

"It's not a question of the quality of the iron. Any iron would have the same effect. Coldmoon told me so himself. So let's not quibble about that."

"Coldmoon? Is that the fellow we found polishing a glass bead? A sad case, that. For he is very young. Surely there must be something better he could do."

"Well," said Waverhouse, "I suppose it is pretty heart-rending, but that's his speciality and, once he's got his polishing right, he can look forward to a fine future as a scholar."

"How very extraordinary. If one can become a fine scholar by rubbing away at a glass bead, the road to intellectual eminence must be open to us all. Even to me. Indeed the owners of toy shops that sell glass marbles to schoolboys would be particularly well advantaged in the quest for professorships. You know," he went on, turning to my master as if seeking the concurrence of that noted academic, "in old Cathay such polishers of stony baubles were known as lapidaries and, I fancy rightly, their standing in the social scale was really rather low."

My master lets his head droop slowly downward in a gesture of respectful assent. "Quite so," he said.

"Nowadays all learning seems to be concentrated on the physical sciences which, though there's superficially nothing wrong with them, are, when it comes to the crunch, totally useless. In the old days it was different. One trained for the profession of arms at literal risk of one's life, and one consequently disciplined one's mind to ensure that in moments of supreme effort or danger one did not lose one's head. I imagine you would agree that such a training was noticeably more rigorous than buffing up beads or winding wires around an armature."

"Quite so," my master once again observes with the same air of respect.

"Tell me, uncle, that discipline of the mind which you mentioned, wasn't it a matter, totally different of course from buffing up beads, of sitting around dead still with your hands tucked into your bosom?"

"There you go again! No, the disciplining of the mind was not just a simple matter of sitting still and saying nothing. More than two thousand years ago Mencius is said to have impressed upon his pupils that a freed mind must then be returned to examine its liberator's self. This wisdom was reiterated, at least in part, by Shao K'ang-chieh, that eminent scholar of the Sung dynasty, who insisted that the highest achievement of human aspiration was the liberated mind. He, of course, was a Confucian, but even among the Chinese Buddhists you will find that such worthies as the Zen master Chung Feng have always taught that a steady and devoted mind was all important. Such teachings, as I'm sure you will agree, are by no means easy to understand."

"If you're asking me," said Waverhouse, "I'd say they were absolutely incomprehensible. What are the recipients of such teachings supposed to do with it?"

"Have you ever read Priest Takuan's discourses upon Zen doctrines?"

"No, I've never even heard of him, let alone his book."

"Takuan, who also wrote importantly upon the seasoning of turnips, was basically concerned with the focusing of mind. If, he says, one focuses one's mind upon the movements of an enemy, then the mind will be entrammeled by and subject to such movements. If upon a foeman's sword, then mind will be subjected to that sword. Correspondingly, if one's mind is concentrated upon the thought of wishing to kill an enemy, that thought will dominate all else. If concentrated upon one's own sword, then it will become effectively possessed by one's own sword. If one's mind centers upon the idea that one does not wish to be killed, then it becomes possessed by that idea. If one's mind is bent solely upon someone's posture, then one's mind will be absorbed to be that posture. In brief there is nowhere that a mind can be directed without ceasing to be itself. Thus, wherever the mind is, it becomes, by definition, non-existent."

"Quite remarkable. Uncle, you must have astonishing powers of memory to be able to quote such complicated stuff at such impressive length. Now, tell me, Sneaze, did you follow the reasoning of that turnip pickling priest?"

"Quite so," replied my master, employing his stock answer to good defensive effect.

"But don't you agree with its truth? Where indeed should one place one's mind? If one focuses one's mind upon the movements of an enemy, then the mind will be entrammeled by and subject to such movements. If upon a foeman's sword. . ."

"Come now, uncle. Mr. Sneaze is already deeply versed in such concepts. In fact, he's only just emerged from his study where he was busy training his mind. As you may yourself have noticed, he's getting so regularly to abandon his mind that he wouldn't even answer the door to a visitor. So don't worry about Sneaze. He's perfectly all right."

"I'm relieved to hear what you say. It's highly commendable that he should so often go out of his mind. You'd do well to do as he does."

Waverhouse giggled, half in horror, half in embarrassment, but then, as ever, rose to the occasion. "Alas," he said, "I haven't got the time. Just because you, uncle, live in a leisurely style, you shouldn't assume that others can afford to fritter their hours away."

"But are you not, in truth, idling your life away?"

"On the contrary. I manage to cram busy moments into my leisured life."

"There you go again. You're a scallywag and a scatterbrain. That's why I keep telling you to discipline your mind. One often hears it said that someone manages to secure odd moments of leisure in a busy life, but I've never heard anyone brag of his ability to cram busy moments into his leisured life. Have you, Mr. Sneaze, ever heard such a thing before?"

"I don't believe I have."

Waverhouse laughed again, this time in genuine amusement. "I'd hoped that wouldn't happen, you two ganging up on me. By the way, uncle," he immediately continued, "how about having some Tokyo eels? It's a long time since you tried them. I'll stand you a meal at the Chikuyo. If we take the tram, we can be there in next to no time."

"Eels would be delightful, and that eel restaurant is undoubtedly the best. Unfortunately, however, I have an appointment with Suihara, and indeed I must be off immediately."

"So you're seeing Mr. Sugihara? Is that old fellow keeping well?"

"Not Sugihara—Suihara. Once again, I catch you in an error, and it's especially rude to make errors about a person's name. You should be more careful."

"But it's written Sugihara."

"It is indeed written Sugihara but it is pronounced Suihara."

"That's odd."

"Not odd at all. It's technically known as a nominal reading. The common stonechat for instance, is called a wheatear, but its name has nothing to do with either wheat or ears. The bird is really a kind of sparrow with particularly pallid feathers on its rump. Its name, in fact, means white arse."

"How extraordinary!"

"Similarly, the magpie was originally a maggot pie, not because it had anything to do with either maggots or meat pies, but because this pied, this black-and-white crow, was still earlier named a Margaret pie; just as the sparrow was dubbed Phillip, the redbreast Robin, and some tits Tom. Margaret and its associated nicknames seem to have been particularly fruitful in this field of linguistics, for it was also from that name that the owl came to be called a madge. So to go around referring to Suihara as Sugihara marks you as a provincial, as much a laughable yokel as someone from the backwoods who still clumps round counting maggot pies for luck."

"All right, all right. I defer to your superior knowledge of patavinities. But if you're going off to see your old friend, how shall we arrange things?"

"If you don't want to come, you needn't. I'll go by myself"

"Can you manage alone?"

"I doubt that I could walk so far. But if you would be so kind as to call a rickshaw, I'll go directly from here."

My master bowed respectfully and quickly arranged for O-san to go and find a rickshaw. When it arrived, the old man delivered the expectedly long-winded speech of departure and, having settled his bowler hat comfortably over his top-knot, left. Waverhouse stayed behind.

"So that's your famous uncle."

"The very one."

"Quite so," said my master who, reseating himself on a cushion, then sank back into thought with his hands tucked back in his bosom.

"Isn't he an astonishing old fellow? I'm lucky to have such an uncle. He carries on like that wherever he goes. You must have been a bit surprised, eh?" Waverhouse evidently likes the idea that my master should have been taken aback.

"No, not at all surprised."

"If that old uncle of mine didn't at least startle you, you must have uncommonly steady nerves."

"It seems to me that there's something magnificent about your uncle. For instance, one could but admire, admire and deeply respect, his insistence on the necessity of training the mind."

"You think that admirable? Maybe when you're well into your sixties, like my uncle, you will be able to afford to be old-fashioned. But for the time being you'd do better to keep your wits about you. You'll do yourself no good if you get yourself known as devoted to old-fashioned notions."

"You worry too much about being considered old-fashioned. Sometimes, in particular cases, being old-fashioned is far more admirable than being up-to-date. Modern education, for instance, attempts too much, and people, ever grasping for more and more, never once question the wisdom of its limitless spread. By comparison, a traditional, even an old-fashioned, Oriental education is less aggressive and, by its very passivity, produces a more discriminating taste. For the traditional education trains the mind itself." Glibly exact, my master trots out as his own views the twaddle that he has only recently picked up from his philosophizing friend.

"This," said Waverhouse in genuine concern, "is getting serious. You sound like Singleman Kidd."

At mention of that name a look of real shock came over my master's face. For the sage philosopher who so recently visited the Cave of the Sleeping Dragon and who, having there converted my master to new styles of thinking, then serenely went upon his way, bore that very name. And Waverhouse had been dead right in his comparison, for my master's words, solemnly spoken as his own original conclusions, were in fact all straight cribs from Kidd's unhinging homily. Since my master had not realized that Waverhouse knew Kidd, the speed with which Waverhouse attributed such ideas to their true source reflected unflatteringly on the superficiality of my master's grasp of them. Indeed, my master actually seems bright enough to regard Waverhouse's comment as a slight upon himself. To establish how much Waverhouse really knew, my master point blank asked him, "Have you ever heard him explaining his ideas?"

"Have I ever heard him! That man's ideas haven't changed one whit in the long ten years since first I heard them in our own undergraduate days."

"Since truth does not change, perhaps that very lack of variance at which you sneer is, in fact, a point in favor of his theories."

"Oh dear, oh dear. Look, it's because men like you lend a sympathetic ear to his ravings that he keeps on raving away. But just consider the man. His family name suggests that he's descended from goats, and that straggly beard, a billy's goatee even in college days, confirms his bloodstock. And his own name too, is singular beyond the point of simple idiosyncrasy. Now let me tell you a story. One day some years ago he came to visit me and, as usual, lectured me at length on the marvels of his mental training and his consequent passive discipline. He went on and on. All the same old tripe and he simply wouldn't stop talking. Eventually I suggested it was getting late, but he wouldn't take the hint. He said he didn't feel at all sleepy and, to my intense annoyance, rattled ever on about his cranky notions. He became so much of a nuisance that I finally told him that, however wakeful he might feel, I was dead tired. I begged and coaxed him to go to bed, and at long last he went. So far, so good. But in the middle of the night there was a major disturbance. A rat, I'm almost sorry to say, came and bit him on the nose. Now, although he'd worn my ears off with his repetitive accounts of his spiritual enlightenment, of the way his training had lifted him above all concern with merely mundane matters, as soon as the rat had nipped his nose he displayed a tremendous interest in worldly realities. He was even worried lest his life should be in danger. What, he demanded, if the rat's teeth were infected? The poison, he whimpered, would be spreading through his system while we wasted time in idle talk. Do something, he pestered me, do something and do it quickly. Well, I didn't know what to do. But, after racking my brains, I staggered off into the kitchen and pressed some grains of boiled rice onto a piece of paper, and that did the trick."

"How can boiled rice grains cure a rat bite?"

"I told him that the gooey mash was an imported ointment recently invented by a famous German doctor and that it had proved an immediate and sovereign cure when applied, in, I think, the State of Hyderabad, to persons fanged by venomous serpents. Provided you clap this on, your life, I told him from the bottom of my heart, will be entirely safe."

"So even in those early days you had a knack for bamboozlement."

"Well, it set Kidd's precious mind at rest. The simpleton believed me and dropped off, smiling, into sleepy-byland. When I woke next morning, I was particularly delighted to notice that a trickle from my ointment had dried into a thread and solidified among the darker threads of his daft goatee."

"I see your point. But he was younger then. It seems to me that he has matured into a man of serious worth."

"Have you seen him lately?"

"He was here about a week ago, and spoke for some long time."

"Ah, that explains why you've been so actively brandishing the childish negativities of the Kidd School."

"It so happens that I was much impressed by his ideas, and I am currently considering whether I myself should make the effort demanded by his mental discipline."

"Making an effort is always a good thing. But you'll only make a fool of yourself if you persist in swallowing every tinseled tale that's flashed in front of you. The trouble with you is that you believe anything and everything that anyone says. Though Kidd talks loftily about freeing himself from coarse realities by the disciplined power of his mind, the truth is that, in a real crisis, he'd be no different from the rest of us. You remember that big earthquake about nine years ago? The only person who jumped from an upstairs window and so broke his leg was your imperturbable Kidd."

"But, as I recall it, he has his own explanation of that incident."

"Of course he has. And a wonderful explanation naturally it is! Kidd's version of that scaredy-cat reality is that the working of the Zen-trained mind is so sharp that, when faced with an emergency, it reacts with the terrifying speed of a bullet fired from a rifle. While all the others, he says, were fleeing helter-skelter during the earthquake, he simply leapt down from an upstairs window. This pleased him very much, for it was a proof that his training had resulted in a truly fantastic immediacy of reaction. Kidd was thus pleased but limping. He refuses to admit defeat. As a matter of fact, you may have noticed that those who make the greatest fuss about the unworldliness bestowed upon them by Zen practices and even by ordinary Buddhism are always the least reliable of men."

"Do you really think so?" asks my master who is patently beginning to wobble.

"When Kidd was here the other day I'll bet he said all sorts of things which you'd only expect from a Zen priest babbling in his sleep. Well, didn't he?"

"In a way, yes. He emphasized the particular significance of a phrase which went something like, 'As a Bash of lightning, the sword cuts through the spring wind.'"

"That same old flash of lightning. It's pitiful to think upon, but that's been his pet stock phrase throughout the last ten years. Not his own phrase, of course. He lifted it from the sayings of Wu Hsüeh, who thought it up in China more than a thousand years ago. We even nicknamed Kidd with an appropriate pun on the sound in Japanese of Wu Hsüeh's Chinese name; and I do assure you that the Reverend No-perception left scarcely one of his fellow lodgers in our student boarding house unstruck by his tedious lightning. We used to tease him into a frenzy because he then got his patter so properly mixed up that he became quite funny. 'As a flash of spring,' he would shout at us, 'the sword cuts through the lightning.' Try it on him the next time he calls around. When he sits there calmly propounding nonsense, interrupt and contradict him. Keep it up until he gets rattled and in no time at all he'll start spouting the most amazing balderdash you've ever heard."

"Nobody's safe with a tricky rascal like you around."

"I wonder who, really, is the trickster. As a rational man, I very much dislike Zen priests and all that riff-raff with their preposterous claims to intuitive enlightenment. Living in a temple near my house there's an old retired priest, maybe eighty-years-old. The other day when we had a heavy shower, a thunderbolt fell in the temple yard, where it splintered a pine tree in the old man's garden. People were at pains to tell me how calm, how unperturbed throughout that frightful happening the good, old man had been, how in his spiritual strength he had shown himself serenely indifferent to a terrifying act of nature, which had scared everyone else clean out of their wits. But I found out later that this spiritual colossus was in fact stone deaf. Naturally, he wasn't shaken by the fall of a thunderbolt of which he was totally unaware. And all too often that's how it really is. I'd have no quarrel with Kidd if he did no more than derange himself in his efforts to find enlightenment, but the trouble is that he goes around involving other people. I know of at least two persons who, thanks to Kidd, are now stark raving mad."

"Who, for instance?"

"Who? One was Rino Tōzen. Thanks to Kidd, he became a fanatic Zen believer, and went to the Zen center at Kamakura and there became a lunatic. As you may know, there's a railway crossing in Kamakura right in front of the Engaku Temple. Well, one day poor old Rino went and sat down there to do his meditation. He made a thorough nuisance of himself telling everyone not to worry because, such were his spiritual powers, he could bring to a halt any train that dared to approach him. In the event, since the train stopped of itself, his stupid life was spared, but he then went around saying that he had a holy body of immortal strength which could neither be burnt with fire nor drowned in water. He actually went so far as to submerge himself in the temple's lotus pond where he bubbled about below the water for quite some time."

"Did he drown?"

"Again he was lucky. He was hauled out by a student priest who happened to be passing. After that he returned to Tokyo and eventually died of peritonitis. It is true, as I've just said, that he died of peritonitis, but the cause of his sickness was that he ate nothing but boiled barley and pickles throughout his time at the temple. Thus, though at several removes, it was Kidd who killed him."

"Overenthusiasm is not, it seems, an unmixed blessing," said my master looking as if he suddenly felt a bit creepy.

"Yes, indeed. And there is yet another of my classmates whom Kidd's meddlesome ministrations brought to an unhappy end."

"How terrible! Who was that?"

"Poor old Pelham Flap. He, too, was egged on into intemperate enthusiasms by that cranky Kidd, and used to come out with pronouncements such as 'The eels are going up to Heaven'; in a sense, they eventually did."

"What d'you mean by that?"

"Well, he was obsessed by food, the most gluttonous man I've ever met. So when his gluttony became linked with the Zen perversities he learnt from Kidd, there wasn't much hope for him so far as this world is concerned. At first, we didn't notice anything, but, now that I come to think back upon it, he was, even from the beginning, given to saying the strangest things. For instance, on one occasion when he was visiting me at home, he warned me somewhat ponderously that beef cutlets might soon be coming to roost in my pine trees. On another occasion he mentioned that in the country district where his people lived it was not uncommon for boiled fish-paste to come floating down the river on little wooden boards. It was still all right when he contented himself with mere bizarre remarks, but when one day he urged me to join him in digging for sugared chestnuts and mashed potatoes in a ditch that ran in front of the house, then I reckoned things had gone too far. A few days later they carted him off to the loony bin at Colney Hatch and he's been there ever since. To tell the truth, an earth-bound, greedy pig like Flap wasn't entitled to rise so high in the spiritual hierarchy as even to qualify to become a lunatic, so I suppose he ought to thank Kidd for that ludicrous measure of advancement. Yes, indeed, the influence of Singleman Kidd is quite something."

"Well, well. So Flap is still confined in an asylum?"

"Oh yes; he's very much at home in there. He's now become a megalomaniac, and finds full scope in that institution for the exercise of his latest bent. He recently came to the conclusion that Pelham Flap was an unimpressive name; so, in the conviction that he is an incarnation of Divine Providence, he's now decided to call himself Mr. Providence Fair. He's really putting on a terrific performance. You ought to go and see him one of these days."

"Did you say 'Providence Fair?'"

"Yes, that's his latest moniker. I must say that, considering he's a certified lunatic, he's picked on a clever name. Anyway, his fancy is that we are all living in darkness, a condition from which he yearns to rescue us. Accordingly, he fires off enlightening letters to his friends or, in fact, to just anyone. I myself have several of his demented encyclicals. Some are extremely long, so long that I've even found myself obliged to pay postage due."

"Then the letter I've just received must have come from this unbalanced Flap!"

"Ah, so you've heard from him, too. That's odd. I bet it came in a scarlet envelope."

"Red in the center and white on both sides, a rather unusual looking envelope."

"D'you know, I'm told he has them specially imported from China. The color scheme is supposed to symbolize one of his pottier maxims: that Heaven's way is white, Earth's way is white, and that the human way turns red between them."

"I see. Even the envelope is pregnant with transcendental meaning."

"Being that of a lunatic, his symbolism is incredibly elaborate. But the quaint thing is that, even though he's gone completely out of his mind, his stomach seems to have maintained its gluttonous appetites. All his letters somewhere mention food. Did he refer to food in his letter to you?"

"Well, yes, he did say something about sea slugs."

"Quite. He was very partial to sea slugs. It's only natural he still should think about them. Anything else?"

"The letter did contain some passing references to blowfish and Korean ginseng."

"That combination is rather clever. Perhaps in his lunatic way he's trying to advise you to take infusions of ginseng when you poison yourself by eating blowfish."

"I don't think that was quite what he meant."

"Never mind if he didn't. He's a lunatic anyway. Nothing more?"

"One thing more. There was a bit toward the end of his letter where he advised me, most respectfully, to drink tea."

"That's amusing. Advising you to drink tea, eh? Pretty tough talk, that, at least when it comes from Flap. I imagine he sees himself as having snubbed you. Well done, Providence Fair!!" Goodness knows what Waverhouse finds so funny, but it certainly makes him laugh.

My master, having now realized that the writer of that letter which he had read and re-read with such immense respect is a notorious maniac feels distinctly annoyed with himself not least because his recent enthusiasm and his spiritual endeavourings have all been a waste of time. He is also somewhat ashamed of himself for having, after assiduous study of the material, so strongly admired the scribblings of an insane person. And to top off his discomforture, he harbors a sneaking suspicion that anyone so impressed by a madman's work is himself likely to be not altogether right in the head. He consequently sits there looking decidedly upset in a mixed condition of anger, humiliation and worry.

Just at that moment we heard a sound of the entrance door being roughly opened and the sound of heavy boots crunching on the step stone. Then a loud voice shouted, "Hello! Excuse me. Is there anyone at home?"

Unlike my sluggish master, Waverhouse is a buoyant person. Without waiting for O-san to answer the caller, he calls out, "Who is it ?" Up on his feet in a flash, he sweeps through the neighboring anteroom in a couple of strides and disappears into the entrance hall. The way he comes barging right into someone else's house without being announced or invited is, of course, annoying, but, once inside, he generally makes himself useful by performing such houseboy functions as answering the door. Still, though Waverhouse does in truth make himself useful, the fact remains that in this house he's a guest; it is not proper that, when a guest flits out to the entrance hall, the master of the house should just stay sitting, disturbingly undisturbed, on the drawing room floor. Any normal person would at least get up and follow a guest, any guest, out to the entrance hall. But Mr. Sneaze is and always will be his own obdurate self. Seemingly totally unconcerned, he sits there with his bottom planted on a cushion, but though such steadiness of bottom might be thought to imply some steadiness of nerve, he was inside a simmer of emotions.

Waverhouse can be heard conducting an animated conversation at the entrance, but eventually he turns to shout back into the drawing room. "Sneaze," he yells, "you're wanted. You'll have to come out here. Only you can cope with this."

My master sighs in resignation and, his hands still tucked inside his robe, slowly shuffles his way to the entrance. There he finds Waverhouse, holding the visitor's card in his hand, crouched down in the polite posture for receiving visitors. Seen from the back, however, that posture looks extremely undignified. The visiting card informs my master that his latest visitor is Police Detective Yoshida Torazō from the Metropolitan Police Office. Standing beside Torazō is a tall young man in his mid-twenties, smartly dressed in a kimono ensemble of fine striped cotton. Quaintly enough, this personable young fellow is like my master in that, similarly silent, he also stands with his hands kept tucked inside his robe. The face strikes me as vaguely familiar and, looking at him a little more closely, I suddenly realize why. Of course! It's the man who burgled us a short while back and made off with that box of yams. And here he is again, by broad daylight, standing there as calm as you please, this time, too, at the front entrance.

"Sneaze," says Waverhouse, "this person is a police detective. He has called specially to tell you that the man who burgled you the other night has now been caught. So he wants you to come to the police station."

My master seems at last to understand why he is being raided by the police, and accordingly, turning to face the burglar, bows politely. An understandable mistake, since the burglar looks decidedly more presentable than the detective. The burglar must have been very surprised but, since he can hardly be expected to identify himself as a burglar, he just stands there calmly. He still keeps his hands buried in the fold of his kimono but, being handcuffed, he cannot take his hands out even if he wants to. Any sensible person could correctly interpret the situation by the appearances of the individuals concerned but my master, out of touch with modern trends, still makes much too much of officials and the police. He thinks the power of the authorities is really terrifying. Though he is just capable of grasping that, in theory at least, policemen and other such creatures are no more than watchmen employed by us and paid by us, in actual practice he is ready to drop on his hands and knees at the first sight of a uniform. My master's father, the headman of a district on the outskirts of some minor town, quickly developed the ugly habit of creeping to his superiors. Perhaps as an act of divine justice, his son was born with that cringing streak which one can but notice in my master's character. I find this very pitiful.

The police detective must have had a sense of humor, for he was grinning when he said, "Please be at the Nihon-zatsumi police substation tomorrow morning at nine o'clock. Would you also please tell me precisely what goods were stolen from you?"

"The stolen goods," my master promptly responded, "consisted of. . ." but having forgotten most of them, his voice petered out. All he could remember was that ridiculous box of yams. He didn't really care about the yams, but he thought he would look silly and undignified if having started to identify the property stolen, he suddenly had to stop dead. After all, it was he who had been burgled, and he was conscious of a certain responsibility deriving from his burgled status. If he could not give a precise answer to the policeman's question, he would feel himself to be somehow less than a man. Accordingly, with sturdy resolution, he completed his sentence. "The stolen goods," he said, "consisted of a box of yams."

The burglar seemed to think this answer was terribly funny, for he looked down and buried his chin in his kimono collar. Waverhouse was less restrained and burst into hoots of laughter. "I see," he squawked, "the yams were really precious, eh?"

Only the policeman looked at all serious. "I don't think you'll recover the yams," he said, "but most of the other things will be returned. Anyway, you can find out about all that at the station tomorrow. Of course, we shall need a receipt for everything you repossess, so don't forget to bring your personal seal. You must arrive no later than nine in the morning at the aforementioned substation, which lies within the jurisdiction of the Asakusa Police Office. Well, goodbye." His mission completed, the policeman walked out of the front door. The burglar followed him. Since he couldn't take his hands out of his kimono, the burglar couldn't close the door behind him, so after he'd gone, it just stood open. Though my master had conducted himself throughout the incident with awe-filled diffidence towards the police, he seemed annoyed by that parting rudeness: for, looking unpleasantly sullen, he closed the door with a vicious sliding slam.

"Well, well," said Waverhouse, "you do seem awed by detectives. I only wish you'd always behave with such remarkable diffidence. You'd be a marvel of good manners. But the trouble with you is that you're civil only to coppers."

"But he'd come a long way out of his way to bring me that good news."

"It's his job to come and tell you. There was no need whatsoever to treat him as anyone special."

"But his is not just any ordinary job."

"Of course it's not an ordinary job. It's a disgusting job called 'being a detective.' An occupation lower and dirtier than any ordinary job."

"If you talk like that, you'll land yourself in trouble."

Waverhouse snorted disrespectfully. "Very well then," he grunted, "I'll lay off slandering detectives. But, you know, it's not really a matter of respecting or not respecting those insufferable sneakers. What really is shocking is this business of being respectful to burglars."

"Who showed respect to a burglar?"

"You did."

"How could I conceivably number a burglar among my friends? Quite impossible!"

"Impossible, is it? But you actually bowed to a burglar."

"When?"

"Just now, you bowed down like a hoop before him."

"Don't be silly. That was the detective."

"Detectives don't wear clothes like that."

"But can't you see, it's precisely because he is a detective that he disguises himself in clothes like that."

"You're being very pig-headed."

"It's you who's being very pig-headed."

"Now do just think. To start with, when a detective visits someone, do you honestly imagine he will just stand there with his hands in his robes?"

"Are you suggesting detectives are incapable of keeping their hands in their robes?"

"If you get so fierce, I'll simply have to break this conversation off. But think, man. While you were bowing to him, didn't he just stand there?"

"Not surprising if he did. After all, he is a detective."

"What glorious self-assurance! You're totally deaf to reason, aren't you?"

"No, I'm not. You keep saying that fellow was a burglar, but you didn't actually see him committing burglary. You just imagine he did so, and you're being extraordinary obstinate about it."

It was at this point that Waverhouse abandoned hope and accepted my master as dim beyond redemption. He fell unwontedly silent. My master, interpreting that silence as an admission of defeat, looks uncommonly pleased with himself. But in proportion to my master's self-elation, Waverhouse's assessment of the wretched man has dropped. In Waverhouse's view my master's fat-headed obstinacy has considerably lowered his value as a man. But in my master's view his firmness of mind has, by a corresponding amount, lifted him above the level of such pifflers as poor Waverhouse. Such topsy-turveydoms are not unusual in this imperfect world. A man who sees himself as magnified by his display of determination is, in fact, dimnished in the public estimation by that demonstration of his crass willfulness. The strange thing is that, to his dying day, the mulish bigot regards his dull opiniatrety as somehow meritorious, a characteristic worthy to be honored. He never realizes that he has made himself a despised laughing stock, and that sensible people want nothing more to do with him. He has, in fact, achieved happiness. I understand that such joy, the wallowing well-being of a pig in its sty, is even called pig's happiness.

"Anyway," said Waverhouse, "do you intend to go to the copper shop tomorrow?"

"Of course. I've been asked to be there by nine o'clock, so I'll leave the house at eight."

"What about school?"

"I'll take a day off. That school—who cares!" retorts my master with almost venomous vigor.

"My, my! What a roaring boy we have become, and all of a sudden too! But will it really be all right to take the day off?"

"Of course it'll be all right. My salary's paid on a monthly basis, so there's no danger of them deducting a day's wages. It's quite safe." There is, of course, something unpleasantly sly in these remarks, but the very frankness of his comments reveals that my master is more simple than dishonest. Though he is, alas, both.

"Fine. But do you know how to get there?"

"Why should I know the way to a police station?" My master is clearly narked. "But it will presumably be quite easy to get there by rickshaw."

"Your knowledge of Tokyo seems no better than that of my uncle from the provinces. I give up."

"You're welcome."

Waverhouse responded to this petty spitefulness with another burst of laughter. "Don't you realize that the police station you'll be visiting is not in any ordinary district. It's down in Yoshiwara."

"Where?"

"In Yoshiwara."

"You mean in the red light district?"

"That's right. There's only one Yoshiwara in Tokyo. Well, now do you still want to go?" Waverhouse starts teasing him again.

On realizing that Yoshiwara meant the Yoshiwara, my master flinched and seemed to hesitate, but, quickly thinking it over, he decided to put on a quite unnecessarily bold front. "Wherever it may be, red light district or not, I've said I'll go, so go I will." In circumstances of this kind any fool is like to prove pig-headed.

Waverhouse, unimpressed, coolly remarked, "It may prove interesting. You really ought to see that place."

The ructions caused by the detective incident died away, and, in the subsequent conversation, Waverhouse displayed his inexhaustible gift for amusing banter. When it began to grow dark, he got up and, explaining that his uncle would be annoyed if he stayed out unduly late, took his departure. After he'd gone, my master downed a hurried dinner and withdrew to the study. There, again with his arms close-folded, he started to muse aloud.

"According to Waverhouse, Singleman Kidd, whom I admired and whose example I very much wanted to follow, is not in truth a person worthy of imitation. On the contrary, the theory he advocates seems sadly lacking in common sense and, as Waverhouse insists, contains features that strongly suggest lunacy, a suggestion which appears all the more well founded when one remembers that two of Kidd's most enthusiastic disciples are incontrovertibly mad. An extremely dangerous situation. If I become too much involved with him, I myself am liable to be regarded as unbalanced. What's more, that Providence Fair fellow, whose writings really impressed me so much that I believed him to be a great man with enormous depths of knowledge and insight, has turned out to be an unadulterated certified maniac, confined, under his real name of Pelham Flap, in a well-known lunatic asylum. Even allowing for the probability that Waverhouse's portrait of the unfortunate fellow is a distorted caricature, it still seems likely that he's having a high, old time in that loony bin under the impression that he's superintending Heaven. Am I, perhaps, myself a little potty? They say that birds of a feather flock together and that like attracts like. If those old sayings are true, my admiration of a loony's thinking, well, let's say my generous sympathy for his writings, suggest that I myself must be a borderline case at least. Even if I'm not yet clearly certifiable, if I freely choose to live next door to a madman, there's an obvious risk that one fine day I might, perhaps unwittingly, topple across into his demented territory and end up, like my neighbor, completely around the bend. What a terrifying prospect! Now that I come to think of it, I confess that I've been more than a little surprised at the very peculiar way in which my brain has recently been functioning. Perhaps some spoonful of my brain cells has suffered a chemical change. Even if nothing like that has happened, it's still true that, of my own free will, I've been doing and saying immoderate things, things that lack balance. I don't feel, yet, anything queer on my tongue or under my armpits, but what's this maddening smell at the roots of my teeth, these crazy muscular tics? This is no longer a joke. Perhaps I've already gone stark staring mad, and it's only because I've been lucky enough not to have hurt anybody or to have become an obvious public nuisance that I'm still allowed to quietly live on in this district as a private citizen. This is indeed no time to be fooling about with negatives and positives, passive or active training of the mind. First of all, let's check my heart rate. My pulse seems normal. Is my brow fevered? No, temperature normal; no sign there of any rush of blood to the brain. Even so, I'm still not satisfied there's nothing wrong."

For a little while my master sat in worried silence, straining his wits about what strains his wits could bear. Then, after a few anxious minutes, his mumblings started up again.

"I've been comparing myself solely with lunatics, concentrating on the similarities between deranged persons and myself. That way I shall never escape from the atmosphere of lunacy. Obviously, I've tackled the problem in the wrong way. I've been accepting lunacy as the norm, and I've been measuring myself by the wonky standards of insanity. Inevitably, I've been coming to lunatic conclusions. If instead, I now start measuring myself by the normal standards of a healthy person, perhaps I'll come to happier results. Let me then start by comparing myself to those close to me, those whom I know best. First, what about that old uncle in a frock coat who came visiting today? But wasn't it he who kept demanding where one should place one's mind? I doubt if he could really be counted as normal. Secondly then, what about Coldmoon? He's so mad on polishing glass beads that, for fear lest lunch should deprive him of one moment's friction, he hoiks a lunchbox down to the laboratory. Hardly normal either. Thirdly, Waverhouse? That man thinks his only function in life is to go around rollicking everywhere. Such a madcap must be a completely positive kind of lunatic. Fourthly, the wife of that man Goldfield. Her disposition is so totally poisonous as to leave no nook for common sense. I conclude that she also must be stark staring mad. Fifthly, Goldfield himself. Though I haven't had the pleasure of meeting him, it is obvious that he must be less than normal because he has achieved conjugal harmony by conforming with the warped characteristics of so abnormal a woman. Such a degree of conformity with the abnormal amounts to lunacy, so he's as bad as she. Who else? Well, there are those charming little gentlemen from Cloud Descending Hall. Though they are still mere sprouts, their raving madness could very easily disrupt the entire universe. They're mad as young March hares, the whole boiling lot of them. Thus, as I review the list of my friends and acquaintances, most of them emerge as stained with maniac stigmata of one sort or another. l begin to feel considerably reassured. The truth may simply be that human society is no more than a massing of lunatics. Perhaps our vaunted social organization is merely a kind of bear-garden, where lunatics gather together, grapple desperately, bicker and tussle with each other, call each other filthy names, tumble and sprawl all over each other in mindless muckiness. This agglomeration of lunatics thus becomes a living organism which, like cells, disintegrates and coalesces, crumbles again to nothing and again reintegrates. Is that not the actual nature of our marvelous human society? And within that organism, such few cells as are slightly sensible and exhibit symptoms of discretion inevitably prove a nuisance to the rest. So they find themselves confined in specially constructed lunatic asylums. It would follow that, objectively speaking, those locked up in mental homes are sane, while those careering around outside the walls are all as mad as hatters. An individual lunatic, so long as he's kept isolated, can be treated as a lunatic, but when lunatics get together and, so massed, acquire the strength of numbers, they also automatically acquire the sanity of numbers. Many lunatics are, by their maniness, healthy persons. It is not uncommon that a powerful lunatic, abusing the authority of his wealth and with myriad minor madmen in his pay, behaves outrageously, but is nevertheless honored and praised by all and sundry as a paragon of human virtue. I just don't understand anything any more."

I have not altered a word of my master's sad soliloquies as he sat there, all that evening, deep in twitchless meditation, under the forlorn light of his solitary lamp. If further evidence were needed, his drooling words confirm the dullness of his brain. Though he sports a fine moustache like Kaiser Bill, he is so preternaturally stupid that he can't even distinguish between a madman and a normal person. Not only that, but after he has given himself the heartache and excruciating mental torment of considering lunacy as an intellectual problem, he finishes up by dropping the matter without reaching any conclusion whatsoever. He lacks the brain power to think through a problem. Any problem. In any field. He's a poor old blithering mutt. The only thing worth noting about the whole of his evening's performance is that, characteristically, his conclusions are as vague and as elusive as the grayish cigarette smoke leaking from his nostrils.

I am a cat. Some of you may wonder how a mere cat can analyze his master's thoughts with the detailed acumen which I have just displayed. Such a feat is a mere nothing for a cat. Quite apart from the precision of my hearing and the complexity of my mind, I can also read thoughts. Don't ask me how I learned that skill. My methods are none of your business. The plain fact remains that when, apparently sleeping on a human lap, I gently rub my fur against his tummy, a beam of electricity is thereby generated, and down that beam into my mind's eye every detail of his innermost reflections is reflected. Only the other day, for instance, my master, while gently stroking my head, suddenly permitted himself to entertain the atrocious notion that, if he skinned this snoozing moggy and had its pelt made up into a waistcoat, how warm, how wonderfully warm, that Kittish Warm would be. I at once sensed what he was thinking, and felt an icy chill creep over me. It was quite horrible. Anyway, it is this extrasensory gift which has enabled me to tell you not only what my master said but even what he thought throughout this dreary evening.

But, as you now must know, he's a pretty feeble specimen of his unperceptive kind. When he'd got as far as telling himself that he just doesn't understand anything any more, his energies were exhausted and he dropped off into sleep. Sure as eggs are eggs, when he wakes tomorrow he'll have forgotten everything he's just been thinking, even why he thought it. If the matter of lunacy ever again occurs to him, he'll have to start anew, right from scratch. But if that ever does happen, I cannot guarantee that his thinking will follow the same lines in order to arrive at the conclusion that he just doesn't understand anything any more. However, no matter how often he ponders these problems, no matter how many lines of thought he develops, one thing I can guarantee with absolute assurance. I give you my feline word that he will invariably conclude, just before dropping asleep, with an admission that he just doesn't understand anything any more.

III

MY DEAR, it's seven already," his wife called out from the other side of the sliding door. It is difficult to say whether my master is awake or asleep: he lies facing away from me and makes no answer. It is, of course, his habit not to give answers. When he absolutely has to open his mouth, he says, "Hmm." Even this non-committal noise does not easily emerge. When a man becomes so lazy that he finds it a nuisance even to give an answer, he often acquires a certain curiously individual tanginess; a certain personal spice which, however, is never appreciated by women. Even his life partner, the less-than-fussy Mrs. Sneaze, seems to set low store upon her husband; so one can readily imagine what the rest of the world thinks about him. There's a popular song which asks, "How can a fellow shunned by both his parents and his brothers possibly be loved by some tart who's a perfect stranger?" How, then, can a man found unattractive even by his own wife expect to be favored by ladies in general? There is, of course, no call upon me to go out of my way gratuitously to expose my master as a creature repulsive to females of his own kind. But I cannot just sit by while he cultivates illusions, blurring reality with such nitwitted notions as the happy thought that it is only some unlucky disposition of their stars which preordains his wife's dislike of him. It is thus purely my kind-hearted anxiety to help my master to see the world as it really is, to realize his own reality, which has induced me to provide the foregoing account of his sexual repulsiveness.

Mrs. Sneaze is under strict instructions to rouse him at a set time. Accordingly, when that time arrives, she tells him so. If he chooses to disregard her call, offering not even his normal subhuman "Hmm" of an acknowledgement, that, she concludes, is his affair. Let him lump the consequences. With an eloquent gesture disclaiming all responsibility if her husband proves late for his appointment, she goes off into the study with her broom in her hand and a dust cloth slung lightly over her shoulder. Soon I heard sounds of the duster flap-flapping all over the study. The daily housework has begun. Now, since it is not my job to clean rooms, I naturally do not know if doing a room is a form of fun or a means of taking exercise. It's certainly no concern of mine, but I cannot forbear to comment that this woman's method of cleaning is totally pointless—unless, that is, she goes through the motions of cleaning for their own ritualistic sake. Her idea of doing a room is to flip the duster curtly over the paper surfaces of the sliding doors and let the broom glide once along the floor. With respect to these activities she shows no interest whatsoever in any possible relation of cause and effect. As a result, the clean places are always clean, while dusty spots and grimy corners remain eternally dusty and begrimed. However, as Confucius pointed out when rebuking a disciple who proposed abandonment of the wasteful and senseless practice of sacrificing a sheep on the first day of every month, a meaningless gesture of courtesy is better than no courtesy at all. It may be that Mrs. Sneaze's style of cleaning a room should be recognized as minimally better than doing nothing at all. In any event, her activities bring my master no benefit. Nevertheless, day after day, she takes the trouble to perform her pointless rite. Which is, alas, the sole redeeming feature. Mrs. Sneaze and room cleaning are, by the custom of many years, firmly linked in a mechanical association; however, their combination has in practice achieved no more actual cleaning than in those old days before she was born and in those even older days before brooms and dusters had been invented. One might indeed say that the relation between Mrs. Sneaze and the cleaning of rooms resembles that of certain terms in formal logic which, totally unrelated in their nature, are nevertheless formally linked.

Unlike my master, I am an early riser, so by this time I was already feeling distinctly peckish. There is, of course, no question of a mere cat expecting to get its breakfast before the human members of the household had sat themselves down at the table. Yet I remain a cat, with all a cat's pure appetites and instincts. And once I had begun to wonder if there could possibly be a delicious smell of soup drifting out of that abalone shell, which serves as my feeding platter, I was simply unable to remain still. When, knowing its hopelessness, one yet hopes on against hope, it is always wisest to concentrate on thinking about that hope and to discipline oneself into silent immobility. But it's easier said than done. One cannot help wanting to check whether one's hope has, or has not, been fulfilled in reality. Even when it is absolutely certain that a check must bring disappointment, one's mind will not stop fidgeting until it has been fully and finally disappointed. I could no longer hold myself in check and accordingly crept out to investigate the kitchen. First, I peep into my abalone shell in its usual place behind the kitchen furnace. Sure enough, the shell is empty, just as it was last night after I'd licked it clean. This morning, that shell looks singularly desolate, chillily reflecting the weird glow of the autumn sunlight filtering down through the skylight. O-san has already transferred the boiled rice into the serving container and is now stirring soup in the saucepan on the stove. Rice-rich liquid that had boiled over in the cooking-pot has dried into hard streaks, some of them looking like stuck-on strips of high-class paper, down the sides of the pot. Since both rice and soup are now ready, I thought my own breakfast should be served at once. It's silly to be backward at such times and, even if I don't succeed in getting what I want, I shan't lose anything by trying. After all, even a hanger-on is as much entitled as anyone else to feel the pangs of hunger; so why shouldn't I call out for my breakfast? First I tried a coaxing kind of mew; an appealing, even a mildly reproachful, noise. O-san does not take the slightest notice. Since she was born polygonal, I am perfectly well aware that her heart is as cold as a clock, but I am counting on my mewing skills to move her rusty sympathies. Next I tried my most pitiable miaowing. I believe this voice of entreaty has a tone so pathetic in its loneliness that it should make a wanderer in a strange land feel that his heart is being torn in pieces. O-san ignores it completely. Can this woman actually be deaf? Hardly. For were she deaf, she'd not be able to hold down her job as a maidservant. Perhaps she is deaf only to cat voices. I understand that there are persons who are colorblind. Though such persons may think their eyesight perfect, from the medical point of view they are in fact deformed. This O-san creature could be voice blind, and persons so deformed are no less freaks than their colorblind homologues. For a mere monstrosity, she's a jolly sight too lordly. Take the nights, for instance, however hard I plead with her that I need to go outside, never once has she opened the door. If by some perversion of her character she should once let me out, there's not a wax cat's chance in hell that she'd ever let me in again. Even in summer, the night dew is bad for one's health, and winter frost is naturally much worse. You can't imagine the agony of staying awake under the eaves and waiting for the sun to rise. The other evening when I chanced to be shut out, some foul stray dog attacked me and only by the skin of my teeth did I manage to escape onto the roof of the tool shed, there to shiver the whole long night away. All such evil hours are brought upon me by the endless wintriness of that hard woman's heart. I know well enough that from such a person my miaowing performance will evoke no kindness, but just as in the proverb a hungry man will turn to God, a man in want will turn to robbery and a lovelorn loon will take to writing songs, so in my extremity will I try anything once. Accordingly, in a last attempt to catch her attention, my third effort was an especially intricate interweaving of mews and muted yowling, which, though, at least in my unshakable judgement, a music no less moving than that of Beethoven, produces no effect whatsoever within that implacable creature's unsociably savage breast. Suddenly, O-san sinks down to her knees and, sliding out a removable floorboard, extracts from the cavity below a stick of charcoal roughly four inches long. Rapped sharply against the corner of the stove, the length broke into some three main pieces and the surrounding area was liberally showered with black dust. A plentiful powdering of charcoal seems to have been added to the soup, but O-san is not the kind of woman to be bothered by such trifles. She quickly shoved the three main pieces under the bottom of the saucepan and so into the stove. I see little prospect of her interrupting her sullen chores to give ear to my symphony. Well, that's the way it is.

Dejected, I set off back to the living room and, as I passed by the bathroom door, I noticed that my master's three small daughters were there busily engaged in washing their faces. Though I say they were washing their faces, the two older girls are still at the kindergarten stage, while the youngest is so tiny that she cannot even trail along with her sisters to their place of schooling. It follows that not one of them can yet properly wash her face or make herself presentable. The baby, having hauled a tangle of damp floor rags out of the mop bucket, is happily using it to stroke her face. I would have thought it most unpleasant to wash one's face with floor rags, but one cannot be surprised at any oddness in this child who regularly responds to earthquakes with outcries of pure joy. Which may, of course, only demonstrate that she is a more enlightened being than Singleman Kidd. Now the eldest girl takes the responsibilities of her seniority with expectedly officious seriousness. Accordingly, she drops her gargling cup and starts trying to part her baby sister from the latter's precious floor rags. "Baby-dear," she tells her, "that's for wiping floors."

But Baby-dear, a self-opinionated tot, is not so easily persuaded and, with a piercing shout of "No, babu," she tugs at the floor-cloth which her sister has just grabbed. Nobody knows what "babu" means or how its use originated, but Baby-dear lets fly with it whenever she loses her temper. As the children tug at the ends of that sodden rag, water squeezed from its center portion starts pitilessly dripping down on Baby-dear's twee tooters. Were it only a matter of wet feet, that would be no great shakes, but soon her knees are also sopping wet. Baby-dear is wearing a backhammon. I've been trying to find out the meaning of that word, and it would seem that to the children it signifies any kind of pattern, in this case patterned clothing, of a medium size. Where they got this information, alas, I could not say.

"Baby-dear," the eldest girl is saying, "your backhammon's getting wet. Be a good baby, Baby-dear, and let go of this cloth." This is remarkably intelligent advice, especially from a girl who herself until just recently thought backhammon was a kind of game. Which reminds me that this eldest girl is constantly misusing words and that her malapropisms not infrequently amuse her adult listeners. The other day she remarked that cornflakes were sparking up from the fire and again, when being dosed with castor oil, asked whether the medicine had been squeezed from the brother of bollocks. She once haughtily announced that she was no common plum child, and it was several days before I discovered that she was in fact bragging that she'd not been born in some back slum. My master sniggers whenever he hears such errors, but I'm prepared to bet that when he's teaching English in his school, he makes in sober earnest far sillier mistakes than his daughter ever does.

Baby-dear, who incidentally always refers to herself as Baby-beer, at last notices that her backhammon is now soaking wet and, bawling out that "Baby-beer's backhammon is got cold," begins to howl her head off. Of course, a cold backhammon is a pretty serious matter, so here comes O-san running from the kitchen. Quickly she dispossesses the squabbling children of their treasured floor rag and cleans the baby up. Throughout the hullaballoo, the second daughter, Sunko, has remained suspiciously quiet. Standing with her back toward us, she has got hold of a small jar of her mother's cosmetic which has tumbled off its shelf and is now busy plastering white paste on her face. First, having poked her finger into the jar, she drags a broad white line down the length of her nose. Which at least makes it easier to see where her nose is. Next, with her finger liberally reloaded, she daubs thick blobs on her cheeks and rubs the stuff around until two white lumps are sticking out from her face. Her beautifying self-adornment had reached this interesting stage when O-san bustled up to deal with Baby-dear. Once Baby-dear was set to rights, Sunko, too, was wiped back into human semblance. She emerged from the white paste looking distinctly peeved.

Leaving this distressing scene behind me, I moved through the living room to inspect my master's bedroom and so to ascertain whether or not he has at last got up. Stealthily I squinny into the room, but my master's head is nowhere to be seen. Instead, one large and high-arched sole is sticking out from the bottom end of the old-fashioned sleeved bed quilt. He seems to have burrowed down to avoid the unpleasantness of being woken up. He looks, in fact, like a not too clever tortoise. At this point Mrs. Sneaze, who had finished cleaning the study, returned to the bedroom with her broom and duster shouldered. Halting at the entrance, she called out as before, "Haven't you got up yet?" then stood there for a while, gazing in disgust at the lump of headless bedding. As before, her question brought no answer.

Mrs. Sneaze advanced a short way into the room. Planting her broom upright with a slightly menacing plunk, she pressed again for an answer. "Not yet woken up, dear?"

This time, my master is awake all right. Indeed, it is precisely because he is awake that he is now, head and body tucked well down, entrenched within the bedclothes against the expected onslaught from his wife. He seems to be relying on some silly notion that, so long as he keeps his head concealed, his wife may fail to notice that he's still snugged down in bed. She shows no disposition to let him off so slightly. Her first call, reckoned my master, had come from the threshold, so there should still be a reasonably safe distance, perhaps as much as six feet, between himself and her. He was consequently shaken when the plunk of her grounded broom-haft came from less than three feet off. Worse still, her solicitous, "Not yet woken up, dear?" sounded, even under the bedclothes, twice more menacing than before. Seeing no hope for it, my master thereupon surrendered, and his small voice answered, "Hmm."

"You said you'd be there by nine o'clock. Hurry up, or you'll be late."

"You don't have to tell me. I'm getting up," replied my master with his face spectacularly visible through the cuff of one sleeve of the bedclothes. His wife is used to this old trick. Once he has managed to convince her that he's going to get up, he usually goes straight back to sleep again. So she's learnt to keep a sharp eye on his morning gambits and therefore answers his mumbled promises with a curt, "Well, get up now." It's annoying, when one's said one's getting up, to be told then to get up. For a selfish man like my master, it is even more than annoying. In one wild, angry gesture, he thrusts aside the pile of bedclothes that he's been keeping over his head, and I note that his eyes are staringly wide-open.

"Don't make all that fuss. If I say I'm getting up, then I'm getting up."

"But you always say you're getting up, and then you never do."

"Nonsense! When have I ever told a ridiculous lie like that?"

"Why, always."

"Don't be so silly."

"Who are you calling silly? Answer me that." She looks quite dashingly militant as she stands there beside the bed with her broomstick planted like a spear shaft. But at this very moment, Yatchan, the child of the rickshawman who lives in the street behind us, suddenly burst out crying with a most tremendous, "Waa!" That Yatchan should start crying as soon as my master gets angry is the responsibility of his ghastly mother. For the wife of the rickshawman is paid to make her baby scream every time my master gets into a fury. Which is fine for the money grubbing mother, but pretty hard on Yatchan. With a mother like that, a child could well have cause to cry around the clock. If my master realized the way things have been rigged and made the little effort needed to control himself, then Yatchan might live longer than seems likely. Even though the victim's mother is being handsomely rewarded by the Goldfields for her torturing of her child, only a person far more dangerously mad than Providence Fair would do such a lunatic thing. Were Yatchan only made to cry on the occasions of my master's anger, he could probably survive, but every time that Goldfield's hireling hooligans come shouting round the house, then too the wretched infant is hurt until he screams. It is taken for granted that the hooligan catcalls will infuriate my master; so, whether or not my master does flare up, Yatchan catches hell in expectation of my master's anger. Every vulgar yell asserting that my master is a terracotta badger is thus invariably matched by a heart-felt yell from Yatchan. Indeed, it has become difficult to distinguish between Yatchan and my master. It is simple to start my master off by indirect approaches. One only needs to torment Yatchan briefly to produce the same effect on my master as slapping him directly in the face. I understand that years ago in Europe whenever a condemned criminal escaped to a foreign land and could not be recaptured, it was the custom to fashion a simulacrum of the fugitive which was then burnt in his stead. Among these hooligans of Goldfield's there seems to be a tactician well acquainted with such ancient European practices, and I must confess he's certainly worked out some very clever ploys. Both the little louts from Cloud Descending Hall and Yatchan's mother represent real problems for my master who, when all is said and done, is a man of limited abilities. There are many other equally awkward customers to be coped with. One might even say that, from my master's point of view, the entire district is populated with awkward customers; since these others are not immediately relevant to this story, I'll introduce them later as developments require. For the moment, I will return you to my master quarreling in the bedroom with his wife.

On hearing Yatchan cry and at such an early hour, my master must have felt really angry. He jerked sharply up into a sitting position among the bedclothes, for at times of such stress no years of mental training, not even the presence of Singleman Kidd himself, could exercise the least restraint. Then with both hands he began to scratch his scalp with such vicious violence that nearly every square inch of its skin was clawed away. A month's accumulated dandruff came floating down to settle nastily on his neck and pajama collar. It is a sight not easily forgotten. Yet another shock greeted my wondering eyes when they fell upon his bristling moustache. Perhaps that ragged growth felt it would be less than seemly to be calm when its owner was so savagely distraught but, whatever the reason, each individual hair has gone completely berserk and, forgetting all sense of co-operation in the frightful vigor of their self-expression, the various hairs are jutting out like the bayonets of ill-trained conscripts in whichever wild direction takes their frantic fancy. This, too, constitutes a sight not easily forgotten. Only yesterday, out of regard for the bathroom mirror and in deference to the German Emperor, these hairs had obediently mustered themselves into disciplined formation, but after no more than a single night's repose all the benefits of their training have been scattered to the winds. Each separate conscript hair has reverted to its aboriginal nature and has resumed that individuality which reduces the moustache to the condition of a rabble. The same sad process of rapid degeneration may be observed in my master. In the space of a single night his mental training loses all effect, and his inborn boorishness comes bristling back into view through every pore in his skin. When one pauses to wonder how such a wildly whiskered tusker has managed to keep his job as a teacher, then for the first time one grasps the varied vastness of Japan. Indeed, only a land of such true enormity could find room for Goldfield and his pack of snooping curs and rabid bitches to pass themselves off as human beings. My master seems to believe that in a society where those monstrosities can indeed pass for human, there is no conceivable reason why his own modest eccentricities should lead to his dismissal. In the last analysis one could always obtain an enlightening explanation of the whole crazy set-up by sending a postcard of enquiry to that noble pile which shelters Providence Fair.

At this point my master opened his ancient eyes, whose drifting cloudiness I have previously described in detail, as wide as they can stretch and, with an unaccustomedly sharp dance, stared at the cupboard in the wall that faced him. This cupboard is about six feet in height, divided horizontally into top and bottom halves, each half having two sliding paper-doors. The bottom end of my master's bedclothes reached almost to the lower part of the cupboard so that, having just sat up, he cannot help but focus, as soon as his lids are lifted, on the picture-painted paper of the cupboard's sliding doors. Here and there the paper skin has peeled or been torn away, and the curious underlayers, the flattened intestines of the panels, are distinctly visible. These innards are of many different sorts. Some are printed papers, others are handwritten; some have been pasted face-side in, others upside-down. The sight of this displayed anatomy of paper stirred in my master a sudden urge to read what was written there. The fact that my master, who until but a moment ago was so frenetically incensed that he could happily have grabbed the wife of the rickshawman and ground her nose against a pine tree, now suddenly wishes to read old scraps of paper may seem a little strange, but actually such conduct is not all that unusual in an extrovert so easily entered. It is another version of the squalling baby who starts to coo as soon as he is given sweets. Years ago in his student days, when my master lodged in a temple, there were five or six nuns living in the room next to his with nothing but the sliding paper-doors between them. Now, nuns are by nature the cattiest of all cat-natured women. These nuns seem quickly to have perceived the true and inmost character of my master, for they made it their practice to chant, tapping out the rhythm on the rim of their cooking-pot, that jingle parents use to tease a child about its changeable moods:

> The little crow that cried and cried
> Has grown a grin six inches wide.

My master, I've been told, has loathed nuns ever since. They may well be detestable, but their chanting told a truth. For, though none of his moods is lasting, my master contrives to weep, to laugh, to rollick, and be downcast more frequently than anyone else in the world. Putting it kindly, one might say he shows a certain lack of tenacity and is inclined to change his mind for insufficient reason. Translated into simple everyday language, that merely means that my master is a shallow, stubborn, spoiled brat. Now, being a spoiled brat, it's not at all surprising that, full of fighting spirit, he should jerk his torso fiercely up from the bed and then, balanced on his bottom, suddenly change his mind and begin to read the flattened intestines of a damaged cupboard door.

The first thing he noticed was a photograph of Itō Hirobumi standing on his head. By twisting his neck to study the date associated with this irreverently pasted picture, my master found it to be September 28, 1878. So, even as long as twenty-seven years ago, the present Resident-General in Korea was already doing somersaults. Wondering how the Resident-General might have occupied himself before Korea was available to reside in, my master crooks himself sufficiently to decipher "Finance Minister." This certainly is a great man. Even when he's standing on his head, he's a Finance Minister. A bit to the left of that information, the Minister again appears. This time he is lying down, having a siesta. Which is very understandable. One cannot be expected to stand on one's head for any protracted period. Near the bottom of the exposed area, the two words "You are" can be seen written in large ideographs. My master naturally wanted to read the rest of such an aggressively sized sentence but, alas, nothing more was visible. Of the next line down, all that can be read is "quickly" and, once again, there's no clue to the rest of the text. If my master were a detective of the Metropolitan Police Board, he might have satisfied his curiosity by ripping off the rest of the top layer of paper even though the cupboard door, its skin and its intestines, all belonged to somebody else. Since no detective has been properly educated, such barbarous persons will do anything to sate their lust for facts. Which is a lamentable state of affairs. I wish they would behave with a little more civilized reserve. Matters would be improved if a rule were established that all facts should be withheld from detectives whose conduct lacks reserve. I understand that these disreputable servants of the public sometimes arrest innocent citizens on the basis of false accusations and manufactured evidence. That public servants, employed and paid for by honest citizens, should be given scope to pin crimes on those who pay and employ them is yet another example of the lunatic condition of human society.

My master next studies the center part of the exposed paper where a map of Oita Prefecture has been pasted upside-down. Since the Resident-General in Korea is standing on his head, it's not surprising that Oita Prefecture should join him in his somersaults. When my master's eyes had taken in the overthrow of Oita, he clenched both hands and thrust his fists on high toward the ceiling. These mantic gestures foretell a coming yawn. His yawning, too, is signally abnormal: less a human yawn than the yowling of a whale. That performance over, my master pulled some clothes on and lurched off into the bathroom for a wash. His wife, who had been impatiently waiting for this moment, quickly gathered up the quilt, folded it and put the bedclothes in the cupboard. Then, as usual, she began to clean the room. Just as Mrs. Sneaze's cleaning system has become a stylized drill, so too over the years her husband has established a routine pattern for washing his face. I think I earlier mentioned his noisy morning gargling, its variations of bass and treble bubblement, and today he's doing it as usual. Finally, having made the usual careful parting in his hair, he appeared in the living room with a hand towel draped across one shoulder. There, with a lordly air, he sat himself down beside the oblong brazier.

Mention of that object may lead some of you to imagine an oblong brazier made from fine zelkova wood. Some perhaps may picture a brazier of black persimmon wood, its inner sides entirely copper plated, against the lip of which a sexy-looking charmer with long and freshly washed tresses, sitting with one knee raised, seductively taps out her long slim tobacco pipe. But poor old Sneaze's brazier is sadly less than picturesque. It is, in fact, so ancient that none but an expert could guess what wood was used to make it. The fine point about any such oblong brazier is the quality and brilliance of the gloss acquired by years of patient polishing, but this brazier is not only undetermined as to its material, which could as well be cherry as zelkova and paulownia as cherry, but has never once been polished. It is consequently a gloomy and most repellent object. Where, I wonder, could he have gotten it? He would certainly not have bought it. Could it, then, have been a present? Not that I've ever heard. Which leaves us with the possibility that he stole it, and at this point all histories of the brazier become a little vague. Many years ago, among my master's relatives there was an old, old man. When that ancient died, my master was asked to live in the dead man's house and just look after it. Some years later when my master moved out to occupy his own, new house, he simply took along with him, possibly unthinkingly, the oblong brazier which he had used so often that he had come to regard it as his personal property. Usufruct decaying into usucaption, which sounds a little wicked. Indeed, when one considers the matter, his act was certainly wrong. However, such happenings are common enough. For instance, I understand that bankers grow so accustomed to handling other people's money that they come to regard it as their own. Similarly, public officials are the servants of the people and can reasonably be regarded as agents to whom the people have entrusted certain powers to be exercised on the people's behalf in the running of public affairs. But as these officials grow accustomed to their daily control of affairs, they begin to acquire delusions of grandeur, act as though the authority they exercise was in fact their own and treat the people as though the people had no say in the matter. Since the world is thus demonstrably full of such usurpers, one cannot brand my master as a thief just because of this business with the oblong brazier. However, if you insist that he has a thievish disposition, an evidenced inclination to theft, then the plain fact is that he shares that criminal cant with everyone else in the world.

I had got as far as saying that my master sat down beside the oblong brazier, but I have not yet explained that, in doing so, he was in fact seating himself at the dining table. Seated around the other three sides and already tucking into their breakfasts were Baby-dear, who cleans her face with floor rags; Tonko, whose learning includes the starry phenomena of Castor and Bollocks; and sweet little Sunko, who pokes about into make-up jars. My master looks at his three daughters with impartial distaste. Tonko's face is flat and round like the steel guard on some old-fashioned sword. Sunko takes after her elder sister so far as face shape is concerned, but its color immediately puts me in mind of those round red lacquer trays from Okinawa. Baby-dear's face is the odd one out, and very odd it is: long and square at the corners, with the long sides of the oblong stretching sideways. Of themselves, oblong heads are not uncommon but in such cases the greater length is vertical. An oblong head like Baby-dear's, horizontally long, is, I think, unheard of. However vertiginous the variance of fashion, I cannot believe that a square face squashed out sideways will ever prove the rage. My master suffers random spasms of concern about his growing daughters. Their growth is unpreventable, and they are certainly all growing. Indeed, the speed of their growth reminds one of the sheer blue force of a bamboo shoot accelerating into sapling size in the garden of some Zen-purveying temple. Every time my master notices an increase in his children's size, he becomes as nervous as if an inexorable pursuer were catching up behind him. Though an inordinately vague person, my master does realize that these three daughters are all females. He also understands that, being females, proper arrangements for their disposition must be made. He understands, yes, but that is all, for he further realizes that he is quite incapable of getting them married off. Therefore, though they are indeed his very own offspring, he finds them more than he cares for. If he's the kind of father who finds his children a bit too much, then he should never have produced them. But such behavior is all too typically human. It is painfully easy to define human beings. They are beings who, for no good reason at all, create their own unnecessary suffering.

But children are terrific. Not even dreaming that their father is thus worried stiff about what to do with them, they go on eating happily. The only unmanageable one is Baby-dear. Baby-dear is now nearly three-years-old, so her mother, seeking to be kind, has provided for her mealtime use a pair of chopsticks and a rice bowl, all of size appropriate to her age. But Baby-dear will have none of it. First she grabs her eldest sister's chopsticks, then her rice bowl. Though they are too large for her, she struggles to control these quite unmanageable things. One finds in this sad world that among mean-spirited persons, the greater their incompetence and inefficiency, the sharper their sense of self-importance and the more virulent their ambition to occupy unsuitably high official posts.

This style of character always begins to develop at the stage now reached by Baby-dear; and, since the roots of these defects of character run down so deeply into babyhood, wise persons quickly resign themselves to the wretched truth that no subsequent discipline or education can eradicate such flaws. Baby-dear positively wallows in her tiny tyrannies, refusing to surrender the enormous rice bowl and the hefty chopsticks that she's looted from her sister. Perhaps, since she is seeking by sheer violence to control objects far too big for her to handle, she has no choice but to play the tyrant. In any event, she begins by clamping both chopsticks tight together in a firm grip applied too far down toward their lower ends. She then rams this wooden wedge into the bottom of the rice bowl, which is about four-fifths full of rice topped up to its brim with bean-paste soup. The rice bowl had managed, somewhat precariously, to retain its balance throughout Baby-dear's initial raid but, as soon as it felt the force of her chopstick battering ram, it tilted some thirty degrees out of the true and poured a sluice of still-hot soup all down the front of its assailant. But Baby-dear is not to be daunted by such a petty setback. For Baby-dear's a tyrant. Accordingly, she yanks the chopsticks savagely out of the bowl, shoves her rosebud mouth right up against the rice bowl's lip, and then proceeds to shovel masses of soggy rice into her slurping maw. Grains that escape her wild style of engulfment joined the soup in its bid for freedom and, with a happy shout, alighted variously on her nose tip, on her cheeks, and on her chin. Those, and they were many, that missed their human target finished up on different parts of the floor. This is a most reckless manner in which to eat rice. I respectfully advise all persons in positions of power, including that infamous Goldfield fellow, that if they persist in treating people with the same crude violence that Baby-dear applies to the rice bowl and the chopsticks, they too will finish up with only a spattering of rice grains in their mouths. The only grains that will, in fact, land up in their gullets will not be those on whom pressure has been applied, but merely those that have lost all sense of direction. I do most earnestly entreat all persons of influence to reflect deeply upon this matter. Men who are truly wise in this world never act so stupidly.

The eldest girl, her bowl and chopsticks snitched by the baby, has been obliged to make do with Baby-dear's dwarf versions, but the baby's bowl can hold so little rice that three quick mouthfuls empty it. Forced into frequent replenishments, she has already downed her fourth helping and is apparently going to take a fifth. She lifts the lid of the rice-container and, holding the broad rice scoop momentarily poised, stares at the bunkered grains as though undecided whether or not to help herself to more. In the end she plumps for another bowlful and carefully scoops out a dollop of rice that looks unburnt. So far, so good. However, as she brought the laden scoop up toward the rim of her bowl, she accidentally banged the two together, with the result that a largish lump of rice fell down onto the floor. Looking not the least put out, she began to pick it up again with almost finicking care. Naturally, I wondered what she was going to do with it. She put it all, every single grain, back into the container. Which seems a dirty thing to do. The conclusion of this ugly business came at the same moment as the climax of Baby-dear's performance with the shoveling chopsticks. And an eldest sister can hardly be expected to overlook a face as foully spattered with rice as Baby-dear's.

"Baby-dear, you look terrible with your face all covered in rice." She begins to clean up the mess. First, she disengaged the rice grain sticking on the baby's nose but, instead of throwing it away, popped it, much to my surprised disgust, into her own mouth. Next she tackles the cheeks. Here the grains, some twenty altogether, are clotted in scattered groups. One by one, her eldest sister picked the kernels off the baby's cheeks, and one by one she ate them.

At this point, the middle sister, Sunko, who hitherto has demurely busied herself with crunching pickled radish, suddenly scooped from her brimming soup bowl a broken gobbet of sweet potato and slung that wretched object straight into her widely opened mouth. As my readers are no doubt aware, nothing can sear the mouth more painfully than sweet potato cooked in bean-paste soup. Unless very careful, even a hardened adult can give himself a truly nasty burn. It is thus understandable that a mere beginner in the art of eating such sweet potatoes should feel scorched, as certainly did Sunko, out of her tiny mind. With a fearful squawking, "Waa," she spat the burning gobbet out upon the table. This slightly mangled object skidded across the table surface, coming at last to rest within convenient grabbing distance of Baby-dear. Now Baby-dear, as tough-mouthed as a carthorse, just dotes on sweet potatoes. Seeing her favorite goody skid to a steaming halt only a hand's stretch from her rice-stripped face, she pitched away her chopsticks, snatched the sweet potato and gobbled it gladly down.

My master, a fully conscious witness of all these ghastly happenings, watches them as dispassionately as if they were occurring on some other planet. Without saying a word, he has quietly got on with eating his own rice and soup, and is now engaged in probing his jaws with a toothpick. He seems to be following a policy of complete non-intervention, even of masterly inactivity, in the rearing of his daughters. One fine day in the not too distant future this trio of bright college girls may be fated to find themselves wild lovers with whom, for the sake of passion, they'll run away from home. If that in fact should happen, I expect that, calmly continuing to eat his rice and soup, my master will just watch them as they go upon their ways. He is certainly a man of little resource, but I've noticed that those who are nowadays regarded as most admirably resourceful know nothing, in fact, except how to deceive their fellows with lies, how to sneak up upon the unwary, how to jump queues, how to create a sensation by bluffing, and by what tricks to ensnare the simple-minded. Even boys at the middle school level, influenced by such conduct, get the idea that only by such means can they expect to make their way in the world. Indeed they seem to think that they can only become fine gentlemen by the successful perpetration of acts of which they ought, in truth, to be thoroughly ashamed. Of course, these imitative loutlings do not display resource, and are in fact no more than hooligans. Being a Japanese cat, I have a certain amount of patriotic sentiment and, every time I see these allegedly resourceful creatures I wish I had the chance to give them a right, good hiding. Each new creature of that type weakens the nation to the degree of his presence. Such students are a disgrace to their school, and such adults a disgrace to their country. Nonetheless, disgraceful as they are, there are lots of them about. Which is really inexplicable. The human beings in Japan, shamefully enough, seem less mettlesome than the cats. One must admit that, compared with hooligans, my master is a very superior model of humankind. He is superior because he is weak-minded. His very uselessness makes him their superior. He is their clear superior because he is not smart.

Having thus uneventfully, and with a show of no resource whatever, finished his breakfast, my master put on his suit, climbed into a rickshaw and left to keep his appointment with the police. As he climbed aboard, he'd asked the rickshawman if he knew the location of Nihon-zutsumi. The rickshawman just grinned. I thought it rather silly of my master to make a point of reminding the rickshawman that his destination lay in the brothel quarter.

After my master's unusual departure—unusual, that is, because he left in a rickshaw—Mrs. Sneaze had her own breakfast and then started nagging at the children. "Hurry up," she says, "or you'll be late for school."

But the children pay no heed. "There isn't," they answer back, "any school today," and they make no effort to get themselves ready.

"Of course there is," she snaps in a lecturing tone of voice. "Hurry and get ready."

"But yesterday the teacher said, 'We have no school tomorrow,'" the eldest girl persists.

It was probably at this point that Mrs. Sneaze began to suspect that the children might be right. She went to the cupboard, lifted out a calendar and checked the date. Today is marked in red, the sign of a national holiday. I fancy that my master was unaware of this fact when he sent a note to his school advising them of his absence. I fancy, too, that Mrs. Sneaze was similarly unaware when she put his note in the post. As for Waverhouse, I can't make up my mind whether he, too, was unaware or whether he simply found it diverting to keep quiet.

Mrs. Sneaze, surprised and softened by this discovery, told the children to go out and play. "But please," she bade them, "just behave yourselves." She then settled down, as she daily does, to get on with her sewing.

For the next half hour peace reigned throughout the house, and nothing happened worth my bother to record. Then, out of the blue, an unexpected visitor arrived: a young girl, student aged, I would guess, perhaps seventeen or eighteen. The heels of her shoes had worn crooked and her long, purple skirt trailed along the ground. Her hair was quaintly dressed in two big bulges above the ears, so that her head resembled an abacus bead. Unannounced, she walked in through the kitchen entrance. This apparition is my master's niece. They say she is a student. She's always liable to drop in on a Sunday, and she usually contrives to have some kind of row with her uncle. This young lady possesses the unusually beautiful name of Yukie but, far from reminding its viewers of a snowy river, her ruddy features are of that dull normality which you can see in any street if you take the trouble to walk a hundred yards.

"Hullo, Auntie!" she casually remarked as, marching straight into the living room, she plonked herself down beside the sewing box.

"My dear, how early you are. . ."

"Because today's a national holiday. I thought I'd come and see you in the morning, so I left home in a hurry about half past eight."

"Oh? For anything special?"

"No, but I haven't seen you for such a long time, and I just wanted to say hullo."

"Well then, don't just say hullo but stay for a bit. Your uncle will soon be back."

"Has Uncle gone out already? That's unusual!"

"Yes, and today he's gone to rather an unusual place. In fact, to a police station. Isn't that odd?"

"Whatever for?"

"They've caught the man who burgled us last spring."

"And Uncle's got to give evidence? What a bore."

"Not altogether. We're going to get our things back. The stolen articles have turned up and we've been asked to go and collect them. A policeman came around yesterday especially to tell us."

"I see. Otherwise Uncle wouldn't have gone out as early as this. Normally he'd still be snoring."

"There's no one quite such a lie-abed as your uncle, and if one wakes him up he gets extremely cross. This morning, for instance, because he'd asked me to wake him up at seven, that's when I woke him up. And d'you know, he promptly crept inside the bed clothes and didn't even answer. Naturally, I was worried about his appointment with the police, but when I tried to wake him up for the second time, he said something rather unkind through a sleeve of the padded bed clothes. Really, he's the limit."

"I wonder why he's always so sleepy. Perhaps," said his niece in almost pleasured tones, "his nerves are shot to pieces."

"I don't know, I'm sure."

"He does lose his temper far too easily. It surprises me that they keep him on as a teacher at that school."

"Well, I'm told he's awfully gentle at the school."

"Which only makes things worse. A blow-hard in the house and all thistledown at school."

"What d'you mean, dear?" asks my mistress.

"Well, don't you think it's bad that he should act around here like the King of Hell and then appear at school like some quaking jelly?"

"And of course it's not just that he's so terribly bad tempered. He's also an ornery man. When one says right, he immediately says left; if one says left, then he says right. And he never, but never, does anything that he's been asked to do. He's as stubborn and crank-minded as a mule."

"Cantankerous, I call it. Being plain contrary is his whole-time hobby. For myself if I ever want him to do something, I just ask him to do the opposite. And it always works. For instance, the other day I wanted him to buy me an umbrella. So I purposely kept on telling him that I didn't want one. 'Of course you want an umbrella,' he exploded and promptly went and bought me one."

Mrs. Sneaze broke out in a womanly series of giggles and titters. "Oh, how clever you are," she said, "I'll do the same in future."

"You certainly should. You'll never get anything out of that old skinflint if you don't."

"The other day an insurance man called around and he tried hard to persuade your uncle to take out an insurance policy. He pointed out this and that advantage and did his very best for about an hour to talk your uncle around. But your obstinate, old uncle was not to be persuaded, even though we have three children and no savings. If only he would take out even the most modest insurance, we'd naturally all feel very much more secure. But a fat lot he cares for things like that."

"Quite so. If anything should happen, you could be very awkwardly placed." This girl doesn't sound like a teenager at all, but more, and most unbecomingly, like an experience-hardened housewife.

"It was really rather amusing to hear your uncle arguing with that wretched salesman. Your uncle said, 'All right, perhaps I can concede the necessity of insurance. Indeed, I deduce that it is by reason of that necessity that insurance companies exist.' Nevertheless he persisted in maintaining that 'nobody needs to get insured unless he's going to die.'"

"Did he actually say that?"

"He did indeed. Inevitably, the salesman answered, 'Of course, if nobody ever died, there'd be no need for insurance companies. But human life, however durable it may sometimes seem, is in fact a fragile and precarious thing. No man can ever know what hidden dangers menace his tenuous existence.' To which your uncle retorted, 'I've decided not to die, so have no worry on my account.' Can you imagine anyone actually saying such an idiotic thing?"

"How extremely silly! One dies even if one decides not to. Why, I myself was absolutely determined to pass my exams, but, in fact, I failed."

"The insurance man said the same thing. 'Life,' he said, 'can't be controlled. If people could prolong their lives by strength of resolution, nobody anywhere would ever leave this earth.'"

"The insurance man makes sense to me."

"I certainly agree. But your uncle cannot see it. He swears he'll never die. 'I've made a vow,' he told that salesman with all the pride of a nincompoop, 'never, never to die.'"

"How very odd."

"Of course he's odd, very odd indeed. He looks entirely unconcerned as he announces that, rather than paying premiums for insurance, he prefers to hold his savings in a bank."

"Has he got any savings?"

"Of course not. He just doesn't give a damn what happens after his death."

"That's very worrisome for you. I wonder what makes him so peculiar. There's no one like him among his friends who come here, is there?"

"Of course there's not. He's unique."

"You should ask someone like Suzuki to give him a talking-to. If only he were as mild and manageable as Suzuki, he would be so much easier to cope with."

"I understand what you mean, but Mr. Suzuki is not well thought of in this house."

"Everything here seems upside-down. Well, if that's no good, what about that other person, that person of such singular self-possession?"

"Singleman Kidd?"

"Yes, him."

"Your uncle recognizes Singleman's superiority, but only yesterday we had Waverhouse around here with some dreadful tales to tell of Singleman's behavior and past history. In the circumstances, I don't think Singleman could be much help."

"But surely he could do it. He's so generously self-possessed, such a winning personality. The other day he gave a lecture at my school."

"Singleman did?"

"Yes."

"Does he teach at your school?"

"No, he's not one of our teachers, but we invited him to give a lecture to our Women's Society for the Protection of Female Virtue."

"Was it interesting?"

"Well, not all that interesting. But he has such a long face and he sports such a spiritual goatee, so everyone who hears him is naturally much impressed."

"What sort of things did he talk about?" Mrs. Sneaze had barely finished her sentence when the three children, presumably drawn by the sound of Yukie's voice, came bursting noisily across the veranda and into the living room. I imagine they had been playing outside in the open space just beyond the bamboo fence.

"Hurray, it's Yukie," shouted the two elder girls with boisterous pleasure.

"Don't get so excited, children," said Mrs. Sneaze. "Come and sit down quietly. Yukie is going to tell us an interesting story." So saying, she shoved her sewing things away into a corner of the room.

"A story from Yukie?" says the eldest. "Oh, I do love stories."

"Will you be telling us again that tale of Click-Clack Mountain?" asks the second daughter.

"Baby-dear a story!" shouts the baby as she rams her knee forward between her squatting sisters. This does not mean that she wants to listen to a story. On the contrary, it means she wants to tell one.

"What! Baby-dear's story yet again!" scream her laughing sisters.

"Baby-dear, you shall tell us your story afterward," says Mrs. Sneaze cajolingly, "after Yukie has finished."

But Baby-dear is in no mood for sops or compromises. "No," she bellows, "now!" And to establish that she's totally in earnest, she adds her gnomic warning of a tantrum. "Babu," she thundered.

"All right, all right. Baby-dear shall start," says Yukie placatingly. "What's your story called?"

"'Bōtan, Bōtan, where you going?'"

"Very good, and what next?"

"I go rice field, I cut rice"

"Aren't you a clever one!"

"If you tum there, rice go rotten"

"Hey, it's not 'tum there,' it's 'if you *come* there.'" One of the girls butts in with a correction. The baby responds with her threatening roar of "Babu," and her interrupting sister immediately subsides. But the interruption has broken the baby's train of remembrance so that, stuck for words, she sits there in a glowering silence.

"Baby-dear, is that all?" asks Yukie at her sweetest.

The baby pondered for a moment and then exclaimed, "Don't want fart-fart, that not nice."

There was a burst of unseemly laughter. "What a dreadful thing to say! Whoever's been teaching you that?"

"O-san," says the treacherous brat with an undisarming smirk.

"How naughty of O-san to say such things," says Mrs. Sneaze with a forced smile. Quickly ending the matter, she turned to her niece. "Now, it's time for Yukie's story. You'll listen to her, won't you, Baby-dear? Yes?" Tyrant though she is, the baby now seems to be satisfied, for she remained quiet.

"Professor Singleman's lecture went like this," Yukie began at last. "Once upon a time a big stone image of the guardian god of children stood smack in the middle of the place where two roads crossed. Unfortunately, it was a very busy place with lots of carts and horses moving along the roads. So this big stone Jizō, interfering with the flow of traffic, was really an awful nuisance. The people who lived in that district therefore got together and decided that the best thing to do would be to move the big stone image to one corner of the crossroads."

"Is this a story of something that actually happened?" asks Mrs. Sneaze.

"I don't know. The Professor did not mention whether the tale was real or not. Anyway, it seems that the people then began to discuss how the statue could in fact be moved. The strongest man amongst them told them not to worry, for he could easily do the job. So off he went to the crossroads, stripped himself to the waist and pushed and pulled at the big stone image until the sweat poured down his body. But the Jizō did not move."

"It must have been made of terribly heavy stone."

"Indeed it was. So terribly heavy that in the end that strongest man of them all was totally exhausted and trudged back home to sleep. So the people had another meeting and talked it over again. This time it was the smartest man amongst them who said, 'Let me have a go at it,' so they let him have a go. He filled a box with sweet dumplings and put it down on the ground a little way in front of the Jizō. 'Jizō,' he said, pointing to the dumpling box, 'come along here.' For he reckoned that the big stone fellow would be greedy enough to be lured forward in order to get at the goodies. But the Jizō did not move. Though the clever man could see no flaw in his style of approach, he calculated that he must have misjudged the appetites of Jizō. So he went away and filled a gourd with *saké* and then came back to the crossroads with the drink-filled gourd in one hand and a *saké* cup in the other. For about three hours he tried to tease the Jizō into moving. 'Don't you want this lovely *saké*?' he kept shouting. 'If you want it, come and get it! Come and drink this lovely *saké*. Just a step and the gourd's all yours.' But the Jizō did not move."

"Yukie," asks the eldest daughter, "doesn't Mr. Jizō ever get hungry?"

"I'd do almost anything," observed her younger sister, "for a boxful of sweet dumplings."

"For the second time the clever man got nowhere. So he went away again and made hundreds and hundreds of imitation banknotes. Standing in front of the big stone god, he flashed his fancy money in and out of his pocket. 'I'll bet you'd like a fistful of these bank notes,' he remarked, 'so why not come and get them?' But even the flashing of bank notes did no good. The Jizō did not move. He must, I think, have been quite an obstinate Jizō."

"Rather like your uncle," said Mrs. Sneaze with a sniff.

"Indeed so, the very image of my uncle. Well, in the end the clever man also gave up in disgust. At which point along came a braggart who assured the people that their problem was the simplest thing in the world and that he would certainly settle it for them."

"So what did the braggart do?"

"Well, it was all very amusing. First, he rigged himself out in a policeman's uniform and a false moustache. Then he marched up to the big stone image and addressed it in a loud and pompous voice. 'You there,' he bellowed, 'move along now, quietly. If you don't move on, you'll find yourself in trouble. The authorities will certainly purpose the matter with the utmost rigor.' This must all have happened long ago," said Yukie by way of comment, "for I doubt whether nowadays you could impress anyone by pretending to be a policeman."

"Quite. But did that old-time Jizō move?"

"Of course it didn't. It was just like Uncle."

"But your uncle stands very much in awe of the police."

"Really? Well, if the Jizō wasn't scared by the braggart's threatenings, they couldn't have been particularly frightening. Anyway, the Jizō was unimpressed and stayed where it was. The braggart then grew deucedly angry. He stormed off home, took off his copper's uniform, pitched his false moustache into a rubbish bin and reappeared at the crossroads got up to look like an extremely wealthy man. Indeed, he contorted his face to resemble the features of Baron Iwasaki. Can you imagine anything quite so potty?"

"What sort of face is Baron Iwasaki's?"

"Well, probably very proud. Toffee-nosed, you know. Anyway, saying nothing more, but puffing a vast cigar, the braggart took no further action but to walk around and around the Jizō."

"Whatever for?"

"The idea was to make the Jizō dizzy with tobacco smoke."

"It all sounds like some storyteller's joke! Did he succeed in dizzying the Jizō?"

"No, the idea didn't work. After all, he was puffing against stone. Then, instead of just abandoning his pantomimes, he next appeared disguised as a prince. What about that?"

"As a prince? Did they have princes even in those days?"

"They must have, for Professor Kidd said so. He said that, blasphemous as it was, this braggart actually appeared in the trappings of a prince. I really think such conduct most irreverent. And the man nothing but a boastful twerp!"

"You say he appeared as a prince, but as which prince?"

"I don't know. Whichever prince it was, the act remains irreverent."

"How right you are."

"Well, even princely power proved useless. So, finally stumped, the braggart threw his hand in and admitted he could do nothing with the Jizō."

"Served him right!"

"Yes indeed, and, what's more, he ought to have been jailed for his impudence. Anyway, the people in the town were now really worried, but though they got together for a further pow-wow, no one could be persuaded to take another crack at the problem."

"Is that how it all finished?"

"No, there's more to come. In the end, they paid whole gangs of rickshawmen and other riff-raff to mill around the Jizō with as much hullaballoo as possible. The idea was to make things so unbearably unpleasant that the Jizō would move on. So, taking it in turns, they managed to keep up an incredible din by day and night."

"What a painful business!"

"But even such desperate measures brought no joy, for the Jizō, too, was stubborn."

"So what happened?" asks Tonko eagerly.

"Well, by now everyone was getting pretty fed up because, though they kept the racket going for days and nights on end, the din had no effect. Only the riff-raff and the rickshawmen enjoyed the row they made, and they of course were happy because they were getting wages for making themselves a nuisance."

"What," asked Sunko, "are wages?"

"Wages are money."

"What would they do with money?"

Yukie was flummoxed. "Well, when they have money. . ." she began and then dodged the question first by a loud false laugh and then by telling Sunko how naughty she was. "Anyway," she continued, "the people just went on making their silly noises all through the day and all through the night. Now it so happened that at that time there was an idiot boy in the district whom they all called Daft Bamboo. He was, as the saying goes, simple. He knew nothing, and nobody had anything to do with him. Eventually, even this simpleton noticed the terrible racket. 'Why,' he asked 'are you making all that noise?' When someone explained the situation, the idiot boy remarked, 'What idiots you are, trying for all these years to shift a single Jizō with such idiotic tricks.'"

"A remarkable speech from an idiot.'"

"He was indeed a rather remarkable fool. Of course nobody thought he could do any good but, since no one else had done better, why not, they said, why not let him have a go at it? So Daft Bamboo was asked to help. He immediately agreed. 'Stop that horrible noise,' he said, 'and just keep quiet.' The riff-raff and the rickshawmen were packed off somewhere out of sight, and Daft Bamboo, as vacuous as ever, then walked up to the Jizō with utter aimlessness."

"Was Utter Aimlessness a special friend of Daft Bamboo?"

Mrs. Sneaze and Yukie burst into laughter at Tonko's curious question.

"No, not a friend."

"Then, what?"

"Well, utter aimlessness is. . . impossible to describe."

"'Utter aimlessness' means 'impossible to describe'?"

"No, that's not it. Utter aimlessness means. . ."

"Yes?"

"You know Mr. Sampei, don't you?"

"Yes, he's the one who gave us yams."

"Well, utter aimlessness means someone like Mr. Sampei."

"Is Mr. Sampei an utter aimlessness?"

"Yes, more or less. . . Now, Daft Bamboo ambled up to the Jizō with his hands in his pockets and said, 'Mr. Jizō, the people in this town would like you to move. Would you be so kind as to do so?' And the

Jizō promptly replied, 'Of course I'll do so. Why ever didn't they come and ask before?' With that he slowly moved away to a corner of the crossroads."

"What a peculiar statue!"

"Then the lecture started."

"Oh! Is there more to come?"

"Most certainly. Professor Kidd went on to say that he had opened his address to the women's meeting with that particular story because it illustrated a point he had in mind. 'If I may take the liberty of saying so,' he said, 'whenever women do something, they are prone to tackle it in a roundabout way instead of coming straight to the point. Admittedly, it is not solely women who beat about the bush. In these so-called enlightened days, debilitated by the poisons of Western civilization, even men have become somewhat effeminate. There are, alas, all too many now devoting their time and effort to an imitation of Western customs in the totally mistaken conviction that aping foreigners is the proper occupation of a gentleman. Such persons are, of course, deformed, for, by their efforts to conform with alien ways, they deform themselves. They deserve no further comment. However, I would wish you ladies to reflect upon the tale I've told today so that, as occasion may arise, you, too, will act with the same clear-hearted honesty as was shown by Daft Bamboo. For if all ladies did so act, there can be no doubt that one-third of the abominable discords between husbands and wives and between wives and their mothers-in-law would simply disappear. Human beings are, alas, so made that the more they indulge in secret schemes, schemes whose very secrecy breeds evil, the deeper they drive the wellsprings of their own unhappiness. And the specific reason why so many ladies are so much less happy than the average man is precisely because ladies over indulge themselves in secret schemes. Please,' he begged us as his lecture ended, 'turn yourselves into Daft Bamboos.'"

"Did he, indeed! Well, Yukie, are you planning to follow his advice?"

"No fear! Turn myself into a Daft Bamboo! That's the last thing I would do. Miss Goldfield, too, she was very angry. She said the lecture was damned rude."

"Miss Goldfield? The girl who lives just round the corner?"

"Yes. Little Miss Popinjay in person."

"Does she go to the same school as you, Yukie?"

"No, she just came to hear the lecture because it was a Women's Society meeting. She certainly dresses up to the nines. Really astonishing."

"They say she's very good looking. Is it true?"

"She's nothing special, in my opinion. Certainly not the knock-out that she fancies herself. Almost any girl would look good under that much make-up."

"So if you, Yukie, daubed on the same amount of make-up, you'd look twice as pretty as she does? Right?"

"What a thing to say! But truly, Auntie, she puts on far too much. Rich she may be, but really she overdoes it."

"Well, it's pleasant to be rich, even if one does consequently overdo the paints and powder. Wouldn't you agree?"

"Yes, perhaps you're right. But if anyone needs to take lessons from Daft Bamboo, that Goldfield girl's the one. She is so terribly stuck-up. Only the other day she was swanking to all the other girls that some poet or other had just dedicated to her a collection of his new-style poetry."

"That was probably Mr. Beauchamp."

"Really? He must be a bit flighty."

"Oh no, Mr. Beauchamp is very sober-minded man. He would think such a gesture the most natural thing in the world."

"A man like that shouldn't be allowed to. . . Actually there is another amusing thing. It seems that somebody recently sent her a love letter."

"How disgusting! Whoever did such a thing?"

"Apparently nobody knows who sent it."

"Wasn't there a name?"

"It was signed, but with a name that no one's ever heard of. And it was a very, very long letter, about a yard long, full of the weirdest things. For instance, it said, 'I love you in the same way that a saintly man loves God.' It said, 'Gladly for your sake would I die like a lamb sacrificed on the altar; for me, so to be slaughtered would be the greatest of all honors.' It said, 'My heart is shaped like a triangle in the center of which, like a bull's eye pierced by a blowgun dart, is Cupid's arrow stuck!'"

"Is all that meant to be serious?"

"It would seem to be. Three of my own friends have actually seen the letter."

"I do think she's awful to go around showing people such a letter. Since she intends to marry Mr. Coldmoon, she could get into trouble if that sort of story begins to get around."

"On the contrary, she'd be terribly pleased if everyone should know about it. I'm sure she'd say you'd be welcome to pass the news to Mr.

Coldmoon when next he pays a visit. I don't suppose he's heard about it yet. Or do you think he has?"

"Probably not, since he spends his entire time polishing little glass beads at the university."

"I wonder if Mr. Coldmoon really intends to marry that girl. Poor man!"

"Why? With all her money she'll be of real help to him on some rainy day in the future. So why should you think he's doing badly?"

"Auntie, you are so vulgar, always talking about money, money, money. Surely love is more important than money. Without love no real relation between husband and wife is possible."

"Indeed? Then tell me, Yukie, what sort of man do you intend to marry?"

"How should I know? I've no one in mind."

Though she had hardly understood a word of what was being said, my master's eldest daughter had listened attentively while her mother and Cousin Yukie launched out upon their earnest discussion of the question of marriage. But suddenly, out of the blue, the little girl opened her mouth. "I," she announced, "would also like to get married." Though Yukie is herself so brimming with youthful ardor that she could well be expected to sympathize with Tonko's feelings, she was in fact struck dumb by such reckless lust. Mrs. Sneaze, however, took it all in her stride and, smiling at her daughter, simply asked, "To whom?"

"Well, shall I tell you? I want to marry Yasukuni Shrine. But I don't like crossing Suidō Bridge, so I'm wondering what to do."

Both Mrs. Sneaze and Yukie were distinctly taken aback by this unexpected declaration of an ambition to marry the shrine dedicated to the departed spirits of those who'd fallen in war for the sake of the fatherland. Words failed them, and all they could do was shake with laughter. They were still laughing when the second daughter said to her eldest sister. "So you'd like to marry Yasukuni Shrine? Well, so would I. I'd love it. Let's both do just that. Come on. No? All right then, if you won't join me, I'll take a rickshaw and go get married by myself"

"Babu go, too," piped up the smallest of my master's daughters. Indeed, such a triple marrying-off would suit him very well.

At that moment there came the sound of a rickshaw stopping in front of the house, followed by the lively voice of a rickshawman announcing the arrival of my master. It would seem he has got back safely from the police station. Leaving the rickshawman to hand over a large parcel to the maid, my master came into the living room with an air of perfect composure. Greeting his niece with a friendly, "Ah, so there you are," he flung down beside the family's famous oblong brazier some bottle shaped object he'd brought back. An object of that shape is not necessarily a bottle, and it certainly doesn't look much like a vase. Being so odd a specimen of earthenware, for the time being I'll content myself with calling it a bottle shaped object.

"What a peculiar bottle! Did you bring it back from the police station?" asks Yukie, as she stands it up on its base.

Glancing at his niece, my master proudly comments, "Isn't it a beautiful shape?"

"A beautiful shape? That thing? I don't think it beautiful at all. What ever made you bring home such an awful oil jar?"

"How could this treasure possibly be an oil jar! What a vulgar comment! You're hopeless."

"What is it then?"

"A vase."

"For a vase, its mouth is too small and its body far too wide."

"That's exactly why it's so remarkable. You have absolutely no artistic taste. Almost as bad as your aunt." Holding the oil jar up toward the paper-window, he stands and gazes at it.

"So, I have no artistic sense. I see. I certainly wouldn't come home from a police station bearing an oil jar as a present. Auntie, what do you think?"

Her aunt is far too engrossed to be bothered. She has opened the parcel and is now frantically checking the goods.

"Gracious me! Burglars seem to be making progress. All these things have been washed and ironed. Just look, dear," she says.

"Who said I was given an oil jar at the police station? The fact is that I got so bored with waiting that I went out for a walk and, while I was walking, I saw this splendid vessel in a shop and picked it up for a song. You, of course, wouldn't see it, but it's a rare object."

"It's too rare. And tell me, where was it that you walked about?"

"Where? Around Nihon-zutsumi, of course. I also visited Yoshiwara. It's quite a lively place, that. Have you ever seen the iron gate? I bet you haven't."

"Nothing would ever induce me to go and look at it. I have no cause to traipse around a brothel area like Yoshiwara. How could you, a teacher, go to such a place? I am deeply shocked. What d'you say, Auntie? Auntie!"

"Yes, dear. I rather think there's something missing. Is this the lot?"

"The only item missing is the yams. They instructed me to be there by nine o'clock and then they kept me waiting until eleven. It's outrageous. The Japanese police are plainly no good at all."

"The Japanese police may be no good, but trotting about in Yoshiwara is very decidedly worse. If you're found out, you'll get the sack. Won't he, Auntie?"

"Yes, probably. My dear," she went on turning to her husband, "the lining of my obi is gone. I knew there was something missing."

"What's so serious about an obi lining? Just forget it. Think about me. For three long hours they kept me waiting. A whole half-day of my precious time completely wasted." My master has now changed into Japanese clothes and, leaning against the brazier, sits and gawps entrancedly at his ghastly oil jar. His wife, recovering rapidly from her loss, replaces the returned articles in a cupboard and comes back to her seat.

"Auntie," says the persistent Yukie, "he says this oil jar is a rare object. Don't you think it dirty?"

"You bought that thing in Yoshiwara? Really!"

"What do you mean by 'Really!'? As if you understand anything!"

"But surely, a jar like that! You could find one anywhere without cavorting off to Yoshiwara."

"That's just where you're wrong. This isn't an object you could find any where."

"Uncle does take after that stone Jizō, doesn't he?"

"None of your cheek, now. The trouble with college girls today is their far too saucy tongues. You'd do better to spend time reading the *Proper Conduct of a Woman*."

"Uncle, it's a fact, isn't it, that you don't like insurance policies? But tell me, which do you dislike more, college girls or insurance policies?"

"I do not dislike insurance policies. Insurance is a necessary thing. Anyone who gives even half a thought to the future is bound to take out a policy. But college girls are good-for-nothings."

"I don't care if I am a good-for-nothing. But you can talk! You aren't even insured!"

"As of next month, I shall be."

"Are you sure?"

"Of course I'm sure."

"Oh, you shouldn't. It's silly to get insured. It would be much better to spend the premium money on something else. Don't you agree, Auntie?"

Mrs. Sneaze grins, but my master, looking serious, retorts, "You only say such irresponsible things because you imagine you're going to go on living until you're a hundred years old. Even two hundred. But when you've grown a little more mature, you'll come to realize the necessity of insurance. From next month, I shall definitely insure myself."

"Oh, well. Can't be helped then. Actually, if you can afford to throw away cash on an umbrella as you did the other day, you might as well waste your wealth on insuring yourself. You bought it for me even though I kept saying I didn't want it."

"You really didn't want it?"

"No. I most certainly did not want any umbrella."

"Then you can give it back to me. Tonko needs one badly, so I'll give it to her. Have you brought it with you today?"

"But that's really mean. How could you! It's terrible to make me give it back after you've bought it for me."

"I asked you to return it only because you clearly stated that you didn't want it. There's nothing terrible about that."

"It's true I don't need it. But you're still terrible."

"What nonsense you do talk. You say you don't want it, so I ask you to return it. Why should that be terrible?"

"But. . ."

"But what?"

"But that's terrible."

"You're making no sense at all, just repeating the same irrational assertion."

"Uncle, you too are repeating the same thing."

"I can't help that if you initiate the repetitions. You did definitely say you didn't want it."

"Yes, I did say that. And it's true that I don't need it. But I don't like to return it."

"Well, I am surprised. You're not only irrational and unreasonable but downright obstinate. A truly hopeless case. Don't they teach you logic at your school?"

"Oh, I don't care. I am uneducated anyway. Say anything you like about me! But to ask me to return my own thing. . . Even a stranger wouldn't make such a heartless request. You could learn a thing or two from poor old Daft Bamboo."

"From whom?"

"I mean you should be more honest and frank."

"You're a very stupid girl and uncommonly obstinate. That's why you fail to pass your exams."

"Even if I do fail, I shan't ask you to pay my school fees. So there!" At this point Yukie appeared to be shaken by uncontrollable emotions. Tears gushed out of her eyes and, pouring down her cheeks, fell to stain her purple dress.

My master sat there stupefied. As though he believed it might help him understand what mental processes could produce such copious tears, he sat and blankly stared, sometimes at the top of her skirt, sometimes, at her down-turned face. Just then, O-san appeared at the door where, squatting with her hands spread out on the matting, she announced, "There is a visitor, Sir."

"Who is it?" asks my master.

"A student from your school," answers O-san, casting a sharp sidelong glance at Yukie's tear-stained face.

My master took himself off to the drawing room. In pursuit of further material for this book, in particular as it might bear upon my study of the human animal, I sneaked out after him by way of the veranda. If one is to make a worthwhile study of mankind, it is vital to seize upon eventful moments. At ordinary times, most human beings are wearisomely ordinary; depressingly banal in appearance and deadly boring in their conversation. However, at certain moments, by some peculiar, almost supernatural, process their normal triviality can be transformed into something so weird and wonderful that no feline scholar of their species can afford to miss any occasion when that transformation seems likely to take place. Yukie's sudden deluge of tears was a very good example of this phenomenon. Though Yukie possesses an incomprehensible and unfathomable mind, she gave no evidence of it in her chattering with Mrs. Sneaze. However, as soon as my master appeared and flung his filthy oil jar into the situation, Yukie was instantly transfigured. Like some sleeping dragon startled into its draconian reality by torrents of water pumped upon it by some idiotic fire engine, unbelievably Yukie suddenly revealed the depths of her wonderfully devious, wonderfully beautiful, wonderfully wondrous character in all its exquisite subtlety. Such wonderful characteristics are, in fact, common among women throughout the world, and it is regrettable that women so seldom make them manifest. On reflection, it would perhaps be more accurate to say that, while these characteristics do continuously manifest themselves, they rarely appear in such uninhibited form, so purely, openly and unconstrainedly, as they did in Yukie's outburst. No doubt I owe it to my master—that commendably crotchety crank who harbors no ill-heartedness when he strokes my fur in the wrong direction—that I have been privileged to witness such a revelation of the female soul. As I tag along through life behind him, wherever we go he provokes more drama than any of the protagonists ever realize. I am fortunate to be the cat of such a man, for, thanks to him, my short cat's life is crammed with incident. Now, who, I wonder, is the visitor awaiting us?

It proved to be a schoolboy of about the same age as Yukie, perhaps sixteen or seventeen. His hair is cropped so short that the skin of his skull, a truly massive skull, shines through it. With a dumpy nose in the middle of his face, he sits despondently waiting in a corner of the room. Apart from his enormous skull, there is nothing remarkable in his features. However, since that head looks huge in its virtually hairless state, it will certainly catch the eye when he lets his hair grow long as does my master. It is one of my master's private theories that heads so vast are always addled. He may, of course, be right, but heads of such Napoleonic grandeur remain indeed impressive. The lad's kimono, like that of any houseboy, is made out of common, dark blue cotton with patterns splashed in white. I cannot identify the style of the pattern, possibly Satsuma, possibly Kurume, even perhaps plain Iyo, but he is undoubtedly wearing a lined kimono of dark blue cotton patterned with splotches of white. Its sleeves seem somewhat short, and he would appear to be wearing neither a shirt nor any underwear. I understand that it is currently considered very stylish, positively dandified, to go about in a lined kimono without underwear and even without socks, but this particular young man, far from seeming stylish, gives a strong impression of extreme shabbiness. In particular I notice that, barefooted like our recent burglar, he has marked the matting with three dirty footprints and now, doing his best to look respectful and certainly looking ill at ease, sits uncomfortably upon the fourth of them. It is in no way extraordinary to see respectable persons behaving respectfully, but when some wild, young hooligan with his skinhead hairstyle and his too-small clothing seats himself in a reverent posture, the effect is distinctly incongruous. Creatures who have the effrontery even to be proud of their insolent refusal to bow to their teachers when they meet them in the street must find it very painful to sit up properly like anyone else, even for so little as half an hour. Moreover, since this particular yahoo is actually trying to behave as if he were a gentleman by birth, a man of natural modesty and of cultivated virtue, the comic incompetence of his performance must surely add to his sufferings. I marvel at the agonizing self-control by which a lout so boisterous both in the classroom and on the playground can bring himself to endure such a laughable charade. It is pitiful but, at the same time, funny. In confrontations of this sort, however stupid my master may be, he still seems to carry rather more weight than any individual pupil. Indeed, my master must be feeling pretty pleased with himself.

The saying goes that even motes of dust, if enough of them pile up, will make a mountain. One solitary schoolboy may well be insignificant, but schoolboys ganged together can be a formidable force, capable of agitating for the expulsion of a teacher, even of going on strike. Just as cowards grow aggressive under the spur of grog, so may students emboldened by mere numbers into stirring up a riot be regarded as having lost their senses by becoming intoxicated with people. How else can one explain how my master, who, however antiquated and decrepit he may be, is nevertheless a teacher, could in his own schoolroom have been reduced to an object of derision by this scruffy little runt now making himself small, dejected perhaps rather than truly humbled, in a corner of our room? Even so, l find it hard to credit that so miserable a snivelard could ever have dared to rag or mock my master.

That noble figure, shoving a cushion toward the drooping crophead, bade him sit on it, but the latter, though he managed to mumble a nervous "thank you," made no move at all. It's quaint to see a living being, even this bighead, sitting blankly with a partly faded cushion rammed up against his knees. The cushion, of course, says nothing, not even, "Sit on me." But cushions are for sitting on. Mrs. Sneaze didn't go to a market stall and buy this particular cushion in order that it should be looked at. It follows that anyone who declines to sit on the cushion is, in effect, casting a slur on its cushionly good name. Indeed, when my master has specifically offered the cushion for sitting upon, a refusal to do so extends the insult to the cushion into a slight upon my master. This crop-head glaring at the cushion and thereby slighting my master does not, of course, have any personal dislike for the cushion itself. As a matter of fact, the only other occasion in his life when he sat in a civilized manner was during the memorial rites for his grandfather, so his present sally into decorum is bringing on pins and needles in his feet while his toes, excruciated by the pressures of propriety, have long been signaling blue murder. Nevertheless, the clot won't sit on the cushion. He will not do so, though the cushion, clearly embarrassed by the situation, yearns to be sat on. Even though my master requests he use the cushion, still this oaf declines it. He is a very wearisome young man. If he can be so over-weeningly modest on a visit, he ought to trot out a little more of his precious modesty when roistering around with his cronies in the school-room and at his lodgings. He positively reeks of decorous reserve when it's totally uncalled for; yet, when just a touch of self-depreciation would hardly come amiss, he's raucous, coarse, and cocky. What an irk-some, cross-grained, crophead this young rascal is.

At that moment the sliding door behind him quietly slid open and Yukie came in formally to place a cup of tea before the silent youth. In normal circumstances, he would have greeted the appearance of such refreshment with jeering catcalls about poor, old Savage Tea, but today, already wilting under my master's immediate presence, he suffers further agony as a priss-ily conducted young lady serves him tea with all that affected ceremonial-ity which has only recently been drilled into her at school. As Yukie closed the sliding door she allowed herself, safe behind the young man's back, to break into a broad grain. Which shows that a female is remarkably more self-possessed than a male of the same age. Indeed, Yukie very evidently has far more spirit to her than this cushion shunning twit. Her bare-faced grin is all the more remarkable when one remembers that, only a few minutes ago, tears of resentment were pouring down her cheeks.

After Yukie had left, a long silence fell. Eventually my master, feeling that the interview was in danger of becoming some kind of dour religious exercise, took the initiative and opened his mouth.

"Your name. . . what did you say it was?"

"Yore."

"Yore? Yore and what else? What's your first name?"

"Lancelot."

"Lancelot Yore. . . I see. Quite a resounding name. Certainly not modern, a somewhat old-fashioned name. You are in your fourth year, aren't you?"

"No."

"Your third year?"

"No, my second year."

"And in Class A?"

"In Class B."

"In B? Then, you're in my class. I see." My master appeared impressed. He had taken note of this particularly monstrous head since its bearer first joined the school, and had recognized it immediately. In fact, that head has so long and so deeply impressed my master that, every so often, he actually dreams about it. However, being of a totally impractical nature, he had never connected that extraordinary head with that odd old-fashioned name, and had somehow failed to connect either with his own second-year Class B. Consequently, when he realized that the impressive head that haunted his dreams actually belonged to one of his own pupils, he was genuinely startled. All the more so since he cannot imagine why this big headed and oddly named member of his own class should now have come to see him. My master is unpopular, and hardly a single schoolboy ever comes near him, even at the New Year. As a matter of fact, this Lancelot Yore is the very first such visitor, and my master is understandably puzzled by his call. It is inconceivable that the visit could be purely social, for how could my master be of the faintest interest to any of his pupils? It seems equally inconceivable that a boy of this kind could need advice about his personal affairs. Of course, it is just conceivable that Lancelot Yore might come around to urge my master into resigning, but in such a case one would expect him to be, if not blatantly aggressive, at least defiant. My master, unable to make heads or tails of the situation, is at a complete loss and, to judge by his appearance, it would seem that Lancelot Yore is himself by no means certain why he has made his visit. In the end my master was driven to asking point-blank questions.

"Have you come here for a chat?"

"No, not for that."

"Then you have something to tell me?"

"Yes."

"About school?"

"Yes, I wanted to tell you something about. . ."

"What is it? Tell me."

"Right, then."

Lancelot lowers his eyes and says nothing. Normally, considered as a second-year student at middle school, Lancelot is talkative. Though his brain is undeveloped in comparison with his skull, he expresses himself rather more effectively than most of his fellow students in Class B. In fact, it was he who recently made my master look rather a fool by asking him how to translate "Columbus" into Japanese. That such a tricky questioner should be as reluctant to start speaking as some stammering princess suggests that something very weird must be involved. Hesitation so prolonged and so entirely out of character cannot possibly be due to modesty. Even my simple master thought the matter really rather odd.

"If you have something to say, go ahead and say it. Why do you hesitate?"

"It's a bit difficult to explain. . ."

"Difficult?" says my master peering across to study Lancelot's face. But his visitor still sits with his eyes lowered, and my master finds it impossible to read anything from their expression. Changing his tone of voice, he added, "Don't worry. Tell me anything you like. Nobody else is listening, and I won't pass on a single word to anyone."

"Could I really tell you?" Lancelot is still wavering.

"Why not?" says my master, taking a sort of plunge.

"All right, I'll tell you." Abruptly lifting up his close-cropped head the boy glanced diffidently at my master. His eyes are triangular in shape. My master puffed out his cheeks with cigarette smoke and, slowly expelling it, looked at his visitor sideways.

"Well, actually. . . things have become awkward. . ."

"What things?"

"Well, it's all terribly awkward, and that's why I've come."

"Yes, but what is it that you find so awkward?"

"I really didn't mean to do such a thing, but as Hamada urged and begged me to lend it. . ."

"When you say Hamada, do you mean Hamada Heisuke?"

"Yes."

"Did you lend him money for board and lodging?"

"Oh, no, I didn't lend him that."

"Then, what did you lend him?"

"I lent him my name."

"Whatever was he doing borrowing your name?"

"He sent a love letter."

"He sent what?"

"I explained I'd rather do the posting than the lending of my name."

"You're not making much sense. Who did what anyway?"

"A love letter was sent."

"A love letter? To whom?"

"As I said, it's so difficult to tell you."

"You mean you've sent a love letter to some woman? Is that it?"

"No, it wasn't me."

"Hamada sent it?"

"It wasn't Hamada either."

"Then who did send it?"

"That's not known."

"None of this makes sense. Did no one send it?"

"Only the name is mine."

"Only the name is yours? I still don't understand. You'll have to explain what's happened clearly and logically. In the first place, who actually received the love letter?"

"A girl named Goldfield who lives just round the corner."

"Goldfield? The businessman?"

"Yes, his daughter."

"And what do you mean when you say you lent only your name?"

"Because that girl is such a dolled-up and conceited pinhead, we decided to send her a love letter. Hamada said it had to be signed. But when I told him to sign it himself, he argued that his name wasn't sufficiently interesting, that Lancelot Yore would be very much more impressive. So I ended up by lending my name."

"And do you know the girl? Are you friends?"

"Friends? Of course not. I've never set eyes on her."

"How very imprudent! Fancy sending a love letter to someone you've never even seen! What made you do such a thing?"

"Well, everyone said she was stuck-up and pompous, so we thought we'd make a fool of her."

"That's even more rash! So you sent the letter clearly signed with your name?"

"Yes. The letter itself was written by Hamada. I lent my name, and

Endo took it round to her house at night and stuck it in the letter box."

"Then all three of you are jointly responsible?"

"Yes, but afterward, when I thought about being found out and possibly expelled from school, I got so worried that I haven't been able to sleep for the last two or three nights. That's why I'm not my usual self."

"It's a quite unbelievably stupid thing you've done. Tell me, when you signed that letter did you give the school's address?"

"No, of course I made no mention of the school."

"Well, that's something. If you had and it ever came out, the good name of our school would be disgraced."

"Do you think I'll be expelled?"

"Well, I don't know. . ."

"My father is very strict and my mother is only a stepmother, so if anything happened such as being expelled, I'd really be in the soup. Do you reckon I'll get expelled?"

"You must understand, you shouldn't have done a thing like that."

"I didn't mean to really, but somehow I just did. Couldn't you save me from being expelled?" With the tears running down his face, the pathetic Lancelot implores my master's help.

For quite some time behind the sliding door Mrs. Sneaze and her niece have been convulsed with silent giggles. My master, doggedly maintaining an air of importance, keeps on repeating his, "Well, I don't know." Altogether a facinating experience.

It is possible that some of you human beings might, and very reasonably, ask me what I find so fascinating about it. For every living being, man or animal, the most important thing in this world is to know one's own self. Other things being equal, a human being that truly knows himself is more to be respected than a similarly enlightened cat. Should the humans of my acquaintance ever achieve such self-awareness, I would immediately abandon, as unjustifiedly heartless, this somewhat snide account of their species as I know them. However, just as few human beings actually know the size of their own noses, even fewer know the nature of their own selves, for if they did, they would not need to pose such a question to a mere cat whom they normally regard, even disregard, with contempt. Thus, though human beings are always enormously pleased with themselves, they usually lack that self-perception which, and which alone, might justify their seeing themselves, and their boasting of it wherever they go, as the lords of all creation. To top things off, they display a brazenly calm conviction in their role which is positively laughable. For there they are, making a great nuisance of themselves with their fussing entreaties to be taught where to find their own fool noses, while at the same time strutting around with placards on their backs declaring their claim to be lords of creation. Would common logic or even common sense lead any such patently loony human being to resign his claim to universal lordship? Not on your life! Every idiot specimen would sooner die than surrender his share in the fantasy of human importance. Any creature that behaves with such blatant inconsistency and yet contrives never to recognize the least minim of self-contradiction in its behavior is, of course, funny. But since the human animal is indeed funny, it follows that the creature is a fool.

The foregoing events occurred precisely as I have recorded them and, as external realities, they left their quaint, little ripples on the stream of time. But in this particular case it was not their manifested conduct which made my master, Yukie, and Yore strike me as amusing. What tickled me was the differing quality of reaction in their inmost hearts, which the same external events evoked in these several persons. First of all, my master's heart is rather cold, and so was his reaction to these happenings. However strictly Yore's harsh father may treat the boy, however hurtfully his stepmother may pick on him, my master's heart would not be moved. How could it be? Yore's possible expulsion from school does not raise any of the issues that would be involved if my master were dismissed. Of course, if all the pupils, nearly a thousand of them, were simultaneously expelled, then the teachers might find it hard to earn a living: but whatever fate befalls this wretched single pupil, the daily course of my master's own life will be totally unaffected. Obviously, where there is no self-interest there is not going to be much sympathy. It is just not natural to knit one's brows, to blow one's nose, or to draw great sighs over the misfortunes of complete strangers. I simply do not believe the human animal is capable of showing such understanding and compassion. People sometimes squeeze out a few tears or try looking sorry as a kind of social obligation, a sort of tax-payment due in acknowledgement of having been born into a community. But such gestures are never heart felt, and their effective performance, like any other act of chicanery, does in fact demand a high degree of skill. Persons who perform these trickeries most artfully are regarded as men of strong artistic feelings and earn the deepest respect of their less-gifted fellows.

It follows, of course, that those who are most highly esteemed are those most morally dubious, an axiom which can easily be proved by putting it to the test. My master, being extremely ham-handed in matters of this kind, commands not the least respect and, having no hope of winning respect by crafty misrepresentation of his true feelings, is quite open in expressing his inner cold-heartedness. The sincerity of his indifference emerges very clearly from the way in which he fobs off poor young Yore's repeated pleas for help with repetitions of the same old formulae: "Well, I don't know" and "Hmm, I wonder." I hasten to comment that I trust my readers will not begin to dislike so good a man as my master just because he happens to be cold-hearted. Coldness is the inborn natural condition of the human heart, and the man who does not hide that fact is honest. If in circumstances such as I've described, you really are expecting something more than cold-heartedness, then I can only say that you have sadly overestimated the worth of humankind. When even mere honesty is in notably short supply, it would be absolutely ridiculous to expect displays of magnanimity. Or do you seriously believe that the Eight Good Men have stepped out of the pages of Bakin's silly novel in order to take up residence in our neighborhood?

So much for my master. Let us now consider his womenfolk tittering away together in the living room. They, in fact, have gone a stage beyond the pure indifference of my master and, naturally adapted as they are to the comic and the grotesque, are thoroughly enjoying themselves. These females regard the matter of the love letter, a matter of excruciating concern to that miserable crophead, as a gift from a kindly heaven. There is no particular reason why they regard it as a blessing. It just seems like one to them. However, if one analyzes their mirth, the simple fact is that they are glad that Yore's in trouble. Ask any female whether she finds it amusing, even a cause for outright laughter, when other people are in trouble, and she will either call you mad or affect to have been deliberately insulted by a question so demeaning to the dignity of her sex. It may well be true that she feels she's been insulted, but it is also true that she laughs at people in trouble. The reality of this ladylike position is that, inasmuch as the lady intends to do something that would impugn her character, no decent person should draw attention to the fact. Correspondingly, the gentleman's position is to acknowledge that he steals but to insist that nobody should call him immoral because an accusation of immorality would involve a stain on his character, an insult to his good name. Women are quite clever: they think logically. If one has the ill luck to be born a human being, one must prepare oneself not to be distressed that other people will not so much as turn to look when you are being kicked and beaten up. And not just that. One must learn to think it a pleasure to be spat upon, shat upon, and then held up to be laughed at. If one cannot learn these simple lessons, there is no chance of becoming a friend of such clever creatures as women. By an understandable error of judgement the luckless Lancelot Yore has made a sad mistake and is now greatly humiliated. He might possibly feel that it is uncivilized to snigger at him behind his back when he is thus humiliated, but any such feeling on his part would simply be a demonstration of pure childishness. I understand that women call it narrow-mindedness if one gets angry with persons who commit a breach of etiquette. So, unless young Yore is prepared to acquire that further humiliation, he'd best belt up.

Finally, I will offer a brief analysis of Yore's own inward feelings. That infantile suppliant is a living lump of quivering anxiety. Just as Napoleon's massive head was bulgy with ambitions, so Yore's gurt skull is bursting with anxiety. The occasional puppylike quivering of his pudgy nose betrays that this inner distress has forced a connection with his nasal nerves so that, by the nastiest of reflex actions, he twitches without knowing it. Now for several days he has been at the end of his tether, going around with a lump in his stomach as though he'd swallowed a cannon ball. Finally, at his wits' end and in the extremity of his desperation, he has come to humble his head before a teacher he most cordially dislikes. I imagine the addled thinking behind this desperate act was that, since teachers are supposed to look after their pupils, perhaps even the loathed Sneaze might somehow help him. Lost in the miasma of his inner agony is any recollection of his habitual ragging of my master; forgotten, too, is the fact that he spent his witless days in egging on his fellow hooligans to hoot and mock old Savage Tea. He seems to believe that, however much he's made a nuisance of himself he's actually entitled to his teacher's help for the single reason that he happens to be a member of that teacher's class. He is indeed a very simple soul. My master did not choose the class he teaches: he was directed to that work by order of the headmaster. I am reminded of that bowler hat of Waverhouse's uncle. It was no more than a bowler hat in name. The idea of my master as a teacher who is also the mentor of his pupils is equally unreal. Teacher, sneacher. A name means nothing. If it did, any marriage broker would by now have been able to interest some aspiring bachelor in a girl with a name as beautiful as that snow river name of Yukie's. The dismal Yore is not only daftly egocentric but, daftly overestimating human kindliness, assumes that his fellow creatures are under some form of obligation to be nice to him. I'm sure he has never dreamt that he might be laughed at, so at least he's learning some useful home truths about his species from his visit to the home of the "person in charge." As a result, he will himself become more truly human. His heart, benignly chilled, will grow indifferent to other people's troubles and, in time, he'll even learn to jeer at the distressed. The world will come to swarm with little Yores, all doing their best to stretch themselves into full-blown Goldfields. For the lad's sake, I do hope he learns his lesson quickly and grows up soon into his full humanity. Otherwise, no matter how hard he worries, no matter how bitterly he repents, no matter how fervently his heart may yearn to be reformed, he can never so much as hope to be able to achieve the spectacular success of that model of humanity, the highly respected Goldfield. On the contrary, he will be banished from human society. Compared with that, expulsion from some piddling middle school would be as nothing.

I was idly amusing myself with these reflections when the sliding door from the hall was roughly jerked aside and half a face suddenly appeared at the opening. My master was mumbling, "Well, I really don't know," when this half-face called his name. He wrenched his head around to find a shining segment of Avalon Coldmoon beaming down upon him.

"Why, hello," says my master making no move to get up, "come along in."

"Aren't you busy with a visitor?" the visible half of Coldmoon asks politely.

"Never mind about that. Come on in."

"Actually, I've called to ask you to come out with me."

"Where to? Akasaka once again? I've had enough of that district. You made me walk so much the other day that my legs are still quite stiff."

"It will be all right today. Come on out and give those legs a stretch."

"Where would we go? Look, don't just stand there. Come along in."

"My idea is that we should go to the zoo and hear their tiger roar."

"How dreary. I say, old man, do come in if only for a few minutes."

Coldmoon evidently came to the conclusion that he would not succeed by negotiating from a distance so, reluctantly removing his shoes, he slouched into the room. As usual, he is wearing gray trousers with patches on the seat. These patches, he is always telling us, are not there either because the trousers are old or because his bottom is too heavy. The reason is that he has just started to learn how to ride a bicycle, and the patches are needed to resist the extra friction involved. Greeting Yore with a nod and a brief hello, he sits down on the veranda side of the room. He has, of course, no idea that he is now sitting down with a direct rival in the lists of love, with the very person who has sent a love letter to that damsel now regarded by all and sundry as the future Mrs. Coldmoon.

"There's nothing particularly interesting about a tiger's roar," observed my master.

"Well, not just at this exact moment. But my idea is that we should walk about for a bit and then go on to the zoo around eleven."

"So?"

"By then, the old trees in the park will be darkly frightening like a silent forest."

"Well, possibly. Certainly, it will be a little more deserted than by daytime."

"We'll follow a path as thickly wooded as possible, one where even in daytime few people pass. Then, before you know it, we'll find ourselves thinking we're far away from the dusty city and a feeling, I'm sure, will grow within us that we've somehow wandered away into far-off mountains."

"What does one do with a feeling like that?"

"Feeling like that, we'll just stand there, silent and motionless for a little while. Then, suddenly, the roar of a tiger will burst upon us."

"Is the tiger trained to roar precisely at that moment?"

"I guarantee he'll roar. Even in broad day that fearsome sound can be heard all the way over at the Science University. So, after dark, in the very dead of night, when not a soul's about in the deep-hushed loneliness, when death can be felt in the air and one breathes the reek of evil mountain spirits. . ."

"Breathing the reek of evil mountain spirits? Whatever does that mean?"

"I understand it's an expression used to signify a condition of extreme terror."

"Is it indeed. Not an expression in common use. I don't believe I've ever heard it before. Anyway, what then?"

"Then the tiger roars. A savage shattering roar that seems to strip each shaking leaf from the ancient cedar trees. Really, it's terrifying."

"I can well believe it is."

"Well then, how about joining me for such an adventure? I'm sure we'll enjoy it. An experience to be treasured. Everyone, sometime, that's how I see it, really ought to hear a tiger roar from the depths of night."

"Well," says my master, "I don't know. . . " He drops on Coldmoon's enthusiastic proposal for an expedition the same wet blanket of indifference with which he has muzzled Yore's agonized entreaties.

Up until this moment that dim nincompoop has been listening, enviously and in silence, to the talk about the tiger, but as a hypnotist's key phrase will bring his subject to his senses, my master's repetition of his indifference snapped Yore smartly back into remembrance of his own dilemma. "Revered teacher," he muttered from his broken trance, "I'm worried sick. What, what, shall I do?"

Coldmoon, puzzled, stares at that enormous head. As for me, I feel suddenly moved, for no particular reason but the feeling, to leave this trio to themselves. Accordingly, I excuse myself from their company and sidle around to the living room.

There I find Mrs. Sneaze with the giggles. She has poured tea into a cheap china cup and, placing that cup on a nasty antimony saucer, says to her niece, "Would you please take this to our guest?"

"I'd rather not."

"Why not?" The mistress sounds surprised and her giggling stops abruptly.

"I'd just rather not," says Yukie. She suddenly adopts a peculiarly supercilious expression and, firmly seating herself on the matting, bends forward and low to study some rag of a daily newspaper.

Mrs. Sneaze immediately resumes negotiations. "What a funny person you are. It's only Mr. Coldmoon. There's no reason to act up."

"It's simply that I really would prefer not to." The girl's eyes remain fixed on the newspaper, but it's obvious that she's too het up to be able to read a word of it. What's more, if anyone points out that she isn't reading, there'll be another flood of maidenly tears.

"Why are you being so shy?" This time, laughing, Mrs. Sneaze deliberately pushes the cup and saucer right onto the newspaper as it lies there flat on the floor.

"What a nasty thing to do!" Yukie tries to yank the paper out from under the tea things, knocks them flying and the spilled tea shoots all over the paper and the living room matting.

"There, now!" says the mistress.

With a cry expressing a curious mixture of anger, shock, and embarrassment, Yukie scrambles to her feet and runs out into the kitchen. I imagine she's gone to fetch a mop. I find this little drama rather amusing.

Mr. Coldmoon, totally unaware of the female flurry which his visit appears to have stirred up in the living room, continues, somewhat oddly, his conversation with my master.

"I notice," he says, "that you've had new paper fixed on that sliding door. Who did it, if I may ask?"

"The women. Quite a good job they made of it, don't you think?"

"Yes, very professional. You say 'the women.' Does that include that college girl who sometimes comes here visiting?"

"Yes, she lent a hand. In fact she was boasting that, since she can make such an obviously splendid job of papering a sliding door, she is also obviously well qualified to get married."

"I see," says Coldmoon still studying the door. "Down the left side, there," he eventually continued, "the paper has been fixed on taut and smooth, but along the right-hand edge it seems to have been inadequately stretched. Hence those wrinkles."

"That was where they started the job, before they'd really got the hang of it."

"I see. It's certainly less well done. The surface forms an exponential curve irrelatable to any ordinary function." From the abyss of his scientific training Coldmoon dredges up monstrosities.

"I dare say," says my master, indifferent as ever.

That dispassionate comment, it would seem, at last brings home to our hooligan scribe the complete hopelessness of hoping that even the most searing of his supplications could ever melt my master's chilly disconcern. Suddenly lowering his huge skull to the matting, Yore in total silence made his farewell salutation.

"Ah," said my master, "you're leaving?"

Yore's crestfallen appearance provided his only answer. We heard him dragging his heavy cedar clogs even after he'd gone out through the gate. A pitiable case. If someone doesn't come to his rescue, he could well compose one of those rock-top suicide poems and then fling his stupid body over the lip of Kegon Falls. Come what may, the root-cause of all this trouble is the flibbertigibbet self-conceit of that insufferable Miss Goldfield. If Yore does do himself in, it is to be hoped that his ghost will find the time to scare that girl to death. No man need regret it if a girl like that, even a brace or more of them, were removed from this already sufficiently troubled world. It seems to me that Coldmoon would be well advised to marry some more ladylike young person.

"Was that, then, one of your pupils?"

"Yes."

"What an enormous head. Is he good at his work?"

"Rather poor for that size of head. But every now and again he asks original questions. The other day he caught me off balance by asking for a translation of the meaning of Columbus."

"Maybe the improbable size of his braincase leads him to pose such an improbable question. Whatever did you answer?"

"Oh, something or other off the cuff."

"So you actually did translate it. That's remarkable."

"Children lose faith in a language teacher who fails to provide them, on demand, with a translation of anything they may ask."

"You've become quite a politician. But to judge by that lad's look, he must be terribly run down. He seemed ashamed to be bothering you."

"He's just managed to get himself into something of a mess. Silly young ass!"

"What's it all about? The mere sight of him moves one's sympathy. What's he done?"

"Rather a stupid thing. He's sent a love letter to Goldfield's daughter."

"What? That great numbskull? Students nowadays seem to stop at nothing. Quite astonishing! Really, I am surprised."

"I hope this news has not upset you?"

"Not in the very least. On the contrary, I find it most diverting. I do assure you, it's quite all right by me, however, many love letters may come pouring in upon her."

"If you feel that self-assured perhaps it doesn't matter. . ."

"Of course it doesn't matter. I really don't mind at all. But isn't it rather remarkable that that great muttonhead should take to writing love letters?"

"Well, actually, it all started as a kind of joke. Because that girl was so stuck-up and conceited, my precious trio got together and. . ."

"You mean that three boys sent one love letter to Miss Goldfield? This business grows more whacky by the minute. Such a joint letter sounds rather like three people settling down to share one portion of a Western-style dinner. Don't you agree?"

"Well, they did divide the functions up between them. One wrote the letter, another posted it, and the third loaned his name for its signature. That young blockhead whom you saw just now, quite the silliest of them all, he's the one who lent his name. Yet he actually told me that he's never even set eyes on the girl. I simply can't imagine how anyone could do such a ludicrous thing."

"Well, I think it's spectacular, a wonder of our times, a real masterpiece of the modern spirit! That that oaf should have it in him to fire off a love letter to some unknown woman. . . Really, it's most amusing!"

"It could lead to some very awkward misunderstandings."

"What would it matter if it did? It would be skin off nobody's nose but the Goldfields'."

"But this daughter of theirs is the very girl you may be marrying."

"True, but I only may be marrying her. Don't be so concerned. Really, I do not mind in the least about the Goldfields."

"You may not mind but. . ."

"Oh, I'm quite sure the Goldfields wouldn't mind. Honest!"

"All right, then, if you say so. Anyway, after the deed was done and the letter delivered, that boy suddenly began to get qualms of conscience. More precisely, he became scared of being found out and therefore came sheepishly around here to ask me for advice."

"Really? Was that why he looked so very down in the mouth? He must, at heart, be a very timid boy. You gave him some advice, I suppose?"

"He's scared silly of being expelled from school. That's his chief worry."

"Why should he be expelled from school?"

"Because he has done such a wicked and immoral thing."

"You can't call sending a love letter, even in joke, either wicked or immoral. It's just not that important. In fact, I'd expect the Goldfields to take it as an honor and to go around boasting about it."

"Oh, surely not!"

"Anyway, even if it was wrong to do such a thing, it's hardly fair to let that poor boy worry himself sick about it. You could be sending him to his death. Though his head is grotesque, his features are not evil. He was twitching his nose, you know. Rather sweet, really."

"You're becoming as irresponsible as Waverhouse in the breezy things you say."

"Well, that's no more than the current style. It's a bit old-fashioned to take things quite as seriously as you do."

"It's hardly a question of being up-to-date or out-of-fashion. Surely, at any time, anywhere, only a complete fool could think it funny to send a love letter to an unknown person. It flies in the face of common sense."

"Come now. The vast majority of all jokes depends on the reversal of ordinary common sense. Ease up on the lad. If only in common charity, do what you can to help him. From what I saw he was already on his way to Kegon Falls."

"Perhaps I should."

"Indeed you should. After all, the world is stiff with full-grown men, men with older and presumably wiser heads, who nevertheless spend all their lives in practical jokes which risk disaster for their fellow men. Would you punish an idiot schoolboy for signing a love letter when men whose jokes could wreck the world go totally unpenalized? If you expel him from school, you can do no less than banish them from civilized society."

"Well, perhaps you're right."

"Good. Then that's settled. Now, how about going out and listening to a tiger?"

"Ah, the tiger."

"Yes. Do come out. As a matter of fact, I've got to leave Tokyo in a few days' time and go back home to attend to some business. Since it will be quite a while before we'll be able again to go out anywhere together, I called today in the express hope we could make some little expedition this evening."

"So you're going home. And on business?"

"Yes, something I myself must cope with. Anyway, let's go out."

"All right, I'll come."

"Splendid. Today, dinner's on me. If, after that, we walk across to the zoo, we should arrive at exactly the right time." Coldmoon's enthusiasm is infectious and, by the time they bustled out together, my master himself was scarcely less excited.

Mrs. Sneaze and Yukie, ever, eternally feminine, just went on with their chit-chat and their sniggering.

IV

IN FRONT OF the alcove, Waverhouse and Singleman sit facing each other with a board for playing *go* set down between them. "Damned if I'm playing for nothing," says Waverhouse forcefully. "The loser stands a dinner. Right?"

Singleman tugs at his daft goatee. "In my experience," he murmurs, "to play for gain, for food or filthy lucre, cheapens this noble pastime. It maims the mind to burden its cells with thoughts of loss or profit. Betting's a scruffy business. I feel, don't you, that the true value of a game encounter is only really appreciated in an atmosphere of leisurely calm where, all considerations of success or failure set aside, one lets things run their own sweet, natural course. Then, and only then, can the finer points of the game be properly savored by its connoisseurs."

"There you go again. Harping away on the same old metaphysical drivel. It's really quite impossible to have any sort of sensible game with a man who carries on as if he'd stepped from the pages of some ancient Chinese tome recording the maunderings of the scholar-hermits of remote antiquity."

"If I harp at all," says Singleman with quite surprising spirit, "it is, as Yüan Ming so neatly put it, that I play on a harp that has no strings."

"Ah," says Waverhouse dryly, "like wiring messages on wireless sets, I suppose."

"Now then, Waverhouse, you can do better than that. But please don't try. Let's get on with the game."

"Will you be black or white?"

"Suit yourself. Either."

"As one might expect of a hermit, you are transcendentally generous. If you'll take white, I'm necessarily black. Right. Let's get cracking. Now then, off you go. Place your first piece anywhere you like."

"The rule is that black starts."

"Really? Is that so? Very well, being a modest fellow, my opening gambit shall be a black piece somewhere around here."

"You can't do that."

"Why not?"

"It's against the rules."

"Never mind them. It's a brand new opening gambit, one I've just invented."

Since I know so little of the world outside my master's house, it was only recently that I first clapped eyes on a *go* board. It's a weird contraption, something no sensible cat would ever think up. It's a smallish square divided into myriad smaller squares on which the players position black and white stones in so higgledy-piggledy a human fashion that one's eyes go askew to watch them. Thereafter, the devotees of this strange cult work themselves up into a muck-sweat, excitedly shouting that this or that ridiculous little object is in danger, has escaped, has been captured, killed, rescued, or whatever. And all this over a bare square foot of board where the mildest tap with my right, front paw would wreak irreparable havoc. As Singleman might quote from his compendium of Zen sermons, one gathers grasses and with their thatch creates a hermitage only to find the same old field when the thatch is blown away. You set the pieces out and then you take them off. A silly occupation. Why don't the players keep their hands in the folds of their kimonos and simply stare at an empty board? In the earlier stages of the game, with only thirty or forty pieces in place, one could not honestly describe the effect as an eyesore, but as things move to a climax, the scrimmage of black and white becomes an offense to the civilized mind. The black and white pieces are so crammed together that they squeak and grate in a jostle of stones. The ones at the edges seem bound to be pushed clean off the board. No piece can get its neighbors to make room. None has the right to order those in front to offer gangway to the crush behind. All they can do is to crouch down where they are and, without stirring, resign themselves to their fate. *Go* is a product of the mind of man and, just as human taste is accurately mirrored in this ever-more-restrictive game, so one may see in the cramping of the pieces an image of the human urge to be jammed up tight together. In that ugly crowding one may fairly read man's mean antipathy to openness, his deliberate squeezing and diminishment of the very universe, his passion for territorial limitation within such dwarfish boundaries that he rarely steps beyond his own immediate shadow. He wallows in the rigors of constriction, in the painful inhibitions of his choice. He is, in short, a masochist.

Heaven knows why the flippant minded Waverhouse and his Zen

besotted friend have chosen today for their game, but chosen it they have. They dug the board out from some dusty cupboard, found the necessary playing stones and eventually settled down to the crass fatuity of *go*. As might be expected of them, they began by playing almost skittishly, plonking down their blacks and whites in a random scatter across the board. But the board has only just so many squares and it wasn't long before flippancy and otherworldliness found themselves in conflict. As the pressure increased, so did the verbal exchanges, spiced, as is their wont, with scarcely relevant quotations from the minor Chinese classics.

"Waverhouse, your play is simply awful. Can't you see it's crazy to place your piece there? Take it away and try it somewhere else."

"A mere Zen zealot may choose to think it crazy, but I learned that ploy from studying the practice of the great *go* master Hon'imbō. You must learn to live with greatness."

"But the piece will be slaughtered."

"Did not the noble Hankai accept not only death for the sake of his lord but even pork on a poignard? Consider me no less sporting. Fair enough? Right then, that's my move."

"So that's your decision. All right. It soothes my troubled brow. As the poet said, 'A balmy breeze has blown in from the south and the palace grows a shade more cool.' Now," says Singleman, "if I link my chain of pieces with another piece, just here, lo and behold, I'm safe."

"Aha, so you've linked them. My, what a clever old thing you are. I never thought you'd see that one. But there you go, quick as a flash, bang, bang, and you think I'm dead. I'd hoped you'd be guided by the good old folk song 'Don't Bang Bells at the Hachiman Shrine.' So what do I do now?" Waverhouse sought to look crafty. "I'll tell you what I'll do. I'll put one here. And what will poor pussy do next?"

"Poor pussy will next do something both simple and daring, like this. Which blocks your line like 'a sword that points up sharply at the sky.'"

"Steady on, old man. If you do that, I've had it. Hang on a moment, now. Really, that's not funny."

"I warned yon not to make that move."

"I offer my abject apologies. You were quite right, and I'll take that move back. So, while I ponder, take your white off, will you?"

"What! Is this another of your sorry-I-wasn't-really-ready gambits?"

"And while you're at it, you might remove the piece right next to it, too."

"You've got a damn nerve."

"You couldn't be suggesting that I'm cheating, eh? Oh, come on, Singleman, what's a stone or two between friends? Don't act so stuffy. Just be a good chap and take the damn things off. It could hardly matter to a lofty soul like you, but to me it's a matter of life and death. Like that moment of supreme crisis in Kabuki plays when some character comes bounding on stage with shouts of 'Hang on, hold it.'"

"I fail to see the similarity."

"Never mind what you see or don't see. Just be a decent fellow and take those pieces off the board."

"This is the sixth time you've asked to have your move back."

"What a remarkable memory you have. When we play next, I'll double it up to a good, round dozen. Anyway, all I'm asking now is that yon should remove a couple of miserable stones, and I must say you're being pretty stubborn about it. I would have thought that, with all your years of contemplating your navel, you'd have learnt by now to show a bit more give."

"But if I let you off, that daring risk I took just now will stack the odds against me."

"I thought I heard you prating that you pay no heed to such mundane considerations as winning or losing."

"I certainly don't mind losing, but I don't want you to win."

"Singleman, you dazzle me with the sophistication of your spiritual enlightenment. I positively gawp at this further manifestation of your gift for cutting through lightning by 'dashing your sword at the winds of spring.'"

"You've got that wrong. It should be the other way around —cutting through the spring winds with a sword flash sharp as lightning."

"Indeed, indeed, a laughable mistake. Only I somehow feel my version sounds the better of the two. I see myself as the last of the great diaskenasts. But let that pass. 'That passed,' the poet said, 'so may this too.' Since I see you've still got all your wits about you, it looks as though I'm done for on this part of the board, so I'd best give up the ghost."

"We have it from the patriarchs that, sharply different as they are, in ultimate reality there's little to differentiate the quick from the dead. I think you're dead, and you'd be wise to be quick to accept it."

"Amen," says Waverhouse, slapping down with a savage clack the piece in his hand on a different part of the board.

While Waverhouse and Singleman are thus slugging it out in front of the alcove, Coldmoon and Beauchamp are sitting side-by-side near the entrance to the room. My wretched master with his yellow face sits with them. Neatly lined up on the matting of the floor, just in front of Coldmoon and eyeing him fishily, three dried bonitos present an extraordinary spectacle. He'd brought them around in the breast of his kimono and, though now exposed in all their nakedness, they still look warm from their walk. Beauchamp and my master were sitting staring at them with a finely balanced mixture of repulsion and curiosity when Coldmoon finally opened his mouth. "As a matter of fact, I got back to Tokyo from my visit home about four days ago, but I've been so rushed off my feet with this and that that I couldn't call around sooner."

"There was no need to hurry here," observes my master with his usual lack of any social grace.

"I wouldn't have hurried, but for my anxiety to give you these fish as quickly as possible."

"But, they're properly dried, aren't they?"

"Oh, yes indeed! Dried bonitos are the speciality of my hometown."

"A speciality?" says my master. "But I fancy one may find excellent dried bonito right here in Tokyo." He lifts the largest fish and, bending slightly, sniffs it.

"One cannot judge the quality of a dried bonito by smelling it."

"Are they special because they're that much bigger?"

"Eat one and see."

"Certainly I shall eat one. But this one here seems to have an edge chipped off."

"That's precisely why I was in a hurry to get them to you."

"I don't understand."

"Well, actually it was slightly gnawed by rats."

"But that's dangerous! Anyone eating that could blacken with the plague."

"Not at all, it's perfectly safe. Such modest gnawings, mere nips and nibbles, never hurt anyone."

"How on earth did the rats get at it?"

"On board ship."

"Ship? What ship? How?"

"I took passage here from home and, having nothing in which to carry your dried bonitos, I popped them into my violin's cloth carrier-bag. And it was there, that night, that the damage was done. Frankly, I'd not have cared if the rats had kept to the fish but unfortunately, perhaps mistaking it for another dried bonito, they also gnawed away at the frame of my precious instrument."

"What idiotic creatures! Perhaps the life at sea blunts their sense of taste. All that salt, you know: the coarseness of the sea-gone soul." Having delivered himself of these odd remarks, my master sat and stared, fish-eyed and ictrine, at Coldmoon's wrinkled gift.

"It's in the nature of rats, wherever they may happen to be living, not to discriminate in their rapacity. Hence, even when I'd gotten the dried fish to my Tokyo lodgings, I worried for their safety. It kept me awake at night. So in the end I took them into my bed and slept with them."

"How revolting. Surely a danger to health?"

"Yes, I agree. You'd better wash them thoroughly before you eat them."

"I doubt if just washing will do."

"Perhaps you should soak them in lye and then, for good measure and to restore the color, polish them up a bit."

"Aside from sleeping with ratty fish, did you also take your violin to bed?"

"The violin's too bulky to sleep with in one's arms and. . ."

At this point the conversation was interrupted from the other side of the room by delighted shouts from Waverhouse. "Do you mean you've been to bed with a violin? How truly romantic! I recall a little poem from the past:

> The spring is passing. Arms can feel
> The weight of the lute
> Becoming real.

"That, of course, is just an old-fashioned *haiku*. If he wants to outdo the ancients, the bright young man of today has no choice but to sleep with a violin in his arms. Beauchamp, lend me your ears. How about this for a modern variation on the theme?

> Beneath this quilted coverlet,
> Warm to one's skin,
> Night-long held safe, frets free from fret:
> My treasured violin.

Of course violins don't have frets, but what of that? One can't expect a nitpicking accuracy of detail in such a splendid example of new-style poetry."

Beauchamp, poor fellow, is a literal-minded youth and his serious mold of character cannot accommodate itself to the verve and shimmers of frivolity. "I'm afraid," he says, "that, unlike *haiku*, new-style poems cannot be constructed off the cuff. They need deep thought, deep feeling, arduous fabrication. But once they're properly composed, their exquisite tonation, working on the inmost soul, can call up spirits from the vasty deep."

"Can they really? Well, I never," says Waverhouse at his falsely ingenuous best. "I'd always thought that only the smoke of hemp stalks, correctly burnt at the Feast of the Hungry Dead, could lure souls back to earth. Do you mean to say that new-style poetry is equally efficacious?" Letting his game go hang, he concentrates on teasing Beauchamp.

"You'll get trounced again if you keep on babbling rubbish," my master warns him.

But Waverhouse takes no notice. "I myself am quite indifferent to winning or losing, but it just so happens that my opponent is now immobilized, squashed up tight like an octopus in a saucepan. And it's only to while away the tedium of waiting for him to decide upon his next wee wriggle of a move that I am forced to join you in your concourse of violins."

Singleman snorts in his exasperation. "For goodness sake, Waverhouse, it's your move now. I'm the one who's being kept waiting."

"Ah? So you've made a move?"

"Of course I have—ages ago."

"Where?"

"I've extended this diagonal of whites."

"So you have. . .

> Diagonal and white
> His hand extends
> The line that in disaster ends.

"Well, in that case my response shall be. . . shall be. . . I know not what, but it shall be the terror of this earth.

> As I was saying, 'I plan, I plan,'

Daylight darkened
And the night began.

"I tell you what. Out of the extreme kindness of my heart I shall grant you an extra move. Place a stone anywhere you like."

"You can't play *go* like that."

"You refuse my generosity? Then you leave me no choice but to. . . what? Suppose I set a piece down here, over in this relatively unsettled territory, right in the corner. Incidentally, Coldmoon, your fiddle can't be up to much if even the rats don't like it. Why don't you splash out on a better one? Shall I get one of those antique models, at least three hundred years old, from Italy?"

"I could never thank you enough—especially if you were also so kind as to foot the bill."

"How could anything as old as that be any use whatever?" His ignorance does not stop my master from speaking his mind.

"I think, Sneaze, you're comparing antique fiddles with antiquated men. They're not the same, you know. Yet even among men, some of the older models—Goldfield for example—become more valuable with age. And when it comes to violins it's invariably a case of the older the better. . . Now, Singleman, will you please get a move on. Being myself no windbag, indeed a man succinct if not actually terse in speech, I will not waste time on a full quotation from the relevant Kabuki play, but have we not been warned by Keimasa that autumn days draw swiftly to their close?"

"It's pure agony playing *go* with a feckless galloper like you. There's never time to think. Well, if you insist on headlong play, that's the way of it. I shall place one here."

"What a pity! You've escaped my clutches after all. I had so hoped you wouldn't make that move, and I've been racking my brains to think up enough rubbish to distract you. All, I fear, in vain."

"Naturally. Some of us concentrate on the game, not on trying to cheat."

"Sir, I never cheat. I may pay less regard to the game than to gamesmanship, but that is precisely the teaching of the school of Hon'imbō, of the Goldfield School, and of the School of Modern Gentlemen. I say, Sneaze, you remember those sharpish pickles that Singleman gobbled down at Kamakura? They seem, after all, to have done him good. He's not much use at *go*, but nothing now seems able to perturb him. I take my hat off to his pickled nerves. They're steady as steel."

"Then why," says my master with his back still turned toward Waverhouse, "doesn't an inconsequential fidget like yourself make the effort to imitate his steadiness and sense?"

Waverhouse, unusually, said nothing but just stuck out a large, red tongue.

Singleman, seemingly unconcerned by these exchanges, tries once again to interest Waverhouse in their game. "It's you to go," he says.

As Waverhouse takes back his tongue and looks down at the board, Beauchamp turns to Coldmoon. "Tell me, when did you start playing the violin? I'd very much like to learn, but they say it's terribly difficult."

"Anyone can learn to play a little."

"It's always been my sneaking hope that, given the similar nature of all arts, persons with an aptitude for poetry ought to be quick at mastering music. Do you think there's anything in it?"

"Perhaps. I'm sure you'd do all right: indeed, very well."

"When did you start your own study of the art?"

"In high school. Have I ever told you," said Coldmoon turning to my master, "how I first came to learn the violin?"

"No, not yet."

"Was it perhaps," asks Beauchamp, "that you had some high school music teacher who encouraged you to learn?"

"No, no teacher; in fact no human encouragement at all. I simply taught myself."

"Quite a genius."

"Being self-taught doesn't necessarily mean that one's a genius," says Coldmoon looking sour. He is, I think, the only being who'd resent being called a genius.

"The point's irrelevant. Just tell us how you taught yourself. It would he useful to know."

"And I'd be happy to tell you. Sir," he addresses my master, "have I your permission to do so?"

"Of course. Please carry on."

"The streets these days are chock-a-block with bright, young men walking along with violin cases in their hands. But when I was a high school lad, very few of us could play any Western instrument whatsoever. My own particular school was way out in the sticks where, since life was lived in accordance with a strong tradition of extreme simplicity, nary a student played the violin."

"An interesting story seems to have started over there, Singleman, so let's pack up this game right now."

"There are still a few points left undecided."

"Forget them all. I'm only too happy to make you a present of the lot."

"But I can't accept that."

"What a meticulous man you are, totally insensitive to that broad approach one expects from a scholar of Zen. All right then, we'll finish it off in double quick time. Coldmoon, my dear fellow, I'm fascinated by your account of that high school. Am I right in thinking yours must be that one where all the students went barefoot?"

"It's true, I attended the school about which so many such lying yarns have been told."

"But I've heard you drilled without shoes and that, from a thousand about-turns, the soles of your feet grew inches thick."

"Absolute nonsense! Whoever stuffed you up with such a ludicrous canard?"

"Never mind who. But they also said that every student brings in for his lunch an enormous rice-ball, as big as a summer orange, hanging from his hip on a string. Is that a canard too? It's further said that the students gobble the rice like mad, unsalted though it is, in order to get at the pickled plum allegedly buried inside. They certainly sound an extremely vigorous and hardy group of youngsters. Are you listening, Singleman? This is exactly the sort of story that appeals to you."

"I'm not at all sure that I get the story's point, but I do indeed approve of simplicity and sturdiness."

"As to simplicity, there's yet another characteristic of that area which should earn your praise. It is, in fact, so simple that they've not yet heard of making ashtrays by sectioning bamboo. A friend of mine who was once on the staff of Coldmoon's school tried to buy such an ashtray, even one of the roughest hew, and the shopkeeper simply told him that, since anyone could go and cut himself an ashtray in the forest, there was no point in trying to make them as objects for sale. Now that's what I call true simplicity. True sturdiness as well. Singleman, you agree?"

"Yes, yes, of course I do. But if you're going to secure your position, Waverhouse, you must immediately put down a reinforcing piece."

"Right. I'll make assurance doubly, doubly sure. A stone placed there should finish the game. You know, Coldmoon, when I heard your account of your early struggles I was frankly amazed. It's quite astonishing that in such a backward place you should, unaided, have taught yourself to play the violin. More than two thousand years ago, in the high days of the Han, that marvelous man Ch'üYüan was writing poems, still unmatched, about the wonders of a life withdrawn from the madding crowd. It could be, Coldmoon, you were born to be our new Ch'ü Yüan."

"That I should very much dislike."

"Well than, how about being the Werther of our times? What's that, Singleman? You want me to pick up my stones and count them? What a pernickety bore you are! There's no need for counting. It's perfectly obvious that I've lost."

"But one cannot leave things hanging in the air. One wants to know the score."

"All right, then. Be so good as to do my counting for me. I really can't be bothered with such a dull accountant's chore when it is my solemn aesthetic duty to learn how the most gifted Werther of our day started learning to play the violin. Would you have me shunned by my ancestors? Therefore," says Waverhouse, "you must excuse me." Sliding his cushion away from the gameboard, Waverhouse moved to sit near Coldmoon. Singleman stayed where he was, methodically gathering stones and marshaling them in little armies to be counted. Coldmoon resumes the telling of his story.

"It was not only that the land was rugged, its inhabitants were philistine and coarse. They considered that any student with even the mildest interest in the arts would get them all laughed at for effeminacy by the students of other prefectures, so their persecution of anyone guilty of refinement was unremittingly merciless."

"It's a sad fact," says Waverhouse, "but the students in Coldmoon's part of the country really are uncouth. Why, for instance, are they always dressed in those dark blue, skirted trousers? The color itself is odd enough, but it looks unpleasantly worse against their near-black skin which is, presumably, occasioned by the high degree of sea salt in the local air. Of course, it doesn't greatly matter how dark the men become, but, if their women-folk are similarly blighted, it must affect their marriage prospects." As usual, when Waverhouse joins in a conversation, its original drift is soon diverted into new and unlikely channels.

"The women there are no less black than the men."

"Do the men show any wish to marry them?"

"Since they're all as black as each other, no one seems to notice."

"What a ghastly state of affairs. One's heart bleeds, doesn't it, Sneaze, for all those muddy women."

"Well, if you're asking me, my opinion of women is that the blacker they are the better. A light skinned female tends to grow more and more conceited every time she sees herself in a mirror. And all women, all the time, are incorrigible, so anything," says my master with a heavy sigh, "that makes them less delighted with themselves is very much to be wished for."

"But if the entire population is dark skinned, won't black become beautiful and the blackest most fair?" Beauchamp puts his Finger on a tricky point.

"The world would be a better place if we were only rid of them all." My master puts his view in a nutshell.

"If you go around saying things like that," laughs Waverhouse, "your wife will give you what-for later on."

"No danger of that."

"She's out?"

"Yes, she went out quite some while ago with the children."

"No wonder it's been quiet. Where's she gone?"

"I haven't the faintest idea. She goes out where and when she likes."

"And she comes home as she likes?"

"More or less. You two don't know how lucky you are to be single. I envy you both from the bottom of my heart."

Beauchamp looks slightly uncomfortable, but Coldmoon keeps on grinning.

"All married men grow to feel like that," says Waverhouse. "What about you, Singleman? Does your wife drive you crazy?"

"Eh? Hang on a tick. Six fours are twenty-four, plus one and one and one makes twenty-seven. Waverhouse, you managed to do better than it looked from the layout on the board. The margin in my favor is no more than a measly eighteen stones. Now then, what was that you asked?"

"I asked if you, too, were driven crazy by a troublesome wife."

"You must be joking again. But, to answer your question, I'm not particularly troubled by my wife, perhaps because she loves me."

"Oh, I do beg your pardon. How typical of Singleman to have a loving wife."

"Singleman's no singleton. The world is full of loving wives."

Coldmoon, a somewhat unlikely champion of the ladies, pipes up sturdily in their defense.

"Coldmoon's right," says Beauchamp. "As I see it, there are only two roads by which a man may come to perfect bliss: by the road of love, and by the road of art. Of all the forms of love, married love is perhaps the noblest. It therefore seems to me that to remain unmarried is to flout the will of Heaven. And what," asks Beauchamp, bending upon Waverhouse his sad and serious gaze, "do you, sir, think of that?"

"I think you have stated an unanswerable case. I fear that this old bachelor will never enter the sphere of perfect bliss."

"If you get yourself a wife, you'll have made it doubly sure that bliss will not be yours." My master croaks from the bottom of the grim well of experience.

"Be that as it may," says Beauchamp, "we young bachelors will never grasp the meaning of life unless we open our hearts and minds to the elevating spirituality of the arts. That is why, in the hope that I might learn to improve myself by playing the violin, I am so particularly interested to hear more of Coldmoon's interrupted account of his actual experience."

"Ah, yes," says Waverhouse, "we were going to hear the tale of our own young Werther's fiddling. Please tell us now. I promise, no more interruptions." With this belated acknowledgement of his habitual failing, Waverhouse at last shut up.

But the spirit of Waverhouse, like the monstrous Hydra itself, is not easily suppressed. Cut off one head, and in its place grow two. Silence Waverhouse, and Singleman gives tongue. "No man ever," he waffled, "became a better man by virtue of a violin. It would be intolerable if universal truth were accessible through self-abandonment to mere fun. Truly to lose the self and thus to achieve the ultimate reality of the identity of self and non-self, a man must be willing to hang by his nails from a cliff, to let go, and to fall to that death in which his spirit may be reborn." With these pomposities Singleman sought to reprove Beauchamp's frivolous materialism; however, he might as well have saved his breath, for Beauchamp knows nothing of Zen and, as his next dry words revealed, has no desire to do so.

"Really?" he comments. "You may be right, but I remain convinced that art is the clearest expression of the highest human aspirations, and I am not to be shaken in that conviction."

"Good for you," says Coldmoon. "I shall be glad to speak of my artistic experience to so congenial a soul. Well, as I was saying, I had great difficulties to contend with before I could even start learning the violin. Can you imagine, Mr. Sneaze, the agonies I suffered merely to buy a violin?"

"Well, I assume that in a place so generally God forsaken as not to have even hemp soled sandals for sale, it can't have been easy to find a shop that offered violins."

"Oh, there was shop, alright. And I'd saved up cash enough for a purchase. But it wasn't as simple as that."

"Why not?"

"Because if I bought a fiddle in a dorp that small, everyone would know, and its brute inhabitants would immediately have made my life unbearable. Believe you me, anyone out there who was thought to be the least bit arty had a very thin time."

"Genius is always persecuted," sighed Beauchamp with deep sympathy.

"There you go again. I do wish you'd stop calling me a genius. It's an embarrassment. Anyway, every day as I passed that shop where the fiddles were displayed, I'd say to myself, 'Ah, how wonderful it would be just to hold one in my arms, to be the owner of a fiddle. Oh, how I wish and wish that one of them were mine.'"

"Quite understandable," commented Waverhouse.

"But it's distinctly odd," my master mused in a voice where his usual bilious perversity was overlaid with genuine wonder, "that some otherwise sensible lad should wander about a backwoods hamlet drooling over a violin."

"It simply proves what I've just been saying. Drooling's a sign of genius."

Only Singleman held aloof, vouchsafing nothing and twisting his foolish beard.

"Perhaps you're wondering how there came to be violins available in such a graceless place, but the explanation's quite simple. There was, you see, a ladies academy in the neighborhood, and, since the curriculum included daily violin-practice, the local shopkeepers were quick to exploit such a captive market. Of course, the violins were of poor quality; more rustic gues than genuine violins. And the shop-folk treated them very roughly, hanging them up at the shop entrance in bunches of two or three, like so many vegetables. Yet, as one passed the shop, one could hear them humming in the wind or, in response to some shopboy's casual finger, quivering into sound. Their singular timbre, every time I heard it, thrilled my heart to such a pitch of excitement that I felt it could but burst."

"That sounds dangerous. There are, of course, many varieties of epilepsy, such as that brought on by the sight of water and that provoked by the presence of crowds. But our young Werther," says Waverhouse—never one to miss an opportunity to wallow in the absurd—seems unique in suffering seizures at the thrumming of fiddle strings."

But the plodding Beauchamp, prosaic even in his passion for the poetic, wouldn't recognize a flight of fancy if it landed on his nose. "It's not a matter for mockery," he snaps. "No man can truly be an artist unless he has sensitivities as keen as Coldmoon's. I say again, Coldmoon is a genius."

Coldmoon still looks restless to have such greatness thrust upon him. "No, no," he says, "maybe it really is some epileptic variant; but the fact remains that the timbre of those sounds moved me to the core. I've played and heard the violin time and again since then, but nothing ever has matched the beauty of that random music. There are no words to convey the faintest echo of its magic. . ."

Nobody paid the slightest attention to Singleman when, rather aptly as it seemed to me, he quoted from an obscure Taoist text: "Only from gems, the jewels in its hilt, could such sweet sounds have issued from the sword." I felt sorry, not only for Singleman but for Chuang-tzu, too, that the words were left to die.

"Day after day for many months, I walked past that shop, but I heard that marvelous music only thrice. On the third occasion I decided that, come what might, I would have to buy a violin. Reproof from the people of my own district, sneers from the slobs in neighboring prefectures, thumpings organized by my fellow students, fist-lynchers to a man, not even formal expulsion from the school could budge me from my resolution. I had no choice but to satisfy my all-consuming need. I would buy a violin."

"How characteristic of genius. That drive, that total concentration upon fulfillment of an inner need. Ah, Coldmoon, how I envy you! How I have longed, lifelong and always in vain, to experience feelings of such vehemence. I go to concerts and I strain my ears until they ache in an effort to be carried away, but for all my full-hearted striving, nothing seems to happen. How you must pity," said Beauchamp in tones that mixed black sadness and green envy, "us earth-bound clods."

"Count yourself lucky," Coldmoon answers. "I can speak of my enthrallment now with relative calm. But then it was pure agony. Excruciating agony. Anyway, my masters, in the end I took the plunge and bought a violin."

"Say on."

"It was the eve of the Emperor's birthday, in November. Everyone in my lodgings had gone off to some hot spring for the night, and the place was empty. I'd reported sick that day and, absenting myself from school, had stayed in bed, where, all day long, I nursed the single thought: this evening I'll go out and get that violin."

"You mean you played truant by shamming illness?"

"That's right."

"Talent indeed," says Waverhouse lost in wonder. "Perhaps he really is a genius."

"As I lay with my head sticking out of the bedclothes, I grew impatient for the nightfall. To break the tension, I ducked beneath the covers and, with my eyes closed tight, entreated sleep; which did not come. So I pulled my head back out, only to find the fierce autumn sun still fully ablaze on the paper-window six feet long. Which niggled me. I then noticed, high up on the paper-window, a long stringy shadow which, every so often, wavered in the autumn wind."

"What was that long, stringy shadow?"

"Peeled, astringent persimmons strung like beads on raffia cords suspended from the eaves."

"Hmm. What happened next?"

"Next, having nothing else to do, I got up from bed, opened the paper-window and went out onto the veranda. There I detached one of the persimmons that had dried to sweetness, and ate it."

"Did it taste good?" My master can be trusted, whatever the subject, to find some childish question to be asked.

"Excellent. Persimmons down there really are superb. You will not taste their like anywhere in Tokyo."

"Never mind the persimmons. What did you do next?" This time it was Beauchamp who was pressing for clarification.

"Next, I ducked back into bed again, closed my eyes and breathed a silent prayer to all the gods and Buddhas for nightfall to come soon. It then seemed that three, perhaps four, long hours had passed; so thinking the evening must have come, I brought my head out from under the bed clothes. To my surprise, the fierce autumn sun was still fully ablaze on the six-foot paper-window, and, on its upper part, those long and stringy shadows were still swaying."

"We've heard all that."

"The same sequence happened again and again. In any event, I got up from bed, opened the paper-window, ate one persimmon that had dried to sweetness, went back to bed, and breathed a silent prayer to all the gods and Buddhas for nightfall to come soon."

"We don't seem to be making much progress with that promised story about learning to play the violin."

"Don't rush me. Just listen, please. Well, having endured the next three, or perhaps four, hours in my bed until, I thought, surely it must now be evening, I popped my head up out of the covers only to find the fierce, autumn sun still fully ablaze on the paper window while, on its upper part, the long stringy shadows were asway."

"You're getting us nowhere."

"Then, I got up from bed, opened the paper-window, went out onto the veranda, ate one persimmon dried to sweetness and. . ."

"So you ate another one? Is there no end to your dreary guzzle of persimmons dried to sweetness?"

"Well, my impatience grew worse."

"*Your* impatience! What about ours?"

"You want everything so rushed along that I find it hard to continue my story."

If Coldmoon finds it hard, so does his audience; even the devoted Beauchamp makes little whimpers of complaint.

"If you all find listening too hard, I have no choice but to bring my story abruptly to its end. In short, I repeated this oscillation between eating persimmons and ducking into bed until all the fruit were gone."

"By the time you'd guzzled that lot the sun must surely have gone down."

"As a matter of fact, it hadn't. After I'd eaten the last persimmon I ducked back into bed, and in due course popped my head out yet again, only to find the fierce autumn sun still fully ablaze upon that six-foot paper-window. . ."

"I've had enough of this. It just goes on and on."

"Me too. I'm bored stiff with the way you tell your tiresome story."

"But it isn't easy on me, you know."

"With the degree of perseverance you have already proven you possess, no enterprise whatsoever could be too difficult. If we had sat here uncomplaining, your autumn sun would have gone on blazing until tomorrow morning. Tell me this: do you, and if so when, intend to buy that violin?" Even the indefatiguable Waverhouse is showing signs of wear. Singleman alone seems unaffected by the slow unrolling (or rather the slow unrolling and rerolling) of Coldmoon's quaint account. For all he cared, Coldmoon's autumn sun could go on blazing all through the night; even, perhaps, until the day, or days, beyond tomorrow.

Coldmoon, too, shows no sign of strain. Calm and composed, he drones on with his story. "Someone has asked me when I intend to buy my violin. The answer is that I intend to go out and buy it just as soon as the sun has set. It is hardly my fault that, whenever I peer out from the bedclothes, the autumn sun is still so brilliantly ablaze. Oh, how I suffered! It was far, far worse, that deep impatience in my soul, than this superficial irritation which seems, so pettily, to irk you all. After I'd eaten the last of the hanging persimmons and saw the day still bright, I could not help but perish into tears. Beauchamp, my dear fellow, I felt so reft of hope that I wept, I wept."

"I'm not at all surprised. Your weeping does you credit. All artists are essentially emotional and their tears are distillations of the truth of things. Nevertheless, one does rather wish that you could speed things up a bit." Beauchamp's a decent-hearted creature and, even when he's knee deep in absurdities, maintains his earnest manner.

"Much as I'd like to speed it up, that laggard sun won't set. Its hang-up is most hard to bear."

"Your endlessly unsetting sun is no less hard on us, your tanned and sweating audience. So, let's forget the whole interminable tale before its lentor kills us. Scrub it, Coldmoon," says my master who is now quite clearly nearing the end of his tether.

"You'd find it harder still if we stopped at this point. For we are now coming to the really interesting part of the story."

"All right then. We're prepared to listen, but only on condition that the sun goes down."

"That's a pretty tall order, but all things yield to my revered teacher, and lo the sun has set."

"How extraordinarily convenient." Singleman uttered his toneless comment with so much nonchalance that everyone broke into laughter.

"So night, at last, had fallen. You can perhaps imagine my relief. With great stealth I slipped out of my lodgings into the quietness of Saddletree, for so that huddle of poor dwellings had been named. My nature shrinks from noisy places so that, despite the obvious conveniences of a city life, I had at that time chosen to withdraw from the whirl of the world and to live secluded in a snail shell of a dwelling, a farmhouse miles from anywhere in a corner of the countryside scarce trodden by the foot of man."

"That 'scarce trodden by the foot of man' seems to be piling it on a bit," objects my master.

"And that touch about the 'snail shell dwelling,'" adds Waverhouse, "is insufferably bombastic. Why don't you say, 'in a tiny room, too small even to have an alcove?' That would sound much better, if only because a great deal less affected."

But Beauchamp, as he immediately makes clear, finds the description praiseworthy. "Whatever the facts of the room's dimensions, Coldmoon's phrasing is poetic. I find it very pleasing."

The meticulous Singleman chips in with a serious enquiry. "It must have been an exhausting business trudging there and back to school from such a remote shack. How many miles, roughly, would you say?"

"Perhaps five hundred yards. You see, the school itself was in the remote village. . ."

"In that case, many of its students would have been boarded in nearby lodgings. Is that correct?" asks Singleman in relentless tones which suggest the far-off baying of bloodhounds.

"Yes. Most of the farm dwellings had one or two student lodgers."

"Yet, did you not describe the place as scarcely trodden by the foot of man?" Singleman moves in for the kill.

"I did indeed. But for the school the place would have been virtually uninhabited. Now, let me tell you how I was dressed as I slipped out into lonely Saddletree in that deepening dusk. Over a padded handwoven cotton kimono, I wore the brass-buttoned overcoat of my school uniform. With the overcoat's hood pulled well down over my head to make sure I'd not be recognized, I drifted along the road in such a way as not to attract attention. Being November, the road from my lodgings to the Southern Highway was thick with fallen persimmon leaves. Every step I took set the dead leaves scurrying, and their rustle behind me seemed proof that I was being followed. When I turned and looked back, the dense mass of the Tōrei Temple, blacker even than its surrounding forest, loomed up black above me. As you may know, that temple is the family shrine of the Matsudaira Clan. An extremely quiet and little-visited building, it lies at the foot of Mount Kōshin not more than a hundred yards from where I was then living. Above the forest trees the sky's vast hollow glittered with moonlit stars, while the Milky Way, slicing across the River of Long Rapids, stretched east and ever east toward. . . now let me see, toward. . . well yes, Hawaii."

"Hawaii? That's quite startling," said a startled Waverhouse.

"I walked some two hundred yards along the Southern Highway, entered the township from Eagle Lane, turned into Old Castle Street, up Great Bushel Road and so past First Street, Second Street, and Third Street, all running off Main Street which itself runs parallel to the Road of the Cost of Food. From there I took Owari Street, Nagoya Street, and the Street of the Magic Dolphin into Fishball Lane and thence. . ."

"You can spare us the topography. What we want to know," my master rudely interrupts, "is whether or not you bought a violin."

"The man who sells musical instruments is Kaneko Zenbei so, using parts of his own name, he calls his shop Kane-zen. But to reach the shop, sir, we've still some way to go."

"Forget the distance. Just go and buy a violin. And do it quickly."

"Your wish, sir, is, as always, my command. Well, when I got to Kane-zen, the shop was ablaze with lantern light and. . ."

"Ablaze? Oh no. Not that again. How often this time are you going to scorch us with the blazing repetition?" On this occasion it was Waverhouse who raised the fire alarm.

"Friends, have no fear. It's only a passing kind of blaze that lights your immediate horizon. It will, I do assure you, flicker and die down. Well, as I peer through the light blaze from the shop, I can see a faint reflection of that glare shining from the polished body of a violin while the roundness of its pinched-in waist gleams almost coldly. So falls the lantern's light across its tightly drawn strings that only a section of the fiddle's stringing flings out at me its glistening darts of silver."

"Now that," says Beauchamp almost moaning in his pleasure at the words, "is a truly masterly piece of description."

"That's the one, I thought, that's the one for me. The blood began pounding in my head and my legs so weakened they could barely hold me up."

Behind a scornful smile, Singleman grunted.

"Instinctively, and with no further thought, I rushed into the shop, yanked out my purse, pulled from it a couple of five-yen notes and. . ."

"So in the end you bought it?" asked my master.

"I was certainly going to do so, but then I thought to myself, 'Wait. This is the moment of crisis. If I act rashly I may bungle things. Should I not pause for deeper reflection?' So, at the eleventh hour, I reined myself in."

"Sweet heaven," groaned my master, "d'you mean to say that even now, after we've slogged along behind you across such veritable Australias of balderdash, you've still not bought your fiddle. You really do drag things out. And all for some piddling contraption of cheap wood and catgut."

"It is not, sir, my intention to drag things out. I can't help being unable to buy it."

"Why can't you?"

"Why can't I? Because it's still too early in the evening. There were still too many people passing by."

"What does it matter if there are two or even three hundred people in the streets? Coldmoon, you really are an extraordinary man," my master shouted in his anger and frustration.

"If they were just people," says Coldmoon, "even a thousand, even two thousand of them, of course it wouldn't matter. But many of them were in fact my fellow students; prowling about with their sleeves rolled up and with bludgeons in their hands. There's a particular group, the Dregs, who pride themselves on being permanently at the bottom of the class. I had to be careful because louts of that kind are invariably good at judo, and I dared not take the risk of any kind of tangle with them. For who knows where even the most trivial brush with violence may end? Of course, I yearned to have that violin, but I was also fairly anxious to remain alive. I preferred to go on breathing without playing a violin to lying dead for having played it."

"Then am I right in thinking that you didn't buy a fiddle?" My master struggles on in search of certainties.

"Oh, but I did make a purchase."

"Coldmoon, you're driving me mad. If you're going to buy a fiddle, buy it; if you don't want to buy one, don't. But for the sake of my sanity, please settle the matter one way or the other."

Coldmoon grinned. "Things settle themselves," he said, "and all too rarely in the way one had most hoped." With careless care he lit a cigarette and blew out smoke at the ceiling.

I think it was the smoke which finally snapped my master's patience.

In any event, it was at this point that he abruptly rose to his feet, went off into his study and, returning with a musty-looking, foreign book, lay down flat on his stomach and began to read. Singleman had earlier slipped away unremarked, and is now sitting in front of the alcove playing *go* by himself. The plain fact is that Coldmoon's story has proved so boringly long that, one by one, his listeners have abandoned him. Only two of them are still sticking it out: Beauchamp with his unquenchable faith in art and Waverhouse to whom longeur is second nature. Coldmoon somewhat crudely blew out a last long stream of smoke and resumed telling his story at the same leisurely pace.

"Having decided that an immediate purchase of that violin would be ill timed, I now had to decide upon a suitable timing. The early part of the evening had already been found too dangerous and the shop would of course be closed if I came too late. Clearly the ideal time would be somewhere before closing time but after the prowling students had all retired to their lairs. Yet to identify the precise best moment of purchase was not, as I'm sure you, Beauchamp, will appreciate, at all easy."

"I can see it would be difficult."

"Eventually, I fixed upon ten o'clock as the best time for action. But what should I do until then? I didn't much like the idea of going back to my lodgings only to sneak out again; while visiting some friend for a time-wasting chat struck me as too selfish. I accordingly decided to pass the waiting period in a simple stroll around town: two or three hours, I thought, could always be quickly and congenially consumed in such a leisured ramble. But on this particular evening so leadenly the time dragged by that I understood as deeply in my heart as if I myself had coined that ancient line which says, 'A single day seems long as a thousand autumns.'" Coldmoon twisted his features into a pattern which he presumably considered expressive of the agonies of waiting and, confident of some suitable reaction from Waverhouse, turned the full glare of his faked distress upon that subtle aesthete.

Nor was he disappointed. Waverhouse would interrupt the announcement of his own death sentence for the sake of hearing himself babble, and Coldmoon's look of open invitation was utterly irresistible. "As I recall," he immediately responded, "the old song tells us not only that it is painful to be kept waiting by the beloved but also, as one might of course expect, that the waiter feels more pain than the awaited. So perhaps that eaves-strung violin actually experienced more bitter pains of waiting than did you on your aimless and dispirited wandering around town like some clueless detective. 'Dispirited' is a splendid word. Isn't it the Chinese who say, 'dispirited as an unfed dog in a house of mourning?' Indeed, there's nothing more dismal than the whining of a homeless dog."

"A dog? That's cruel. I've never before been likened to a dog."

"As I listen to your story I feel as though I were reading the biography of some ancient, master artist, and my heart brims with sympathy for your sufferings. Our tame comedian Waverhouse was only trying to be funny when he compared you with a dog. Take no notice of his nonsense but pray continue with your story." Beauchamp pours oil on potentially troubled waters, but Coldmoon in truth needs neither encouragement nor consolation. Come what may, he's going to tell his story

"Well," he continues, "I wandered up Infantry Road and, along the Street of a Hundred Houses and thence, through Money-changers' Alley, into the Street of the Falconers. There I counted first the withered willows in front of the prefectural office, and then the lighted windows in the side-wall of the hospital. I smoked two cigarettes on Dyer's Bridge and then I looked at my watch. . ."

"Was it yet ten o'clock?"

"Not yet, I'm sorry to say. I drifted across Dyer's Bridge and as I walked eastward along the river path I passed a home bound group of three masseurs. Somewhere in the distance dogs were howling at the moon."

"To hear, on an autumn night by the riverside, the distant barking of dogs. . . That sounds like some scene-setting speech from a Kabuki play. You, Coldmoon, are cast as the fugitive hero."

"Have I done anything wrong?"

"You are about to do something frightful."

"That's a bit much. All I'm going to do is to buy a violin. If that's to be considered criminal, every student at every school of music must be guilty of crime."

"Criminality is not determined by any absolute standard of good or evil. The acts of a criminal may actually be good in absolute terms but, since they have not been recognized as good by the consensus of public opinion enshrined in the law, they will be treated, and punished, as crimes. It is extremely difficult to establish what, in truth, is a crime. For what is truth? Christ himself in the context of his society was a criminal and was punished as a criminal. Of the bloodline from King David, he was accused by his fellow Jews of wishing to be a king. He did not deny the charge, which naturally was very serious to the Roman governor of that conquered province, and the plaque on his crucifix, 'The King of the Jews,' identified his crime. Now, does our handsome Coldmoon deny being an artist in a society where artists are regarded as offensive? Of lusting after a violin in a community where such a filthy emotion is virtually criminal?"

"All right," says Coldmoon. "I acknowledge my guilt. But what worries me is how to pass the time until ten o'clock finally deigns to arrive."

"Nonsense," replies Waverhouse. "You can run through, yet again, that time consuming naming of the names of streets. If that doesn't work, you can haul up your dear, old autumn sun for a few more bouts of blazing. And what about those persimmons, sun-dried, of course, to sweetness? I'm sure you could eat at least another three dozen. That sort of stuff will keep you going until ten, and I'm prepared to listen for as long as you like."

Coldmoon had the grace to break into a broad grin. "Since you've taken the very words from my mouth, I won't insist on using them myself. So, by an artistic distortion of the truth, all of a sudden it's ten o'clock. Right on that appointed hour I returned to Kane-zen. The streets were deserted, and the sound of my wooden clogs was desperately lonely. The big outer shutters had already been hoisted into place across the front of the shop and only the paper sliding door of its small side entrance was still available for use. As I slid that light door open, I was again assailed by a vaguely uneasy feeling that some sneaky dog was still slinking along behind me."

At this point, my master glanced up from his grubby-looking book and asked, "Have you bought that violin yet?"

"He's just going to buy it now," said Beauchamp.

"What! He still hasn't bought it after all this time? Buying fiddles must be an arduous business," my master mutters to himself and turns back to his reading. Singleman, who has by now practically covered the whole board with black and white pieces, maintains his disinterested silence.

"Summoning up my courage, I dived into the shop and, with my head buried in my hood, said that I wanted a violin. Several shop boys and young assistants who were sitting chattering around a brazier looked up in surprise and stared at my half hidden face. Automatically, with my right hand, I tugged the hood still lower. When I had asked for a second time to be shown a violin, the boy sitting nearest me, who'd been trying to peer up under my hood, got to his feet and, with a half-hearted 'Certainly, sir,' slouched off to the front of the shop and came back with a tied cluster of some four or five. In response to my question, he said a violin cost five yen and twenty sen.

"'As cheap as that? These must be only toys. Are they all the same price?'

"'Yes,' he answered, 'all the same price. All exactly the same and all strongly and carefully constructed.'

"I took out my purse and extracted from it one five-yen note and a twenty-sen silver coin. Then I wrapped the violin in a big cloth I'd specially brought for that purpose. Apart from myself and the inquisitive shop boy, no one in the shop had spoken a word since I entered. They just sat there watching me. Since my face was well concealed, I knew there was no risk of being recognized, but I still felt nervous and anxious to get back out to the street as quickly as possible. At long last, with my cloth wrapped treasure tucked inside my overcoat, I left the shop. 'Thank you, sir,' they chorused as I did so, and my blood ran cold. Outside, I glanced quickly up and down the street. It was pretty well empty; except that, perhaps a hundred yards away, I could hear some two or three voices quoting Chinese poems at each other in accents so loud as to waken the whole town. Edgy as ever and fearing lest the loudness of the voices forewarned of a troublesome incident with argumentative drunks, I slipped away westward around the corner of the shop, hurried along beside the moat until I came out on to Drug King's Temple Road. Then, passing through Alder Village to the foot of Mount Kōshin, I at last got back to my lodgings. And the time was ten to two."

"Then you've been walking practically the whole night long," exclaimed Beauchamp with his usual admiring sympathy.

"So! At long, long last it's over," says Waverhouse with impolitely obvious relief. "The way it went on and on, it was like traveler's backgammon."

"But it's only now," protests Coldmoon, "that we come to the really interesting part. So far it's only prelude."

"More to come? But that's terrible. You can't expect the patience of your audience to last out through a full recital after such an exhausting prelude."

"I only hope that, for their own sakes, my audience will bear with me.

To break off now would be, as the saying has it, to have plowed a field and then to forget to sow the seed. I shall therefore press on."

"My dear chap," says Waverhouse, "what you decide to say is entirely up to you. For my part, I shall simply sit and hear whatever it is I'll hear."

"What about you, my revered master? Will you consent to be so gracious as to hearken to my stumbling tale? May I mention, sir, that I have already bought a violin."

"So what are you now proposing? To sell it? I see no reason to listen to an odyssey of sale."

"I am far from selling it."

"In that case there's even less need to listen."

"Your decision grieves me. Well then, Beauchamp, it seems that only you have the kindness and discriminating taste to hear me out. I confess it's all a bit discouraging. But never mind. I'll do my best to be brief."

"You needn't be brief. Take your time. I Find your story fascinating."

"Well now, where was I? Ah yes, back safely in my lodgings, the proud possesser after so many vicissitudes of my precious violin. But my troubles were not over. First, I didn't know where to keep it. All sorts of visitors were accustomed to dropping in on me, so I couldn't just leave it about the place where they would immediately spot it. If I dug a hole and buried it, it would have been tiresome to dig it up whenever I wanted to play."

"Quite so. Could you perhaps hide it up in the ceiling?"

"I was lodged in a farmhouse, so the ceilings had no boards."

"That was hard. Where did you put it then?"

"Where do you think I put it?"

"I've no idea. In the space where the storm boards for the windows can be slid away?"

"No."

"Wrapped up in your bed clothes and tucked away in the bedding cupboard?"

"No."

While Beauchamp and Coldmoon continue with their guessing game, my master and Waverhouse become engrossed in a totally separate conversation. "How do you read these lines?" my master asked.

"Which lines?"

"These two lines here."

"What's this then? *Quid aliud est mulier nisi amicitie inimica*. . . But it's

Latin."

"I know it's Latin. But how do you read it?"

"Come off it, Sneaze," says Waverhouse evasively as his sensitive nose scents danger, "you're always bragging about your knowledge of dead languages. Can't you read it yourself?"

"Of course I can. Quite easily. But I'm asking you for your reading of this particular text."

"You know how to read it, and yet you ask me what it means. That's a bit thick, you know."

"Never mind if it's thick or thin. Just translate the Latin into English."

"Tut-tut. Such giving of orders, such military ways. D'you take me for your batman or something?"

"Don't slide away from the question behind a military smoke screen. Just be so good as to let me hear your version of these two lines."

"Let's leave your Latin problems for the moment. I'm keen—aren't you?—to keep up with developments in Coldmoon's extraordinary story. He's just coming to a crisis point, trembling between discovery and the successful caching of his treasure. Am I not right, Coldmoon? Well, how then did you cope with your dilemma?" Waverhouse evinces a sudden new enthusiasm for Coldmoon's fantasy on a violin and moves over to rejoin the fiddle group. My wretched master, I regret to say, is left alone with his text.

Encouraged by this unexpected attention, Coldmoon proceeded to explain where he'd hidden his violin. "I ended up," he said, "by smuggling it away into the old, varnished, wicker box that my grandmother had given me for storing clothes when I'd first left home. It was her parting gift to me, and she herself I seem to remember, brought it into the family as part of her own bridal gear."

"Such an antique would hardly seem to sort with a brand-new violin. What do you think, Beauchamp?"

"I agree they sound a poor match."

"But you yourself suggested the ceiling, and that," said Coldmoon, squashing Beauchamp, "is hardly a good match either."

"Despite the oddity of Coldmoon's hideyhole, his decision strikes me as the very stuff of *haiku*. So let's not start a squabble. How about this?

In an ancient, wicker box a hidden violin:
A feeling of utter lonesomeness

As the autumn closes in."

"Today you're fairly oozing with little squibs."

"Not just today. Day in, day out, they well up in my mind. My knowledge of the art is so profound that even the late, great Masaoka Shiki was struck dumb by its depth."

"Goodness, did you know Shiki?" asked the honest-hearted Beauchamp. His voice rose in serious enquiry and he sounded thrilled actually to know someone who had known the late, great, master poet.

"We were never physically close," said Waverhouse, "but we were always directly in warm contact by a kind of spiritual telepathy." Shocked, even disgusted, by this ridiculous answer, Beauchamp fell silent.

Coldmoon merely smiled and went on with his own improbable story. "Having decided on how to hide it, my next problem was how to make use of it. I foresaw no trouble about taking it out from its wicker box and looking at it, but such mere gloating would hardly suffice. I needed to be able actually to play it. But the resulting sounds would scarcely pass unnoticed. Therein lay a particular danger because the leading bully-boy of those damnable Dregs happened to lodge in the boarding house immediately south of mine: the two buildings were, in fact, separated only by a scrawny hedge consisting of a single row of Roses of Sharon."

"That was stinking luck," Beauchamp chimes in sympathetically.

"Stinking luck indeed. For one cannot mask a telltale sound. As we all well know, the whereabouts of the luckless Lady Kogō were betrayed to the vengeful Taira by the sound of her harp. If," says Waverhouse, "you were merely guzzling stolen food or faking paper money, that could be managed, but one cannot scrape a fiddle and keep one's presence hidden."

"If only my fiddle made no sound, I could have gotten away with it. . ."

"You speak as though sound were the only betrayer, but there are soundless things which still can not be hidden. I remember that years ago, when we were self-catering students lodging in a temple over in Koishikawa, one of our gang, a certain Suzuki Tō, was passionately fond of sweetened, cooking *saké*. He used to keep it in a beer bottle, never offered it around but swigged it all by himself. One day, when Suzuki was out for a walk, the otherwise decent Sneaze, very unwisely, nicked Suzuki's bottle, took a couple of gulps and then. . ."

"That's a flat lie. I never touched Suzuki's stuff. It was always you who were knocking it back," exclaimed my master suddenly and in a loud voice.

"Oh, so you're still with us, are you? I'd thought you were so busy in your book that I could safely tell these terrible truths without fear of interruption by the guilty party. But all the time you were listening. Which just shows what a sneaky, *saké* sneaking sort of fellow you are. One talks of people who are equally skilled in thought and action. Thought and faction are more your style. I don't deny that, now and again, I took a modest nip from Suzuki's bottle. But you were the villain who got found out. And how did you come to be caught? Just listen to this, you two. We all know, don't we, that our miserable host is anyway incapable of serious drinking. Alcohol! He just can't take it. But just because that cooking *saké* belonged to someone else, he slugged it down as though his life depended on it. Imagine what inevitably followed. His face swelled up and turned a ghastly red. It was a most fearsome sight."

"Pipe down, Waverhouse! You can't even read Latin."

"That's a laugh! You want a laugh? Then listen to the sequel. When Suzuki got back, he made a beeline for his grog, lifted the bottle, shook it, and immediately discovered it was more than half empty. Sneaze had really given it a hammering. Of course Suzuki realized that someone had been at it and, when he looked around, there was Sneaze flat out in a corner, as stiff and dully scarlet as some crude, clay doll."

Remembering that ludicrous incident, Waverhouse exploded into raucous laughter and the others joined in. Even my master chuckled into his book. Only Singleman seems proof against low comedy. He's probably overstrained his Zen-besotted mind with all those bits of stone. In any event, slumped down across the board, he's fallen fast asleep.

When his guffaws had ended, Waverhouse began again, "I remember another occasion when a noiseless action nevertheless betrayed itself. I'd gone," he said, "to a hot spring inn at Ubako where I found myself sharing a room with some old man who was, I believe, a retired draper from Tokyo. Since he was no more to me than a temporary roommate, it hardly matters whether he was a retired draper or a practicing second-hand clothes dealer, but I thought you'd like a bit of background detail. In any event, he got me into trouble. That is to say, after some three days at the inn I ran out of cigarettes. Ubako is an out-of-the-way place, miles up in the mountains with only a single inn and absolutely nothing else. One can eat and one can bathe in the hot springs. But that's all. Imagine what it's like to run out of fags in Ubako. It put me under strain. When one is deprived of something, one begins to crave for it as never before. Though I'm not much of a smoker, the moment I realized I was out of cigarettes I found myself aching for a puff. What made it worse was that the old man had brought with him a big stock of cigarettes carefully bundled up in a carrying cloth, from which he would take out several at a time, squat down right in front of me, and chain-smoke like a sooted chimney. If he'd smoked in an ordinary decently human sort of way, I would not have hated him so passionately, but he flaunted his tobacco wealth. He made smoke rings, blew the fumes out forward, sideways, straight up at the ceiling, in and out of his nostrils, and almost out of his ears until I could have killed him. Some men are born show-offs. This man was a smoke-off."

"What d'you mean, a smoke-off?"

"If you flaunt your clothes or jewelry, you're a show-off; if you flaunt your fags, you're a smoke-off."

"If it put you through such agony, why didn't you simply ask him to let you have a few of his cigarettes?"

"There are things a man can't do. To beg, I am ashamed."

"So it's wrong to ask for a cigarette?"

"Perhaps not actually sinful, but I could never beg."

"Then what did you do?"

"As a matter of fact, I stole."

"Oh, dear!"

"When the old man, clutching his personal hand towel, tottered off for a hot spring bath, I knew my chance had come. I looted his hoard and I smoked and smoked and smoked as fast as I could go. Just as I was smirking to myself, partly with the pleasure of smoking, partly with the even greater self-satisfaction of the successful thief the door opened and there he was again."

"What happened to his bath?"

"Oh, he was certainly planning to take it, but when he'd gone some way down the corridor he suddenly remembered he'd left his purse behind so he came back to get it. Damn cheek! As if I'd steal someone's purse. . ."

"Well, wouldn't you? You seem to have been pretty quick with his cigarettes."

"You must be joking. That's not the same at all. Anyway, apart from his disgraceful behavior in that matter of the purse, the old man proved a person of real feeling. When he opened the door, the room was thick with at least two days worth of cigarette smoke. Ill news travels fast, they say. It didn't take him long to read the situation."

"Did he say anything?"

"He hadn't lived all those years without growing more shrewd than that. Saying nothing, he wrapped some fifty or sixty cigarettes in a piece of paper; then, turning to me, he courteously observed, 'Do please forgive their miserable quality, but if these cigarettes could be of any use to you, I'd be honored if you'd accept them.' Then he went off down to the bath."

"Perhaps that's what's meant by 'the Tokyo style.'"

"I don't know if it's Tokyo style or draper's style; anyway, after that incident, the old man and I became firm friends and we spent a most enjoyable two weeks together."

"With free fags for a fortnight?"

"Since you ask me, yes."

My master finds it difficult to give in gracefully, but he sometimes tries. He accordingly closed his book, rolled off his stomach and said, as he sat up, "Have you finished with that violin?"

"Not yet. We're just coming to the interesting part, so do please listen. As for that person flaked out on the *go* board—what was his name?—What? Singleman? Well, I'd like him to listen, too. It's bad for him to sleep so much. Surely it's time we woke him up."

"Hey, Singleman, wake up. Wake up. This is an interesting story. Do wake up. They say it's bad for you to sleep so much. Your wife is getting anxious."

"Eh?" Singleman lifted up his face. Slobber had dribbled down his goatee to leave a long shining line as if a slug had trailed its slime across him. "I was sleeping," he managed to get out, "like a white cloud on the mountain top. I've had a delightful nap."

"We've all seen how delightfully you sleep. Suppose you wake up now."

"I expect it's time I woke. Has anyone had anything to say worth hearing?"

"Coldmoon's been telling us about his violin. He's just about to. . . What was it he was going to do? Come on, Sneaze. What was it?"

"I haven't the foggiest idea."

Coldmoon intervened. "I am," he said, 'just about to play it."

"He's going to play his violin at last. Come over here and join us as we listen."

"Still that violin? Bother."

"You've no cause to be bothered because you're one of those people who only play on stringless harps; Coldmoon here has every reason to be bothered out of his tiny skull because his screeching squawks are heard all over the neighborhood."

"Ah, yes? Coldmoon, don't you yet know how to play a violin without being heard by your neighbors?"

"No, I don't. If there is such a way, I'd very much like to learn about it."

"There's really nothing to learn. Just concentrate, as all the Zen masters advise, on the pure, white cow which stands there in the alley. Desire will drop away from you and, as enlightenment occurs, you'll find you already know how soundless music can be played. And because you'll already know, you'll have no need to learn." Singleman's distorted messages from the Gateless Gate, even when he's wide awake, are usually incomprehensible.

But Coldmoon simply assumed that the man babbled like that because his brains were still floating about somewhere in the land of Nod. So he deliberately ignored him and continued with his story. "After long thought I devised a plan. The next day, being the Emperor's Birthday, was a national holiday and I proposed to spend it in bed. But I felt restless all day long and I kept getting up, first to lift and then to replace the lid of my wicker box. When, in due course, the daylight faded and the crickets in the bottom of my grandmother's parting gift began to chirrup, I took my courage in both hands and lifted the violin and its bow from their biding place."

"At wonderful last," chirruped Beauchamp, "Coldmoon's going to play."

"Take it easy, now," warns Waverhouse. "Gently, gently, Coldmoon. Don't do anything hasty. Let caution rule your twilight."

"First I took out the bow and examined it from its tip to its guard. . ."

"You sound like some half-witted seller of swords," chaffed Waverhouse.

"If you can take a bow in your hands and feel that it is your own soul that you're holding, then you will have achieved that same spiritual condition which transfuses a *samurai* when he unsheathes his white-honed blade and dotes upon it in the failing light of autumn. Holding that bow in my hands I trembled like a leaf."

"Ah, what a genius!" sighs Beauchamp.

"Ah, what an epileptic," adds Waverhouse tartly.

"Please," said my master, "please get on with playing it. And right away. Now."

Singleman makes a wry face as though acknowledging the pointlessness of trying to bring light to the invincibly ignorant.

"Happily the bow proved in perfect condition. Next I took the violin and, holding it close under the lamp, examined its front and back. All these preparations had taken about five minutes. Please now try to picture the scene. Tirelessly, from the bottom of their box, the crickets are still chirruping. . ."

"We'll imagine anything you like. Set your mind at rest, take up your precious instrument and play."

"No, not yet. Now I have checked it over and, like its bow, the violin is flawless. All is wonderfully well. I spring to my feet. . ."

"Are you going out?"

"Oh, do keep quiet and listen. I cannot tell this story if you keep interrupting every single phrase. . ."

"Gentlemen! We are to be silent. Hush!" calls Waverhouse commandingly.

"It's you yourself who do the interrupting."

"Oh, I see. I beg your pardon. Pray carry on."

"With the violin beneath my arm, soft-soled sandals on my feet, I had taken some few steps beyond the outer glass door of my lodgings when. . ."

"I knew it. I knew it. I knew in my bones there was going to be a breakdown. Coldmoon cannot walk two steps or breathe two minutes without a hitch or hang-up."

"I suppose you do realize," said my master at his most sarcastic, "that there are no more dried persimmons hanging from the eaves. Even if you're now very hungry there's no point in turning home for them."

"It is highly regrettable that two such scholars as you and you"— Coldmoon nodded at Waverhouse and Sneaze— "should persist in behaving like common hecklers. I shall have to address my further remarks to Mr. Beauchamp only. Now, Beauchamp, as I was saying, though I had left my lodgings, I was obliged to turn back for something I should need. Thereafter, having draped around my head a scarlet blanket (for which I'd paid three yen and twenty sen in my own hometown before I left it years before), I blew out the lamp. Unfortunately, in the consequent pitch darkness I could not find my sandals."

"But why did you want to go out? Where were you off to?"

"Patience, patience. I shall come to that. At long last, outside in my scarlet blanket, my violin beneath my coat, I again found myself as on the previous night, ankle deep in fallen leaves under a star lit sky. I turned away to the right and, as I came to the foot of Mount Kōshin, the boom of the temple bell on Eastern Peak struck through my blanket shrouded ears and penetrated to my inmost head. Beauchamp, can you guess what time it was?"

"This is your story, Coldmoon. I've no idea what the time was."

"Beauchamp, it is nine; nine and the evening chill. I am now climbing through the early autumn darkness along a mountain path which rises nearly three thousand feet to a sort of terrace plateau which the locals call Big Flat. Timid as I am, at any other time I'd have been scared clean out of my wits, but it's one of those strange things that, when the mind is truly concentrated upon one specific aim, all sense of being frightened or not frightened is wiped from one's heart. Odd as it must sound, I had become a lion-heart by virtue of my single-minded lust to play a fiddle. This place, Big Flat, is a famous beauty spot on the south flank of Mount Kōshin. Looking down from there on a fine day, one can see through the red pines the whole layout of the castle town below. I'd guess the level area must cover some four hundred square yards and, smack in the middle of it, a large, flat rock protrudes to form a low fifteen-square-yard platform. On the north side of Big Flat there's a swampy pond called Cormorant's Marsh, and around the pond there's nothing but a thick stand of quite enormous camphor trees, each one no less than three arm-spans around. The place is deep in the mountains and the only sign of man is a small hut used by the camphor gatherers. Even by day the pond oppresses the visitor with its air of sodden gloom. Remote as it is, Big Flat is not too hard to visit because, on some long-ago maneuvres, the Corps of Engineers cut a pathway up the mountainside. When I finally reached the flat rock, I spread out my scarlet blanket and sat down on it. I'd never climbed up here before on a night so cold and, as my pulse steadied, I began to feel the surrounding loneliness encroach upon me as a kind of cramp creeping ever deeper into my belly. When one is thus alone in the mountains the sheer intensity of that loneliness can fill the mind with a feeling of terror; but if that feeling can be emptied away, all that remains in the mind is an extraordinary sense of icy crystalline clarity. For some twenty minutes I sat there on my scarlet rug completely abstracted from my normal self and feeling as though I were totally alone in a palace of pure crystal. It was as though every bit of me, my body, even my soul, had become transparent, as if made of some kind of quartz, and I could no longer tell whether I was inside that palace of crystal or that freezing palace was within my belly."

Not quite sure how to react to Coldmoon's strange account, Waverhouse contented himself with a style of teasing more demure than his mocking wont. "How terrible," he said. Singleman, however, was genuinely impressed by Coldmoon's personal report of a state of consciousness not unknown to many meditation sects. "Quite extraordinary," he observed. "Most interesting."

"Had my condition of cold translucency persisted, I might well have stayed frozen on that rock until I melted in the morning sun. Then I should never have played my violin."

"Have there been any earlier reports," Beauchamp asked, "to suggest that Big Flat might be haunted? You know, by foxes, badgers, or any other such shape-changing creatures?"

"As I was saying, I couldn't even tell whether I was my own self or not, and I scarcely knew if I were alive or dead when suddenly I heard a harsh screaming cry from the far end of the old marsh."

"Aha," says Waverhouse, "things are happening."

"This awful cry, like a blast of autumn wind tossing the treetops, echoed away far and deep across the entire mountain; at its sound, I came to myself with a jerk."

"What a relief!" sighed Waverhouse, heaving a grotesquely simulated sigh.

"As the masters say, 'One must perish into life.' Isn't that so, Coldmoon?" Even Singleman, who winked as he offered his observation, now seems disposed to treat his friend's spiritual experience in the spirit of light farce. However, his Zen reference was completely lost on Coldmoon.

"Having been thus startled back into my usual self, I looked around me. The whole vast mountain was now dead quiet: nothing, not even the drip of a raindrop, could be heard. What then was that ghastly cry? Too piercing to have been human, too loud for any bird. Could it have been a monkey? But around there there aren't any monkeys. What on earth could it have been? Once that question had entered my head and I began to search around for its answer, all the demons of misgiving who had hitherto lain quiet in the crannies of my mind erupted into pandemonium. You remember how the city crowds went wild, people running here and there and even all over each other in a lunacy of welcome, when Prince Arthur of Connaught came to Tokyo in February 1906? Well, inside my head it was worse than that. And then things suddenly came to a crisis. I felt my very pores gape open and through their yawn my body's flightiest visitors—Courage, Pluck, Prudence, and Composure departed from me. Like cheap alcohol blown in a spray on hairy shins to cool them, my visitors evaporated. Under my ribs my heart began to hammer. It leapt and danced like a red frog. My legs trembled like the humming strings of a kite. And my nerve broke. In mindless panic I grabbed my scarlet blanket around my head and, with the violin clutched beneath one arm, I scrambled down from the low flat rock and helter-skelter fled away down the rough mountain path. When, scampering like a rat through the layers of dead leaves, I came at last to my lodgings, I crept in quietly and hid myself in my bed. I had been so exhausted by terror that I fell immediately asleep. D'you know, Beauchamp, that was the most terrifying experience of my whole life."

"And then?"

"That's it. There isn't any more."

"No playing of the violin?"

"How could I possibly have played? If you had heard that eldritch cry, I bet my boots the last thing you'd have thought about would be playing a violin."

"I find your story less than satisfactory."

"Perhaps so, but it was the truth." Coldmoon, vastly pleased with himself, surveyed his audience. "Well," he said, "and what did you think of it?"

"Excellent. A point well taken," laughed Waverhouse. "You really must have gone through great travail to bring your story to that remarkable conclusion. In fact, I've been following your account with the closest attention, for it seemed increasingly clear to me that, in the person of yourself, these Eastern climes have perhaps been visited by a male reincarnation of Sandra Belloni." Waverhouse paused in the obvious hope that someone would give him an opportunity to air his knowledge of Meredith's heroine by asking for clarification of this obscure reference. But all the members of his audience, having been caught that way before, held their peace; so Waverhouse, regrettably uncued, simply rattled on. "Just as Sandra Belloni's harp playing and Italian song in a moonlit forest called down the goddess of that silver orb, so Coldmoon's near performance with a violin upon the ledges of Mount Kōshin called up some phantom badger from a fen. There is, of course, a difference of degree but the principle's the same. What I find peculiarly interesting is that such a slight difference in degree should produce so vast a difference in result: in Sandra's case a manifestation of ethereal beauty, but in Coldmoon's nothing but crude and earthy farce. That must have been a painful disappointment to you."

"No disappointment at all," said Coldmoon who seemed genuinely uninterested, perhaps not in his own weird experience, but certainly in Waverhouse's question.

"Trying to play a violin on a mountain top! What effete behavior! It serves you right that you got scared silly." My master's scathing comment showed his usual lack of sympathy with anything beyond the world of his own wizened imagination.

Singleman piped in:

"How more than pitiful it is to find
That one must live one's human life confined
Within a world of an inhuman kind."

None of Singleman's mangled quotations from the works of deluded medieval metaphysicians ever makes the least sense to Coldmoon. Or to anyone else. Perhaps not even to Singleman. His words were left to float away into the nothingness of a long silence.

After a while, Waverhouse changed the subject by asking, "Incidentally, Coldmoon, are you still haunting the university in order to polish your little, glass balls?"

"No. My visit home rather interrupted things. Indeed, I doubt if I'll ever resume that line of research. It was always, if you'll pardon the joke, something of a grind, and lately I've been finding it a real bore."

"But without your polished beads, you won't get your doctorate," says my master, looking slightly worried.

Coldmoon seems no more concerned about his doctorate than he was with his failure to become a Japanese version of Sandra Belloni. "Oh that," he says with a careless laugh. "I've no longer any need for a degree."

"But then the marriage will be canceled and both sides will be upset."

"Marriage? Whose marriage?"

"Yours."

"To whom am I supposed to be getting married?"

"To the Goldfield girl."

"Really?"

"But surely you've already plighted your troth?"

"I've never plighted anything. I had no part in the spread of that particular rumor."

"That's a bit thick," says my master. "I say, Waverhouse, you, too, remember that incident, don't you?"

"Incident? You mean that business when the Nose came shoving herself in here? If so, it's not just you and I who've heard about the engagement, but the world and his wife have long been in on the secret. As a matter of fact, I'm constantly being pestered by some quite respectable newspapers who want me to let them know when they may have the honor of printing photographs of Coldmoon and his blushing Opula in their Happy Couples column. What's more, Beauchamp there finished his epic epithalamium, 'A Song of Lovebirds,' at least three months ago and has since been waiting anxiously to learn the right date for its publication. You don't want your masterpiece to rot in the ground like buried treasure just because Coldmoon's grown bored with buffing up his little, glass beads, do you, Beauchamp, eh?"

"There's no question of pushing for early publication. Of course, my very heart and soul have gone into that poem, but I am happily convinced that it will remain suitable for publication at any appropriate time."

"There, you see: the question of whether or not you take your degree has wide and potentially painful repercussions. So, pull yourself together. Get those beads rubbed spherical. Polish the whole thing off."

"I like the joke in your phrasing, and I'm truly sorry if I've given any of you cause to worry. But I really do not any longer need a doctorate."

"Why not?"

"Because I have already got my own wife."

"I say, that's grand! When did this secret marriage take place? Life is certainly full of surprises. Well, Sneaze, as you've just heard, Coldmoon has apparently acquired a wife and children."

"No children yet. It would be terrible if a child were born after less than a month of marriage."

"But when and where did you ever get married?" demanded my master as though he were the presiding judge at some official court of inquiry.

"As a matter of fact, during my recent trip home. She was there waiting for me. Those dried bonitos were one of the wedding presents from her relatives."

"Three miserable dried bonitos! That was rather a stingy gift."

"No, no. There were scads of them. I only brought you three."

"So your bride is from your own home district? Does it then follow that she's on the dark skinned side?"

"Yes, she's dark complexioned. Exactly right for me."

"And what are you going to do about the Goldfields?"

"Nothing."

"But you can't just leave things, poof like that," my master bleated. "What do you think, Waverhouse?"

"I think he can. The girl will marry someone else. After all, marriage is little more than two people bumping against each other in the dark. If they cannot manage such bumping by themselves, other people contrive their blind collision. It doesn't much matter who bumps whom. In my opinion, the only person deserving our tears and pity is the unfortunate author of 'A Song of Lovebirds.'"

"Thank you, but please don't worry. My epithalamium, as it stands, is perfectly suitable for dedication to Coldmoon on the already achieved occasion of his marriage. I can easily write another when Opula gets wed."

"Ah, that marvelous, heartless professionalism of the true poet," sighed Waverhouse, "whipping out a masterpiece at the drop of a hat. Easy as a wink of an eye. One's heart is cramped with jealousy."

"Have you notified the Goldfields?" My master is still touchingly concerned about the feelings of that granite clan.

"No, and why should I? I never proposed to the girl or asked her father for her hand in marriage. I have no reason whatsoever to say a single word to either of them. Moreover, I'm sure they've already learned the last least detail from those dozens of detectives they employ."

My master's face, as the word "detectives" entered his ear, immediately turned sour. "You're right, Coldmoon, tell such people nothing," and he proceeded to offer the following comments on detectives as though they were all weighty arguments against observing the proprieties in handling a broken engagement. "Persons who snatch property from the unwary in the streets are called pickpockets; those who snitch the thoughts of the unwary are called detectives. Those who jimmy open your doors and windows are called thieves; those who use leading questions to lever out one's private thoughts are called detectives. Those who threateningly jab their swords into one's floor matting as a way of forcing the surrender of money are called armed burglars; those who by the jabbing menace of their words force one into admissions against one's will are called detectives. To my way of thinking, it inexorably follows that pickpockets, thieves, armed burglars, and detectives are all spawn of the same subhuman origin, things unfit to be treated even as men. Their every endeavor should be thwarted and they themselves quite mercilessly put down."

"Don't work yourself into such a lather. I'm not frightened by detectives, even though they should appear by the battalion. Let all be warned with whom they will be dealing. Am I not the King of the Glass Ball Polishers, Avalon Coldmoon B.Sc.?"

"Bravo! Well spoken! That's the stuff to give 'em! Just the spirited words one would expect from a newly married bachelor of science. However, Sneaze," Waverhouse continued, "if you categorize detectives with such grubs as pickpockets, thieves, and common robbers, where do you place a creature such as Goldfield who gives employment to such vermin?"

"Perhaps a modern version of that long departed villain, Kumasaka Chōhan."

"Oh yes, I like that. Chōhan, as I recall it, was said to have disappeared when he was sliced in half. But our modern version over the way, squatting on a fortune made by blatant usury, is so intensely alive in his meanness and sharp greediness that, cut in a million pieces, he'd reappear as a million Chōhan clones. It would be a lifelong source of trouble if such a blood-sucking creature ever came to believe he had a bone to pick with you. So be careful, Coldmoon."

"To hell with that! I shall face him down with the sort of speech you hear from heros of the Hōshō style of Noh play. You know what I mean. 'Pretentious thief though well aware of my fearsome reputation, you yet dare break into my house.' That should stop him short." Coldmoon, unwisely careless of the real dangers he might have to cope with from a vengeful Goldfield, strikes a series of dramatic poses.

"Talking of detectives, I wonder why it is that nearly everyone nowadays tends to behave as detectives do." In strict accordance with his usual style, Singleman begins his observations by reference to the matters under discussion and then veers off into complete irrelevance.

"Perhaps," says Coldmoon kindly, "it's because of the high cost of living."

Beauchamp mounts his hobbyhorse. "I myself believe it's because we have lost our feeling for art."

"It's because the horns of modern civilization are sprouting from the human head and the irritations of that growth, like nettles in one's underwear, are driving us mad." It's a pity that Waverhouse, who is both well-read and intelligent, still should strive to be merely clever.

When it came to my master's turn, he opened the following lecture with an air of enormous self-importance. "I have, of late, devoted considerable thought to this topic and I have concluded that the current marked trend toward detective-mindedness is entirely caused by the individual permitting himself too strong a realization of the self. By that I do not mean self-realization of the spiritual nature which Singleman pursues in his Zen search for his 'unborn face,' that self he was before he contrived to be born. Nor do I mean that other form of Zen self-realization where, by either gradual or sudden enlightenment, the mind perceives its own identity with heaven and earth. . ."

"Dear, dear, this is becoming rather heavy going. But if Sneaze, you really do propose to make an exhaustive and scholarly analysis of the psychological maladies of our times, I feel that I, Waverhouse in person, must be granted an opportunity to lodge a full complaint against the civilization I seek to grace."

"You are always free to say what you like. But generally you don't say anything. You just talk."

"On the contrary, I have a very great deal to say. It was you, Sneaze, who, only a brief week back, fell down and worshiped a police detective. Yet here you are today, making ugly comparisons between detectives and pickpockets. You are an incarnation of the principle of contradiction. Whereas I am a man who, through every earlier life right to this present day of my present incarnation, has never wavered in the certitudes of my opinions."

"Police detectives are police detectives. The other day is the other day. And today's today. Never to change one's opinions is to demonstrate a petrifaction of mind that prevents its least development. To be, as Confucius put it in the *Analects*, willfully ignorant beyond all hope of education, is, my dear Waverhouse, to be you."

"That's really rather rude. Still, even a detective when he tries to speak his honest mind can be rather sweet."

"Are you calling me a detective?"

"I simply meant to say that, since you are not a detective, you're an honest man, and that that's good. There, there. No more quarrels. Let's listen to the rest of your formidable argument."

"The heightened self-awareness of our contemporaries means that they realize only too well the wide gap between their own interests and those of other people; as the advance of civilization daily widens that gap, so this so-called self-awareness intensifies to a point where everyone becomes incapable of natural or unaffected behavior. William Henley, the English poet, once said that his friend Robert Louis Stevenson was so continuously unable to forget himself that, if he happened to be in a room with a mirror on the wall, he could not pass in front of the glass without stopping to study his reflection. Stevenson's condition is a telling example of the general modern trend. Because this overweening consciousness of self never lets up, not even when one sleeps, it is inevitable that our speech and behavior should have become forced and artificial. We impose constrictions on ourselves and, in that process, inhibitions on society. In short, we conduct our whole lives as if we were two young people at their first meeting in the context of a marriage negotiation. Words such as serenity and self-composure have become no more than so many meaningless strokes of a writing brush. It is in this sense that people nowadays have become like detectives and burglars. A detective's job is essentially to make profit by being sneaky and self-effacing; only by cultivating an intense awareness of himself can he even believe in his own existence. To no less a degree the rapacious burglar is obsessed with me, me, me, because the thought of what will happen to him if he's caught is never out of his mind. Modern man, even in his deepest slumber, never stops thinking about what will bring him profit or, even more worrying, loss. Consequently, as with the burglar and the detective, his self-absorption grows daily more absolute. Modern man is jittery and sneaky. Morning, noon, and night he sneaks and jitters and knows no peace. Not one single moment's peace until the cold grave takes him. That's the condition to which our so-called civilization has brought us. And what a mess it is."

"Most interesting. A penetrating analysis of our case," says Singleman who rarely resists any opportunity to thicken the clouds when high flown, cloudy matters are discussed. "I consider Sneaze's explanation is very much to the point. In the old days, a man was taught to forget himself. Today it is quite different: he is taught not to forget himself and he accordingly spends his days and nights in endless self-regard. Who can possibly know peace in such an eternally burning hell? The apparent realities of this awful world, even the beastliness of being, are all symptoms of that sickness for which the only cure lies in learning to forget the self. This dire situation is well summarized in that ancient Chinese poem whose author was one of those

> Who simply sit and, sitting all night through
> Under a drifting moon, themselves withdrew
> Themselves from Self and thereby came to be
> Free of the world and from all Being free.

Modern man lacks naturalness even when performing acts of genuine kindness. The English, as is well-known, are vastly proud of being nice, both in the sense of their refined behavior and in the sense of common kindness; however, one may fairly suspect the hearts behind the niceness of the English as packed with self-regard. Perhaps I might remind you of the story of that member of the English royal family who, during some visit to India, was invited to a banquet. Among those present was an Indian prince who, momentarily forgetful of the nature of the occasion but perfectly naturally in terms of Indian custom, reached out for a potato, picked it up in his fingers and put it on his plate. Realizing his gaffe, he was terribly ashamed. But the English gentleman, immediately and with apparently equal naturalness, proceeded to help himself to potatoes with his fingers. An act of the most refined and kindly politeness? Or an act so-seeming but ultimately taken in order that it should be remembered, as it clearly has been, to the enhancement of English royalty?"

"Is it the English custom," asks Coldmoon, missing the point of the story, "to eat potatoes with their fingers?"

Disregarding Coldmoon's question, my master spoke. "I've heard another such story about the English. On some occasion at their barracks in England a group of regimental officers gave a dinner in honor of one of their non-commissioned officers. Toward the end of the meal, when finger bowls filled with water were placed in front of each diner, the non-commissioned officer, a man not used to banquets, lifted the bowl to his mouth and swallowed the water down in a single gulp. Immediately, the colonel of the regiment raised his own finger bowl in a toast to the non-commissioned officer's health and gulped its water down. His lead was promptly followed by every officer present."

"I wonder if you've heard this one," says Waverhouse who does not like to remain silent. "When Carlyle was presented to the queen, he, being an eccentric and anyway a man totally unschooled in court procedures, suddenly sat down on a chair. All the chamberlains and ladies-in-waiting standing ranged behind the queen began to giggle. Well, not quite. They were about to start giggling when the queen turned around toward them and signaled them also to be seated. Carlyle was thus saved from any embarrassment. I confess I find this courtly courtesy somewhat elaborate."

"I don't suppose," said Coldmoon rather shortly, "that, being the man he was, Carlyle would have been the least embarrassed if only he and the queen were seated while all the rest stayed standing."

"To be self-aware when one is actually being kind to other people may be all right," Singleman started up again, "but being self-aware does make it that much harder to be genuinely kind. It is widely held that the advance of civilization brings with it a moderation of combative spirit and a general easing of relationships between individuals. But that's all nonsense. When individual awareness grows so strong, how can mutual gentleness be expected? It's true of course that modern relationships seem superficially calm and easy-going, but they are in fact extremely tough; rather like the relationship between two *sumo* wrestlers who, immobilized by cross-grips in the middle of the ring, are nevertheless butting each other with their vast potbellies as hard as they can heave."

"In former times disputes were settled by the relatively healthy means of brute force, whereas nowadays the means and mentality have become so specialized that the intensity of the combatant's self-awareness has inevitably increased," says Waverhouse, taking it to be now his turn to talk. "Sir Francis Bacon observed in his *Novum Organum* that one can only triumph over nature by obeying the laws of nature. Is it not peculiar that modern quarrels so closely follow the pattern identified by Bacon in that, as in a *jūjutsu* contest, one defeats one's opponent by an exploitation of that opponent's own strength."

"Or again, it is, I suppose, something like the generation of hydroelectricity. One makes no effort to oppose the flow of water, but merely diverts its force into the production of power."

Coldmoon had obviously only just begun to express an interesting idea, but Singleman butted in to add, "And therefore, when one is poor, one is tied by poverty; when rich, entrapped in wealth; when worried, tangled by anxiety; and when happy, dizzied by happiness. A talented man falls at the hand of talent, a man of wisdom is defeated by wisdom, and a quick-tempered man like Sneaze is quickly provoked into rashness and goes rushing headlong out into the deadfalls dug by his artful enemies."

"Here, here," cried Waverhouse clapping his hands. And when my master, actually grinning, said, "Well, you won't in practice catch me quite as simply as that," everyone burst out laughing.

"By the way, I wonder what sort of thing would finish off a fearful fellow like Goldfield?"

"His wife will obviously be toppled over by the weight of her nose, while the hardness of his heart will crush that usurer to death. His henchmen will be trampled to death by stampeding detectives."

"And the daughter?"

"Well, I'm not sure about her, and I have never in fact clapped eyes on her. But it seems likely that she'll be suffocated by clothes or food or even drinking. I can't imagine that she'll die of love, though I suppose she might end up as a roadside beggar like that fabled beauty Ono-no-Komachi."

"That's a bit unkind," objected Beauchamp who, after all, had written some new-style poems for the girl.

"And therein lies the importance of the moral injunction that one must have a merciful heart and never lose one's subjectivity. Unless one reaches and sustains that condition of mind, one will suffer torment throughout eternity." That benighted Singleman waffles on as usual as though he were the sole proprietor of enlightenment.

"Don't be such a moralizing twerp. The chances are," said Waverhouse, "that you will meet your just deserts upside-down in one of your own oft-quoted flashes of Zen lightning. In the spring, of course."

"One thing at least is certain," said my master. "If civilization continues its rapid development along its present lines, I would not wish to live and witness it."

"The choice is yours. As Seneca advises, no man should carp at life when the road to freedom runs down every vein. Why don't you do yourself in?" Waverhouse helpfully enquired.

"I care rather less for dying than I do for living."

"No one seems to pay much attention when he's being born, but everybody makes no end of a fuss about his departure." Coldmoon offers his own cool comment.

"It's the same with money," says Waverhouse. "When one borrows money, one does so lightly, but everyone worries like crazy when it comes to paying it back."

"Happy are they who don't worry about repayment; as happy as those who do not worry about death," intoned Singleman in his most lofty and unworldly style.

"I suppose you'd argue that the bravest in the face of death are those who are most enlightened?"

"Most certainly. Perhaps you know the Zen phrase 'The iron-ox-heart of an iron-ox-face: the ox-iron-heart of an ox-iron-face?'"

"And are you claiming to be so ox-and-iron-hearted?" Waverhouse, who happened to know that the phrase meant to have a heart so strong as to be undisturbed by anything, doubted that Singleman would dare make such a claim.

"Well, no, I wouldn't go that far. But," said Singleman for no very obvious reason, "the fact remains that neurasthenia was an unknown ailment until after people became worried about death."

"It's plain that you must have been born and bred before the invention of nervous prostration."

This weird dialogue held so little interest for Coldmoon and Beauchamp that my master had no difficulty in retaining them as an audience for a further airing of his grievances against civilization. "The key question," he announced, "is how to avoid repaying borrowed money."

"But surely no such question can arise. Anything borrowed must always be repaid."

"All right, all right. Don't get so up in the air. This is just a discussion between intelligent men, so listen and don't interrupt. I ask how can one borrow without repaying in order to lead in to the parallel question as to how can one contrive to avoid dying. Though it is no longer much pursued, that used to be the key question: hence the ancient concern with alchemy. However, the alchemists achieved no real success and it soon became deadly clear that no human being could ever dodge death."

"It was deadly clear long before the alchemists confirmed it."

"All right, but since this is just an argument, you just listen. Right? Now, once it became clear that everyone was bound to die, then the second question arose."

"Indeed?"

"If one is certain to die, what's the best way to do so? That is the second question. Once this second question had been formulated, it was only a matter of time before the Suicide Club would be founded."

"I see."

"It is hard to die, but it is much harder if one cannot die. Victims of neurasthenia find living far more painful than any death. Yet they remain obsessed with death; not because they shun it, but because they fret to discover the best means to that much desired end. The majority will lack the common sense to solve the problem. They will give up and leave nature to solve it for them or society itself will bully them to death. But there will also be a handful of awkward customers who will be unwilling to endure the slow death of such bullying. They will study the options into death and their research will lead to marvelous new ideas. Beyond all doubt, the main characteristic of the future will be a steady rise in suicides and, almost certainly, every self-destructor will be expected to work out his own original method of escape."

"People will be put to a great deal of trouble."

"Yes, they most certainly will. Henry Arthur Jones has already written a play in which the leading figure is a philosopher who strongly advocates suicide."

"Does he kill himself?"

"Regrettably, no. But within a thousand years everyone will be doing it, and I am prepared to bet that in ten thousand years time nobody will even think of death except in terms of suicide."

"But that will be terrible."

"Indeed it will. By that time the study of suicide, on a foundation of years of detailed research, will have been raised to the level of a highly respected and fully institutionalized science. At middle schools such as the Hall of the Descending Clouds the study of suicide will have replaced ethics as a compulsory subject."

"An intriguing prospect. A lecture course on the theory and practice of suicide might well be worth attending. Hey, Waverhouse, have you been listening to Sneaze on the destiny of man?"

"Yes I have. By the time of which he has just been speaking the ethics teacher at the Hall of the Descending Clouds will be holding our current concepts of public morality up to reproof and ridicule. The young men of that far world will be instructed to abandon the barbarous customs of the ancients and to recognize that suicide is the first duty of every decent person. Moreover, since it is eternally right to do unto others as one would wish done to oneself the moral obligation to commit suicide implies an equally moral obligation to commit murder. Consider, the teacher will say, the case of Mr. Peke Sneaze, that wretched, struggling scholar dragging out his miserable existence just across from our school. Is he not obviously agonized by his persistent breathing yet lacks the ordinary physical courage to fulfill his moral duty to do away with himself? Is it not therefore, in common humanity, your compassionate duty to do him in? Not, of course, in any of the ancient cowardly ways involving such crudities as spears, halberds or any kind of firearm. In this day and age we are surely civilized beyond such coarse atrocities. No, he should be harassed unto death. Only the most refined techniques of verbal assassination should be employed. Which will be not only an act of charity toward that luckless sufferer but a credit to yourselves and to the school."

"This extension lecture, Waverhouse upon Sneaze, is deeply interesting. I am truly moved by the high-mindedness of our descendants."

"Yes, but there's even more upon which to laud our unborn heirs. In our ill-governed times the police are intended to safeguard the lives and property of citizens. But in the happier times of our enlightened future, the police will carry cudgels, like dog-catchers, and go around clubbing the citizens to death."

"Why that?"

"Because today we value our lives and the police accordingly protect them. When in the future, living is recognized for the agony it is, then the police will be required to club the agonized to a merciful death. Of course, anyone in his right mind will already have committed suicide; so the necessary objects of police attention will be only the gutless milksops, those mentally impaired or deranged and any persons so pitifully disabled as to be unable to destroy themselves. Additionally, anyone in need of help or assistance will, as today, just stick up a notice to that effect on the gate to his house. The police will call around at some convenient time and promptly supply to the man or woman concerned the assistance requested. The dead bodies? Collected in hand drawn carts by the police on their regular rounds. The police themselves? Recruited from criminals guilty of acts so hideous they've been condemned to life. And that's not all. Consider this further interesting aspect of. . ."

"But is there no end to this joke?" exclaims Beauchamp from the daze of his admiration. Before an answer could be given, Singleman began to speak, very slowly and with great deliberation, even though he still continued worrying away at his ridiculous tuft of beard.

"You may call it a joke, but it might well, and better, be called a prediction. Those whose minds are not unwaveringly concentrated upon the pursuit of ultimate truth are normally misled by the mere appearances, however unreal, of the phenomenal world. They tend to accept what they directly see and feel, not as some empty froth of illusion but as manifestations of an eternal reality. Consequently, if someone says anything even slightly out of the ordinary, such prisoners of their senses have no choice but to treat the communication as a joke."

"Do you mean," says Coldmoon, deeply impressed, "something like that Chinese verse about small birds being unable to understand the minds of greater birds?

The swallow and the sparrow see no use
In things that, to the eagle and the goose,
Are plainly useful. It could even be
That from their littleness the little see
Nothing whatever of Immensity."

And he smirks with delight when Singleman, with an approving inclination of his head, says, "Something like that."

Singleman, the even plodding of his speech unspurred even by adulation, slowly continues. "Once, years ago, there was a place in Spain called Cordoba. . ."

"Once? It's still there, isn't it?"

"That may be. The question of time past or present is immaterial. In any event, in Cordoba it used to be the custom that at the time of the angelus, the evening striking of the bells of churches, all the women came out of their houses and bathed in the river. . ."

"Even in winter?"

"I'm not sure about that, but in any case, every female in the place—young or old—jumped into the river, and no man was allowed to join them. The men simply looked on from a distance, and all they could see in the evening twilight were the women's whitish forms dimly moving above the rippling waters."

"That's poetic. It could be made into a new-style poem. What did you say the place was called?" Beauchamp always shows interest whenever female nudity is mentioned.

"Cordoba. Now, the young men thought it a pity that they could neither swim with the women nor study their form in a better light. So, one fine day, they played a little trick. . ."

"Oh really? Tell me more," says Waverhouse immediately. The mention of any kind of trick has, upon him, the same invigorating effect as nudity works upon Beauchamp.

"They bribed the bell-ringer to sound the angelus one hour early. The women, being such sillies, all trooped down to the riverbank as soon as they heard the bells, and there, one after another in their various states of undress, they jumped off into the water. And then, too late, they at last realized that it was still broad day."

"Are you sure that there wasn't a fierce autumn sun ablaze?"

"A great number of men were standing watching from the bridge. The women didn't know what to do and felt terribly ashamed."

"And then?"

"The moral is simply this: that one should always be wary of the common human failing of allowing oneself to be blinded by habit to basic realities."

"Not a bad little sermon. A tale worth remembering. But let me give you another example, from a magazine story which I recently read, of someone rendered blind by an accustomed habit. Imagine that I've opened an antique shop and that, up at the front, I've put on display some particularly excellent scrolls and works of art. No fakes, nothing shabby, only genuine, first-class stuff. Naturally the prices are very high. In due course along comes some art fancier who stops and enquires about the price of a certain scroll. I point out that the scroll is by Motonobu, that son of Masanobu who founded the Kano school in the early sixteenth century, and I then quote some quite astronomical sum, say, six thousand. The customer replies that he likes the scroll very much but, at such a price, and not carrying such large sums of money on his person, he'll have to let it go."

"How can you possibly know," asks my master, ever the wet blanket, "that the customer will answer like that?"

"Don't worry, he will. And anyway it's only a story, so I can make my customer answer as I like. So I then say to him, 'Please, for those of us who appreciate Motonobu, payment is hardly the point. If you like it, take it with you.' The customer can hardly do that. So he hesitates. I proceed in my friendliest manner to say that, confident that I shall be enjoying his future patronage, I would be happy to settle any difficulties about payment by accepting small sums paid monthly over a long period. 'Please don't feel under any obligation. But how about a hundred a month? Or shall we say fifty?' Finally, after a few more questions and answers, I end up selling him the Motonobu scroll for six thousand paid in monthly installments of only a hundred."

"Sounds like that scheme in 1898 for buying the ninth edition of the *Encyclopedia Britannica Through the Times*."

"*The Times* is reliable, an honest sort of broker, but my scheme is of a very different character. As, if you listen carefully, you'll see. Now, Coldmoon, suppose you pay a hundred a month for my Motonobu, how long will you be paying installments?"

"For five years? Of course, isn't it?"

"Five years, of course. Now, Singleman, do you think five years is a long time or a short time?"

Singleman raised his head into its best position for the drone of Zen wisdom and intoned:

> "A single minute may be felt to be
> As sempeternal as eternity,
> While ten millenia can at times go by
> In the mere flicker of an adder's eye.

"By which I mean your five years could be either long or short or simultaneously both."

"You're at it again, Singleman. Is there some deep moral message in that quotation? A sense of morals totally detached from common sense, eh? Anyway, a hundred a month for five years involves sixty separate payments, and therein lies the danger of habit. If one repeats the same action sixty times over, month after month, one is likely to become so habituated to payment that one also coughs up on the sixty-first occasion. And on the sixty-second. And on the sixty-third and so on because the breaking of an established habit irks the habitue. Men are supposed to be clever, but they all have the same weakness: they follow established patterns without questioning the reason for their establishment. My scheme simply exploits that weakness to earn me a hundred a month until my customer finally drops dead."

"Though I like your joke," tittered Coldmoon, "I doubt if you'll find a great many customers so profitably forgetful."

My master, however, did not seem to find the story funny. In a serious voice he said, "That sort of thing does actually happen. I used to pay back my university loan, month after month on a regular basis, and I kept no count of the number of payments. In the end I only stopped because the university told me to stop." My master seems almost to brag of his half-wittedness as though it were the benchmark of humanity.

"There you are," cries Waverhouse. "You see, the reality of my imagined customer is sitting right here in front of us. Yet that very same person, a self-confessed slave to human habit, has the effrontery to laugh at my projection of his own vision of our future civilization into its likely and unlaughable reality. Inexperienced young fellows like Beauchamp and Coldmoon, if they are not to be defrauded of their human rights, should listen very carefully for the wisdom in our words."

"I hear and shall obey. Never, never shall I commit myself to any installment plan that involves more than sixty repayments."

"I know you still think it's all just a joke but I do assure you, Coldmoon, that it was a truly instructive story," said Singleman turning directly to face him. "For instance, suppose that someone as wise and experienced as either Sneaze or Waverhouse told you that you had acted improperly in going off and getting married without advising any of the interested parties of your intentions? Should they advise that you ought to go and apologize to that Goldfield person, what would you do? Would you go and make your apologies?"

"I should beg to be excused. I would not demur if they wished to go and offer an explanation of my behavior. But to go myself, no."

"What if the police ordered you to apologize?"

"I should refuse all the more strongly."

"If a minister of the government or a peer of the realm asked you to apologize?"

"Then, yet more firmly still, I would refuse."

"There, you see how times have changed. Not so long ago the power of those in authority was unlimited. Then came a time when there were certain things which even they could not demand. But nowadays there are strict limits upon the power of peers and even ministers to compel the individual. To put the matter bluntly, we are witnessing a period when, the greater the power of the authorities, the greater the resistance they'll encounter. Our fathers would be astonished to see how things which the authorities clearly want done, and have ordered should be done, nevertheless remain undone. This era takes for granted any number of things which elderly people would once have thought unthinkable. It is quiet extraordinary how quickly and how totally both men and their concept of society can change. So, though you may of course laugh as much as you like at Waverhouse's version of the future, you would be wise not to laugh so hard that you fail to consider how much of it might prove true."

"Flattered as I am to have found so appreciative a friend, I feel that much more obliged to continue with my forecast of the future. First I would emphasize, as Singleman has already indicated, that anyone nowadays who proudly thinks himself powerful by reason of delegated authority, or who seeks to maintain an outdated power by marching around with a troop of a hundred henchmen brandishing bamboo spears, can only be compared to that antiquated bigot who imagined that his spanking palanquin could travel faster than a railway train. I fancy that the best local example of such a fathead might actually be that usurer Goldfield, whom I consider the master fathead of them all. So perhaps we should simply relax and leave time to slide over him. Anyway, my forecast of the future is not so much concerned with such minor transitional matters as with a particular social phenomenon that will determine the long-term destiny of the entire human race. My friends, if you will take a long-term view of the trends already obvious in the development of our civilization, you will have no choice but to share my view that marriage has had it. Are you surprised? That the sacred institution of marriage should be so summarily written off? Well, the grounds for my forecast have already been stated and, I think, accepted: that modern society is centered, to the exclusion of all else, upon the idea of individuality. When the family was represented by its head, the district by its magistrate and the province by its feudal lord, then those who were not representatives possessed no personalities whatsoever. Even if exceptionally, they actually did have personalities, those characteristics, being inappropriate to their place in society, were never recognized as such. Suddenly everything changed. We were all discovered to possess personalities, and every individual began to assert his newfound individuality. Whenever two persons chanced to meet, their attitudes betrayed a disposition to quarrel, an underlying determination to insist that 'I am I, and you are you,' and that no human being was any more human than any other. Obviously, each individual grew a little stronger by reason of this new individuality. But, of course, precisely because everyone had grown stronger, everyone had also grown proportionately weaker than their fellow-individuals. Because it's now harder for people to oppress you, certainly you're stronger; but because it's now a lot more difficult for you to meddle in other folk's affairs, you're clearly that much weaker. Everyone, naturally, likes to be strong, and no one, naturally, likes to be weak. Consequently, we all vigorously defend the strong points in our position in society, scrapping like fiends over the merest trifles, and at the same time, in an unremitting effort to undermine the position of our fellows, we lever away at their weakest points at every opportunity. It follows that men have no genuine living space left between them which is not occupied by siege engines and counterworks. Too cramped to live at ease, the constant pressure to expand one's individual sphere has brought mankind to a painful bursting point and, having arrived by their own machinations at such an unpleasant state of affairs, men thereupon devised a means to relieve the unbearable pressure: they developed that system under which parents and their married offspring live separately. In the more backward parts of Japan, among the wilder mountains, you can still find entire families, including their lesser cousinage, all living together, perfectly contentedly, in one single house. That lifestyle was only viable because, apart from the head of the family, no member of the group possessed any individuality to assert; while any member who, exceptionally, happened to possess it, took good care never to let it show. However, in more up-to-date and civilized communities the individual members of families are struggling amongst themselves, no less fiercely than do other and totally unrelated members of modern society, both to guard their own positions and to undermine those of their so-called nearest and dearest. There is, therefore, little real choice but to live separately.

"In Europe, where the modernization of society has proceeded much further than has yet happened in Japan, this necessary disintegration of the multi-generation family unit has long been common. If by chance European parents and sons do live in the same house, the sons pay, as they would elsewhere, for board and lodging. Similarly, if sons borrow money from their father, they pay it back with interest as they would if they had borrowed from a bank. This sort of laudable arrangement is only possible when fathers recognize and pay proper respect to sons' individualities. Sooner or later such customs must be adopted in Japan. It is many years now since uncles, aunts, and cousins moved out of the family unit to establish their separate lives: the time is now coming for fathers and sons to separate, but the development of individuality and of a feeling of respect toward individuality will go on growing endlessly. We shall never be at peace unless we move farther apart and give each other room for that growth. But when parents, sons, brothers, and sisters have all so eased apart, what further easement can be sought? Only the separation of husband and wife. Some people today still persist in the mistaken view that a husband and wife are a husband and wife because they live together. The point is that they can only live together if their separate individualities are sufficiently harmonious. No question of disharmony arose in the old days because, being in the Confucian phrase 'two bodies but one spirit,' husband-and-wife was a single person. Even after death they remained inseparable, haunting the world as two badgers from a single sett. That barbarous state of affairs is now all changed. A husband now is simply a man who happens to be married, a wife a woman in the same lamentable condition. This wife person went to a girls' school from which, after an excellent education designed to strengthen her individuality, she comes marching out in a Western hairstyle to be a bride. No wonder the man she marries cannot make her do what he likes. If such a woman did, in fact, accommodate herself to her husband's beck and call, people would say she's not a wife but a doll. The harder she works to become an intelligent helpmate, the greater the space demanded by her individuality and the less her husband can abide her. Quarreling begins. The brighter the wife, the more bitter and incessant are the quarrels, and there's no sense in boasting of intelligence in a wife if all it produces is misery for both of you. Now within this marriage a boundary is established, a boundary as distinct as that between oil and water. Even that would not be too awful if only it were steady, but in practice the line of marital friction bounces up and down so that the whole domestic scene is in a constant condition of earthquake. By such experiences the human race has come to accept that it is unprofitable to both parties that married couples should live together."

"So what do they do?" asks Coldmoon. "Divorce on the scale you imply is a worrying prospect."

"Yes, they part. What else can they do? It's clear to me that, eventually, all married couples will get divorced. As things still stand, those who live together are husband and wife, but in the future those who live together will be generally considered to have disqualified themselves from being a normal married couple."

"I suppose that a man like myself will be one of the disqualified. . ." Coldmoon misses no chance to remind us of his recent marriage.

"You are lucky to have been born in the days of the Emperor Meiji when traditional ways are still observed. Being a gifted prophet of things to come, I am inevitably two or three stops ahead of my contemporaries in all matters of any importance; that, of course, is why I am already a bachelor. I know there are people who go around saying that I remain unmarried because of some early disappointment in love, but one can only pity such persons for their shallow minds and their inability to see further than the ends of their snooping noses." Waverhouse paused for breath. "But to return to my farsighted vision of the future. . . A philosopher will descend from heaven. He will preach the unprecedented truth that all members of mankind, both men and women, are essentially individuals. Impairment of their individuality can only lead to the destruction of the human race. The purpose of human life is to maintain and develop individuality, and, to attain that end, no sacrifice is too great. It is thus contrary to the nature and needs of mankind that the ancient, evil, barbarous practice of marriage should continue. Such primitive rites were, perhaps, understandable before the sacrosanctity of individuality was recognized, but to allow the continuation of these dreadful customs into our own civilized era is quite unthinkable. The deplorable habit of marriage must be broken. In our developed culture there is no reason whatsoever why two individuals should be bound to each other in the highly abnormal intimacy of the traditional marriage relationship. Once the revelations of the heaven sent philosopher have been clearly understood, it will be regarded as extremely immoral of young uneducated men and women to allow themselves to be so carried away by base and fleeting passions that they even stoop to low indulgence in wedding ceremonies. Even today we must do our best to get such tribal customs discontinued."

"Sir," said Beauchamp so very firmly that he even slapped his kneecap, "I totally reject your vile prognostication. In my opinion, nothing in this world is more precious than love and beauty. It is entirely thanks to these two things that we can be consoled, be made perfect, and be happy. Again, it is entirely due to them that our feelings can be gracefully expressed, our characters made noble, and our sympathies refined. Therefore, no matter where or when one is born, here or in Timbuktu, now or in the future, love and beauty remain the eternal guidestars of mankind. When they manifest themselves in the actual world, love is seen in the relationship between husband and wife, while beauty shines forth either as poetry or music. These are the expressions, at its highest level, of the very humanity of the human race; I do not believe, so long as our kind exists upon the surface of this planet, that either the arts or our current ideal of the married couple will perish therefrom."

"It would be well, perhaps, if it were so. But, for the reasons which the heaven sent philosopher has just given for his forecast, both love and beauty are bound to perish. You will just have to accept the inevitable. You spoke of the imperishable glories of art, but they will go the same way as the married couple: into oblivion. The irreversible development of individuality will bring ever greater demands by individuals for recognition of their singular identity. In a world where I and you both insist that 'I am I, and you are you,' how can any art perdure? Surely the arts now flourish by reason of a harmony between the individualities of the artist and of each appreciative member of his public. That harmony is already being crushed to death. You may protest until the cows come home that you are a new-style poet, but if no one shares your conviction of the worth of your poems, I'm afraid you'll never be read. However many epithalamia you compose, your work will be dying as you write it. It is thus especially gratifying that, writing as you do in Meiji times, the whole world may still rejoice in its excellence."

"I'm not all that well-known."

"If already today your splendid efforts are not all that well-known, what do you imagine will be their fate in the future when civilization has advanced yet further and that heaven sent philosopher has knocked the stuffing out of marriage? No one at all will read your poems. Not because the poems are yours and you are a bad poet, but because individuality has intensified to such an extent that anything written by other people holds no interest for anyone. This stage of the literary future is already evidenced in England where two of their leading novelists, Henry James and George Meredith, have personalities so strong and so strongly reflected in their novels that very few people care to read them. And no wonder. Only readers with personalities of matching force could find such works of any interest. That trend will accelerate and, by the time that marriage is finally recognized as immoral, all art will have disappeared. Surely you can see that, when anything that either of us might write has become quite meaningless to the other, then there will be nothing, let alone art, which we can share. We shall all be excommunicated from each other."

"I suppose you're right; but somehow, intuitively, I cannot believe the fearful picture you have painted."

"If you can't grasp it intuitively, then try it discursively."

"Discursive or intuitive," Singleman blurts out, "what's it matter? The point is that it's true. It's quite obvious that the greater the freedom of the individuality permitted to human beings, the less free their interrelations must become. I consider that all Nietzsche's glorification of a Superman is nothing but a philosophical attempt to talk a way out of the dead-end facing mankind. You might at first sight think that Nietzsche was enunciating some cherished ideal, but on reflection you'll recognize that he's simply voicing his bitter discontent. Twisting about in his bed, niggled by his neighbors, worried by their developing individualities, Nietzsche funked even the nineteenth century. Pouring out such jeremiads, he must have lived in an agony of despair. Reading his works, one does not feel inspired, merely sorry for their wretched author. That voice of his is not the voice of intrepidity and determination; it is nothing more than the whine of grievance and the screams of indignation. It was, perhaps, an understandable reaction in a rejected philosopher. When in ancient times a truly great man appeared, all the whole world flocked to gather under his banner. Which was no doubt very gratifying, certainly sufficiently gratifying for the great man in question to feel no need to resort to pen and paper with all that virulence one finds in Nietzsche. The superhuman characters portrayed in Homer's epics and in the *Ballad of Chevy Chase* are not demon-driven. Unlike Nietzsche's Superman, they are alive with life, with gaiety and just plain fun. Their times were truly merry and the merriment is recreated in the writing. Naturally, in days like that there was no trace of Nietzsche's atrabilious venom. But in Nietzsche's period things were sadly different. No hero shone on his horizons and, even if a hero had appeared, no one would have honored, respected, or even noticed him. When, in a much earlier period, Confucius made his appearance, it was relatively easy for him to assert his importance because he had no equals as competitors. Today they're ten a penny and possibly the whole wide world is packed with them. Certainly no one nowadays would be impressed if you claimed to be a new Confucius, and you, because you had failed to impress, would become waspish in your discontent, in precisely the sort of discontent which leads to books which brandish Superman about our ears. We sought freedom and now we suffer from the inconveniences that freedom can but bring. Does it not follow that, though Western civilization seems splendid at first glance, at the end of the day it proves itself a bane? In sharp contrast, we in the East have always, since long, long, long ago, devoted ourselves not to material progress but to development of the mind. That Way was the right way. Now that the pressures of individuality are bringing on all sorts of nervous disorders, we are at last able to grasp the meaning of the ancient tag that 'people are carefree under firm rule.' And it won't be long before Lao Tzu's doctrine of the activating effect of inactivity grows to seem less of a paradox. By then, of course, it will be too late to do anything more than recognize our likeness to addicted alcoholics who wish they'd never touched the stuff."

"All you fellows," said Coldmoon, "seem hideously pessimistic about the future, but none of your moans and groans depress me in the least. I wonder why."

"That's because you've just got married," said Waverhouse hastening to explain away the mildest manifestation of hope.

Then, suddenly, my master began to talk. "If my dear Coldmoon, you're thinking yourself fortunate to have found a wife, you're making a big mistake. For your particular information, I shall now read out something of pertinent interest." Opening that antique of a book which he'd brought from his study a short time back, my master then continued. "As you can see, this is an old book but it was perfectly clear, even in those early days, that women were terrible."

"Sir, you surprise me. But may I ask when the book was written?" said Coldmoon.

"In the sixteenth century, by a man called Thomas Nashe."

"I'm even more surprised. You mean to say that even in those early days someone spoke ill of my wife?"

"The book contains a wide variety of complaints about women, some of which will certainly apply to your wife. So you'd better listen carefully."

"All right. I am listening. Very honored, too."

"The book begins by saying that all men must heed the views of womanhood propounded down the ages by recognized sages. You follow me? Are you listening?"

"We are all listening. Even I, a bachelor, am listening."

"Aristotle says that, since all women are good-for-nothings anyway, it is best, if you must get married, to choose a small bride, because a small good-for-nothing is less disastrous than a large one."

"Coldmoon, is this wife of yours hefty or petite?"

"She's one of the heftier good-for-nothings."

They all laughed, more at the suddenness with which Coldmoon had rejoined the eternal conspiracy of males than at anything inherently funny in his answer.

"Well," said Waverhouse, "that's an interesting book, I must say. Read us some more."

"A man once asked what might be a miracle, and the sage replied, 'A chaste woman.'"

"Who, sir, is this sage?"

"The book doesn't give his name."

"I'll bet he was a sage who had been jilted."

"Next comes Diogenes who, when asked at what age it was best to take a wife, replied, 'For a young man, not yet; for the old man, never.'"

"No doubt that miserable fellow thought that up in his barrel," observed Waverhouse.

"Pythagoras says that there are three evils not to be suffered: fire, water, and a woman."

"I didn't know," said Singleman, "that any Greek philosopher was responsible for such an ill-considered apothegm. If you ask me, none of them are evil: one can enter fire and not be burnt, enter water and not be drowned, enter. . ." Here he got stuck until Waverhouse helped him out by adding, "And entertain a woman without being bewitched, eh?"

Paying no regard to his friends interjections, my master went on with his reading. "Socrates says that a man's most difficult task is to try to control women and children. Demosthenes says that the greatest torment a man can invent for his enemy's vexation is to give him his own daughter in marriage 'as a domestical Furie to disquiet him night and day' until he dies of it. The eminent Seneca says that there be two especial troubles in this world: a wife and ignorance. The Emperor Marcus Aurelius compares women to ships because 'to keep them well in order, there is always somewhat wanting.' Plautus claims that women 'deck themselves so gorgeously and lace themselves so nicely' because, and I paraphrase, such a mean trick disguises their natural ugliness. Valerius Maximus in a letter to one of his friends advises him that almost nothing is impossible for a woman, and goes on to entreat God Almighty that 'his sweet friend be not entrapped by woman's treacherie.' It was this same Valerius Maximus who answered his own question about the nature of woman by saying, 'She is an enemy to friendship, an inevitable pain, a necessary evil, a natural temptation, a desired calamity, a honey-seeming poison.' He also remarked that, if it is a sin to put a woman away, it is surely a much greater torment to keep her still."

"Please, sir," pleaded Coldmoon, "that's enough. I cannot bear to hear any more awful things about my wife."

"There are still several more pages. How about listening to the end?"

"Oh, have a heart," said Waverhouse, "and anyway isn't it about time for your own good lady to come home?" He had hardly started his usual style of teasing when from the direction of the other room there came the sound of Mrs. Sneaze calling sharply for the maid.

"I say, that's torn it," Waverhouse whispered. "Had you realized she was back?"

My master permitted himself a spasm of muffled laughter. "What's it matter if she is?"

But Waverhouse was not to be dissuaded. "Oh, Mrs. Sneaze," he called, "how long have you been home?"

Answer, as the poets put it, came there none.

"Did you happen to hear what your noble spouse was just telling us, Mrs. Sneaze?"

Still no answer.

"I hope you understand he wasn't speaking his own thoughts. Just reading out the opinions of a Mr. Nashe from the sixteenth century. Nothing personal. Please don't take it to heart."

"It hardly matters to me," came the curt response in a voice so faint and distant that Mrs. Sneaze might well have been away in the sixteenth century pursuing the issue with Mr. Nashe himself. Coldmoon giggled nervously.

"Well, of course it hardly matters to me, either. I'm sorry to have mentioned it." Waverhouse was now laughing out loud when we heard the sound of the outside gate being opened and heavy footsteps entering the house. Next moment, and with no further announcement, the sliding door of the room was yanked aside and the face of Tatara Sampei peered in through the gap.

Sampei hardly looked himself. His snow-white shirt and his spanking new frock-coat were surprises in themselves but he was also carrying, their necks string-tied together, a clutch of bottles of beer. He set the bottles down beside the dried bonitos, and himself, without even a nod of greeting, hunkered down heavily on his hams with all the self-confident resolution of a warrior. "Mr. Sneaze, sir," he immediately began, "has your stomach trouble gotten any better lately? It's all this staying at home, you know; it does you no good."

"I haven't said whether my stomach was better or worse," my master tartly objected.

"No, I know you haven't. But your complexion speaks for itself. It's not good, yellow like that. This is the right time of year to go fishing. Why not hire a boat at Shinagawa? Bracing. I went out last Sunday."

"Did you catch anything?"

"No, nothing."

"Is it any fun when you don't catch a sausage?"

"The idea is to buck yourself up, to get the old juices flowing again. How about all of you? Have you ever been out fishing? It's terrific fun. You see," he began speaking to them as a group, somewhat loftily as though to a ring of children, "you set off in this tiny boat across the vast blue ocean. . ."

"My preference," said the irrepressible Waverhouse, "would be to set off in a vast blue boat across the smallest possible ocean."

"I can see no point," said Coldmoon in his most detached voice, "no fun at all in setting off on a fishing expedition unless one expects to catch at least a whale. Or a mermaid."

"You can't catch whales from cockleshells and mermaids don't exist. You scribbling men of letters have no common sense whatever."

"I'm not a man of letters."

"No? Then what the devil are you? I'm a businessman, and for us businessmen the one thing you must have is common sense." He turned toward my master and addressed him directly. "You know, sir, over the last few months I have amassed a very great stock of common sense. Of course, working as I do in a great business center, it's only natural that I should become like this."

"Like what?"

"Take, for instance, cigarettes. One can't expect to get very far in business if one goes around smoking trashy brands like Shiki-shima or Asahi." At this point, he produced a pack of Egyptian cigarettes, selected a gold-tipped tube, lit it ostentatiously and began to puff its scented smoke.

"Can you really afford to chuck your money around like that? You must be rolling in the stuff."

"No. No money yet, but something will turn up. Smoking these cigarettes builds one's image, confers considerable prestige."

"It's certainly an easier way to gain prestige than by polishing glass balls. A real short cut to fame. Far less troublesome than all your labors, wouldn't you say, Coldmoon?"

Waverhouse had scarcely closed his mouth, and before Coldmoon could utter a syllable, Sampei turned and said, "So, you are Mr. Coldmoon. The chap who's given up on his doctorate. For which reason it's become me."

"You're studying for a degree?"

"No, I'm marrying Miss Goldfield. To tell the truth, I felt rather sorry for you, missing a chance like that, but they pressed me so hard that I've agreed to marry her. Nevertheless, I can't help feeling that somehow I've wronged Mr. Coldmoon. Can you follow my feelings, Mr. Sneaze?"

"But please, my dear sir," said Coldmoon, "you are most welcome to the match."

"If she's what you want," my master mumbled vaguely, "then I suppose you might as well marry her."

"How absolutely splendid," burbles Waverhouse. "All's well that ends well, and all that. It just goes to show that nobody need ever worry about getting his daughters married. Wasn't I saying only just now that someone suitable would quickly come along and, sure enough, she's already found this very cool customer to be her unblushing bridegroom. Think of it, Beauchamp, and rejoice. It's a gift of a theme for one of your new-style poems. Waste no time. Get going." Waverhouse was off again.

"And are you," asked Sampei somewhat obsequiously, "the poet Mr.

Beauchamp? I should be deeply grateful if you would deign to compose something for our wedding. I could have it printed right away and have it sent out to all concerned. I will also arrange for it to be printed in the daily press."

"I'd be happy to oblige. When would you like to have it?"

"Any time. And any piece which you already have on hand would do. And for that I'll invite you to our wedding reception. We'll be having champagne. Have you ever tried it? It tastes delicious. I'm planning, Mr. Sneaze, to hire an orchestra, a small one, for the occasion. Perhaps we could get Mr. Beauchamp's poem set to music and then it could be played while the guests are eating. How about that, Mr. Sneaze? What do you think?"

"You do as you like."

"But Mr. Sneaze, could you write the musical setting for me?"

"Don't be silly."

"Isn't there anyone among you who could handle the music?"

"Mr. Coldmoon, the unsuccessful marriage candidate and failed ball polisher, happens also to be a fine violinist. Ask him if he'll oblige. But I doubt if he'll squander his wealth of soul in return for a mere sipping of champagne."

"But there are champagnes and champagnes. I shan't be offering anything cheap or nasty. No filthy pops. Nothing but the best. Won't you help me out?"

"Of course, and with pleasure. I'll write the music even if your champagne is mere cider. Indeed, if you like, I'll do the job for nothing."

"I wouldn't dream of asking you to aid me unrewarded. If you don't enjoy champagne, how about this for payment?" Reaching into his jacket pocket, Sampei pulled out some seven or eight photographs and scattered them on the floor-matting. One was half-length, one was full-length, one standing, another sitting, one dressed somewhat casually, another very correctly in a long-sleeved kimono and yet another wearing a formal Japanese hairdo. All of them were photographs of young girls.

"Mr. Sneaze, sir, these were all prospective brides in whom I am, of course, no longer interested. But if any of these marriage candidates happened to interest Mr. Coldmoon or Mr. Beauchamp, I would gladly, in recognition of their assistance to myself act as their agent in effecting introductions to any of these fanciable ladies. How about this one here?"

he asks, thrusting a photograph under Coldmoon's nose.

"Oh nice," says Coldmoon, "very nice. I rather fancy that one."

"And how about this?" He shoves another picture into Coldmoon's hand.

"Very nice, too. Quite charming. Yes, I certainly fancy her."

"But which one do you want?"

"I don't mind which."

"You seem a bit feckless," Sampei commented dryly. Then, turning to my master, he went on with his sales pitch. "This one, actually, is the niece of a doctor."

"I see."

"This next one is extremely good-natured. Young, too. Only seventeen. . . And this one carries a whacking great dowry. . . While this one here is a daughter of a provincial governor." All alone with his imaginings, Sampei rattles on.

"Do you think I could marry them all?"

"All? That's plain gluttonous. Are you some kind of polygamist or something?"

"No, not a polygamist. But a carnivore, of course."

"Never mind what you are. Sampei, put those snaps away at once. Can't you see," said my master in a tone of sharp scolding, "that he's only leading you on?"

"So you don't want an introduction to any of them," said Sampei, half in question and half in statement, as, one by one, slowly, giving Beauchamp and Coldmoon a last chance to relent, he put the pictures back into his pocket.

There was no response.

"Well now, what are those bottles for?"

"A present. I bought them just now at the dramshop on the corner so that we might drink to my forthcoming marriage. Come, let's start."

My master clapped his hands for the maid and asked her to open the bottles. Then the five of them, my master, Waverhouse, Singleman, Coldmoon, and Beauchamp, solemnly lifting their glasses, congratulated Sampei on his good fortune in love. Sampei fairly glowed with self-esteem and assured them, "I shall invite you all to the ceremony. Can all of you come? I do hope so."

"No," my master answered promptly. "I shan't."

"Why ever not? It'll be the grandest once-in-a-lifetime day of my life.

And you won't attend it? Seems a bit heartless."

"I'm not heartless. But I won't attend."

"Ah, you haven't got the things to wear? Is that the snag? I can gladly arrange for the right kit to be made available. You really ought to go out more and meet people. I'll introduce you to some well-known persons."

"That's the very last thing I would wish."

"It might even cure your stomach troubles."

"I don't care if they never get better."

"Well, if you can't be budged, you can't. But how about you others? Will you be able to come?"

"Me? I'd love to," said Waverhouse. "I would even be delighted to play the role of the honored go-between. A verse leaps to my lips:

Evening in spring:
The marriage rite
And nuptial bonds made champagne-tight.

"What's that you said? Suzuki's going to be the go-between? I might have known it. Well, in that case, I'm sorry, but there it is. I suppose that it really would be a bit too much to have two lots of go-betweens. So I'll attend your party as an ordinary human being."

"And how about you? Will you come with your friends?"

"Me?" said Singleman apparently surprised.

"Having this fishing rod to be my friend,
I live at ease in nature and am free
Of every care the red-dust world might send
Like some hooked promise to entangle me."

"And what the hell is that?" asked Waverhouse. "Something from the hallowed guide on how to write a poem in Chinese?"

"I really can't remember where I picked it up."

"You really can't remember? How tiresome for you. Well, come if your fishing rod can spare you. And you, Mr. Coldmoon, I hope I may count on you. After all, you have a special status in this matter."

"Most certainly I'll be there. It would be a pity to miss the chance of hearing my own music played by an orchestra."

"Of course. And what about you, Mr. Beauchamp?"

"Well, yes. I'd like to be there to read my new-style poem in front of the couple themselves."

"That's wonderful. Mr. Sneaze, sir, I've never before in all my life felt so pleased with the world. And, to mark the moment, I'll have another glass of that beer." He filled a tumbler to the brim and sank it at one go. Slowly his face turned shining red.

The short autumn day has grown dark. The charcoal fire in the brazier has long ago burnt out and its crust of ash is studded and strewn with an ugly mess of cigarette ends. Even these happy-go-lucky men seem to have had enough of their merriment and in the end it was Singleman who, climbing stiffly to his feet, remarked, "It's getting late. Time to be on our way." The others followed suit and, politely apopemptic, vanished into the night. The drawing room grew desolate, like a variety hall when the show is over.

My master ate his dinner and went off into his study. His wife, feeling the autumn chill, tightens her collar, settles over her sewing box, and gets on with her remodeling of a worn-out kimono. The children, lying in one row, are fast asleep. The maid has gone out to a bathhouse.

If one tapped the deep bottom of the hearts of these seemingly lighthearted people, it would give a somewhat sad sound. Though Singleman behaves as though enlightenment had made him a familiar of the skies, his feet still shuffle, earthbound, through this world. The world of Waverhouse, though it may be easy-going, is not the dreamworld of those painted landscapes which he loves. That winsome donzel Coldmoon, having at last stopped polishing his little globes of glass, has fetched from his far home province a bride to cheer his days. Which is pleasant and quite normal, but the sad fact is that long-continued, pleasant normality becomes a bore. Beauchamp too, however golden-hearted he is now, will have come in ten years' time to realize the folly of giving away for nothing those new-style poems that are the essence of his heart. As for Sampei, I find it difficult to judge whether he'll finish up on top of the pile or down the drain, but I'd like to think he'll manage to live his life out proud and happy in the ability to souse his acquaintance in champagne. Suzuki will remain the same eternal groveling creeper. Grovelers get covered in mud, but, even so be-sharned, he'll manage better than those who cannot creep at all.

As for me, I am a cat, still nameless though born two years ago, who has lived his life among men. I have always thought myself unique in my knowledge of mankind, but I was recently much surprised to meet another cat, some German mog called Kater Murr, who suddenly turned up and started sounding off in a very high-falutin' manner on my own special subject. I subsequently made enquiries and discovered that my visitor was in fact the ghost of a cat who, though he'd been in Hell since dying a century ago, had become so piqued with curiosity about my reputation that he rematerialized for the express purpose of upsetting me. This cat, I learned, was a most unfilial creature. On one occasion when he was going to meet his mother, he was carrying a fish in his mouth to give her as a present. However he failed to control his animal appetites and broke his journey to guzzle the fish. His combination of talents and greed was such as to make him virtually human, and he even once astonished his master by writing a poem. If such a feline culture-hero was already demonstrating superior cat skills so long as a century ago, perhaps a good-for-nothing specimen like me has already outlived its purpose and should no more delay its retirement into nothingness.

My master, sooner or later, will die of his dyspepsia. Old man Goldfield is already doomed by his greed. The autumn leaves have mostly fallen. All that has life must lose it. Since there seems so little point in living, perhaps those who die young are the only creatures wise. If one heeds the sages who assembled here today, mankind has already sentenced itself to extinction by suicide. If we don't watch out, even cats may find their individualities developing along the lethal crushing pattern forecast for these two-legged loons. It's an appalling prospect. Depression weighs upon me. Perhaps a sip of Sampei's beer would cheer me up.

I go around to the kitchen. The backdoor is half-open and rattles in the autumn wind. Which seems to have blown the lamp out, for the room's unlit. Still, there are shadows tilting inward through the window. Moonrise, I suppose. On a tray there are three glasses, two of them half-filled with a brownish liquid. Even warm water, if kept in a glass, looks cold. Naturally this liquid, standing quietly beside the jar of charcoal existinguisher, looks, in the icy moonlight, chill and uninviting. However, anything for experience. If Sampei, as I recall, could after drinking it become a bright, warm red and start breathing as heavily as a man who's run a mile, perhaps it's not impossible for a cat that drinks it to feel livelier. Anyway, some day I, too, must die so l might as well try everything before I do. Once I'm dead, I tell myself, it will be too late in the grave to regret that I never tasted beer. So, take courage and drink up!

I flicked my tongue into the stuff but, as I began to lap, I got a sharp surprise. The tip of my tongue, as though it had been pricked with needles, stung and tingled painfully. What possible pleasure can human beings find in drinking such unpleasant stuff? I've heard my master describe revolting food as not fit for a dog, but this dark drink is truly not fit for a cat. There must be some fundamental antipathy between cats and beer. Conscious of danger, I quickly withdrew my tongue. But then, on reflection, I remembered that men have a pet saying about good medicines always tasting filthy and that the drafts they down to cure their colds invariably make them grimace with disgust. I've never worked out whether they get cured by drinking muck or whether they'd get well anyway without the face-making business. Now's my chance to find out. If drinking beer poisons my entire intestines, well, that will be just too bad: but if like Sampei, I grow so cheerful as to forget everything around me, then I'll accept the experience as an unexpected joy and even, perhaps, I'll teach all the cats of the neighborhood how sweet it is to drown one's woes in drink. Anyway, let's take a chance and see. The decision made, I drooped my tongue out cautiously. But if I can actually see the bitter liquid I find it hard to drink it; so closing my eyes tight shut, I began to lap.

When, by sheer strength of will and tigerlike perseverance, I'd lapped away the beer-lees in the first glass, a strange phenomenon occurred. The initial agony of my needled tongue began to ease off and the ghastly feeling in my mouth, a feeling as if some hand were squeezing my cheeks together from the outside, was pleasurably relieved. By the time I'd dealt with the first glass, beer swilling was no longer much of a problem. I finished off the second glass so painlessly that, while I was about it, I even lapped up all the spill on the tray and slurped the whole lot down into my stomach.

That done, in order to study my body's reactions, I crouched down quietly for a while. My body is gradually growing warm. I feel hot around my eyes and my ears are burning. I feel like singing a song. I feel like dancing the Cat's High Links. I feel like telling my master, Waverhouse, and Singleman that they can all go to hell. I feel like scratching old man Goldfield. I feel like biting his wife's vast nose off. I feel like doing lots of things. And in the end I felt I'd like to wobble to my feet. As I stood up, I felt I'd like to walk. Highly pleased with myself I felt like going out. And as I staggered out, I felt like shouting, "Moon, old man, how goes it?" So I did. Oh, but I felt wonderful!

So this, I thought, is how it feels to be gloriously drunk. Radiant with glory, I persevered in setting my unsteady feet one in front of each other in the correct order. Which is very difficult when you have four feet. I made no effort to travel in any particular direction but just kept going in long, slow wayward totter. I'm beginning to feel extremely sleepy, and indeed I hardly know if I'm still walking or already sunk in sleep. I try to open my eyes, but their lids have grown unliftably heavy. Ah, well, it can't be helped. Confidently telling myself that nothing in this world, neither seas nor mountains nor anything else, could now impede my cat-imperial progress, I put a front paw forward when suddenly I hear a loud, sloppy splash. . . As I come to my senses, I know that I'm done for. I had no time to work out how I'd been done for because, in the very moment that I realized the fact of it, everything went haywire.

When I again came to myself I found I was floating in water. Because I was also in pain I clawed at what seemed its cause, but scratching water had no effect except to result in my immediate submersion. I struck out desperately for the surface by kicking with my hind-legs and scrabbling with my fore-paws. This action eventually produced a sort of scraping sound and, as I managed to thrust my head just clear of the water, I saw that I'd fallen into a big clay jar against whose side my claws had scraped. All through the summer this jar had contained a thick growth of water-hollyhocks, but in the early autumn the crows had descended first to eat the plants and then to bathe in the water. In the end their splashing about and the heat of the sun had so lowered the water level that the crows found it difficult either to bathe or to drink, and they had stopped coming. I remember that only the other day I was thinking that the water must have gone down because I'd seen no birds about. Little did I then dream that I myself would be the next to splash about in that jar.

From the water's surface to the lip of the jar, it measures some five inches. However much I stretch my paws I cannot reach the lip. And the water gives no purchase for a jump. If I do nothing, I just sink. If I flounder around, my claws scrabble on the clay sides but the only result is that scraping sound. It's true that when I claw at the jar I do seem to rise a little in the water but, as soon as my claws scrape down the clay, I slide back deep below the surface. This is so painful that I immediately start scrabbling again until I break surface and can breathe. But it's a very tiring business, and my strength is going. I become impatient with my ill success, but my legs are growing sluggish. In the end I can hardly tell whether I am scratching the jar in order to sink or am sinking to induce more scratching.

While this was going on and despite the constant pain, I found myself reasoning that I'm only in agony because I want to escape from the jar. Now, much as I'd like to get out, it's obvious that I can't: my extended front leg is scarcely three inches long and even if I could hoist my body with its outstretched fore-paws up above the surface, I still could never hook my claws over the rim. Accordingly, since it's blindingly clear that I can't get out, it's equally clear that it's senseless to persist in my efforts to do so. Only my own senseless persistence is causing my ghastly suffering. How very stupid. How very, very stupid deliberately to prolong the agonies of this torture.

"I'd better stop. I just don't care what happens next. I've had quite enough, thank you, of this clutching, clawing, scratching, scraping, scrabbling, senseless struggle against nature." The decision made, I give up and relax: first my fore-paws, then my hind-legs, then my head and tail.

Gradually I begin to feel at ease. I can no longer tell whether I'm suffering or feeling grateful. It isn't even clear whether I'm drowning in water or lolling in some comfy room. And it really doesn't matter. It does not matter where I am or what I'm doing. I simply feel increasingly at ease. No, I can't actually say that I feel at ease, either. I feel that I've cut away the sun and moon, they pull at me no longer; I've pulverized both Heaven and Earth, and I'm drifting off and away into some unknown endlessness of peace. I am dying, Egypt, dying. Through death I'm drifting slowly into peace. Only by dying can this divine quiescence be attained. May one rest in peace! I am thankful, I am thankful. Thankful, thankful, thankful.